AGAIN, DANGEROUS VISIONS I

EDITED BY
Harlan Ellison

ILLUSTRATIONS BY ED EMSHWILLER

A SIGNET BOOK
NEW AMERICAN LIBRARY
TIMES MIRROR

Library of Congress Catalog Card Number: 70-123689

This is an authorized reprint of a hardcover edition
published by Doubleday & Company, Inc.

 SIGNET TRADEMARK REG. U.S. PAT. OFF. AND FOREIGN COUNTRIES
REGISTERED TRADEMARK—MARCA REGISTRADA
HECHO EN CHICAGO, U.S.A.

SIGNET, SIGNET CLASSICS, SIGNETTE,
MENTOR AND PLUME BOOKS
are published by The New American Library, Inc.,
1301 Avenue of the Americas,
New York, New York 10019

First Printing, November, 1973

3 4 5 6 7 8 9

PRINTED IN THE UNITED STATES OF AMERICA

For Brian & Lauraine Kirby
. . . and baby makes three.

CONTENTS

INTRODUCTION

An Assault of New Dreamers

Dumas wrote *The Three Musketeers* in 1844. Popular demand compelled him to write two sequels, *Vingt Ans Après* in 1845 and *Le Vicomte de Bragelonne* in 1848. Arthur Conan Doyle grew tired of Sherlock Holmes and ended his career as a criminologist (as well as that of Professor Moriarty as a master criminal) with a tumble over the Reichenbach Falls in "The Final Problem." The public would have none of it. Doyle, pressed to the wall, revived his immortal sleuth three years later with "The Adventure of the Empty House." In 1959 Evan S. Connell, Jr. wrote *Mrs. Bridge* and it became an instant classic of contemporary fiction. No sequel was possible, but the name became a literary catchphrase, and in 1969 Mr. Connell wrote *Mr. Bridge.* The creators of Captain America killed off that star-spangled warrior for Democracy and the American Way near the end of World War II. In the early Sixties the Sub-Mariner, Prince Namor of Atlantis, found Cap floating around perfectly preserved in a block of ice, and revived him. Isaac Asimov has had to suffer sequelization many times. No one will let him stop telling stories of Dr. Susan Calvin and her U.S. Robots and Mechanical Men, Inc.; stories of the Foundation; stories of Lije Bailey and R. Daneel Olivaw. Ike is resigned. They have lives of their own.

I did not want to edit another *Dangerous Visions.*

A man may enter the Valley of the Shadow once because he has a taste for danger or because he simply doesn't recognize the terrain. But once having gone and come back, only a fool returns. In November of 1965 I began work on what I thought would be an interesting little project, the creation of an anthology of new stories, in a new mode, for the field of speculative fiction. Four and a half years later, fifty thousand hardcovers and God only knows how many paperbacks later, *Dangerous Visions* has become a landmark (for once my ego-dreams came true) and somehow, magically, as though it had a life of *its* own, *Dangerous Visions* has forced the creation of a companion volume, bigger than the original, and I sit here in lonely desperation, trying to beat a publication deadline, writing another Introduction. We both arrive at the same conclusion: I am a monumental fool.

Let me tell you how it happened.

No, wait a minute. Let me first tell you what *Dangerous Visions* did, apart from selling more copies of an sf anthology than any other in recent memory.

First, the awards.

Fritz Leiber's "Gonna Roll the Bones" and Chip Delany's "Aye, and Gomorrah . . ." won the 1967 Nebula Awards of the Science Fiction Writers of America in the categories of best novelette and best short story, respectively—incidentally beating out nominees by this editor in both categories. (Seldom has a man so willingly aided his executioners.)

At the 26th World SF Convention in Oakland, in 1968, Philip José Farmer tied for the Hugo Award in the Best Novella category with "Riders of the Purple Wage" from *Dangerous Visions* (for purists, he tied with Anne McCaffrey's "Weyr Search"); and Fritz took a Hugo with "Gonna Roll the Bones" for Best Novelette. (I got two Hugos that year, so I didn't feel the need to bitch or begrudge.)

And the Oakland convention gave me a plaque for editing "the most significant and controversial sf book published in 1967."

Dangerous Visions appeared on BOOK WORLD's list of the best paperbacks of 1969. It was reprinted by the Science Fiction Book Club and sold over 45,000 copies. The Literary Guild offered it as a bonus selection. It has had—or will shortly have—translations or editions in Great Britain, Germany, Japan, Spain, Italy and France. It almost single-handedly helped bring into being a counter-revolutionary movement in the genre called "The Second Foundation," dedicated to eradicating all that *Dangerous Visions* stood for. Whatever that is.

I personally received over two thousand letters from readers of the book ranging from a telegram from an influential New York editor who said *Congratulations on publication day of the most important sf book of the decade* to a Mrs. S. Blittmon of Philadelphia who wrote, in part: "When I picked up your book 'Dangerous Visions' at the library & read the 2 introductions I thought it was going to be great. I cannot tell you how sick I feel after reading [and she named two stories, one my own]. You say you had a Jewish grandmother (so did I) but I think not; she must have been Viet Cong, otherwise how could you think of such atrocities. Shame, shame on you! Science fiction should be beautiful. With your mind

(?) you should be cleaning latrines & that's too nice. Sincerely . . ."

Go please the world.

Mostly, everyone was dazzled and delighted. The men and women who contributed the thirty-three original stories for *Dangerous Visions* went where no one had gone before and came back whispering of new tomorrows, many of them in ways the field of speculative fiction had never thought possible. Many people said my intention of publishing stories that were unpublishable in the commercial magazine markets because of taboos and editorial restrictions was only partially achieved. Others said only seventy per cent of the stories were top-grade. Others said sixty-two per cent, and one fan magazine found only twelve per cent of merit. Somehow, for all the pissing and moaning, the book managed to sell like ice cubes in Rio, managed to stand the field on its ear and alter its direction, managed to puff the prides of the writers who appeared therein, and became, as I say, a landmark. Ask anyone.

But when the dust settled, I was about eighteen hundred dollars out of pocket.

Through no frugality on the part of Doubleday, our publisher, I assure you. Strictly due to my own grandiose belief that the book was never big enough, never startling enough, never innovative enough. So I spent and spent. And as I said, when the dust cleared, I was in the hole. To date, I haven't yet hit the black on *Dangerous Visions* and I'm still repaying author Larry Niven for the loan he gave the book to purchase the last few stories. It doesn't matter. It was a prideful thing to assemble that book.

Only one author has vocally confessed to being upset with his participation in the project. I learned of that discontent only recently, and at risk of annoying the author and his agent, I really *must* relay the anecdote.

J.G. Ballard—easily one of the most innovative and serious contributors to the genre of speculative fiction—mentioned in an interview that he considered *Dangerous Visions* a hypocritical volume because I had asked writers to submit stories they felt could not be published in the traditional markets due to controversial content or approach, but when presented with it I had rejected "The Assassination of John Fitzgerald Kennedy Considered as a Downhill Motor Race."

The interview, in a magazine called *Cypher*, quoted Jim Ballard as saying I had rejected the story—ostensibly written specially for *Dangerous Visions*—on the grounds it would offend too many American readers.

When I read that item, I was horrified and stricken with a sinking-gut feeling ... for I'd never *seen* the story. Though Ballard had, indeed, written it for the book, his agent in New York, instead of sending it on to me here in Los Angeles, had made a prejudgment that the story was offensive, and drawered it till they could return it to Ballard. Whether or not they contrived to advise Ballard I'd bounced it, I do not know, to this day. Subsequently, Michael Moorcock published the story in *New Worlds* in England, and it instantly drew the praise it deserved.

As one of the most exciting and controversial stories written in the field in recent memory, it would have been perfect for *Dangerous Visions,* and when I learned that I'd missed buying the piece because of a wholly unjustified clerical judgment, I ground my teeth in frustration. But to be accused of hypocrisy on top of the loss, was more than I could bear. Jim Ballard's story "The Recognition" in *Dangerous Visions* was a good story, a laudable piece of fantasy, but it simply wasn't in the same time-zone with "Downhill Motor Race," one of the germinal stories of the past decade.

When I met Jim Ballard—in Rio de Janeiro in March of 1969—we rehashed what had happened, and I thought we'd gotten the matter discussed, with mutual commiseration. Then came that *Cypher* quote. And though I've written him reminding him of the circumstances surrounding the "submission" of the story, there's been no reply. So if any of you out there run into J.G. Ballard, would you kinda sorta tell him what happened? I'd hate for him, or any of you, to grow much older thinking I was stupid enough to reject a story that clearly brilliant and noteworthy.

I've been known to be stupid, but I refuse to cop to a charge of brain damage.

And while we're on the subject of my stupidity, I have to own up to stupidity in having arbitrarily denied a space in *Dangerous Visions* to Thomas Disch, whose work these past four years has elevated him to the top level of sf writers. Because of personal blindness, I rejected a Disch story that *should* have been in the book and, when later I got to know Tom better, regretted my prejudice bitterly.

Fortunately, Disch is a better man than your now-humble editor, and he has written for *this* volume an even better story. We'll get to that in due time, but the mention of that omission on my part brings us to the next phase of this introduction:

Why another *Dangerous Visions* collection?

Well, Disch is one reason. Piers Anthony is another. And the forty other writers herein nail it down finally.

Even so, even though there were handfuls of authors who never made it into *Dangerous Visions*, I was quite literally dragged, kicking and screaming, to *Again, Dangerous Visions*. I'll tell you about it.

After DV came out (you'll excuse me if I resort to initial-ese; the book is long enough as it stands, over 250,000 words, without having to write out *Dangerous Visions* every time), in 1967, and the memory of what aggravation it had been to get the damned thing together had faded from Doubleday editor Larry Ashmead's mind, he considered the sales figures, added them to the amount of prestige the book had brought to the otherwise foundering Doubleday empire, and he decided there should be a companion volume.

I am too much the gentleman to comment on the history of congenital insanity in the Ashmead ancestry, save to report Larry is inordinately proud of a spinster Ashmead aunt who was said to have had repeated carnal knowledge of a catamaran, and a paternal great-grandfather who introduced the peanut-butter-and-tuna-fish ice cream sundae in the Hebrides.

For my part, I was still recuperating from DV, both physically and financially. The high praise and bitter denunciations of the book were totaling at that time, and I was sitting back, breathing deeply, and thinking how good it was that the entire DV affair was ended. That was early in June of 1968.

The phone rang.

It was Ashmead.

"Hi, Harlan!" He always opens his conversations that way with me. As though he's really genuinely pleased to be talking to me. Sneaky sonofabitch.

"Hi, Larry," I responded, "what's happening? How's the latest Allen Drury disaster doing?"

"Making a fortune," he said.

"You ought to be ashamed of yourself, actually taking money for *dreck* like that. Why don't you get into a decent line of work, like racehorse doping or pre-pubescent white slavery?"

"We also publish Irving Stone, Leon Uris and Taylor Caldwell. Any one of whom makes more than you make in a year, in any five minute period."

"I only wish on you plagues of mice, locusts, salamanders, Irving Wallace, Jacqueline Susann and Harold Robbins. Also you should never be able to get a good point on your pencils." I'd have wished Erich Segal on him, but who knew about *that* horror in 1968? We Jews have a fine mind for curses.

"Just called to tell you we're putting DV out of print."

"Terrific," I said. "It's the hottest selling anthology in sf history, nothing but rave reviews, colleges are starting to use it as a text and you put it out of print. What corporate genius came up with *that* one?"

"It's Doubleday policy."

"That's what Adolf Eichmann said. Do you broast chickens on the side?"

"How'd you like to do another *Dangerous Visions?*"

I hung up on him.

He called me back. "We were cut off."

"We weren't cut off. I hung up on you."

"Oh. What I said was: 'How'd you like to do another *Dangerous Visions?'* "

I hung up on him again.

So he called me back again and before I could say anything he screamed very shrilly, "DON'T HANG UP ON ME!"

"Okay," I said, "I won't hang up on you, but don't *you* use filthy language to me over the phone. I'm of a delicate nature."

"But why *not*? I think it would be a marvelous idea."

"I'll hang up on you again."

"Think of all the writers who've been influenced by the book. Writers who need that kind of showcase, writers who need a break, writers who want to spread their wings, writers who . . ."

"Ashmead, knock it off. I used that hype on *you* when I was trying to sell you *Dangerous Visions* in '65."

"I know. I was using the memo you sent me. You misspelled fledgling."

"Go away, I'm retired from the editing business."

But he persisted. Lawrence Ashmead is a very persistent man. Anyone who publishes Asimov has *learned* to be persistent. Also comatose.

So I decided the surest, quickest way to scare him off was to demand three times as much money as Doubleday had ever offered for a science fiction book. So I demanded it. (No, I'm not going to tell you how much that was, so stop bugging me.)

"It's a deal!" Larry chirruped. When he has swallowed a canary he *always* chirrups.

I sank instantly and completely out of sight in a funk of watertight absoluteness.

"You has done me, Ashmead," I muttered, chewing my armpit. I felt like a satyr condemned to a hell of sex-crazed nymphomaniacs, each with her own special spirochete or Oriental fungus.

"Just remember how happy you were when DV won all those awards," he said. "Don't you remember how happy you were?" My mind's camera quickly flashed the memory behind my eyes. I remembered those Nebula citations Larry and I had picked up for the award-winning Leiber and Delany stories. I saw again my expression. It didn't look happy to me. It looked like a man who has just eaten a ripe persimmon.

I shrugged away the ghastly after-image of myself (in corrupted missionary tuxedo shirt and ludicrous facial stricture), of Ashmead (dapper, smug, already plotting my future horror) and said, "Okay, I'll do another volume of the damned thing, *but I'll do it at my own pace.* You have *got* to promise on the lives of your cats that you won't *noodge* me about deadlines. I can take ten years if I want to."

"Sure, Harlan," he said. The voice of the asp.

On June 28th, 1968 the contracts were signed and I began soliciting manuscripts for the book you now hold in your hands. Or propped against your belly. Or whatever.

(As an aside, I also made sure no book club or paperback editions of *Again, Dangerous Visions* could be sold without my agreement, thereby assuring that the writers who contributed to this volume would have a good long trade edition run for their royalties before those deadbeats among you who wait for cheaper editions could obtain marked-down incarnations. The point of this aside is to assure those of you reading this book over the shoulders of your friends, that you won't be obtaining a cheapo version for some time, so you'd better rush out right now and buy this edition at full-price. Or rip it off from the bookstore. Either way it counts for full royalties.)

As I got into the editing of this book, I found my greatest joy was in seeing stories by new writers who were just starting to flex their literary muscles. An only slightly less joyful joy was in seeing older writers, who'd established reputations for doing one certain kind of story, trying something new.

The word had gotten around because of DV that asking for really far-reaching innovative fiction was not mouth-to-mouth resuscitation. And (despite what happened with Ballard) the writers responded.

As a consequence, I find this second book in the DV trilogy *much* more daring and, well, "dangerous" than the first. Lupoff and Anthony and Nelson and Vonnegut and O'Donnell and Bernott and Parra and Tiptree get it on in ways I don't think would have been possible before the advent of *Dangerous Visions*.

Now I realize that smacks of hoopla, and I've been pilloried repeatedly in the fan press for steadfastly and endlessly committing the crime. Understanding in front that this explanation contains not one scintilla of defense, let me advise all who will review or comment on *this* DV that I will do it again—the hyper-ventilating hurrah—because whatever uglies are laid at *my* door, it gets the word out for the rest of the men and women in this book. You see, in a very real sense, I am the custodian of this wonderland. It is my responsibility to see that every writer in this book gets the widest possible exposure for his or her work. It is a trust which I assume with considerable gratitude, and with a naked intent to smash down doors and bang on drums and buttonhole critics and beat on the ears of potential readers till they scream all right, all right, already, I'll *read* it . . . and then first-story writers in this book like Evelyn Lief and Ken McCullough and Jim Hemesath will have their chance, as well as established names like Ursula Le Guin and Ben Bova and Tom Sherred.

It's not the gentlemanly way to do it, I suppose, but in a world where Evelyn Lief and Al Parra have to compete with Jacqueline Susann and Erich Segal, having the services of a flack commando can be a necessary evil.

How it pains my mother to hear me called evil.

The introduction to *Dangerous Visions* talked about that book (hopefully) being the opening shot of a revolution in the literary genre of speculative fiction. From that simple phrase came endless reams of criticism and artificial controversy. The phrase gave birth to another phrase: The New Wave.

A few words should be expended here on the subject.

We are a small but closely-tied community, we readers and writers of sf. We fight and love and honor and hate one another the way any small family does, and whenever one of us has the audacity to suggest that things here in the household might be run a little differently, ah, then we have recrimination, vitriol, backbiting, remorse. Danger threatens. Tarahhh! The lancers lurch to the rescue. The dragoons deploy. The hussars hurtle forward. To protect the reputations of Arthur C. Clarke and Hal Clement and Robert Heinlein. Oh, come *on*! Is someone putting us on? Does Norman Spinrad *really* threaten Isaac Asimov? Can John Jeremy Pierce truly believe that? No one in his right mind ever said "the new wave," whatever the hell that might be, was going to drive Murray Leinster or Poul Anderson or Frank Herbert off the printed page. In fact, Frank will have a story in *The Last Dangerous Visions*. (More about that later. Let's stick to the subject.) Poul was in the original DV. It's all bullshit. (Oops. There go a hundred library sales of this book. Ah well.)

The New Wave is as much myth as The Old Wave, unless we choose to postulate The Old Wave as forming back around the time of Aristophanes and cresting out with, say, Randall Garrett.

It's all bullshit, kiddies, and let's hear no more about it.

DV and A,DV are composed of almost a *hundred* New Waves, each one just a single writer in depth, and each one going its own way, against the tides. Take it or leave it, we are a family of mavericks and toads and pteranodons, and I cannot see *any*one driving Bob Heinlein *any*where he doesn't want to go.

Does it parse? Hopefully.

Onward.

Even casual observers of the DV series will see that no one who appeared in DV appears in this book. Nor will any of those found in DV or A,DV be found in the final book of the trilogy, *The Last Dangerous Visions*. When I took on the job of editing this second book, and said there would be no repeats, I was advised I'd lost my mind, there weren't—simply weren't—enough *other* good writers to fill out a second book. Bullshit again, my children. Not only were there enough to fill *this* book with more writers than we saw in DV, but the overflow had to be put into a third volume. And we *still* haven't used up the riches.

When DV was published, I thought I'd gathered in all the important writers. But since then Piers Anthony and Gregory Benford and Richard Lupoff and Gene Wolfe and Thomas Disch and the amazing James Tiptree, Jr. have burst on us, and there are more where *they* came from. Ours is a field of constant growth, of fresh thoughts and new dreams. Were I to edit a DV every month for the next ten years I wouldn't be able to keep up with the influx of writers.

So why, the question will be asked, are certain writers conspicuous by their absence? Why no Bester, why no de Camp, why no Heinlein, why no George P. Elliott or Wilson Tucker or Alexei Panshin? Because I've asked each of these writers at least once, and most many times, to contribute to the books, but things just didn't work out. Bob Heinlein is into

xviii   AGAIN, DANGEROUS VISIONS I

new novels and he hasn't been well. Alfred Bester is editing
Holiday. George Elliott was offered a better showcase and
more money by *Esquire* and he quite rightly took the deal.
Alex Panshin tried to please me with a story but I didn't like
it, probably because I had to read it in a restaurant in the
company of twenty shrieking sf writers and their ladies (as
well as some shrieking sf writers who were, themselves,
ladies) and I was half coherent from an oncoming flu bout
. . . but then again, maybe it just wasn't a very good story. In
any case, he didn't try me again, for which I'm sorry. Alex is
a fine writer.

As for Wilson Tucker, well, that's another story:

I don't know whether you've ever heard of Richard Geis,
but in the event you aren't that much into sf, he is a very talented writer who also edited a magazine called *Science Fiction Review* for many years. It was a gathering-place and
watering-hole for fans and professionals, where opinion and
information was offered in between the name-calling. Well, in
issue #32 of SFR, in August of 1969, Piers Anthony got into
a hassle with Wilson (Bob) Tucker, and the following extract
from an Anthony letter appeared:

"In reply to my urging that he publish a good new sf story
in *Again, Dangerous Visions* (so as not to let the volume go
entirely to pot by being filled with the crud of neo writers
like me), Bob Tucker says he would not have a fair chance
with Harlan Ellison . . . Since it is important to me that
Tucker be in that volume, I am forced to rear back on my
hind limbs and tackle the bull by the balls:

"Harlan Ellison—are you there? I challenge you, by the
authority vested in me as one of the youngest and turkiest of
the young turks, to publish the excellent sf story Bob Tucker
offers you for *Again, Dangerous Visions*, to pay him at least
3¢ per word against hard and paper royalties, and not to
tamper with one single word in it. (You may say what you
please in your introduction, however.) Kindly signify your
abject acceptance of these rigorous terms by so stating publicly in this fanzine.

"OK, Bob, you're on your own now. Submit your story. (I
always like to give the tired old timers a helping hand in
coping with today's more demanding market.)"

Well, Piers did it again.

Foot in mouth, he did a no-no.

Understand, I have nothing but respect for most of what
Piers has written these last five years, but if he thinks that
kind of challenge really incites either Tucker or me, he's
wrong. I'd been in contact with Tucker long before Piers set

his teeth on edge. In fact, Bob had submitted an excellent short novel for my consideration. After reading and enjoying it, however, I reluctantly came to the conclusion it was not right for this book.

Again understand, it was a *good* book. It just wasn't off-beat enough for *this* particular madhouse. It could have been published by any mainstream publisher (unlike Piers's story or Lupoff's or Nelson's or Vonnegut's) and so I *very* reluctantly returned it to Tucker. Since then, Bob has written and seen published to wide acclaim, *The Year of the Quiet Sun*, a novel that should have satisfied Piers as to Tucker's continued strength as a writer.

But you see, that's an example of the kind of challenge the DV books have come to represent, and it explains with one instance why some writers are not present here.

Randy Garrett isn't here because, though he called one frantic November night and tried to hype me into sending him an advance against a story he *would* write, he never submitted a manuscript.

Barry Weissman isn't here because his submission, a short story about a snot vampire was too vomitous even for *me*! You want to know what taboo turns me right around: snot vampires. *Now* pillory the editor for a closed mind.

Alfred Bester isn't here because he hasn't been writing fiction, and Arthur C. Clarke isn't here because he made this movie with Kubrick and he's just now getting back into fiction, and Algis Budrys isn't here because ... well, that's another story. But forty-two marvelous writers *are* here, and maybe another fifty will appear in *The Last Dangerous Visions* and perhaps even a few of the men and women I've mentioned here will pull free and submit something before TLDV closes.

But one shot is all anyone gets. The DV writers aren't represented a second time here in A,DV because they had their chance, and most of them took it. With all the gunslinging newcomers coming at us, we have very little time to wait for others to get a second-wind. And besides, some of those stories they've written for the DV books can win awards when they show up in *Orbit* or *Quark* or *New Worlds* or *Infinity* or the other all-original antholgies that have proliferated since publishers saw how well DV did. (At this point we pause to let the generosity of my nature saturate the air. No, thank you, a shpritz of Glade will *not* be necessary.)

It occurs to me at this point in the general introduction that a word or three might be proffered about my introduc-

tions. Opinion is split. Critics who review the book, and fans
who read it, seem divided neatly into two camps: those who
dote on the introductions and feel they offer amusing and in-
sightful asides on the writers and their work; and those who
flat-out despise the supplementary material that surrounds the
fiction. The former view is typified by readers like Sherry
Colston of Hannibal, Ohio who wrote, "I relished the candid
verbosity in your *Dangerous Visions* prefaces. If you can't do
anything else, you can communicate." The latter position is
defined by comments like those of Mr. Edmund Cooper, a
writer of considerable talent himself, who said (in the London *Sunday Times* of 2 May 71, reviewing the English edition of DV, containing the first half of the American edition,
the second part to come later in the year): "*Dangerous
Visions* does not seem to contain any dangerous visions. It
does contain one foreword, two introductions, and sixteen
stories, each with an introduction and afterword." Mr. Cooper
didn't think much of the book, but in as brief a review as he
gave it, to dote on the supplementary material strikes me as
putting him in the latter group of introduction-assayers.

As a well-known chowderhead has said, let me make one
thing perfectly clear. People who don't care for the introductions should skip over them. It's that simple, really. They
come free. There are over a quarter of a million words of
fiction in this book, each word paid for and consequently reflected in the price you pay for the total volume. The intro-
ductory stuff is written by me, and I write it free of charge. I
sit here for endless days and hammer out lead-ins to the stories that include as complete biographical and bibliographical
information as the writers have provided me, and I spice it
up with personal reminiscence and observations about the authors. Putting aside the purely factual information, there's
maybe another forty thousand words of absolutely free wordage, provided for your possible amusement and edification. If
introductions—and notably *my* introductions—bug you . . .
turn to the stories. I don't like *Bonanza* much, but unlike the
people who drove *The Smothers Brothers Comedy Hour* off
the air because it tinkered with their ideas of what other
folks should view, I simply twiddle the dial and get another
program.

Because of the mixed reactions to the introductions, I had
serious thoughts about simply presenting the stories without
any attendant gimcrackery. But it occurred to me that that
was censoring the pleasures of one group to satisfy the prejudices of another, and frankly, that idea stinks on ice. So in
advance, to those fan critics and newspaperfolk who'll be get-

ting this book for review (and most of you get the *entire* tome for free, so who the hell gave *you* the right to bitch?) may I suggest you worry about evaluating the fiction and leave the curlicues and gingerbread to those who care about such things? I mayn't? Well ...

And for those of you who are curious as to why I spend all this time *doing* the introductions, when I only get banged on the head for my trouble, understand this: I *enjoy* writing about my friends, about the writers of sf, about the real and very fallible human beings behind those flawless fictions. And as long as I'm going in debt, spending years cobbling up this monster, I'm damned well going to enjoy myself while I'm about it.

There is much to be said for making oneself as happy as possible. Even if it means making Edmund Cooper miserable.

Let's see, what else is there to talk about? I guess I should do some lofty number about how sf has come of age and how Kurt Vonnegut is on the cover of *Saturday Review* and how some of us are even asked to lecture at institutions of higher education, and all the textbooks now featuring sf stories along with Thomas Hardy and George Eliot, and all that jive, but frankly it's a drag; this is a book of good stories (I think), and you were all called here this evening to enjoy them. So I'll skip all the proofs that speculative fiction is hotter than sliced bread, and make just a few comments about TLDV, and we can all pass on through to the KEYNOTE ENTRY by Mr. Heidenry and the stories that follow him.

The Last Dangerous Visions will be published, God willing, approximately six months after this book. It was never really intended as a third volume. What happened was that when A,DV hit half a million words and seemed not to be within containment, Ashmead and I decided rather than making A,DV a boxed set of two books that would cost a small fortune, we'd split the already-purchased wordage down the middle and bring out a final volume six months after this one.

In that book will be such authors as Clifford Simak, Wyman Guin, Doris Pitkin Buck, Graham Hall, Chan Davis, Mack Reynolds, Avram Davidson, Ron Goulart, Fred Saberhagen, Charles Platt, Anne McCaffrey, John Jakes, Michael Moorcock, Howard Fast, James Gunn, Frank Herbert, Thomas Scortia, Robert Sheckley, Gordon Dickson and a gaggle of others. I'm waiting on stories from Daniel Keyes and a new kid named James Sutherland and Laurence Yep and a few more, but this is only a partial taste. There will be novels by Richard Wilson and John Christopher (yeah, that's right, full novels) and short stories by Bertram Chandler and Franklin Fisher, and really fine work by newcomers like Vonda McIntyre and Octavia Estelle Butler and George Alec Effinger and Steve Herbst and Russell Bates and . . .

I grow excited. Let me compose myself.

The four and more years since DV hit have been electric ones for our little field of literary endeavor. Previously, anthologies tended to contain almost exclusively the work of "recognized names" in the genre. Damon Knight's *Orbit* series and Chip Delany's *Quark* series and the others, and DV, made it obvious that names are no longer the important commodity we have to sell. The newer writers, the ones who grew up on sf since the Forties, these are the ones who are taking our carefully-nurtured ideas and turning them inside out to show us visions of tomorrows we never dreamed ourselves.

We're constantly being assaulted by these new dreamers, and if nothing else is accomplished by the DV books, it will be satisfying to me merely to know that by the time all three volumes are racked on your shelf—pushing off everything else there with size if not quality—we'll have given half a hundred young turks their turn.

Hopefully, somewhere in this book there are more Hugo and Nebula winners, but that isn't the important dream. The important one is that herein contained are names you may never have heard before, of men and women who will dazzle and delight you, not merely for the time it takes to read this book (or as *Liberty* magazine would have put it in 1937: reading time, 2 years—6 months—2 weeks—11 days—19 hours—45 minutes—13 seconds) but for all the years to come in which speculative fiction will figure more and more prominently as a fiction for our times.

In case you hadn't noticed, there are ugly and evil things happening all around us, and while I'm not wimp enough to think the answer lies solely with everyone under-30, I believe very firmly that our best hope lies with the *young in imagination*, and they are the ones for whom and to whom sf speaks most clearly.

For them, for the new dreamers, this book is sent on its way with enormous amounts of love by the writers, artists, designers, editors and ancillary folk who made it all happen, and with great weariness by its editor,

HARLAN ELLISON

Sherman Oaks, California
6 May 1971

Once again, the Editor wishes to express his gratitude to, and acknowledge the assistance of, the many writers, editors, agents and aficionados of speculative fiction and *Dangerous Visions,* whose contributions of time, money, suggestions and empathy, and whose response to the original project (necessitating a companion volume), made this book possible:

Mr. Lawrence P. Ashmead
Ms. Judith Glushanok
Ms. Julia Coopersmith
Ms. Diane Cleaver
Mr. Ed Bryant
Mr. George P. Elliott
Mr. Ed Emshwiller
Ms. Louise Farr
Ms. Janet Freer
Ms. Virginia Kidd
Mr. Damon Knight
Professor Willis E. McNelly
Mr. Robert P. Mills
Mr. Ted Chichak
Mr. Richard Posner
Mr. Charles Platt
Mr. Michael Moorcock
Ms. Barbara Silverberg
Mr. Robert Silverberg
Mr. Norman Spinrad
Mr. James Sutherland
Ms. Michele Tempesta
Ms. Helen Wells
Mr. Ted White
Ms. Kate Wilhelm
Dr. Robin Scott Wilson

As with all projects of this size and scope, stretching over five years, the aid and kindness of many people blurs together at the rushed last moments as one roseate glow of encouragement. Thomas Disch and David Gerrold and Harry Harrison recommended writers; Lester del Rey and JudyLynn Benjamin del Rey of *Galaxy* offered invaluable suggestions and encouragement; only Don Congdon gave me a hard time. If I've overlooked giving any their due, chalk it up to exhaustion and encroaching senility.

HARLAN ELLISON

Sherman Oaks, California
11 November 71

AGAIN, DANGEROUS VISIONS 1

Introduction to

THE COUNTERPOINT OF VIEW:

Introducing a "keynote entry" is the sheerest Newcastle-coaling. By its very nature, the piece is intended to set the tone and mood for what is to follow. And yet, symmetry is much to be desired; a certain reliability of order; and why should John Heidenry get jobbed out of a few words of introduction just because he wrote a surreal set-piece that somewhichway cornerstones the intent and attitude of the book? Surely we can't begrudge him such a miniscule pleasure; his due, in fact.

Heidenry came to me late in the assemblage of this book via Larry Ashmead of Doubleday.

The chain of goodword put in for Heidenry illustrates the incestuous nature of the New York publishing daisy-chain. Mr. Heidenry was Managing Editor of Herder and Herder in New York, publishers of weighty tomes on theology and philosophy. He writes various stuff on the side. Not the least stuff are three novels he describes as "a lovely dream-flecked pastoral romance, another (for practice) on the black days of fear and trembling, and a third on which I am still receiving mystical revelations." In some arcane manner beyond explication, Mr. Heidenry came to the attention of Miss Elizabeth Bartelme at Doubleday; and though Heidenry had no contract for the books—he says he doesn't want to submit outlines or sample chapters, the fool—Miss Bartelme took an interest in his work and mentioned him to Ashmead. So Ashmead looked at some of it and wrote to me, suggesting Heidenry might be a good bet. So when Mr. Heidenry sent me "The Counterpoint of View" I knew who he was. I was enthused about the piece, and wanted to include it, but the money had run out.

So I let Larry know the sad state of affairs, and he suggested the cost of buying the story might be equivalent to a good meal bought by him, as my editor, for me, as his author, at one of the posher watering-holes in Manhattan. So he put Heidenry on the expense account as a lunch date with me, and sent me his personal check, and now I've spilled it

1

all and Nelson Doubleday will fire Larry, which serves him right for pushing me on deadlines.

But that's how Heidenry came to lead off this book.

"The Counterpoint of View" is his first actual *story*, though he tells me he has always considered himself a writer, in the manner of Andre Gide who expected others to know from a mere glance at his eyes that he was an artist. (He is allegedly working on a second short story, however, working-titled, "Yaw, Dizzy," which, to use a sort of metaphor, is about "the time Arthur Rimbaud used to play right field for the old St. Louis Browns.")

Though I have not pressed Heidenry on this last—discretion being next to cleanliness, which as we all know lives next door to godliness, thereby depreciating the land values in the neighborhood—I feel it incumbent on me to urge all readers who enjoy what follows to petition Doubleday to give him a contract or two, and some cash, without his having to submit some sample sides of beef.

Speaking of beef, here are John Heidenry's particulars: born in St. Louis, Missouri, on May 15, 1939; mediocre education; started reading books in nineteenth year; decided to study theology, and majored in same at St. Louis University; swears he never intended to be a priest (man who'd screw around with God like that can't be believed nohow); completed studies but declined degree; mediocre education; 1960-61, super-simultaneous editor of *Social Justice Review*, *Catholic Women's Journal* and *The Call to Catholic Youth*, three monthlies with a combined circulation of 3000; 1961, a charming change-of-pace, a breakdown and some time spent in New Orleans (having spent some time in New Orleans myself, on tour with Three Dog Night, I can assure you it is a fine and juicy town in which to recover from a breakdown while acquiring an altogether different and more debilitating breakdown); 1962-63, super-writer for *St. Louis Review;* wrote practically everything but the editorials (Heidenry assures me it is a generally good paper . . . except for the editorial page); 1971, finished a novel titled *Dearly Beloved,* became unemployed, and began accepting alms; married and father of three children, thereby helping to insure not only his status as a solid Catholic, but an expansion of the circulation of *The Call to Catholic Youth*.

The final entry necessary here to flesh out Heidenry for you is an excerpt from a marvelous Nabokovian analysis he wrote for *The Commonweal* in May of 1969. Titled "Vladimir in Dreamland," section one reads as follows:

Vla-di-mir: the tip of the tongue taking a trip down the palate to stop, at three, on the teeth: Vla. De. Mirror. You can always count on a Nabonut for a fancy prose style.

And quite apart from the utter fecundity of the keynote item you are about to read, so you shouldn't think this editor is merely trying to maintain the nepotism of the New York editorial ingroup, the editors of *The Commonweal*—light-years above and beyond the reach of corruption, as we all know—identified John in a one-line *précis*, as follows: "John Heidenry is at work on a famous novel."

More distinguished a keynote speaker we could not have found had we engaged the Pope himself.

● **KEYNOTE ENTRY:**

John Heidenry

THE COUNTERPOINT OF VIEW

Enacraos, one of the scholars of Tlön, the most heretical—and wisest—hermeneutist of his time, discovered, perhaps accidentally, during his research into obscure Massoretic palimpsests relating to the *qabbalah* and its apocrypha, that William Shakespeare was indeed among the company of translators assigned by James I of England in the early 1600's to work out a new version of the Scriptures, so that "it may speake like it selfe." He enlisted as one of his five proofs the translation of Psalm 46, where undeniably Shakespeare had signatured his composition with the forty-sixth words counting from both beginning and end. (A sixth proof has since been offered by an anonymous Tlönian computer: that the chance of those two words, *shake* and *spear,* falling into their respective positions by haphazard versification was 4,600,-000,000 to 1. That larger number, the computer reasoned, did not even exist in Shakespeare's day.)

At the same time that Shakespeare was introducing[1] cryptography into English letters (having earlier practiced with fictional fiction in *The Comedy of Errors* and other plays), in Spain, land of dark and dangerous experiments, Miguel Saavedra de Cervantes had already begun to allude to characters who had read the actual book of which they were a part, and knew its author. This involution into artifice reached its culmination in recent years with Pierre Menard's heroic attempt—without reading into the life of Cervantes or the history of Spanish culture—to recreate the poetical experience of Cervantes himself: to produce a few pages of manuscript which would coincide, word for word and line for line, with the *Quixote.* Menard's superior text was the first example of art successfully imitating, and finally transcending, mere art.

During its complex and imperspicuous development into *genre* there were times (as Enacraos has shown) when fantastic writing was the idiosyncrasy of philosophy, and lost to art: most ingenuiously in the lucid speculations of the neo-Platonic divine, George Berkeley, who attained such mastery that of his subtleties Hume could say, "They admit of no answer and produce no conviction."[2] Intermittently too there were hiatus and regression: the ornate skill cheapened into gaudy technique, the clear optic exchanged for (as in Lewis Carroll) the looking glass and jabberwocky. Yet in the brave and finally pitiful person of Edgar Allen Poe—in his essay on cipher writing and in his grotesque, enigmatical tales—the true awful possibilities of illusory truth were, if scantly established, asserted nonetheless for evermore. Poe, at last no longer able to persevere in his investigations, turned finally to the saner unrealities of laudanum and alcohol;—dying, at five o'clock in the morning of October 7, 1849, with the cry, "God help my poor soul!"

Other practitioners of this subterfuge or art are, of course, Shams Joist, the newclear punman, who split the syllable of reality; Vladimir Nabokov, assembler of Zembla and dissembler of deceit; and Jorge Luis Borges himself.

Enacraos, in an appendix to his edition of *The Targum of Onkelos and Its Massoretic Revision,* both anticipated and defined the direction of literary art in his enumeration of the one hundred and three primary types of ambiguity, and in his formulation of the "trifold principle of moving viewpoint," the first and last parts of which read, "Everything that is what it seems is what it seems it is not that is not." By not punctuating his dictum, Enacraos was able to give it both many truths and many lies. Jorge Luis Borges, reflecting on the feat of Menard, saw a further logical insinuation of fantastic writing. Menard's achievement, he has suggested, prompts us to read, for instance, the *Odyssey* as though it were posterior to the *Aeneid;* the *Imitatio Christi* as though it were the work of Louis Ferdinand Celine or James Joyce. Yet a more frightening possibility—revealed now to the world for the first time, plagiarized from secret Tlönian analysis which even that land's most liberal censors would not allow to be published—is that the reader of language becomes its writer, and the writer the reader.

Let us take as our example the nearest piece of writing at hand—this fiction. Supposedly, in the ordinary space-time continuum, I am its writer and you the reader. But in the Enacraotic scheme of things, things are not only what they scheme to be, but are, or can be (among other things), precisely the opposite. Anagrammatic resolution of the opening paragraph shows thus that in the first and third sentences I have given evidence that it is not myself alone who is at work composing these words. A textual refraction of paragraph 2 clearly raises the likelihood of the reader's identity coinciding with my own; and (inexorably) the deciphered transcription of paragraphs 3, 4, 5, and 7, and the title of this tale, irrefutably verifies the premonition that I am not, in fact, its author, and that you, the reader, probably are. (I say *probably* because certain details of the solution point also to a contradictory and utterly fantastic alternative. I have come to my conclusion, however, proceeding upon the basis of Sherlock Holmes's observation that when you have excluded the impossible, whatever remains, however improbable, must be the truth.)

Thus now that I have finished "writing"—inflected, punctuated, parenthesized to the counterpoint of having neither identity nor purpose nor even knowledge—I propose to sit back and read this story at my ease and learn just what it is that you (its true and onlie author) wish to have me know.

NOTES

[1] Chaucer's sage puzzles and palindromes are, of course, though pleasing, innocently contrived.

[2] David Hume, *An Enquiry Concerning Human Understanding*, Section XII, Part I, note. William Butler Yeats had very nearly the same insight, writing of his kinsman, "Though he [Berkeley] could not describe mystery—his age had no fitting language—his suave

glittering sentences suggest it. We feel perhaps for the first time that eternity is always at our heels or hidden from our eyes by the thickness of a door." Introduction to J. M. Hone and M. M. Rossi, *Bishop Berkeley. His Life, Writings, and Philosophy* (London, Faber & Faber Ltd, 1931), pp. xxi–xxii.

Afterword:

I have lost track of this story, but think I wrote it in 1612. There was a third footnote, excised in deference to some ambiguous rules of style, or stylish rules of ambiguity, which inquired into Ben Jonson's perhaps patriotic, but certainly treacherous reasons for denigrating Shakespeare's immense knowledge of Latin and Greek—or of any language for that matter.

Alternate titles for this little tale are *The Counterview of Counterpoint* and *The Viewpoint of View*. These at any rate are the only ones that I have been told about.

Further information on this story, or on Joseph Conrad, or preferably on the lost land of Raintree County, may be gotten by writing to my father in care of the Imperial Bar, 10th and Pine Streets, St. Louis, Missouri; or by visiting him personally on Wednesday mornings from ten o'clock till noon.

Introduction to

CHING WITCH!:

In the ghastly, seemingly endless and (quite obviously to me) artificial brouhaha about "old wave science fiction" vs. "new wave speculative fiction," the majority of those putting in their unnecessary comments have overlooked one salient and saddening fact. By creating a paper tiger and fleshing it with reams of copy so it *seemed* a threat, many older, long-established writers have taken into themselves feelings of inadequacy. On half a dozen occasions during the preparations for DV and A,DV when I approached men and women who had been my personal favorites when I was doing the reading necessary to catch up with the field since 1926, I was confronted with a shamefaced (again the word pops up), saddening response that "I can't write that new stuff."

Three of the most potent, formative talents in our genre in the Forties, refused even to *attempt* a story for these volumes, having convinced themselves that they were fit only to write what they'd been writing for years; that no one wanted to see them experiment; that if they *tried* some experimental writing, they'd fail miserably. No amount of cajoling or reassurance could sway them from that sad state of mind.

I conceive of it as the greatest single evil of the "new/old wave" nonsense. And I suggest to those writers that they consider now Ross Rocklynne.

Ross Rocklynne is fifty-seven years old. He was born during the First Balkan War in which Montenegro, Bulgaria, Greece and Serbia fought Turkey. He was born in the year President Francisco Madero of Mexico was murdered by Huerta and civil war broke out between Huerta's and Carranza's forces, resulting in Pancho Villa's taking over as a dictator in the north. Woodrow Wilson was President of the United States when Ross was born, the year King George of Greece was assassinated. That was 1913, just one year before Archduke Ferdinand and his wife, the Duchess of Hohenberg, were assassinated at Sarajevo. Ross contends he was conceived at the same time as Tarzan, sometime in 1912. Fifty-seven years old, friends and self-deprecating writers.

The first Rocklynne story to appear in print was "Man of Iron," a short piece in *Astounding Stories* for August of 1935. He was twenty-two at the time. I encountered Rocklynne's work late in the game, 1951, when I read with considerable awe, "Revolt of the Devil Star" in the now-defunct *Imagination: Stories of SF & Fantasy*, a story about sentient stars. It was well beyond the terms and intents of what was being written in the field. It was—Ross will excuse the phrase, I hope—very *avant-garde*. It was also exquisitely written. I rummaged through used magazine shops in Cleveland to find other Rocklynne stories and read with delight "Jackdaw," "Collision Course," "The Bottled Men," "Exile to Centauri," "Time Wants a Skeleton" and later, others in magazines whose names are merely memories to the young writers of today: *Planet Stories, Future Science Fiction, Startling Stories;* Archduke Ferdinand, Woodrow Wilson, Francisco Madero.

The latest story by Rocklynne to appear in print is the one that follows. "Ching Witch!" is as fresh and original and *now* as anything turned out by the young turks I tout so heavily in these pages.

Most men fifty-seven years old whom I encounter, spend their time telling me what a sorry state the youth of today are in, how no one has any respect for law and order, how Dr. Spock has created generations of sniveling, self-indulgent, anarchistic snots. When I met Ross Rocklynne, at last, five years ago, I thought he was in his thirties and somehow had acquired the secret of mastery over aging. He is as young and forthright and forward-looking in his view of life as the most *au courant* campus intellectual.

Is there a message in the life-style of Ross Rocklynne for the writers who said they couldn't write for A,DV because they were too old-time? Is that message clearly present for those of us who think we're with it today and forever "of our time"?

In the event the reader misses the deep respect of the editor for Rocklynne in these words, let me hasten to add it goes far beyond the fact that the editor is 5'5" and Rocklynne is 6'2"; the testament of constant growth to which Ross Rocklynne's life attests is solidly encapsulated in the story that follows, written with the talent and insight denied to many of the younger writers whom we laud regularly.

I would say more about Rocklynne, but the biographical information he sent me for this introduction is so fine, so much *of the man*, that I think no one could introduce you to the creator of "Ching Witch!" better than the creator himself.

Snotnoses of the world, I give you Ross Rocklynne the man . . . after which Ross Rocklynne the writer will speak his marvelous piece.

"In 1953 L. Sprague de Camp wrote me for information for his book SCIENCE-FICTION HANDBOOK. I stalled. At the time I was studying under a black-bearded guru, and my vows precluded discussion of the ego. Besides, I thought it ridiculous that Sprague wanted to write about me, as I had stopped writing; I wished he wouldn't. Back came another request. Egomania leaked through, and I finally wrote a weak-kneed account of myself. Sprague returned a postcard which was a fire hazard, saying I had been one of eighteen writers on whom he'd intended to devote a chapter, but my contribution had arrived far too late, so that now he could only insert my name. I suppose it's too late to apologize, but looking back, I would have appreciated being a chapter in that book. At the time, however, the world was coming to an end. Being dramatic about it (mystery herewith injected) I died for more than ten years. The black-bearded guru became white-bearded and I had achieved neither death nor rebirth. Still, Gurdjieff and Ouspensky and the eastern pantheon are the pivots of my Beliefs today; that and the Teaching of the black-bearded one who became white-bearded. But I departed with What I Knew, or Thought I Knew, and went to see what was Outside. Science fiction was.

"I was conceived when Tarzan was. (Philip José Farmer overlooked this angle.) I was no Tarzan, being red-headed and freckled and starting out kind of plump. Nonetheless, at age seven I was swinging through the trees over the old canal which ran through Cincinnati and saw a canal boat being pulled by mules. This could make a person historical. I was the almost typical barefoot boy roaming a vast yard composed of woods, meadows, dairy, canal, and lands beyond.

"At home, my father, a machinist, entered an occasional story contest. He also invented; and worked at the problem of perpetual motion. One invention, which was not developed or patented by him, was the hydroplane, which he thought might lift ships out of the water to escape World War I torpedoes. Another device was the half-gear, which though it revolved in one direction, caused a back-and-forth motion in the mechanism to which it was attached; I saw this one at work in a General Motors exhibit in New York City in 1939.

"Later my father and I developed two inventions and sold

the rights to *Popular Mechanics* for $3.00 apiece: the funnel-shaped keyhole, and the upside-down pocket.

"My mother was a hard-working and conscientious woman who in the evenings played the piano, or the mandolin in duet with my father on the guitar. Holidays such as Christmas and Easter always had all the trimmings of candle-lighted trees and eggs, and always gifts. Today, she maintains the early traditions. When crossword puzzles came in, she worked the first one; still does them. This interest in words therefore cuts across three or four generations, for my two sons have no trouble beating almost anybody at Scrabble.

"At age twelve, the product-sob-of-a-broken-home, I was placed into a boys' school called the Kappa Sigma Pi where I stayed five years. A Tarzan-like friend threw me about in an effort to develop my skinny self. He also introduced me to the Edgar Rice Burroughs books, which became a fixation. At night in bed we threw feathered darts at each other across the room until one lodged in my chest. We also crawled and leaped at night on the steep outside of the old building, an art which was called 'ramification.'

"In that same school I inherited a subscription to *Amazing Stories*. The covers were by Frank R. Paul, who, unknown to our present culture, invented color and knee-pants. I entered, at this age level, a manuscript in the new *Science Wonder Stories* cover contest.

"New York City, 1939. First World Science Fiction Convention. There are fans here who will become big names. People here I will know right up to the present, and others I will meet again for the first time in thirty years at the Baycon in '68. Now comes 1940 and the Chicon. Charles R. Tanner, Dale Tarr and I, who did not then realize we were one of the early fan groups ('The Hell Pavers'), made the Chicago scene. And then, for me, marriage. California. War work. There were interims of writing, these interims being productive in other fields beside science fiction.

"But an old nervous ailment began recharging its batteries. There were two sons. Four years work in story analysis at Warner Bros. Then divorce. I worked for a literary agency. My brain grew peach fuzz. A variety of work was to follow, selling and repairing sewing machines, driving and dispatching for a taxi outfit, operating machines in a machine shop, salesman in an art shop, a brief stint lumbering.

"Suddenly: 1950, and dear old Ron cleared the way for all of us in *Astounding*, and I was well into dianetics. From there it was only a step or two to the black-bearded guru who became white-bearded. Suddenly, again: it was 1964, and I was walking *free* in Westlake Park. By mid-1967 I started, slowly, to write again. It came about like this, a brilliant thought, 'I betcha I could write a story and have it published. I *betcha!*'

"Writing is still slow. The story I like in the morning is hateful at night. The see-saw is time-consuming, and often I think I had better look for some other kind of fun, except that I've already been on the merry-go-round. So I don't know. I should mention one writing project having to do with my study of the somesthetic senses (using myself as the authentic and self-authorized laboratory). The somesthetic senses tell us about what goes on inside our bodies, and are pressure, pain, and warmth or cold. Our old ideas on the meaning of pain, for instance, will be reversed in this here now book I'm thinking about. It will be shown that the pain and the injury, or the pain and the illness, are opposite things. The pain is investigative and coordinating, not only a 'warning.' As such it could be used on purpose to reverse some changes in morphology. This set of ideas would be presented as a tool some people might find useful. I ride the see-saw on this one, too."

Ellison again. There is an old Chinese curse that wishes on the recipient that he "live in interesting times." In these days and nights during which we find ourselves (as Rod McKuen would phrase it, God help us) "trapped in the angry," we live in the most interesting times of all. Wilson and Sarajevo seem, and are, far behind us in what was, even as hostile as it might have been, a much quieter time. We tend to accept as truth the proposition that if we aren't deeply committed to change and action, we have no soul.

Ross Rocklynne grew up in that quieter time and has, by his own words, paid his dues. But he is not a shouter or an antagonist or even a jingoistic radical. He is merely, and with substantial glory, a fine writer who has come through all the years of his life with his talent intact, as now he unarguably proves.

Ross Rocklynne

CHING WITCH!

The tintinabula was very ching that night, just before old Earth blew.

The dance appropriately enough was the ching-maya.

Captain Ratch Chug pin-wheeled, somewhere up there in the misty blue-green of the dance-globe. He threw his hip up in the crawfish modification of the dance which he himself had invented just last week in Rangoon, right in the middle of the war. To his own distaste, he heard his purr-engine wind up when the bundle of groomed pink flesh hanging onto his fingertips glowed her delight.

"You are ching," she squealed rather noisily into his pointy ear, "ching," but this was merely part of the dance and may not have been admiration at all. There is no question but that the slitted glitter of his eyes was a fascination to her, though, no less than the fabulous whiskery waxed mustache he wore in defiance of all the customs. "How ching," she hooted dreamily, free-falling against him from five feet up at the convulsive reechoing conclusion of the tintinabular construction. She would give him thirty seconds of her life lying here, and during this time he could say pretty much what he pleased.

"How's 'bout going off this planet with me?" was what Chug said, the air around him warbling and humming the last notes of that ching wappo.

"How far off this planet with you?" she pouted, calculating, using the final echoes of uranium-borrowed music to ride the question in. "Just how far would you say, old man of space? How far?" That was ten seconds right there!

"Ten light years, no less."

Chug was startled. Something had started screaming at him, inside him.

"To Zephyrus!" he cried.

Then he caught himself. He crooned, enticing, "Voyage with me to the god of the south!"

His runty thick brown fingers, curved of claw, tightened around her naked pink shoulders so that her eyes smiled and her pouty sweet lips writhed.

"What's the tear drops for, man of space? What are they, tears for me, 'cause you know I ain't going with you? You got the face of a crazy. This dance is over. You used your thirty. I go find another man."

"You ain't got time to find another man," he moaned, letting the tears squeeze out. "They pulled *that lever*! The war's gonna be over! Earth's gonna blow! I'm getting off!

"You got to go with me, young pink thing. I ain't no human, you know, one-fifth of me ain't, and there ain't nobody like me on Earth, and that's the reason I *know*! Coming with me? How's about it, you gonna keep that pink skin? You won't regret it. I'm nice, you'll like me, and there ain't no time for me to find another squud. Give up!"

But no approach would work. She slid away still pink, and he watched her float in the reduced field toward a group of watching couples, who smiled at what seemed a familiar scene. Chug pulled his shiny black and green 2nd Repellor Corps uniform jacket down around his trim hips, and kicked himself smartly by habit toward the floating bar.

Lights glinted in racing rippling patterns off glasses and goblets as the bar whirled around him in an improvised dance-step which enticed the numb Captain Ratch Chug into an allemande left. He stopped that, and ordered two drinks. The tomatoed bartender paid him, but Chug left the cards hanging, and drank fast. Then he began to cry in earnest, his thin pocked brown face worked, and his teeth began chattering; and his nose twitched as the ends of his whiskery mustache vibrated. He left the great room, and went toward the spaceport about three miles up.

"I'm gonna be dancing and watching Earth in the mirror when she blows," vowed Chug, staring at his swollen eyes and vexed lips. "When the first alphas and gammas hit, I'm gonna be doing a Hopi rain jig. Or the Lambeth Walk.

Maybe the Bunny Hop! That's what I think of you, ol' Earth. So give me another drink."

He had reduced his speed to just below a light. His fast track from Earth was a dotted line as the ship sewed itself in and out of space. Earthlight soon would catch up with him. He drank the drinks the tomatoed equipment dutifully prepared. Wowie, he thought, dreaming. That ching-maya was a wappo! But how about the Irish Lilt? Particularly when you got a tomato knows how to manufacture good Irish whipskey—let's try again, ol' man of space, Irich whiskey. About that time, he saw old Earth blow. Captain Ratch Chug, late of the late 2nd Repellor Corps, saw it blow in the pick-up mirror. He cried horribly, in spite of the fact he didn't give a damn. Also, he didn't dance. And he told the tomato to quit making those stupid drinks. And he turned off the mirror, thinking of the young pink thing.

She wasn't very pink.

Her fault.

Captain Ratch Chug made a correction in his flight to Zephyrus, setting his effective speed at one and one-half times the speed of light, this being commensurate with his fuel supply.

Chug would arrive on Zephyrus how many years before the wave-front of fractured light arrived from Earth? Interesting question.

Just before he went into his long sleep, Chug lay weeping alcoholically on his pallet. Suddenly he shouted at the winding tubes of freezing gel advancing toward him, "What the hell! There's other planets, and other women to play with! And that's what I'm gonna be doing a good long time before I break the news to them Zephrans. I tell you, this is a sad business. I feel like hell!"

Zephyrus was named after the gentle and lovable god of the south wind, because it was the only human-populated planet south of the ecliptic plane.

Earth was on the outs with Zephyrus—had been for one hundred and three years. No Earth ship climbing the thready beams of space had pulled itself to Zephyrus in all that time. Furthermore, Earth had disrupted its communicator systems, making it a radio-hole in the sky so far as Zephyrus was concerned, and had departed with all its high-speed ships and the secrets of manufacturing same. Zephyrus was isolated!

Why was this? Simple. Make up all the fancy political and socio-economic reasons you want to, it all boils down to the prime fact that Earth people, every man, woman, and child of them, were mean, sneaky, commercial, undernourished and puny, and pleasure-loving. Not fun-loving—pleasure-loving. The Zephrans were noble, generous, tall, godly, and worshipful of the Mother Planet. Naturally they were an affront to the worthless, degraded Earthlings, so the Earthlings snubbed them out of practical existence. This was not a kind thing to do, but that was old Earth for you.

The sight of an Earth ship coming to the Zephran skies woke up the whole planet. It was as if every person on that planet bloomed, turning his petals toward the vast surprise. Not that they were flower-people, don't get me wrong; they were as human as you or I—or as human as we used to be; (but that's another story.)

"Hail Zephrans," said Chug weakly as the last remnants of the preserving gel slid away. "I bring you greetings from the home planet. As the solely constituted representative of Earth—" But he hadn't meant to say that. He was still drunk, his alcoholic state having been preserved intact by the process. He arose staggering.

A pleasant voice now said: "We hear you, Earthman. We'll get your ship docked in—oh, say an hour; so why not lie down again and sleep it off?"

"What?"

Chug felt his back arching.

He felt curling sensations in his fingernails.

"Look," he said. "Whoever you—"

"You're drunk, son," interrupted the pleasant voice. "But that's all right. That's just between you and me. And we aren't going to tell anybody, are we? Of course not, old chap, old buddy."

"Whyn't you talk *English!*" Chug spat. "You got a hell of a accent." He weaved under the bright lights in his cabin filled with a ghastly surprise. First, there was that arching of his spine, and the feeling of claws on the ends of his fingers. He'd overcome that! He had, had! But now it was back, the first time somebody caught him at a disadvantage. Second, here was this supposedly worshipful Zephran, who wasn't worshipful at all, but was blowing a distinct north wind.

"You ain't no Zephran!"

"But also I ain't no Earthling," the other said. "Please listen, my dear man. I'm entrusted with the task of bringing your ship in. It is not my purpose to spoil your little game."

"WHAT GAME? What the hell game you talking about?" There it was again—and Chug almost wept—the feeling of long eye-teeth, of lips drawn back; damn damn damn.

"Oh my." The other sighed and rolled his eyes; it was a gesture that had to be there. "Look, son. Do it *my* way. Get yourself sobered up and cleaned up. Look smart! Back straight! Shoes shined! Hup!"

"Oh-h-h-h-h," groaned Chug, sagging to a seat droop-shouldered.

"Be not alarmed, dear boy. Zephran society is eagerly awaiting you. My, what a treasure you will be to the worshipful elders and teeming teenagers of Zephyrus who even now are assembling to welcome you!

"One hour."

The blankness following this gave ample indication that communication had been cut off.

One hundred top-ranking Zephrans variously stood or sat in the great auditorium of the floating winged palace of the mayor of the city of Matchley. Chug, having been transported in style from his ship on, naturally, a winged green horse, stood facing them. Thin television screens, also equipped with wings, dipped and dived by the hundreds through the air and each screen was packed with intent teenage faces.

Captain Ratch Chug, late of the 2nd Repellor Corps, was a triumph! He looked splendid. Where else in the universe could you find anybody wearing a uniform these days, and particularly a uniform edged and pinked in gold and red, and with moppish epaulets that as they swung seemed to beat out a martial air? Nowhere but on someone from Earth, because that was the only place anybody had wars.

Chug was striking a pose. Something was humming away inside him, the product of a vast, anticipatory content. He stood gracefully with one polished boot stiffly ahead of the other one. He twirled and twirled his dandy whiskery waxed mustache. His eyes glittered and appraised and swept the murmuring crowds of notables, as well as the clouds of bewinged thin television screens bursting with the excited faces of worshiping Zephran teenagers. He felt fine for now, having overcome for the moment his terrible grief over the blow-up of Mother Earth, and he was determined to bask in the glowing worship these Zephrans radiated.

He already had been asked some questions, all about Earth.

"Wars? wars? Nope, ain't no more wars on Earth," Chug answered truthfully.

"This is splendid," he was told.

(Everybody on the planet was listening to this conversation, except that it was the gort season, and therefore a hundred

thousand Zephrans were out hunting gorts. These gorts—
however, that is not a part of this story.)

"What can you tell us in general terms about the possible
future relations of Earth and Zephyrus?"

"The relations will be the very best," Chug assured them.
Ya damn betcha: No Earth.

"Is it perhaps true that you, acting for Earth, will return
to us the secret of faster-than-light ships?"

A question to flutter the heart. Avowed Chug, crossing a
finger, "I aim to give it to ya!"

"Is it perhaps true that our ships will then be allowed in
Earth's skies?"

"Better not make it for a couple Zephran years!" Chug
said, hastily computing. "And approach kinda slow in case
there's some kind of—er—flare-up!"

"Then our age-old offense against the Mother World has
been forgiven?"

"Ain't nobody holding a thing against ya!"

His questioner, an elderly and most handsome man who
was in the position of mayor of the welcoming city of
Matchley, said apologetically, "If you will speak more slowly.
The refinements of the mother tongue have been lost to us."

While he talked, while he equivocated, the contented purring in Chug stopped. In fact, his purr-engine had been running down for some time. Because there was someone in this
room who made his fur—*what the hell!* who made his skin
crawl. He knew who it was: the non-Zephran who had
brought his ship in and who had made unkind remarks that
no Zephran would make to a worshiped Earthling. Where
was he, who was he?

In that crowd of worshiping faces, Chug had no idea.

If he could just find somebody who wasn't worshiping him.

Just then a small warm hand slipped into Chug's hand.
Startled at first, he looked down into the peachiest face he
had ever seen; peachy and creamy and plump all the way
down to its pink toes. "Why, hul*lo!*" said Chug, showing his
delight at this intrusion by instantly clicking around facing
her, and giving her all the attention he had given the officials
crowding the room. "I am delighted!" he said for emphasis.
It never failed! Here he was, crowding forty, and a bachelor,
and this eighteen-year-old knew what he was: she *knew!*

"Hi hi," she said. "Ips!"

"Ips!" said Chug.

"Rightly. What we want to know, we, the teeming teenagers of our worshiping planet, what we want to know is, what
does it on Earth?"

"What—uh—*does* it?"

"Yah. Flickly. What's the WORD?"

"The word," said Chug. "Hah! The WORD!?? Ah." Out of his intuition, he desperately selected the answer. "Ching—that's the word!"

"Ching!" she screamed on sudden tip-toe, then clapping her hand over her mouth. "Halla-hoo! I'm sorry!" she said to the assembled officials who nonetheless watched her and listened to her with what seemed a supreme indulgence. She raised her voice again, however, and she had one of those healthy, tingly, musical female voices that could knock over fences.

"Hah, all witches," she shouted. "Ching's the WORD! That's what does it!"

The bewinged television screens flipped and sailed and a myriad thin screams sounded.

Chug realized she must be getting her message across to all the teenagers on the planet (except those who might be out hunting gorts).

"This is miraculous," she said, still snuggling her warm hand in his. "You've come all the way from Earth to give us the WORD. Already ching is the big thing. I myself am already a ching-witch, if you follow. My name is Alise."

"And my name is Humpty Dumpty."

"Break a leg," she acknowledged. "By any chance, Sir Chug, would you happen to know, uh, *just one Earth dance?*"

"Just one? I ain't no peanut-vender, girl! Watch this!" Chug's legs moved in entrechat and cabriole, his feet and knees jiggered, and his arms were all over, finally clapping his hips. "See that? Up in the air and down on the ground, all in one breath." She became very faint at this. Her eyes crossed. Chug took the opportunity to try to settle a nagging fear. He turned smartly to his host, the mayor of Matchley.

"As you can see, sir," he began, "I ain't up on the pecking order in this situation. Here are you gentlemen, and here's this very ching young lady, really a credit to the teeming teenagers of Zephyrus—"

"There is really no difficulty, here," he was assured. "Our teenagers are alert, kind, and intelligent, and outnumber us. Ips!"

"Ips," said Chug, and was fascinated by the chorus of "ips" that ran around the room. Moreover, the mayor of Matchley's feet were tapping, and his eyes were bright and glistening as if in anticipation, or some other emotion Chug failed to recognize. Chug's own feet were tingling. His fingers were feeling a little snappy. Zephyrus, what a place. "Mr. Mayor," he hummed, "you people were ching before *I* ever got here. And I'm glad of that, I'm glad of that."

"He's glad of that, he's glad of that," hummed Alise, by this time standing very close and examining his chest medals.

"And I want to thank you, yes, all of you, indeed I do, before I demonstrate, before I do, a few of the more popular dance numbers they used to have—well, that they got on Earth. But in particular I would like to thank the wappo gentleman who brought my ship to dock."

"Wappo," mused Alise warmly. "*Wappo!*" Her index finger shot up into the air.

"And I would like to thank him personal," amended Chug, tapping his foot unconsciously to some hot music suddenly coming from *somewhere!*

Chug's host nodded somewhat dubiously, and spoke to an aide; who moved a few steps to another aide, who then spoke to his aide, who disappeared through a door. A minute later another aide hurried back into the room, and spoke hurriedly to the mayor, who then began to turn very red. The elements of the small comic opera did not escape Chug.

What the hell! he thought, astonished. They ran questions around in circles. Nobody knows nothing. "Your pardon, sir," he said out loud while he felt his fingers snapping uncontrollably in his head, "it don't matter right now, not when we got to show this here young miss some of the vital folk dances of old Earth. But—"

"You see," the mayor of Matchley said, wiping his face, "nobody seems to know *who* was on the landing board at that hour. Now on a civilized planet like Earth, tomatoed equipment would have brought your craft in, but here on Zephyrus we still work—sometimes as much as an hour a day. It's possible that some records have been kept, and that the man or woman who brought you in—"

"A man!" said Chug. "A man's voice!"

"Well, perhaps not, Sir Chug, if you'll pardon me. You see, the voder is usually programmed in the masculine range—"

Chug felt giddy. Of a sudden his population of possible enemies was doubled. Somebody who was *very knowledgeable* knew things about him. How much did that person know? Maybe old Chug better give up and give them the bad news. About Earth. About there ain't no Earth, kiddies, there ain't no ching dances, there ain't no Earth left to forgive you! Then what becomes of old Chug? Old Chug—a dried-out piece of Earth dung, that's what! He almost wept at the thought.

But the way things were—ah!

He snapped his fingers and twittered his feet to the beat of the invisible music that ching-witch Alise turned on.

The way things were, he was a hot-shot and duly constituted representative of Earth's billions. Let it be.

"Let it be," he told his charmed audience who were watching his twittering feet and quite forgetting that they were notables greeting the duly constituted representative of Earth's billions. "Let it be," said Chug, becoming motionless in a slight crouch. "That's the name of the newest hot-shot dance on old Earth. You don't do *nothing!* You do all your dancing with your thinking, and your thinking moves your muscles around inside 'til you think you're gonna tear apart.

"The tintinabula is tearing the air apart meanwhile, and then we come to the last eight bars, and that's when we can let go. We're wound up like springs, and we go flying up in the air, if the anti-gravs are on, pin-wheeling and gyring and gimbaling in the wabe.

"And then there's the ching-honey-cha-cha."

"Ching-honey-cha-cha!" screamed Alise, clapping her hand to her mouth. "Halla-hoo! I'm sorry!" she said to everybody.

"The ching-honey-cha-cha goes like this," said Chug, calling it out in rhythm. "Begging your pardon, Your Honor."

"Ips, ips," protested His Honor the mayor. "We quite understand." He pressed back, creating a space.

"Come on in, young pink thing," droned Chug, snapping his fingers. "Watch my feet. You come on in now."

Alise came in. That girl knew what she was doing. She and old Chug danced for the whole planet, except for the gort-hunters. Alise came in and knew what she was doing. Those feet with the peachy pink toes had been around.

Alise was under his chin, giggling, her thready red hair scalloped in front to the unexpected shape of two devil's horns.

"Sir Chug, you got the pointiest ears!"

That was unsettling.

"Not *that* pointy," said Chug, growling. "You watch your language, miss."

"Pointy!" giggled Alise. "Like a cat!"

"I got claws, too, if you wanna know. And you're gonna get scratched!"

"I've been scratched before, mister! You got sharper claws?"

So that was the way it was gonna be.

That *was* the way it was with Sir Captain Ratch Chug and the ching-witch Alise.

Alise was a witch, besides being very ching, and you could well believe it if you had seen them nights taking off on degravitized brooms whizzing through the sky to their rendezvous with ching teenagers who wore faddy black peakéd hats and twirled sorcerers' mustachios. Sir Captain Ratch Chug, sallow and pocked of face, runty and stunted, mean and sneaky to the core, was a fair representative of the glory of old Earth. The Zephran kids in no time at all reflected this significant collision with another and superior culture by wearing smart uniforms, sporting pointy ears, and looking sallow.

"I'm gonna crash!" moaned Chug early in his Zephran career steering his broom one night over the spitting sparkling lights of Puckley, a fun-city run by teenagers. "We're gravving down too fast!"

"All the extra lives *you* got," the whizzing Alise informed him, "you don't have to worry!"

"*What!*" gasped Chug. "*Who's* got extra lives?"

"*You* have, else you wouldn't *purr afterwards*! Halla-hoo," cried the whizzing Alise to the packed teenagers on the roof below as she upended and landed with Chug safe behind her. "Hah, all witches! Tonight Sir Captain Ratch Chug of the worshiped Mother World brings us the California Schottishe! The Badger Gavotte! The Patty Cake Polka! The Chingadaidy-do! Position, varsouvienne!"

"I don't know no Badger Gavotte," snarled Chug in her peachy pink ear. "How come you know what I don't know half the time?"

"I know," said Alise, bobbing her hairy horns wisely, "I read it in a book in a place I happen to know name of Flora," as the worhsipful Zephran kids swarmed around and the 4/4 beat took over.

So that was the way it was, until hyacinthus-time.

Hyacinthus-time, however, was of the future, and Chug was by his nature very much of the present.

A lot could be said about the life of Sir Captain Ratch Chug on the planet Zephyrus. He was the sensation of the season and the season after that, and then the one after that. What he did was to sustain a pitch, and just before it broke bring in some drums; and then he wouldn't let those drums get quite off the ground until he was manufacturing new sounds. In fact, he did help some music technicians build a tintinabula (translates random atomic motion into orchestrated sound) just so he could dance the ching-maya. Those split sounds drove the Zephran kids wild.

"All is illusion," Chug told the Zephran kids. "That's what the ching-maya and the tintinabula are telling you. You don't really hear that music, you don't really do them steps. The sound is just split up to sound in your head, and what you think is motion is just repetitive creation."

"All hail Chug the guru!" cried the sometimes too-spirited Alise.

Chug lived in a palace, a floating palace, with big golden eagle wings that flapped him around the planet. Quite a sight. Of course, the flapping wings were illusion too, because anti-gravs were built into the wings and everytime they flapped they nullified gravity in certain directions so that he went where he wanted to or up or down.

He was down most of the time, sampling the wild social life of the planet. But he was up much of the time too, receiving visitors, all of whom worshiped him. He had thirty rooms to receive people in, rooms thick with the green and yellow furs of gorts on floors and walls, and with big roomy couches, and pillows of soft eider in every corner, and numerous mirrors which caught slanting beams of soft and sometimes whirling light proceeding out of mysterious alcoves set into the ceilings and walls. Here and there were pools with fountains where fish swam, and cages where canaries flew, and goldfish bowls. Truly, Chug's palace was a place to relax in. And Chug, when he wasn't out bringing Earth culture to Zephyrus, or conferring with historians, or fending off some of the delicately probing inquiries of Zephran scientists, usually could be found relaxing, his purr-engine revved up, sunk into a couch surrounded by pillows, or in bed with eyes half-closed, listening for the soundless approach of a servant announcing visitors. Ah, Chug was happy happy happy. *This* was what he had been looking for all his life.

Only sour note was that non-Zephran, whoever he-she was, who knew *all about him*.

Ugh! Better forget that.

Until Earth's wave-front of tell-tale light caught up with him and wrote across the sky for all to see:

LIAR!

And so, at last, came hyacinthus-time.

"You're such a fibber," said Alise, peachier than ever and two Zephran years (equal to one Earth year) older. "Last night you was out *prowling*—catting around, as it were; and you told me you was having a interview with the scientist fellas. That's all right."

"Well," said Chug. "Come here."

"Thank you," said Alise.

Indeed he had been out prowling and catting around but it had been with the scientist fellas themselves after an exhausting interview. They went into a whiz-bar where the worshipful Zephrans fought to buy him drinks. What with the drinks and the fact that the whiz-bar actually was whizzing through the air with fascinating changes of liquor-sloshing grav-speed Chug almost offered to take them for a ride in his faster-than-light space-ship!

He groaned to think about it.

"*Then* what happened?" asked Alise, delightfully pulling at his whiskery mustache. "What happened after you said you wouldn't?"

"Nothing happened!"

Except somebody ordered drinks from the tomato and everybody in the bar crowded around toasting Chug, the revered man from the Mother World.

"What *kind* of a drink?"

"A Blue Hyacinth."

"To Sir Captain Ratch Chug!" the worshipful Zephrans cried, hoisting the drinks high, and after that the revellers worshipfully helped Chug back to his sky-high home, and flew for a while outside his door chanting a drunken song which went, "AI! AI! AI!"

"Flickly," said Alise, "I never heard of no song like that, and I never heard of no drink like that! Tomorrow night at the Skitterly festival we'll order Blue Hyacinths and find somebody that knows AI! AI! AI!"

"No!" said Chug, stiffening. "Look, girl, I do the ordering and I do the singing. I don't want no Blue Hyacinth and I don't want no song that goes AI! AI! AI!"

"Why not?" asked Alise. "What's wrong with a Blue Hyacinthus?" she asked, mispronouncing. "What's wrong with a song goes AI! AI! AI!" she asked, crooning into his pointy ear so it sounded like a Greek lament.

Hyacinthus! Hyacinthus! Hyacinthus! Very nearly inaudible, the name beat against Chug's micro-consciousness with the chat-a-chat flutter of tiny wings.

Then he awoke one morning and things were very bad.

Hyacinthus!

He was feeling it. Something was wrong, not like before old Earth blew, but something different. Like music, old music, thinly off in the distance, calling him awake like a broken bugle. Like the old days, when the screamers were coming!

Here he was, safe, high above the city in his floating flying palace, halfway out of his lovely dreams, and something was terribly wrong.

"Hi hi, Old Hump," said Alise, sitting with a thump on his bed with its golden coverlets while he opened a slitted eye.

"You used to call me Sir Chug," said Chug. "Now you call me Old Hump. What you got there?"

"I brung you a present," said Alise, who prided herself on having learned the new *lingua* Ge which Chug brought to this planet almost three Earth years ago. "It's that bowl of gold-fish you was admiring in the shop in Stickley last weeklette when we was on that party where you taught us worshipful Zephrans the Charleston."

"The Charleston? That wasn't supposed to be for six months," he groaned out loud, sitting up. "I was drunk! I'm gonna run out of dances!"

"You know lots of dances." Alise patted her red hairy horns and turned a mirror on to view herself in. "What about the Jarabe Tapatio? That's the Mexican Hat dance."

"I know! But how do *you* know?"

"I read it in a book, up on a planet I know named Flora."

"Flora! Ain't no planet named Flora!"

"It's a kind of invisible planet which I just happen to know. Then there's the Chug Step. Kinda pushy."

He glared.

"Then," she went on, one-half an eye on him, "there's a waltz they had in a place they used to call Denmark called Little Man In A Fix."

"WHAT?"

Here was this girl, this peachy, creamy girl, this adored, lovely, once-in-a-lifetime girl, needling and prodding him. He was certain of it. She knew things about him! She was the one who brought his ship in! It couldn't be; no, no!

"How's about some square dances?" she asked brightly. "There's one called Somebody Goofed!

"How's about Birdie In A Cage?" She chanted, talking it up,

"Up and down and around and around
Allemande left and allemande aye
Ingo, Bingo, six penny high,
Big cat *little* cat
Root hog or DIE!

"Besides," she said, catching one of his astounded eyes in the mirror, "do you *have* six months?"

"Do I have six months," Chug croaked from a dry throat.

The tiny wings were the pinions of bats, flapping in the caverns of his intuition. Hyacinthus, they flapped, before he was able to close off the hideous sound.

"Whaddya mean, do I have six months?" he snarled, swinging out of bed in his silken glitter of mandarin pajamas. Then in fright he squeezed the thought back. HYACIN-THUS!!

"And whaddya mean, giving me *goldfish for a present?*" he gasped. "I'm onto you, girl. You're after me. You always have been!

"Here I am, the most respected man on the planet. I'm a goldmine of information about the Mother World. Savants have written books about me. I'm important. Big. Beloved. I've changed the cultural life of the teeming teenagers of Zephyrus. Given 'em fads, whooped 'em up, taught 'em jitter-bugging—"

She was under his chin and pressing his nose in with a curved forefinger. She cooed, "I know. You're a cool cat."

"And whaddya give me?" he raved. "Goldfish!"

"But you *like* goldfish!"

"Only to look at!"

"That's what I brung 'em for, to look at. What else do you do with 'em?"

"Eat 'em!" snarled Chug. "Like I'm gonna eat you one of these days!"

She giggled. "You *are* a cat," she said. "I knowed that when I first seen you. They took your mom and dad's chromosomes and tweezered in some cat genes, now didn't they? You come out of a laboratory, Old Hump. You come out mewing and spitting and clawing. Then they passed a law because they didn't want any more human cats.

"You're a cat, Old Hump. And that's the reason you always land on your feet!"

Old Chug was on his feet and stalking and circling and spitting and pulling frustratedly at the long hairs of his dandy, waxed, whiskery mustache.

"You're a little bit telepathic?" he inquired.

"A little bit," she admitted. "Like you! Flickly, you *know* when there's trouble ahead—like now.

"Wanna meet my father?"

"I guess I better," said Chug trailing stupidly after her through the thirty rooms of his cushion-strewn furry-rugged palace with its whispering tinkling fountains and its shiny gold canary cages where he had lived his dream of purring contentment when he had been able to stop thinking of that demon wave-front of shattered Earth's light catching up with him! Now! soon!—it would all explode out of time, like the plaint of a brook, like the juice of a leaf!

Soon Alise was lashing her horse-and-buggy across the sunny skies of Zephyrus. Every time those anti-grav hooves kicked at the air the buggy shot ahead. "Gee!" cried Alise, hanging onto the reins. "Haw!" she said, and "Haw!" again for a left U-turn, and finally, "Whoa!" The motors quieted down.

Alise's father had horns growing out of his head.

"They aren't real horns," the slim father confessed shyly, taking off his head-piece and hanging it on an air-peg where it bobbed fitfully. "My real ones were sawed off when they sent us from Flora to study the cultural life of Zephyrus."

"Flora was nowhere," said Alise helpfully, standing close to Chug and stroking his arm. "We didn't have nothing to do. *Nothing*. We come here, flickly, to bring back some dances and some fads and *wild* things. And guess what, Old Hump? We found you! Wasn't we lucky?"

Chug was sweating, gazing upon these two who gazed back upon him benignly and pleasantly and most alarmingly. He attempted to move away from Alise and her stroking hand.

"Aw," she said, her peachy pink lips drooping. Chug sat weakly down, his head throbbing. Now he was really feeling it, the terrible thing that had gone wrong with his world. "Flora," he muttered.

"Yes," said the father in his shy manner. "Flora, wife of Zephyrus, but divorced for some time, as it were. We keep our planet shielded from the Zephrans, invisible to them, one might say, to keep them from destroying us."

Chug's head came up. "Zephrans? Destroy you?"

"Oh, yes," said Alise, happily placing herself on Chug's knee and diddling her fingers under his ear. "The Zephrans would tear us apart like that if they knew we were on their planet. So we had to saw off our horns.

"Oh, yes. We grow horns. Something about the climate, I'm sure."

Chug looked askance at the beauteous head and then shuddered his glance away. "The Zephrans are noble, gentle, tall, courteous and godly. They wouldn't hurt anybody!"

Both Alise and her father laughed gently.

"Hyacinthus," said the father, removing his headpiece from the air-peg and placing it back on his head and then turning on a mirror while he fitted it. "Surely you remember the Greek god Zephyrus who was jealous of Hyacinthus and caused his death. Zephrans think of Earth as Hyacinthus."

Chug was ill. He looked past Alise into the mirror, where

he saw the horned man who suddenly looked very sinister. "You're him," cried Chug hysterically, all his accumulated fears centered on this apparition. "The one who brung me in." He leaped up as if to flee a terrible danger, but caught Alise so she wouldn't fall and stood trembling.

"Yes," said the father, nodding, and smiling inwardly as if at himself. "You'll forgive me my rudeness, but it was necessary to sharpen you up so you could put on a convincing show."

"WHAT show?" Chug cried.

"Oh," said the father, flinching. "That again."

Alise snuggled against the mandarin pajamas Chug still wore. She said dreamily, "We knew all about you, but it didn't matter. You were what we were looking for, so we tested you. Here on Zephyrus. But it's time to go now. To Flora. You'll probably grow horns. You understand, Hyacinthus?"

"Don't call me Hyacinthus!" Chug pushed her away, spitting his fury. His hair again felt as if it were standing up like fur, and again he could feel retractile muscles pulling at his fingernails. He crouched and arched his back and lashed out a paw at the smiling peachy pink girl.

"Zephrans ain't gonna kill *me!*" he said. "Zephrans worship *me!*"

"Their worship was a barrier to keep you from penetrating to their hate. You were too quick to drink the Blue Hyacinth," said the father, now seeming not quite so shy.

His finger ran sharply through the air and the mirror in which he ostensibly was admiring himself turned into a television screen.

"All over the planet the word has gone out," he said. "Hyacinthus, they are screaming, Hyacinthus!"

Chug could not believe eyes or ears. He was looking at his floating palace with its lazy golden eagle wings. It was surrounded by winged cars, and the cars were full of worshipful Zephrans.

They were not too worshipful.

"Hyacinthus!" they were screaming. Weapons in their hands were discharging projectiles and rays at the floating palace. "Hyacinthus!" the terrible screaming came. Chug's palace was coming down.

Tears were in Chug's eyes. Sympathetically Alise petted the back of his head.

"They've been hating us for a long time," she said, "but they've been hating Earth *longer!* They've been out into space, Old Hump. While you were entertaining us worshipful teenagers and making things really ching, they were stealing

the faster-than-light secret from your ship. They've seen
Earth explode at last—only about six months from here.
They know you've been fooling them. They know they don't
have to be afraid of Earth anymore.

"We're going back to Flora, Old Hump. The teeming teenagers of Flora need fads, dances, and songs and a tintinabula
or two. Everybody will love you. You can come and go as
you please. Stay out at night and yowl, as it were. Ips."

"Ips," said Chug weakly. He was drained, watching the destruction of his august mansion of the air. Then he could
watch no longer. The doom he had closed out of his mind for
so long at last was upon him. His purr-engine seemed dead,
Earth was gone, and what was left? Strangely enough, plenty
and everything. Almost as fast as old Chug reached bottom,
he started back up. Uncomplicated by worry and fear, a new
destiny beckoned.

Already he was beginning to hum again. Already, the dread
moment of betrayal from the hateful Zephrans was being
put behind him. He opened an eye, sadly, to watch the burning eagle wings.

Moreover, maybe that witch Alise at last saw in him a person of talents and importance.

He hoped.

"You'll go with us?" cried Alise, steepling her hands en-
treatingly under his nose.

"Let it be," sighed Chug blackly as his palace crashed.

"Let it be," cried Alise, whirling into an excited pirouette
and fouette, then flinging herself into old Chug's arms for an
ecstatic sashay. "You'll love your new home, Old Hump.
You'll be warm and cozy, and we'll take care of you—"

Chug preened a bit, but dour experience flashed signals.
"You mean," he inquired suspiciously, "you're gonna take me
to Flora like some blue-ribbon, prize-winning *cat?*"

"Halla-hoo!" cried Alise wide-eyed. "We wasn't thinking of
no *prize*-winning cat! What we had in mind was, more like a
house-pet!"

(So that was the way it was gonna be.)

Afterword:

Haight-Ashbury, 1966. I visited there for 10 days in November of that year, staying in a semi-hippie type apartment run
by my two sons and one other. One son worked, the other
went to school at San Francisco State, and the other boy

worked at night and tried to sleep during the day. Bodies came and went at all hours. There was a stereo. The cow-moo voice of Bob Dylan blew on the wind; and Joan Baez guitared. After the first shock, I appreciated both of them and do. There was also Mozart, Beethoven, Bach, played quiet. There was food eaten by anybody and provided by anybody. Disarray in kitchen and bedroom was the rule; suddenly someone would clean up the joint. Pot there was not (that I knew). The older son handed me a stack of Marvel comics and remarked, incredibly, that Stan Lee and what he was saying was part of the religion of the Berkeley/Haight-Ashbury scene. I was entranced with The Hulk, with Prince Namor of Atlantis, with The Fantastic Four, with Doctor Strange, the Mighty Thor, and others. I lay on the bed face close to the floor and read and glutted myself in leisure.

On the first day, a Sunday, that I was there, I walked with sons and their friends drinking beer down to the Panhandle of Golden Gate Park where a love-in was in progress. The flower children were beginning now. Girls with painted faces and bare soiled feet. Naked-to-the-waist painted men gyrating in dances to strange Eastern instruments. Paints, brushes, and frames with paper thumb-tacked on them were there for those who wanted to express themselves artistically. A rock band tore the air. Couples danced, roiled, sprawled. Older people, very cubic like me, looked on. Children ran, screamed, danced, sang, automatically knew what their thing was: anybody over ten had to think it out.

On the second day, the older son hesitantly asked if I minded riding pillion on the motorcycle. "It's the only transportation we've got." I did mind. As the motorcycle started off, me tethered behind, it made a sound which went "ratch-chug." My son explained, his voice blowin' back in the wind, "The kind of sound you can expect from our machine-oriented culture." We chugged on down Cole St., past the psychedelic shops and the little food shops and ice-cream shops run by young people with humble shoulders and Indian head-dress, young and older girls smiling hopefully that love had come to stay, not knowing that the cycle would swing as it does with all things—but that's another story.

The next day, having plenty of time, and having chased a tomcat off the back porch where it was stealing the little cat's food, I sat down with a typewriter and some paper and without too much trouble wrote ten silly pages. My older son read the pages, and jolted me with, Did I get my inspiration from the Marvel Comics? "Not that I know of," I replied. Younger son said, "You going back to writing, Dad? Maybe you should finish this one." I told him I definitely would finish it . . . someday; that was a promise.

The above indicates how the elements of the story may have fused together. The story is not supposed to have any theme, or any significance, nor does it seem to attempt to solve any social problems. I tried *not* to make it timely.

The story was finished up, and rewritten a bit for *Again, Dangerous Visions*, but it was not the story I started to write. That story dealt with a priest who scoffed at the idea of light-speed being the limiting velocity in our universe, and with God's help got to Alpha Centauri in *no time at all*. The difficulties in this theme became enormous, and I turned to the almost forgotten ten pages turned out in a lost San Francisco world. To Keith and Jeff, here 'tis.

Introduction to

THE WORD FOR WORLD
IS FOREST:

The problem isn't *what* to say about the incredible Ursula Le Guin, it's where to *start*.

Should I, he said, begin with the observation that she is without question the most elegant writer in the sf world? Perhaps. If for no other reason, then surely to expand on the proposition that on certain people in this life a gift of grace and *style* is bestowed that makes all the rest of us look like garden slugs. Being in Ursula's company for any extended period is an enriching experience, but one gets the impression that oneself and everyone else in the room are on the grace level of a paraplegic's basketball team being trained by Fred Astaire.

She is witty, strong, emphatic and empathic, wise, knowledgeable, easygoing and electric, seraphic, gracious, sanguine and sane. Without sacrificing the finest scintilla of femininity she dominates a group with her not inconsiderable strengths as an individual; it is Ursula Le Guin, as a model, I'm sure, women's liberationists are most striving to emulate. In short, she's dynamite.

She also smokes a pipe . . . in private.

She also writes one helluva stick.

Ursula won a Nebula in 1969 for her novel *The Left Hand of Darkness*. You've read it, of course, so there's no need to dwell on its level of excellence. Yet it can truly be said, no award in that category in recent years has done the Nebula more credit.

Ursula Kroeber Le Guin was born in Berkeley, California in 1929; daughter of anthropologist Alfred L. Kroeber and Theodora K. Kroeber, author of *Ishi in Two Worlds, The Inland Whale*, and several other tomes of an equally awe-inspiring nature. (Interestingly enough, I find my own listing in *Contemporary Authors*, volumes 5–8, along with Ursula's mother's listing. But no Ursula. Would someone kindly point out their oversight to them.)

Ursula grew up in Berkeley and in the Napa Valley. She received her B.A. from Radcliffe and her Masters from Columbia, in French and Italian Renaissance literature.

She met and married Charles A. Le Guin (pronounced *Luh Gwinn*) while they were both on Fulbrights in France. He is now a Professor of French History at Portland State College, Oregon; they have lived in Portland for ten years. They have three children: Elisabeth, Caroline, Theodore.

In 1968–69, Ursula and her husband went on Sabbatical to England; they returned in July of 1969, to Portland, but out of the journey came some marvelous letters, portions of which I include here as examples of purest Ursula.

Here's an example:

"You know London buses have 2 storeys with a sort of half-circular staircase, smoking allowed on the top deck—in winter, between Woodbines & Bronchitis, it's like an Advanced T.B. Ward crossed with a Sauna Bath on fire, all lurching through dark Dickensian alleys jammed with Minicars and Miniskirts—Well, you never get up the stairs before the bus plunges off again, so the conductor/tress shouts, 'Eol pridi daeneow!' or 'Eoldon toit luv!'—or, if West Indian, sings out in the picturesque native dialect (English), 'Hold on pretty tight now!' And if you don't, you've *had* it. There's no door."

Or how about this summation of the English encounter: "We were on sabbatical, except the kids, who went to the local school and got a splendid education and a Cockney accent. We lived in a drab old North London borough called Islington, long rows of high houses like dirty toffees all stuck together staring at the row of dirty toffees opposite. By the time we left, we found these streets very beautiful, and inhaled the exhaust gases of a double-decker red London bus deeply, like sea air. This was essentially a result of the kindliness of the English (including Pakistani Indian Greek Italian, etc.) among whom we lived in Islington. It was the Spirit we were breathing in. London air causes asthma in many, but it is worth it. The English are slightly more civilized than anyone else has yet been. Also England is a good country for introverts; they have a place in society for the introvert, which the United States has not. In fact there is a place in London for everything; you can find what you want there, from organized diabolical perversity *à la* Baron Charlus, to the kind of lollipops that change color as you proceed inwards. I mean it has *everything*. But the best thing, the finest thing, is the kindliness."

Kindliness is something of a central concern with Ursula Le Guin, and as soon as I tend to her bibliography here, I'll tell you of a gratuitous kindness she did me which sums up for me the wonder of Le Guin.

Apart from *The Left Hand of Darkness* and the brilliant *Playboy* story, "Nine Lives," Ursula Le Guin has written the following novels (all available in Ace paperback editions): *Rocannon's World, Planet of Exile, City of Illusions* and *A Wizard of Earthsea*. These in addition to poems in various of the "little" magazines and short stories in magazines and collections like QUARK and ORBIT. Her latest titles are *Tombs of Atuan* (Atheneum) and *The Lathe of Heaven* (Scribner's). That taken care of, let me tell you an Ursulincident that made me forever her slave.

In 1970, in Berkeley, the Science Fiction Writers of America saw fit to award both Ursula and myself Nebula awards, which I've mentioned before (not only to assert *her* gloriousness, but to balm my own ego-needs as well). One splendid evening during that Nebula weekend was spent in the company of Ursula, sf-writer Norman Spinrad, Miss Terry Champagne (authoress of the world's foremost cockroach horror sf story), the ever-popular Miss Louise Farr, and a couple that memory vaguely reminds me were Greg Benford and his lovely wife. We went to an Afghanistani restaurant where, to my again flawed memory, I did *not* cause a scene, thereby making it an historic occasion. And afterward, we went up into the Berkeley hills to the magnificent all-wood home of Ursula's mother. Seeing the latter, it is easy to understand where the former obtained her elegance and style. It was one of the most pleasant evenings I've ever spent, rife with *bon mots* and lucid conversation, but I had the undercurrent feeling (totally self-generated, I assure you) that I was a guttersnipe among royalty. Nothing in the manner of Ursula or her family contributed to forming that little nubbin of self-flagelation . . . it was just one of the many niggling little doubts about personal worthiness that all of us have when we are in the company of the very talented, the very beautiful, the very rich or the very landed gentry. It interfered in no way with my enjoyment of the evening.

The next night, when the Nebulas were awarded, a ceremony of singular traumatic content, Ursula Le Guin proved by one single gesture how senseless it is for even the most secure of us to harbor such lack of self-worth.

Among the nominees sitting in that small dining room at the Claremont Hotel that night, were Norman Spinrad (who was up against Ursula with his novel *Bug Jack Barron*), Fritz Leiber (who was vying with me for the novella Nebula with his "Ship of Shadows"), Chip Delany, Greg Benford and

Norman again, all up against Ursula's "Nine Lives" for the novelette award, and Larry Niven (whose short story "Not Long Before the End" was up against my "Shattered Like A Glass Goblin"). It was a tense situation. When Ursula's *The Left Hand of Darkness* beat out Zelazny, Brunner, Silverberg, Vonnegut and Spinrad ... Norman went into a funk that spread its miasmic pall throughout the time-zone. When I copped mine, a very lovely lady sitting with Fritz Leiber burst into tears and Karen Anderson, authoress and wife of Poul Anderson, looked as though she wanted to cut my throat. When Samuel R. Delany took the novelette Nebula, Greg and Ursula were a study in conflicting emotions, and Norman went under the table. Thank God Silverberg grabbed the short story award, because Larry Niven would have cheerfully knifed me, had I won two that night. Those of us who were there—Ursula, Chip and myself—(Silverberg accepted his award at the East Coast banquet in New York, safe from his competition) slunk up and took our trophies with a few mumbled, embarrassed words, and crawled away again. All in all, it was horrendous. Never have I felt so guilty winning an award.

Shortly thereafter, when the crowd broke up into small groups, I detached myself from the well-wishers to go over and congratulate Ursula on winning what is surely the first of many awards to come. She was sitting at a table with a clot of people standing around. Her Nebula was on the table. Mine was in my arms. Hers was prettier than mine. I switched them. (Since our names and the stories we'd written to win the trophies were engraved on the plinth of each, it was clearly a gag of the moment.) I waited for that moment when Ursula would realize she had my Nebula and I had hers, and it would be my way of saying good-for-you. But that moment never came.

One of the ladies standing there, a lady with a penchant for hysteria, began shrieking at the top of her lungs, "Ursula! Ursula! He stole your Nebula! He stole your Nebula, Ursula, Ursula!!!" and she began weeping convulsively.

I panicked and quickly switched them back as Ursula, suddenly jerked into a wild scene, tried to get her bearings to establish what was happening.

"Hey, take it easy, it was only a joke," I said to the trembling lady, "they're both Nebulas, you know."

To which the lady responded, "Yes, but *hers* is for a *novel*, not a story." Since I have never won an award for a novel—and the lady knew it—that was what we of the jet set call a consummate downer. It dropped a shroud over the joy of the evening, such as it was, and added to Fritz Leiber's companion's tears, it made me feel like a pound and a half of mandrill shit.

I started to lurch away, when I felt a hand on my arm. It was Ursula. I looked back down at her and she was staring at me with an expression that said I understand, forget it, it doesn't matter what she says, all's right with the world.

It instantly brought me up like the Goodyear blimp. And it saved the evening for me.

One gesture of kindliness, that tells more about Ursula K. Le Guin than all the biographies anyone could write.

And as a final note, check the placement of her very long and very fine novella in these pages. It is the second actual *story* in the book (Heidenry's is, as stated, a keynote entry). The wise editor, I was informed early in my career as a compiler of anthologies, puts his very strongest stuff at the beginning and the end of the book. I started off with the Rocklynne because of its strength and because of his personal meaning for the field. And since I had three extra-long pieces for inclusion here, one to start, one in the middle, and one to close, I wanted to make it a story that would zonk the readership.

Her wonderfulness aside, it am the words of Ursula Le Guin what wins the heart and memory, and the hot spot in this book.

Ursula K. Le Guin

THE WORD FOR WORLD IS FOREST

1.

Two pieces of yesterday were in Captain Davidson's mind when he woke, and he lay looking at them in the darkness for a while. One up: the new shipload of women had arrived.

Believe it or not. They were here, in Centralville, twenty-seven lightyears from Earth by NAFAL and four hours from Smith Camp by hopper, the second batch of breeding females for the New Tahiti Colony, all sound and clean, 212 head of prime human stock. Or prime enough, anyhow. One down: the report from Dump Island of crop failures, massive erosion, a wipe-out. The line of 212 buxom beddable breasty little figures faded from Davidson's mind as he saw rain pouring down into ploughed dirt, churning it to mud, thinning the mud to a red broth that ran down rocks into the rainbeaten sea. The erosion had begun before he left Dump Island to run Smith Camp, and being gifted with an exceptional visual memory, the kind they called eidetic, he could recall it now all too clearly. It looked like that bigdome Kees was right and you had to leave a lot of trees standing where you planned to put farms. But he still couldn't see why a soybean farm needed to waste a lot of space on trees if the land was managed really scientifically. It wasn't like that in Ohio; if you wanted corn you grew corn, and no space wasted on trees and stuff. But then Earth was a tamed planet and New Tahiti wasn't. That's what he was here for: to tame it. If Dump Island was just rocks and gullies now, then scratch it; start over on a new island and do better. Can't keep us down, we're Men. You'll learn what that means pretty soon, you godforsaken damn planet, Davidson thought, and he grinned a little in the darkness of the hut, for he liked challenges. Thinking Men, he thought Women, and again the line of little figures began to sway through his mind, smiling, jiggling.

"Ben!" he roared, sitting up and swinging his bare feet onto the bare floor. "Hot water get-ready, hurry-up-quick!" The roar woke him satisfyingly. He stretched and scratched his chest and pulled on his shorts and strode out of the hut into the sunlit clearing all in one easy series of motions. A big, hard-muscled man, he enjoyed using his well-trained body. Ben, his creechie, had the water ready and steaming over the fire, as usual, and was squatting staring at nothing, as usual. Creechies never slept, they just sat and stared. "Breakfast. Hurry-up-quick!" Davidson said, picking up his razor from the rough board table where the creechie had laid it out ready with a towel and a propped-up mirror.

There was a lot to be done today, since he'd decided, that last minute before getting up, to fly down to Central and see the new women for himself. They wouldn't last long, 212 among over two thousand men, and like the first batch probably most of them were Colony Brides, and only twenty or thirty had come as Recreation Staff; but those babies were

real good greedy girls and he intended to be first in line with
at least one of them this time. He grinned on the left, the
right cheek remaining stiff to the whining razor.

The old creechie was moseying round taking an hour to
bring his breakfast from the cookhouse. "Hurry-up-quick!"
Davidson yelled, and Ben pushed his boneless saunter into a
walk. Ben was about a meter high and his back fur was more
white than green; he was old, and dumb even for a creechie,
but Davidson knew how to handle him. A lot of men couldn't
handle creechies worth a damn, but Davidson had never had
trouble with them; he could tame any of them, if it was
worth the effort. It wasn't, though. Get enough humans here,
build machines and robots, make farms and cities, and nobody would need the creechies any more. And a good thing
too. For this world, New Tahiti, was literally made for men.
Cleaned up and cleaned out, the dark forests cut down for
open fields of grain, the primeval murk and savagery and ignorance wiped out, it would be a paradise, a real Eden. A
better world than worn-out Earth. And it would be his world.
For that's what Davidson was, way down deep inside him: a
world-tamer. He wasn't a boastful man, but he knew his own
size. It just happened to be the way he was made. He knew
what he wanted, and how to get it. And he always got it.

Breakfast landed warm in his belly. His good mood wasn't
spoiled even by the sight of Kees Van Sten coming towards
him, fat, white, and worried, his eyes sticking out like blue
golf-balls.

"Don," Kees said without greeting, "the loggers have been
hunting red deer in the Strips again. There are eighteen pair
of antlers in the back room of the Lounge."

"Nobody ever stopped poachers from poaching, Kees."

"You can stop them. That's why we live under martial law,
that's why the Army runs this colony. To keep the laws."

A frontal attack from Fatty Bigdome! It was almost
funny. "All right," Davidson said reasonably, "I could stop
'em. But look, it's the men I'm looking after; that's my job,
like you said. And it's the men that count. Not the animals.
If a little extra-legal hunting helps the men get through this
godforsaken life, then I intend to blink. They've got to have
some recreation."

"They have games, sports, hobbies, films, teletapes of every
major sporting event of the past century, liquor, marijuana,
hallies, and a fresh batch of women at Central. For those un-
satisfied by the Army's rather unimaginative arrangements
for hygienic homosexuality. They are spoiled rotten, your
frontier heroes, and they don't need to exterminate a rare na-

tive species 'for recreation.' If you don't act, I must record a major infraction of Ecological Protocols in my report to Captain Gosse."

"You can do that if you see fit, Kees," said Davidson, who never lost his temper. It was sort of pathetic the way a euro like Kees got all red in the face when he lost control of his emotions. "That's your job, after all. I won't hold it against you; they can do the arguing at Central and decide who's right. See, you want to keep this place just like it is, actually, Kees. Like one big National Forest. To look at, to study. Great, you're a spesh. But see we're just ordinary joes getting the work done. Earth needs wood, needs it bad. We find wood on New Tahiti. So—we're loggers. See, where we differ is that with you Earth doesn't come first, actually. With me it does."

Kees looked at him sideways out of those blue golf-ball eyes. "Does it? You want to make this world into Earth's image, eh? A desert of cement?"

"When I say Earth, Kees, I mean people. Men. You worry about deer and trees and fibreweed, fine, that's your thing. But I like to see things in perspective, from the top down, and the top, so far, is humans. We're here, now; and so this world's going to go our way. Like it or not, it's a fact you have to face; it happens to be the way things are. Listen, Kees, I'm going to hop down to Central and take a look at the new colonists. Want to come along?"

"No thanks, Captain Davidson," the spesh said, going on towards the Lab hut. He was really mad. All upset about those damn deer. They were great animals, all right. Davidson's vivid memory recalled the first one he had seen, here on Smith Land, a big red shadow, two meters at the shoulder, a crown of narrow golden antlers, a fleet, brave beast, the finest game-animal imaginable. Back on Earth they were using robodeer even in the High Rockies and Himalaya Parks now, the real ones were about gone. These things were a hunter's dream. So they'd be hunted. Hell, even the wild creechies hunted them, with their lousy little bows. The deer would be hunted because that's what they were there for. But poor old bleeding-heart Kees couldn't see it. He was actually a smart fellow, but not realistic, not tough-minded enough. He didn't see that you've got to play on the winning side or else you lose. And it's Man that wins, every time. The old Conquistador.

Davidson strode on through the settlement, morning sunlight in his eyes, the smell of sawn wood and woodsmoke sweet on the warm air. Things looked pretty neat, for a logging camp. The two hundred men here had tamed a fair patch of wilderness in just three E-months. Smith Camp: a couple of big córruplast geodesics, forty timber huts built by creechie-labor, the sawmill, the burner trailing a blue plume over acres of logs and cut lumber; uphill, the airfield and the big prefab hangar for helicopters and heavy machinery. That was all. But when they came here there had been nothing. Trees. A dark huddle and jumble and tangle of trees, endless, meaningless. A sluggish river overhung and choked by trees, a few creechie-warrens hidden among the trees, some red deer, hairy monkeys, birds. And trees. Roots, boles, branches, twigs, leaves, leaves overhead and underfoot and in your face and in your eyes, endless leaves on endless trees.

New Tahiti was mostly water, warm shallow seas broken here and there by reefs, islets, archipelagoes, and the five big Lands that lay in a 2500-kilo arc across the Northwest Quartersphere. And all those flecks and blobs of land were covered with trees. Ocean: forest. That was your choice on New Tahiti. Water and sunlight, or darkness and leaves.

But men were here now to end the darkness, and turn the tree-jumble into clean sawn planks, more prized on Earth than gold. Literally, because gold could be got from seawater and from under the Antarctic ice, but wood could not; wood came only from trees. And it was a really necessary luxury on Earth. So the alien forests became wood. Two hundred men with robosaws and haulers had already cut eight mile-wide Strips on Smith Land, in three months. The stumps of the Strip nearest camp were already white and punky; chemically treated, they would have fallen into fertile ash by the time the permanent colonists, the farmers, came to settle Smith Land. All the farmers would have to do was plant seeds and let 'em sprout.

It had been done once before. That was a queer thing, and the proof, actually, that New Tahiti was intended for humans to take over. All the stuff here had come from Earth, about a million years ago, and the evolution had followed so close a path that you recognised things at once: pine, oak, walnut, chestnut, fir, holly, apple, ash; deer, bird, mouse, cat, squirrel, monkey. The humanoids on Hain-Davenant of course claimed they'd done it at the same time as they colonised Earth, but if you listened to those ETs you'd find they claimed to have settled every planet in the Galaxy and invented everything from sex to thumbtacks. The theories about Atlantis were a lot more realistic, and this might well be a lost Atlantean colony. But the humans had died out. And the nearest thing that had developed from the monkey line to replace them was the creechie—a meter tall and covered with green fur. As ETs they were about standard, but as men they were a bust, they just hadn't made it. Give 'em another million years, maybe. But the Conquistadors had arrived first. Evolution moved now not at the pace of a random mutation once a millennium, but with the speed of the starships of the Terran Fleet.

"Hey Captain!"

Davidson turned, only a microsecond late in his reaction, but that was late enough to annoy him. There was something about this damn planet, its gold sunlight and hazy sky, its mild winds smelling of leafmould and pollen, something that made you daydream. You mooched along thinking about conquistadors and destiny and stuff, till you were acting as thick and slow as a creechie. "Morning, Ok!" he said crisply to the logging foreman.

Black and tough as wire rope, Oknanawi Nabo was Kees's physical opposite, but he had the same worried look. "You got half a minute?"

"Sure. What's eating you, Ok?"

"The little bastards."

They leaned their backsides on a split rail fence. Davidson lit his first reefer of the day. Sunlight, smoke-blued, slanted warm across the air. The forest behind camp, a quarter-mile-wide uncut strip, was full of the faint, ceaseless, cracking, chuckling, stirring, whirring, silvery noises that woods in the morning are full of. It might have been Idaho in 1950, this clearing. Or Kentucky in 1830. Or Gaul in 50 B.C. "Te-whet," said a distant bird.

"I'd like to get rid of 'em, Captain."

"The creechies? How d'you mean, Ok?"

"Just let 'em go. I can't get enough work out of 'em in the mill to make up for their keep. Or for their being such a damn headache. They just don't work."

"They do if you know how to make 'em. They built the camp."

Oknanawi's obsidian face was dour. "Well, you got the touch with 'em, I guess. I don't." He paused. "In that Applied History course I took in training for Far-out, it said that slavery never worked. It was uneconomical."

"Right, but this isn't slavery, Ok baby. Slaves are humans. When you raise cows, you call that slavery? No. And it works."

Impassive, the foreman nodded; but he said, "They're too little. I tried starving the sulky ones. They just sit and starve."

"They're little, all right, but don't let 'em fool you, Ok. They're tough; they've got terrific endurance; and they don't feel pain like humans. That's the part you forget, Ok. You think hitting one is like hitting a kid, sort of. Believe me, it's more like hitting a robot for all they feel it. Look, you've laid some of the females, you know how they don't seem to feel anything, no pleasure, no pain, they just lay there like mattresses no matter what you do. They're all like that. Probably they've got more primitive nerves than humans do. Like fish. I'll tell you a weird one about that. When I was in Central, before I came up here, one of the tame males jumped me once. I know they'll tell you they never fight, but this one went spla, right off his nut, and lucky he wasn't armed or he'd have killed me. I had to damn near kill him before he'd even let go. And he kept coming back. It was incredible the beating he took and never even felt it. Like some beetle you have to keep stepping on because it doesn't know it's been squashed already. Look at this." Davidson bent down his close-cropped head to show a gnarled lump behind one ear. "That was damn near a concussion. And he did it after I'd broken his arm and pounded his face into cranberry sauce. He just kept coming back and coming back. The thing is, Ok, the creechies are lazy, they're dumb, they're treacherous, and they don't feel pain. You've got to be tough with 'em, and stay tough with 'em."

"They aren't worth the trouble, Captain. Damn sulky little green bastards, they won't fight, won't work, won't nothing. Except give me the pip." There was a geniality in Oknanawi's grumbling which did not conceal the stubbornness beneath. He wouldn't beat up creechies because they were so much smaller; that was clear in his mind, and clear now to Davidson, who at once accepted it. He knew how to handle his men. "Look, Ok. Try this. Pick out the ringleaders and tell 'em you're going to give them a shot of hallucinogen. Mesc, lice, any one, they don't know one from the other. But they're scared of them. Don't overwork it, and it'll work. I can guarantee."

"Why are they scared of hallies?" the foreman asked curiously.

"How do I know? Why are women scared of rats? Don't look for good sense from women or creechies, Ok! Speaking of which I'm on the way to Central this morning, shall I put the finger on a Collie Girl for you?"

"Just keep the finger off a few till I get my leave," Ok said grinning. A group of creechies passed, carrying a long 12×12 beam for the Rec Room being built down by the river. Slow, shambling little figures, they worried the big beam along like a lot of ants with a dead caterpillar, sullen and inept. Oknanawi watched them and said, "Fact is, Captain, they give me the creeps."

That was queer, coming from a tough, quiet guy like Ok.

"Well, I agree with you, actually, Ok, that they're not worth the trouble, or the risk. If that fart Lyubov wasn't around and the Colonel wasn't so stuck on following the Code, I think we might just clean out the areas we settle, instead of this Voluntary Labor routine. They're going to get rubbed out sooner or later, and it might as well be sooner. It's just how things happen to be. Primitive races always have to give way to civilised ones. Or be assimilated. But we sure as hell can't assimilate a lot of green monkeys. And like you say, they're just bright enough that they'll never be quite trustworthy. Like those big monkeys used to live in Africa, what were they called."

"Gorillas?"

"Right. We'll get on better without creechies here, just like we get on better without gorillas in Africa. They're in our way. . . . But Daddy Ding-Dong he say use creechie-labor, so we use creechie-labor. For a while. Right? See you tonight, Ok."

"Right, Captain."

Davidson checked out the hopper from Smith Camp HQ: a pine-plank 4-meter cube, two desks, a watercooler, Lt. Birno repairing a walkytalky. "Don't let the camp burn down, Birno."

"Bring me back a Collie, Cap. Blonde. 34-22-36."

"Christ, is that all?"

"I like 'em neat, not floppy, see." Birno expressively outlined his preference in the air. Grinning, Davidson went on up to the hangar. As he brought the helicopter back over camp he looked down at it: kid's blocks, sketch-lines of paths, long stump-stubbled clearings, all shrinking as the machine rose and he saw the green of the uncut forests of the great island, and beyond that dark green the pale green of the sea going on and on. Now Smith Camp looked like a yellow spot, a fleck on a vast green tapestry.

He crossed Smith Straits and the wooded, deep-folded ranges of north Central Island, and came down by noon in Centralville. It looked like a city, at least after three months in the woods; there were real streets, real buildings, it had been there since the Colony began four years ago. You didn't see what a flimsy little frontier-town it really was, until you looked south of it a halfmile and saw glittering above the stumplands and the concrete pads a single golden tower, taller than anything in Centralville. The ship wasn't a big one but it looked so big, here. And it was only a launch, a lander, a ship's boat; the NAFAL ship of the line, *Shackleton*, was half a million kilos up, in orbit. The launch was just a hint, just a fingertip of the hugeness, the power, the golden precision and grandeur of the star-bridging technology of Earth.

That was why tears came to Davidson's eyes for a second at the sight of the ship from home. He wasn't ashamed of it. He was a patriotic man, it just happened to be the way he was made.

Soon enough, walking down those frontier-town streets with their wide vistas of nothing much at each end, he began to smile. For the women were there, all right, and you could tell they were fresh ones. They mostly had long tight skirts and big shoes like galoshes, red or purple or gold, and gold or silver frilly shirts. No more nipplepeeps. Fashions had changed; too bad. They all wore their hair piled up high, it must be sprayed with that glue stuff they used. Ugly as hell, but it was the sort of thing only women would do to their hair, and so it was provocative. Davidson grinned at a chesty little euraf with more hair than head; he got no smile, but a wag of the retreating hips that said plainly, Follow follow follow me. But he didn't. Not yet. He went to Central HQ: quickstone and plastiplate Standard Issue, 40 offices 10 watercoolers and a basement arsenal, and checked in with New Tahiti Central Colonial Administration Command. He met a couple of the launch-crew, put in a request for a new semirobo bark-stripper at Forestry, and got his old pal Juju Sereng to meet him at the Luau Bar at fourteen hundred.

He got to the bar an hour early to stock up on a little food before the drinking began. Lyubov was there, sitting with a couple of guys in Fleet uniform, some kind of speshes that had come down on the *Shackleton*'s launch. Davidson didn't have a high regard for the Navy, a lot of fancy sunhoppers who left the dirty, muddy, dangerous on-planet work to the Army; but brass was brass, and anyhow it was funny to see Lyubov acting chummy with anybody in uniform. He was talking, waving his hands around the way he did. Just in passing Davidson tapped his shoulder and said, "Hi, Raj old pal, how's tricks?" He went on without waiting for the scowl, though he hated to miss it. It was really funny the way Lyubov hated him. Probably the guy was effeminate like a lot of intellectuals, and resented Davidson's virility. Anyhow Davidson wasn't going to waste any time hating Lyubov, he wasn't worth the trouble.

The Luau served a first-rate venison steak. What would they say on old Earth if they saw one man eating a kilogram of meat at one meal? Poor damn soybeansuckers! Then Juju arrived with—as Davidson had confidently expected—the pick of the new Collie Girls: two fruity beauties, not Brides, but Recreation Staff. Oh the old Colonial Administration sometimes came through! It was a long, hot afternoon.

Flying back to camp he crossed Smith Straits level with the sun that lay on top of a great gold bed of haze over the sea. He sang as he lolled in the pilot's seat. Smith Land came in sight hazy, and there was smoke over the camp, a dark smudge as if oil had got into the waste-burner. He couldn't even make out the buildings through it. It was only as he dropped down to the landing-field that he saw the charred jet, the wrecked hoppers, the burned-out hangar.

He pulled the hopper up again and flew back over the camp, so low that he might have hit the high cone of the burner, the only thing left sticking up. The rest was gone, mill, furnace, lumberyards, HQ, huts, barracks, creechie compound, everything. Black hulks and wrecks, still smoking. But it hadn't been a forest fire. The forest stood there, green, next to the ruins. Davidson swung back round to the field, set down and lit out looking for the motorbike, but it too was a black wreck along with the stinking, smouldering ruins of the hangar and the machinery. He loped down the path to camp. As he passed what had been the radio hut, his mind snapped back into gear. Without hesitating for even a stride he changed course, off the path, behind the gutted shack. There he stopped. He listened.

There was nobody. It was all silent. The fires had been out a long time; only the great lumber-piles still smouldered, showing a hot red under the ash and char. Worth more than gold, those oblong ash-heaps had been. But no smoke rose from the black skeletons of the barracks and huts; and there were bones among the ashes.

Davidson's brain was super-clear and active, now, as he crouched behind the radio shack. There were two possibilities. One: an attack from another camp. Some officer on King or New Java had gone spla and was trying a coup de planète. Two: an attack from off-planet. He saw the golden tower on the space-dock at Central. But if the *Shackleton* had gone privateer why would she start by rubbing out a small camp, instead of taking over Centralville? No, it must be invasion, aliens. Some unknown race, or maybe the Cetians or the Hainish had decided to move in on Earth's colonies. He'd never trusted those damned smart humanoids. This must have been done with a heatbomb. The invading force, with jets, aircars, nukes, could easily be hidden on an island or reef anywhere in the SW Quartersphere. He must get back to his hopper and send out the alarm, then try to look around, reconnoiter, so he could tell HQ his assessment of the actual situation. He was just straightening up when he heard the voices.

Not human voices. High, soft, gabble-gobble. Aliens.

Ducking on hands and knees behind the shack's plastic roof, which lay on the ground deformed by heat into a bat-wing shape, he held still and listened.

Four creechies walked by a few yards from him, on the path. They were wild creechies, naked except for loose leather belts on which knives and pouches hung. None wore the shorts and leather collar supplied to tame creechies. The Volunteers in the compound must have been incinerated along with the humans.

They stopped a little way past his hiding-place, talking their slow gabble-gobble, and Davidson held his breath. He didn't want them to spot him. What the devil were creechies doing here? They could only be serving as spies and scouts for the invaders.

One pointed south as it talked, and turned, so that Davidson saw its face. And he recognised it. Creechies all looked alike, but this one was different. He had written his own signature all over that face, less than a year ago. It was the one that had gone spla and attacked him down in Central, the homicidal one, Lyubov's pet. What in the blue hell was it doing here?

Davidson's mind raced, clicked; reactions fast as always, he stood up, sudden, tall, easy, gun in hand. "You creechies. Stop. Stay-put. No moving!"

His voice cracked out like a whiplash. The four little green creatures did not move. The one with the smashed-in face looked at him across the black rubble with huge, blank eyes that had no light in them.

"Answer now. This fire, who start it?"

No answer.

"Answer now: hurry-up-quick! No answer, then I burn-up first one, then one, then one, see? This fire, who start it?"

"We burned the camp, Captain Davidson," said the one from Central, in a queer soft voice that reminded Davidson of some human. "The humans are all dead."

"You burned it, what do you mean?"

He could not recall Scarface's name for some reason.

"There were two hundred humans here. Ninety slaves of

my people. Nine hundred of my people came out of the forest. First we killed the humans in the place in the forest where they were cutting trees, then we killed those in this place, while the houses were burning. I had thought you were killed. I am glad to see you, Captain Davidson."

It was all crazy, and of course a lie. They couldn't have killed all of them, Ok, Birno, Van Sten, all the rest, two hundred men, some of them would have got out. All the creechies had was bows and arrows. Anyway the creechies couldn't have done this. Creechies didn't fight, didn't kill, didn't have wars. They were intraspecies non-aggressive, that meant sitting ducks. They didn't fight back. They sure as hell didn't massacre two hundred men at a swipe. It was crazy. The silence, the faint stink of burning in the long, warm evening light, the pale-green faces with unmoving eyes that watched him, it all added up to nothing, to a crazy bad dream, a nightmare.

"Who did this for you?"

"Nine hundred of my people," Scarface said in that damned fake-human voice.

"No, not that. Who else? Who were you acting for? Who told you what to do?"

"My wife did."

Davidson saw then the telltale tension of the creature's stance, yet it sprang at him so lithe and oblique that his shot missed, burning an arm or shoulder instead of smack between the eyes. And the creechie was on him, half his size and weight yet knocking him right off balance by its onslaught, for he had been relying on the gun and not expecting attack. The thing's arms were thin, tough, coarse-furred in his grip, and as he struggled with it, it sang.

He was down on his back, pinned down, disarmed. Four green muzzles looked down at him. The scarfaced one was still singing, a breathless gabble, but with a tune to it. The other three listened, their white teeth showing in grins. He had never seen a creechie smile. He had never looked up into a creechie's face from below. Always down, from above. From on top. He tried not to struggle, for at the moment it was wasted effort. Little as they were, they outnumbered him, and Scarface had his gun. He must wait. But there was a sickness in him, a nausea that made his body twitch and strain against his will. The small hands held him down effortlessly, the small green faces bobbed over him grinning.

Scarface ended his song. He knelt on Davidson's chest, a knife in one hand, Davidson's gun in the other.

"You can't sing, Captain Davidson, is that right? Well,

then, you may run to your hopper, and fly away, and tell the Colonel in Central that this place is burned and the humans are all killed."

Blood, the same startling red as human blood, clotted the fur of the creechie's right arm, and the knife shook in the green paw. The sharp, scarred face looked down into Davidson's from very close, and he could see now the queer light that burned way down in the charcoal-dark eyes. The voice was still soft and quiet.

They let him go.

He got up cautiously, still dizzy from the fall Scarface had given him. The creechies stood well away from him now, knowing his reach was twice theirs; but Scarface wasn't the only one armed, there was a second gun pointing at his guts. That was Ben holding the gun. His own creechie Ben, the little grey mangy bastard, looking stupid as always but holding a gun.

It's hard to turn your back on two pointing guns, but Davidson did it and started walking towards the field.

A voice behind him said some creechie word, shrill and loud. Another said, "Hurry-up-quick!" and there was a queer noise like birds twittering that must be creechie laughter. A shot clapped and whined on the road right by him. Christ, it wasn't fair, they had the guns and he wasn't armed. He began to run. He could outrun any creechie. They didn't know how to shoot a gun.

"Run," said the quiet voice far behind him. That was Scarface—Selver, that was his name. Sam, they'd called him, till Lyubov stopped Davidson from giving him what he deserved and made a pet out of him, then they'd called him Selver. Christ, what was all this, it was a nightmare. He ran. The blood thundered in his ears. He ran through the golden, smoky evening. There was a body by the path, he hadn't even noticed it coming. It wasn't burned, it looked like a white balloon with the air gone out. It had staring blue eyes. They didn't dare kill him, Davidson. They hadn't shot at him again. It was impossible. They couldn't kill him. There was the hopper, safe and shining, and he lunged into the seat and had her up before the creechies could try anything. His hands shook, but not much, just shock. They couldn't kill him. He circled the hill and then came back fast and low, looking for the four creechies. But nothing moved in the streaky rubble of the camp.

There had been a camp there this morning. Two hundred men. There had been four creechies there just now. He hadn't dreamed all this. They couldn't just disappear. They were there, hiding. He opened up the machinegun in the hopper's nose and raked the burned ground, shot holes in the green leaves of the forest, strafed the burned bones and cold bodies of his men and the wrecked machinery and the rotting white stumps, returning again and again until the ammo was gone and the gun's spasms stopped short.

Davidson's hands were steady now, his body felt appeased, and he knew he wasn't caught in any dream. He headed back over the Straits, to take the news to Centralville. As he flew he could feel his face relax into its usual calm lines. They couldn't blame the disaster on him, for he hadn't even been there. Maybe they'd see that it was significant that the creechies had struck while he was gone, knowing they'd fail if he was there to organise the defense. And there was one good thing would come out of this. They'd do like they should have done to start with, and clean up the planet for human occupation. Not even Lyubov could stop them from rubbing out the creechies now, not when they heard it was Lyubov's pet creechie who'd led the massacre! They'd go in for rat-extermination for a while, now; and maybe, just maybe, they'd hand that little job over to him. At that thought he could have smiled. But he kept his face calm.

The sea under him was greyish with twilight, and ahead of him lay the island hills, the deep-folded, many-streamed, many-leaved forests in the dusk.

2.

All the colors of rust and sunset, brown-reds and pale greens, changed ceaselessly in the long leaves as the wind blew. The roots of the copper willows, thick and ridged, were moss-green down by the running water, which like the wind moved slowly with many soft eddies and seeming pauses, held back by rocks, roots, hanging and fallen leaves. No way was clear, no light unbroken, in the forest. Into wind, water, sunlight, starlight, there always entered leaf and branch, bole and root, the shadowy, the complex. Little paths ran under the branches, around the boles, over the roots; they did not go straight, but yielded to every obstacle, devious as nerves. The ground was not dry and solid but damp and rather springy, product of the collaboration of living things with the long, elaborate death of leaves and trees; and from that rich graveyard grew ninety-foot trees, and tiny mushrooms that sprouted in circles half an inch across. The smell of the air was subtle, various, and sweet. The view was never long, unless looking up through the branches you caught sight of the stars. Nothing was pure, dry, arid, plain. Revelation was lacking. There was no seeing everything at once: no certainty. The colors of rust and sunset kept changing in the hanging leaves of the copper willows, and you could not say even whether the leaves of the willows were brownish-red, or reddish-green, or green.

Selver came up a path beside the water, going slowly and often stumbling on the willow roots. He saw an old man dreaming, and stopped. The old man looked at him through the long willow-leaves and saw him in his dreams.

"May I come to your Lodge, my Lord Dreamer? I've come a long way."

The old man sat still. Presently Selver squatted down on his heels just off the path, beside the stream. His head drooped down, for he was worn out and had to sleep. He had been walking five days.

"Are you of the dream-time or of the world-time?" the old man asked at last.

"Of the world-time."

"Come along with me then." The old man got up promptly and led Selver up the wandering path out of the willow grove into dryer, darker regions of oak and thorn. "I took you for a god," he said, going a pace ahead. "And it seemed to me I had seen you before, perhaps in dream."

"Not in the world-time. I come from Sornol, I have never been here before."

"This town is Cadast. I am Coro Mena. Of the White-thorn."

"Selver is my name. Of the Ash."

"There are Ash people among us, both men and women. Also your marriage-clans, Birch and Holly; we have no women of the Apple. But you don't come looking for a wife, do you?"

"My wife is dead," Selver said.

They came to the Men's Lodge, on high ground in a stand of young oaks. They stooped and crawled through the tunnel-entrance. Inside, in the firelight, the old man stood up, but Selver stayed crouching on hands and knees, unable to rise. Now that help and comfort was at hand his body, which he had forced too far, would not go farther. It lay down and the eyes closed; and Selver slipped, with relief and gratitude, into the great darkness.

The men of the Lodge of Cadast looked after him, and their healer came to tend the wound in his right arm. In the night Coro Mena and the healer Torber sat by the fire. Most

of the other men were with their wives that night; there
were only a couple of young prentice-dreamers over on the
benches, and they had both gone fast asleep. "I don't know
what would give a man such scars as he has on his face,"
said the healer, "and much less, such a wound as that in his
arm. A very queer wound."

"It's a queer engine he wore on his belt," said Coro Mena.

"I saw it and didn't see it."

"I put it under his bench. It looks like polished iron, but
not like the handiwork of men."

"He comes from Sornol, he said to you."

They were both silent a while. Coro Mena felt unreason-
ing fear press upon him, and slipped into dream to find the
reason for the fear; for he was an old man, and long adept.
In the dream the giants walked, heavy and dire. Their dry
scaly limbs were swathed in cloths; their eyes were little and
light, like tin beads. Behind them crawled huge moving things
made of polished iron. The trees fell down in front of them.

Out from among the falling trees a man ran, crying aloud,
with blood on his mouth. The path he ran on was the door-
path of the Lodge of Cadast.

"Well, there's little doubt of it," Coro Mena said, sliding
out of the dream. "He came oversea straight from Sornol, or
else came afoot from the coast of Kelme Deva on our own
land. The giants are in both those places, travellers say."

"Will they follow him," said Torber; neither answered the
question, which was no question but a statement of possibility.

"You saw the giants once, Coro?"

"Once," the old man said.

He dreamed; sometimes, being very old and not so strong
as he had been, he slipped off to sleep for a while. Day
broke, noon passed. Outside the Lodge a hunting-party went
out, children chirped, women talked in voices like running
water. A dryer voice called Coro Mena from the door. He
crawled out into the evening sunlight. His sister stood outside,
sniffing the aromatic wind with pleasure, but looking stern all
the same. "Has the stranger waked up, Coro?"

"Not yet. Torber's looking after him."

"We must hear his story."

"No doubt he'll wake soon."

Ebor Dendep frowned. Headwoman of Cadast, she was
anxious for her people; but she did not want to ask that a
hurt man be disturbed, nor to offend the Dreamers by insisting on her right to enter their Lodge. "Can't you wake him,
Coro?" she asked at last. "What if he is . . . being pursued?"

He could not run his sister's emotions on the same rein with his own, yet he felt them; her anxiety bit him. "If Torber permits, I will," he said.

"Try to learn his news, quickly. I wish he was a woman and would talk sense. . . ."

The stranger had roused himself, and lay feverish in the halfdark of the Lodge. The unreined dreams of illness moved in his eyes. He sat up, however, and spoke with control. As he listened Coro Mena's bones seemed to shrink within him trying to hide from his terrible story, this new thing.

"I was Selver Thele, when I lived in Eshreth in Sornol. My city was destroyed by the yumens when they cut down the trees in that region. I was one of those made to serve them, with my wife Thele. She was raped by one of them and died. I attacked the yumen that killed her. He would have killed me then, but another of them saved me and set me free. I left Sornol, where no town is safe from the yumens now, and came here to the North Isle, and lived on the coast of Kelme Deva in the Red Groves. There presently the yumens came and began to cut down the world. They destroyed a city there, Penle. They caught a hundred of the men and women and made them serve them, and live in the pen. I was not caught. I lived with others who had escaped from Penle, in the bogland north of Kelme Deva. Sometimes at night I went among the people in the yumen's pens. They told me that that one was there. That one whom I had tried to kill. I thought at first to try again; or else to set the people in the pen free. But all the time I watched the trees fall and saw the world cut open and left to rot. The men might have escaped, but the women were locked in more safely and could not, and they were beginning to die. I talked with the people hiding there in the boglands. We were all very frightened and very angry, and had no way to let our fear and anger free. So at last after long talking, and long dreaming, and the making of a plan, we went in daylight, and killed the yumens of Kelme Deva with arrows and hunting-lances, and burned their city and their engines. We left nothing. But that one had gone away. He came back alone. I sang over him, and let him go."

Selver fell silent.

"Then," Coro Mena whispered.

"Then a flying ship came from Sornol, and hunted us in the forest, but found nobody. So they set fire to the forest; but it rained, and they did little harm. Most of the people freed from the pens and the others have gone farther north and east, towards the Holle Hills, for we were afraid many yumens might come hunting us. I went alone. The yumens know me, you see, they know my face; and this frightens me, and those I stay with."

"What is your wound?" Tober asked.

"That one, he shot me with their kind of weapon; but I sang him down and let him go."

"Alone you downed a giant?" said Torber with a fierce grin, wishing to believe.

"Not alone. With three hunters, and with his weapon in my hand—this."

Torber drew back from the thing.

None of them spoke for a while. At last Coro Mena said, "What you tell us is very black, and the road goes down. Are you a Dreamer of your Lodge?"

"I was. There's no Lodge of Eshreth any more."

"That's all one; we speak the Old Tongue together. Among the willows of Asta you first spoke to me calling me Lord Dreamer. So I am. Do you dream, Selver?"

"Seldom now," Selver answered, obedient to the catechism, his scarred, feverish face bowed.

"Awake?"

"Awake."

"Do you dream well, Selver?"

"Not well."

"Do you hold the dream in your hands?"

"Yes."

"Do you weave the shape, direct and follow, start and cease at will?"

"Sometimes, not always."

"Can you walk the road your dream goes?"

"Sometimes. Sometimes I am afraid to."

"Who is not? It is not altogether bad with you, Selver."

"No, it is altogether bad," Selver said, "there's nothing good left," and he began to shake.

Torber gave him the willow-draught to drink and made him lie down. Coro Mena still had the headwoman's question to ask; reluctantly he did so, kneeling by the sick man. "Will the giants, the yumens you call them, will they follow your trail, Selver?"

"I left no trail. No one has seen me between Kelme Deva and this place, six days. That's not the danger." He struggled to sit up again. "Listen, listen. You don't see the danger. How can you see it? You haven't done what I did, you have never dreamed of it, making two hundred people die. They will not follow me, but they may follow us all. Hunt us, as hunters drive coneys. That is the danger. They may try to kill us. To kill us all, all men."

"Lie down—"

"No, I'm not raving, this is true fact and dream. There were two hundred yumens at Kelme Deva and they are dead. We killed them. We killed them as if they were not men. So will they not turn and do the same? They have killed us by ones, now they will kill us as they kill the trees, by hundreds, and hundreds, and hundreds."

"Be still," Torber said. "Such things happen in the fever-dream, Selver. They do not happen in the world."

"The world is always new," said Coro Mena, "however old its roots. Selver, how is it with these creatures, then? They look like men and talk like men, are they not men?"

"I don't know. Do men kill men, except in madness? Does any beast kill its own kind? Only the insects. These yumens kill us as lightly as we kill snakes. The one who taught me said that they kill one another, in quarrels, and also in groups, like ants fighting. I haven't seen that. But I know they don't spare one who asks life. They will strike a bowed neck, I have seen it! There is a wish to kill in them, and therefore I saw fit to put them to death."

"And all men's dreams," said Coro Mena, cross-legged in shadow, "will be changed. They will never be the same again. I shall never walk again that path I came with you yesterday, the way up from the willow grove that I've walked on all my life. It is changed. You have walked on it and it is utterly changed. Before this day the thing we had to do was the right thing to do; the way we had to go was the right way and led us home. Where is our home now? For you've done what you had to do, and it was not right. You have killed men. I saw them, five years ago, in the Lemgan Valley, where they came in a flying ship; I hid and watched the giants, six of them, and saw them speak, and look at rocks and plants, and cook food. They are men. But you have lived among them, tell me, Selver: do they dream?"

"As children do, in sleep."

"They have no training?"

"No. Sometimes they talk of their dreams, the healers try to use them in healing, but none of them are trained, or have any skill in dreaming. Lyubov, who taught me, understood me when I showed him how to dream, and yet even so he called the world-time 'real' and the dream-time 'unreal,' as if that were the difference between them."

"You have done what you had to do," Coro Mena repeated after a silence. His eyes met Selver's, across shadows.

The desperate tension lessened in Selver's face; his scarred mouth relaxed, and he lay back without saying more. In a little while he was asleep.

"He's a god," Coro Mena said.

Torber nodded, accepting the old man's judgment almost with relief.

"But not like the others. Not like the Pursuer, nor the Friend who has no face, nor the Aspen-leaf Woman who walks in the forest of dreams. He is not the Gatekeeper, nor the Snake. Nor the Lyre-player nor the Carver nor the Hunter, though he comes in the world-time like them. We may have dreamed of Selver these last few years, but we shall no longer; he has left the dream-time. In the forest, through the forest he comes, where leaves fall, where trees fall, a god that knows death, a god that kills and is not himself reborn."

The headwoman listened to Coro Mena's reports and prophecies, and acted. She put the town of Cadast on alert, making sure that each family was ready to move out, with some food packed, and litters ready for the old and ill. She sent young women scouting south and east for news of the yumens. She kept one armed hunting-group always around town, though the others went out as usual every night. And when Selver grew stronger she insisted that he come out of the Lodge and tell his story: how the yumens killed and enslaved people in Sornol, and cut down the forests; how the people of Kelme Deva had killed the yumens. She forced women and undreaming men who did not understand these things to listen again, until they understood, and were frightened. For Ebor Dendep was a practical woman. When a Great Dreamer, her brother, told her that Selver was a god, a changer, a bridge between realities, she believed and acted. It was the Dreamer's responsibility to be careful, to be certain that his judgment was true. Her responsibility was then to take that judgment and act upon it. He saw what must be done; she saw that it was done.

"All the cities of the forest must hear," Coro Mena said. So the headwoman sent out her young runners, and headwomen in other towns listened, and sent out their runners. The killing at Kelme Deva and the name of Selver went over North Island and oversea to the other lands, from voice to voice, or in writing; not very fast, for the Forest People had no quicker messengers than footrunners; yet fast enough.

They were not all one people on the Forty Lands of the world. There were more languages than lands, and each with

a different dialect for every town that spoke it; there were infinite ramifications of manners, morals, customs, crafts;
physical types differed on each of the five Great Lands. The
people of Sornol were tall, and pale, and great traders; the
people of Rieshwel were short, and many had black fur, and
they ate monkeys; and so on and on. But the climate varied
little, and the forest little, and the sea not at all. Curiosity,
regular trade-routes, and the necessity of finding a husband
or wife of the proper Tree, kept up an easy movement of
people among the towns and between the lands, and so there
were certain likenesses among all but the remotest extremes,
and half-rumored barbarian isles of the Far East and South.
In all the Forty Lands, women ran the cities and towns, and
almost every town had a Men's Lodge. Within the Lodges the
Dreamers spoke an old tongue, and this varied little from
land to land. It was rarely learned by women or by men who
remained hunters, fishers, weavers, builders, those who
dreamed only small dreams outside the Lodge. As most writing was in this Lodge-tongue, when headwomen sent fleet
girls carrying messages, the letters went from Lodge to
Lodge, and so were interpreted by the Dreamers to the Old
Women, as were other documents, rumors, problems, myths,
and dreams. But it was always the Old Women's choice
whether to believe or not.

Selver was in a small room at Eshsen. The door was not
locked, but he knew if he opened it something bad would
come in. So long as he kept it shut everything would be all
right. The trouble was that there were young trees, a sapling
orchard, planted out in front of the house; not fruit or nut
trees but some other kind, he could not remember what kind.
He went out to see what kind of trees they were. They all lay
broken and uprooted. He picked up the silvery branch of one
and a little blood ran out of the broken end. No, not here,
not again, Thele, he said: O Thele, come to me before your
death! But she did not come. Only her death was there, the
broken birchtree, the opened door. Selver turned and went
quickly back into the house, discovering that it was all built
above ground like a yumen house, very tall and full of light.
Outside the other door, across the tall room, was the long
street of the yumen city Central. Selver had the gun in his
belt. If Davidson came, he could shoot him. He waited, just
inside the open door, looking out into the sunlight. Davidson
came, huge, running so fast that Selver could not keep him in
the sights of the gun as he doubled crazily back and forth
across the wide street, very fast, always closer. The gun was

heavy. Selver fired it but no fire came out of it, and in rage and terror he threw the gun and the dream away.

Disgusted and depressed, he spat, and sighed.

"A bad dream?" Ebor Dendep inquired.

"They're all bad, and all the same," he said, but the deep unease and misery lessened a little as he answered. Cool morning sunlight fell flecked and shafted through the fine leaves and branches of the birch grove of Cadast. There the headwoman sat weaving a basket of blackstem fern, for she liked to keep her fingers busy, while Selver lay beside her in half-dream and dream. He had been fifteen days at Cadast, and his wound was healing well. He still slept much, but for the first time in many months he had begun to dream waking again, regularly, not once or twice in a day and night but in the true pulse and rhythm of dreaming which should rise and fall ten to fourteen times in the diurnal cycle. Bad as his dreams were, all terror and shame, yet he welcomed them. He had feared that he was cut off from his roots, that he had gone too far into the dead land of action ever to find his way back to the springs of reality. Now, though the water was very bitter, he drank again.

Briefly he had Davidson down again among the ashes of the burned camp, and instead of singing over him this time he hit him in the mouth with a rock. Davidson's teeth broke, and blood ran between the white splinters.

The dream was useful, a straight wish-fulfilment, but he stopped it there, having dreamed it many times, before he met Davidson in the ashes of Kelme Deva, and since. There was nothing to that dream but relief. A sip of bland water. It was the bitter he needed. He must go clear back, not to Kelme Deva but to the long dreadful street in the alien city called Central, where he had attacked Death, and had been defeated.

Ebor Dendep hummed as she worked. Her thin hands, their silky green down silvered with age, worked black fern-stems in and out, fast and neat. She sang a song about gathering ferns, a girl's song: I'm picking ferns, I wonder if he'll come back. . . . Her faint old voice trilled like a cricket's. Sun trembled in birch leaves. Selver put his head down on his arms.

The birch grove was more or less in the center of the town of Cadast. Eight paths led away from it, winding narrowly off among trees. There was a whiff of woodsmoke in the air; where the branches were thin at the south edge of the grove you could see smoke rise from a house-chimney, like a bit of blue yarn unravelling among the leaves. If you looked closely

among the live-oaks and other trees you would find
houseroofs sticking up a couple of feet above ground, between a hundred and two hundred of them, it was very hard
to count. The timber houses were three-quarters sunk, fitted
in among tree-roots like badgers' setts. The beam roofs were
mounded over with a thatch of small branches, pinestraw,
reeds, earth-mould. They were insulating, waterproof, almost
invisible. The forest and the community of eight hundred
people went about their business all around the birch grove
where Ebor Dendep sat making a basket of fern. A bird
among the branches over her head said, "Te-whet," sweetly.
There was more people-noise than usual, for fifty or sixty
strangers, young men and women mostly, had come drifting
in these last few days, drawn by Selver's presence. Some were
from other cities of the North, some were those who had
done the killing at Kelme Deva with him; they had followed
rumor here to follow him. Yet the voices calling here and
there and the babble of women bathing or children playing
down by the stream, were not so loud as the morning bird-
song and insect-drone and under-noise of the living forest of
which the town was one element.

A girl came quickly, a young huntress the color of the pale
birch leaves. "Word of mouth from the southern coast,
mother," she said. "The runner's at the Women's Lodge."

"Send her here when she's eaten," the headwoman said
softly. "Sh, Tolbar, can't you see he's asleep?"

The girl stooped to pick a large leaf of wild tobacco, and
laid it lightly over Selver's eyes, on which a shaft of the
steepening, bright sunlight had fallen. He lay with his hands
half open and his scarred, damaged face turned upward, vulnerable and foolish, a Great Dreamer gone to sleep like a
child. But it was the girl's face that Ebor Dendep watched. It
shone, in that uneasy shade, with pity and terror, with adoration.

Tolbar darted away. Presently two of the Old Women
came with the messenger, moving silent in single file along
the sun-flecked path. Ebor Dendep raised her hand, enjoining
silence. The messenger promptly lay down flat, and rested;
her brown-dappled green fur was dusty and sweaty, she had
run far and fast. The Old Woman sat down in patches of sun,
and became still. Like two old grey-green stones they sat
there, with bright living eyes.

Selver, struggling with a sleep-dream beyond his control,
cried out as if in great fear, and woke.

He went to drink from the stream; when he came back he
was followed by six or seven of those who always followed

him. The headwoman put down her half-finished work and said, "Now be welcome, runner, and speak."

The runner stood up, bowed her head to Ebor Dendep, and spoke her message: "I come from Trethat. My words come from Sorbron Deva, before that from sailors of the Strait, before that from Broter in Sornol. They are for the hearing of all Cadast but they are to be spoken to the man called Selver who was born of the Ash in Eshreth. Here are the words: There are new giants in the great city of the giants in Sornol, and many of these new ones are females. The yellow ship of fire goes up and down at the place that was called Peha. It is known in Sornol that Selver of Eshreth burned the city of the giants at Kelme Deva. The Great Dreamers of the Exiles in Broter have dreamed giants more numerous than the trees of the Forty Lands. These are all the words of the message I bear."

After the singsong recitation they were all silent. The bird, a little farther off, said, "Whet-whet?" experimentally.

"This is a very bad world-time," said one of the Old Women, rubbing a rheumatic knee.

A grey bird flew from a huge oak that marked the north edge of town, and went up in circles, riding the morning up-draft on lazy wings. There was always a roosting-tree of these grey kites near a town; they were the garbage service.

A small, fat boy ran through the birch grove, pursued by a slightly larger sister, both shrieking in tiny voices like bats. The boy fell down and cried, the girl stood him up and scrubbed his tears off with a large leaf. They scuttled off into the forest hand in hand.

"There was one called Lyubov," Selver said to the head-woman. "I have spoken of him to Coro Mena, but not to you. When that one was killing me, it was Lyubov who saved me. It was Lyubov who healed me, and set me free. He wanted to know about us; so I would tell him what he asked, and he too would tell me what I asked. Once I asked how his race could survive, having so few women. He said that in the place where they come from, half the race is women; but the men would not bring women to the Forty Lands until they had made a place ready for them."

"Until the men made a fit place for the women? Well! they may have quite a wait," said Ebor Dendep. "They're like the people in the Elm Dream who come at you rump-first, with their heads put on front to back. They make the forest into a dry beach"—her language had no word for 'desert'—"and call that making things ready for the women? They should have sent the women first. Maybe with them the women do the Great Dreaming, who knows? They are backwards, Selver. They are insane."

"A people can't be insane."

"But they only dream in sleep, you said; if they want to dream waking they take poisons so that the dreams go out of control, you said! How can people be any madder? They don't know the dream-time from the world-time, any more than a baby does. Maybe when they kill a tree they think it will come alive again!"

Selver shook his head. He still spoke to the headwoman as if he and she were alone in the birch grove, in a quiet hesitant voice, almost drowsily. "No, they understand death very well. . . . Certainly they don't see as we do, but they know more and understand more about certain things than we do. Lyubov mostly understood what I told him. Much of what he told me, I couldn't understand. It wasn't the language that kept me from understanding; I know his tongue, and he learned ours; we made a writing of the two languages together. Yet there were things he said I could never understand. He said the yumens are from outside the forest. That's quite clear. He said they want the forest: the trees for wood, the land to plant grass on." Selver's voice, though still soft, had taken on resonance; the people among the silver trees listened. "That too is clear, to those of us who've seen them cutting down the world. He said the yumens are men like us, that we're indeed related, as close kin maybe as the Red Deer to the Grey-buck. He said that they come from another place which is not the forest; the trees there are all cut down; it has a sun, not our sun, which is a star. All this, as you see, wasn't clear to me. I say his words but don't know what they mean. It does not matter much. It is clear that they want our forest for themselves. They are twice our stature, they have weapons that outshoot ours by far, and fire-throwers, and flying ships. Now they have brought more women, and will have children. There are maybe two thousand, maybe three thousand of them here now, mostly in Sornol. But if we wait a lifetime or two they will breed; their numbers will double and redouble. They kill men and women; they do not spare those who ask life. They cannot sing in contest. They have left their roots behind them, perhaps, in this other forest from which they came, this forest with no trees. So they take poison to let loose the dreams in them, but it only makes them drunk or sick. No one can say certainly whether they're men or not men, whether they're sane or insane, but that does not matter. They must be made to leave the forest, because they are dangerous. If they will not go they must be

burned out of the Lands, as nests of stinging-ants must be
burned out of the groves of cities. If we wait, it is we that
will be smoked out and burned. They can step on us as we
step on stinging-ants. Once I saw a woman, it was when they
burned my city Eshreth, she lay down in the path before a
yumen to ask him for life, and he stepped on her back and
broke the spine, and then kicked her aside as if she was a
dead snake. I saw that. If the yumens are men they are men
unfit or untaught to dream and to act as men. Therefore they
go about in torment killing and destroying, driven by the
gods within, whom they will not set free but try to uproot
and deny. If they are men they are evil men, having denied
their own gods, afraid to see their own faces in the dark.
Headwoman of Cadast, hear me." Selver stood up, tall and
abrupt among the seated women. "It's time, I think, that I go
back to my own land, to Sornol, to those that are in exile
and those that are enslaved. Tell any people who dream of a
city burning to come after me to Broter." He bowed to Ebor
Dendep and left the birch grove, still walking lame, his arm
bandaged; yet there was a quickness to his walk, a poise to
his head, that made him seem more whole than other men.
The young people followed quietly after him.

"Who is he?" asked the runner from Trethat, her eyes following him.

"The man to whom your message came, Selver of Eshreth,
a god among us. Have you ever seen a god before, daughter?"

"When I was ten the Lyre-Player came to our town."

"Old Ertel, yes. He was of my Tree, and from the North
Vales like me. Well, now you've seen a second god, and a
greater. Tell your people in Trethat of him."

"Which god is he, mother?"

"A new one," Ebor Dendep said in her dry old voice. "The
son of forest-fire, the brother of the murdered. He is the one
who is not reborn. Now go on, all of you, go on to the
Lodge. See who'll be going with Selver, see about food for
them to carry. Let me be a while. I'm as full of forebodings
as a stupid old man, I must dream. . . ."

Coro Mena went with Selver that night as far as the place
where they first met, under the copper willows by the stream.
Many people were following Selver south, some sixty in all,
as great a troop as most people had ever seen on the move at
once. They would cause great stir and thus gather many
more of them, on their way to the sea-crossing to Sornol.
Selver had claimed his Dreamer's privilege of solitude for this

one night. He was setting off alone. His followers would catch him up in the morning; and thenceforth, implicated in crowd and act, he would have little time for the slow and deep running of the great dreams.

"Here we met," the old man said, stopping among the bowing branches, the veils of dropping leaves, "and here part. This will be called Selver's Grove, no doubt, by the people who walk our paths hereafter."

Selver said nothing for a while, standing still as a tree. the restless leaves about him darkening from silver as clouds thickened over the stars. "You are surer of me than I am," he said at last, a voice in darkness.

"Yes, I'm sure, Selver. . . . I was well taught in dreaming, and then I'm old. I dream very little for myself any more. Why should I? Little is new to me. And what I wanted from my life, I have had, and more. I have had my whole life. Days like the leaves of the forest. I'm an old hollow tree, only the roots live. And so I dream only what all men dream. I have no visions and no wishes. I see what is. I see the fruit ripening on the branch. Four years it has been ripening, that fruit of the deep-planted tree. We have all been afraid for four years, even we who live far from the yumens' cities, and have only glimpsed them from hiding, or seen their ships fly over, or looked at the dead places where they cut down the world, or heard mere tales of these things. We are all afraid. Children wake from sleep crying of giants; women will not go far on their trading-journeys; men in the Lodges cannot sing. The fruit of fear is ripening. And I see you gather it. You are the harvester. All that we fear to know, you have seen, you have known: exile, shame, pain, the roof and walls of the world fallen, the mother dead in misery, the children untaught, uncherished. . . . This is a new time for the world: a bad time. And you have suffered it all. You have gone farthest. And at the farthest, at the end of the black path, there grows the Tree; there the fruit ripens; now you reach up, Selver, now you gather it. And the world changes wholly, when a man holds in his hand the fruit of that tree, whose roots are deeper than the forest. Men will know it. They will know you, as we did. It doesn't take an old man or a Great Dreamer to recognise a god! Where you go, fire burns; only the blind cannot see it. But listen, Selver, this is what I see that perhaps others do not, this is why I have loved you: I dreamed of you before we met here. You were walking on a path, and behind you the young trees grew up, oak and birch, willow and holly, fir and pine, alder, elm, white-flowering ash, all the roof and walls of the world, forever renewed. Now farewell, dear god and son, go safely."

The night darkened as Selver went, until even his night-seeing eyes saw nothing but masses and planes of black. It began to rain. He had gone only a few miles from Cadast when he must either light a torch, or halt. He chose to halt, and groping found a place among the roots of a great chestnut tree. There he sat, his back against the broad, twisting bole that seemed to hold a little sun-warmth in it still. The fine rain, falling unseen in darkness, pattered on the leaves overhead, on his arms and neck and head protected by their thick silk-fine hair, on the earth and ferns and under-growth nearby, on all the leaves of the forest, near and far. Selver sat as quiet as the grey owl on a branch above him, unsleeping, his eyes wide open in the rainy dark.

3.

Captain Raj Lyubov had a headache. It began softly in the muscles of his right shoulder, and mounted crescendo to a smashing drumbeat over his right ear. The speech centers are in the left cerebral cortex, he thought, but he couldn't have said it; couldn't speak, or read, or sleep, or think. Cortex, vortex. Migraine headache, margarine breadache, ow, ow, ow. Of course he had been cured of migraine once at college and again during his obligatory Army Prophylactic Psychotherapy Sessions, but he had brought along some ergotamine pills when he left Earth, just in case. He had taken two, and a superhyperduper-analgesic, and a tranquillizer, and a digestive pill to counteract the caffeine which counteracted the ergotamine, but the awl still bored out from within, just over his right ear, to the beat of the big bass drum. Awl, drill, ill, pill, oh God. Lord deliver us. Liver sausage. What would the Athsheans do for a migraine? They wouldn't have one, they would have daydreamed the tensions away a week before they got them. Try it, try daydreaming. Begin as Selver taught you. Although knowing nothing of electricity he could not really grasp the principle of the EEG, as soon as he heard about alpha waves and when they appear he had said, "Oh yes, you mean this," and there appeared the unmistakable alpha-squiggles on the graph recording what went on inside his small green head; and he had taught Lyubov how to turn on and off the alpha-rhythms in one half-hour lesson. There really was nothing to it. But not now, the world is too much with us, ow, ow, ow above the right ear I always hear

Time's winged chariot hurrying near, for the Athsheans had burned Smith Camp day before yesterday and killed two hundred men. Two hundred and seven to be precise. Every man alive except the Captain. No wonder pills couldn't get at the center of his migraine, for it was on an island two hundred miles away two days ago. Over the hills and far away. Ashes, ashes, all fall down. And amongst the ashes, all his knowledge of the High Intelligence Life Forms of World 41. Dust, rubbish, a mess of false data and fake hypotheses. Nearly five E-years here, and he had believed the Athsheans to be incapable of killing men, his kind or their kind. He had written long papers to explain how and why they couldn't kill men. All wrong. Dead wrong.

What had he failed to see?

It was nearly time to be going over to the meeting at HQ. Cautiously Lyubov stood up, moving all in one piece so that the right side of his head would not fall off; he approached his desk with the gait of a man underwater, poured out a shot of General Issue vodka, and drank it. It turned him inside out: it extraverted him: it normalized him. He felt better. He went out, and unable to stand the jouncing of his motorbike, started to walk down the long, dusty main street of Centralville to HQ. Passing the Luau he thought with greed of another vodka; but Captain Davidson was just going in the door, and Lyubov went on.

The people from the *Shackleton* were already in the conference room. Commander Yung, whom he had met before, had brought some new faces down from orbit this time. They were not in Navy uniform; after a moment Lyubov recognised them, with a slight shock, as non-Terran humans. He sought an introduction at once. One, Mr Or, was a Hairy Cetian, dark grey, stocky, and dour; the other, Mr Lepennon, was tall, white, and comely: a Hainishman. They greeted Lyubov with interest. and Lepennon said, "I've just been reading your report on the conscious control of paradoxical sleep among the Athsheans, Dr Lyubov," which was pleasant, and it was pleasant also to be called by his own, earned title of doctor. Their conversation indicated that they had spent some years on Earth, and that they might be hilfers, or something like it; but the Commander, introducing them, had not mentioned their status or position.

The room was filling up. Gosse, the colony ecologist, came in; so did all the high brass; so did Captain Susun, head of Planet Development—logging operations—whose captaincy like Lyubov's was an invention necessary to the peace of the military mind. Captain Davidson came in alone, straight-backed and handsome, his lean, rugged face calm and rather stern. Guards stood at all the doors. The Army necks were all stiff as crowbars. The conference was plainly an Investigation. *Whose fault?* My fault, Lyubov thought despairingly; but out of his despair he looked across the table at Captain Don Davidson with detestation and contempt.

Commander Yung had a very quiet voice. "As you know, gentlemen, my ship stopped here at World 41 to drop you off a new load of colonists, and nothing more; *Shackleton's* mission is to World 88, Prestno, one of the Hainish Group. However, this attack on your outpost camp, since it chanced to occur during our week here, can't be simply ignored; particularly in the light of certain developments which you would have been informed of a little later, in the normal course of events. The fact is that the status of World 41 as an Earth Colony is now subject to revision, and the massacre at your camp may precipitate the Administration's decisions on it. Certainly the decisions *we* can make must be made quickly, for I can't keep my ship here long. Now first, we wish to make sure that the relevant facts are all in the possession of those present. Captain Davidson's report on the events at Smith Camp was taped and heard by all of us on ship; by all of you here also? Good. Now if there are questions any of you wish to ask Captain Davidson, go ahead. I have one myself. You returned to the site of the camp the following day, Captain Davidson, in a large hopper with eight soldiers; had you the permission of a senior officer here at Central for that flight?"

Davidson stood up. "I did, sir."

"Were you authorised to land and to set fires in the forest near the campsite?"

"No, sir."

"You did, however, set fires?"

"I did, sir. I was trying to smoke out the creechies that killed my men."

"Very well. Mr Lepennon?"

The tall Hainishman cleared his throat. "Captain Davidson," he said, "do you think that the people under your command at Smith Camp were mostly content?"

"Yes, I do."

Davidson's manner was firm and forthright; he seemed indifferent to the fact that he was in trouble. Of course these Navy officers and foreigners had no authority over him; it was to his own Colonel that he must answer for losing two hundred men and making unauthorized reprisals. But his Colonel was right there, listening.

"They were well fed, well housed, not overworked, then, as well as can be managed in a frontier camp?"

"Yes."

"Was the discipline maintained very harsh?"

"No, it was not."

"What, then, do you think motivated the revolt?"

"I don't understand."

"If none of them were discontented, why did some of them massacre the rest and destroy the camp?"

There was a worried silence.

"May I put in a word," Lyubov said. "It was the native hilfs, the Athsheans employed in the camp, who joined with an attack by the forest people against the Terran humans. In his report Captain Davidson referred to the Athsheans as 'creechies.' "

Lepennon looked embarrassed and anxious. "Thank you, Dr Lyubov. I misunderstood entirely. Actually I took the word 'creechie' to stand for a Terran caste that did rather menial work in the logging camps. Believing, as we all did, that the Athsheans were intraspecies non-aggressive, I never thought they might be the group meant. In fact I didn't realise that they cooperated with you in your camps.—However, I am more at a loss than ever to understand what provoked the attack and mutiny."

"I don't know, sir."

"When he said the people under his command were content, did the Captain include native people?" said the Cetian, Or, in a dry mumble. The Hainishman picked it up at once, and asked Davidson, in his concerned, courteous voice, "Were the Athsheans living at the camp content, do you think?"

"So far as I know."

"There was nothing unusual in their position there, or the work they had to do?"

Lyubov felt the heightening of tension, one turn of the screw, in Colonel Dongh and his staff, and also in the starship commander. Davidson remained calm and easy. "Nothing unusual."

Lyubov knew now that only his scientific studies had been sent up to the *Shackleton*; his protests, even his annual assessments of 'Native Adjustment to Colonial Presence' required by the Administration, had been kept in some desk drawer deep in HQ. These two N.-T.H.'s knew nothing about the exploitation of the Athsheans. Commander Yung did, of course; he had been down before today and had probably seen the creechie-pens. In any case a Navy commander on Colony runs wouldn't have much to learn about Terran-hilf relations. Whether or not he approved of how the Colonial Administration ran its business, not much would come as a shock to him. But a Cetian and a Hainishman, how much would they know about Terran colonies, unless chance brought them to one on the way to somewhere else? Lepennon and Or had not intended to come on-planet here at all. Or possibly they had not been intended to come on-planet, but, hearing of trouble, had insisted. Why had the commander brought them down: his will, or theirs? Whoever they were they had about them a hint of authority, a whiff of the dry, intoxicating odor of power. Lyubov's headache had gone, he felt alert and excited, his face was rather hot. "Captain Davidson," he said, "I have a couple of questions, concerning your confrontation with the four natives, day before yesterday. You're certain that one of them was Sam, or Selver Thele?"

"I believe so."

"You're aware that he has a personal grudge against you."

"I don't know."

"You don't? Since his wife died in your quarters immediately subsequent to sexual intercourse with you, he holds you responsible for her death; you didn't know that? He attacked you once before, here in Centralville; you had forgotten that? Well, the point is, that Selver's personal hatred for Captain Davidson may serve as a partial explanation or motivation for this unprecedented assault. The Athsheans aren't incapable of personal violence, that's never been asserted in any of my studies of them. Adolescents who haven't mastered controlled dreaming or competitive singing do a lot of wrestling and fist-fighting, not all of it good-tempered. But Selver is an adult and an adept; and his first, personal attack on Captain Davidson, which I happened to witness part of, was pretty certainly an attempt to kill. As was the Captain's retaliation, incidentally. At the time, I thought that attack an isolated psychotic incident, resulting from grief and stress, not likely to be repeated. I was wrong.—Captain, when the four Athsheans jumped you from ambush, as you describe in your report, did you end up prone on the ground?"

"Yes."

"In what position?"

Davidson's calm face tensed and stiffened, and Lyubov felt a pang of compunction. He wanted to corner Davidson in his lies, to force him into speaking truth once, but not to humiliate him before others. Accusations of rape and murder supported Davidson's image of himself as the totally virile man, but now that image was endangered: Lyubov had called up a picture of him, the soldier, the fighter, the cool tough man, being knocked down by enemies the size of six-year-olds. . . . What did it cost Davidson, then, to recall that moment when he had lain looking up at the little green men, for once, not down at them?

"I was on my back."

"Was your head thrown back, or turned aside?"

"I don't know."

"I'm trying to establish a fact here, Captain, one that might help explain why Selver didn't kill you, although he had a grudge against you and had helped kill two hundred men a few hours earlier. I wondered if you might by chance have been in one of the positions which, when assumed by an Athshean, prevent his opponent from further physical aggression."

"I don't know."

Lyubov glanced round the conference table; all the faces showed curiosity and some tension. "These aggression-halting gestures and positions may have some innate basis, may rise from a surviving trigger-response, but they are socially developed and expanded, and of course learned. The strongest and completest of them is a prone position, on the back, eyes shut, head turned so the throat is fully exposed. I think an Athshean of the local cultures might find it impossible to hurt an enemy who took that position. He would have to do something else to release his anger or aggressive drive.— When they had all got you down, Captain, did Selver by any chance sing?"

"Did he what?"

"Sing."

"I don't know."

Block. No go. Lyubov was about to shrug and give it up when the Cetian said, "Why, Mr Lyubov?" The most winning characteristic of the rather harsh Cetian temperament was curiosity, inopportune and inexhaustible curiosity; Cetians died eagerly, curious as to what came next.

"You see," Lyubov said, "the Athsheans use a kind of ritualised singing to replace physical combat. Again it's a universal social phenomenon that might have a physiological foundation, though it's very hard to establish anything as 'innate' in human beings. However the higher primates here all go in for vocal competing between two males, a lot of howling and whistling; the dominant male may finally give the other a cuff, but usually they just spend an hour or so trying to outbellow each other. The Athsheans themselves see the similarity to their singing-matches, which are also only between males; but as they observe, theirs are not only aggression-releases, but an art-form. The better artist wins. I wondered if Selver sang over Captain Davidson, and if so, whether he did because he could not kill, or because he preferred the bloodless victory. These questions have suddenly become rather urgent."

"Dr Lyubov," said Lepennon, "how effective are these aggression-channelling devices? Are they universal?"

"Among adults, yes. So my informants state, and all my observation supported them, until day before yesterday. Rape, violent assault, and murder virtually don't exist among them. There are accidents, of course. And there are psychotics. Not many of the latter."

"What do they do with dangerous psychotics?"

"Isolate them. Literally. On small islands."

"The Athsheans are carnivorous, they hunt animals?"

"Yes, meat is a staple."

"Wonderful," Lepennon said, and his white skin paled further with pure excitement. "A human society with an effective war-barrier! What's the cost, Dr Lyubov?"

"I'm not sure, Mr Lepennon. Perhaps change. They're a static, stable, uniform society. They have no history. Perfectly integrated, and wholly unprogressive. You might say that like the forest they live in, they've attained a climax state. But I don't mean to imply that they're incapable of adaptation."

"Gentlemen, this is very interesting but in a somewhat specialist frame of reference, and it may be somewhat out of the context which we're attempting to clarify here—"

"No, excuse me, Colonel Dongh, this may be the point. Yes, Dr Lyubov?"

"Well, I wonder if they're not proving their adaptability, now. By adapting their behavior to us. To the Earth Colony. For four years they've behaved to us as they do to one another. Despite the physical differences, they recognised us as members of their species, as men. However, we have not responded as members of their species should respond. We have ignored the responses, the rights and obligations of non-violence. We have killed, raped, dispersed, and enslaved the native humans, destroyed their communities, and cut down their forests. It wouldn't be surprising if they'd decided that we are not human."

"And therefore can be killed, like animals, yes yes," said the Cetian, enjoying logic; but Lepennon's face now was stiff as white stone. "Enslaved?" he said.

"Captain Lyubov is expressing his personal opinions and

theories," said Colonel Dongh, "which I should state I consider possibly to be erroneous, and he and I have discussed this type of thing previously, although the present context is unsuitable. We do not employ slaves, sir. Some of the natives serve a useful role in our community. The Voluntary Autochthonous Labor Corps is a part of all but the temporary camps here. We have very limited personnel to accomplish our tasks here and we need workers and use all we can get, but on any kind of basis that could be called a slavery basis, certainly not."

Lepennon was about to speak, but deferred to the Cetian, who said only, "How many of each race?"

Gosse replied: "2641 Terrans, now. Lyubov and I estimate the native hilf population very roughly at 3 million."

"You should have considered these statistics, gentlemen, before you altered the native traditions!" said Or, with a disagreeable but perfectly genuine laugh.

"We are adequately armed and equipped to resist any type of aggression these natives could offer," said the Colonel. "However there was a general consensus by both the first Exploratory Missions and our own research staff of specialists here headed by Captain Lyubov, giving us to understand that the New Tahitians are a primitive, harmless, peace-loving species. Now this information was obviously erroneous—"

Or interrupted the Colonel. "Obviously! You consider the human species to be primitive, harmless, and peace-loving, Colonel? No. But you knew that the hilfs of this planet are human? As human as you or I or Lepennon—since we all came from the same, original, Hainish stock?"

"That is the scientific theory, I am aware—"

"Colonel, it is the historic fact."

"I am not forced to accept it as a fact," the old Colonel said, getting hot, "and I don't like opinions stuffed into my own mouth. The fact is that these creechies are a meter tall, they're covered with green fur, they don't sleep, and they're not human beings in my frame of reference!"

"Captain Davidson," said the Cetian, "do you consider the native hilfs human, or not?"

"I don't know."

"But you had sexual intercourse with one—this Selver's wife. Would you have sexual intercourse with a female animal? What about the rest of you?" He looked about at the purple colonel, the glowering majors, the livid captains, the cringing specialists. Contempt came into his face. "You have not thought things through," he said. By his standards it was a brutal insult.

The Commander of the *Shackleton* at last salvaged words from the gulf of embarrassed silence. "Well, gentlemen, the tragedy at Smith Camp clearly is involved with the entire colony-native relationship, and is not by any means an insignificant or isolated episode. That's what we had to establish. And this being the case, we can make a certain contribution towards easing your problems here. The main purpose of our journey was not to drop off a couple of hundred girls here, though I know you've been waiting for 'em, but to get to Prestno, which has been having some difficulties, and give the government there an ansible. That is, an ICD transmitter."

"What?" said Sereng, an engineer. Stares became fixed, all round the table.

"The one we have aboard is an early model, and it cost a planetary annual revenue, roughly. That, of course, was 27 years ago planetary time, when we left Earth. Nowadays they're making them relatively cheaply; they're SI on Navy ships; and in the normal course of things a robo or manned ship would be coming out here to give your colony one. As a matter of fact it's a manned Administration ship, and is on the way, due here in 9.4 E-years if I recall the figure."

"How do you know that?" somebody said, setting it up for Commander Yung, who replied smiling, "By the ansible: the one we have aboard. Mr Or, your people invented the device, perhaps you'd explain it to those here who are unfamiliar with the terms?"

The Cetian did not unbend. "I shall not attempt to explain the principles of ansible operation to those present," he said. "Its effect can be stated simply: the instantaneous transmission of a message over any distance. One element must be on a large-mass body, the other can be anywhere in the cosmos. Since arrival in orbit the *Shackleton* has been in daily communication with Terra, now 27 lightyears distant. The message does not take 54 years for delivery and response, as it does on an electromagnetic device. It takes no time. There is no more time-gap between worlds."

"As soon as we came out of NAFAL time-dilatation into planetary space-time, here, we rang up home, as you might say," the soft-voiced Commander went on. "And were told what had happened during the 27 years we were travelling. The time-gap for bodies remains, but the information lag does not. As you can see, this is as important to us as an interstellar species, as speech itself was to us earlier in our evolution. It'll have the same effect: to make a society possible."

"Mr Or and I left Earth, 27 years ago, as Legates for our respective governments, Tau II and Hain," said Lepennon.

His voice was still gentle and civil, but the warmth had gone out of it. "When we left, people were talking about the possibility of forming some kind of league among the civilised worlds, now that communication was possible. The League of Worlds now exists. It has existed for 18 years. Mr Or and I are now Emissaries of the Council of the League, and so have certain powers and responsibilities we did not have when we left Earth."

The three of them from the ship kept saying these things: an instantaneous communicator exists, an interstellar supergovernment exists. . . . Believe it or not. They were in league, and lying. This thought went through Lyubov's mind; he considered it, decided it was a reasonable but unwarranted suspicion, a defense-mechanism, and discarded it. Some of the military staff, however, trained to compartmentalize their thinking, specialists in self-defense, would accept it as unhesitatingly as he discarded it. They must believe that anyone claiming a sudden new authority was a liar or conspirator. They were no more constrained than Lyubov, who had been trained to keep his mind open whether he wanted to or not.

"Are we to take all—all this simply on your word, sir?" said Colonel Dongh, with dignity and some pathos; for he, too muddleheaded to compartmentalize neatly, knew that he shouldn't believe Lepennon and Or and Yung, but did believe them, and was frightened.

"No," said the Cetian. "That's done with. A colony like this had to believe what passing ships and outdated radiomessages told them. Now you don't. You can verify. We are going to give you the ansible destined for Prestno. We have League authority to do so. Received, of course, by ansible. Your colony here is in a bad way. Worse than I thought from your reports. Your reports are very incomplete; censorship or stupidity have been at work. Now, however, you'll have the ansible, and can talk with your Terran Administration; you can ask for orders, so you'll know how to proceed. Given the profound changes that have been occurring in the organisation of the Terran Government since we left there, I should recommend that you do so at once. There is no longer any excuse for acting on outdated orders; for ignorance; for irresponsible autonomy."

Sour a Cetian and, like milk, he stayed sour. Mr Or was being overbearing, and Commander Yung should shut him up. But could he? How did an "Emissary of the Council of the League of Worlds" rank? Who's in charge here, thought Lyubov, and he too felt a qualm of fear. His headache had returned as a sense of constriction, a sort of tight headband over the temples.

He looked across the table at Lepennon's white, long-fingered hands, lying left over right, quiet, on the bare polished wood of the table. The white skin was a defect to Lyubov's Earth-formed aesthetic taste, but the serenity and strength of those hands pleased him very much. To the Hainish, he thought, civilisation came naturally. They had been at it so long. They lived the social-intellectual life with the grace of a cat hunting in a garden, the certainty of a swallow following summer over the sea. They were experts. They never had to pose, to fake. They were what they were. Nobody seemed to fit the human skin so well. Except, perhaps, the little green men? the deviant, dwarfed, over-adapted, stagnated creechies, who were as absolutely, as honestly, as serenely what they were. . . .

An officer, Benton, was asking Lepennon if he and Or were on this planet as observers for the (he hesitated) League of Worlds, or if they claimed any authority to . . . Lepennon took him up politely: "We are observers here, not empowered to command, only to report. You are still answerable only to your own government on Earth."

Colonel Dongh said with relief, "Then nothing has essentially changed—"

"You forget the ansible," Or interrupted. "I'll instruct you in its operation, Colonel, as soon as this discussion is over. You can then consult with your Colonial Administration."

"Since your problem here is rather urgent, and since Earth is now a League member and may have changed the Colonial Code somewhat during recent years, Mr Or's advice is both proper and timely. We should be very grateful to Mr Or and Mr Lepennon for their decision to give this Terran colony the ansible destined for Prestno. It was their decision; I can only applaud it. Now, one more decision remains to be made, and this one I have to make, using your judgment as my guide. If you feel the colony is in imminent peril of further and more massive attacks from the natives, I can keep my ship here for a week or two as a defense arsenal; I can also evacuate the women. No children yet, right?"

"No, sir," said Gosse. "482 women, now."

"Well, I have space for 380 passengers; we might crowd a hundred more in; the extra mass would add a year or so to the trip home, but it could be done. Unfortunately that's all I can do. We must proceed to Prestno; your nearest neighbor, as you know, 1.8 lightyears distant. We'll stop here on the way home to Terra, but that's going to be three and a half more E-years at least. Can you stick it out?"

"Yes," said the Colonel, and others echoed him. "We've had warning now and we won't be caught napping again."

"Equally," said the Cetian, "can the native inhabitants stick it out for three and a half Earth-years more?"

"Yes," said the Colonel. "No," said Lyubov. He had been watching Davidson's face, and a kind of panic had taken hold of him.

"Colonel?" said Lepennon, politely.

"We've been here four years now and the natives are flourishing. There's room enough and to spare for all of us, as you can see the planet's heavily underpopulated and the Administration wouldn't have cleared it for colonisation purposes if that hadn't been as it is. As for if this entered anyone's head, they won't catch us off guard again, we were erroneously briefed concerning the nature of these natives, but we're fully armed and able to defend ourselves, but we aren't planning any reprisals. That is expressly forbidden in the Colonial Code, though I don't know what new rules this new government may have added on, but we'll just stick to our own as we have been doing and they definitely negative mass reprisals or genocide. We won't be sending any messages for help out, after all a colony 27 light-years from home has come out expecting to be on its own and to in fact be completely self-sufficient, and I don't see that the ICD really changes that, due to ship and men and material still have to travel at near lightspeed. We'll just keep on shipping the lumber home, and look out for ourselves. The women are in no danger."

"Mr Lyubov?" said Lepennon.

"We've been here four years. I don't know if the native human culture will survive four more. As for the total land ecology, I think Gosse will back me if I say that we've irrecoverably wrecked the native life-systems on one large island, have done great damage on this subcontinent Sornol, and if we go on logging at the present rate, may reduce the major habitable lands to desert within ten years. This isn't the fault of the colony's HQ or Forestry Bureau; they've simply been following a Development Plan drawn up on Earth without sufficient knowledge of the planet to be exploited, its life-systems, or its native human inhabitants."

"Mr Gosse?" said the polite voice.

"Well, Raj, you're stretching things a bit. There's no denying that Dump Island, which was overlogged in direct contravention to my recommendations, is a dead loss. If more than a certain percentage of the forest is cut over a certain area, then the fibreweed doesn't reseed, you see, gentlemen, and the fibreweed root-system is the main soil-binder on clear land; without it the soil goes dusty and drifts off very fast under wind-erosion and the heavy rainfall. But I can't agree that our basic directives are at fault, so long as they're scrupulously followed. They were based on careful study of the planet. We've succeeded, here on Central, by following the Plan: erosion is minimal, and the cleared soil is highly arable. To log off a forest doesn't, after all, mean to make a desert—except perhaps from the point of view of a squirrel. We can't forecast precisely how the native forest life-systems will adapt to the new woodland-prairie-plowland ambiance foreseen in the Development Plan, but we know the chances are good for a large percentage of adaptation and survival."

"That's what the Bureau of Land Management said about Alaska during the First Famine," said Lyubov. His throat had tightened so that his voice came out high and husky. He had counted on Gosse for support. "How many Sitka spruce have you seen in your lifetime, Gosse? Or snowy owl? or wolf? or Eskimo? The survival percentage of native Alaskan species in habitat, after 15 years of the Development Program, was .3%. It's now zero.—A forest ecology is a delicate one. If the forest perishes, its fauna may go with it. The Athshean word for *world* is also the word for *forest*. I submit, Commander Yung, that though the colony may not be in imminent danger, the planet is—"

"Captain Lyubov," said the old Colonel, "such submissions are not properly submitted by staff specialist officers to officers of other branches of the service but should rest on the judgment of the senior officers of the Colony, and I cannot tolerate any further such attempts as this to give advice without previous clearance."

Caught off guard by his own outburst, Lyubov apologised and tried to look calm. If only he didn't lose his temper, if his voice didn't go weak and husky, if he had poise. . . .

The Colonel went on. "It appears to us that you made some serious erroneous judgments concerning the peacefulness and non-aggressiveness of the natives here, and because we counted on this specialist description of them as non-aggressive is why we left ourselves open to this terrible tragedy at Smith Camp, Captain Lyubov. So I think we have to wait until some other specialists in hilfs have had time to study them, because evidently your theories were basically erroneous to some extent."

Lyubov sat and took it. Let the men from the ship see

them all passing the blame around like a hot brick: all the better. The more dissension they showed, the likelier were these Emissaries to have them checked and watched over. And he was to blame; he had been wrong. To hell with my self-respect so long as the forest people get a chance, Lyubov thought, and so strong a sense of his own humiliation and self-sacrifice came over him that tears rose to his eyes.

He was aware that Davidson was watching him.

He sat up stiff, the blood hot in his face, his temples drumming. He would not be sneered at by that bastard Davidson. Couldn't Or and Lepennon see what kind of man Davidson was, and how much power he had here, while Lyubov's powers, called "advisory," were simply derisory? If the colonists were left to go on with no check on them but a super-radio, the Smith Camp massacre would almost certainly become the excuse for systematic aggression against the natives. Bacteriological extermination, most likely. The *Shackleton* would come back in three and a half or four years to "New Tahiti," and find a thriving Terran colony, and no more Creechie Problem. None at all. Pity about the plague, we took all precautions required by the Code, but it must have been some kind of mutation, they had no natural resistance, but we did manage to save a group of them by transporting them to the New Falkland Isles in the southern hemisphere and they're doing fine there, all sixty-two of them. . . .

The conference did not last much longer. When it ended he stood up and leaned across the table to Lepennon. "You must tell the League to do something to save the forests, the forest people," he said almost inaudibly, his throat contricted, "you must, please, you must."

The Hainishman met his eyes; his gaze was reserved, kindly, and deep as a well. He said nothing.

4.

It was unbelievable. They'd all gone insane. This damned alien world had sent them all right round the bend, into bye-bye dreamland, along with the creechies. He still wouldn't believe what he'd seen at that 'conference' and the briefing after it, if he saw it all over again on film. A Starfleet ship's commander bootlicking two humanoids. Engineeers and techs cooing and ooing over a fancy radio presented to them by a Hairy Cetian with a lot of sneering and boasting, as if ICD's hadn't been predicted by Terran science years ago! The humanoids had stolen the idea, implemented it, and called it an 'ansible' so nobody would realise it was just an ICD. But the worst part of it had been the conference, with that psycho Lyubov raving and crying, and Colonel Dongh letting him do it, letting him insult Davidson and HQ staff and the whole Colony; and all the time the two aliens sitting and grinning, the little grey ape and the big white fairy, sneering at humans.

It had been pretty bad. It hadn't got any better since the *Shackleton* left. He didn't mind being sent down to New Java Camp under Major Muhamed. The Colonel had to discipline him; old Ding Dong might actually be very happy about that fire-raid he'd pulled in reprisal on Smith Island, but the raid had been a breach of discipline and he had to reprimand Davidson. All right, rules of the game. But what wasn't in the rules was this stuff coming over that overgrown TV set they called the ansible—their new little tin god at HQ.

Orders from the Bureau of Colonial Administration in Karachi: *Restrict Terran-Athshean contact to occasions arranged by Athsheans.* In other words you couldn't go into a creechie warren and round up a workforce any more. *Employment of volunteer labor is not advised; employment of forced labor is forbidden.* More of same. How the hell were they supposed to get the work done? Did Earth want this wood or didn't it? They were still sending the robot cargo ships to New Tahiti, weren't they, four a year, each carrying about 30 million new-dollars worth of prime lumber back to Mother Earth. Sure the Development people wanted those millions. They were businessmen. These messages weren't coming from them, any fool could see that.

The colonial status of World 41—why didn't they call it New Tahiti any more?—*is under consideration. Until decision is reached colonists should observe extreme caution in all dealings with native inhabitants. ... The use of weapons of any kind except small side-arms carried in self-defense is absolutely forbidden*—just as on Earth, except that there a man couldn't even carry side-arms any more. But what the hell was the use coming 27 lightyears to a frontier world and then get told No guns, no firejelly, no bugbombs, no no, just sit like like nice little boys and let the creechies come spit in your faces and sing songs at you and then stick a knife in your guts and burn down your camp, but don't you hurt the cute little green fellers, no sir!

A policy of avoidance is strongly advised; a policy of aggression or retaliation is strictly forbidden.

That was the gist of all the messages actually, and any fool could tell that that wasn't the Colonial Administration talking. They couldn't have changed that much in thirty years.

They were practical, realistic men who knew what life was like on frontier planets. It was clear, to anybody who hadn't gone spla from geoshock, that the 'ansible' messages were phoneys. They might be planted right in the machine, a whole set of answers to high-probability questions, computer run. The engineers said they could have spotted that; maybe so. In that case the thing did communicate instantaneously with another world. But that world wasn't Earth. Not by a long long shot! There weren't any men typing the answers onto the other end of that little trick: they were aliens, humanoids. Probably Cetians, for the machine was Cetian-made, and they were a smart bunch of devils. They were the kind that might make a real bid for interstellar supremacy. The Hainish would be in the conspiracy with them, of course; all that bleeding-heart stuff in the so-called directives had a Hainish sound to it. What the long-term objective of the aliens was, was hard to guess from here; it probably involved weakening the Terran Government by tying it up in this 'league of worlds' business, until the aliens were strong enough to make an armed takeover. But their plan for New Tahiti was easy to see. They'd let the creechies wipe out the humans for them. Just tie the humans' hands with a lot of fake 'ansible' directives and let the slaughter begin. Humanoids help humanoids: rats help rats.

And Colonel Dongh had swallowed it. He intended to obey orders. He had actually said that to Davidson. "I intend to obey my orders from Terra-HQ, and by God, Don, you'll obey my orders the same way, and in New Java you'll obey Major Muhamed's orders there." He was stupid, old Ding Dong, but he liked Davidson, and Davidson liked him. If it meant betraying the human race to an alien conspiracy then he couldn't obey his orders, but he still felt sorry for the old soldier. A fool, but a loyal and brave one. Not a born traitor like that whining, tattling prig Lyubov. If there was one man he hoped the creechies did get, it was bigdome Raj Lyubov, the alien-lover.

Some men, especially the asiatiforms and hindi types, are actually born traitors. Not all, but some. Certain other men are born saviors. It just happened to be the way they were made, like being of euraf descent, or like having a good physique; it wasn't anything he claimed credit for. If he could save the men and women of New Tahiti, he would; if he couldn't, he'd make a damn good try; and that was all there was to it, actually.

The women, now, that rankled. They'd pulled out the 10 Collies who'd been in New Java and none of the new ones were being sent out from Centralville. "Not safe yet," HQ bleated. Pretty rough on the three outpost camps. What did they expect the outposters to do when it was hands off the she-creechies, and all the she-humans were for the lucky bastards at Central? It was going to cause terrific resentment. But it couldn't last long, the whole situation was too crazy to be stable. If they didn't start easing back to normal now the *Shackleton* was gone, then Captain D. Davidson would just have to do a little extra work to get things headed back towards normalcy.

The morning of the day he left Central, they had let loose the whole creechie work-force. Made a big noble speech in pidgin, opened the compound gates, and let out every single tame creechie, carriers, diggers, cooks, dustmen, houseboys, maids, the lot. Not one had stayed. Some of them had been with their masters ever since the start of the colony, four E-years ago. But they had no loyalty. A dog, a chimp would have hung around. These things weren't even that highly developed, they were just about like snakes or rats, just smart enough to turn around and bite you as soon as you let 'em out of the cage. Ding Dong was spla, letting all those creechies loose right in the vicinity. Dumping them on Dump Island and letting them starve would have been actually the best final solution. But Dongh was still panicked by that pair of humanoids and their talky-box. So if the wild creechies on Central were planning to imitate the Smith Camp atrocity, they now had lots of real handy new recruits, who knew the layout of the whole town, the routines, where the arsenal was, where guards were posted, and the rest. If Centralville got burned down, HQ could thank themselves. It would be what they deserved, actually. For letting traitors dupe them, for listening to humanoids and ignoring the advice of men who really knew what the creechies were like.

None of those guys at HQ had come back to camp and found ashes and wreckage and burned bodies, like he had. And Ok's body, out where they'd slaughtered the logging crew, it had had an arrow sticking out of each eye like some sort of weird insect with antennae sticking out feeling the air, Christ, he kept seeing that.

One thing anyhow, whatever the phoney 'directives' said, the boys at Central wouldn't be stuck with trying to use 'small side-arms' for self-defense. They had fire throwers and machine guns; the 16 little hoppers had machine guns and were useful for dropping firejelly cans from; the five big hoppers had full armament. But they wouldn't need the big stuff.

Just take up a hopper over one of the deforested areas and catch a mess of creechies there, with their damned bows and arrows, and start dropping firejelly cans and watch them run around and burn. It would be all right. It made his belly churn a little to imagine it, just like when he thought about making a woman, or whenever he remembered about when that Sam creechie had attacked him and he had smashed in his whole face with four blows one right after the other. It was eidetic memory plus a more vivid imagination than most men had, no credit due, just happened to be the way he was made.

The fact is, the only time a man is really and entirely a man is when he's just had a woman or just killed another man. That wasn't original, he'd read it in some old books; but it was true. That was why he liked to imagine scenes like that. Even if the creechies weren't actually men.

New Java was the southernmost of the five big lands, just north of the equator, and so was hotter than Central or Smith which were just about perfect climate-wise. Hotter and a lot wetter. It rained all the time in the wet seasons anywhere on New Tahiti, but in the northern lands it was a kind of quiet fine rain that went on and on and never really got you wet or cold. Down here it came in buckets, and there was a monsoon-type storm that you couldn't even walk in, let alone work in. Only a solid roof kept that rain off you, or else the forest. The damn forest was so thick it kept out the storms. You'd get wet from all the dripping off the leaves, of course, but if you were really inside the forest during one of those monsoons you'd hardly notice the wind was blowing; then you came out in the open and wham! got knocked off your feet by the wind and slobbered all over with the red liquid mud that the rain turned the cleared ground into, and you couldn't duck back into the forest quick enough; and inside the forest it was dark, and hot, and easy to get lost.

Then the C.O., Major Muhamed, was a sticky bastard. Everything at N. J. was done by the book: the logging all in kilo-strips, the fibreweed crap planted in the logged strips, leave to Central granted in strict non-preferential rotation, hallucinogens rationed and their use on duty punished, and so on and so on. However, one good thing about Muhamed was he wasn't always radioing Central. New Java was his camp, and he ran it his way. He didn't like orders from HQ. He obeyed them all right, he'd let the creechies go, and locked up all the guns except little popgun pistols, as soon as the orders came. But he didn't go looking for orders, or for advice.

Not from Central or anybody else. He was a self-righteous type: knew he was right. That was his big fault.

When he was on Dongh's staff at HQ Davidson had had occasion sometimes to see the officers' records. His unusual memory held on to such things, and he could recall for instance that Muhamed's IQ was 107. Whereas his own happened to be 118. There was a difference of 11 points; but of course he couldn't say that to old Moo, and Moo couldn't see it, and so there was no way to get him to listen. He thought he knew better than Davidson, and that was that.

They were all a bit sticky at first, actually. None of these men at N. J. knew anything about the Smith Camp atrocity, except that the camp C.O. had left for Central an hour before it happened, and so was the only human that escaped alive. Put like that, it did sound bad. You could see why at first they looked at him like a kind of Jonah, or worse, a kind of Judas even. But when they got to know him they'd know better. They'd begin to see that, far from being a deserter or traitor, he was dedicated to preventing the colony of New Tahiti from betrayal. And they'd realise that getting rid of the creechies was going to be the only way to make this world safe for the Terran way of life.

It wasn't too hard to start getting that message across to the loggers. They'd never liked the little green rats, having to drive them to work all day and guard them all night; but now they began to understand that the creechies were not only repulsive but dangerous. When Davidson told them what he'd found at Smith; when he explained how the two humanoids on the Fleet ship had brainwashed HQ; when he showed them that wiping out the Terrans on New Tahiti was just a small part of the whole alien conspiracy against Earth; when he reminded them of the cold hard figures, twenty-five hundred humans to three *million* creechies—then they began to really get behind him.

Even the Ecological Control Officer here was with him. Not like poor old Kees, mad because men shot red deer and then getting shot in the guts himself by the sneaking creechies. This fellow, Atranda, was a creechie-hater. Actually he was kind of spla about them, he had geoshock or something; he was so afraid the creechies were going to attack the camp that he acted like some woman afraid of getting raped. But it was useful to have the local spesh on his side anyhow.

No use trying to line up the C.O.; a good judge of men, Davidson had seen it was no use almost at once. Muhamed was rigid-minded. Also he had a prejudice against Davidson which he wouldn't drop; it had something to do with the Smith Camp affair. He as much as told Davidson he didn't consider him a trustworthy officer.

He was a self-righteous bastard, but his running N. J. camp on such rigid lines was an advantage. A tight organization, used to obeying orders, was easier to take over than a loose one full of independent characters, and easier to keep together as a unit for defensive and offensive military operations, once he was in command. He would have to take command. Moo was a good logging-camp boss, but no soldier.

Davidson kept busy getting some of the best loggers and junior officers really firmly with him. He didn't hurry. When he had enough of them he could really trust, a squad of ten lifted a few items from old Moo's locked-up room in the Rec House basement full of war toys, and then went off one Sunday into the woods to play.

Davidson had located the creechie town some weeks ago, and had saved up the treat for his men. He could have done it singlehanded, but it was better this way. You got the sense of comradeship, of a real bond among men. They just walked into the place in broad open daylight, and coated all the creechies caught above-ground with firejelly and burned them, then poured kerosene over the warren-roofs and roasted the rest. Those that tried to get out got jellied; that was the artistic part, waiting at the rat-holes for the little rats to come out, letting them think they'd made it, and then just frying them from the feet up so they made torches. That green fur sizzled like crazy.

It actually wasn't much more exciting than hunting real rats, which were about the only wild animals left on Mother Earth, but there was more thrill to it; the creechies were a lot bigger than rats, and you knew they could fight back, though this time they didn't. In fact some of them even lay down instead of running away, just lay there on their backs with their eyes shut. It was sickening. The other fellows thought so too, and one of them actually got sick and vomited after he'd burned up one of the lying-down ones.

Hard up as the men were, they didn't leave even one of the females alive to rape. They had all agreed with Davidson beforehand that it was too damn near perversity. Homosexuality was with other humans, it was normal. These things might be built like human women but they weren't human, and it was better to get your kicks from killing them, and stay *clean*. That had made good sense to all of them, and they stuck to it.

Every one of them kept his trap shut back at camp, no boasting even to their buddies. They were sound men. Not a word of the expedition got to Muhamed's ears. So far as old Moo knew, all his men were good little boys just sawing up logs and keeping away from creechies, yes sir; and he could go on believing that until D-Day came.

For the creechies would attack. Somewhere. Here, or one of the camps on King Island, or Central. Davidson knew that. He was the only officer in the entire colony that did know it. No credit due, he just happened to know he was right. Nobody else had believed him, except these men here whom he'd had time to convince. But the others would all see, sooner or later, that he was right.

And he was right.

5.

It had been a shock, meeting Selver face to face. As he flew back to Central from the foothill village, Lyubov tried to decide why it had been a shock, to analyse out the nerve that had jumped. For after all one isn't usually terrified by a chance meeting with a good friend.

It hadn't been easy to get the headwoman to invite him. Tuntar had been his main locus of study all summer; he had several excellent informants there and was on good terms with the Lodge and with the headwoman, who had let him observe and participate in the community freely. Wangling an actual invitation out of her, via some of the ex-serfs still in the area, had taken a long time, but at last she had complied, giving him, according to the new directives, a genuine 'occasion arranged by the Athsheans.' His own conscience, rather than the Colonel, had insisted on this. Dongh wanted him to go. He was worried about the Creechie Threat. He told Lyubov to size them up, to 'see how they're reacting now that we're leaving them strictly alone.' He hoped for reassurance. Lyubov couldn't decide whether the report he'd be turning in would reassure Colonel Dongh, or not.

For ten miles out of Central, the plain had been logged and the stumps had all rotted away; it was now a great dull flat of fibreweed, hairy grey in the rain. Under those hirsute leaves the seedling shrubs got their first growth, the sumacs, dwarf aspens, and salviforms which, grown, would in turn protect the seedling trees. Left alone, in this even, rainy climate, this area might reforest itself within thirty years and reattain the full climax forest within a hundred. Left alone.

Suddenly the forest began again, in space not time: under the helicopter the infinitely various green of leaves covered the slow swells and foldings of the hills of North Sornol.

Like most Terrans on Terra, Lyubov had never walked among wild trees at all, never seen a wood larger than a city block. At first on Athshe he had felt oppressed and uneasy in the forest, stifled by its endless crowd and incoherence of trunks, branches, leaves in the perpetual greenish or brownish twilight. The mass and jumble of various competitive lives all pushing and swelling outwards and upwards towards light, the silence made up of many little meaningless noises, the total vegetable indifference to the presence of mind, all this had troubled him, and like the others he had kept to clearings and to the beach. But little by little he had begun to like it. Gosse teased him, calling him Mr. Gibbon; in fact Lyubov looked rather like a gibbon, with a round, dark face, long arms, and hair greying early; but gibbons were extinct. Like it or not, as a hilfer he had to go into the forests to find the hilfs; and now after four years of it he was completely at home under the trees, more so perhaps than anywhere else.

He had also come to like the Athsheans' names for their own lands and places, sonorous two-syllabled words: Sornol, Tuntar, Eshreth, Eshsen—that was now Centralville—Endtor, Abtan, and above all Athshe, which meant the Forest, and the World. So earth, terra, tellus mean both the soil and the planet, two meanings and one. But to the Athsheans soil, ground, earth was not that to which the dead return and by which the living live: the substance of their world was not earth, but forest. Terran man was clay, red dust. Athshean man was branch and root. They did not carve figures of themselves in stone, only in wood.

He brought the hopper down in a small glade north of the town, and walked in past the Women's Lodge. The smell of an Athshean settlement hung pungent in the air, woodsmoke, dead fish, aromatic herbs, alien sweat. The atmosphere of an underground house, if a Terran could fit himself in at all, was a rare compound of CO_2 and stinks. Lyubov had spent many intellectually stimulating hours doubled up and suffocating in the reeking gloom of the Men's Lodge in Tuntar. But it didn't look as if he would be invited in this time.

Of course the townsfolk knew of the Smith Camp massacre, now six weeks ago. They would have known of it soon, for word got around fast among the islands, though not so fast as to constitute a 'mysterious power of telepathy' as the loggers liked to believe. The townsfolk also knew that the 1200 slaves at Centralville had been freed soon after the

Smith Camp massacre, and Lyubov agreed with the Colonel that the natives might take the second event to be a result of the first. That gave what Colonel Dongh would call 'an erroneous impression,' but it probably wasn't important. What was important was that the slaves had been freed. Wrongs done could not be righted, but at least they were not still being done. They could start over: the natives without that painful, unanswerable wonder as to why the 'yumens' treated men like animals; and he without the burden of explanation and the gnawing of irremediable guilt.

Knowing how they valued candor and direct speech concerning frightening or troublous matters, he expected that people in Tuntar would talk about these things with him, in triumph, or apology, or rejoicing, or puzzlement. No one did. No one said much of anything to him.

He had come in late afternoon, which was like arriving in a Terran city just after dawn. Athsheans did sleep—the colonists' opinion, as often, ignored observable fact—but their physiological low was between noon and four p.m., whereas with Terrans it was usually between two and five a.m.; and they had a double-peak cycle of high temperature and high activity, coming in the two twilights, dawn and evening. Most adults slept five or six hours in 24, in several catnaps; and adept men slept as little as two hours in 24; so, if one discounted both their naps and their dreaming-states as 'laziness,' one might say they never slept. It was much easier to say that than to understand what they actually did do.—At this point, in Tuntar, things were just beginning to stir again after the late-day slump.

Lyubov noticed a good many strangers. They looked at him, but none approached; they were mere presences passing on other paths in the dusk of the great oaks. At last someone he knew came along his path, the headwoman's cousin Sherrar, an old woman of small importance and small understanding. She greeted him civilly, but did not or would not respond to his inquiries about the headwoman and his two best informants, Egath the orchard-keeper and Tubab the Dreamer. Oh, the headwoman was very busy, and who was Egath, did he mean Geban, and Tubab might be here or perhaps he was there, or not. She stuck to Lyubov, and nobody else spoke to him. He worked his way, accompanied by the hobbling, complaining, tiny, green crone, across the groves and glades of Tuntar to the Men's Lodge. "They're busy in there," said Sherrar.

"Dreaming?"

"However should I know? Come along now, Lyubov, come

see . . ." She knew he always wanted to see things, but she couldn't think what to show him to draw him away. "Come see the fishing-nets," she said feebly.

A girl passing by, one of the Young Hunters, looked up at him: a black look, a stare of animosity such as he had never received from any Athshean, unless perhaps from a little child frightened into scowling by his height and his hairless face. But this girl was not frightened.

"All right," he said to Sherrar, feeling that his only course was docility. If the Athsheans had indeed developed—at last, and abruptly—the sense of group enmity, then he must accept this, and simply try to show them that he remained a reliable, unchanging friend.

But how could their way of feeling and thinking have changed so fast, after so long? And why? At Smith Camp, provocation had been immediate and intolerable: Davidson's cruelty would drive even Athsheans to violence. But this town, Tuntar, had never been attacked by the Terrans, had suffered no slave-raids, had not seen the local forest logged or burned. He, Lyubov himself, had been there—the anthropologist cannot always leave his own shadow out of the picture he draws—but not for over two months now. They had got the news from Smith, and there were among them now refugees, ex-slaves, who had suffered at the Terrans' hands and would talk about it. But would news and hearsay change the hearers, change them radically?—when their unaggressiveness ran so deep in them, right through their culture and society and on down into their subconscious, their 'dream time,' and perhaps into their very physiology? That an Athshean could be provoked, by atrocious cruelty, to attempt murder, he knew: he had seen it happen—once. That a disrupted community might be similarly provoked by similarly intolerable injuries, he had to believe: it had happened at Smith Camp. But that talk and hearsay, no matter how frightening and outrageous, could enrage a settled community of these people to the point where they acted against their customs and reason, broke entirely out of their whole style of living, this he couldn't believe. It was psychologically improbable. Some element was missing.

Old Tubab came out of the Lodge, just as Lyubov passed in front of it. Behind the old man came Selver.

Selver crawled out of the tunnel-door, stood upright, blinked at the rain-greyed, foliage-dimmed brightness of daylight. His dark eyes met Lyubov's, looking up. Neither spoke. Lyubov was badly frightened.

Flying home in the hopper, analysing out the shocked

nerve, he thought, why fear? Why was I afraid of Selver? unprovable intuition or mere false analogy? Irrational in any case.

Nothing between Selver and Lyubov had changed. What Selver had done at Smith Camp could be justified; even if it couldn't be justified, it made no difference. The friendship between them was too deep to be touched by moral doubt. They had worked very hard together; they had taught each other, in rather more than the literal sense, their languages. They had spoken without reserve. And Lyubov's love for his friend was deepened by that gratitude the savior feels toward the one whose life he has been privileged to save.

Indeed he had scarcely realised until that moment how deep his liking and loyalty to Selver were. Had his fear in fact been the personal fear that Selver might, having learned racial hatred, reject him, despise his loyalty, and treat him not as 'you,' but as 'one of them'?

After that long first gaze Selver came forward slowly and greeted Lyubov, holding out his hands.

Touch was a main channel of communication among the forest people. Among Terrans touch is always likely to imply threat, aggression, and so for them there is often nothing between the formal handshake and the sexual caress. All that blank was filled by the Athsheans with varied customs of touch. Caress as signal and reassurance was as essential to them as it is to mother and child or to lover and lover; but its significance was social, not only maternal and sexual. It was part of their language. It was therefore patterned, codified, yet infinitely modifiable. "They're always pawing each other," some of the colonists sneered, unable to see in these touch-exchanges anything but their own eroticism which, forced to concentrate itself exclusively on sex and then repressed and frustrated, invades and poisons every sensual pleasure, every humane response: the victory of a blinded, furtive Cupid over the great brooding mother of all the seas and stars, all the leaves of trees, all the gestures of men, Venus Genetrix. . . .

So Selver came forward with his hands held out, shook Lyubov's hand Terran fashion, and then took both his arms with a stroking motion just above the elbow. He was not much more than half Lyubov's height, which made all gestures difficult and ungainly for both of them, but there was nothing uncertain or childlike in the touch of his small, thin-boned, green-furred hand on Lyubov's arms. It was a reassurance. Lyubov was very glad to get it.

"Selver, what luck to meet you here. I want very much to talk with you—"

"I can't, now, Lyubov."

He spoke gently, but when he spoke Lyubov's hope of an unaltered friendship vanished. Selver had changed. He was changed, radically: from the root.

"Can I come back," Lyubov said urgently, "another day, and talk with you, Selver? It is important to me—"

"I leave here today," Selver said even more gently, but letting go Lyubov's arms, and also looking away. He thus put himself literally out of touch. Civility required that Lyubov do the same, and let the conversation end. But then there would be no one to talk to. Old Tubab had not even looked at him; the town had turned its back on him. And this was Selver, who had been his friend.

"Selver, this killing at Kelme Deva, maybe you think that lies between us. But it does not. Maybe it brings us closer together. And your people in the slave-pens, they've all been set free, so that wrong no longer lies between us. And even if it does—it always did—all the same I . . . I am the same man I was, Selver."

At first the Athshean made no response. His strange face, the large deepset eyes, the strong features misshapen by scars and blurred by the short silken fur that followed and yet obscured all contours, this face turned from Lyubov, shut, obstinate. Then suddenly he looked round as if against his own intent. "Lyubov, you shouldn't have come here. You should leave Central two nights from now. I don't know what you are. It would be better if I had never known you."

And with that he was off, a light walk like a long-legged cat, a green flicker among the dark oaks of Tuntar, gone. Tubab followed slowly after him, still without a glance at Lyubov. A fine rain fell without sound on the oak-leaves and on the narrow pathways to the Lodge and the river. Only if you listened intently could you hear the rain, too multitudinous a music for one mind to grasp, a single endless chord played on the entire forest.

"Selver is a god," said old Sherrar. "Come and see the fishing-nets now."

Lyubov declined. It would be impolite and impolitic to stay; anyway he had no heart to.

He tried to tell himself that Selver had not been rejecting him, Lyubov, but him as a Terran. It made no difference. It never does.

He was always disagreeably surprised to find how vulnerable his feelings were, how much it hurt him to be hurt. This sort of adolescent sensitivity was shameful, he should have a tougher hide by now.

The little crone, her green fur all dusted and besilvered with raindrops, sighed with relief when he said goodbye. As he started the hopper he had to grin at the sight of her, hop-hobbling off into the trees as fast as she could go, like a little toad that has escaped a snake.

Quality is an important matter, but so is quantity: relative size. The normal adult reaction to a very much smaller person may be arrogant, or protective, or patronising, or affectionate, or bullying, but whatever it is it's liable to be better fitted to a child than to an adult. Then, when the child-sized person was furry, a further response got called upon, which Lyubov had labelled the Teddybear Reaction. Since the Athsheans used caress so much, its manifestation was not inappropriate, but its motivation remained suspect. And finally there was the inevitable Freak Reaction, the flinching away from what is human but does not quite look so.

But quite outside of all that was the fact that the Athsheans, like Terrans, were simply funny-looking at times. Some of them did look like little toads, owls, caterpillars. Sherrar was not the first little old lady who had struck Lyubov as looking funny from behind. . . .

And that's one trouble with the colony, he thought as he lifted the hopper and Tuntar vanished beneath the oaks and the leafless orchards. We haven't got any old women. No old men either, except Dongh and he's only about sixty. But old women are different from everybody else, they say what they think. The Athsheans are governed, in so far as they have government, by old women. Intellect to the men, politics to the women, and ethics to the interaction of both: that's their arrangement. It has charm, and it works—for them. I wish the Administration had sent out a couple of grannies along with all those nubile fertile high-breasted young women. Now that girl I had over the other night, she's really very nice, and nice in bed, she has a kind heart, but my God it'll be forty years before she'll say anything to a man. . . .

But all the time, beneath his thoughts concerning old women and young ones, the shock persisted, the intuition of recognition that would not let itself be recognised.

He must think this out before he reported to HQ.

Selver: what about Selver, then?

Selver was certainly a key figure to Lyubov. Why? Because he knew him well, or because of some actual power in his personality, which Lyubov had never consciously appreciated?

But he had appreciated it; he had picked Selver out very soon as an extraordinary person. 'Sam,' he had been then, bodyservant for three officers sharing a prefab. Lyubov remembered Benson boasting what a good creechie they'd got, they'd broke him in right.

Many Athsheans, especially Dreamers from the Lodges, could not change their polycyclic sleep-pattern to fit the Terran one. If they caught up with their normal sleep at night, that prevented them from catching up with the REM or paradoxical sleep, whose 120-minute cycle ruled their life both day and night, and could not be fitted in to the Terran workday. Once you have learned to do your dreaming wide awake, to balance your sanity not on the razor's edge of reason but on the double support, the fine balance, of reason and dream, once you have learned that, you cannot unlearn it any more than you can unlearn to think. So many of the men became groggy, confused, withdrawn, even catatonic. Women, bewildered and abased, behaved with the sullen listlessness of the newly enslaved. Male non-adepts and some of the younger Dreamers did best; they adapted, working hard in the logging camps or becoming clever servants. Sam had been one of these, an efficient, characterless bodyservant, cook, laundry-boy, butler, backsoaper and scapegoat for his three masters. He had learned how to be invisible. Lyubov borrowed him as an ethnological informant, and had, by some affinity of mind and nature, won Sam's trust at once. He found Sam the ideal informant, trained in his people's customs, perceptive of their significances, and quick to translate them, to make them intelligible to Lyubov, bridging the gap between two languages, two cultures, two species of the genus Man.

For two years Lyubov had been travelling, studying, interviewing, observing, and had failed to get at the key that would let him into the Athshean mind. He didn't even know where the lock was. He had studied the Athsheans' sleeping-habits and found that they apparently had no sleeping-habits. He had wired countless electrodes onto countless furry green skulls, and failed to make any sense at all out of the familiar patterns, the spindles and jags, the alphas and deltas and thetas, that appeared on the graph. It was Selver who had made him understand, at last, the Athshean significance of the word 'dream,' which was also the word for 'root,' and so hand him the key of the kingdom of the forest people. It was with Selver as EEG subject that he had first seen with comprehension the extraordinary impulse-patterns of a brain entering a dream-state neither sleeping nor awake: a condition

which related to Terran dreaming-sleep as the Parthenon to a
mud hut: the same thing basically, but with the addition of
complexity, quality, and control.

What then, what more?

Selver might have escaped. He stayed, first as a valet, then
(through one of Lyubov's few useful perquisites as a Spesh)
as Scientific Aide, still locked up nightly with all other
creechies in the pen (the Voluntary Autochthonous Labor
Personnel Quarters). "I'll fly you up to Tuntar and work with
you there," Lyubov had said, about the third time he talked
with Selver, "for God's sake why stay here?"—"My wife
Thele is in the pen," Selver had said. Lyubov had tried to get
her released, but she was in the HQ kitchen, and the ser-
geants who managed the kitchen-gang resented any interference from 'brass' and 'speshes'. Lyubov had to be very careful, lest they take out their resentment on the woman. She
and Selver had both seemed willing to wait patiently until
both could escape or be freed. Male and female creechies
were strictly segregated in the pens—why, no one seemed to
know—and husband and wife rarely saw each other. Lyubov
managed to arrange meetings for them in his hut, which he
had to himself at the north end of town. It was when Thele
was returning to HQ from one such meeting that Davidson
had seen her and apparently been struck by her frail, frightened grace. He had had her brought to his quarters that
night, and had raped her.

He had killed her in the act, perhaps; this had happened
before, a result of the physical disparity; or else she had
stopped living. Like some Terrans the Athsheans had the
knack of the authentic death-wish, and could cease to live. In
either case it was Davidson who had killed her. Such murders
had occurred before. What had not occurred before was what
Selver did, the second day after her death.

Lyubov had got there only at the end. He could recall the
sounds; himself running down Main Street in hot sunlight; the
dust, the knot of men. The whole thing could have lasted
only five minutes, a long time for a homicidal fight. When
Lyubov got there Selver was blinded with blood, a sort of toy
for Davidson to play with, and yet he had picked himself up
and was coming back, not with berserk rage but with intelligent despair. He kept coming back. It was Davidson who was
scared into rage at last by that terrible persistence; knocking
Selver down with a side-blow he had moved forward lifting
his booted foot to stamp on the skull. Even as he moved,
Lyubov had broken into the circle. He stopped the fight (for
whatever blood-thirst the ten or twelve men watching had

had, was more than appeased, and they backed Lyubov when he told Davidson hands off); and thenceforth he hated Davidson, and was hated by him, having come between the killer and his death.

For if it's all the rest of us who are killed by the suicide, it's himself whom the murderer kills; only he has to do it over, and over, and over.

Lyubov had picked up Selver, a light weight in his arms. The mutilated face had pressed against his shirt so that the blood soaked through against his own skin. He had taken Selver to his own bungalow, splinted his broken wrist, done what he could for his face, kept him in his own bed, night after night tried to talk to him, to reach him in the desolation of his grief and shame. It was, of course, against regulations.

Nobody mentioned the regulations to him. They did not have to. He knew he was forfeiting most of what favor he had ever had with the officers of the colony.

He had been careful to keep on the right side of HQ, objecting only to extreme cases of brutality against the natives, using persuasion not defiance, and conserving what shred of power and influence he had. He could not prevent the exploitation of the Athsheans. It was much worse than his training had led him to expect, but he could do little about it here and now. His reports to the Administration and to the Committee on Rights might—after the roundtrip of 54 years—have some effect; Terra might even decide that the Open Colony policy for Athshe was a bad mistake. Better 54 years late than never. If he lost the tolerance of his superiors here they would censor or invalidate his reports, and there would be no hope at all.

But he was too angry now to keep up his strategy. To hell with the others, if they insisted on seeing his care of a friend as an insult to Mother Earth and a betrayal of the colony. If they labelled him 'creechie-lover' his usefulness to the Athsheans would be impaired; but he could not set a possible, general good above Selver's imperative need. You can't save a people by selling your friend. Davidson, curiously infuriated by the minor injuries Selver had done him and by Lyubov's interference, had gone around saying he intended to finish off that rebel creechie; he certainly would do so if he got the chance. Lyubov stayed with Selver night and day for two weeks, and then flew him out of Central and put him down in a west coast town, Broter, where he had relatives.

There was no penalty for aiding slaves to escape, since the Athsheans were not slaves at all except in fact: they were Voluntary Autochthonous Labor Personnel. Lyubov was not even reprimanded. But the regular officers distrusted him to-tally, instead of partially, from then on; and even his col-leagues in the Special Services, the exobiologist, the ag and forestry coordinators, the ecologists, variously let him know that he had been irrational, quixotic, or stupid. "Did you think you were coming on a picnic?" Gosse had demanded.

"No. I didn't think it would be any bloody picnic," Lyubov answered, morose.

"I can't see why any hilfer voluntarily ties himself up to an Open Colony. You know the people you're studying are going to get plowed under, and probably wiped out. It's the way things are. It's human nature, and you must know you can't change that. Then why come and watch the process? Maso-chism?"

"I don't know what 'human nature' is. Maybe leaving de-scriptions of what we wipe out is part of human nature.—Is it much pleasanter for an ecologist, really?"

Gosse ignored this. "All right then, write up your descrip-tions. But keep out of the carnage. A biologist studying a rat colony doesn't start reaching in and rescuing pet rats of his that get attacked, you know."

At this Lyubov had blown loose. He had taken too much. "No, of course not," he said. "A rat can be a pet, but not a friend. Selver is my friend. In fact he's the only man on this world whom I consider to be a friend." That had hurt poor old Gosse, who wanted to be a father-figure to Lyubov, and it had done nobody any good. Yet it had been true. And the truth shall make you free. ... I like Selver, respect him; saved him; suffered with him; fear him. Selver is my friend.

Selver is a god.

So the little green crone had said as if everybody knew it, as flatly as she might have said So-and-so is a hunter. "Selver sha'ab." What did sha'ab mean, though? Many words of the Women's Tongue, the everyday speech of the Athsheans, came from the Men's Tongue that was the same in all com-munities, and these words often were not only two-syllabled but two-sided. They were coins, obverse and reverse. Sha'ab meant god, or numinous entity, or powerful being; it also meant something quite different, but Lyubov could not remember what. By this stage in his thinking, he was home in his bungalow, and had only to look it up in the dictionary which he and Selver had compiled in four months of exhaust-ing but harmonious work. Of course: sha'ab, translator.

It was almost too pat, too apposite.

Were the two meanings connected? Often they were, yet not so often as to constitute a rule. If a god was a translator, what did he translate? Selver was indeed a gifted interpreter, but that gift had found expression only through the fortuity of a truly foreign language having been brought into his world. Was a *sha'ab* one who translated the language of dream and philosophy, the Men's Tongue, into the everyday speech? But all Dreamers could do that. Might he then be one who could translate into waking life the central experience of vision: one serving as a link between the two realities, considered by the Athsheans as equal, the dream-time and the world-time, whose connections, though vital, are obscure. A link: one who could speak aloud the perceptions of the subconscious. To 'speak' that tongue is to act. To do a new thing. To change or to be changed, radically, from the root. For the root is the dream.

And the translator is the god. Selver had brought a new word into the language of his people. He had done a new deed. The word, the deed, murder. Only a god could lead so great a newcomer as Death across the bridge between the worlds.

But had he learned to kill his fellowmen among his own dreams of outrage and bereavement, or from the undreamed-of actions of the strangers? Was he speaking his own language, or was he speaking Captain Davidson's? That which seemed to rise from the root of his own suffering and express his own changed being, might in fact be an infection, a foreign plague, which would not make a new people of his race, but would destroy them.

It was not in Raj Lyubov's nature to think, "What can I do?" Character and training disposed him not to interfere in other men's business. His job was to find out what they did, and his inclination was to let them go on doing it. He preferred to be enlightened, rather than to enlighten; to seek facts rather than the Truth. But even the most unmissionary soul, unless he pretend he has no emotions, is sometimes faced with a choice between commission and omission. "What are they doing?" abruptly becomes, "What are we doing?" and then, "What must I do?"

That he had reached such a point of choice now, he knew, and yet did not know clearly why, nor what alternatives were offered him.

He could do no more to improve the Athsheans' chance of survival at the moment; Lepennon, Or, and the ansible had done more than he had hoped to see done in his lifetime. The Administration on Terra was explicit in every ansible communication, and Colonel Dongh, though under pressure from some of his staff and the logging bosses to ignore the directives, was carrying out orders. He was a loyal officer; and besides, the *Shackleton* would be coming back to observe and report on how orders were being carried out. Reports home meant something, now that this ansible, this *machina ex machina*, functioned to prevent all the comfortable old colonial autonomy, and make you answerable within your own lifetime for what you did. There was no more 54-year margin for error. Policy was no longer static. A decision by the League of Worlds might now lead overnight to the colony's being limited to one Land, or forbidden to cut trees, or encouraged to kill natives—no telling. How the League worked and what sort of policies it was developing could not yet be guessed from the flat directives of the Administration. Dongh was worried by these multiple-choice futures, but Lyubov enjoyed them. In diversity is life and where there's life there's hope, was the general sum of his creed, a modest one to be sure.

The colonists were letting the Athsheans alone and they were letting the colonists alone. A healthy situation, and one not to be disturbed unnecessarily. The only thing likely to disturb it was fear.

At the moment the Athsheans might be expected to be suspicious and still resentful, but not particularly afraid. As for the panic felt in Centralville at news of the Smith Camp massacre, nothing had happened to revive it. No Athshean anywhere had shown any violence since; and with the slaves gone, the creechies all vanished back into their forests, there was no more constant irritation of xenophobia. The colonists were at last beginning to relax.

If Lyubov reported that he had seen Selver at Tuntar, Dongh and the others would be alarmed. They might insist on trying to capture Selver and bring him in for trial. The Colonial Code forbade prosecution of a member of one planetary society under the laws of another, but the Court Martial over-rode such distinctions. They could try, convict, and shoot Selver. With Davidson brought back from New Java to give evidence. Oh no, Lyubov thought, shoving the dictionary onto an overcrowded shelf. Oh no, he thought, and thought no more about it. So he made his choice without even knowing he had made one.

He turned in a brief report next day. It said that Tuntar was going about its business as usual, and that he had not been turned away or threatened. It was a soothing report, and the most inaccurate one Lyubov ever wrote. It omitted everything of significance: the headwoman's non-appearance,

Tubab's refusal to greet Lyubov, the large number of strangers in town, the young huntress' expression, Selver's presence. . . . Of course that last was an intentional omission, but otherwise the report was quite factual, he thought; he had merely omitted subjective impressions, as a scientist should. He had a severe migraine whilst writing the report, and a worse one after submitting it.

He dreamed a lot that night, but could not remember his dreams in the morning. Late in the second night after his visit to Tuntar he woke, and in the hysterical whooping of the alarm-siren and the thudding of explosions he faced, at last, what he had refused. He was the only man in Centralville not taken by surprise. In that moment he knew what he was: a traitor.

And yet even now it was not clear in his mind that this was an Athshean raid. It was the terror in the night.

His own hut had been ignored, standing in its yard away from other houses; perhaps the trees around it protected it, he thought as he hurried out. The center of town was all on fire. Even the stone cube of HQ burned from within like a broken kiln. The ansible was in there: the precious link. There were fires also in the direction of the helicopter port and the Field. Where had they got explosives? How had the fires got going all at once? All the buildings along both sides of Main Street, built of wood, were burning; the sound of the burning was terrible. Lyubov ran towards the fires. Water flooded the way; he thought at first it was from a fire-hose, then realised the main from the river Menend was flooding uselessly over the ground while the houses burned with that hideous sucking roar. How had they done this? There were guards, there were always guards in jeeps at the Field. . . . Shots: volleys, the yatter of a machine gun. All around Lyubov were small running figures, but he ran among them without giving them much thought. He was abreast of the Hostel now, and saw a girl standing in the doorway, fire flickering at her back and a clear escape before her. She did not move. He shouted at her, then ran across the yard to her and wrested her hands free of the doorjambs which she clung to in panic, pulling her away by force, saying gently, "Come on, honey, come on." She came then, but not quite soon enough. As they crossed the yard the front of the upper storey, blazing from within, fell slowly forward, pushed by the timbers of the collapsing roof. Shingles and beams shot out like shell-fragments; a blazing beam-end struck Lyubov and knocked him sprawling. He lay face down in the firelit lake of mud. He did not see a little green-furred huntress leap at the girl, drag her down backwards, and cut her throat. He did not see anything.

6.

No songs were sung that night. There was only shouting and silence. When the flying ships burned Selver exulted, and tears came into his eyes, but no words into his mouth. He turned away in silence, the fire thrower heavy in his arms, to lead his group back into the city.

Each group of people from the West and North was led by an ex-slave like himself, one who had served the yumens in Central and knew the buildings and ways of the city.

Most of the people who came to the attack that night had never seen the yumen city; many of them had never seen a yumen. They had come because they followed Selver, because they were driven by the evil dream and only Selver could teach them how to master it. There were hundreds and hundreds of them, men and women; they had waited in utter silence in the rainy darkness all around the edges of the city, while the ex-slaves, two or three at a time, did those things which they judged must be done first: break the water-pipe, cut the wires that carried light from Generator House, break into and rob the Arsenal. The first deaths, those of guards, had been silent, accomplished with hunting weapons, noose, knife, arrow, very quickly, in the dark. The dynamite, stolen earlier in the night from the logging camp ten miles south, was prepared in the Arsenal, the basement of HQ Building, while fires were set in other places; and then the alarm went off and the fires blazed and both night and silence fled. Most of the thunderclap and tree-fall crashing of gunfire came from the yumens defending themselves, for only ex-slaves had taken weapons from the Arsenal and used them; all the rest kept to their own lances, knives, and bows. But it was the dynamite, placed and ignited by Reswan and others who had worked in the loggers' slave-pen, that made the noise that conquered all other noises, and blew out the walls of the HQ Building and destroyed the hangars and the ships.

There were about seventeen hundred yumens in the city that night, about five hundred of them female; all the yumen females were said to be there now, that was why Selver and the others had decided to act, though not all the people who wished to come had yet gathered. Between four and five thousand men and women had come through the forests to the Meeting at Endtor, and from there to this place, to this night.

The fires burned huge, and the smell of burning and of butchering was foul.

Selver's mouth was dry and his throat sore, so that he could not speak, and longed for water to drink. As he led his group down the middle path of the city, a yumen came running towards him, looming huge in the black and dazzle of the smoky air. Selver lifted the fire thrower and pulled back on the tongue of it, even as the yumen slipped in mud and fell scrambling to its knees. No hissing jet of flame sprang from the machine, it had all been spent on burning the airships that had not been in the hangar. Selver dropped the heavy machine. The yumen was not armed, and was male. Selver tried to say, "Let him run away," but his voice was weak, and two men, hunters of the Abtan Glades, had leapt past him even as he spoke, holding their long knives up. The big, naked hands clutched at air, and dropped limp. The big corpse lay in a heap on the path. There were many others lying dead, there in what had been the center of the city. There was not much noise any more except the noise of the fires.

Selver parted his lips and hoarsely sent up the home-call that ends the hunt; those with him took it up more clearly and loudly, in carrying falsetto; other voices answered it, near and far off in the mist and reek and flame-shot darkness of the night. Instead of leading his group at once from the city, he signalled them to go on, and himself went aside, onto the muddy ground between the path and a building which had burned and fallen. He stepped across a dead female yumen and bent over one that lay pinned down under a great, charred beam of wood. He could not see the features obliterated by mud and shadow.

It was not just; it was not necessary; he need not have looked at that one among so many dead. He need not have known him in the dark. He started to go after his group. Then he turned back; straining, lifted the beam off Lyubov's back; knelt down, slipping one hand under the heavy head so that Lyubov seemed to lie easier, his face clear of the earth; and so knelt there, motionless.

He had not slept for four days and had not been still to dream for longer than that—he did not know how long. He had acted, spoken, travelled, planned, night and day, ever since he left Broter with his followers from Cadast. He had gone from city to city speaking to the people of the forest, telling them the new thing, waking them from the dream into the world, arranging the thing done this night, talking, always talking and hearing others talk, never in silence and never alone. They had listened, they had heard and had come to follow him, to follow the new path. They had taken up the fire they feared into their own hands: taken up the mastery over the evil dream: and loosed the death they feared upon their enemy. All had been done as he said it should be done. All had gone as he said it would go. The lodges and many dwellings of the yumens were burnt, their airships burnt or broken, their weapons stolen or destroyed: and their females were dead. The fires were burning out, the night growing very dark, fouled with smoke. Selver could scarcely see; he looked up to the east, wondering if it were nearing dawn. Kneeling there in the mud among the dead he thought, This is the dream now, the evil dream. I thought to drive it, but it drives me.

In the dream, Lyubov's lips moved a little against the palm of his own hand; Selver looked down and saw the dead man's eyes open. The glare of dying fires shone on the surface of them. After a while he spoke Selver's name.

"Lyubov, why did you stay here? I told you to be out of the city this night." So Selver spoke in dream, harshly, as if he were angry at Lyubov.

"Are you the prisoner?" Lyubov said, faintly and not lifting his head, but in so commonplace a voice that Selver knew for a moment that this was not the dream-time but the world-time, the forest's night. "Or am I?"

"Neither, both, how do I know? All the engines and machines are burned. All the women are dead. We let the men run away if they would. I told them not to set fire to your house, the books will be all right. Lyubov, why aren't you like the others?"

"I am like them. A man. Like them. Like you."

"No. You are different—"

"I am like them. And so are you. Listen, Selver. Don't go on. You must not go on killing other men. You must go back ... to your own ... to your roots."

"When your people are gone, then the evil dream will stop."

"*Now*," Lyubov said, trying to lift his head, but his back was broken. He looked up at Selver and opened his mouth to speak. His gaze dropped away and looked into the other time, and his lips remained parted, unspeaking. His breath whistled a little in his throat.

They were calling Selver's name, many voices far away, calling over and over. "I can't stay with you, Lyubov!" Selver said in tears, and when there was no answer stood up and tried to run away. But in the dream-darkness he could go only very slowly, like one wading through deep water. The Ash Spirit walked in front of him, taller than Lyubov or any yumen, tall as a tree, not turning its white mask to him. As Selver went he spoke to Lyubov: "We'll go back," he said. "I will go back. Now. We will go back, now, I promise you, Lyubov!"

But his friend, the gentle one, who had saved his life and betrayed his dream, Lyubov did not reply. He walked somewhere in the night near Selver, unseen, and quiet as death.

A group of the people of Tuntar came on Selver wandering in the dark, weeping and speaking, overmastered by dream; they took him with them in their swift return to Endtor.

In the makeshift Lodge there, a tent on the river-bank, he lay helpless and insane for two days and nights, while the Old Men tended him. All that time people kept coming in to Endtor and going out again, returning to the Place of Eshsen which had been called Central, burying their dead there and the alien dead: of theirs more than three hundred, of the others more than seven hundred. There were about five hundred yumens locked into the compound, the creechie-pens, which, standing empty and apart, had not been burnt. As many more had escaped, some of whom had got to the logging camps farther south, which had not been attacked; those who were still hiding and wandering in the forest or the Cut Lands were hunted down. Some were killed, for many of the younger hunters and huntresses still heard only Selver's voice saying *Kill them*. Others had left the night of killing behind them as if it had been a nightmare, the evil dream that must be understood lest it be repeated; and these, faced with a thirsty, exhausted yumen cowering in a thicket, could not kill him. So maybe he killed them. There were groups of ten and twenty yumens, armed with logger's axes and hand-guns, though few had ammunition left; these groups were tracked until sufficient numbers were hidden in the forest about them, then overpowered, bound, and led back to Eshsen. They were all captured within two or three days, for all that part of Sornol was swarming with the people of the forest, there had never in the knowledge of any man been half or a tenth so great a gathering of people in one place; some still coming in from distant towns and other Lands, others already going home again. The captured yumens were put in among the others in the compound, though it was overcrowded and the huts were too small for yumens. They were watered, fed twice daily, and guarded by a couple of hundred armed hunters at all times.

In the afternoon following the Night of Eshsen an airship
came rattling out of the east and flew low as if to land, then
shot upward like a bird of prey that misses its kill, and circled the wrecked landing-place, the smouldering city, and the
Cut Lands. Reswan had seen to it that the radios were
destroyed, and perhaps it was the silence of the radios that
had brought the airship from Kushil or Rieshwel, where
there were three small towns of yumens. The prisoners in the
compound rushed out of the barracks and yelled at the machine whenever it came rattling overhead, and once it dropped
an object on a small parachute into the compound: at last it
rattled off into the sky.

There were four such winged ships left on Athshe now,
three on Kushil and one on Rieshwel, all of the small kind
that carried four men; they also carried machine guns and
flamethrowers, and they weighed much on the minds of
Reswan and the others, while Selver lay lost to them, walking
the cryptic ways of the other time.

He woke into the world-time on the third day, thin, dazed,
hungry, silent. After he had bathed in the river and had
eaten, he listened to Reswan and the headwoman of Berre
and the others chosen as leaders. They told him how the
world had gone while he dreamed. When he had heard them
all, he looked about at them and they saw the god in him. In
the sickness of disgust and fear that followed the Night of
Eshsen, some of them had come to doubt. Their dreams were
uneasy and full of blood and fire; they were surrounded all
day by strangers, people come from all over the forests, hundreds of them, thousands, all gathered here like kites to car-
rion, none knowing another: and it seemed to them as if the
end of things had come and nothing would ever be the same,
or be right, again. But in Selver's presence they remembered
purpose; their distress was quietened, and they waited for
him to speak.

"The killing is all done," he said. "Make sure that everyone
knows that." He looked round at them. "I have to talk with
the ones in the compound. Who is leading them in there?"

"Turkey, Flapfeet, Weteyes," said Reswan, the ex-slave.

"Turkey's alive? Good. Help me get up, Greda, I have eels
for bones. . . ."

When he had been afoot a while he was stronger, and
within the hour he set off for Eshsen, two hours' walk from
Endtor.

When they came Reswan mounted a ladder set against the
compound wall and bawled in the pidgin-English taught the
slaves, "Dong-a come to gate hurry-up-quick!"

Down in the alleys between the squat cement barracks, some of the yumens yelled and threw clods of dirt at him. He ducked, and waited.

The old Colonel did not come out, but Gosse, whom they called Weteyes, came limping out of a hut and called up to Reswan, "Colonel Dongh is ill, he cannot come out."

"Ill what kind?"

"Bowels, water-illness. What you want?"

"Talk-talk.—My lord god," Reswan said in his own language, looking down at Selver, "the Turkey's hiding, do you want to talk with Weteyes?"

"All right."

"Watch the gate there, you bowmen!—To gate, Mis-ter Goss-a, hurry-up-quick!"

The gate was opened just wide enough and long enough for Gosse to squeeze out. He stood in front of it alone, facing the group led by Selver. He favored one leg, injured on the Night of Eshsen. He was wearing torn pajamas, mud-stained and rain-sodden. His greying hair hung in lank festoons around his ears and over his forehead. Twice the height of his captors, he held himself very stiff, and stared at them in courageous, angry misery. "What you want?"

"We must talk, Mr Gosse," said Selver, who had learned plain English from Lyubov. "I'm Selver of the Ash Tree of Eshreth. I'm Lyubov's friend."

"Yes, I know you. What have you to say?"

"I have to say that the killing is over, if that be made a promise kept by your people and my people. You may all go free, if you will gather in your people from the logging camps in South Sornol, Kushil, and Rieshwel, and make them all stay together here. You may live here where the forest is dead, where you grow your seed-grasses. There must not be any more cutting of trees."

Gosse's face had grown eager: "The camps weren't attacked?"

"No."

Gosse said nothing.

Selver watched his face, and presently spoke again: "There are less than two thousand of your people left living in the world, I think. Your women are all dead. In the other camps there are still weapons; you could kill many of us. But we have some of your weapons. And there are more of us than you could kill. I suppose you know that, and that's why you have not tried to have the flying ships bring you fire-throwers, and kill the guards, and escape. It would be no good; there really are so many of us. If you make the promise with

us it will be much the best, and then you can wait without
harm until one of your Great Ships comes, and you can leave
the world. That will be in three years, I think."

"Yes, three local years—How do you know that?"

"Well, slaves have ears, Mr Gosse."

Gosse looked straight at him at last. He looked away, fidg-
eted, tried to ease his leg. He looked back at Selver, and
away again. "We had already 'promised' not to hurt any of
your people. It's why the workers were sent home. It did no
good, you didn't listen—"

"It was not a promise made to us."

"How can we make any sort of agreement or treaty with a
people who have no government, no central authority?"

"I don't know. I'm not sure you know what a promise is.
This one was soon broken."

"What do you mean? By whom, how?"

"In Rieshwel, New Java. Fourteen days ago. A town was
burned and its people killed by yumens of the Camp in
Rieshwel."

"What are you talking about?"

"About news brought us by messengers from Rieshwel."

"It's a lie. We were in radio contact with New Java right
along, until the massacre. Nobody was killing natives there or
anywhere else."

"You're speaking the truth you know," Selver said, "I the
truth I know. I accept your ignorance of the killings on
Rieshwel; but you must accept my telling you that they were
done. This remains: the promise must be made to us and
with us, and it must be kept. You'll wish to talk about these
matters with Colonel Dongh and the others."

Gosse moved as if to re-enter the gate, then turned back
and said in his deep, hoarse voice, "Who are you, Selver? Did
you—was it you that organised the attack? Did you lead
them?"

"Yes, I did."

"Then all this blood is on your head," Gosse said, and with
sudden savagery, "Lyubov's too, you know. He's dead—your
'friend Lyubov.' "

Selver did not understand the idiom. He had learned murder, but of guilt he knew little beyond the name. As his gaze
locked for a moment with Gosse's pale, resentful stare, he
felt afraid. A sickness rose up in him, a mortal chill. He tried
to put it away from him, shutting his eyes a moment. At last
he said, "Lyubov is my friend, and so not dead."

"You're children," Gosse said with hatred. "Children, savages. You have no conception of reality. This is no dream,

this is real! You killed Lyubov. He's dead. You killed the women—the *women*—you burned them alive, slaughtered them like animals!"

"Should we have let them live?" said Selver with vehemence equal to Gosse's, but softly, his voice singing a little. "To breed like insects in the carcase of the World? To overrun us? We killed them to sterilise you. I know what a realist is, Mr Gosse. Lyubov and I have talked about these words. A realist is a man who knows both the world and his own dreams. You're not sane: there's not one man in a thousand of you who knows how to dream. Not even Lyubov and he was the best among you. You sleep, you wake and forget your dreams, you sleep again and wake again, and so you spend your whole lives, and you think that is being, life, reality! You are not children, you are grown men, but insane. And that's why we had to kill you, before you drove us mad. Now go back and talk about reality with the other insane men. Talk long, and well!"

The guards opened the gate, threatening the crowding yumens inside with their spears; Gosse re-entered the compound, his big shoulders hunched as if against the rain.

Selver was very tired. The headwoman of Berre and another woman came to him and walked with him, his arms over their shoulders so that if he stumbled he should not fall. The young hunter Greda, a cousin of his Tree, joked with him, and Selver answered light-headedly, laughing. The walk back to Endtor seemed to go one for days.

He was too weary to eat. He drank a little hot broth and lay down by the Men's Fire. Endtor was no town but a mere camp by the great river, a favorite fishing place for all the cities that had once been in the forest round about, before the yumens came. There was no Lodge. Two fire-rings of black stone and a long grassy bank over the river where tents of hide and plaited rush could be set up, that was Endtor. The river Menend, the master river of Sornol, spoke ceaselessly in the world and in the dream at Endtor.

There were many old men at the fire, some whom he knew from Broter and Tuntar and his own destroyed city Eshreth, some whom he did not know; he could see in their eyes and gestures, and hear in their voices, that they were Great Dreamers; more dreamers than had ever been gathered in one place before, perhaps. Lying stretched out full length, his head raised on his hands, gazing at the fire, he said, "I have called the yumens mad. Am I mad myself?"

"You don't know one time from the other," said old Tubab, laying a pine-knot on the fire, "because you did not dream either sleeping or waking for far too long. The price for that takes long to pay."

"The poisons the yumens take do much the same as does the lack of sleep and dream," said Heben, who had been a slave both at Central and at Smith Camp. "The yumens poison themselves in order to dream. I saw the dreamer's look in them after they took the poisons. But they couldn't call the dreams, nor control them, nor weave nor shape nor cease to dream; they were driven, overpowered. They did not know what was within them at all. So it is with a man who hasn't dreamed for many days. Though he be the wisest of his Lodge, still he'll be mad, now and then, here and there, for a long time after. He'll be driven, enslaved. He will not understand himself."

A very old man with the accent of South Sornol laid his hand on Selver's shoulder, caressing him, and said, "My dear young god, you need to sing, that would do you good."

"I can't. Sing for me."

The old man sang; others joined in, their voices high and reedy, almost tuneless, like the wind blowing in the water-reeds of Endtor. They sang one of the songs of the ash-tree, about the delicate parted leaves that turn yellow in autumn when the berries turn red, and one night the first frost silvers them.

While Selver was listening to the song of the Ash, Lyubov lay down beside him. Lying down he did not seem so monstrously tall and large-limbed. Behind him was the half-collapsed, fire-gutted building, black against the stars. "I am like you," he said, not looking at Selver, in that dream-voice which tries to reveal its own untruth. Selver's heart was heavy with sorrow for his friend. "I've got a headache," Lyubov said in his own voice, rubbing the back of his neck as he always did, and at that Selver reached out to touch him, to console him. But he was shadow and firelight in the world-time, and the old men were singing the song of the Ash, about the small white flowers on the black branches in spring among the parted leaves.

The next day the yumens imprisoned in the compound sent for Selver. He came to Eshsen in the afternoon, and met with them outside the compound, under the branches of an oak tree, for all Selver's people felt a little uneasy under the bare open sky. Eshsen had been an oak grove; this tree was the largest of the few the colonists had left standing. It was on the long slope behind Lyubov's bungalow, one of the six or eight houses that had come through the night of the burning undamaged. With Selver under the oak were Reswan, the headwoman of Berre, Greda of Cadast, and others who wished to be in on the parley, a dozen or so in all. Many bowmen kept guard, fearing the yumens might have hidden weapons, but they sat behind bushes or bits of wreckage left from the burning, so as not to dominate the scene with the hint of threat. With Gosse and Colonel Dongh were three of the yumens called officers and two from the logging camp, at the sight of one of whom, Benton, the ex-slaves drew in their breaths. Benton had used to punish 'lazy creechies' by castrating them in public.

The Colonel looked thin, his normally yellow-brown skin a muddy yellow-grey; his illness had been no sham. "Now the first thing is," he said when they were all settled, the yumens standing, Selver's people squatting or sitting on the damp, soft oak-leaf mould, "the first thing is that I want first to have a working definition of just precisely what these terms of yours mean and what they mean in terms of guaranteed safety of my personnel under my command here."

There was a silence.

"You understand English, don't you, some of you?"

"Yes. I don't understand your question, Mr Dongh."

"Colonel Dongh, if you please!"

"Then you'll call me Colonel Selver, if you please." A singing note came into Selver's voice; he stood up, ready for the contest, tunes running in his mind like rivers.

But the old yumen just stood there, huge and heavy, angry yet not meeting the challenge. "I did not come here to be insulted by you little humanoids," he said. But his lips trembled as he said it. He was old, and bewildered, and humiliated. All anticipation of triumph went out of Selver. There was no triumph in the world any more, only death. He sat down again. "I didn't intend insult, Colonel Dongh," he said resignedly. "Will you repeat your question, please?"

"I want to hear your terms, and then you'll hear ours, that's all there is to it."

Selver repeated what he had said to Gosse.

Dongh listened with apparent impatience. "All right. Now you don't realise that we've had a functioning radio in the prison compound for three days now." Selver did know this, as Reswan had at once checked on the object dropped by the helicopter, lest it be a weapon; the guards reported it was a radio, and he let the yumens keep it. Selver merely nodded. "So we've been in contact with the three outlying camps, the two on King Land and one on New Java, right along, and if we had decided to make a break for it and escape from that prison compound then it would have been very simple for us

to do that, with the helicopters to drop us weapons and covering our movements with their mounted weapons, one flamethrower could have got us out of the compound and in
case of need they also have the bombs that can blow up an
entire area. You haven't seen those in action of course."

"If you'd left the compound, where would you have gone?"

"The point is, without introducing into this any beside the
point or erroneous factors, now we are certainly greatly outnumbered by your forces, but we have the four helicopters at
the camps, which there's no use you trying to disable as they
are under fully armed guard at all times now, and also all the
serious fire-power, so that the cold reality of the situation is
we can pretty much call it a draw and speak in positions of
mutual equality. This of course is a temporary situation. If
necessary we are enabled to maintain a defensive police action to prevent all-out war. Moreover we have behind us the
entire fire-power of the Terran Interstellar Fleet, which could
blow your entire planet right out of the sky. But these ideas
are pretty intangible to you, so let's just put it as plainly and
simply as I can, that we're prepared to negotiate with you,
for the present time, in terms of an equal frame of reference."

Selver's patience was short; he knew his ill-temper was a
symptom of his deteriorated mental state, but he could no
longer control it. "Go on, then!"

"Well, first I want it clearly understood that as soon as we
got the radio we told the men at the other camps not to
bring us weapons and not to try any airlift or rescue attempts, and reprisals were strictly out of order—"

"That was prudent. What next?"

Colonel Dongh began an angry retort, then stopped; he
turned very pale. "Isn't there anything to sit down on," he
said.

Selver went around the yumen group, up the slope, into
the empty two-room bungalow, and took the folding desk-
chair. Before he left the silent room he leaned down and laid
his cheek on the scarred, raw wood of the desk, where
Lyubov had always sat when he worked with Selver or alone;
some of his papers were lying there now; Selver touched
them lightly. He carried the chair out and set it in the rain-
wet dirt for Dongh. The old man sat down, biting his lips, his
almond-shaped eyes narrow with pain.

"Mr Gosse, pehaps you can speak for the Colonel," Selver
said. "He isn't well."

"I'll do the talking," Benton said, stepping forward, but
Dongh shook his head and muttered, "Gosse."

With the Colonel as auditor rather than speaker it went more easily. The yumens were accepting Selver's terms. With a mutual promise of peace, they would withdraw all their outposts and live in one area, the region they had forested in Middle Sornol: about 1700 square miles of rolling land, well watered. They undertook not to enter the forest; the forest people undertook not to trespass on the Cut Lands.

The four remaining airships were the cause of some argument. The yumens insisted they needed them to bring their people from the other islands to Sornol. Since the machines carried only four men and would take several hours for each trip, it appeared to Selver that the yumens could get to Eshsen rather sooner by walking, and he offered them ferry service across the straits; but it appeared that yumens never walked far. Very well, they could keep the hoppers for what they called the 'Airlift Operation.' After that, they were to destroy them.—Refusal. Anger. They were more protective of their machines than of their bodies. Selver gave in, saying they could keep the hoppers if they flew them only over the Cut Lands and if the weapons in them were destroyed. Over this they argued, but with one another, while Selver waited, occasionally repeating the terms of his demand, for he was not giving in on this point.

"What's the difference, Benton," the old Colonel said at last, furious and shaky, "can't you see that we can't use the damned weapons? There's three million of these aliens all scattered out all over every damned island, all covered with trees and undergrowth, no cities, no vital network, no centralised control. You can't disable a guerrilla type structure with bombs, it's been proved, in fact my own part of the world where I was born proved it for about thirty years fighting off major super-powers one after the other in the twentieth century. And we're not in a position until a ship comes to prove our superiority. Let the big stuff go, if we can hold on to the side-arms for hunting and self-defense!"

He was their Old Man, and his opinion prevailed in the end, as it might have done in a Men's Lodge. Benton sulked. Gosse started to talk about what would happen if the truce was broken, but Selver stopped him. "These are possibilities, we aren't yet done with certainties. Your Great Ship is to return in three years, that is three and a half years of your count. Until that time you are free here. It will not be very hard for you. Nothing more will be taken away from Centralville, except some of Lyubov's work that I wish to keep. You still have most of your tools of tree-cutting and ground-moving; if you need more tools, the iron-mines of Peldel are in your territory. I think all this is clear. What remains to be known is this: When that ship comes, what will they seek to do with you, and with us?"

"We don't know," Gosse said. Dongh amplified: "If you hadn't destroyed the ansible communicator first thing off, we might be receiving some current information on these matters, and our reports would of course influence the decisions that may be made concerning a finalised decision on the status of this planet, which we might then expect to begin to implement before the ship returns from Prestno. But due to wanton destruction due to your ignorance of your own interests, we haven't even got a radio left that will transmit over a few hundred miles."

"What is the ansible?" The word had come up before in this talk; it was a new one to Selver.

"ICD," the Colonel said, morose.

"A kind of radio," Gosse said, arrogant. "It put us in instant touch with our home-world."

"Without the 27-year waiting?"

Gosse stared down at Selver. "Right. Quite right. You learned a great deal from Lyubov, didn't you?"

"Didn't he just," said Benton. "He was Lyubov's little green buddyboy. He picked up everything worth knowing and a bit more besides. Like all the vital points to sabotage and where the guards would be posted, and how to get into the weapon stockpile. They must have been in touch right up to the moment the massacre started."

Gosse looked uneasy. "Raj is dead. All that's irrelevant now, Benton. We've got to establish—"

"Are you trying to infer in some way that Captain Lyubov was involved in some activity that could be called treachery to the Colony, Benton?" said Dongh, glaring and pressing his hands against his belly. "There were no spies or treachers on my staff, it was absolutely handpicked before we ever left Terra and I know the kind of men I have to deal with."

"I'm not inferring anything, Colonel. I'm saying straight out that it was Lyubov stirred up the creechies, and if orders hadn't been changed on us after that Fleet ship was here, it never would have happened."

Gosse and Dongh both started to speak at once. "You are all very ill," Selver observed, getting up and dusting himself off, for the damp brown oak-leaves clung to his short body-fur as to silk. "I'm sorry we've had to hold you in the creechie-pen, it is not a good place for the mind. Please send for your men from the camps. When all are here and the large weapons have been destroyed, and the promise has been spoken by all of us, then we shall leave you alone. The gates of the compound will be opened when I leave here to-day. Is there more to be said?"

None of them said anything. They looked down at him. Seven big men, with tan or brown hairless skin, cloth-covered, dark-eyed, grim-faced; twelve small men, green or brownish-green, fur-covered, with the large eyes of the semi-nocturnal creature, with dreamy faces; between the two groups, Selver, the translator, frail, disfigured, holding all their destinies in his empty hands. Rain fell softly on the brown earth about them.

"Farewell then," Selver said, and led his people away.

"They're not so stupid," said the headwoman of Berre as she accompanied Selver back to Endtor. "I thought such giants must be stupid, but they saw that you're a god, I saw it in their faces at the end of the talking. How well you talk that gobble-gubble. Ugly they are, do you think even their children are hairless?"

"That we shall never know, I hope."

"Ugh, think of nursing a child that wasn't furry. Like trying to suckle a fish."

"They are all insane," said old Tubab, looking deeply distressed. "Lyubov wasn't like that, when he used to come to Tuntar. He was ignorant, but sensible. But these ones, they argue, and sneer at the old man, and hate each other, like this," and he contorted his grey-furred face to imitate the expressions of the Terrans, whose words of course he had not been able to follow. "Was that what you said to them, Selver, that they're mad?"

"I told them that they were ill. But then, they've been defeated, and hurt, and locked in that stone cage. After that anyone might be ill and need healing."

"Who's to heal them." said the headwoman of Berre, "their women are all dead. Too bad for them. Poor ugly things—great naked spiders they are, ugh!"

"They are men, men, like us, men," Selver said, his voice shrill and edged like a knife.

"Oh, my dear lord god, I know it, I only meant they *look* like spiders," said the old woman, caressing his cheek. "Look here, you people. Selver is worn out with this going back and forth between Endtor and Eshsen, let's sit down and rest a bit."

"Not here," Selver said. They were still in the Cut Lands, among stumps and grassy slopes, under the bare sky. "When we come under the trees. . . ." He stumbled, and those who were not gods helped him to walk along the road.

7.

Davidson found a good use for Major Muhamed's tape recorder. Somebody had to make a record of events on New Tahiti, a history of the crucifixion of the Terran Colony. So that when the ships came from Mother Earth they could learn the truth. So that future generations could learn how much treachery and cowardice and folly humans were capable of, and how much courage against all odds. During his free moments—not much more than moments since he had assumed command—he recorded the whole story of the Smith Camp Massacre, and brought the record up to date for New Java, and for King and Central also, as well as he could with the garbled hysterical stuff that was all he got by way of news from Central HQ.

Exactly what had happened there nobody would ever know, except the creechies, for the humans were trying to cover up their own betrayals and mistakes. The outlines were clear, though. An organised bunch of creechies, led by Selver, had been let into the Arsenal and the Hangars, and turned loose with dynamite, grenades, guns, and flamethrowers to totally destruct the city and slaughter the humans. It was an inside job, the fact that HQ was the first place blown up proved that. Lyubov of course had been in on it, and his little green buddies had proved just as grateful as you might expect, and cut his throat like the others. At least, Gosse and Benton claimed to have seen him dead the morning after the massacre. But could you believe any of them, actually? You could assume that any human left alive in Central after that night was more or less of a traitor. A traitor to his race.

The women were all dead, they claimed. That was bad enough, but what was worse, there was no reason to believe it. It was easy for the creechies to take prisoners in the woods, and nothing would be easier to catch than a terrified girl running out of a burning town. And wouldn't the little green devils like to get hold of a human girl and try experiments on her? God knows how many of the women were still alive in the creechie warrens, tied down underground in one of those stinking holes, being touched and felt and crawled over and defiled by the filthy, hairy little monkeymen. It was unthinkable. But by God sometimes you have to be able to think about the unthinkable.

A hopper from King had dropped the prisoners at Central a receiver-transmitter the day after the massacre, and

Muhamed had taped all his exchanges with Central starting that day. The most incredible one was a conversation between him and Colonel Dongh. The first time he played it Davidson had torn the thing right off the reel and burned it. Now he wished he had kept it, for the records, as a perfect proof of the total incompetence of the C.O.'s at both Central and New Java. He had given in to his own hotbloodedness, destroying it. But how could he sit there and listen to the recording of the Colonel and Major discussing total surrender to the creechies, agreeing not to try retaliation, not to defend themselves, to give up all their big weapons, to all squeeze together onto a bit of land picked out for them by the creechies, a reservation conceded to them by their generous conquerors, the little green breasts. It was incredible. Literally incredible.

Probably old Ding Dong and Moo were not actually traitors by intent. They had just gone spla, lost their nerve. It was this damned planet that did it to them. It took a very strong personality to withstand it. There was something in the air, maybe pollens from all those trees, acting as some kind of drug maybe, that made ordinary humans begin to get as stupid and out of touch with reality as the creechies were. Then, being so outnumbered, they were pushovers for the creechies to wipe out.

It was too bad Muhamed had had to be put out of the way, but he would never have agreed to accept Davidson's plans, that was clear; he'd been too far gone. Anyone who'd heard that incredible tape would agree. So it was better he got shot before he really knew what was going on, and now no shame would attach to his name, as it would to Dongh's and all the other officers left alive at Central.

Dongh hadn't come on the radio lately. Usually it was Juju Sereng, in Engineering. Davidson had used to pal around a lot with Juju and had thought of him as a friend, but now you couldn't trust anybody any more. And Juju was another asiatiform. It was really queer how many of them had survived the Centralville Massacre; of those he'd talked to, the only non-asio was Gosse. Here in Java the fifty-five loyal men remaining after the reorganization were mostly eurafs like himself, some afros and afrasians, not one pure asio. Blood tells, after all. You couldn't be fully human without some blood in your veins from the Cradle of Man. But that wouldn't stop him from saving those poor yellow bastards at Central, it just helped explain their moral collapse under stress.

"Can't you realise what kind of trouble you're making for

us, Don?" Juju Sereng had demanded in his flat voice. "We've made a formal truce with the creechies. And we're under direct orders from Earth not to interfere with the hilfs and not to retaliate. Anyhow how the hell can we retaliate? Now all the fellows from King Land and South Central are here with us we're still less than two thousand, and what have you got there on Java, about sixty-five men isn't it? Do you really think two thousand men can take on three million intelligent enemies, Don?"

"Juju, fifty men can do it. It's a matter of will, skill, and weaponry."

"Batshit! But the point is, Don, a truce has been made. And if it's broken, we've had it. It's all that keeps us afloat, now. Maybe when the ship gets back from Prestno and sees what happened, they'll decide to wipe out the creechies. We don't know. But it does look like the creechies intend to keep the truce, after all it was their idea, and we have got to. They can wipe us out by sheer numbers, any time, the way they did Centralville. There were thousands of them. Can't you understand that, Don?"

"Listen, Juju, sure I understand. If you're scared to use the three hoppers you've still got there, you could send 'em over here, with a few fellows who see things like we do here. If I'm going to liberate you fellows singlehanded, I sure could use some more hoppers for the job."

"You aren't going to liberate us, you're going to incinerate us, you damned fool. Get that last hopper over here to Central now: that's the Colonel's personal order to you as Acting C.O. Use it to fly your men here; twelve trips, you won't need more than four local dayperiods. Now act on those orders, and get to it." Ponk, off the air—afraid to argue with him any more.

At first he worried that they might send their three hoppers over and actually bomb or strafe New Java Camp; for he was, technically, disobeying orders, and old Dongh wasn't tolerant of independent elements. Look how he'd taken it out on Davidson already, for that tiny reprisal-raid on Smith. Initiative got punished. What Ding Dong liked was submission, like most officers. The danger with that is that it can make the officer get submissive himself. Davidson finally realized, with a real shock, that the hoppers were no threat to him, because Dongh, Sereng, Gosse, even Benton were *afraid* to send them. The creechies had ordered them to keep the hoppers inside the Human Reservation: and they were obeying orders.

Christ, it made him sick. It was time to act. They'd been

waiting around nearly two weeks now. He had his camp well defended; they had strengthened the stockade fence and built it up so that no little green monkeymen could possibly get over it, and that clever kid Aabi had made lots of neat home-made land mines and sown 'em all around the stockade in a hundred-meter belt. Now it was time to show the creechies that they might push around those sheep on Central but on New Java it was men they had to deal with. He took the hopper up and with it guided an infantry squad of fifteen to a creechie-warren south of camp. He'd learned how to spot the things from the air; the giveaway was the orchards, concentrations of certain kinds of tree, though not planted in rows like humans would. It was incredible how many warrens there were once you learned to spot them. The forest was crawling with the things. The raiding party burned up that warren by hand, and then flying back with a couple of his boys he spotted another, less than four kilos from camp. On that one, just to write his signature real clear and plain for everybody to read, he dropped a bomb. Just a firebomb, not a big one, but baby did it make the green fur fly. It left a big hole in the forest, and the edges of the hole were burning.

Of course that was his real weapon when it actually came to setting up massive retaliation. Forest fire. He could set one of these whole islands on fire, with bombs and firejelly dropped from the hopper. Have to wait a month or two, till the rainy season was over. Should he burn King or Smith or Central? King first, maybe, as a little warning, since there were no humans left there. Then Central, if they didn't get in line.

"What are you trying to do?" said the voice on the radio, and it made him grin, it was so agonsied, like some old woman being held up. "Do you know what you're doing, Davidson?"

"Yep."

"Do you think you're going to subdue the creechies?" It wasn't Juju this time, it might be that bigdome Gosse, or any of them; no difference; they all bleated baa.

"Yes, that's right," he said with ironic mildness.

"You think if you keep burning up villages they'll come to you and surrender—three million of them. Right?"

"Maybe."

"Look, Davidson," the radio said after a while, whining and buzzing; they were using some kind of emergency rig, having lost the big transmitter, along with that phoney ansible which was no loss. "Look, is there somebody else standing by there we can talk to?"

"No; they're all pretty busy. Say, we're doing great here,

but we're out of dessert stuff, you know, fruit cocktail, peaches, crap like that. Some of the fellows really miss it. And we were due for a load of maryjanes when you fellows got blown up. If I sent the hopper over, could you spare us a few crates of sweet stuff and grass?"

A pause. "Yes, send it on over."

"Great. Have the stuff in a net, and the boys can hook it without landing." He grinned.

There was some fussing around at the Central end, and all of a sudden old Dongh was on, the first time he'd talked to Davidson. He sounded feeble and out of breath on the whining shortwave. "Listen, Captain, I want to know if you fully realize what form of action your actions on New Java are going to be forcing me into taking. If you continue to disobey your orders. I am trying to reason with you as a reasonable and loyal soldier. In order to ensure the safety of my personnel here at Central I'm going to be put into the position of being forced to tell the natives here that we can't assume any responsibility at all for your actions."

"That's correct, sir."

"What I'm trying to make clear to you is that means that we are going to be put into the position of having to tell them that we can't stop you from breaking the truce there on Java. Your personnel there is sixty-six men, is that correct, well I want those men safe and sound here at Central with us to wait for the *Shackleton* and keep the Colony together. You're on a suicide course and I'm responsible for those men you have there with you."

"No, you're not, sir. I am. You just relax. Only when you see the jungle burning, pick up and get out into the middle of a Strip, because we don't want to roast you folks along with the creechies."

"Now listen, Davidson, I order you to hand your command over to Lt. Temba at once and report to me here," said the distant whining voice, and Davidson suddenly cut off the radio, sickened. They were all spla, playing at still being soldiers, in full retreat from reality. There were actually very few men who could face reality when the going got tough.

As he expected, the local creechies did absolutely nothing about his raids on the warrens. The only way to handle them, as he'd known from the start, was to terrorise them and never let up on them. If you did that, they knew who was boss, and knuckled under. A lot of the villages within a thirty-kilo radius seemed to be deserted now before he got to them, but he kept his men going out to burn them up every few days.

The fellows were getting rather jumpy. He had kept them logging, since that's what forty-eight of the fifty-five loyal survivors were, loggers. But they knew that the robo-freighters from Earth wouldn't be called down to load up the lumber, but would just keep coming in and circling in orbit waiting for the signal that didn't come. No use cutting trees just for the hell of it; it was hard work. Might as well burn them. He exercised the men in teams, developing fire-setting techniques. It was still too rainy for them to do much, but it kept their minds busy. If only he had the other three hoppers, he'd really be able to hit and run. He considered a raid on Central to liberate the hoppers, but did not yet mention this idea even to Aabi and Temba, his best men. Some of the boys would get cold feet at the idea of an armed raid on their own HQ. They kept talking about "when we get back with the others." They didn't know those others had abandoned them, betrayed them, sold their skins to the creechies. He didn't tell them that, they couldn't take it.

One day he and Aabi and Temba and another good sound man would just take the hopper over, then three of them jump out with machine guns, take a hopper apiece, and so home again, home again, jiggety jog. With four nice egg-beaters to beat eggs with. Can't make an omelet without beating eggs. Davidson laughed aloud, in the darkness of his bungalow. He kept that plan hidden just a little longer, because it tickled him so much to think about it.

After two more weeks they had pretty well closed out the creechie-warrens within walking distance, and the forest was neat and tidy. No vermin. No smoke-puffs over the trees. Nobody hopping out of bushes and flopping down on the ground with their eyes shut, waiting for you to stomp them. No little green men. Just a mess of trees and some burned places. The boys were getting really edgy and mean; it was time to make the hopper-raid. He told his plan one night to Aabi, Temba, and Post.

None of them said anything for a minute, then Aabi said, "What about fuel, Captain?"

"We got enough fuel."

"Not for four hoppers; wouldn't last a week."

"You mean there's only a month's supply left for this one?"

Aabi nodded.

"Well then, we pick up a little fuel too, looks like."

"How?"

"Put your minds to it."

They all sat there looking stupid. It annoyed him. They

looked to him for everything. He was a natural leader, but he liked men who thought for themselves too. "Figure it out, it's your line of work, Aabi," he said, and went out for a smoke, sick of the way everybody acted, like they'd lost their nerve. They just couldn't face the cold hard facts.

They were low on maryjanes now and he hadn't had one for a couple of days. It didn't do anything for him. The night was overcast and black, damp, warm, smelling like spring. Ngenene went by walking like an ice-skater, or almost like a robot on treads; he turned slowly through a gliding step and gazed at Davidson, who stood on the bungalow porch in the dim light from the doorway. He was a power-saw operator, a huge man. "The source of my energy is connected to the Great Generator I cannot be switched off," he said in a level tone, gazing at Davidson.

"Get to your barracks and sleep it off!" Davidson said in the whipcrack voice that nobody ever disobeyed, and after a moment Ngenene skated carefully on, ponderous and graceful. Too many of the men were using hallies more and more heavily. There was plenty, but the stuff was for loggers relaxing on Sundays, not for soldiers of a tiny outpost marooned on a hostile world. They had no time for getting high, for dreaming. He'd have to lock the stuff up. Then some of the boys might crack. Well, let 'em crack. Can't make an omelet without cracking eggs. Maybe he could send them back to Central in exchange for some fuel. You give me two, three tanks of gas and I'll give you two, three warm bodies, loyal soldiers, good loggers, just your type, a little far gone in bye-bye dreamland. . . .

He grinned, and was going back inside to try this one out on Temba and the others, when the guard posted up on the lumberyard smoke stack yelled. "They're coming!" he screeched out in a high voice, like a kid playing Blacks and Rhodesians. Somebody else over on the west side of the stockade began yelling too. A gun went off.

And they came. Christ, they came. It was incredible. There were thousands of them, thousands. No sound, no noise at all, until that screech from the guard; then one gunshot; then an explosion—a land mine going up—and another, one after another, and hundreds and hundreds of torches flaring up lit one from another and being thrown and soaring through the black wet air like rockets, and the walls of the stockade coming alive with creechies, pouring in, pouring over, pushing, swarming, thousands of them. It was like an army of rats Davidson had seen once when he was a little kid, in the last Famine, in the streets of Cleveland, Ohio, where he grew up.

Something had driven the rats out of their holes and they had come up in daylight, seething up over the wall, a pulsing blanket of fur and eyes and little hands and teeth, and he had yelled for his mom and run like crazy, or was that only a dream he'd had when he was a kid? It was important to keep cool. The hopper was parked in the creechie-pen; it was still dark over on that side and he got there at once. The gate was locked, he always kept it locked in case one of the weak sisters got a notion of flying off to Papa Ding Dong some dark night. It seemed to take a long time to get the key out and fit it in the lock and turn it right, but it was just a matter of keeping cool, and then it took a long time to sprint to the hopper and unlock it. Post and Aabi were with him now. At last came the huge rattle of the rotors, beating eggs, covering up all the weird noises, the high voices yelling and screeching and singing. Up they went, and hell dropped away below them: a pen full of rats, burning.

"It takes a cool head to size up an emergency situation quickly," Davidson said. "You men thought fast and acted fast. Good work. Where's Temba?"

"Got a spear in his belly," Post said.

Aabi, the pilot, seemed to want to fly the hopper, so Davidson let him. He clambered into one of the rear seats and sat back, letting his muscles relax. The forest flowed beneath them, black under black.

"Where you heading, Aabi?"

"Central."

"No. We don't want to go to Central."

"Where do we want to go to?" Aabi said with a kind of womanish giggle. "New York? Peking?"

"Just keep her up a while, Aabi, and circle camp. Big circles. Out of earshot."

"Captain, there isn't any Java Camp any more by now," said Post, a logging-crew foreman, a stocky, steady man.

"When the creechies are through burning the camp, we'll come in and burn creechies. There must be four thousand of them all in one place there. There's six flamethrowers in the back of this helicopter. Let's give 'em about twenty minutes. Start with the jelly bombs and then catch the ones that run with the flamethrowers."

"Christ," Aabi said violently, "some of our guys might be there, the creechies might take prisoners, we don't know. I'm not going back there and burn up humans, maybe." He had not turned the hopper.

Davidson put the nose of his revolver against the back of

Aabi's skull and said, "Yes, we're going back; so pull yourself together, baby, and don't give me a lot of trouble."

"There's enough fuel in the tank to get us to Central, Captain," the pilot said. He kept trying to duck his head away from the touch of the gun, like it was a fly bothering him. "But that's all. That's all we got."

"Then we'll get a lot of mileage out of it. Turn her, Aabi."

"I think we better go on to Central, Captain," Post said in his stolid voice, and this ganging up against him enraged Davidson so much that reversing the gun in his hand he struck out fast as a snake and clipped Post over the ear with the gun-butt. The logger just folded over like a Christmas card, and sat there in the front seat with his head between his knees and his hands hanging to the floor. "Turn her, Aabi," Davidson said, the whiplash in his voice. The helicopter swung around in a wide arc. "Hell, where's camp, I never had this hopper up at night without any signal to follow," Aabi said, sounding dull and snuffly like he had a cold.

"Go east and look for the fire," Davidson said, cold and quiet. None of them had any real stamina, not even Temba. None of them had stood by him when the going got really tough. Sooner or later they all joined up against him, because they just couldn't take it the way he could. The weak conspire against the strong, the strong man has to stand alone and look out for himself. It just happened to be the way things are. Where was the camp?

They should have been able to see the burning buildings for miles in this blank dark, even in the rain. Nothing showed. Grey-black sky, black ground. The fires must have gone out. Been put out. Could the humans have driven off the creechies? After he'd escaped? The thought went like a spray of icewater through his mind. No, of course not, not fifty against thousands. But by God there must be a lot of pieces of blown-up creechie lying around on the minefields, anyway. It was just that they'd come so damned thick. Nothing could have stopped them. He couldn't have planned for that. Where had they come from? There hadn't been any creechies in the forest anywhere around for days and days. They must have poured in from somewhere, from all directions, sneaking along in the woods, coming up out of their holes like rats. There wasn't any way to stop thousands and thousands of them like that. Where the hell was camp? Aabi was tricking, faking course. "Find the camp, Aabi," he said softly.

"For Christ's sake I'm trying to," the boy said.

Post never moved, folded over there by the pilot.

"It couldn't just disappear, could it, Aabi. You got seven minutes to find it."

"Find it yourself," Aabi said, shrill and sullen.

"Not till you and Post get in line, baby. Take her down lower."

After a minute Aabi said, "That looks like the river."

There was a river, and a big clearing; but where was Java Camp? It didn't show up as they flew north over the clearing. "This must be it, there isn't any other big clearing is there," Aabi said, coming back over the treeless area. Their landing-lights glared but you couldn't see anything outside the tunnels of the lights; it would be better to have them off. Davidson reached over the pilot's shoulder and switched the lights off. Blank wet dark was like black towels slapped on their eyes. "For Christ's sake!" Aabi screamed, and flipping the lights back on slewed the hopper left and up, but not fast enough. Trees leaned hugely out of the night and caught the machine.

The vanes screamed, hurling leaves and twigs in a cyclone through the bright lanes of the lights, but the boles of the trees were very old and strong. The little winged machine plunged, seemed to lurch and tear itself free, and went down sideways into the trees. The lights went out. The noise stopped.

"I don't feel so good," Davidson said. He said it again. Then he stopped saying it, for there was nobody to say it to. Then he realised he hadn't said it anyway. He felt groggy. Must have hit his head. Aabi wasn't there. Where was he? This was the hopper. It was all slewed around, but he was still in his seat. It was so dark, like being blind. He felt around, and so found Post, inert, still doubled up, crammed in between the front seat and the control panel. The hopper trembled whenever Davidson moved, and he figured out at last that it wasn't on the ground but wedged in between trees, stuck like a kite. His head was feeling better, and he wanted more and more to get out of the black, tilted-over cabin. He squirmed over into the pilot's seat and got his legs out, hung by his hands, and could not feel ground, only branches scraping his dangling legs. Finally he let go, not knowing how far he'd fall, but he had to get out of that cabin. It was only a few feet down. It jolted his head, but he felt better standing up. If only it wasn't so dark, so black. He had a torch in his belt, he always carried one at night around camp. But it wasn't there. That was funny. It must have fallen out. He'd better get back into the hopper and get it. Maybe Aabi had taken it. Aabi had intentionally crashed the hopper, taken Davidson's torch, and made a break for it. The slimy little bastard, he was like all the rest of them. The air was black and full of moisture, and you couldn't tell where to put your feet, it was all roots and bushes and tangles. There were noises all around, water dripping, rustling, tiny noises, little things sneaking around in the darkness. He'd better get back up into the hopper, get his torch. But he couldn't see how to climb back up. The bottom edge of the doorway was just out of reach of his fingers.

There was a light, a faint gleam seen and gone away off in the trees. Aabi had taken the torch and gone off to reconnoiter, get orientated, smart boy. "Aabi!" he called in a piercing whisper. He stepped on something queer while he was trying to see the light among the trees again. He kicked at it with his boots, then put a hand down on it, cautiously, for it wasn't wise to go feeling things you couldn't see. A lot of wet stuff, slick, like a dead rat. He withdrew his hand quickly. He felt in another place after a while; it was a boot under his hand, he could feel the crossings of the laces. It must be Aabi lying there right under his feet. He'd got thrown out of the hopper when it came down. Well, he'd deserved it with his Judas trick, trying to run off to Central. Davidson did not like the wet feel of the unseen clothes and hair. He straightened up. There was the light again, black-barred by near and distant tree-trunks, a distant glow that moved.

Davidson put his hand to his holster. The revolver was not in it.

He'd had it in his hand, in case Post or Aabi acted up. It was not in his hand. It must be up in the helicopter with his torch.

He stood crouching, immobile; then abruptly began to run. He could not see where he was going. Tree-trunks jolted him from side to side as he knocked into them, and roots tripped up his feet. He fell full length, crashing down among bushes. Getting to hands and knees he tried to hide. Bare, wet twigs dragged and scraped over his face. He squirmed farther into the bushes. His brain was entirely occupied by the complex smells of rot and growth, dead leaves, decay, new shoots, fronds, flowers, the smells of night and spring and rain. The light shone full on him. He saw the creechies.

He remembered what they did when cornered, and what Lyubov had said about it. He turned over on his back and lay with his head tipped back, his eyes shut. His heart stuttered in his chest.

Nothing happened.

It was hard to open his eyes, but finally he managed to. They just stood there: a lot of them, ten or twenty. They carried those spears they had for hunting, little toy-looking things but the iron blades were sharp, they could cut right through your guts. He shut his eyes and just kept lying there.

And nothing happened.

His heart quieted down, and it seemed like he could think better. Something stirred down inside him, something almost like laughter. By God they couldn't get him down! If his own men betrayed him, and human intelligence couldn't do any more for him, then he used their own trick against them—played dead like this, and triggered this instinct reflex that kept them from killing anybody who took that position. They just stood around him, muttering at each other. *They couldn't hurt him.* It was as if he was a god.

"Davidson."

He had to open his eyes again. The resin-flare carried by one of the creechies still burned, but it had grown pale, and the forest was dim grey now, not pitch-black. How had that happened? Only five or ten minutes had gone by. It was still hard to see but it wasn't night any more. He could see the leaves and branches, the forest. He could see the face looking down at him. It had no color in this toneless twilight of dawn. The scarred features looked like a man's. The eyes were like dark holes.

"Let me get up," Davidson said suddenly in a loud, hoarse voice. He was shaking with cold from lying on the wet ground. He could not lie there with Selver looking down at him.

Selver was emptyhanded, but a lot of the little devils around him had not only spears but revolvers. Stolen from his stockpile at camp. He struggled to his feet. His clothes clung icy to his shoulders and the backs of his legs, and he could not stop shaking.

"Get it over with," he said. "Hurry-up-quick!"

Selver just looked at him. At least now he had to look up, way up, to meet Davidson's eyes.

"Do you wish me to kill you now?" he inquired. He had learned that way of talking from Lyubov, of course; even his voice, it could have been Lyubov talking. It was uncanny.

"It's my choice, is it?"

"Well, you have lain all night in the way that means you wished us to let you live; now do you want to die?"

The pain in his head and stomach, and his hatred for this horrible little freak that talked like Lyubov and that had got him at its mercy, the pain and the hatred combined and set his belly churning, so he retched and was nearly sick. He shook with cold and nausea. He tried to hold on to courage.

He suddenly stepped forward a pace and spat in Selver's face.

There was a little pause, and then Selver, with a kind of dancing movement, spat back. And laughed. And made no move to kill Davidson. Davidson wiped the cold spittle off his lips.

"Look, Captain Davidson," the creechie said in that quiet little voice that made Davidson go dizzy and sick, "we're both gods, you and I. You're an insane one, and I'm not sure whether I'm sane or not. But we are gods. There will never be another meeting in the forest like this meeting now between us. We bring each other such gifts as gods bring. You gave me a gift, the killing of one's kind, murder. Now, as well as I can, I give you my people's gift, which is not killing. I think we each find each other's gift heavy to carry. However, you must carry it alone. Your people at Eshsen tell me that if I bring you there, they have to make a judgment on you and kill you, it's their law to do so. So, wishing to give you life, I can't take you with the other prisoners to Eshsen; and I can't leave you to wander in the forest, for you do too much harm. So you'll be treated like one of us when we go mad. You'll be taken to Rendlep where nobody lives any more, and left there."

Davidson stared at the creechie, could not take his eyes off it. It was as if it had some hypnotic power over him. He couldn't stand this. Nobody had any power over him. Nobody could hurt him. "I should have broken your neck right away, that day you tried to jump me," he said, his voice still hoarse and thick.

"It might have been best," Selver answered. "But Lyubov prevented you. As he now prevents me from killing you.—All the killing is done now. And the cutting of trees. There aren't trees to cut on Rendlep. That's the place you call Dump Island. Your people left no trees there, so you can't make a boat and sail from it. Nothing much grows there any more, so we shall have to bring you food and wood to burn. There's nothing to kill on Rendlep. No trees, no people. There were trees and people, but now there are only the dreams of them. It seems to me a fitting place for you to live, since you must live. You might learn how to dream there, but more likely you will follow your madness through to its proper end, at last."

"Kill me now and quit your damned gloating."

"Kill you?" Selver said, and his eyes looking up at Davidson seemed to shine, very clear and terrible, in the twilight of the forest. "I can't kill you, Davidson. You're a god. You must do it yourself."

He turned and walked away, light and quick, vanishing among the grey trees within a few steps.

A noose slipped over Davidson's head and tightened a little on his throat. Small spears approached his back and sides. They did not try to hurt him. He could run away, make a break for it, they didn't dare kill him. The blades were polished, leaf-shaped, sharp as razors. The noose tugged gently at his neck. He followed where they led him.

8.

Selver had not seen Lyubov for a long time. That dream had gone with him to Rieshwel. It had been with him when he spoke the last time to Davidson. Then it had gone, and perhaps it slept now in the grave of Lyubov's death at Eshsen, for it never came to Selver in the town of Broter where he now lived.

But when the great ship returned, and he went to Eshsen, Lyubov met him there. He was silent and tenuous, very sad, so that the old carking grief awoke in Selver.

Lyubov stayed with him, a shadow in the mind, even when he met the yumens from the ship. These were people of power; they were very different from all yumens he had known, except his friend, but they were much stronger men than Lyubov had been.

His yumen speech had gone rusty, and at first he mostly let them talk. When he was fairly certain what kind of people they were, he brought forward the heavy box he had carried from Broter. "Inside this there is Lyubov's work," he said, groping for the words. "He knew more about us than the others do. He learned my language and the Men's Tongue; we wrote all that down. He understood somewhat how we live and dream. The others do not. I'll give you the work, if you'll take it to the place he wished."

The tall, white-skinned one, Lepennon, looked happy, and thanked Selver, telling him that the papers would indeed be taken where Lyubov wished, and would be highly valued. That pleased Selver. But it had been painful to him to speak his friend's name aloud, for Lyubov's face was still bitterly sad when he turned to it in his mind. He withdrew a little from the yumens, and watched them. Dongh and Gosse and others of Eshsen were there along with the five from the ship. The new ones looked clean and polished as new iron. The old ones had let the hair grow on their faces, so that they looked a little like huge, black-furred Athsheans. They still wore clothes, but the clothes were old and not kept clean. They were not thin, except for the Old Man, who had been ill ever since the Night of Eshsen; but they all looked a little like men who are lost or mad.

This meeting was at the edge of the forest, in that zone where by tacit agreement neither the forest people nor the yumens had built dwellings or camped for these past years. Selver and his companions settled down in the shade of a big ash-tree that stood out away from the forest eaves. Its berries were only small green knots against the twigs as yet, its leaves were long and soft, labile, summer-green. The light beneath the great tree was soft, complex with shadows.

The yumens consulted and came and went, and at last one came over to the ash-tree. It was the hard one from the ship, the Commander. He squatted down on his heels near Selver, not asking permission but not with any evident intention of rudeness. He said, "Can we talk a little?"

"Certainly."

"You know that we'll be taking all the Terrans away with us. We brought a second ship with us to carry them. Your world will no longer be used as a colony."

"This was the message I heard at Broter, when you came three days ago."

"I wanted to be sure that you understand that this is a permanent arrangement. We're not coming back. Your world has been placed under the League Ban. What that means in your terms is this: I can promise you that no one will come here to cut the trees or take your lands, so long as the League lasts."

"None of you will ever come back," Selver said, statement or question.

"Not for five generations. None. Then perhaps a few men, ten or twenty, no more than twenty, might come to talk to your people, and study your world, as some of the men here were doing."

"The scientists, the Speshes," Selver said. He brooded. "You decide matters all at once, your people," he said, again between statement and question.

"How do you mean?" The Commander looked wary.

"Well, you say that none of you shall cut the trees of Athshe: and all of you stop. And yet you live in many places. Now if a headwoman in Karach gave an order, it would not be obeyed by the people of the next village, and surely not by all the people in the world at once. . . ."

"No, because you haven't one government over all. But we do—now—and I assure you its orders are obeyed. By all of us at once. But, as a matter of fact, it seems to me from the story we've been told by the colonists here, that when *you* gave an order, Selver, it was obeyed by everybody on every island here at once. How did you manage that?"

"At that time I was a god," Selver said, expressionless.

After the Commander had left him, the long white one came sauntering over and asked if he might sit down in the shade of the tree. He had tact, this one, and was extremely clever. Selver was uneasy with him. Like Lyubov, this one would be gentle; he would understand, and yet would himself be utterly beyond understanding. For the kindest of them was as far out of touch, as unreachable, as the cruellest. That was why the presence of Lyubov in his mind remained painful to him, while the dreams in which he saw and touched his dead wife Thele were precious and full of peace.

"When I was here before," Lepennon said, "I met this man, Raj Lyubov. I had very little chance to speak with him, but I remember what he said; and I've had time to read some of his studies of your people, since. His work, as you say. It's largely because of that work of his that Athshe is now free of the Terran Colony. This freedom had become the direction of Lyubov's life, I think. You, being his friend, will see that his death did not stop him from arriving at his goal, from finishing his journey."

Selver sat still. Uneasiness turned to fear in his mind. This one spoke like a Great Dreamer.

He made no response at all.

"Will you tell me one thing, Selver. If the question doesn't offend you. There will be no more questions, after it. . . . There were the killings: at Smith Camp, then at this place, Eshsen, then finally at New Java Camp where Davidson led the rebel group. That was all. No more since then. . . . Is that true? Have there been no more killings?"

"I did not kill Davidson."

"That does not matter," Lepennon said, misunderstanding; Selver meant that Davidson was not dead, but Lepennon took him to mean that someone else had killed Davidson. Relieved to see that the yumen could err, Selver did not correct him.

"There has been no more killing, then?"

"None. They will tell you," Selver said, nodding towards the Colonel and Gosse.

"Among your own people, I mean. Athsheans killing Athsheans."

Selver was silent.

He looked up at Lepennon, at the strange face, white as the mask of the Ash Spirit, that changed as it met his gaze.

"Sometimes a god comes," Selver said. "He brings a new way to do a thing, or a new thing to be done. A new kind of singing, or a new kind of death. He brings this across the bridge between the dream-time and the world-time. When he has done this, it is done. You cannot take things that exist in the world and try to drive them back into the dream, to hold them inside the dream with walls and pretenses. That is insanity. What is, is. There is no use pretending now, that we do not know how to kill one another."

Lepennon laid his long hand on Selver's hand, so quickly and gently that Selver accepted the touch as if the hand were not a stranger's. The green-gold shadows of the ash leaves flickered over them.

"But you must not pretend to have reasons to kill one another. Murder has no reason," Lepennon said, his face as anxious and sad as Lyubov's face. "We shall go. Within two days we shall be gone. All of us. Forever. Then the forests of Athshe will be as they were before."

Lyubov came out of the shadows of Selver's mind and said, "I shall be here."

"Lyubov will be here," Selver said. "And Davidson will be here. Both of them. Maybe after I die people will be as they were before I was born, and before you came. But I do not think they will."

Afterword:

Writing is usually hard work for me, and enjoyable; this story was easy to write, and disagreeable. It left me no choice. Writing it was a little like taking dictation from a boss with ulcers. What I wanted to write about was the forest and the dream; that is, I wanted to describe a certain ecology from within, and to play with some of Hadfield's and Dement's ideas about the function of dreaming-sleep and the uses of dream. But the boss wanted to talk about the destruction of ecological balance and the rejection of emotional balance. He didn't want to play. He wanted to moralize. I am not very fond of moralistic tales, for they often lack charity. I hope this one does not. I can only say—having been forced to endure the experience—that it is even more painful to be Don Davidson than it is to be Raj Lyubov.

Introduction to

FOR VALUE RECEIVED:

andy offutt tells me this story was turned down by myriad
publishers because they were afraid of it. That may be true, I
don't know. It seemed to me the instant I read it, one of the
cleverest ways to screw up The System ever invented. For
those of us who daily grapple with the monstrousness of The
System, stories such as andy's come as reaffirmation of our
silent, increasingly more dangerous and difficult mission: the
tossing of spanners into the machinery of The Corporate
State, what Reich calls in *The Greening of America*, "a mindless juggernaut, destroying the environment, obliterating human values, and assuming domination over the lives and
minds of its subjects. To the injustices and exploitation of the
nineteenth century, the Corporate State has added deperson-
alization, meaninglessness, and repression, until it has threatened to destroy all meaning and all life."

I've written elsewhere, and at great length about the ways
in which the mindless juggernaut debases and manhandles us,
and I've even written of the few legitimate and legal steps
I've taken to slow its crushing inertia. The illegal and illegiti-
mate steps I've taken will go to my grave with me, probably
very soon if I keep at them.

But overpaying one's telephone bill by something just under a dollar (so it costs them many more dollars to clear it on
their computers) and remitting one's telephone bill in the return envelope *without* postage ... writing to the giant food
companies telling them you found a dead fly or a cockroach
in their breakfast food, so they send you a case of the crap
just to appease you ... conscientious objecting or joining the
Peace Corps to screw the war machine out of another warm
body ... suing the automobile manufacturers when their cars
fall to pieces, or suing in general because they pollute the air
... these, and the thousands of other ripoffs, both legal and
illegal ... these are manna in the desert to those of us who
see the snowball roll of the Corporate State flattening individuality and reason and humanity in these Dark Days of our
civilization's decline.

So andy offutt offers another one here. A lovely and original one.

Which sort of says it about andy offutt.

You've noticed his name always appears in lower-case, no initial-caps. How about that. It's the way andrew j. offutt signs his letters and heads his stationery, and bylines his stories and in general continues to annoy people. He's annoyed me ever since 1954 when his short story, "And Gone Tomorrow," won first place in a College SF Contest sponsored by *If: Worlds of Science Fiction*. I'd entered that contest myself, being in an impoverished state (Ohio) at the time, working my way through Ohio State Impoverished cadging off my mother, waiting table, writing term papers (on which I guaranteed a "B" or better) and shoplifting to obtain the little luxuries like books and records. When the contest was won by an "A. J. Offutt" I thought, *flash in the pan; stupid sonofabitch'll never write another word.*

Didn't hear from the clown again till 1959 when "Blacksword" appeared in *Galaxy*. But by that time I'd been writing professionally for three years, I was out of the Army, and I could afford to be charitable. Still didn't know or care much about anything named Offutt (in those days the name was capped).

Who he was, and where he came from is contained in this revealing and semi-literate biography, presented here without comment by your editor, who is still working on the grudge from 1954 . . .

"The first thing we did was move from Louisville to this farm, where i grew up with a couple of coonhounds, 35 or so Holstein cattle, a bull with manners like a NYC editor, some horses, lots of tobacco and hay (fever for me), and a cat named Papa who went coon-hunting with Dad. (Racoons. We i mean us Kentuckians don't consider ourselves Southerners. Ohioans do. Tennesseeans consider us damyanks. What are you going to do? We supplied the leaders to BOTH sides of that godawful war.)

"I had a damned unhappy childhood during which i attended a 1-room, 8-grade schoolhouse for 4 years; waited at the mailbox every day after we sent off the Sears order; reigned as the most unathletic kid in the county (i got chosen next to last when we played ball; the little fat girl was chosen last, bless her, i was always sent to right field. That's where the balls don't come); was very short until i was 17 or worse, when i grew 8 inches in 10 months; committed the unpardonable sincrime of being awfully smart, as well as Catholic in a community devoted to stupidity and where the KKK had rid-den only 23 years earlier—against Catholics! (The community was too small to afford Jews or Blacks, who keep Catholics safe in big cities.)

"We were also pore.

"At 17 i took a lot of tests and skipped my senior year of high school to enter the U. of Louisville on a Ford Foundation Scholarship. I graduated at 20. In the meanwhile i did a lot of stuff like playing bridge and poker and cutting lots of classes and being a virgin and president of my fraternity and the Newman Club and on the student council and editor of the Air Farce ROTC paper and Mng Editor of the school weekly. Uncle andy's Advice column was a popular feature, honest to Abby! I also had lots of jobs; 3 in my senior year, simultaneously. In '54 or '55 i entered IF's College SF Contest and won because Ellison had dropped out of college to become Symington's aide, or something. My story 'And Gone Tomorrow,' laid in 2054, predicted trial marriages (would you believe it started happening a little earlier, like 90 years?) and other earthshaking stuff. I also said that there was no perfect government, but that a dictatorship comes closest. I still believe that, but prefer freedom and so write things that try to show how my favorite form of government could be better. You know, the one America used to have. I took no business courses, so i went to work with Proctor & Gamble until i outgrew it. I went into the life and health insurance business and by Fall of '68 i had agencies in three towns. Fortunately i was able to outgrow that, too. Oh, at around age 28 i also outgrew the Roman Church; Vardis Fisher helped a lot.

"I was always a slow starter. My second story was published in 1959, in *Galaxy*. (Despite the fact that it was mostly written on my honeymoon, my wife is still with me.) It was called 'Blacksword' and was about a man named that, not a weapon. Another one called 'Population Implosion' was picked for Ace's WORLD'S BEST in '68, and you can now read it in Japanese if you've a mind to. There were other stories. My stories usually involve satire and resistance to Authority and attacks on Established Faiths (AMA, ABA, USA, ETC), which i guess indicates i must have had funny feelings about my coonhunten daddy who ran the house as if he were the Sheriff of Nottingham.

"I love to talk first and write second, and i do both because i have to. I've sold a lot of novels, under several names; i'm John Cleve, usually, when i write about goodole sex (which maybe i like better than writing and eating, come to think). I like to drink, too, and prefer Maker's Mark and soda with lemon in season and gin 'n' tonic in the other season. I put lemon in everything i drink except beer and the gallon or so of saccariny coffee i store away daily.

"Ours is an enormous old white elephant of a house with a living room the size of the standard FHA/VA house of the '50's. It is on 3½ acres on a high hill in Haldeman, 8 miles from Morehead (which is about 8 miles from Salt Lick and 15 from Flemingsburg, so you'll know). We call the place Funny Farm because there's a wife i'm crazy about and four offutt-spring i endeavor to tolerate and a coonhound named Pompeius Magnus who prays to me every night because black-and-tans are like that (coonhounds, not Irish, of which my wife is one). (We don't raise anything except hell and kids.) I fully expect to have to defend the damned place from you lebensrauming scum from NYC and places like that, anyday soon. I fully expect LA to solve its own problem, and i will miss Atlanteans Kirby and Ellison and Geis and a few others."

offutt is the author of any number of novels, about sixty totaled. He's even managed to sell about forty of them. When I sat down to write this introduction, however, I found that offutt had cleverly avoided giving me the titles of any of them, and since only one (as of this writing) has appeared under his name—*Evil Is Live Spelled Backwards*—and a pretty fair country novel it is, too—I got on the phone and called him in Morehead, Kentucky, or wherever the hell he is. He was rather annoyed.

I see no reason why a man should be annoyed that you call him at 12:30 a.m. Los Angeles time, that is. In Kentucky it was 3:30 in the morning, and his wife, Jodie, answered the phone, so I said, "Happy Mother's Day," thinking that might placate her. I must say, for all that, andy offutt is crummy company at 3:30 in the morning. All he does is grumble.

But I managed to get some titles out of him. He was very reluctant. He felt my including the titles of his "erotic" novels was a cheapjack trick of yellow journalism. Not so. I happen to think the contemporary "erotica" scene has produced some very heady writing (if you'll pardon the term) and some very interesting writers. Like David Meltzer and Michael Perkins and Hank Stine . . . and John Cleve, who is andrew j. offutt.

So he gave me a few titles. *Barbarana, The Seductress, Mongol!, Black Man's Harem, the Devoured* and something he says should be written like so: *the great 24 hour THING.*

He's also got some more sf novels coming out under his

own name—*The Castle Keeps* from Berkley and *Messenger of Zhuvastou* from the same place, and Dell is publishing *Ardor on Aros.* As you can see, offutt writes a lot, and he writes a lot of "erotica." (When *I* was writing that stuff, we called it "stiffeners," but then, *we* weren't Artists.)

Which brings me to the second large chunk of comment out of offutt himself. I include it here, recognizing that the introduction will be almost as long as the story it introduces, because it offers some very amusing and perceptive insights into the way a *professional* works.

Look: A,DV is something of a living entity. It is not merely a batch of stories cobbled up by a faceless dude trying to fill in the lag-time between his own books, with another group of faceless dudes submitting at random and hoping to make a buck. It is a great wild bunch of us sitting about and rapping till well into the wee hours, and when one of us gets it on in a sufficiently fascinating manner, we like to let him ramble on. So for all of you out there who think writing is this or that or the other thing, who have writing blocks and want to know what the mind of the writer is like, here's offutt on his habits behind the typewriter. I think you'll find it highly readable. Take it, andy:

"i have defined a writer as the happiest man alive, because he gets paid for doing his thing, his hobby. i wrote a novel when i was nine (cowboys, what else?), and stories right along, and a novel when i was 13 or so (Edgar Rice Burroughs, what else?). i wrote three novels while in college (pretending to be taking notes during dull lectures). Two of them still read pretty well. i graduated at 20.

"Cut to 1967. i had published a few short stories, solo and in unlikely collaborations; had put in several years with Proctor & Gamble until i outgrew that; had put in a year in the life insurance business and then had gone into that same business for myself; had begun managing. Suddenly, after saying No about seven times, i finally said yes and took up the management of three insurance agencies in three different cities. Ripping up and down the highways. Holding meetings here and there. Playing Executive in motels (that's a fun game too, and most players never outgrow it). i was a member in good standing of the crisis-of-the-day club. i was exhausting myself, mentally and physically. Too, i knew what my twice-daily Alka-Seltzering for that fluttery gut was in all likelihood leading to. Yet with the exhaustion came extreme mental stimulation.

"On weekends i was in sore need of relaxation.

"i relaxed in front of the Selectric. (i like the best machinery, too; the Mercedes and the Selectric are, although the Underwood P-48 and the SCM-250 i had for a year each were Bhad Nhews.) In six months of such heavyweight management, capped—and made bearable by—Saturday-and-Sunday writing, i created three short stories and 5½ novels. They started selling. i closed the out-of-Morehead agencies. Four months later i made certain other arrangements, and took a back seat in *andrew offutt associates* (unltd).

"Finally, in August 1970, i left the insurance business altogether. i did some designs, spent a lot of money, and had an office built in here at home, Funny Farm.

"i had been in the life/hospitalization insurance business seven years. In the final 20 months i managed, selling nothing because i did not try to (that's true capitalism). In that same period i sold sixteen 50,000-word novels. Settings, times, subject matter, 'type' and even styles—I did a Victorian, for instance—varied.

"Since August 1967 i've sold just under two million words. In 1969 10 novels sold, over a half-million words. In 1970 12 novels, four of which, finally, were sf with my own name on them, and a couple of shorts and an underground-newspaper article. (Well, all right: *Screw*.)

"Until very recently, all my work was done on weekends, on the IBM. i would start at about 1:30 PM, sometimes a little earlier, on Saturdays. And write until dinner call: between 6:30 and 7:30. Interruptions were (1) frequent bellows for more coffee; (2) bathroom; (3) lunch: cheese and a little wine. Sunday's schedule was the same, without lunchbreak. i wrote at a secretary's metal typing table, at the top of the steps in the hallway of this huge old house.

"During the week there were other things to do: research, editing first-drafts and proofreading submission drafts. Sure, there are spurts; one Monday night in October i had an idea, and hand-outlined a novel while watching the NBC movie. Next day i typed that outline. Following night i read/changed/expanded that, while watching election returns. Wednesday i typed *that*: a long outline of 6500 or so words. Thursday i typed the first chapter, but had to stop to go make a speech. Friday-Saturday-Sunday-Monday i wrote on it, and finished it Tuesday. That novel's writing was a happening, to me, and i enjoyed rereading it because it was created so fast i hardly noticed what it was about!

"Last summer, June 1970, i experienced my first Block, that ancient writer's devil i'd heard about. Stupid; it was MY fault. The novel was 2/3 outlines, see, with the ending decided (although it got changed when i reached it), and the previous weekend had seen completion of a chapter, a section, and the outline. Simultaneously. Very neat. Very stupid. That's the WORST place to stop. Stupid. i HANDED myself a block. It's a book i feel deeply about, too; it came a little less easily than some. It's the pretty-immediate future, as i see it, and regional (i live in Appalachia and most people who write about Kentucky ruralites don't know what the holy hell they are typing about), drawing strongly, aside from personal observations/notes/thinking, from three books: *(The) Territorial Imperative, Naked Ape,* and *Environmental Handbook.*

"Anyhow, i blocked. When i came back to it the following weekend, for the first time in my life i could NOT pick up and get going.

"i fought. My brain fought back. i bathroomed three times, washed a pair of corfam boots, wished it were Winter so i could chop wood, separated original and carbon of the novel just finished for submission, got up and down, fixed more coffee. It was awful. i sweated. (i do not perspire, i have never perspired. i sweat. And no, you're wrong: i weight 154 at 6' 1".)

"i fought. i kept sitting down and trying to type. i snarled, cursed, cussed, obscenitized. Kept on fingering keys. (i use three fingers, one of which is on my left hand. It gets sorest.) i kept on. Come *on,* damn you!

"i PREVAILED! It had been awful. It had lasted 45 minutes, and now i know what a block is. i'd liefer forget, and i will never ever stop at a stopping point again!

"i can't see that a block ever need be longer, assuming one has any control over himself at all. Ideas come out of the woodwork, daily, and who writes something he doesn't WANT to write?"

Ellison again. Now you understand why I have allowed offutt to go on at such length. As a man who is just emerging from a very long Writer's Block (for me), a Block that's lasted about three months, I know how the poor soul felt during those terrible 45 minutes.

offutt, you arrogant sonofabitch, there are writers around whose pencil cases we can't carry, who've been in blocks for *years!* Sturgeon has been through at least three that I know of, each one about three years long. Sheckley goes into blocks that drive him to the Costa Brava and keep him off the typer for a year at a time. William Tenn has been in a Block for at least the last ten years that *I* know of, living off the teaching abilities of Phil Klass. There are fans who jest about me and Silverberg "blocking"—for half an hour. But one day will come, smartass; one frightening, mouth-drying day when *nothing* comes. And then you'll know what it is to suffer the torments of a hell you can't even name. It's like being nibbled to death by mice in Philadelphia. You straighten the desk, you clean the house, you listen to music, you re-read Tolstoy, you pray, you go get laid, you come back and . . . nothing.

And it goes on and on.

You try to explain it to yourself and your friends and those who have you fish-hooked with deadlines, and they won't believe you, because you've been arrogantly productive all your writing life. And you exist there all alone, trapped out on the edge of your mind; gone suddenly black and empty. It's not that you don't have ideas. Oh, hell, you have thousands of those. You're as articulate, as clever, as facile as you ever were. You just don't *want to work*. You stare at the machine and it's loathsome.

And then, one day, for no reason you can discern, it breaks. The Block vanishes and you start bamming the keys again.

And at that moment, ANDREW J. CAPITALS AND ALL DAMNED OFFUTT, and all of you dainty dilettantes out there reading this, who think writing is something *any* schlepp can do, remember the words of Hemingway, who said, "There are three conditions for becoming a writer. He must write today, he must write tomorrow, he must write the day after that . . ."

offutt's a writer. He writes. As this story, at long last, attests.

andrew j. offutt

FOR VALUE RECEIVED

Mary Ann Barber, M.D., was graduated from medical school at the tender age of 23. Her Boards score set a new high. No, she isn't a genius. You don't know about her? Where've you been? There have been Hospital Board Meetings and Staff Meetings and even discussions of her case in the AMA and the AHA. Most important medical case in American history; frightening precedent. She's been written up, with pictures, in LIFE, LOOK, PARENTS, THE JOURNAL OF THE AMA, HOSPITAL NEWS, TODAY'S HEALTH, READER'S DIGEST—and FORTUNE. Her father has turned down movie offers. He's also been interviewed by THE INDEPENDENT, PSYCHOLOGY TODAY, RAMPARTS, THE OBJECTIVIST NEWSLETTER, and PLAYBOY.

It started twenty-three years ago when Robert S. Barber won a sales contest and received a very healthy company bonus. That was just before his wife Jodie was due to present him with their third child. Feeling expansive, Bob Barber suggested a private room for Jodie's confinement. She agreed, with enthusiasm. Last time she had shared a room with Philomena, a mother of nine. Philomena had complained constantly about the horror of being a breeding machine. Jodie told her to have faith—and stop. Philomena advised her that her Faith was the source of her problem.

Jodie entered the Saint Meinrad Medical Center in a room all to herself, rather than sharing one with another new mother in the American Way. The room cost ten dollars a day more than the money provided by the Barber's group hospitalization insurance; privacy's expensive! Nevertheless the ID card got them past the Warder of the Gates, a suspicious matron at the Admittance desk whose job it was to admit all patients impartially—provided they either possessed insurance ID cards or were visibly and provably destitute. There wasn't any middle ground.

The baby, a hairless girl—at least she showed certain evidences of insipidly incipient femalehood—was born with the usual number of arms, legs, fingers, etcetera after a brief period of labor. She proved with gusto the proper functioning of her lungs and larynx. She also took immediately to breast-feeding as if it were the normal method. She throve without seeming to realize that her infantile neighbors wouldn't recognize a mammary if they saw one.

Meanwhile the girls in the nursery went about their job: spoiling the infants entrusted to them by parents who had no choice and who would wonder in a few days how it was possible for a child to be born spoiled. The second part of the job of all hospital personnel involved, then as now, keeping the male of the species from both his chosen mate and the fruit of his loins. Robert Barber objected to this. Why his presence was forbidden while Jodie nursed the baby was beyond him. He'd seen 'em before. As a matter of fact he considered them his.

The nun he asked failed to reply.

Ostensibly, visiting hours were to protect the patients from disturbances in the form of Aunt Martha ("Yaas, I knew someone who had the selfsame operation, my dear. She died, poor soul.") and the like. But new mothers were not sick. It was obvious to Robert Barber that the prescribed hours—and the far greater number of proscribed ones—were for the convenience of a hospital staff whose mystique suffered from a surfeit of Commoners noticing their humanness. Naturally this assumption was strengthened by the fact that physicians, nurses, interns, residents, orderlies, Candy-Stripers, Gray Ladies, Pink Ladies, and the Lady pushing the cart peddling magazines and tissues disturbed the patients far more than "lay" visitors.

The inescapable prayers on the loudspeaker every night were rather disturbing, too.

But Robert Barber was a determined man. He had noticed that there were two kinds of people in hospitals, aside from the patients: Those Who Belong, and Others. The Others visited and indeed seemed to exist only by the sufferance of anyone who wore white shoes or a lab coat. Or carried a little black satchel. All one had to do, Bob Barber decided, was to act as if one Belonged.

So he adopted protective coloration. Carrying his black briefcase and striding purposefully, he traversed the hallowed and antiseptic halls.

"Good-evening-nurse," he said briskly, barely deigning to see the deferential girls who ducked respectfully out of his way. "Sister," he said to the nuns who were not quite so deferential: after all, doctor or no doctor, he was only a man, and a layman at that. But they nodded and rustled aside nevertheless.

Thus did the fiercely independent Bob Barber disregard Visiting Hours for four days running.

The fateful day arrived without portentous occurrence in the skies. Jodie Barber was pronounced ready to go home by a duly authorized member of the American Magicians Association. Thanking the kindly old AMA shaman-priest, Bob went down to settle with the cashier. She ruled a smallish domain separated from the world by a counter-*cum*-window that reminded him of a bank. She regarded him with the usual expression: as if he had committed a crime.

He had not.

He was about to.

"You seem to have placed your wife in a better room than your hospitalization covers, Mister Barber." Her tone was the same you've heard in movies when the prosecutor says, "Then you were indeed at or near the scene of the crime on the night of March 21st!"

Bob Barber smiled and nodded. "Yes. I should owe you about forty dollars, right?"

She nodded wordlessly, giving him an exemplary imitation of the gaze of the legendary basilisk.

Frowning a little, wondering if it were a communicable disease, Robert Barber also nodded, again. "Uh, well . . ."

"Would-you-like-to-pay-the-balance-by-cash-or-check, Mister Barber?"

He hesitated, he told an interviewer years later, waiting for the words THIS IS A RECORDING. He had recognized good salesmanship; the room was "better," not "more costly" than his insurance covered. Now he'd been given the standard "fatal choice": cash or check. "Send me a bill, please. You have my address."

"Mister Barber, our policy is that all bills are handled upon the release of the patient."

He remarked on that word "handled" later, too. Not "paid." She *had* taken a course in salesmanship/semantics!

"Yes, well, you've got $237.26 coming from the hospitalization and $40 from me. Just send me a bill at the end of the month like everyone else, will you?"

His smile failed to bring one in return. "We have a policy, Mister Barber, of not dismissing the patient until the bill has been settled in full."

"We've got an out then, ma'm. My wife isn't a patient here. We merely came here because it's a more convenient place for our doctor to watch the baby being born. Now ... my car is back by the Emergency Door, and my wife's all packed." He gave her his very best boyish smile. "Am I supposed to sign something?"

It didn't work. She sighed. "Mister Barber, you just don't seem to understand. It's a *rule*, Mister Barber. A *hospital* rule. We cannot dismiss the patient until the bill has been settled."

Bob Barber shoved his hands into his trouser pockets and squared his shoulders. She not only hadn't a cerebral cortex, he thought, she was missing her ovaries and needed a heart transplant! He firmed his mouth. "OK," he said. "If you must keep hostages, that's your business. But I'm sure one will do. Mrs. Barber and I are leaving in a few minutes. We are nursing the baby, so my wife will be coming back six times daily. The baby's name is Mary Ann, by the way." He smiled in his confidence, enjoying her shocked look. "When she's big enough to go to college we'll send you the tuition money." He grinned and waited for the backdown. He was without doubt the first man in history to call her bluff.

When Mary Ann Barber was six years old her father picked her up at the hospital each day to transport her to school. Each Friday she brought him a bill. It had passed $9000 when she was partly through the first grade.

She entered the tenth grade at age fourteen. On her fourth day as a Junior, she handed her daddy a bill for $106,378.23. She was one of the brightest girls in high school, and one of the healthiest. She had absorbed a tremendous amount of knowledge and sophistication, talking with interns. And it was easy to remain healthy, living in a hospital.

She had been moved from Nursery to Pediatrics to Children's Ward to Second Floor. Then the interns had doubled up to make her a gift: a private room away from the patients. Her parents visited her twice daily, usually. At visiting hours.

There were the Staff and Board Meetings, the magazine and newspaper articles, the interviews. Offers to pay Mary

Ann Barber's daily-increasing bill had come from all over the country, as well as from seventeen foreign nations and the governments of two. The hospital had offered to settle for ninety cents on the dollar. Then seventy-five. Fifty cents. Forty. Bob Barber said he was holding out for the same terms the Feds had given James Hoffa.

On her fourteenth birthday Mary Ann received one thousand, two hundred seventy-one cards. Shortly thereafter she received 1,314 Christmas cards. Her clothing came from one manufacturer, her shoes from another, her school books from two others. Her tuition arrived anonymously each year. Bob Barber solemnly invested it in an insurance annuity in his daughter's name. Most of the clothing she never wore; the parochial school she attended required sexless, characterless uniforms of navy-blue jumpers over white blouses. And black shoes. And white socks, rolled just to here.

She was graduated from college at nineteen and entered medical school at once. The doctors had won; the nuns had tried to sell her on the convent, the nurses on being an airline stewardess or secret agent. Mary Ann was far too fond of interns.

On his daughter's twenty-first birthday Robert Barber received his now-monthly itemized bill. It was thirty-seven feet long, neatly typed by the hated machine he called an Iron Brain, Malefic. The bill totalled $364,311.41, very little of which was for anything other than room and board. The discount had been applied and figured for him as usual, although this time he noticed he was asked for only twenty cents on the dollar. Still, $72,862.28 was more than he had available. He sent the usual note:

> I agreed to forward the forty dollars outstanding on my daughter's bill at the end of the month of her birth. When the bill arrived it was for $130, including ten days at $9 for Nursery Care. I returned it, requesting a corrected total of $40. Had you responded I would have had a daughter all these years, like other people. You chose to advise that I owed you for the time she spent in the hospital past the day I took my wife home. I disagreed then and I disagree today; those additional ten days were spent in your institution at your request, not mine. And not hers. Thus, since you claim to be a nonprofit organization and the courts have refused to uphold me in prosecuting for kidnap-at-ransom, I am still willing to pay the $40. However I cannot do this un-

til I receive a proper bill for that amount, so that I can account for it on my income tax return.

—Robert S. Barber

PS: The enclosed check is to cover all expenses for my daughter's recent tonsillectomy. Actually, had I had a choice I would have chosen another hospital providing better care, but she advises your service was satisfactory.

—RSB.

It was signed, as usual, with a flourish. You can see for yourself; the hospital threw away the first few, but they have a file of 243 of those letters. Two hundred thirty-seven of them are printed.

There was another Board Meeting. The vote still went against bowing to Barber's request for a total bill of $40, although Board members calculated that the bookkeeping had cost them $27.38 a year. But—in the first place, What Would People Think if they learned hospitals are fallible, and admit errors? In the second, Eli R. Hutchinson, president of the biggest bank in town and a board member for thirty-six years, absolutely refused to agree to the $40 settlement unless it included interest. Simple interest on the original amount came to $50.40. Barber had rejected that six years ago.

As they left the Board Meeting William Joseph Spaninger, MD, was heard to mutter to Sister Mary Joseph, OP, RN, "Well, Hutch can't live forever."

Sister Mary Joseph shook her head and rattled her beads. "You're a sinful man, Doctor Spaninger. Besides, Mister Hutchinson had a complete physical last week. He's in ridiculously good health."

Mary Ann Barber, as noted, graduated from Med School at 23 and made an extraordinary grade on her Boards. By that time she had turned down seven offers from six magazines to be photographed as their Nubile Young (semi) Nude (semi) Virgin of the month; three major studios who wanted to film her life story—two with herself in the starring role; seven hundred twenty-four written, wired, and cabled offers of matrimony, and six offers of the same from fellow medical students. There were other offers, most of them from fellow med students, most of them less formal.

Special arrangements were made for her to intern at home: Saint Meinrad Medical Center. The interns are salaried at exactly one hundred twenty dollars monthly. Doctor M. A. Barber began on the first of September.

At exactly midnight on the tenth she moved her possessions out of the hospital and just as quietly moved into a long-empty room at her parents' home. At two AM she returned to the hospital to go on duty.

Her departure was discovered at 8:30, while she was assisting—medicalese for watching—Doctor Spaninger perform a Pilonidal Cystectomy on a nineteen-year-old college student. Dr. Spaninger glanced up at the frantically-signaling nun in the doorway, then looked at Doctor Barber. Her eyes smiled at him above her mask. He shook his head at the nun and pulled his brows down at her as ferociously as possible. Doctor Mary Ann Barber smiled sweetly at her.

"What's she want?" Dr. Spaninger asked as they smoked a cigaret in the Physicians' Lounge after what he called a Tailectomy. He was very popular among nurses, residents, and interns, who called him the nearest-human doctor in town.

"Probably discovered I moved out last night. At midnight."

"Moved out of the hospital? My god, girl! You've run away from home!"

She shook her very blonde hair. "No doctor. I moved *to* home. It's quite a lovely room, although it certainly *smells* odd."

He nodded. "That's air. O_2 and some other stuff, nitrogen, hydrogen; you know. No antiseptics. No medicines. Possibly a little chintz, and some mothballs. Take some getting used to, I guess." He gazed at her, brows down. "But you're a . . . *resident* here. A resident resident, I mean, not a medical one. Let's don't go into it; I've been on the damned Hospital Board twenty years, and I've been living with the infamous Barber case all twenty of 'em. You can't leave. You have a hell of a bill here. Or your irascible, independent, atavistic, heroic old S.O.B. of a father does."

She pulled off the surgery cap and her hair flew as she shook her head with a very bright smile. "Nope. He doesn't. I signed some papers assuming all my own bills, debts, etcetera etcetera the day I turned twenty-one. I'm his daughter, you know; I agree with him. He didn't much like that, but I used the word 'independent' and he shut up pretty fast. That's Sacrament at his—my house. Then I told him my plan. That *really* shut him up, after he stopped laughing."

Dr. Spaninger waited. Then he sighed, looked at his watch, and leaned back, lighting another cigaret. She also had a cigaret out; he pushed the lighter back into his pocket.

"Don't play woman with me, Doctor," he said. "You're much too independent, competent and professional for me to insult you by lighting your cigaret. Besides, I've diapered you a few times. Never sent a bill, either." He watched a snake of smoke writhe up to the ceiling. "All right Mary Ann, I'll bite. What's your Plan?"

"Was. It's completed. I started here on the first of September, at $120 a month. September hath thirty days. That's four whole U.S. rasbuckniks a day."

"Um-hm. Shameful. We do everything we can to keep you yunkers out of the profession, including starve you out."

"We won't go into that either, overworked but wealthy old physician. Well, as of midnight last night I had worked ten days. That's forty dollars worth. I moved out. And left a note at the desk; I'm to receive only eighty dollars this month. We're even."

He leaned back and laughed. Loudly. Long. Eventually he grew rather red in the face and leaned over to slap his knee. His concerned young ward warned him about his blood pressure. He nodded, gasping and choking.

"Wait till they hear THIS! Wait'll Eli Hutch hears this! Oh, wonderful! We're shut of the Barber case at last!" He looked at her and frowned again. "Unless the rest of the Board decides to sue you . . . hm. I'll take care of that in *advance*. The only Barber I want to hear about hereafter is Doctor Barber. I hope I never hear the name Robert S. Barber again!"

"That's not very charitable, but Daddy and I are opposed to charity anyhow. I promise you this: my son won't be named Rober—what you said. He will be named William Robert Joseph Barber, OK?"

Dr. William Joseph Spaninger stared at her. "What . . . son?"

She shrugged. "Oh, the one I'll eventually have. I'm trying to decide now which of my fellow interns is the most promising-looking." She smiled at him. "No, I will *not* be an OB patient any ways soon. Not till I've finished up here, anyhow. And probably not till after I'm married."

"Thank god. But that's a dang lie—you're stuck on young Chris Andrews and you know it." He studied her thoughtfully. "Well. How the devil do you plan to exist on eighty bucks this month?"

"I won't have to. I am receiving forty dollars from Daddy. He says the bill was his responsibility, anyhow. We accept our responsibilities in my family."

Dr. Spaninger waved a hand at the hospital. "Nonsense. This is your family, and I haven't found two people here willing to accept responsibility in the past twenty years. And I hope you will allow me, as a token of an old girl-watcher's admiration for a very good-looking one, to give you a check for exactly $40 for your birthday. Your father's giving you the forty sounds suspiciously like charity, and I really hate to see the old bas—rascal start changing, now. He's a great man. Just for god's sake don't ever tell him so. And . . . carry on his work."

"I intend to. I'll spend the rest of my life bucking the System and marking 'PLEASE' in all those nasty DO NOT WRITE IN THIS SPACE blocks and punching extra holes in computer cards. But he's a greater man than you think, O Reverend Father-image. I said I was *receiving* the money from him, Doctor. I did *not* say anything about charity. It's a business arrangement; Daddy pays only for value received. For the duration of the month, on my hours off-duty from here, I'm on KP at home."

Afterword:

This one wasn't too dangerous because it will probably happen. Only the IR (I do not call them "service" because I do not lie) people are more arrogant than hospital exchequers. They have to be; it's amazing how much costs have risen since free Medicare came along. If it paid *all* the bill for those people who are now going in hospital for rests, your tax bill and mine would be even worse. Since it doesn't, we have to pay for them when we're hospitalized, just like everything at the grocery is a penny or 3 higher because you and I help defray the cost of shoplifters.

Besides, "For Value Received" is half-true. Down to the break, when Bob Barber calls the hospital's bluff. Bob Barber is me. Jodie is my wife. Mary Ann is my daughter Scotty. I wanted to visit my wife when *I* wanted to, not when it was convenient for the hospitaleers. So I carried a black bag, acted brusque and Belonging, and was naturally mistaken for a member of the American Magicians' Association: AMA. The creature at the desk said everything to me the one in the story does. I owed a lousy forty bucks, and was not accustomed to being treated as if I were at a world sf convention or something. So I called her bluff. I said *exactly* what Mary Ann's dad says in the story. After staring at me in shocked silence, she backed apoplectically away and went into a little opaque-glass cubicle. (Just like the guy at the car lot. You know; he *always* has to go ask the boss if he can let you have the cigaret lighter for only $9.95 instead of $10.00.)

I waited. A black-bonneted head came out. Looked me over. I was in Uniform: suit, shirt, tie. Only a fool wears anything else at hospital checkout desks or in traffic court. Head withdrew. The Creature returned. I was let off; all she wanted was name and address and phone number, which she already had. Checking. I started to go, once again having won a Great Victory over an Established Faith (did Harlan tell you about how I got the tax people off my back by writing the President?).

"Uh . . . Mister offutt . . . you WILL pay this, won't you?"

I swear. I gave her my best don't-you-wish-you-knew-who-your-father-was look and departed. With wife and of-futtspring.

That became one of our three favorite stories to tell captive audiences dumb enough to beholden themselves by coming out to drink my liquor. (The other two are how-andy-scared - off - the - prowler - with - a - Daisy - air - rifle - while - scared - to - death - the - bb's - would - rattle, and how - andy - damnear - chopped - off - his - left - thumb - with - a - machete - while - cutting - weeds - and - thank - Mithra - he - types - with - only - the - index - finger - on - that - hand - anyhow.) Come out for a drink and we'll tell you. If you mix with 7-up or cola, you get cheap Ky bourbon. If you drink it bare, or with water or soda, you'll get Maker's Mark and the stories will be painless.

Anyhow, one night we told our friend Bill Hough the hospital story and he didn't laugh and beam at me as if I were god. Before I could snatch his drink and throw him out, he said:

"Ever think what might've happened if they'd called your bluff *back?*"

I gave Bill another drink and wrote the story next day. It was turned down by *Redbook*, *Satevepost* (which immediately went bust), *Atlantic*, *Good House*, and the *agent* I had at that time! Here's what he said:

"I'm sorry but—and I don't believe 'For Value Received' would make it. It has humor and truth to a point, but it's against the rules to spoof the medical profession. . . ."

So, obviously, this IS a dangerous vision. To dwarfs, anyhow. We're surrounded by them.

Introduction to

MATHOMS FROM THE TIME CLOSET:

Gene Wolfe is a quiet, mostly amiable man with a sense of humor that has all the gentility of a carnivorous plant. I like and admire him more than I've ever told him. He is the author of a so-so novel, *Operation Ares*, and a horde of short stories that are well into the category labeled brilliant. He lives on Betty Drive in Hamilton, Ohio, the state from which I came; and when I left, Ohio got Gene, as the act of a benevolent God.

During the 1971 Nebula awards in New York, I sat in front of Gene during one of the most painful incidents it has ever been my gut-wrench to witness, and the way Gene reacted to it says much about the man.

Isaac Asimov had been pressed into service at the last moment to read the winners of the Nebulas. Gene was up in the short story category for his extravagantly excellent "The Island of Doctor Death And Other Stories" from Damon Knight's ORBIT 7 (Gene has appeared nine times in the eight ORBIT collections as of this writing) (thereby attesting to Damon's perspicacity as an editor) (taught the kid everything he knows, except table manners at banquets) (he throws peanuts and peas). Isaac had not been given sufficient time to study the list, which was hand-written, and he announced Gene as the winner. Gene stood up as the SFWA officers on the platform went pale and hurriedly whispered words to Ike. Ike went pale. Then he announced he'd made an error. There was "no award" in the short story category. Gene sat back down and smiled faintly.

Around him everyone felt the rollercoaster nausea of stomachs dropping out backsides. Had it been me, I would have fainted or screamed or punched Norbert Slepyan of Scribner's, who was sitting next to me. Gene Wolfe just smiled faintly and tried to make us all feel at ease by a shrug and a gentle nod of his head.

His three short stories in this book mark a departure in my DV policies: when I started assembling stories, I said no one writer would have more than a single story in the series. One shot and that was it. But I bought "Loco Parentis" in 1968, one of my first purchases, at the Milford SF Writers Conference, and the following year when the Conference was held in Madeira Beach, Gene showed up with "Robot's Story" and "Against the Lafayette Escadrille," neither of which I could resist. So I bought all three and Gene devised an umbrella overtitle for the group, and it subsequently allowed Bernard Wolfe and James Sallis to sell me more than one. There is simply no defense against a Gene Wolfe story.

For me, his is one of the wildest and richest imaginations in the genre.

Here is what he says of himself:

"The usual middle class upbringing for kids born, as I was, in the worst of the depression. No brothers or sisters, the family moving around as my father tried to earn a living. (Mostly, he was trying to sell cash registers, God help him.) He was a man who was home only on weekends, and brought me one or two lead soldiers every time he came, until I had a corrugated board box of them so heavy I could not pick it up. If we're so much richer now, why can't you buy those lead soldiers anymore?

"My mother was from the deep south (North Carolina) descended through *her* mother from one of those real Scarlett O'Hara families that lost it all in the Civil War. (Oddly enough, my father's family also had roots in North Carolina, having come from there north about 1830, and I may be distantly related to Thomas Wolfe.) I remember her taking me to be shown to her parents, and how no one would explain why Grandfather kept those funny chickens that could not be let in with the regular chickens ("Or they'll kill 'em!") or the scarred white dog which had to be chained up when there were other dogs around. Grandfather had a wooden leg he kept out in front of him and was as deaf as a stump when he didn't want to hear you; I wish I could have known him better.

"*Something* must have happened during my school days, but I mostly remember that it was very hot. I am left-handed, and the chairs had their broad arm on the wrong side. My hands were always sweating and sticking to the paper. I remember that.

"The sports for which I showed some ability, boxing and shooting, were unimportant beside such necessities as basketball. I was good at baseball, except for the parts which involve catching or throwing the ball. In Junior High I acquired a distaste for compulsory athletics which has never deserted me.

"My father, who had little money to spare for sending a son to college (he was operating a food business or a restaurant by this time, I'm not quite sure when the change was made), obtained the promise of a senatorial appointment to West Point for me. Unfortunately by the time I graduated from High School in 1949 there had been a readjustment of the power structure, and the new man, a short-sighted fellow named L. B. Johnson, refused to honor his predecessor's commitment.

"A few years later I found myself a private in the 7th Infantry Division, attempting to excavate a foxhole with the buttons of my shirt. I had dropped out of Texas A&M, which is a land grant college and something of a cross between V.M.I. and Tom Disch's CAMP CONCENTRATION but very cheap if you live in the state, and learned to my sorrow the meaning of 'student deferment.' That was the Korean Police Action—remember that?

"The G.I. bill let me return to school at the University of Houston, and I got a B.S.M.E. there in 1956, following which I flew Texas, something I sometimes regret. I still hold the job I took when I graduated—that is to say, I'm working for the same employer, but since the job is Research and Development things change almost from month to month.

"I have a wife and four children. They seem like more."

Gene Wolfe

MATHOMS FROM THE TIME CLOSET

1: Robot's Story

It's a cold night, and the wind comes in so there's no *inside*, only two *outsides:* the one there where it howls up from the river, and the one in here—a little more sheltered, a little warmed by our breath. Che's poster flutters on the wall as though he's trying to talk; the kids would say "rap."

The kids are the older ones, three sitting crosslegged on Candy's mattress. (That's the Chillicothe Candy: there are fifty others up and down Calhoun Street.) The kids are the younger ones, runaways: two virgin (or nearly) girl groupies, and a thin, sad boy who never talks. The kids are Robot, who has been down the hall where the plumbing works (it is stopped up here) and comes in, *step, step, step,* thinking about each move his legs make.

I've talked to Robot more than to any of the others because he is (perhaps) the least hostile and the most interesting. Robot is about nineteen, very tall, with a round, small head and a shock of black hair. Robot was custom-built, he tells me, in the thirty-third century to be the servant of an ugly woman who lived in a house floating on nothingness. Whenever Robot feels depressed he says: "I don't know how good I was made. Maybe I'm going to work for a thousand years; maybe I'm more than half used up already."

Robot says he is five. He escaped, or so he once told me, by spinning the dials of the ugly woman's time closet and stepping in while they were still in motion. This, as he explains, was to prevent his whenabouts (emphasized by his voice so that I'll notice the word) becoming known; but he had hoped to arrive in the thirteenth century B.C., a period which exercises a fascination for him.

Candy and the two boys with her ignore him, and after watching them for a moment he sits on the floor with the groupies (self-proclaimed) and the sad-faced boy and me. The boy is almost asleep, but to get Robot talking I ask, "Don't you wish you were back now, Robot?"

He shakes his head. "This is better. That was a drag all the time." He thinks for a moment, then asks, "Do you mind if I tell a story?" I tell him to go ahead, and so do the groupies, but he still hesitates. "You don't mind? I'm programmed for them, and there wasn't anyone who would listen there, so I never got to get them out. When I get them out they're checked off, you know? It's kind of like being constipated."

The sad boy says, "Go on." This, I think, is what Robot has been waiting for.

"This is a fairy story," Robot begins. "It goes way back to the days when the little one-man scout ships went out from here in every direction looking for habitable spheres, scattering like sperm from semen dropped in the sea."

I had not known Robot possessed such a strain of eloquence, and I look closely at him. His eyes are staring straight ahead and his mouth is a round *O*, the way he holds it when he is pretending there is a speaker in his throat.

"Those days continued for many, many years, you must understand. And every year the ships left in tens or hundreds—up toward the pole star; out like spokes around the sun; down past the Southern Cross. This is about one of the ships that went down.

"It dropped for years, but it didn't count years. The pilot was asleep, and in a hundred days he would breathe three times. In a year, maybe, he would turn over and then plastic hands would come out of the wall and turn him right again. The ship woke him up when they had gotten somewhere.

"He woke up, and it knew he had forgotten almost everything except what he'd been dreaming of, so it explained it all to him while it rubbed him and gave him something to eat. When it was finished he thought, 'What a tourist I was to let them talk me into this.' Then he got up to see what this world he found was.

"It wasn't anything special; as near as he could see mostly high grass—higher than your head. He landed and the air was all right and he got out and did all the things he was supposed to do, but there was really nothing there but all this grass."

(I wondered if the "grass" in the story was an unconscious reflection of the kids' obsession with marijuana; or if for Robot as for Whitman it represented the obliterations of time.)

"Then just when he was getting ready to go, this really lovely chick came out of the grass. No noise, you dig? No drums, no trumpets. She just pushed it back like a chick will push back her hair and came out. He was crazy about her as soon as he saw her, and they made a deal.

"He couldn't take her back in the ship with him and she wouldn't have gone anyway. But she told him she'd live with him there if he'd do three things, and she made him write them out in his own blood. He had to swear first of all that he'd do all the work, and never ask her to do anything. Then that he wouldn't tell people back here what he'd found, and that he wouldn't ask her any questions.

"He wrote it all and he signed it, and she had him build them a house, like out of sod and the grass and pieces of his ship. He dug a cistern and planted some seeds he'd had in the ship to get things started for the colony people who were supposed to come after him. And that was it, except that sometimes she would catch the soft little animals that lived in the grass and eat them. She never gave him any and he never asked for any, and they were too quick for him to catch himself.

"He got older but she didn't, and he thought that was groovy. He was getting to be an old guy but he still had a young wife as pretty as a girl. He had to do everything like he had agreed, but otherwise she was always nice. She sang a lot without words and played a thing like a flute, and she told him all the time what a great guy he was.

"Then one day just after sundown when he'd been out hoeing the crops and was just about to go in he saw a new spark up among the stars. He watched it for a long time, trying to straighten up his back and rubbing the white hair around his face. After that he saw it every night for three nights, moving across the sky. Then on the fourth day, when he was carrying water from the cistern there was a kind of whizz in the air and something big hit the ground a long way off. He was starting to think about that when his wife came down the path. She wasn't carrying anything, or doing anything to make her look different from the way she usually did, and she didn't wear clothes, but there was a kind of glow to her like she'd brushed her hair a little more than usual and maybe toweled herself harder when she washed. She went walking right past him and never said a thing.

"He watched her walk through all the place he'd cleared to grow food and when she got to the grass she just kept going, opening it with her hands and stepping in. Then he yelled, 'Where are you going?'

"She didn't even turn her head, but she yelled back, 'I'm going to get myself a new fool.'"

Robot pauses.

One of the groupies asks, "Is that all there is to it?"

Robot doesn't answer. Candy has come over, and she's saying, "Robot, we want you to go out and cop a nickel for us." Which means: "Buy us five dollars worth of marijuana."

Robot stands and holds out his hand, and one of the boys squatting on Candy's mattress laughs and says, "If we had it we'd cop ourselves." For a moment I think of lending Robot my coat (his own orange one belonged to a hotel doorman, and is so worn in spots that the lining shows through the napless fabric) but the way people usually do, I think too long before saying anything. He goes out, Candy and her two friends settle down on the mattress to wait for him, and now I think we are all going to sleep.

2: Against the Lafayette Escadrille

I have built a perfect replica of a Fokker triplane, except for the flammable dope. It is five meters, seventy-seven centimeters long and has a wing span of seven meters, nineteen centimeters, just like the original. The engine is an authentic copy of an Oberursel UR II. I have a lathe and a milling machine and I made most of the parts for the engine myself, but some had to be farmed out to a company in Cleveland, and most of the electrical parts were done in Louisville, Kentucky.

In the beginning I had hoped to get an original engine, and I wrote my first letters to Germany with that in mind, but it just wasn't possible; there are only a very few left, and as nearly as I could find out none in private hands. The Oberursel Worke is no longer in existence. I was able to secure plans though, through the cooperation of some German hobbyests. I redrew them myself translating the German when they had to be sent to Cleveland. A man from the newspaper came to take pictures when the Fokker was nearly ready to fly, and I estimated then that I had put more than three thousand hours into building it. I did all the airframe and the fabric work myself, and carved the propeller.

Throughout the project I have tried to keep everything as realistic as possible, and I even have two 7.92 mm Maxim "Spandau" machineguns mounted just ahead of the cockpit. They are not loaded of course, but they are coupled to the engine with the Fokker Zentralsteuerung interrupter gear.

The question of dope came up because of a man in Oregon I used to correspond with who flies a Nieuport Scout. The authentic dope, as you're probably aware, was extremely flammable. He wanted to know if I'd used it, and when I told him I had not he became critical. As I said then, I love the Fokker too much to want to see it burn authentically, and if Antony Fokker and Reinhold Platz had had fireproof dope they would have used it. This didn't satisfy the Oregon man and he finally became so abusive I stopped replying to his letters. I still believe what I did was correct, and if I had it to do over my decision would be the same.

I have had a trailer specially built to move the Fokker, and I traded my car in on a truck to tow it and carry parts and extra gear, but mostly I leave it at a small field near here where I have rented hangar space, and move it as little as possible on the roads. When I do because of the wide load I have to drive very slowly and only use certain roads. People always stop to look when we pass, and sometimes I can hear them on the front porches calling to others inside to come and see. I think the three wings of the Fokker interest them particularly, and once in a rare while a veteran of the war will see it—almost always a man who smokes a pipe and has a cane. If I can hear what they say it is often pretty foolish, but a light comes into their eyes that I enjoy.

Mostly the Fokker is just in its hangar out at the field and you wouldn't know me from anyone else as I drive out to fly. There is a black cross painted on the door of my truck, but it wouldn't mean anything to you. I suppose it wouldn't have meant anything even if you had seen me on my way out the day I saw the balloon.

It was one of the earliest days of spring, with a very fresh, really indescribable feeling in the air. Three days before I had gone up for the first time that year, coming after work and flying in weather that was a little too bad with not quite enough light left; winter flying, really. Now it was Saturday and everything was changed. I remember how my scarf streamed out while I was just standing on the field talking to the mechanic.

The wind was good, coming right down the length of the field to me, getting under the Fokker's wings and lifting it like a kite before we had gone a hundred feet. I did a slow turn then, getting a good look at the field with all the new, green grass starting to show, and adjusting my goggles.

Have you ever looked from an open cockpit to see the wing struts trembling and the ground swinging far below? There is nothing like it. I pulled back on the stick and gave it more throttle and rose and rose until I was looking down on the backs of all the birds and I could not be certain which of the tiny roofs I saw was the house where I live or the factory where I work. Then I forgot looking down, and looked up and out, always remembering to look over my shoulder especially, and to watch the sun where the S.E. 5a's of the Royal Flying Corps love to hang like dragonflies, invisible against the glare.

Then I looked away and I saw it, almost on the horizon, an orange dot. I did not, of course, know then what it was; but I waved to the other members of the Jagstaffel I command and turned toward it, the Fokker thrilling to the challenge. It was moving with the wind, which meant almost directly away from me, but that only gave the Fokker a tail-wind, and we came at it—rising all the time.

It was not really orange-red as I had first thought. Rather it was a thousand colors and shades, with reds and yellows and white predominating. I climbed toward it steeply with the stick drawn far back, almost at a stall. Because of that I failed, at first, to see the basket hanging from it. Then I leveled out and circled it at a distance. That was when I realized it was a balloon. After a moment I saw, too, that it was of very old-fashioned design with a wicker basket for the passengers and that someone was in it. At the moment the profusion of colors interested me more, and I went slowly spiraling in until I could see them better, the Easter egg blues and the blacks as well as the reds and whites and yellows.

It wasn't until I looked at the girl that I understood. She was the passenger, a very beautiful girl, and she wore crinolines and had her hair in long chestnut curls that hung down over her bare shoulders. She waved to me, and then I understood.

The ladies of Richmond had sewn it for the Confederate army, making it from their silk dresses. I remembered reading about it. The girl in the basket blew me a kiss and I waved to her, trying to convey with my wave that none of the men of my command would ever be allowed to harm her; that we had at first thought that her craft might be a French or Italian observation balloon, but that for the future she need fear no gun in the service of the Kaiser's Flugzeugmeisterei.

I circled her for some time then, she turning slowly in the basket to follow the motion of my plane, and we talked as well as we could with gestures and smiles. At last when my fuel was running low I signaled her that I must leave. She took, from a container hidden by the rim of the basket, a badly shaped, corked brown bottle. I circled even closer, in a tight bank, until I could see the yellow, crumbling label. It was one of the very early soft drinks, an original bottle.

While I watched she drew the cork, drank some, and held it out symbolically to me.

Then I had to go. I made it back to the field, but I landed dead stick with my last drop of fuel exhausted when I was half a kilometer away. Naturally I had the Fokker refueled at once and went up again, but I could not find the balloon.

I have never been able to find it again, although I go up almost every day when the weather makes it possible. There is nothing but an empty sky and a few jets. Sometimes, to tell the truth, I have wondered if things would not have been different if, in finishing the Fokker, I had used the original, flammable dope. She was so authentic. Sometimes toward evening I think I see her in the distance, above the clouds, and I follow as fast as I can across the silent vault with the Fokker trembling around me and the throttle all the way out; but it is only the sun.

3: Loco Parentis

DAD: He's beautiful, isn't he?

MOM: So new and unscratched! Like a car in the showroom, or a turbine that's never turned! Like a new watch!

DAD: You're just enthusing, aren't you? Are you trying to tell me something?

MOM: I mean he's beautiful, just as you said. Stop scratching yourself.

NURSE: Isn't he lovely? But he's only ten months old. He'll need all sorts of care. Cleaning and feeding.

DAD: Oh, I know all about that. I've watched.

MOM: You mean we know.

NURSE: You'll both learn, I'm sure. (Leaves baby and exits.)

DAD: What did you mean, about the turbine? I've heard that because there are so many couples like us, who want children but can't have them, they build robots, half-living simulacra, like children, to satisfy the instinct. Once a month they come at night and change them for larger so that you think the child's growing. It's like eating wax fruit.

MOM: That's absurd. But they mutate the germ plasm of chimpanzees (Pan satyrus) to resemble the human, producing half-people simians to be cared for. It's as if the organ played its music when there was no one to hear except the organ grinder's monkey.

DAD: (Drawing away the baby blanket) He's not a mutated chimp. See how straight his legs are.

MOM: (Touching) He's not a machine. Feel how warm he is with the real warmth, even when none of his parts are moving.

SON: May I play outside?

MOM: With whom?

SON: With Jock and Ford. We're going to fly kites and climb trees.

MOM: I'd rather you didn't play with Ford. I saw him when he fell and cut his knee. The blood didn't come in proper spurts, but just flowed out, like something draining.

DAD: I'd just as soon you avoided Jock. He eats too much fruit, and I don't approve of his taste in clothing.

SON: He doesn't wear any.

MOM: That's what your father means.

SON: I love his sister. (Goes out)

DAD: Don't cry. They grow up so fast. Hasn't everyone always told you?

MOM: (Still sobbing) It isn't that. Jock's sister!

DAD: She's a lovely girl. Hauntingly beautiful, in fact.

MOM: Jock's sister!

SON: (Re-entering, followed by a middle-aged couple) Mom, Dad, these people tell me that they're my real parents; and now that I've grown enough to be very little trouble, except for tuition, they've come to claim me.

MR. DUMBROUSKI: We've explained to the boy how useful foster parent-things are, allowing real people necessary leisure.

MRS. DUMBROUSKI: I've always said it's an honorable calling and by filling desk space in offices when they're supposed to be at work, the father-things usefully increase the prestige of their nominal supervisors. Don't they, dear?

MR. DUMBROUSKI: Yes indeed. I've got several working for me, although I'd never admit it at the office.

Son: Goodbye, Mom and Dad. I know one or both of you may be a machine or an ape or both, but I'll never forget you. I won't come to see you, because someone might see me coming in, but I'll never forget you. (To Mr. Dumbrouski:) Will I know which is which when I've had time to think about it?

Nurse: Isn't he lovely? But he's only ten months old. He'll need all sorts of care. Cleaning and feeding.

Dad: Like a new bamboo shoot!

Mom: Like a new headlight socket just coming out of the plating tank!

Nurse: You'll learn, I'm sure. (Leaves baby and exits)

Junior: May I just sit here by the clock to eat my banana?

Mom & Dad: *My son!*

Afterword:

Three stories: If you liked them you have three people to thank, of whom you yourself are one. If Harlan and I have messed with your mind in the pages just past it was because you have a mind to mess with. Many of the things you thought I said, you said.

Three ways of playing with time: If you're authentic enough, and so deep up the blue hole nothing contrasts with your authenticity, you've gone back—haven't you? Or, you're mature in an instant (we all were) and Mother is only a tall woman with copper hair, Father a short man with hairy arms. Or, you recite (having arrived from there last night) the enigmatic myths of the future.

Three guesses: Do you need them? I am Robot; I fly the soaring Fokker, though only in my mind (and yours, I hope); my parents were and are as described, and these are some of my Dangerous Visions, my hang-ups. You and I have walked among three wraiths. There are others.

Headup! You may be a prince (or princess) of Mars.

Introduction to

**TIME TRAVEL
FOR PEDESTRIANS:**

Recently, here in Los Angeles, and I presume all around our vital, healthy country, drive-ins and local neighborhood movie theaters played a charming double-bill. The upper, or A feature, was something called *I Suck Your Blood;* the lower half of the bill, the B feature, was *I Eat Your Skin.* After the hysterical convulsions pass, kindly note these two bum flicks were coded GP, which means kids can see them, but only with the consent and accompaniment of an adult. At the same time, a sex film titled *101 Acts of Love* was being shown in the area, with an X rating, meaning if you're a Catholic and go to see it, you'll burn in eternal hellfire. Kids strictly forbidden.

This is hardly an original thought I'm about to lay on you, but doesn't it seem strange to anyone else out there that it's okay for kids to see people having their necks bitten, their flesh eaten and their bodies used for fertilizer, but it is considered corrupting for them to watch two people having sex?

Where I'm going with this is toward Ray Nelson, but I'd like to make a couple of conversational stops on the way.

You see, DV (and surely A,DV will see a repetition of the problem) had some acceptability problems with certain libraries, with some bookstores, and when it was reprinted in the Science Fiction Book Club a number of scoutmasters and outraged mommies and common garden-variety guardians of public morality (like Keating, the head wimp of the Citizens for Decent Literature, on whose squamous skull a curse of succotash!) fired the book back with bleats of horror that their delicate children were being sent such mind-rotting filth that would obviously pollute their precious bodily fluids. In the general introduction I quoted one lady who wrote me directly. She was not alone in her vehemence.

It is to Doubleday's and Larry Ashmead's eternal glory that never once did they warn me away from "controversial" material, either in subject matter or treatment or language. The same has held true with this volume. They said, in fact, get it on, and do what has to be done. As a result, this book contains stories like Ray Nelson's that I'm sure will bleach white the hair of librarians and others invested with the fraudulent chore of protecting delicate young minds.

To simply state that Ray's story is a zinger and needs no further defense than its quality would be the wise course for me here, but as I have never been known to exist in a territory of wisdom, I'll go on and make a few comments about censorship, about protecting those who need no protection, about hypocrisy, and about "dirty" language.

Those of you who've heard these things need not attend. The test afterward only counts for half your grade.

In any case: having traveled around the country a good deal these past few years, lecturing at colleges and high schools, I've found that while people under-thirty are no less susceptible to slogans and simplistic answers than their over-thirty counterparts, *on the whole* they don't have the same hangups about language and topics of forbidden discussion to which their elders subscribe. When I was nineteen I was still a virgin, but when I pass a high school now, and see the fifteen, sixteen and seventeen year old girls, I am struck by the resemblance to a casting call for *Irma La Douce*, and I am hip to the fact that young people are getting it on sexually much earlier than when I was their age. I think that's all to the good. Times have changed. The Pill and mass communications dissemination of hygienic information have made most of the restrictions against pre-marital sex invalid and outdated. Young people are reaching each other in some very natural, normal ways that were *verboten* to generations past, and along with that tacit acceptance of the body and its many uses, comes an acceptance of language. It is, for instance, virtually impossible today to shock kids by a discussion of masturbation. Everyone knows guys masturbate, and so do girls. If it comes up in conversation it's an accepted, like television or the jumbo jet. They grew up with it, and all the taboos about even owning up to the fact that you play with yourself strike them as pointless and hincty.

Which, perforce, brings me to Ray Nelson, "Time Travel for Pedestrians" and the hypocrisy of protecting those who need no protection. Ray's story deals, in small part, with the concept of masturbation as a triggering device for time travel. Its inclusion here, as well as publication of the stories by Piers Anthony, Richard Lupoff and Ben Bova, not to mention just the *title* of the Vonnegut story, promise trouble with bluenoses. Understand *please*, these stories are not to me "dirty" or "offensive" in any way. My contention is that *nothing* should be forbidden to a creator in the pursuit of an idea. But I am not fool enough to think these stories will slip by unnoticed when the hawklike eyes of the NODL and Citizens for Decent Everything get their white sheets on.

We had some of this, as I've said, with DV. In fact, for almost three years we could not get an edition contracted in Great Britain, because the publishers kept turning the book down as "unpublishable." In the light of subsequent books released with ease in England, this now seems wholly ridiculous, but when we first acquired an English publisher, Leslie Frewin, we insisted the book be published as it stood, in its entirety, without deletions or concessions to censorship. Frewin agreed, but when the book was about to go to press, I learned that they were dropping the Theodore Sturgeon story because it dealt with incest, the Philip K. Dick story because it postulated God as a Chinese Communist, my own story because it used the word "fuck" and because it was clinically descriptive of a slaying by Jack the Ripper, and several others, including a story by Miriam Allen de Ford—on grounds I've *yet* to be able to name. Naturally, they were enjoined to cease publication, and the book was yanked away from them.

Fortunately, a more reliable and (one would presume) daring publisher in London, David Bruce & Watson, bought the rights and have published *Dangerous Visions* in two handsome volumes. But this was not the only instance of outright fear on the part of reprint houses to pick up the book. In Germany we were stuck with a wretched house, Heyne, who not only dropped stories without permission, but cut all the prefatory material, altered titles, changed copy beyond the normal considerations of translation into German, and in all botched DV hideously. (I have taken steps to insure there will be no repetitions of this with A,DV, but a pending lawsuit against Heyne is the residue of lack of foresight initially.)

I report all this in the (probably) vain hope that those who have nothing better to do with their time than worry that someone else will read what he wants to read, will think twice before pulling A,DV from library shelves or lobbying against it in their Saturday afternoon purity meetings.

For the rest of you, who can be shocked only by Calleys and Mansons and repression and violence, when you read this story you will more than likely say, "What the hell was all the shouting about? It isn't offensive. Is this Ellison on the hype again?" To you I say, these words were intended for the backward, the frightened, the sexually and emotionally constipated who exist in vast numbers out there.

And I'm sure this long preamble will surprise Ray Nelson,

who never thought his story would be a bone of contention. Which brings me, at long last, to Radell Faraday Nelson himself, and his personal statistics, herewith proffered in his own words:

"When I was about fifteen years old I remembered being born. I didn't know that's what I was remembering until much later. There were no words in the memory, just the feeling of being squeezed rhythmically again and again. It wasn't unpleasant.

"I was born in a hospital in Schenectady, N.Y. on Oct. 3, 1931 at (for those who are astrologically inclined) 2 a.m. I was the fruit of the union of mixed RH factors, and my head was too big for my body. I looked like, they tell me, one of those beings from the distant future, from a time when the body has all but wasted away from disuse. But I lived. I have one brother who lived, too. And many sisters who were still-born.

"Sometimes I think my sisters are near me, whispering things to me, guarding me from harm. I picture them covered with fine soft womb hair, all hunched over with their noses on their knees, floating just at the edge of my field of vision so that I can almost see them but not quite.

"As a child I was carried from place to place by my parents, not seeing the world around me too much, but talking to beings that only I could see. We traveled from one state to another, following my father's work, and as I ran, dreaming, along a stone wall on the edge of the Grand Canyon, I struck my head against a branch and almost fell over the cliff. I still have the scar, just above my left eyebrow.

"The best scar on my body, however, is on one side of my lower stomach (the right side) where my appendix was removed. I had had a bellyache for a long time but I was very brave about it and as a result almost died in the last minute operation that was performed on me after I collapsed on the basketball court at high school. I couldn't do anything rough for over a year after that for fear I might open up again, so I discovered reading. I read science fiction and Little Literary Reviews, neither of which left any visible scars, at least on my body.

"That was how I became a science fiction fan and hippie, though that was before the word hippie had been invented. I was deeply religious and everybody hated me because, when one of my classmates stole a ballpoint pen in a drugstore, I went back and paid for it. They left many little scars all over my torso, particularly the ass. There's another interesting scar on my left forearm, while we're on the subject.

"That's where, after I graduated from college and was working as a silk screen printer in Oakland, California, I held a candleflame under my arm and cooked the flesh until it turned black, in order to show that the spirit need not be troubled by the sufferings of the flesh. Fortunately the friends of mine who were present had promised in advance not to turn me over to the mental authorities. It was interesting to watch the scab form and then, a few months later, crumble and fall away to reveal the image of a perfect egg in white skin on a field of tan.

"There are many other marks on my body ... such as the little brown dots of various shapes all over me. I never noticed them until I dropped acid. Can you imagine that? Here I was, covered with little brown spots and I didn't even know it, then I expanded my consciousness and there they were. It was then that I noticed that my skin was also covered with a network of tiny diamond shaped lines, as if I were made of crystal, and that my flesh was everywhere touched with subtle blending shades of color, like coral. I don't know anything else about myself to speak of, since most of the things I've done have not marked my flesh and thus I can't be sure that they aren't false memories, like the events upon which the story, 'Time Travel for Pedestrians' is based, according to my analyst."

He may not know anything more of himself to speak of, but Your Dauntless Editor, up to his gunwales in Nelsonia, has a few more vitalistics. First, he is the co-author with Philip K. Dick of a novel titled *The Ganymede Takeover,* he had an absolutely sensational story in *The Magazine of Fantasy & Science Fiction* a few years back, called "Turn Off the Sky," and he has written full volumes of material for amateur magazines, not to mention his cartoons which were a staple item of "fanzines" during the years he was a science fiction fan.

And Ray is a classic example of how science fiction, the only kind of fiction that does this, brings up its own new generations of writers from the ranks of amateurs. The list of Big Name SF Writers of today, who started out as fans is endless—Silverberg, Brunner, Benford, Hoffman, Bradbury, Lupoff, Carr, Asimov, Knight, Pohl, Blish, Tucker, White—and both A,DV and *The Last Dangerous Visions* will showcase many of them.

A discussion of fandom is here improper, yet a few words from Nelson of the days when we were both fans, seem nostalgically appropriate, so once again:

"I remember a little café just outside Detroit.

"You and I were there, and George Young and all those other truefans, and we were all underage and we were all (except you, who don't drink) drinking beer and playing the electric bowling machine, and the manager came around and started asking for I.D. cards, and you had on a suit and tie and a large, literary-looking pipe, and when they came to you, you said, 'They're all right. I'll vouch for them.' And they didn't ask you for your I.D., though I believe you were the youngest one there.

"You just stood there drinking ginger ale and smoking and looking like our legal guardian.

"That's what we really are, Harlan. Feuds, the National Fantasy Fan Federation, letters to the prozines, mimeo ink under the fingernails, dreams of the Hugo while high on corflu (which you actually have gotten, at last, old superfan), articles typed straight on stencils, frightful poems and worse fannish imitation profiction, costumes at cons and musical beds, hateful monster movies that we just can't resist, Seventh Fandom, talking philosophy all night in greasy spoons, and that whole wild scene.

"I'm not just me, and you're not just you.

"Whenever I open my trap, the little microcosm that produced me is speaking through me, as if I were a ventriloquist's dummy. If you look down my throat you'll see, way back by the tonsils, the tiny figure of Claude Degler proclaiming in a piping voice, 'Fans are Slans.'

"So write anything about fandom, anything at all, and that will also be about me."

And so that future historians, coming back to this book as a reference, will have *all* the facts, Ray Nelson . . .

Is a graduate of the University of Chicago (1960) where he majored in liberal arts and received his B.A. He has an Operation and Wiring Certificate for IBM machines from the Automation Institute (head of the class, 1961) and is familiar with the IBM 514, 522, 077, 403, 407, 604 and 632. He is presently employed as a Machine Accountant Assistant with the University of California.

He was a translator and administrative assistant to a French author named Linard in Vesoul, France from 1957 to 1960. He has held jobs as a silk screen printer, sign writer, cartoonist, IBM machine programmer and operator, Great Books salesman, fork-lift truck operator, beatnik poet (one slender book of poems published; entitled, *Perdita: Songs of Love, Sex and Self-Pity*) (named for his first wife), movie extra, Abstract Expressionist, interior decorator (with a paint mixing stick in one hand and a bottle of Jack Daniels in the other), Dixieland banjo player, folknik guitar player and singer, bum, and etc.

He briefly attended the Art Institute of Chicago, and The Sorbonne, has lived in or visited all the states in the original 48, plus Canada, Mexico, England, and all the nations of free Europe. He is married to a beautiful Norwegian girl named Kirsten, whom he met while living in Paris. They have a son named Walter and they live in El Cerrito, California.

Married, speaks fluent French, student at The Sorbonne, a father . . . now I ask you, censors and trembling uptights of the world, is *this* the sort of man who could write a dirty story? Shit, no!

Ray Nelson

TIME TRAVEL FOR PEDESTRIANS

Masturbation fantasy is the last frontier.

When we travel to other planets we won't find much that we can't see or guess at from here, but there are things so strange we can hardly get the fingers of our minds around them that are closer to us than our own skin. Martin Esslin said it, in *The Theatre of the Absurd:*

"In a world that has become absurd, transcribing reality with meticulous care is enough to create the impression of extravagant irrationality."

Have you ever seen those photographs in magazines of familiar objects taken from an unfamiliar angle or from very close up? It's hard to recognize even such an everyday thing as the end of a cigarette when you see it up close. Why is this true? Because you never do look at things, not really. The closer a thing is to you, the less you examine it, the more you take it for granted and ignore it. On TV you learn all about the private lives of the famous, but what about your own private life? What do you know about that?

What do you really know, for instance, about the stag films projected on those dark night flights into your own private lost continents, projected against the inner surfaces of your closed eyelids when you sit in the Cock Pit and grasp the Joy Stick in a sweating hand? There's no movie reviewer to tell you whether the film is good for you or not. Perhaps the plot, if written down, would seem rather idiotic, yet this sort of film, that you project for yourself and yourself alone, seems to hold you spellbound. You return to it again and again, never growing weary of repeating the same arbitrary details over and over.

What do you think about when you jack off, or when you "make love"? Is it torture? And if it is, are you the tortured or the torturer? Is it leather clothes? Or rubber clothes? Is it high heels? Or do you dream of dressing in the clothes of the opposite sex, or even of trading bodies with the "loved one"? Is your mother there watching you in your mind, or your father, or someone who once rejected you? Is God watching you, condemning you? Is it silk? Nylon? Huge heaving breasts or wiggling rumps? Or is it the mouth of the womb itself, giving you a bearded kiss or spreading wide open to allow your return to the soft, warm darkness from which you came? Is it little girls or little boys, great round eyes fixed upon your hand as you slowly unzip your fly?

Are you thinking about it now? Is the picture once again flickering before your eyes? If it is, then this time look at it, long and hard. Examine it as if it were a masterpiece of art. Meditate on it as if it were the words of a great teacher. For it is the one thing in the universe that you have made for yourself alone, and not to impress someone else or to gain the approval of the church, the government, or the "respectable community." It may well be the only doorway that will ever open to allow you entrance into your own inner self.

Why do you hang back? Haven't you always thought Socrates was so frightfully wise when he took as his motto, "Know thyself"? Come. Let us enter. "It isn't as easy as all that," you may say. And you're right. There's something blocking your way. Let's put it a little more poetically. There's an angel guarding the entrance, with a flaming sword. He's been there a long time, but he is never tired. Angels don't need to sleep. You'll have to trick him, or drug him, if you want to get past.

I chose to drug him.

I went to the Five-and-Ten at the local shopping center and bought some very ordinary flower seeds. The pusher was a middle-aged Catholic saleslady in the garden department.

I think her name was Eve.

Then I went home and took a hammer and pounded the seeds to powder. I kept them in their packages while I pounded, so that they wouldn't fly all over the place. I had to sift them many times through a tea sieve before they formed a fine enough powder to suit me. Then I spread the powder over the surface of a dish of strawberry ice cream.

The angel in my mind touched me with fear, standing between me and the ice cream, but I knew from the Bible that if you fight an angel and win, the prize can be very great sometimes, so I ate it anyway. The ground seeds tasted like sawdust.

Then I went upstairs to my bedroom, where I had a double bunk all prepared for the occasion. Beside the bunk was a tape recorder on which I had recorded my own voice reading, over and over again, the First Bardo from the *Tibetan Book of the Dead* as translated by Timothy Leary. That's the chapter all about Ego Death. The *Book of the Dead* was the "In Thing" at that time, if you recall.

I lay down on the lower bunk.

From there I could see, scotch-taped to the lower face of the upper bunk, a Hindu hypnograph I had put up there some months ago when I had used it to soothe a toothache through hypnosis. As you can see, everything was "programmed." Did I tell you that I once was an IBM computer programmer?

I turned on the tape recorder and relaxed, listening to my own boring voice droning on and on, waiting for something to happen. (I had "tripped" before, but never with such elaborate preparations.) After a while something did happen. I got sick to my stomach.

I ran down to the bathroom and knelt before the john and threw up once, twice, three times. But it wasn't unpleasant, as it usually is. It was good. It was more than good. It was ecstatic. I was throwing up with my whole body, holding nothing back. It was an orgasm, or at least what an orgasm can be when it's good, when nobody is likely to bust in on you or when nobody is saying "Shhh, someone might hear you."

So I knew I was high.

And the light was different, too. You know, sort of bluewhite, as if everything were under water on a bright day. And the flickers of flame were silently dancing on every polished surface.

I lay down again.

The tape recorder was still talking.

God, I sounded pompous and stupid on the tape!

But still I decided to co-operate with that idiotic other self of mine who had set up this elaborate farce. Like, why not?

I looked at the hypnograph above me, at the dot in the middle you're supposed to concentrate on, and the voice on the tape machine said "Ego Death." I couldn't seem to catch the rest of it. "Ego Death. Ego Death. Ego Death."

Then it was only, "Death. Death. Death. Death."

"For Chrissakes," I thought, in momentary terror. "This is a trap!"

The angel was laughing now, but he was dark, and huge, and monstrous, and I knew that angels and devils are really the same. They are angels if you are on their side and devils if you're against them.

I sprang up, soaked in sweat, and tore off my clothes until I stood naked in the center of the room, panting and licking my salt lips. The titles of the books in my bookcase seemed to be speaking to me, and it was all about death that they were speaking.

I took hold of my dick. It was stiff and hard.

I felt safe, holding it.

I lay down on the lower bunk again, slowly, gently milking Old Dick with a practiced hand.

I looked at the hypnograph. Portions of it were starting to black out from time to time, winking out of reality and back again. The voice on the tape must be obeyed! The voice on the tape was the voice of my angel, perhaps even the voice of God.

"Death," said the pompous voice of absolute authority. "Death. Death. Death."

Then I remembered my favorite masturbation fantasy, the one where I am a girl with beautiful long black hair being fucked by a man with a beard. In an instant the fantasy took hold and I could no longer see the hypnograph, no longer hear the voice that said "Death." I returned to the reality of the bunk in my room just long enough to grab a black candle I had intended to burn later, after dark. I looked at it wildly for an instant, then thrust it brutally up my ass as the room I was in and some other room, where I was that girl with the long black hair, flickered rapidly in and out of my consciousness. The angel was trying to hold me back (Was there something protective about the clawed hand he laid on my arm?) but I shook him off and fell out of twentieth century America into . . . where? And when?

But who cared when the bearded man was so wonderfully rough, thrusting so deep up inside me, kissing my shoulders, my arms, my breasts? To be pierced! To be run through, to be stabbed deep again and again by that hard knife of blood-bloated flesh! Oh my God! How good it was!

My head was suddenly full of Germans. I was German. I was in Germany.

And there were other men and women in the room. I could hear them shout and laugh and struggle. I could smell the stink of bodies long unwashed and sweating. The air was hot and wet and close and full of smoke from torches stuck into the walls that threw dancing shadows on the mass of naked and half-clothed bodies that writhed about me.

Now another man was mounting me, and then another.

Oh, my God, it was good!

And at last the Great One came.

The Great One was a man wearing the skin of an animal.

Or was it the spirit of an animal wearing the body of a man?

"My Lord," I whispered to him.

With a savage snarl, half-rage, half-tenderness, he threw me to the hard earthen floor of the hut and entered me, and it was painful but it was good. The drug in my blood made it good. The Great One was so huge in his dick he almost split me in half, but still it was good.

Then it was morning and I wandered away from the hut, still naked, dancing aimlessly, without rhythm, through the tall, dew-wet weeds. The sun was just coming up. The birds were singing in the autumn trees. Nobody was with me. I came to the coven alone. Alone I left. Marriage is for Christians, not for those who remember the Old Religion, not for a girl who is the wife of the God or the wife of all men or no men. I sang a song against marriage as I walked up the hill.

From the hilltop I looked down on the village and the church in the center of it. Perhaps I was cold. I know not. The drug kept me warm. I could have stood naked in the snow with the drug in me and not felt the cold.

How small the church looked, down there, how small and weak. In their book the Christians claim they once healed the blind and lame with a touch, but if that's true, why can they do it no longer? I can do it. We can do it. I laughed at them, prisoners in their safe little town, for they could not even walk the woods at night, as I could, for all that lives is my friend and their enemy.

Great power is given to the free! The power to cure . . . or kill, with a glance of the eye.

I felt weak. Dizzy.

And this was not right. The dancing with the Great One was more restful than sleep. They know the Great One's wives, down in the town, by the lightness of their step and the song on their red lips. The Christians know us and are afraid. Their skins are pale and they are always sick, knowing not how to eat and drink to live long and fuck merry.

But now I was sick. I was sick! How could that be?

I felt then, for the first time, the wetness on my leg. I looked down and saw the blood running from my cunt down my legs. My blood, and my power, and my life, were running out, and so quickly!

"Oh, must I die so soon?" I said softly.

For when we die we know it. The body tells so many things to those who listen to it. But my angel said, "Your sacrifice was not good."

"Not good?" I cried. "I burned my own newborn babe to the God tonight!"

"Not as one who gives a priceless gift," said the dark angel, "but as one who rids herself of an unwanted burden. As one who gives garbage to the God!"

"No! No! It's not true!" I called out.

The angel saw my lie and only smiled. "The Christians made you ashamed," he said. "Ashamed of being a mother with no husband."

"No!" I shouted again, but it is useless to shout against angels.

"I tell you this," said the angel. "If you falter in your faith, if you listen to the Christians and become ashamed, I shall turn my face away from you and the world will be given to them instead. There is a trial in the other world between the Gods, and you are the jury. I give you knowledge and freedom, while my Brother gives only commands. If your body dies, it is nothing. You'll soon be back in another body. But if your faith dies, the case will be won by the Tyrant, and you and I shall both die the second death from which there is no return."

"No," I cried a third time, for now the fear of death was coming on me. "Help me! Don't let me die!"

"You are losing me," said the angel softly. "Remember. Remember when you were on earth before."

"I remember nothing! *Oh, save me, angel!*"

But the angel was gone.

I wandered down the hill toward the road.

I climbed over a fence of loose-piled stones.

I cried and sobbed and tried to stop the blood with my hand, but it flowed steady and only made my helpless fingers red and sticky. The flies were after me now. I hate flies.

I reached the road, but I was too weak to go on, so I half-fell, half-knelt in the sand. Now I no longer cried. Crying uses precious energy, and I had so little of that left.

Also, I was no longer afraid or unhappy.

While I lived many an animal gave his life to feed me, and many a plant. Even plants have spirits, and animals certainly do, no matter what the foolish Christians say. They died for me. Now I die for them. That is the world's agreement with us. There were some ants in the dust of the road. They began crawling on me. They began to gather around the spreading stain of my blood, like my brothers and sisters in the coven gathering to the great feast of Midsummer's Eve.

"Merry meet, merry part, my darlings," I said to the ants, as I lay down gently in the sand, trying not to crush any of them. The sun came up and warmed my naked flesh, which was good, since as the drug wore off I began to feel the cold in the morning breeze. I lay so still a bee landed close to my nose and I could see the beautiful shifting colors in his wings.

The flies were there too, and they also had pretty wings.

I don't really hate flies.

And then I died.

And dying, I remembered.

I was a boy and I tended goats.

My meat was goat meat. My drink was goat milk. My clothing was goat skins. I tended goats and protected them from wild animals and demons. My God had the face of a goat, and the blood of goats was poured out to Him on the stone before our hut.

When the man with the clothes that were not made of skins came to us and told us of Jesus and showed us the dead man on the cross we were kind to him, as we are kind to all strangers, as it is certainly true that all of us are strangers passing through this world again and again. But we could not believe in the things he said and besides he spoke with such an accent some young men could not help but laugh at him. He then grew angry and went away, this Jesus man.

Before he left, he said, "Those who cannot learn from the word must then learn from the sword." We knew what he meant and were troubled. We have never learned the arts of war in this rough land, depending on the unpleasantness of our climate and the infertility of our soil to discourage invaders. The Jesus man did not want our land, as an ordinary enemy might. He wanted us. He wanted us to become his goats, that he could protect or kill, as he wished.

But months passed with no word of him, and we forgot him in our daily round with the goats and our private feuds between families. (These fights between families rarely produced fatalities, since they were fought almost exclusively with quarterstaffs.)

Then, one afternoon when the sun was warm and the sky without a cloud, I was watering the goats at a stream near the Dun bridge when I heard a horse coming at a slow walk in the distance. I ran up and stood on the bridge, trying to catch a glimpse of the rider, for the truth is that horses are rare things in this country.

In a moment I saw him, coming up the rocky pitted road.

The cross on his shield was plain enough even at a distance, so I knew he was the man with the sword the Jesus man had promised to send after us. I knew also that I was not going to let this man pass over our bridge, save after I was dead. It's little enough our people have, but we do have our pride, and that no man can take from us.

All the same I was scared.

This horseman rode so slow and steady. He must have seen me, standing in the middle of the bridge with my quarterstaff, but he rode neither slower nor faster than he had before sighting me. Perhaps the horse had but one gait, and that a slow one, for he was surely the biggest, heaviest beast that ever bore the name of horse. I suppose he had to be a big one to carry the weight of all the armor the rider wore. When this great monster of a horse and his rider all bound up in metal were within earshot I called out, "Hey, what's your business here?"

"I've come to teach good Christian ways to you and your demon-loving people," he answered, and oh, his voice was cold.

"It's we who may be teaching you manners," I shouted. "We are many and there's but one of you."

"One of us is enough," he said, "with God and cold metal on my side." He raised his lance and kept on coming, neither slower nor faster than before.

"Stop!" I shouted, raising my stick. I had been taught that a well-used quarterstaff could deflect a lance, if you were quick enough with it. "Stop, I say!"

He bent forward slightly in the saddle and gave his horse a

little kick with his heels. The ungainly creature broke into a heavy trot. In an instant those great hoofs sounded on the bridge and that sharp bright point of the lance was bearing down on me. I held my staff in both hands, waiting for the exact instant to jerk it up and send the lancepoint harmlessly to one side. Then, a quick thrust between the horse's legs and . . .

Now!

I brought up my staff smartly, exactly right, but the man in metal was too strong for me. His lance went into my belly, deep in, and came out again through my back. It was painful, being pierced, but not so bad as I had expected. I didn't faint. I didn't even cry out. I was just . . . surprised.

The horseman reined in and backed off, pulling his lance carefully free of me. That's what really hurt! And seeing that point swing up and back, covered with my blood and bits and strings of my guts. It was the thought of it that hurt me, really. The idea of being pierced, stabbed, run through. The idea was what hurt most.

I stepped back, and my foot came down on empty air.

I made a futile try at keeping my balance, but it was too late. Down I went with a rush and a wet thump, into the shallows of the stream under the bridge. I looked up. The horseman was laughing so hard he almost fell off his horse, looking down at me through the slits in his helmet. He was still laughing when he turned his horse and continued on across the bridge.

I tried to move my legs, but they no longer obeyed me. I thought then that perhaps I had broken my back in the fall.

My people could place no blame on me. I had done all I could to stop the invader. Then I thought, "No, I could have run ahead and given warning. Now he will take my people by surprise." Only then did I begin to cry. My bravery had been all for nothing, where my cowardice might have made possible some defense, however feeble.

The water went on flowing over my half-submerged body. I watched, through my tears, the sunlight dancing on the surface like leaping fire, and I said to myself, very softly, "If I return to Earth again, I shall return as one of the strong, like that horseman."

And that thought made me smile as I died.

When I did return to the world it was in Southern France, near the Spanish border. I had, of course, forgotten all about my past life. Or had I? There was something about the passing of mounted men of arms that made me excited beyond belief, and when I saw the sign of the cross a strange emotion, awe mixed with fear and, perhaps, a touch of hate, swept over me.

Once, in a parade, I saw some high church dignitaries riding, all covered with jewels and fine clothing, and I thought, "Some day, I shall be like that."

My parents owned a house and lands, but overseers and servants saw to the running of them. My father worked and studied in one little room in the great house, writing far into the night by candlelight and reading ancient scrolls in Greek and Latin. He was a hard man to talk to, but one day I went to him (I was then in my early teens) and told him I wished to become a priest.

He did not answer me at first, as he sat there in his carved chair, one arm on an octagonal wood-inlaid table and the other hanging loose so his fingertips touched the rug, while I stood tongue-tied before him. At last he slowly shook his head, as if an infinite weariness had come over him.

"Do you think I've cared for you all these years only to hand you over to the Pope?" he demanded, his long, delicate scholar's fingers doubling into fists.

"What's wrong with that?" said I.

"Let me show you," he said, gentle now, no longer angry.

He showed me things he had translated out of the ancient scrolls in Latin and Greek, showed me quotations from the Bible, quotations from Josephus, one dusty scroll after another until my vison blurred and my head was spinning. "You see?" he kept saying eagerly. "You see?"

At last I could contain myself no longer. I cried out, "No, I don't see! I don't understand!"

"But it's so clear," said my father, fixing me with his great dark hollow eyes. "The Pope is the anti-Christ. The Catholic Church is not Christ's mission in the world, but the Devil's."

For a moment I was too stunned to speak, then I shouted, "No! No! I won't listen!" and ran from the room. I knew then, for the first time, that my father was a heretic.

He never spoke to me again on the subject of religion, and rarely on any other subject. It was my sister, two years younger than I, who became from that day forward his constant companion, who now wore boy's clothing and began to be raised as a boy, and I understood that she had taken my place with my father, that he had meant for me to inherit his house and lands and carry on his demon-inspired work with the old books and scrolls, but that now everything, everything would go to her.

When he lay on his deathbed, it was she, not I, that he called to his side, while I stood outside the closed door, straining to hear their whispering. And when he died, it was she who put on his emerald ring and great green cloak and went every day into the little room to work until after midnight behind locked doors. She and I had been so close, when we had been younger, and had played at being knight and lady in the open fields, even at being lovers. (A sister's kiss is the sweetest of any, because it's forbidden.) Now that was all done and finished. The locked door and the piles of ancient manuscripts lay between us like a curse.

I went to the village priest and told him everything, including the demon work of my father and sister, and my own desire to become a priest. It was in my mind that I was really helping her, as if calling in a doctor for someone who is ill, and it was also in my mind that I wanted an education, so that I could read Latin and Greek as my sister could, so that I could become the wise child my father had wanted me to be.

The angel laughs a mocking laugh and says, softly, "Is that all?" No, no, that's not all. Perhaps, perhaps I may have given a few moments' thought to the house and lands, too, that would be mine if she were gone.

I don't know how she knew, but she knew what I had done. She was not angry with me, but only gave herself over more feverishly than ever to her writing and her ancient scrolls in that damned little room. All she said to me was, "If they take me, my brother, you must hide the book I'm working on from them. There's our father's life's work in that book, and you mustn't let them destroy it."

I promised. I could never refuse her anything, to her face.

So, one night, when it was raining hard and the wind was screaming over the rooftops, they did finally come for her. I was in the upstairs hall, leaning my head against the uneven greenish glass window above the front door, feeling the cool glass against my forehead, when I heard the cart in the distance, bumping and rumbling over the cobblestones.

They came to the door.

They knocked, with the great iron doorknocker.

My sister went down to let them in, reaching the door before any of the servants, as if the devil had told her that it was she they were seeking. She went with them without a word, and I listened to the cart rumble away until its sound was drowned in the hiss of the rain.

Then I went to the little room, where all the ancient scrolls in Greek and Latin were hidden, and, one by one, I burned them all in the vast fireplace under the tapestry of the unicorn kneeling before the Tree of Knowledge. Yes, all of them, even the huge book begun by my father and carried on by my sister.

Then I went to bed, but I did not sleep well.

The Church was good to me. The good fathers took me in and taught me Greek and Latin and the Bible and obedience. In return I worked hard for the Church all the rest of my life. They found I had a talent for sniffing out heretics, so that became my work. There were in the land at that time many false Christians who claimed that we are born again and again and that the Pope is not to be obeyed, but rather the spirit of Christ in one's own heart. I cannot count the number of those I brought back to the Church, either through argument or prayer or, all else failing, torture. But there were many who slipped away from me, dying while still in a state of sin, and some were braver than any Christian I have known, and died with a smile on their lips, damning me with their forgiveness. It was those that smiled that haunted my sleep, more than those that screamed and pleaded. Again and again they said to me, with their last breaths, "We do not fear you, who can only harm our bodies." I began to drink more good wine than the worst slave of sin, but nobody reproached me for it. Indeed, all my fellow heretic hunters drank too much, and some, while drunk, more than once broke their vows of chastity.

When I reached the age of fifty, I longed to die, I even prayed to die, but God does not listen to such requests, and I lived on and on and on, as if the alcohol in my blood preserved me from all decay.

I thought more and more often of my sister. I had never seen her again. I did not know if she were alive or dead, though once I heard a rumor that she had died in a nunnery, still faithful to her demonic heresy. I could not ask my superiors about her and, in truth, I preferred not to know her fate, whatever it might be.

Was I in my seventies or my eighties when I found myself at last on my deathbed, surrounded by my withered comrades in their dark robes, their faces all shadows in the candlelight? I don't know. I no longer counted the years, or even the days.

They all knew I was dying, but they tried to cheer me with talk of all we would do when I was "up and around again." Then the Bishop came in to give me final absolution from my sins, and that was the end of the cheerful lies. It was quite an honor, to be thus attended by the Bishop himself, and my ancient friends nodded to each other about it knowingly. I had given my life for the Church, and now I was going to get my reward.

But then, before he could begin, I raised myself on my elbow and croaked out to him, "Stop that! I won't have it! No absolution for me!"

"What?" cried the bishop, amazed. "But then you'll be damned!"

"So let it be!" I rasped out. "But you can't grant me absolution, nor can your Church!"

"Why not?" demanded the Bishop, his face turning livid with anger.

"It's you who have damned me!" I exclaimed, then fell back on my pillow. As if from very far away I heard the Bishop going on with the ceremony, but now I was powerless to stop him, or even to speak.

"I'm damned," I whispered to myself. "Damned. Damned. Damned."

"Hey, don't take it so hard just because you can't get a hard-on," said Marie, lifting her head from where she was uselessly sucking on my dick, my flabby, hopeless, impotent dick.

Outside, in Montmartre, it was raining, but the night people still walked the streets, shouting and laughing and pretending to have fun, and the accordion in the Lapin Agile cabaret down the street played a heavy-footed waltz. I reached over to the bedtable and poured myself a drink.

"That won't help you fuck," said Marie. "That's what's damning you, in fact, if you ask me."

I ignored her and drank deep.

"Hey, my friend," she said. "Were you ever a monk?"

"Hell no," I snapped. "Do I look like one?"

"You drink a lot and can't make love. That's the way it is with a monk, eh?"

"I was born a second-rate piano player," I growled. "That's all I ever was and that's all I ever will be."

"You aren't much of a lover, my friend," she said, sitting up on the edge of the bed and reaching for her bloomers, "but I like the way you play piano, and the songs you sing. They tell the truth about what a shithouse we live in, and besides, people pay good money to hear them. That's the important thing, if you ask me."

"I'm damned," I said again. "I wish I was dead."

"Are you going to get into that? Listen, you promised me you wouldn't try to kill yourself again, right?"

"That's right."

"Well, promise me again."

"I won't try to kill myself," I said, gloomily. "Now how much do I owe you?"

"Listen, my friend. Forget it. Nothing for nothing, right? We've been friends so long we're like brother and sister, eh? It's all in the family."

"Brother and sister? Shit. If you were my sister I wouldn't let you sell your ass for a living."

"How do you know, my friend? Brothers don't always treat their sisters so very well. Now help me into my corset like a good brother. Then you can walk me down to the Gare St. Lazare. I have to catch a train."

"Walk all that way? In the rain? Shit!"

"It'll be good for you, my drunken brother. It'll sober you up."

"Oh, what the hell. All right. I don't give a fuck!"

She stood in front of the mirror, putting on her little silver crucifix.

"What do you wear that thing for?" I asked her as I searched for my pants.

"I know what's good for me," she answered with a shrug.

When we were finally dressed and stumbling down the steep streets trying not to get run over by the passing horses and carriages, I asked Marie, "Where are you going, anyway, on that train?"

"I am going to make my visits," she answered simply, clutching my arm to steady herself, though lord knows I could have used a little steadying myself.

"Visits?'

"To my family. Everyone makes visits, you know."

"I don't," I told her.

"Poor man," she said sadly. "A veritable orphan!"

"I have parents . . . right here in Paris. They have no more wish to see me than I have to see them."

"Poor man," she repeated.

After a while we were in the station. It was crowded as hell.

We stood together on the platform for a while, not speaking, and then she said, "Listen, my friend. I have nothing to read on the train. Can you run down to the stand and buy me a newspaper or something?"

"All right."

"But hurry. The train is due any minute."

I started off through the crowd, but it was slow going.

I saw an old woman sitting on a bench, and I thought she was dead because her skin was so blue, but then she moved.

Old age is always horrible. Only fools see anything good in it.

"You won't be old," said the dark angel in my ear.

I was used to hearing strange voices when I drank too much, so I paid no attention. I just bought a few newspapers at random and started back through the milling mob.

Then I heard the train coming in, puffing and chugging and hissing like a winded dragon. And I saw it . . . or anyway the clouds of smoke it was belching out, so I tried to run, but the crowd was so thick it was like swimming in molasses. At the edge of the platform there seemed to be some clear space, so I tried to get through there.

The locomotive was coming now, drivers pumping with a slow easy roll.

Then someone pushed me.

I went off balance for an instant, then fell onto the tracks, landing on my side with a painful thud. There were two thoughts in my head, before the train hit me. The first was of Marie, that she would think I had done it on purpose. The second was of my songs. "Oh, why didn't I ever write anything down?"

Miriam apo Magdalla, when I spoke of writing down her account of the Master's life and sayings, answered mockingly, "If Jesus had wanted a book written he would have written it himself. It was to free us from a book that He took on flesh! What need have we of a book when God speaks through us directly? Did Jesus not say, 'The letter brings death; the spirit, life'? He who lives by a book is unfaithful to the Holy Spirit within himself, as if God, having spoken once, could never speak again. I say, on the day that men open the book of ink and papyrus, they will close the book of the Spirit, and men will no longer do good, but only devote their lives to catching each other in errors, pointing to the papyrus and saying, 'See! I am right and you are wrong!' Is this faith, to say that God's words may be lost? I say, if all record of God's words is lost, He need but say them again, and those who have ears to hear will hear. And I say further that those who love a book more than God will become murderers and torturers and liars and tyrants and be able to justify every sort of monstrous cruelty by quoting their book. *God is within me, or there is no God!* And if He is within me, He will tell me Himself, directly, all that I should know."

So I left the old woman, Mad Miriam of Magdalla, without the words I had come to record on my scroll, and walked the streets of the Jewish quarter in Alexandria. A grim-faced Roman soldier passed in a chariot, red cape twisting in the hot, sand-laced wind. The wheels of the chariot were bright-painted wood rimmed with iron, and the sound of the iron clattering on the stones of the street lingered in the air long after the chariot had passed. I, an Egyptian by birth but a Greek by education, had no love for the Roman conquerors, but on these streets the sight of a servant of law and order was a welcome sight indeed, what with the riots and violence that filled our streets every night. And now night was almost upon me!

I was dressed as a Jew, and so was fairly safe from the knives of the Jews, but what if I should meet a Greek? Would I have time to tear the Jewish deep blue tassels from the hem of my tunic? What indignity! That the life of a gentleman, a scribe of the Great Library of Serapis, should hang upon a blue tassel!

And yet, would you believe it, I ventured into that lawless, bloodstained quarter again and again, drawn as if by a wizard's spell to that strange old woman who claimed to have kissed the lips of the God-King of the Jews. There were those who said she was a witch. And more who said she was possessed by seven demons.

For my superiors, religion was but an instrument of politics, and a new gospel from this old woman would serve no other purpose than to be another means of holding down the fanatical rebelliousness of the Jews. If they must have a Messiah, let it be a Messiah of Peace, not like the others who spring from every stone in the streets of Jerusalem to raise a sword against Rome.

At first, I felt the same.

And then, who knows? Perhaps she bewitched me.

Why else would I listen to tirades like this one?

"You should have seen how grudgingly the Twelve allowed my presence by the Master's side. Those idiots! How many times did their slow wits try the patience of my Rabbi, my Lord, my King? I, only I, really understood Him, for only the mad can know the mad. His kingdom had three ranks . . . those who know, those who only believe, and those who neither know nor believe, but only wander in ignorance. Only He and I dwelt in the highest rank, for only to us did the voices speak and the visions appear. Because of our visions, this lower world cast us out, and we lived in another, but the Twelve remained in this lower world. They chose which world they'd follow. When my Rabbi went to the stake, they ran and hid themselves while I stayed with Him to the end. In their shame they could not bear to see me or hear my scorn for their cowardice, and they quickly did what they dared not do while the Master was alive. They sent me away, saying that because I was a woman I was not worthy to be one of them. Now we hear talk that they, too, see visions, hear voices and even speak in tongues, yet I know that whoever it is that speaks through them, it is not my Rabbi! My Rabbi, in the flesh, never preached the Jewish virtues of law, work, family and ritual. When He said He had come to fulfil the Law, He meant He'd come to end it! The Law called for an eye for an eye and a tooth for a tooth, but Jesus freed us to become kind."

Or fantastic claims like this?

"The Great Beast, Nero, is not dead forever, but will return, as shall we all, in a new body, when the time is ripe. We all come, the good, the evil, the indifferent, again and again into the world. John, the Baptist, was, before this, Elijah, the prophet, and I was before this the sister of Moses."

No, it was a certain ring, a certain feeling that hooks the mind, in stories she told about Jesus. Like this one:

A certain Zealot asked Jesus, "If the Romans threaten our religion, should we not defend our God with the sword?"

Jesus answered, "Who is stronger, you or God?"

The Zealot said, "God, of course!"

And Jesus said, "Then God has no need of your defense. It is you who need His."

Or another like it, about a Roman Centurion who was questioned by Jesus in the marketplace:

Jesus said to the Centurion, "Why do you need armies?"

The Centurion answered, "To defend the borders of our Empire."

Then Jesus said, "If your Empire had no borders, what, then, would you have to defend?"

Or this one:

Jesus said, "Some build temples by laying one dead stone on another, but how can dead things ever give life? I have made my temple as a living tree is made, growing outward from the seed, and in the fruits of that tree are the seeds of new life."

When she told a story she would then explain it, like this:

Miriam said, "The Master's thought is like a great tree. It has many leaves and branches and bears rich fruit, but it all grew from one little seed, and that seed is that Man was created in the image of God. Everything else grows outward from that."

I managed to write down a few of her stories from memory, but what I really needed was a full story, with a beginning, middle and end, like the scroll the Jew, Mark, had made a few years ago for the followers of Jesus in Alexandria, but more complete and bringing out more the radical pacifism of this particular Messiah. Such a document, with the authority given it by an eyewitness like Miriam, could do more to tame the bloodthirsty Jews than seven legions of Caesar's finest.

All the news was of endless bloodshed in the war between the Romans, led by General Vespasian and his son Titus, and the Jewish fanatics in Judaea, so that at times I wondered if my mission of peace would have any effect, even if I were to produce the manuscript I felt the occasion demanded. And now, with the death of Nero, civil war broke out in Rome itself, where first one emperor, then another, laid claim to the throne of the world.

It was useless to appeal to Miriam on humanitarian grounds. She felt those Jews who put their faith in Herod's defiled temple deserved whatever they got. It was only by chance that I finally hit upon a way to secure her co-operation.

I happened to mention Mark's gospel to her.

"What? Mark wrote a gospel? But he never knew the Master! He was no more than Peter's scribe! How can he write of that which he knows nothing?" she shouted, smashing her withered old fist on the table.

Jealousy! How could I have guessed that saints could be jealous? Yet it had been obvious all along.

"If you were to dictate another," I said carefully, "perhaps Mark's foolish impulsiveness could be corrected."

"You're a sly one," she said to me. "But yes, I'll do it. I'll do it after all!"

I knelt at my writing table, took a reed brush from behind my ear, wet my writing ink, and waited. Miriam's Greek was crude and ungrammatical, but I could polish it as I wrote. Together we might well produce a work of lasting value.

"But first," she said, "you must promise me something."

"Of course," I said, my eagerness overcoming my caution.

"You must promise to defend the truth I give you from all those who would change or corrupt it."

"Of course," I easily agreed.

"Until the end of time," she added.

"Until the end of time? How can I promise that?" I demanded.

"You will remember, from one life to the next, what you have promised to me here, even if you forget me, even if you forget everything else. Is it agreed?"

In my heart I did not believe a man has more lives than one, so why not humor the old woman? "Agreed," I said. And so she began:

"When he was a child, Jesus was brought here to Alexandria to escape Herod, who called himself King of the Jews, though he was neither King nor Jew. Herod slaughtered all who had rightful claim on the Jewish throne, and Jesus was of royal blood, of the House of David. Like Buddha, Jesus was born an earthly ruler, but renounced earthly rule for the other kingdom, that is not of this world. He was a student, not of one religion, but of them all, for that is what it means to be raised in Alexandria, where every god in the universe has at least one follower. From the Buddhist Theraputae by the lake He learned monasticism and meditation, from the Rabbi the whole of Jewish law and tradition, and from the shaven-headed priests of Osirus He learned how a man can save his soul by identification with a sacrificial god, and it was from them, too, that He learned baptism and the wearing of the Cross of Life. Yet He never forgot his people, the Jews, never forgot that He and His brothers and sisters were the true royal family of Judaea, and many were the times, while He was still only a boy, that He spent the whole of the night talking of the sad plight of the Jews with His cousin, John, who was later called 'The Baptist.' He saw, clearer than anyone else, that the Jews could never throw off the Roman rule by force of arms, and that by trying to, they would only bring down upon themselves destruction. He saw, clearer than anyone else, that the Jews had been led away from the religion of their fathers and of the prophets by the false king, Herod, and the false priests Herod appointed, and the false temple Herod built in Jerusalem.

"I knew Him then, but I did not learn holy things from Alexandria. For a young girl who has no money and cannot speak Greek like a lady, Alexander's city of marble has other lessons to teach. I learned that there was something between my legs that I could sell again and again, yet never lose. Jesus said my cunt was like knowledge in that way, or like truth, for though all my family and friends turned away from me because of what I did, Jesus never turned away. You know that a woman is counted lower than a horse or cow in this world, but though I was a woman, and the lowest of women, Jesus spoke to me as if I were a man, and His equal, and defended me from His friends, who were forced to put up with me, at least until Jesus was dead.

"When I returned to my home in Magdalla, on the Sea of Galilee, Jesus and John returned also, and John went south to preach the things he and Jesus had learned in Alexandria, and he soon had a great following, because the people of

Judaea were simple and unlearned, except in the Torah, and John had sharpened his wit in debate with the school-trained philosophers from the Alexandrian library. Even on the subject of the Torah and the Jewish traditions, there was not one Rabbi who could best him in a fair argument, and you should know that the Jews decide all things by learned argument, whether it be the origin of the universe, or the proper preparation of food, or the number of days in a year.

"But the people of that day were not content with a prophet. They called out for a Messiah, and many were the false Messiahs who stepped forward to lead them to destruction against the Romans. In all Judaea, in all the world, there was only one who, by right of blood, could be a true Messiah, and that was Jesus, the eldest prince in the House of David. So Jesus went to join John in Judaea, and I believe it was in His mind to look for some sign from Heaven that would tell Him whether or not He was truly the savior His people longed for and cried out for night and day.

"When it came, the sign was a simple thing. At other times it would have passed without notice, but it came at the exact moment that John was baptizing Him. A bird, I think it was a dove, came down and lighted on Jesus' arm, and He ran from the water into the wilderness like a man possessed by demons."

"Go on!" I cried. "Continue!"

"No, not now," she said, lowering her head into her hands. "I'm an old woman, and tired. Come back again tomorrow."

So I went away, and returned again the next day.

But it was even more dangerous than usual to pass through the streets of the Jewish quarter. The Jewish garments that kept Jewish knives away from me now invited attack not only from the Greeks, but from the Roman soldiers in Vespasian's army, now commanded by the general's son, Titus, since the father had become our new emperor. They had defeated the Jews in Jerusalem, but not before many a good Roman had lost his life, and the sight of a Jew could make a soldier draw his sword, particularly if the soldier was drunk. Titus was young, and the troops did not fear him as they did his father.

I breathed a sigh of relief when I was (as I thought) safely inside the filthy little hole where Old Miriam lived, and sat down to wet my ink and unroll my scroll.

It was then that a great pounding at the door destroyed any feeling of safety I might have had, and a loud, drunken voice shouted out in Latin, *"Open the door, you filthy Jew bastard! We know you're in there!"*

They must have followed me, I realized with horror.

"*If you won't open the door,*" came another brutal voice, "*we'll break it in!*"

Calmly Miriam stepped toward the door.

"Wait!" I shouted, and drew my sword.

But as the soldiers burst in she pushed between me and them, saying scornfully, "How many times shall my Jesus and I be betrayed? How can they hurt us? *Are we not immortal spirits?*" And a moment later my chance to fight had passed and we were both dragged roughly into the street and bound.

Have you ever seen a man nailed to a stake? The crowd cares not how that man has lived, only how he dies, so that the most vicious, brutal, stupid murderer can win the favor of the mob if only he can say something defiant or simply keep silent and not cry out when the nails go through his wrists. Miriam died well, even after torture. Though her eyes had been put out with hot irons, still she said to the man who drove the nails, "It is not I, but you who are the prisoner."

As for me, I thought at first to do honor to Miriam's Jesus by saying something worthy of a gentleman, when my time came.

But instead I . . .

Instead I . . .

Instead I screamed and pleaded and wept and begged and shouted, as the nails went through my flesh and the crowd of drunken Romans and Greeks cheered. "It's all a mistake! I'm not a Jew! I'm not a Christian! I'm an Egyptian and a Roman citizen! No! No! Don't! For God's sake don't do it!"

Soon I could no longer form words, but only screams, like an animal in labor, but nobody listened to me. They only laughed at me, and drank, and threw empty wine jugs at me.

And finally, with a gesture of contempt, one of the soldiers buried his spear in my belly.

To be pierced! To be pierced! Oh, my God, have you any idea what it feels like to be pierced? Yet there's some good in it. There's some good. Because it is a pain that brings release from pain, one big pain that ends all the little ones.

I stood, after a while, on a vast empty plain beneath a gray, overcast sky. I was naked, and it was cold. Some distance ahead of me was a crossroads, with paths that led away from it in all directions like strands in a gigantic spiderweb. There were no trees, no grassy areas, no hills or mountains or streams or bodies of water; just bare dust in all directions as far as the eye could see.

But wait. There was something.

A lone figure was walking slowly toward me from the opposite side of the crossroads. As the figure drew closer I could see that it had wings on its back, and then, a moment later, I could make out that it had a sword in one hand and a silver cup in the other. It had long dark hair, but I could not tell for sure whether it was a man or a woman. Perhaps it was both. Perhaps neither.

It was my angel.

"Drink," said the angel, stopping and holding out the cup to me.

"First tell me, Angel, what's in the cup!"

"Forgetfulness."

"There's nothing I want to forget," I said quickly.

The angel smiled. "Not even what you have done?"

I thought a moment. "No," I answered, but this time with hesitation.

"Not even what was done to you?"

"No."

"Not even the pain?"

I paused. Being pierced. If I could forget that . . .

"You must forget all or nothing," said the angel, apparently reading my thoughts.

So. Then what is *"being-pierced,"* after all? Every day dead things enter my mouth and pass through my body and out my asshole. In every life my spirit pierces a new body and passes through it, coming out the other side.

"Don't you understand?" said the angel. "I am only trying to protect you."

"From what?"

"From the knowledge of good and evil. Only gods and angels can stand to know what evil there is in the best of earthly things. For you it is a forbidden fruit, so drink. Drink and forget."

I needed time to think. Stalling, I asked, "Where are we?"

"This is the land of Woomtoom, beyond time and outside space. All these paths lead back into the world, at different points in history."

"There seem to be thousands of them," I said.

"But all are for your feet and yours alone," said the angel. "Now drink, and return to your body."

"No," I said softly.

"So be it," said the angel, pouring out the cup in the dust at his feet. I stepped forward and the angel raised his sword.

"You cannot return now," said the winged being. "You must remain here. You can never return to the world."

But then I remembered again that according to the Bible it was possible to wrestle with angels, and win! I pretended to lunge forward, and the angel's sword swung downward toward me, but at the last possible split-second I sidestepped and avoided the sword at the same time as I leaned close and grabbed the angel's arm. To his intense amazement, I threw him, with a simple Judo spring-hip throw, then threw myself onto him from the rear, in spite of his wildly thrashing wings. The sword flew harmlessly from his hand and skittered into the dust well out of arm's reach, while I leaned in between his two wings, passed my right arm around his neck and snapped the hand back toward me so that it grasped my left arm just above the elbow. Then I placed the palm of my left hand against the back of the angel's head, pressing forward with it while pulling back with the other.

"Give up?" I demanded.

The angel only struggled all the harder.

I tightened the choke hold.

"What do you say now?" I asked coldly.

There was no answer, only more thrashing and writhing. I squeezed harder, and the struggling grew weaker and finally ceased. I held the choke a little longer, just to make sure, then let go. The angel rolled over in the dust, completely limp.

I listened for his heartbeat, felt for his pulse.

There was nothing. The angel was dead.

I picked up the sword and the empty cup and, choosing a direction at random, began walking.

I opened my eyes and looked up at the Hindu hypnograph on the lower face of the upper bunk above me. Nearby the tape spun uselessly in my tape recorder. Flap flap flap flap.

I sat up and turned the machine off.

By the clock only about an hour had passed. It seemed more like two thousand years.

I was still pretty high, but I knew, somehow, that the peak of the "trip" had passed. I got dressed and went downstairs.

The mail had come. It was lying next to the front door, under the mail slot. I picked it up and glanced over it. There were two form letters, one from the John Birch Society and one from the Peace and Freedom Party. They both wanted me to join their organizations. Each wanted my help in fighting the other.

I took a coin from my pocket and looked at it for a while, smiling to myself.

Then I flipped it.

Afterword:

I have not written much science fiction in the last few years, though the little I have written has been well-received. The reason for this is simple. In spite of regularly repeated claims that the science fiction field enjoys a freedom of thought and speech greater than that found in any other field, my own experience has been that this boasted freedom is a pure illusion. In spite of the courageous efforts of such pioneers as Avram Davidson, Damon Knight, Phil Dick and Judith Merril, not one of my stories has reached print without either minor or major deletions designed to mollify the bluenoses.

There is a constant cry from editorial circles for new ideas and new writing approaches, but when this demand is answered by stories which dare to indicate that the sexual morality or the political system we now enjoy may not last forever, or that even today there may be a rather large leap from where things are to where they officially are said to be, the call for "something new" is instantly replaced by calculations of what middle-western high-school librarians might consider proper. I love the science fiction field. I have loved it ever since childhood, but it seems to me that science fiction only rarely does more than scratch the surface of its potential, so long as it remains contained within the boundaries imposed by such calculations, so, even though, or perhaps because, I love the genre so well, I have turned my hand to other fields for the most part.

It is possible that, had not Harlan dared to break through the Middlewesternlibrarian Barrier, I would never have written another science fiction story. His anthology, *Dangerous Visions*, is the first ray of real hope I have seen in this country. One of the standard cornball plots in the field is the one where one man saves the whole universe. I used the plot once, in *Eight O'Clock in the Morning,* but I never really believed in it until now. It may well turn out that one man, Harlan Ellison, actually will save the dying universe of science fiction writing.

In literature there is only one unforgivable sin, and that is not the portrayal of sex or violence or unpopular religious and philosophical ideas. The one unforgivable sin is boredom. And science fiction, in recent years, has become boring. There have been signs of life in England, but up until *Dangerous Visions* the U.S. has gradually been sinking into the mud. Made-up jargon has passed for technology, allowing the old entrenched fan to feel smug while making the story almost impossible for the new reader to understand. Story after story has revolved around phony "plants" of unimportant or incorrect tidbits of science. Story after story has marched the same old WASP engineer paperdoll through the same old story lines, most of which were very good when they were used by H. G. Wells, but which are now showing signs of wear.

"Time Travel for Pedestrians" is a story I have had in my head for several years, ever since some experiences with LSD and numerous other drugs that showed me, among other things, how limited my views and the views of other SF writers were. When, at the annual science fiction convention in Oakland, Harlan mentioned that he was looking for stories for a second volume of *Dangerous Visions,* I instantly left the convention, went home and wrote "Time Travel" at one sitting, in an ecstasy of freedom and creative delight. I have been off drugs for over a year now, but in writing this story I got zonked out of my mind all over again. I still feel pretty high now, as I write this.

But what I'm high on is hope, the hope that now that Harlan has broken the ice we'll see some real fireworks again in the field . . . we'll see some controversy, some brilliance, some writing that has a real sense of life, some real guts and glory. I like Star Trek a lot, but I can't see tying down magazine and book science fiction to what could easily be broadcast over family TV. Even Star Trek, which feeds off ideas tried and proven in the magazine field, will eventually go stale unless there is a massive influx of new approaches and ideas in the field as a whole. Like, it's no use picking a blank mind.

But now I'm high on hope, fellow fans.

Zonked out of my mind.

Please, baby, don't bring me down.

Ladies and gentlemen, a man who needs no introduction . . .

Probably no other writer in this book could I get away with introducing in that way. But who in the civilized, book-reading world doesn't know the name Ray Bradbury? When the time came to write a few words to preface Ray, I suddenly was struck with the impossibility of the act. There have been whole treatises written on Bradbury, his poetic images, his humanity, his blue period, his chrome period . . . who the hell was I to write about him?

Well, I'm a Bradbury fan, and that's not bad for openers. Not only because it indicates an affection for the man and his work that stretches back over twenty-one years to that first reading of "Pillar of Fire" in a copy of August Derleth's excellent *The Other Side of the Moon* anthology I'd pilfered from the Cleveland Heights High School library, but because too many chuckleheads have taken to balming their own mingey little egos by mumbling Bradbury ain't as good as we thought he was. I sneer at them; may the milk of their mothers turn to yogurt; may all their children be harelipped; may they (in the words of an ancient Yiddish curse) be so poor they come to me for a loan and may I be so poor I haven't got it!

Ray Bradbury is very probably better than we ever imagined him to be in our wildest promotion of him as the first sf writer to escape the ghetto and win approbation from such as Isherwood, Wilder, Fadiman, Algren, Gilbert Highet, Graham Greene, Ingmar Bergman, Francois Truffault and Bertrand Russell, for God's sake!

Let's face it, fellow sf readers, we've been living off Ray Bradbury's success for twenty years. Every time we try to hype some non-believer into accepting sf and fantasy as legitimate *literature*, we refer him or her to the words of Ray Bradbury. Who the hell else have we produced who has approached the level of Bradbury for general acceptance? I mean, there's a *Viking Portable Library* edition of RAY BRADBURY. Sure, Arthur C. Clarke and Isaac Asimov are well-known and much-beloved, but if you go out on the street and buttonhole the average *shmendrik*, and ask him to name a dozen famous American writers, if he isn't a dullard who'd name Erich Segal and Leon Uris and Jacqueline Whats-hername, he'll rattle off Hemingway, Steinbeck, Mickey Spillane, maybe Faulkner, and very probably Bradbury. That's a load of ego-boost for all of us, and it's about time someone said it. When we do the conversion bit with scoffers, we whirl them over to the meager sf racks in most bookstores and we may find no Delany, no Lafferty, no Knight or Disch or Dickson, but by God we always find *The Martian Chronicles*.

And we say, "Here try this. You'll love it." And the chances are we've handed the reluctant one "Small Assassin" or "Mars is Heaven!" or "The Fruit at the Bottom of the Bowl" or *Fahrenheit 451* or "I Sing the Body Electric" or "The Veldt" or "The Long Rain" or "A Sound of Thunder" or "The Jar" or ... jeezus, once you get started it's impossible to stop remembering all those great moments you had from all those fine Bradbury stories, and I don't just mean excitement like seeing "The Kilimanjaro Machine" in *Life* or seeing "The Jar" done so it scared the piss out of you on *The Alfred Hitchcock Hour*. I mean those private blessed moments when you lay up on your back under a tree or on a sofa or down on the floor, and started reading something that began, "It was a warm afternoon in early September when I first met the Illustrated Man."

I mean come *on*, all you smartass literary cynics who make points off other men's careers, can you ever *really* forget that thing that called to the foghorn from the sea? Can you really forget Uncle Einar? Can you put out of your mind all the black folk leaving for Mars, years before the black folk started telling you they wanted out? Can you forget Parkhill in "—And the Moon Be Still as Bright" doing target practice in one of the dead Martian cities, "shooting out the crystal windows and blowing the tops off the fragile towers"? There aren't many guys in our game who've given us so many treasurable memories.

And the really lovely thing about Bradbury is that he started out a fan, a runny-nosed, hungry-to-make-it fan like so many of us. Hung up on Lovecraft and Burroughs and Poe and *Weird Tales* and Walt Disney and Hemingway and Saroyan and Dickens and Malory's *Morte d'Arthur*, homage to all of whom he has paid in his fictions. But he *had* it, he had that extra spark that fired him, and he made it; big enough and good enough and forever enough that now we take him a bit too much for granted.

We see *The Illustrated Man* made into a not-too-distinguished film, and *Fahrenheit 451* and the not-yet-released *Picasso Summer* and maybe even some day (if they lick the script) *The Martian Chronicles*, and it becomes very chic to dismiss Ray Bradbury as though he were a literary snail like Segal. Well, not here, my friends. Here, Ray Bradbury gets his praise, because . . . well, it's my book in large part, and twice I've been in Bradbury's company where great things happened, and anybody wants to put down the author of "Henry IX" (which, under the title "A Final Sceptre, a Lasting Crown" I tried to buy for DV), well they got to fight me first. And I'm mean.

I was going to go into detail about those two swell times I had with Bradbury—one at the newsstand on Cahuenga and Hollywood Boulevards, the other an afternoon we spent on the same podium with Frank Herbert, where the spark-gap was leapt and seven hundred California English teachers wept and laughed and gave us a standing ovation and for one of the rare moments in my life I *truly* believed, down to the gut core of myself, that it was the noblest thing in the world to be a writer—but space doesn't permit, and besides I'd rather tell it to you when we meet and have more time to talk.

So I'll just tag out by saying Ray Bradbury is a man who has written some 300 stories that have been collected in books like *The October Country, Dark Carnival, The Golden Apples of the Sun, The Illustrated Man, Something Wicked This Way Comes, The Anthem Sprinters, I Sing the Body Electric!, The Martian Chronicles, A Medicine for Melancholy, The Machineries of Joy, Dandelion Wine* and *Fahrenheit 451*. He wrote the screenplay for John Huston's production of *Moby Dick* (which, strangely, looks much better on a TV screen than in a theater). He also wrote the script for an animated film history of Hallowe'en in collaboration with Chuck Jones, *The Halloween Tree*, and he's now at work on a stage play titled *Leviathan '99*. He wrote a "space age cantata" dealing with the possible images of Christ on other worlds, *Christus Apollo*, music by Jerry Goldsmith, and he is a very good, kind, committed man who was in no small part responsible for getting LBJ booted out of office.

And he's the only man whose poetry I would have included in this, a book of stories. Well, maybe Robert Graves . . .

Ray Bradbury

CHRIST, OLD STUDENT IN A NEW SCHOOL

O come, please come, to the Poor Mouth Fair
Where the Saints kneel round in their underwear
And say out prayers that most need saying
For needful sinners who've forgotten praying;
And in every alcove and niche you spy
The living dead who envy the long-since gone
Who never wished to die.
Then, see the Altar! There the nailed-tight crucifix
Where Man in place of Christ gives up the ghost,
And priests with empty goblets offer Us
As Host to Jesus Who, knelt at the rail,
Wonders at the sight
Of Himself kidnapped off cross and man nailed there
In spite of all his cries and wails and grievements.
Why, why? he shouts, these nails?
Why all this blood and sacrifice?
Because, comes from the belfries, where
The mice are scuttering the bells and mincing rope
And calling down frail Alleluiahs
To raise Man's hopes, said hopes being blown away
On incensed winds while Christ waits there
So long prayed to, He has Himself forgot the Prayer.
Until at last He looks along a glance of sun
And asks His Father to undo this dreadful work

This antic agony of fun.
No more! He echoes, too. No more!
And from the cross a murdered army cries: No more!

And from above a voice fused half of iron
Half of irony gives a man a dreadful choice.
The role is his, it says, Man makes and loads his dice,
They sum at his behest
He Dooms himself. He is his own jest.
Let go? Let be?
Why do you ask this gift from Me?
When, trussed and bound and nailed,
You sacrifice your life, your liberty,
You hang yourself upon the tenterhook!
Pull free!

Then suddenly, upon that cross immense,
As Christ Himself gives stare
Three billion men-in-one blink wide their eyes, aware!
Look left! Look right!
At hands, as if they'd never seen a hand before,
Or spike struck into palm
Or blood adrip from spike,
No! never seen the like!

The wind that blew the benedictory doors
And whispered in the cove and dovecot sky
Now this way soughed and that way said:
Your hand, your flesh, your spike.
You will to give and take,
Accept the blow, lift the hammer high
And give a thunderous plunge and pound,
You make to die.
You are the dead.
You the assassin of yourself
And you the blood
And you the one Foundation Ground on which red spills
You the whipping man who drives
And you the Son who sweats all scarlet up the hills
to Calvary;
You the Crowd gathered for the thrill and urge
You both composer and dear dread subject of the dirge
You are the jailor and the jailed,
You the impaler and you the one that your own
Million-fleshed self in dreams by night
Do hold in thrall and now at noon must kill.

Why have you been so blind?
Why have you never seen?
The slave and master in one skin
Is all your history, no more, no less,
Confess! This is what you've been!

The crowd upon the cross gives anguished roar;
A moment terrible to hear.
Christ, crouched at the rail, no more can bear
And so shuts up his ears with hands.
The sound of pain he's long since grown to custom in his
wits,
But this! the sound of wilful innocence awake
To self-made wounds, these children thrown
To Revelation and to light
Is too much for his sanity and sight.
Man warring on himself an old tale is;
But Man discovering the source of all his sorrow
In himself,
Finding his left hand and his right
Are similar sons, are children fighting
In the porchyards of the void?!
His pulse runs through his flesh,
Beats at the gates of wrist and thigh and rib and throat,
Unruly mobs which never heard the law.
He answers panic thus:
Now in one vast sad insucked gasp of loss
Man pries, pulls free one hand from cross
While from the other drops the mallet which put in the
nail.
Giver and taker, this hand or that, his sad appraisal
knows
And knowing writhes upon the crucifix in dreadful guilt
That so much time was wasted in this pain.
Ten thousand years ago he might have leapt off down
To not return again!
A dreadful laugh at last escapes his lips;
The laughter sets him free.
A Fool lives in the Universe! he cries.
That Fool is me!
And with one final shake of laughter
Breaks his bonds.
The nails fall skittering to marble floors.
And Christ, knelt at the rail, sees miracle
As Man steps down in amiable wisdom
To give himself what no one else can give:

His liberty.
And seeing there the Son who was in symbol vast
Their flesh and all,
Hands him an empty cup and bades Him drink His fill
And Christ, gone drunk on laughter,
Vents a similar roar,
Three billion voices strong,
That flings the bells in belfries high
And slams, then opens, every sanctuary door;
The bones in vaults in frantic vibrancy of xylophone
Tell tunes of Saints, yes, Saints not marching in but out
At this hilarious shout!
And having given wine to dissolve thrice ancient hair-
balls
And old sin,
Now Man puts to the lips and tongue of Christ
His last Salvation crumb,
The wafer of his all-accepting smile,
His gusting laugh, the joy and swift enjoyment of his
image:
Fool.
It is most hard to chew.
Christ, old student in a new school
Having swallowed laughter, cannot keep it in;
It works itself through skin like slivers
From a golden door
Trapped in the blood, athirst for air;
Christ, who was once employed as single son of God
Now finds himself among three billion on a billion
Brother sons, their arms thrown wide to grasp and hold
And walk them everywhere,
Now weaving this way, now weaving that in swoons,
Snuffing suns, breathing in light of one long
Rambled aeon endless afternoon....

They reach the door and turn
And look back down the aisle of years to see
The rail, the altar cross, the spikes, the red rain,
The sad sweet ecstasy of death and hope
Abandoned, left and lost in pain;
Once up the side of Calvary, now down Tomorrow's
slope,
Their palms still itching where the scar still heals,
Into the marketplace where, so mad the dances
And the reels, Christ the Lord Jesus is soon lost
But found again uptossed now here, now there

In every multi-billioned face! There! See!
Some sad sweet laughing shard of God's old Son
Caught up in crystal blaze fired out at thee.
Ten thousand times a million sons of sons move
Through one great and towering town
Wearing their wits, which means their laughter
As their crown. Set free upon the earth
By simple gifts of knowing how mere mirth can cut the bonds
And pull the blood spikes out;
Their conversation shouts of "Fool!"
That word they teach themselves in every school,
And, having taught, do not like Khayyam's scholars
Go them out by that same door
Where in they went,
But go to rockets through the roofs
To night and stars and space,
A single face turned upward toward all Time,
One flesh, one ecstasy, one peace.

The cross falls into dust, the nails rust on the floor,
The wafers, half-bit through, make smiles
On pavements
Where the wind by night comes round
To sit in aisles in booths to listen and confess
I am the dreamer and the doer
I the hearer and the knower
I the giver and the taker
I am the sword and the wound of the sword.
If this be true, then let the sword fall free from hand.
I embrace myself.
I laugh until I weep
And weep until I smile
Then the two of us, murderer and murdered,
Guilty and he who is without guile
Go off to Far Centauri
To leave off losings, and take on winnings,
Erase all mortal ends, give birth to only new beginnings,
In a billion years of morning and a billion years of
sleep.

Afterword:

What to say about this poem? Say that it is a metaphor of
Christ and Man and the fact of man finding himself trapped

in a flesh where the Beast rends Human and the Human tries
to tame the Beast. Out of this stuff comes War. The trial of
man trying to become truly Human over the centuries, in
spite of his blood-lust, forces him to weep for his lost opportunities, his many murders, his dead children, done in by
those Wars. Christ is the symbol of that failure, and the
promise of new opportunities to have a final winning. So
Bradbury says.

Introduction to

KING OF THE HILL:

One night in College Station, Texas, in the company of Chad Oliver—almost a legendary name in science fiction because of the scarcity and impossibly high quality level of his stories—I demolished a restaurant and turned a formal banquet at which I was speaking into a scene of loot and pillage.

Now. You hear these myth fables about writers. About Scott Fitzgerald's "crazy Sunday" in which he threw himself into the pool at a producer's mansion. About Hemingway tossing his first novel, the one *before The Sun Also Rises*, overboard on the ship back from Paris, because he felt a writer should never publish his first novel. About Steinbeck going into deadly barrooms on the Jersey docks and challenging whole groups of wallopers to bare knuckle contests. About Faulkner when he worked in one of the Hollywood studios, sitting there for hours typing over and over again on the same sheet of paper, "Boy gets girl, boy gets girl, boy gets girl ..." And there are stories told about your Gentle Editor—who does not for one *moment* publicly cop to an ego that puts him in the same league with the gentlemen noted above—and these are stories of rape and ruin that sound like the purest bullshit. Some of them are. But some actually happened, and there is always one person who was there and saw it: Silverberg was there when the drunken giant Puerto Rican came at me with the broken quart beer bottle; Avram Davidson was there when I walked into the middle of a street gang in Greenwich Village as they were getting ready to stomp us; a girl named Toni Feldman was there when I dragged an old woman out of a burning car after it had crashed into a fence and before it blew up; Norman Spinrad was there when I got the crap kicked out of me by a guy who was the muscle for a gang of ripoff artists in Milford, Pennsylvania; and Chad Oliver was there when I mobilized the restaurant.

I treasure these people. Not only because they are the unimpeachable verification that the contretemps in which I find myself actually took place—thereby staving off the label of righteous liar I might otherwise wear—but because they are reference points for me, enabling me to distinguish between the colorful lies I tell about myself to enhance my own image of myself, and the truly unbelievable things that actually happen.

It is my most fervent wish that these people stay alive and well, because if they go, then with them go the few pieces of reality to which I cling ferociously.

So ask Chad about that evening.

It was the only time we've ever been in each other's company, and exhausts my anecdotes about Chad. Except that he is a big, charming, pipe-smoking dude. The rest he can relate for himself:

"DEMOGRAPHIC DOPE. Born in Cincinnati, Ohio, in 1928. All male Olivers were doctors (father, grandfather, uncle). I am therefore a mutant. Moved to Crystal City, Texas, when I was a sophomore in high school. I loved it—played football, edited the school paper, made friends that are still with me. (It's the town used as background in Shadows in the Sun.) Moved around some in Texas since (Galveston, Kerrville, now Austin) but I guess it's fair to say that Texas is Home. Married a Texas girl in 1952; she is known variously as Betty Jane, Beje, and B.J. Have two children: daughter Kim, 17 years, and son Glen, 5½. You might call that spacing them out.

"ACADEMIC. I got my B.A. and M.A. at the University of Texas. Took my Ph.D. (in anthropology) at UCLA. I'm a cultural anthropologist, with particular interests in cultural ecology, the Plains Indians, and the ethnology of East Africa. My rank is Full Professor, not that anyone cares, and I am Chairman of the Department of Anthropology at the University of Texas at Austin. I am peculiar in that I happen to like to teach, especially undergraduates. I normally teach several hundred students each semester; out of that number, maybe 3 or 4 know that I write science fiction. I can recognize them by their beady little eyes.

"WRITING. I discovered science fiction when I was a kid, back in the Paleolithic. I remember the story that hooked me: Edmond Hamilton's 'Treasure on Thunder Moon' in the old, fat Amazing. I hopped on my bicycle and went back to the newsstand and bought every science fiction magazine I could find. I bought a second-hand typewriter and—aged 15—began to Write. Seven years later, Tony Boucher bought my first story. I've sold virtually everything I have written since then—mostly science fiction, but also a few historical westerns for Argosy and The Saturday Evening Post. I fear I have not been terribly prolific—it comes to around 50 short stories and novelettes, most of which have been anthologized.

"Books include *Mists of Dawn* (1952), *Shadows in the Sun* (1954), *Another Kind* (1955), *The Winds of Time* (1957), *Unearthly Neighbors* (1960), and *The Wolf Is My Brother* (1967). The latter won the award as Best Western Historical Novel of 1967 from the Western Writers of America. I have a new science fiction novel, *The Shores of Another Sea*, from NAL (Signet) and a new collection, *The Edge of Forever* (Sherbourne), both published in 1971.

"All of this, I guess, tells you very little about me. Maybe that is just as well. I am serious about my writing and I try to write as well as I can. If there is anything about me worth knowing, I hope it can be found somewhere in all those words I have struggled to put on paper."

And finally, these three items. 1) The full name is Symmes Chadwick Oliver. In anthropology he uses Symmes C. Oliver; for fiction, he uses Chad. 2) *Publishers' Weekly* for 3 May 71 announces, "Sherbourne Press of Los Angeles has signed Chad Oliver for his first hardcover collection of science fiction short stories. All of the stories have an anthropological theme." See above. 3) "King of the Hill" is one of the best, tightest, most memorable stories Chad has ever written and I am deeply honored he sold his first short story in years to this anthology. Now go and enjoy it.

Chad Oliver

KING OF THE HILL

She floated there in the great nothing, still warm and soft and blue-green if you could eyeball her from a few thousand miles out, still kissed under blankets of clouds.

Mama Earth. Getting old now, tired, her blankets soiled with her own secretions, her body bruised and torn by a billion forgotten passions.

Like many a mother before her, she had given birth to a monster. He was not old, not as planets measure time, and there had been other children. But he was old enough. He had taken over.

His name?

You know it: there are no surprises left. Man. Big Daddy of the primates. The ape that walks like a chicken. Homo sap. Ah, the tool-maker, flapper of tongues, builder of fires, sex fiend, dreamer, destroyer, creator of garbage . . .

You know me, Al.

Mirror, mirror, on the wall—

Ant is the name, anthill is the game.

There were many men, too many men. They have names. Try this one on for size: Sam Gregg. Don't like it? Rings no bells? Not elegant enough? Wrong ethnic affiliation?

Few among the manswarm, if any, cared for Sam Gregg. One or two, possibly, gave a damn about his name. A billion or so knew his name.

Mostly, they hated his guts—and envied him.

He was there, Sam Gregg, big as life and twice as ugly.

He stuck out.

A rock in the sandpile.

They were after him again.

Sam Gregg felt the pressure. There had been a time when he had thrived on it; the adrenaline had flowed and the juices bubbled. Sure, and there had been a time when dinosaurs had walked the earth. Sam had been born in the year that men had first walked on the moon. (It had tickled him, when he was old enough to savor it. A man with the unlikely name of Armstrong, no less. And his faithful sidekick, Buzz. And good old Mike holding the fort. Jesus.) That made him nearly a century old. His doctors were good, the best. It was no miracle to live a hundred years, not these days. But he wasn't a kid anymore, as he demonstrated occasionally with Lois.

The attacks were not particularly subtle, but they were civilized. That meant that nobody called you a son of a bitch to your face, and the assassins carried statistics and platitudes instead of knives and strangling cords.

Item. A bill had been introduced in Washington by good old Senator Raleigh, millionaire defender of the poor. Stripped of its stumbling oratorical flourishes, it argued that undersea development was now routine and therefore that there should be no tax dodges for phony risk capital investment. That little arrow was aimed straight at one of Sam's companies—at several of them, in fact, although the somewhat dim-witted Raleigh probably did not know that. Sam could beat the bill, but it would cost him money. That annoyed him. He had an expensive hobby.

Item. Sam retained a covey of bright boys whose only job it was to keep his name out of the communications media. They weren't entirely successful; your name is not known to a billion people on a word-of-mouth basis. Still, he had not been subjected to one of those full-scale, no-holds-barred, dynamic, daring personal close-ups for nearly a year now. One was coming up, on Worldwide. The mystery man—revealed! The richest man in the world—exposed! The hermit—trapped by fearless reporters! Sam was not amused. The earth was sick, blotched by hungry and desperate people from pole to shining pole. There had never been an uglier joke than pinning man's future on birth control. A sick world needs a target for its anger. Sam's only hope was to be inconspicuous. He had failed in that, and it would get him in the end. Still, he only needed a little more time . . .

Item. The U.N. delegate from the Arctic Republic had charged that Arctic citizens of Eskimo descent were being passed over for high administrative positions in franchises licensed to operate in the Republic. "We must not and will not allow," he said, "the well-known technical abilities of our people to serve as a pretext for modern-day colonial exploitation." The accusation was so much rancid blubber, of course; Sam happened to like Eskimos as well as he liked anybody, and in any event he was always very careful about such things. No matter. There would be a hearing, facts would have to be tortured by the computers, stories would have to be planted, money would be spent. The root of all evil produced a popular shrub.

There were other items, most of them routine. Sam did not deal with them himself, and had not done so for fifty years. ("Mr. Gregg never does anything *personally*," as one aide had put it in a famous interview.) Sam routed the problems down to subordinates; that was what they were for. Nevertheless, he kept in touch. A ruler who does not know what is going on in his empire can expect the early arrival of the goon squad that escorts him into oblivion. There were the usual appeals to support Worthy Causes, to contribute to Charity, to help out Old Friends. Sam denied them all without a qualm and without doing anything; his lieutenants had their orders. A penny saved . . .

Sam was not really worried; at worst he was harassed, which was the chronic complaint of executives. *They* were not on to him yet. There was no slightest hint of a leak where it counted. If *that* one ever hit the air cleaner there would be a stink they could smell in the moon labs.

Still, he felt the pressure. He was human, at least in his own estimation. There was a classic cure for pressure, known to students of language as getting away from it all. It was a cure that was no longer possible for the vast majority of once-human beings, for the simple reason that there was nowhere to go.

("To what do you attribute your long and successful life, Mr. Gregg?" "Well, I pension off my wives so that I always have a young one, and I see to it that she talks very little. I drink a lot of good booze, but I never get drunk. I don't eat meat. I count my money when I get depressed. If I feel tense, I knock about the estate until I feel better. I try to break at least three laws every day. I owe it all to being a completely evil man.")

Sam Gregg could take the cure, and he did.

He did not have to leave his own land, of course.

Sam *never* left his Estate. (Well, hardly ever.)

He took the private tube down from his suite in the tower and stepped outside. That was the way he thought of it, but it was not precisely true. There was a miniature life-support pod that arched over a thousand acres of his property. It was a high price to pay for clean air, but it was the only way. Sam needed it and so did the animals.

There were two laws that he broke every day. In a world so strangled by countless tons of human meat that land per capita was measured in square feet, Sam Gregg owned more than a thousand *acres*. Moreover, he did nothing useful with that supremely illegal land. He kept *animals* on it. Even dogs and cats had been outlawed for a quarter of a century, and what passed for meat was grown in factory vats. When people are starving, wasting food on pets is a criminal act. (Who says so? Why, people do.) Most of the zoos were gone now, and parks and forests and meadows were things of the past.

Sam took a deep breath, drinking in the air. It was just right, and not completely artificial either. Cool it was, and fragrant with living smells: trees and wet-green grass and water that glided over rocks and earth that was soft and thick.

This was all that was left, a fact that Sam fully appreciated.

This was the world as it once had been, lost now and forever.

Man had come, mighty man. Oh, he was smart, he was clever. He had turned the seas into cesspools, the air into sludge, the mountains into shrieking cities. Someone had once said that one chimpanzee was no chimpanzee. It was true; they were social animals. But how about ten thousand chimpanzees caged in a square mile? That was no chimpanzee also—that was crazy meat on a funny farm.

Oh, man was clever. He raped a world until he could not live with it, and then he screamed for help.

Don't call me, Al. I'll call you.

Sam shook his head. It was no good thinking about it. He could not ride to the rescue, not with all of his billions. He had no great admiration for his fellow men, and it would not matter if he had.

There was only one thing left to try.

Sam tried to close his mind to it. He had to stay alive a little longer. He had to relax, value, enjoy—

He walked along an unpaved trail, very likely the last one left on the planet. He breathed clean air, he felt the warmth of the sun glowing through the pod, he absorbed . . .

There were squirrels chattering in the trees, rabbits busy at rabbit-business in the brush. He saw a deer, a beautiful buck with moss on his horns; the buck ran when he spotted Sam. He knew who the enemy was. He saw a thin raccoon, a female that stared at him from behind her bandit's mask. She had three young ones with her and they were bold, but Mama herded them up into an oak and out of danger. He could see the three little masks peering down at him from the branches.

The trail wound along a stream of cold, fast water. Sam watched the dark olive shadows lurking in the pools. Trout, of course. Sam drew the line at bass and carp.

He came out of the trees and into a field of tall grass. There were yellow flowers and insects buzzed in the air. He sensed the closeness of shapes and forms, but he could not see them in the breeze-swept grass. There was life here, and death, and life again.

But not for long.

He turned and retraced his steps. He felt a little better.

The raccoons were still in the oak.

Sam went back inside. Back to the salt mine.

He worked hard until dinner.

"What was the exact hour?" Lois asked him, absently stroking one of her remarkable legs. (She had two of them.)

"I don't remember," Sam said. "I was very young."

"Come on, Sam. I'm not stupid. You *can't* tell me that with all the resources of your mysterious enterprises you can't find out the exact time."

"I am telling you. I don't know." Sam looked at her, which was always pleasant in a tense sort of way. Lois was sensual but there was no softness in her. She had a lacquered surface stretched like a drumhead over taut springs. She always looked perfect, but even her casual clothes were somehow formal. She never forgot herself. She was a challenge, which was fine once in a while. Sam was old enough to decline most challenges without dishonor.

Lois did not have to remind Sam that she had a brain. Sam never made *that* mistake. Her little reference to "mysterious enterprises" was an effective threat. At thirty, she had climbed the highest pinnacle on her scale of values: she was the wife of the richest man in the world. She didn't want a settlement. She wanted it all. Sam had no children.

Bright, yes. Cunning, yes. Skilled, certainly. Faithful with her body, yes—Lois took no needless risks. But that fine-boned head enclosed a brain that was all output; not much of significance ever went *in*. The hard violet eyes looked out from jelly that had been molded in Neolithic times.

She would have made a dandy witch.

She spent her days puttering with expensive clothing and obscure cosmetics. She had a library of real books, thus proving her intellectual capacity. They were all about reincarnation and astrology. She considered herself something of an expert with horoscopes. A pun had frequently occurred to Sam in this connection, but he had refrained. He was not a cruel man.

"I want to do it for you," she said. "You have decisions to make. It would help. Really, Sam."

She was quite sincere, like all fanatics. It was a gift she could give him, and that was important to her. It was an ancient problem for women like Lois: what do you give to a man who has everything? The gag presents get pretty thin very quickly, and Sam was not a man who was easily convulsed.

He sipped his drink, enjoying it. He always drank Scotch; the labs could create nothing better. "Well," he said. "I haven't a clue about the minute of my birth. I'd just as soon forget my birthday."

Lois was patient. "It would be so simple to find out."

"But I don't give a damn."

"*I* give a damn. What about me? It's a small thing. I know the day, of course. But if the moons of Saturn were in the right position . . ."

Sam raised his eyebrows and took a large swallow of Scotch before he answered. "They are always in the right position," he said carefully. "That's the way moons are."

"Oh, Sam." She did not cry; she had learned some things.

Sam Gregg stood up to refill his glass. He did not like to have obtrusive robots around the house. Self-reliance and all that.

He was not unaware of himself. He did not look his age. He was a tall, angular man. There was still strength in him. His hair was gray, not white. His craggy face was lined but there was no flab on him. His brown eyes were sharp, like dirty ice.

Sam sometimes thought of himself as a vampire in one of the still-popular epics. ("Ah, my dear, velcome to Castle Mordor. A moment vhile I adjust my dentures.") Splendid looking chap, distinguished even. But then, suddinkly, at the worst possible moment, he dissolves into a puff of primeval dust . . .

"Let's go beddy-bye," Sam said, draining his glass. "Maybe I can remember."

"I'll help you," Lois said, reporting for duty.

"You'll have to," Sam agreed.

Sam worked very hard the next few weeks. He even found time to check the hour and the minute of his birth. He was being very careful indeed, trying to think of everything.

Lois was delighted. She retreated to her mystic stewpot, consulted her illustrated charts, talked it over with several dead Indians, and informed Sam that he was thinking about a long, long journey.

Sam didn't explode into laughter.

His work was difficult because so much of it involved waiting. There were many programs to consider, all of them set in motion years ago. They had to mesh perfectly. They all depended on the work of other men. And they all had to be masked.

It wasn't easy. How, for instance, do you hide a couple of spaceships? Particularly when they keep taking off and landing with all the stealth of trumpeting elephants?

("Spaceship? I don't see any spaceship. Do you see a spaceship?")

Answer: You don't hide them. You account for them. For

all practical purposes, Sam owned the space station that or-
bited the Earth. He controlled it through a mosaic of interlocking companies, domestic and foreign. It was only natural
for him to operate a few shuttle ships. A man has a right to
keep his finger in his own pie.

Owned the space station, Daddy?

Yes, Junior. Listen, my son, and you shall hear . . .

The great space dream had been a bust. A colossal fizzle.
A thumping anticlimax.

The trails blazed by the space pioneers led—quite literally—Nowhere.

Fortunately or otherwise, Mighty Man could not create the
solar system in his own image. The solar system was one hell
of a place, and not just on Pluto. There were no conveniently
verdant worlds. There were just rocks and craters, heat and
cold, lifeless dust and frozen chemicals.

There were other suns, other planets. Big deal. There were
no handy space warps, no faster-than-light drives. Unmanned
survey ships took a very long time to report, and their news
produced no dancing in the streets: rocks, craters, desolation.
Who would spend a lifetime to visit Nothing?

Would you? (Naw, I'd rather go see Grandma.)

Scientific bases had been established on Luna, and they survived. They survived with enormous expense, with highly
trained personnel, with iron discipline. Even the scientific
teams had to be replaced at short intervals.

Radiation, you know. Puts funny kinks in the old chromosomes.

The Mars Colony of half a century ago, widely advertised
as a solution to the population crisis, was a solution only in
the grim sense of a Final Solution. Even with the life-support
pods—Sam had lost a fortune on the early models, but he
had learned a few things—it was no go. Five thousand human beings had gone to Mars to start the New Life. (A drop
in the bucket, to be sure. But there was much talk about Beginnings, and Heroic Ancestors, and First Steps.) A few of
them had gotten back. Most had died or gone mad or both.
Some of them were still there, although this was not generally known. They were no longer human.

The problem was that it was perfectly possible to set up a
scientific base on Mars, or even a military base if there had
been any need for one. But soldiers on Mars are a joke, and
appropriations committees had long since stopped playing the
old game: *Can You Top This?* Scientists could do little on
Mars that they could not do on Luna. And people—plain, ordinary people, the kind that swarmed the Earth and

scratched for a living, the kind that had to go—could not exist on Mars.

And so?

And so, kiddies, what was left of the space program was taken over by what was referred to as the Private Sector of the Economy. Got your decoder badges ready? It works out to S-a-m G-r-e-g-g. Governments could not continue to pour billions into space when there was no *earthly* reason for doing so. But with existing hardware and accumulated expertise it was not prohibitively expensive for Sam Gregg to keep a few things going. There was the matter of motive, of course. Sam Gregg had one, and he made money besides.

There were other projects to conceal, but they were easier than spaceships. Genetics research? Well, cancer was still a killer and everyone wanted to live forever. Such work was downright humanitarian, and therefore admirable. Ecological studies? The whole wretched planet was fouled by its own ecology—a solution *had* to be found. (There was no solution at this late date, but so what? It was a Good Thing. Everyone said so.) Computers, robots, cybernetics? Certainly *they* were beyond reproach. Hadn't they ushered in the Golden Age? Well, hadn't they?

Sam Gregg had his faults—ask anyone—but wishful thinking was not among them. He *knew* that he could succeed if he just had time. He could succeed if they didn't get him first. He could succeed because he had the resources and because the problem was essentially one of technology. No matter how complex they are, technological problems can be solved unless they involve flat impossibilities. You can build a suspension bridge, send a man to Mars or wherever, construct cities beneath the sea.

There are other problems, human problems. How do you build a bridge between people? How do you send a better man to Mars? How do you construct an anthill city that is not a bughouse? Money will not solve those problems. Rhetoric will not solve them. Technology will not solve them.

Therefore, Sam did not fool with them. He used them for protective coloration, but he did not kid himself.

He stuck to the art of the possible.

Oh yes, he had a dream.

There was justice in it, of a sort. But human beings care nothing for justice. They look out for Number One.

Number One?

Sam permitted himself a brief, cold smile.

They would tear him apart if they knew, all those billions of Number Ones . . .

A day came when all the bits and pieces fell into place. The data came back, coded across the empty hundreds of millions of miles. The columns added up. The light turned green.

Sam was exultant, in a quiet sort of way. He had expected it to work, of course. He had checked it all out countless times. But that was theory, and Sam was a skeptic about theories.

This was fact.

It was ready. Not perfect, no—but that too had been anticipated.

Ain't science wunnerful?

He could not stay inside, not when he was this close. He had to get outside, taste what was left of freedom. At times like these, it was not enough to know that it was there. He had to *see* it.

He walked on the Estate.

Lois joined him, which was a pain in the clavicle but Sam did not allow her presence to destroy his mood. Lois had on one of her cunning Outdoor Suits. She always professed to adore what she called Nature, but she walked as though every blade of grass were poison ivy.

(Poison ivy had been extinct for decades. Lois would soon follow suit.)

"It's so peaceful," Lois said. She usually said that here.

Rather to his own surprise, Sam answered her. He wanted to talk to somebody, to celebrate. Failing that, he talked to Lois. "No," he said. "Not really. It only seems peaceful because we are observers, not part of it. And it *is* controlled, to some extent."

Lois looked at him sharply. It had been one of his longer speeches.

"See that cedar?" Sam pointed to it, knowing that she did not know a cedar from a cottonwood. "Tough little tree. It'll grow in poor soil, it doesn't take much water. See how the roots come up near the surface? It's brittle, though. Won't last long. The oak is crowding it, and it's got a century or two to play with. See that little willow—there, the droopy one? It needs too much water and the drainage is wrong. It'll never make it. Am I boring you?"

"No," Lois said truthfully. She was too amazed to be bored.

"See the bunny rabbit?" Sam's voice lapsed into parody. "See bunny run! He'd better run. Lots of things eat bunny rabbits. Hawks, bobcats, wolves. Snakes eat little bunnies—"

"Oh, Sam."

As if to prove his point, a beagle hound stuck his wet nose out of the brush. His white-tipped tail wagged tentatively. His liquid eyes were pools of adoration. (Beagles were originally bred as hunters. Remember?)

Sam turned his back on the dog. "Man's best friend. The supreme opportunist. He figured the odds twenty thousand years ago and threw in with us. K-9, Secret Agent. Con. Fink. Surplus now. Dear old pal."

"I don't understand you sometimes," Lois said with rare perception.

I don't understand them, either, Sam thought. *Animals, not women. Little Forest Friends. Nobody understands them. We were too busy. There wasn't even a decent field study of the chimpanzee until around 1930. Seventy years later there were no chimpanzees. We didn't bother with the animals that were not like men; who cared? We learned exactly nothing about kudus and bears, coons and possums, badgers and buffalo. Too late now. They are gone or going, and so is their world.*

Sam Gregg was not a sentimental man. He was a realist. Still, the facts bothered him. It was hard not to know. He would never know, and that was that. There was no way.

They walked along the trail together. (Arm in arm, lovely couple, backbone of empire.) Sam was a little nervous. It had been a long fight and—as they used to say—victory was at hand.

He felt a little like God and a lot like an old man.

From the branches of a gnarled oak, a masked mother and three small bandits watched them pass.

There were ancient raccoon thoughts in the air.

You are ready.
So do it. Don't wobble.
Sam did it.
Sound dramatic?

It was (in the very long run) and it wasn't (here and now). An extremely well-balanced, insulated, innocuous conveyor left the main lab and hissed gently to the spaceport. A large gray metallic box was loaded into a shuttle ship and locked into place. The box was ten feet square, and it was heavy. It could have been much smaller and lighter—about the size of a jigger glass—except for the refrigeration units, the electronic circuits, the separation cubicles, and the protective layers.

The shuttle lifted to the space station. Strictly routine.

The gray cube of metal was transferred very gingerly to a

larger ship. She (that was surely the proper pronoun) was a special ship, a swimmer of deep space. She was crammed with expensive gear. Say, a billion dollars worth. Maybe more.

She took off. She was completely automated, controlled by computers, powered by atomics.

There were no men on board.

The ship was never coming back.

Sam?

He stayed home.

There was nowhere for him to go.

Remember?

It is curious how a small gesture will offend some people.

There was no more capital punishment, unless living on earth was it, but good men and true were willing to make an exception in Sam's case.

"So you sunk twenty billion into it over a ten-year period," his chief lawyer said. He said it the same way he might have asked, "So you think you're a kumquat, eh?"

"Give or take a few million. Of course, some of the basic research goes back more than ten years. If you figure all that in, it might go to twenty-two billion. Maybe twenty-three."

"Never mind that." The lawyer groaned. He really did.

Lois was not happy and developed a case of severe frigidity. She was not only married to a man confronting bankruptcy, but she was also the wife of a Master Criminal. It does imperil one's social position.

(There was no way to keep it quiet, naturally. Sam had known that. Too many people were involved.)

They had a great time, the venom-spewers: senators and editorialists, presidents and kings, cops and commissions, professors and assorted hotshots. All the Good People.

Sam had, to put it mildly, violated a public trust. (Translation: he hadn't spent his money on what *they* wanted.)

He was guilty of a crime against humanity. (Judge and jury, definer of crime? Humanity. All heart.)

It did not matter in the least that twenty billion dollars (or twenty-two, or twenty-three, or a hundred) could not have saved the Earth. Earth was finished, smothered by her most illustrious spawn. It would take a few years yet, while she gasped for breath and filled the bedpan. But she was through.

Man had never cared overmuch for facts.

He believed what he wanted to believe.

("Things may be bad, but they are getting better. All we have to do is like be relevant, you know? Enforce the Law.

Consult the swami. Have a hearing. Salvation through architecture. When the going gets tough the tough get going. All problems have solutions.")

There was one other thing that made Sam's sin inexcusable.

You see, animals have no votes.

The defense?

It was clear, simple, correct, and beyond dispute. It was therefore doomed.

("We'll give him a fair trial, then hang him.")

Way down deep where convictions solidify, Big Man had expected to meet his counterpart on other worlds. ("Ah, Earthling, you surprise I speak your language so good.") He had failed. He had found only barren rocks at the end of the road.

From this, he had drawn a characteristically modest conclusion.

Man, he decided, was alone in the accessible universe.

This was a slight error. There were primitive men who would not have made it, but there were no more primitive men.

The plain truth was that it was *Earth* that was unique and alone. Earth had produced life. Not just self-styled Number One, not just Superprimate. No. He was a late arrival, the final guest.

("All these goodies just for *me!*")

Alone? Man?

Well, not quite.

There were a million different *species* of insects. (Get the spray-gun, Henry.) Twenty thousand kinds of fish. (I got one, I got one!) Nine thousand types of birds. (You can still see a stuffed owl in a museum.) Fifteen thousand species of mammals. (You take this arrow, see, and fit the string into the notch . . .)

Alone? Sure, except for the kangaroos and bandicoots, shrews and skunks, bats and elephants, armadillos and rabbits, pigs and foxes, raccoons and whales, beavers and lions, moose and mice, oryx and otter and opossum—

Oh well, *them.*

Yes.

They too had come from the earth. Incredible, each of them. Important? Only if you happened to think that the only known life in the universe was important.

Man didn't think so. Not him.

Not the old perfected end-product of evolution.

He didn't kill them all, of course. He hadn't been around

that long. The dinosaurs had managed to become extinct without his help. There were others.

He did pretty well, though. He could be efficient, give him that.

He started early. Remember the ground sloth, the mammoth, the mastodon? You don't? Odd.

He kept at it. He was remarkably objective about it, really. He murdered his own kin as readily as the others. The orang had gone down the tube when Sam was a boy, the gorilla and the chimp and the gibbon a little later.

Sorry about that, gang.

In time, he got them all. It was better than in the old days. He took no risks, dug no traps, fired no guns. He simply crowded them out. When there were billions upon billions of naked apes stacked in layers over the earth, there was no room for anything else.

Goodbye, Old Paint.

So long, Rover.

Farewell, Kitty-cat.

Nothing personal, you understand.

All in the name of humanity. What higher motive can there be?

This is a defense?

What in hell did Sam do?

In hell, he did this:

Sam Gregg decided that mankind could not be saved. Not *should* not (although Sam, it must be confessed, did not get all choked up at the thought of human flesh) but *could* not. It was too late, too late when Sam was born. Man had poisoned his world and there were no fresh Earths.

Man could not survive on other planets, not without drastic genetic modifications.

And man would not change, not voluntarily.

After all, he was perfect, wasn't he?

That left the animals. Earth's other children, the ones pushed aside. The dumb ones. The losers. The powerless.

You might call it the art of the possible.

Did they matter? If they were the only life in the universe? Who knew? Who decided?

Well, there was Sam. A nut, probably. Still, he could play God as well as the next man. He had the money.

Pick a world, then. Not Mars. Too close, and there were still those ex-human beings running around there. Don't want to interfere with *them*.

Sam chose Titan, the sixth moon of Saturn. It was plenty

big enough; it had a diameter of 3550 miles. It had an atmosphere of sorts, mostly methane. He liked the name.

Besides, think of the view.

It was beyond human engineering skill to convert Titan into a replica of Mother Earth in her better days. Tough, but that's the way the spheroid rebounds.

However, with atomic power generated on Titan a great deal could be done. It was, in fact, titanic.

The life-support pods—enormous energy shields—made it possible to create pockets in which breathable air could be born. It just required heat and water and chemical triggers and doctored plants—

A few little things.

A bit of the old technological razzle-dazzle.

Men could not live there, even under the pods. Neither could the animals that had once roamed the earth.

Sam's animals were different, though. He cut them to fit. That was one thing about genetics. When you knew enough about it, you could make alterations. Not many, perhaps. But enough.

Getting the picture?

Sam did not line the critters up two by two and load them into the Ark. (Noah, indeed.) He could not save them all. Some were totally gone, some were too delicate, some were outside the range of Sam's compassion. (Who needs a million kinds of bugs?) He did what he could, within the time he had.

He sent sex cells, sperm and ova, one hundred sets for each species. (Was that what was in the box? Yes, Junior.) Animals learn some things, some more than others, but most of what they do is born into them. Instinct, if you like. There was a staggering amount of information in that little box.

The problem was to get it out.

Parents have their uses, sometimes.

But robots will do, if you build them right. You can build a long, long program into a computer. You can stockpile food for a few years.

So—get the joint ready. Then bring down the ship and reseal the pods. Activate the mechanisms. Fertilize the eggs. Subdivide the zygotes. Put out the incubators. Fill the pens.

And turn 'em loose.

Look out, world.

That was what Sam Gregg did with his money.

They didn't actually execute him, the good people of Earth. There was not even a formal trial. They just confiscated what was left of his money and put him away in a Nice Place with the other crazies.

It would be pleasant to report that Sam died happy and that his dust was peaceful in its urn. In fact, Sam was sorry to go and he was even a littler bitter.

If he could have known somehow, he might—or might not—have been more pleased.

Millions of lonely miles from the dead earth, she floated there in the great nothing. Beneath the shimmering pods that would last for thousands of years, a part of her was cool rather than cold, softer than the naked rocks, flushed with green.

Saturn hovered near the horizon, white and frozen and moonlike.

The ancient lifeways acted out their tiny dramas, strange under an alien sky. They had changed little, most of them.

There was one exception.

It might have been the radiation.

Then again, the raccoon had always been a clever animal. He had adroit hands, and he could use them. He had alert eyes, a quick intelligence. He could learn things, and on occasion he could pass on what he knew.

Within ten generations, he had fashioned a crude chopping tool out of flaked stone.

Within twenty, he had built a fire.

That beat man's record by a considerable margin, and the point was not lost on those who watched.

A short time later, the dog showed up, out in the shadows cast by the firelight. He whined. He thumped his shaggy tail. He oozed friendship.

The raccoons ignored him for a few nights. They huddled together, dimly proud of what they had done. They thought it over.

Eventually, one of the raccoons threw him a bloody bone, and the dog came in.

Don't like the ending?

A trifle stark?

Is there no way we can communicate with them from out of the past? Can't we say something, a few words, now that we are finished?

Ah, man. Ever the wishful thinker.

Still talking.

Sam had tried. He was human; he made the gesture.

There was a small plaque still visible on the outside of the silent ship that had brought them here. It was traditional in spaceflights, but Sam had done it anyhow.

It could not be read, of course.

It could not be deciphered, ever.

But it was there.

It said the only words that had seemed appropriate to Sam:

Good luck, old friends.

Afterword:

I won't write an editorial. I have already cheerfully sinned: there is a message in my story. If you didn't receive it, look out your window. Or pry open the lid on your coffin.

What triggers a story? Harlan triggered this one. If he had not asked for it, I probably would not have written it, at least not now. So he is to blame.

But why this particular story? I can't explain, of course. No writer can. You might be interested in a few personal notes:

It is early in September, 1969. I've just come back from a month in the mountains of Colorado. I consider myself a trout fisherman, dry flies only. (I don't keep many of them; I return them to the streams. Cheers.) I walked a lot, through country that was almost deserted twenty years ago. I can testify that there are few streams so remote that someone has not tossed a beer can into them. Trailers are everywhere, a pox on the land. Kleenex hangs from the bushes, the final mark of man. Beaver dams are ripped apart for sport. Trees are slashed with initials. There are even, so help me, Development Schemes. Ain't nature keen?

When I was in Kenya a few years ago, I did a little demographic work with just one tribe. Back in 1850, the first explorer in the area (a missionary type named Krapf) estimated that there were about 70,000 Kamba. A bit later, in 1911, the British took a kind of a census. There were 230,-000 Kamba. As of right now, the figure is pushing 900,000. This, mind you, is on the same land area. You should see it.

I saw the pictures from Mars. You did too. It does not look one hell of a lot like Barsoom.

The summer is ending and soon the cold winds will blow. When fall comes, we feed the raccoons on our porch. They have to eat a fair amount before winter. They look at me and I look at them. There will be fewer of them this year, and more of them will be hurt and dragging shattered feet. Bulldozers have torn their environment apart. Old men set traps and the kids blaze away with popguns.

This morning, driving to work and trailing exhaust fumes, I saw raw sewage from an overflow line dumped into the lake.

Had enough?

Me too.

I hope someone reads my story, and doesn't like it.

As I sit down to write this introduction to Ed Bryant and his story, he lies sleeping in the blue bedroom with the enormous bird kite hanging from the ceiling, in the "west wing" of my home here in Los Angeles. About half an hour ago he took home his date, a gorgeous lady named Roz, who had too much cheap wine to drink and got kittenish as hell.

It ain't easy to write about Bryant. He has become one of my very closest friends, and all the things I'd like to tell about him, like the morning I'd lost touch with reality and desperately needed to know what day it was, and he told me with grave seriousness that it was "National Mackerel Commemorative Day," won't mean a thing to you. You'd have to know Bryant and his warped, utterly black sense of guillotine humor to know what a trauma that was.

For openers, he is a rare delight as a human being; a genuinely good man with the kind of sensible morality and ethic that Jim Sutherland says is holding the frangible world together. For seconds, he is a joy to the heart of any writer who takes another writer "under his wing" and hopes the acolyte will break away and develop his own voice, his own successful career. On that point, in short, Bryant is getting it on. In one year he's sold twenty-five very good, very professional stories and articles. And he's getting laid regularly now. For a WASP from Wyoming, that's enormous forward-striding.

Yet Bryant is peculiar, and it is this peculiarity that makes him something that should be on display in the Smithsonian. Today, for instance, I said to him, "Ed, you're getting weirder and weirder. I can't put my finger on it, man, but you seem to be getting more surreal." He looked at me from above his ginger-colored mustache with the odd unfocused stare of a Polynesian water bird, and mumbled, "You mean I'm not relating to everyday objects." Yes, I agreed, that was it. "Start relating, Ed. Talk to your rug, listen to your hand, get chummy with a coffee pot and the doorknobs. Make friends." He stared at me.

"I can't talk to my rug," he said sadly, "it's too self-involved. It has piles."

I walked away.

Born 27 August 1945 in White Plains, New York, Edward Winslow Bryant, Jr. moved at the age of six months with his family to southern Wyoming, where the elders took up cattle ranching. He attended a one-room country school for the first four grades and spent the rest of his secondary education in Wheatland, Wyoming (population 2350). Thus far his life parallels that of Lincoln. He attended college at the University of Wyoming, treading water for a year as an embryo aerospace engineer then, recognizing the error of his ways, switched to liberal arts. He received his B.A. in English in 1967 and an M.A. in the same field a year later. In his "official" biography, Bryant lays down all the preceding dull information, neglecting to mention the one truly important act of his otherwise pedestrian life. He noticed, picked up and bought the August 1957 issue of *Amazing Stories* and became a—shhhh!—science fiction fan. Somehow, he managed to keep it a secret from all of those in the literary world who've seen him burst on the scene these last couple of years, who envision him as being untainted by the fannish life, a pure creature of Mainstream Literary Origins. Nonsense. He was a *fan*, a grubby, scrofulous fan who published an illiterate fanmagazine called *Ad Astra*.

(Incidentally, that August 1957 *Amazing Stories* included in its contents one of the classic tales of modern sf, "The Plague Bearers," which opened with these deathless lines:

> I came up behind the Screamie as he grabbed the girl, and shoved the bayonet into his neck. It was a rusty blade, and went in crookedly. I had to stick him again to finish the job. He fell, moaning and clutching at his streaming neck. I kicked him under some rubble.

Modesty forbids me heaping the unstinting praise due the author of that now-classic tale of man's nobility, but it is easy to see where Bryant's deranged inspiration came from. Yechhh.)

Because of this unnatural interest in Things God Never Intended Man to Screw Around With At Toward, he attended the first and second Clarion (Penna.) College Workshops in SF & Fantasy, 1968 and 1969, which is where I first encountered him. Bryant tells it like this:

". . . a traumatic experience which Changed My Life; I received the criticism, instruction and encouragement necessary to make me believe that maybe, just maybe, there was something in my writing worth sharing with the universe."

In actuality, the pathetic quality of his attempts at writing so touched the hearts of all of us on the staff—Robin Scott Wilson, Damon Knight, Kate Wilhelm, Fritz Leiber, Fred Pohl and a lady anthologist whose name escapes me—that we labored harder with him than those who genuinely had talent. You know how it is: you always feel warmth for the retard in the group.

Well, as it turned out, Bryant, this lame, who up till then had been making a precarious living in and around Wheatland, Wyoming as a deejay, shipping clerk in a stirrup buckle factory and as general layabout, fastened leechlike on your editor and the next thing I knew he was inhabiting (like some fetid troglodyte) the blue bedroom here at Ellison Wonderland. Like the man who came to dinner, he ventured out of Wyoming to attend the SFWA banquet, West Coast division, in early 1969, stayed a while and went away till September of that year, when he returned, saying he was just "stopping by." Nine months later I was compelled to hire a young lady of great personal warmth and questionable morality, to lure him away to New York. I wanted to change the linen and air out the blue bedroom. He returned here in March of 1971 and as of this writing he doesn't look like he's *ever* going to leave. The pile of gnawed bones is growing larger in the blue bedroom. The smell is something Lovecraft would have called "a stygian uncleanliness, foul beyond description, spoor of the pit and festooned with moist evil."

Nonetheless, Bryant keeps working, his only saving grace. He's appeared in *Quark, Orbit, National Lampoon, New Dimensions*, the *LA Free Press, Magazine of Fantasy & Science Fiction, Worlds of Tomorrow, If, New Worlds, Infinity, Nova, Universe*, both *Clarion* anthologies and a host of men's magazines, such as the quality periodical *Swingle*, which refuses to run a photo of a woman unless she has 53D breasts.

Appearances in these one-handed publications have so permanently warped Bryant's already twisted view of the universe that when I had a few dates with a young lady who is the current rage of the sexploitation films, he ran amuck and wound up at one of her film producers', and the next thing I knew he had a part in a class epic titled—are you ready for a consummate horror?—FLESH GORDON.

Now he lurches about the house looking like a detail from one of the deranged etchings by the Marquis von Bayros, and tells me about Flesh, Dr. Jerkoff, Prince Precious and something called the giant Penisaurus, which is large and worm-like and slides in and out of a soft, pink, moist, undulating cave.

It is very difficult retaining one's lunch in company of Edward Winslow Bryant, Jr.

The story that follows, however, was his first sale. It was, in fact, the first story bought for this book. Which, because of the time it took to put this book together, makes it four years old. Many there may be among you who will contend this makes it unrepresentative of the advances in technique and tone that have informed Mr. Bryant's subsequent already-published works. Not so. He has made *no* advance in four years, and this is *still* the best thing he ever wrote.

And finally, those out there who have heard unsavory rumors of a novel Bryant is writing, will have to wait a while longer for confirmation. Oh, the novel is almost finished, and he has several publishers nibbling (but then, let's not get into Bryant's sexual proclivities), but as I had written and sold a sensational short story titled "At the Mouse Circus," I felt it a bit crummy of him to title his novel, *The Mouse Circus*. We had quite a go-around about that. He steadfastly refused to change the title, told me, in fact, to fuck off. So I "persuaded" him to change it. I waited till four in the ayem, when he was asleep in his cave, and sneaked in with a wet sponge. Sitting on his chest, I awakened him to face the possibility of clean water actually touching his body. Like the Wicked Witch of the West, the thought of water so terrified him, he acceded to my polite request, and as of this writing the novel is untitled. Until he comes up with a new one, he can't market the book.

So if you like the story that follows, why not send some title suggestions to Bryant. Send them care of General Delivery, Wheatland, Wyoming, because I *swear* by the time this book is released, eight months from now, he ain't gonna be *here!*

Edward Bryant

THE 10:00 REPORT IS BROUGHT TO YOU BY ...

FADE IN:
EXTERIOR SHOT—NIGHT

They cornered her in the alley. The chase had been short and never in doubt; not to the three men who stalked, shadowed, between her and the flickering light of the street. The girl crouched among the garbage pails and tried to hold her breath. She had run too far; her lungs were too starved for oxygen. She attempted to hold back a gasp for air, and choked.

One of the three hunters laughed softly. "Takes your breath away, don't it, chick?" Softer, "Wait, baby, just wait."

The girl cowered deeper into the narrow gap between two pails and the brick flank of a building, the side of her face pressing hard against corrugated chill. Her knees were insensitive to the rough pavement. The three men converged on the stack of pails, making no attempt at stealth. The girl tensed. On three sides of her refuge, leather scuffed on gravel and asphalt.

She broke for the mouth of the alley. Four steps. An explosion of pain hurled her against the bricks. A hand jerked her violently to her feet. The man slapped her again. There was no pain now; only the dull sensation of something sticky trickling down her face. The man shoved her roughly and she sprawled on her side.

Above her loomed three shapes, black on black. The girl whimpered and tried to crawl. The man on the left kicked her in the belly; not too hard, just enough to jackknife her body. Her eyes hazed and this time she felt pain because she could not breathe.

"That's plenty," said the man on the right. "The chick's got to be able to enjoy this. Carl, you're first. Tico, you hold her shoulders."

The girl struggled.

A deer fights briefly before the wolf pack rends it.

"Baby, this'll blow your mind," said Carl.

In the darkness, a whir. Overhead, the scarlet Cyclops stare.

DIRECT CUT TO:

Barney Chandler stared intently at the television screen and tried to keep his attention on the program. Barney wanted out. Not yet, but he would. Or, to be more precise, his wife wanted out. Ella usually got what she wanted.

"Barney," she said, "Hank's not going to keep that job open forever." Hank was Ella's brother; he owned the largest Chevy dealership in Burbank.

A noncommittal grunt. Barney Chandler used his remote-control switch to turn the television set to Channel 34. He upped the volume. Barney picked up his beer and swore in annoyance when the napkin clung to the bottom of the bottle.

"Barney! Will you turn down the set and listen to me? Hank's coming over for supper tomorrow. He's going to want an answer about that manager's job."

"For Chrissake, Ella!" Barney slammed the edge of his hand down on the remote-control and the TV blinked off. "Can't I even watch the competition in peace without you bugging me?"

Ella rolled her faded blue eyes heavenward. "Mister Chandler," she said. "This just happens to be the big chance of your life, and I'm not about to see you blow it." This was a practiced speech. Barney had heard it often enough the past week. "You're almost forty. You've been a millhand, a taxi driver, and a lousy insurance salesman. Now you're a news cameraman for a TV station. Barney, it's just not taking you anywhere. Now Hank's impressed with you. He really is. He thinks you'd make a fine assistant manager. And once you got into management, there'd be no telling where you could end up. Please, Barney, when Hank comes over tomorrow, tell him you'll take it." She turned away and walked into the kitchen.

Barney looked at his beer and said nothing. He liked being a cameraman. He didn't particularly relish the idea of becoming the assistant manager in the largest Chevy dealership in Burbank. But Ella wanted him to take Hank's offer. Barney gulped and drained his bottle. He reached for the opener. Another few beers and he wouldn't feel so badly about telling Ella that he'd say yes to Hank.

He sat back heavily in the chair and flicked the TV switch on. Barney turned the channel selector to 27. It was almost time for "Saga of the Sage." Barney enjoyed watching adventure series. He seldom watched other programs with the exception of newscasts; Barney liked viewing the clips he himself had filmed. Too, he enjoyed keeping up with the work of his competition at the other stations.

In the hall the phone rang. Ella answered it.

"Barney," she called. "It's for you. It's Parker down at the studio. He says it's important."

DISSOLVE TO:

How many forests did it take, Calvin Randall wondered, *to panel all these offices?* So much of the earth had gone into the making of the KNBS-TV Building; mahogany, polished stone, many metals. Randall glanced around the reception room as he had done so many times before. The decor was just a bit too flashy for his taste. He vaguely wished that the mahogany were back alive and growing in its original groves, that the polished granite was once again buried inside rough Colorado mountains.

"Mr. Carmine will see you now, sir," dimpled the blonde receptionist.

"Thank you," said Randall. He picked up his attache case and walked past the prominent brass plaque that indicated the imminent presence of L. J. Carmine, Program Director, KNBS-TV. Randall grimaced at the 36-point tempo bold lettering. Ostentatious.

There was someone new with Carmine today, someone Randall didn't know. Randall had a bad feeling. The stranger was short and pudgy, gray hair thinning above black-rimmed glasses. "Network" was stamped all over him. *Trouble,* Randall thought.

"Cal, baby," said Carmine, enthusiastically clapping Randall on the shoulder. "Come in, boy, come in. Here, I want you to meet Arthur Hedley. Art's with the Public Events Department over at the Network." Randall shook hands with the chubby stranger. Carmine turned and addressed the Network man: "This is the boy I've been telling you about, Art. Cal's one of the bright young talents around here, and he's definitely the best news director this station's ever had."

What's he building up to, the axe? Randall speculated.

"Cal, baby," Carmine continued, "Art suggested that I call you in here today for a little conference."

Public execution? wondered Randall.

"It's like this," said Carmine. "KNBS-TV has one of the best equipped, best staffed, most competent news teams of any station in the metro area—in fact, we probably have *the* best news department. Of course, Cal, the credit's got to go to you for doing such a tremendous job reorganizing the staff and lifting it to where it is now. Naturally we're looking forward to seeing you keep up the good work."

"The point is, Mr. Randall," interjected Hedley, "the good work is going to have to be accelerated. The Network has closely studied your operation here at KNBS and we generally agree with Mr. Carmine's evaluation of your news staff. Unfortunately an external factor has entered the situation. Are you aware of this station's present rating figures, Mr. Randall?"

SHOCK CUT TO:

Naked, the figure of the girl lay motionless. Tico's rough hands pressed heavily against her shoulders and she felt the gravel bite into her back. Carl and the third man stood above her, panting.

"Man, this chick's got a real hang-up about losing her clothes," Carl said. "If I had to work this hard to undress my old lady I'd be too tired for anything else."

"Too tired now?"

"Hell, no." Carl kneeled and unbuckled his belt. "Now relax, baby. This'll be a groove." He touched her hip.

"Christ!" Carl screamed in agony and toppled onto his side on the rough pavement. His body doubled over, he retched in the darkness.

The third man laughed. "Keep hold of her shoulders," he said. He looked down at the girl. "You're a real tiger, aren't you baby. Looks like Carl's going to have to hold your legs when he figures out how to breathe again." His voice was flat, emotionless. "Sorry you did this, baby. I mean it was just going to be good, clean fun and games. But now it's going to be something else, chick. Really something else."

Overhead, the voyeurs.

DIRECT CUT TO:

"The rating figures?" *I knew it,* Calvin Randall thought. *Those goddam ratings.* "More or less," he said.

"Let me refresh your memory, then," said Hedley. "As you are no doubt aware, our new rating system is quite reliable. The electronic equipment we have installed in our aircraft and trucks is quite accurate in detecting and measuring the small amounts of radiation emitted by each and every television set in the city. We can depend upon the computer-evaluated interpretation of this data to get a very clear picture of where we stand in the ratings competition. I'm sorry to say that this station has consistently fallen below par in its averages over the past few months, particularly during the time-slots allotted for news broadcasts."

"And does the Network have a solution?" asked Randall rather stiffly. *Other than firing the news director?* "Do we know exactly why KNBS has fewer viewers during our news-shots?"

"Yes," said the Network man. "NBS Audience Analysis has discovered what they are confident is the root of the problem."

"I'm sure Cal would be interested in hearing about their analysis," Carmine interjected. Hedley shot an annoyed glare at the Program Director.

"It's relatively simple," continued Hedley, "and it is something I truly regret having to say." The Network man's voice took on a distinctly paternal tone, a bit scolding. "Mr. Randall, the Network feels that your news department here at KNBS has been letting the viewing public down."

Randall was startled. "Letting them down? My God, we've broken our necks getting the most comprehensive news coverage possible."

"But you have still failed. *We* have failed," said Hedley. "Let me offer two cases in point. If you will, please recall last November when Congressman Coghill was so tragically murdered. You may remember that Channel 34, as it happened, was on the scene taping the final seconds of the Congressman's speech when the fatal shot was fired. Thirty-four was the only major station present. As a result, they presented the viewing public with a videotape of the assassination a full half-hour before any other metropolitan station could assemble a special newscast. We were one of those other stations. By falling down so badly in our coverage of the tragedy, we did our public a disservice.

"Another case I might mention was that unfortunate disaster at Los Angeles International when that 737 liner exploded on takeoff. By coincidence it was being filmed by a Channel 34 crew engaged in doing promotional shots for an airline. Because of this chance circumstance, Channel 34 was able to beam live, vital coverage of the catastrophe to the public almost immediately. KNBS crews, however, did not reach the area of the crash until minutes after Thirty-four had already aired their first comprehensive report.

"What I am trying to illustrate by these examples, Mr. Randall, is that this station must now make an increased effort to keep abreast of the very immediacy of the news. This is certainly not a problem revolving solely around audience ratings. You must realize that we are licensed by the Federal Communications Commission to broadcast in the public interest. In the public interest, Mr. Randall. Our license obliges us to keep that duty always in view; indeed, obligates us."

"That's all well and good," said Randall. "But the practical aspect of what you're describing depends a lot on the breaks of the game. My staff has a conscious dedication to covering as much news as quickly and comprehensively as is humanly possible. But we can't tell the future and figure out where to assign teams to catch the news as it happens. We're just not—" Randall searched for a word "—not fortune tellers."

"Admittedly," Hedley said, "we cannot foresee the future. But on the other hand, neither can we talk about 'the breaks of the game.' The Network feels that competent news reporting cannot afford to deal in such imprecise concepts. That is for the past. This is 1980, and the key word now is professionalism."

Wasn't it always? Randall thought.

"That's right," said Carmine. "Professionalism. The Public Events Department at the Network has been doing some fine work on this. They've really come up with something exciting, Cal; what I believe are the freshest and most radical innovative concepts in news coverage I've ever seen. Mr. Hedley and I want to bat them around with you." He picked up a yellowed newspaper clipping from his desk and handed it to Randall. "Here," Carmine said. "Read this first."

Less than an hour later, Calvin Randall, News Director of KNBS-TV, resigned his position. Two hours later, he was very drunk.

DIRECT CUT TO:

Sweat flowed and dripped from the florid little man who was mayor of Carroll, California. In the everyday real world he was the owner of a hardware store. Now he cowered shaking in his leather chair in the Carroll City Council chambers. He was stripped of everything that seemed to him important: his clothes, his dignity, his courage.

"What has this town ever done to you and your friends?" he pleaded.

"Nothing," answered the mayor's black-jacketed warden. "Nothing but exist."

"But why us? Why Carroll?"

The mayor's captor grinned wolfishly, his dark glasses glinting above bared teeth. "Why not, man?"

DIRECT CUT TO:

The rest of the team was assembled in the KNBS briefing room when Barney Chandler arrived. The team director, Mike De La Ree, was speaking as Barney seated himself.

"Remember that this is a major coverage operation," said De La Ree. "There'll be three mobile crews placed at strategic positions through the town. They'll use hand-held Sony SonoVid units. Chuck"—he gestured at his assistant—"Chuck and I will be back at the chopper with the monitor equipment. Everyone will be plugged into a central radio link." He checked his watch. "Okay, we're behind schedule already. Let's move out. I'll finish the briefing with you individually in the copter."

The men scrambled to their feet and began picking up equipment cases.

"Hey, Chandler," called De La Ree. "When did you come in? I think you missed out on the first part of the briefing. Get Parker to fill you in while you're getting your gear."

"Okay," responded Barney, unclipping his SonoVid from its rack. "Parker, what gives? How come all the big rush?"

Parker's sandy eyebrows rose and he shrugged his thin shoulders. "Beats me, Barney. De La Ree's been pretty close-mouthed about the whole operation. Apparently there's some kind of cycle gang running around in the hills out west of Barstow. I guess they're hitting a town tonight and we're going to take pretty pictures of the mess."

"Oh great," said Barney. "An all-nighter. Ella's going to kill me."

DISSOLVE TO:

TEASER

"Carroll, California, high in the Santa Mira Hills west of Barstow, was attacked tonight by a rampaging motorcycle gang.

"Hi, this is Irvin Conley. I'll have a complete report on this and other late-breaking events from around the Golden State at ten tonight on the Enerco Ten O'Clock Report."

DIRECT CUT TO:

Slowly and nearly silent, the dirigible swam across the smoggy sky. From the pods of sophisticated equipment freckling the airship's belly, electronic fingers reached down and precisely measured the tiny amounts of energy radiated by each of the millions of television sets scattered through the sprawling city. Telemetry relayed each bit of information to a computer miles to the north. Machines and men teamed in the attempt to read the composite mind of that mythic figure, the average televiewer.

"It's incredible," the night-man at the computer center muttered to himself. "Eighty-seven per cent of the sets in the whole city still on at midnight—and more than ninety per cent of those tuned to one station." He scanned the read-out card again. The numbers hadn't changed. "The KNBS brass'll go out of their skulls when they see these figures."

DISSOLVE TO:

"Violence headlines the news tonight.

"Good evening. This is Irvin Conley with the Friday edition of the Ten O'Clock Report. I'll have news for you from around the state of California right after this word from Enerco, the kerosene fuel that keeps your turbine humming like a top . . ."

DISSOLVE TO:

The dim light from the monitors washed the color out of De La Ree's face. His gaunt features evoked the image of a specter crouched over scenes from hell.

"Two, pull back to cover the whole crowd by the bar. Now pan up to the broken windows. One, get ready to cut in with a close shot of the looters." De La Ree's voice was level and professional. "Three, move to the east edge of your position. Look for an alley below and to your left. There should be some action soon. Switch in your starlight scope; I don't think there'll be enough available light from the burning stores."

Three was the designation for Barney Chandler's SonoVid unit. Parker and Barney crossed to the east edge of the roof. The Farmer's Bank of Carroll was solidly constructed of brick—it wouldn't burn. Barney looked down and to the left as De La Ree had ordered.

"Dark as sin," Barney said. "I'll switch on the scope." The four figures in the alley below sprang into sharp relief in the starlight scope's eyepiece. Barney violently drew in his breath.

"Mike," he whispered into the throat-mike. "You sure you want us to shoot this bit in the alley?"

"Hell yes," returned De La Ree from the KNBS copter. "Shoot everything—they'll edit it back at the studio."

DIRECT CUT TO:

Calvin Randall, one-time KNBS News Director, nursed his drink in morose silence. He had been conserving a steady procession of drinks for almost a day now. Calvin Randall was worried about his future.

You should have gone along with Carmine, he thought wryly. *Stayed with a young station on the make. Stayed on the make yourself. In six months that station will be the highest-rated channel in L.A.*

The TV above the bar was tuned to KNBS. So were most of the television sets in the Los Angeles area. Other stations had rushed teams to Carroll; millions of feet of tape had whirred through cameras and recorders. Everyone had beautiful shots of the aftermath. But only KNBS had footage of the real thing; the actual events as they were occurring. The fires, murders, lootings, rapes.

The men and women seated on either side of Randall watched the screen as though hypnotized. Their eyes reflected the flickering shadows of the television. KNBS was running an in-depth report on the rape of Carroll, California.

"My God," the man on Randall's left hoarsely whispered. "How can they show pictures like that?"

Inside Randall a delayed explosion found release. He jumped to his feet. His arm flailed against his glass, smashed it to diamond tears scattered across the bar.

"Because you bastards watch them!" he screamed. He turned and rushed blindly for the door.

DISSOLVE TO:

CLOSE SHOT—IRVIN CONLEY

". . . and now the news.

"One of the most brutal dramas in the history of California was played out tonight in the sleepy little town of Carroll, high in the Santa Mira Hills west of Barstow. Carroll is customarily a quiet agricultural community of a thousand inhabitants. This evening the summer calm was shattered when a roving gang of black-jacketed motorcycle toughs, estimated to number at least three hundred, invaded Carroll. Preliminary reports from the scene indicate extensive looting and bloodshed. KNBS airlifted a complete news team to Carroll tonight and is on the scene. Here now is correspondent David Parker with an exclusive report videotaped earlier this evening . . ."

SHOCK CUT TO:

They finally left her there in the alley. She didn't note their leaving. She was incapable of that now. The girl never saw the monitor light of the distant SonoVid wink out, never heard the mechanical purr click off. She lay motionless in a swell of pain, hardly breathing. For a brief minute her mind swam close to consciousness. She moved her hand and was vaguely aware of the blood dappling her legs.

DIRECT CUT TO:

CLIPPING (YELLOWED) FROM LOS ANGELES TRIBUNE-OBSERVER, JULY 28, 1966
SET ON BROAD MAHOGANY DESK-TOP
CAMERA MOVES IN:

Rumbles for Rent?

Los Angeles (UniPress) An unidentified spokesman for a major television network today revealed his organization last week was offered "the inside track" in covering the activities of a notorious California motorcycle gang. A man purporting to be the gang's "press officer" approached Hollywood representatives of the network July 13 with the proposal that in exchange for an undisclosed sum of money, the gang would create a "rumble" in any small town the network chose. For its money the network would receive exclusive photographic coverage of the event.

The unidentified network spokesman stated: "We turned down the offer, of course. It was never treated as a serious proposal by any of the network management personnel. If the self-appointed "press officer" were quite sincere in proffering his offer, then his proposition is a deplorable commentary on our times. If he were attempting some sort of hoax, then his effort was in the worst possible taste."

The network spokesman stated further that the man's description has been turned over to Los Angeles County authorities for possible investigation.

DIRECT CUT TO:

MONTAGE:

The Personnel Director was kind, but firm. "I'm sorry, Mr. Randall, but I'm afraid that KNBS cannot see fit to rehire you in any capacity." The Network was not, however, without a sense of largesse. *Don't rock the boat, Cal. We'd hate to put your name on a blacklist.*

"Tell your brother to shove his car-peddling job," Barney told his wife in the morning. "I'm sticking with KNBS. News reporting's gonna be a job with a future."

A still form, white against the darkness of the alley. Not dead yet, but waiting. Hoping.

MATCH DISSOLVE TO:

The plastic flash of capped teeth. Feral, somehow. The television-blue shirt. The pleasantly deep baritone.

" . . . and those are the latest stories currently making headlines in the Golden State. From behind the Enerco News

Desk, this is Irvin Conley saying good night, and have a good weekend."

FADE OUT:

Afterword:

"Ten O'Clock Report" is a story about prostitution. I was angry when I wrote it and I become angry each time I read it again. I am angry with the vast majority of good citizens who sell out their souls for their particular messes of pottage, be they money, prestige, emotional titillation, or whatever. I am angry with everyone who submits peacefully to having his mind seduced by the vast-scaled rotten things that pervade our society. Further, I am angry with all you people who don't even attempt to *do* anything about those aforementioned rotten things. And that includes me. After all, all I did was to write the story.

No, I don't have a thick, black beard and dwell sullenly back in the hills in a cave. My beard is brown and scraggly and I live out in the world, just like the rest of you. But I *have* worked as a broadcast newsman and have had experiences with events such as described in "Ten O'Clock Report," although on a much less spectacular scale. And I *have* grown up as a member of the generation which has seen America adopt violence as a spectator sport second in popularity only to sex (sex as a spectator activity doesn't turn me on either, but that's a theme for another story . . .).

One June evening in 1968 I was seated in a grubby pizza parlor in a small western Pennsylvania town with a little group of both established and would-be SF writers. At the time I was still luxuriating in the warm glow of having made my first professional sale. SF author Chip Delany then intruded into that pleasant glow with an uncomfortably pointed question. "Ed," he asked. "Just why do you want to write?" That was a tough question. It still is. The answer I gave then, after a lot of desperate thinking, was: "I write because I want to tell people something." I think that answer still holds true for me. This story is an embodiment of that thought; it contains elements of both commentary and warning. Beyond that it is designed to be entertainment.

I never intended to become a preacher.

Introduction to

THE FUNERAL:

It is easy to be charmed by the total *womanness* of Kate
Wilhelm, so easy to lose one's perspective of her as a human
being in pure affection and admiration, that I sometimes forget for a moment that she is one of the very finest writers in
America today. She is certainly the very best we have working in the field of speculative fiction. I will not defend that
statement, nor elaborate upon it. Her work speaks most elo-
quently to the point.

Kate is a very private sort of woman, and so the back-
ground data I have at hand is skimpy. She was born in
Toledo, Ohio on June 8th, 1928; she has two semi-adult sons
by her first marriage and a third—Jonathan the Loud—by
her current spouse, Damon Knight. She is on the Visiting
Lecturer staff of the Tulane University Workshop in SF &
Fantasy, as she was on the staff of the original Clarion Col-
lege Workshop. She is the author of *The Mile Long
Spaceship, The Nevermore Affair, The Downstairs Room,
Let the Fire Fall, More Bitter Than Death, The Killer Thing*
and *Abyss*. With Ted Thomas she is the author of *The Clone*
and *The Year of the Cloud*. Her big new novel, *Margaret and
I* is a marvel, despite the uninformed and bestial review in
Newsweek.

She is not only a writer *sui generis*, but a student of the
English language and as sure and incisive a critic as any
writer could be blessed to have appraising his manuscript.
She is also one of the gentlest, toughest creatures God ever
put on this Earth.

"The Funeral" is so good, it hurts. I hope I have not invaded her privacy with these brief comments.

Kate Wilhelm

THE FUNERAL

No one could say exactly how old Madam Westfall was when she finally died. At least one hundred twenty, it was estimated. At the very least. For twenty years Madam Westfall had been a shell containing the very latest products of advances made in gerontology, and now she was dead. What lay on the viewing dais was merely a painted, funereally garbed husk.

"She isn't real," Carla said to herself. "It's a doll, or something. It isn't really Madam Westfall." She kept her head bowed, and didn't move her lips, but she said the words over and over. She was afraid to look at a dead person. *The second time they slaughtered all those who bore arms, unguided, mindless now, but lethal with the arms caches that they used indiscriminately.* Carla felt goose bumps along her arms and legs. She wondered if anyone else had been hearing the old Teacher's words.

The line moved slowly, all the girls in their long gray skirts had their heads bowed, their hands clasped. The only sound down the corridor was the sush-sush of slippers on plastic flooring, the occasional rustle of a skirt.

The Viewing Room had a pale green, plastic floor, frosted-green plastic walls, and floor to ceiling windows that were now slits of brilliant light from a westering sun. All the furniture had been taken from the room, all the ornamentation.

There were no flowers, nothing but the dais, and the bedlike box covered by a transparent shield. And the Teachers. Two at the dais, others between the light strips, at the doors. Their white hands clasped against black garb, heads bowed, hair slicked against each head, straight parts emphasizing bilateral symmetry. The Teachers didn't move, didn't look at the dais, at the girls parading past it.

Carla kept her head bowed, her chin tucked almost inside the V of her collarbone. The serpentine line moved steadily, very slowly. "She isn't real," Carla said to herself, desperately now.

She crossed the line that was the cue to raise her head; it felt too heavy to lift, her neck seemed paralyzed. When she did move, she heard a joint crack, and although her jaws suddenly ached, she couldn't relax.

The second green line. She turned her eyes to the right and looked at the incredibly shrunken, hardly human mummy. She felt her stomach lurch and for a moment she thought she was going to vomit. "She isn't real. It's a doll. She isn't real!" The third line. She bowed her head, pressed her chin hard against her collarbone, making it hurt. She couldn't swallow now, could hardly breathe. The line proceeded to the South Door and through it into the corridor.

She turned left at the South Door, and with her eyes downcast, started the walk back to her genetics class. She looked neither right nor left, but she could hear others moving in the same direction, slippers on plastic, the swish of a skirt, and when she passed by the door to the garden she heard laughter of some Ladies who had come to observe the viewing. She slowed down.

She felt the late sun hot on her skin at the open door and with a sideways glance, not moving her head, she looked quickly into the glaring greenery, but could not see them. Their laughter sounded like music as she went past the opening.

"That one, the one with the blue eyes and straw-colored hair. Stand up, girl."

Carla didn't move, didn't realize she was being addressed until a Teacher pulled her from her seat.

"Don't hurt her! Turn around, girl. Raise your skirts, higher. Look at me, child. Look up, let me see your face . . ."

"She's too young for choosing," said the Teacher, examining Carla's bracelet. "Another year, Lady."

"A pity. She'll coarsen in a year's time. The fuzz is so soft right now, the flesh so tender. Oh, well . . ." She moved away, flicking a red skirt about her thighs, her red-clad legs narrowing to tiny ankles, flashing silver slippers with heels that were like icicles. She smelled ... Carla didn't know any words to describe how she smelled. She drank in the fragrance hungrily.

"Look at me, child. Look up, let me see your face ..." The words sang through her mind over and over. At night, falling asleep she thought of the face, drawing it up from the deep black, trying to hold it in focus: white skin, pink cheek ridges, silver eyelids, black lashes longer than she had known lashes could be, silver-pink lips, three silver spots—one at the corner of her left eye, another at the corner of her mouth, the third like a dimple in the satiny cheek. Silver hair that was loose, in waves about her face, that rippled with life of its own when she moved. If only she had been allowed to touch the hair, to run her finger over that cheek ... The dream that began with the music of the Lady's laughter, ended with the nightmare of her other words: "She'll coarsen in a year's time ..."

After that Carla had watched the changes take place on and within her body, and she understood what the Lady had meant. Her once smooth legs began to develop hair; it grew under her arms, and most shameful, it sprouted as a dark, coarse bush under her belly. She wept. She tried to pull the hairs out, but it hurt too much, and made her skin sore and raw. Then she started to bleed, and she lay down and waited to die, and was happy that she would die. Instead, she was ordered to the infirmary and was forced to attend a lecture on feminine hygiene. She watched in stony-faced silence while the Doctor added the new information to her bracelet. The Doctor's face was smooth and pink, her eyebrows pale, her lashes so colorless and stubby that they were almost invisible. On her chin was a brown mole with two long hairs. She wore a straight blue-gray gown that hung from her shoulders to the floor. Her drab hair was pulled back tightly from her face, fastened in a hard bun at the back of her neck. Carla hated her. She hated the Teachers. Most of all she hated herself. She yearned for maturity.

Madam Westfall had written: Maturity brings grace, beauty, wisdom, happiness. Immaturity means ugliness, unfinished beings with potential only, wholly dependent upon and subservient to the mature citizens.

There was a True-False quiz on the master screen in front of the classroom. Carla took her place quickly and touch-typed her ID number on the small screen of her machine.

She scanned the questions, and saw that they were all simple declarative statements of truth. Her stylus ran down the

True column of her answer screen and it was done. She wondered why they were killing time like this, what they were waiting for. Madam Westfall's death had thrown everything off schedule.

Paperlike brown skin, wrinkled and hard, with lines crossing lines, vertical, horizontal, diagonal, leaving little islands of flesh, hardly enough to coat the bones. Cracked voice, incomprehensible: *they took away the music from the air ... voices from the skies ... erased pictures that move ... boxes that sing and sob ...* Crazy talk. And, *... only one left that knows. Only one.*

Madam Trudeau entered the classroom and Carla understood why the class had been personalized that period. The Teacher had been waiting for Madam Trudeau's appearance. The girls rose hurriedly. Madam Trudeau motioned for them to be seated once more.

"The following girls attended Madam Westfall during the past five years." She read from a list. Carla's name was included on her list. On finishing it, she asked, "Is there anyone who attended Madam Westfall whose name I did not read?"

There was a rustle from behind Carla. She kept her gaze fastened on Madam Trudeau. "Name?" the Teacher asked.

"Luella, Madam."

"You attended Madam Westfall? When?"

"Two years ago, Madam. I was a relief for Sonya, who became ill suddenly."

"Very well." Madam Trudeau added Luella's name to her list. "You will all report to my office at 8 A.M. tomorrow morning. You will be excused from classes and duties at that time. Dismissed." With a bow she excused herself to the class Teacher and left the room.

Carla's legs twitched and ached. Her swim class was at eight each morning and she had missed it, had been sitting on the straight chair for almost two hours, when finally she was told to go into Madam Trudeau's office. None of the other waiting girls looked up when she rose and followed the attendant from the anteroom. Madam Trudeau was seated at an oversized desk that was completely bare, with a mirrorlike finish. Carla stood before it with her eyes downcast, and she could see Madam Trudeau's face reflected from the surface of the desk. Madam Trudeau was looking at a point over Carla's head, unaware that the girl was examining her features.

"You attended Madam Westfall altogether seven times during the past four years, is that correct?"

"I think it is, Madam."

"You aren't certain?"

"I . . . I don't remember, Madam."

"I see. Do you recall if Madam Westfall spoke to you during any of those times?"

"Yes, Madam."

"Carla, you are shaking. Are you frightened?"

"No, Madam."

"Look at me, Carla."

Carla's hands tightened, and she could feel her fingernails cutting into her hands. She thought of the pain, and stopped shaking. Madam Trudeau had pasty, white skin, with peaked black eyebrows, sharp black eyes, black hair. Her mouth was wide and full, her nose long and narrow. As she studied the girl before her, it seemed to Carla that something changed in her expression, but she couldn't say what it was, or how it now differed from what it had been a moment earlier. A new intensity perhaps, a new interest.

"Carla, I've been looking over your records. Now that you are fourteen it is time to decide on your future. I shall propose your name for the Teachers' Academy on the completion of your current courses. As my protege, you will quit the quarters you now occupy and attend me in my chambers . . ." She narrowed her eyes, "What is the matter with you, girl? Are you ill?"

"No, Madam. I . . . I had hoped . . . I mean, I designated my choice last month. I thought . . ."

Madam Trudeau looked to the side of her desk where a records screen was lighted. She scanned the report, and her lips curled derisively. "A Lady. You would be a Lady!" Carla felt a flush fire her face, and suddenly her palms were wet with sweat. Madam Trudeau laughed, a sharp barking sound. She said, "The girls who attended Madam Westfall in life, shall attend her in death. You will be on duty in the Viewing Room for two hours each day, and when the procession starts for the burial services in Scranton, you will be part of the entourage. Meanwhile, each day for an additional two hours immediately following your attendance in the Viewing Room you will meditate on the words of wisdom you have heard from Madam Westfall, and you will write down every word she ever spoke in your presence. For this purpose there will be placed a notebook and a pen in your cubicle, which you will use for no other reason. You will discuss this with no one except me. You, Carla, will prepare to move to my quarters immediately, where a learning cubicle will be awaiting you. Dismissed!"

Her voice became sharper as she spoke, and when she finished the words were staccato. Carla bowed and turned to leave.

"Carla, you will find that there are certain rewards in being chosen as a Teacher."

Carla didn't know if she should turn and bow again, or stop where she was, or continue. When she hesitated, the voice came again, shorter, raspish. "Go. Return to your cubicle."

The first time, they slaughtered only the leaders, the rousers, . . . would be enough to defuse the bomb, leave the rest silent and powerless and malleable . . .

Carla looked at the floor before her, trying to control the trembling in her legs. Madam Westfall hadn't moved, hadn't spoken. She was dead, gone. The only sound was the sush, sush of slippers. The green plastic floor was a glare that hurt her eyes. The air was heavy and smelled of death. Smelled the Lady, drank in the fragrance, longed to touch her. Pale, silvery-pink lips, soft, shiny, with two high peaks on the upper lip. The Lady stroked her face with fingers that were soft and cool and gentle. . . . *when their eyes become soft with unspeakable desires and their bodies show signs of womanhood, then let them have their duties chosen for them, some to bear the young for the society, some to become Teachers, some Nurses, Doctors, some to be taken as Lovers by the citizens, some to be . . .*

Carla couldn't control the sudden start that turned her head to look at the mummy. The room seemed to waver, then steadied again. The tremor in her legs became stronger, harder to stop. She pressed her knees together hard, hurting them where bone dug into flesh and skin. Fingers plucking at the coverlet. Plucking bones, brown bones with horny nails.

Water. Girl, give me water. Pretty, pretty. You would have been killed, you would have. Pretty. The last time they left no one over ten. No one at all. Ten to twenty-five.

Pretty. Carla said it to herself. Pretty. She visualized it as p-r-i-t-y. Pity with an r. Scanning the dictionary for p-r-i-t-y. Nothing. Pretty. *Afraid of shiny, pretty faces. Young, pretty faces.*

The trembling was all through Carla. Two hours. Eternity. She had stood here forever, would die here, unmoving, trembling, aching. A sigh and the sound of a body falling softly to the floor. Soft body crumbling so easily. Carla didn't turn her head. It must be Luella. So frightened of the mummy. She'd had nightmares every night since Madam Westfall's death. What made a body stay upright, when it fell so easily? Take it out, the thing that held it together, and down, down. Just to let go, to know what to take out and allow the body to fall like that into sleep. Teachers moved across her field of vision, two of them in their black gowns. Sush-sush. Returned with Luella, or someone, between them. No sound. Sush-sush.

The new learning cubicle was an exact duplicate of the old one. Cot, learning machine, chair, partitioned-off commode and washbasin. And new, the notebook and pen. Carla had never had a notebook and pen before. There was the stylus that was attached to the learning machine, and the lighted square in which to write, that then vanished into the machine. She turned the blank pages of the notebook, felt the paper between her fingers, tore a tiny corner off one of the back pages, examined it closely, the jagged edge, the texture of the fragment; she tasted it. She studied the pen just as minutely; it had a pointed, smooth end, and it wrote black. She made a line, stopped to admire it, and crossed it with another line. She wrote very slowly, "Carla," started to put down her number, the one on her bracelet, then stopped in confusion. She never had considered it before, but she had no last name, none that she knew. She drew three heavy lines over the two digits she had put down.

At the end of the two hours of meditation she had written her name a number of times, had filled three pages with it, in fact, and had written one of the things that she could remember hearing from the gray lips of Madam Westfall: "Non-citizens are the property of the state."

The next day the citizens started to file past the dais. Carla breathed deeply, trying to sniff the fragrance of the passing Ladies, but they were too distant. She watched their feet, clad in shoes of rainbow colors: pointed toes, stiletto heels; rounded toes, carved heels; satin, sequinned slippers ... And just before her duty ended for the day, the Males started to enter the room.

She heard a gasp, Luella again. She didn't faint this time, merely gasped once. Carla saw the feet and legs at the same time and she looked up to see a male citizen. He was very tall and thick, and was dressed in the blue and white clothing of a Doctor of Law. He moved into the sunlight and there was a glitter from gold at his wrists, and his neck, and the gleam of a smooth polished head. He turned past the dais and his eyes met Carla's. She felt herself go light-headed and hurriedly she ducked her head and clenched her hands. She thought he was standing still, looking at her, and she could feel her heart thumping hard. Her relief arrived then and she crossed the room as fast as she could without appearing indecorous.

Carla wrote: "Why did he scare me so much? Why have I never seen a Male before? Why does everyone else wear colors while the girls and the Teachers wear black and gray?"

She drew a wavering line-figure of a man, and stared at it, and then Xed it out. Then she looked at the sheet of paper with dismay. Now she had four ruined sheets of paper to dispose of.

Had she angered him by staring? Nervously she tapped on the paper and tried to remember what his face had been like. Had he been frowning? She couldn't remember. Why couldn't she think of anything to write for Madam Trudeau? She bit the end of the pen and then wrote slowly, very carefully: *Society may dispose of its property as it chooses, following discussion with at least three members, and following permission which is not to be arbitrarily denied.*

Had Madam Westfall ever said that? She didn't know. but she had to write something, and that was the sort of thing that Madam Westfall had quoted at great length. She threw herself down on the cot and stared at the ceiling. For three days she had kept hearing the Madam's dead voice, but now when she needed to hear her again, nothing.

Sitting in the straight chair, alert for any change in the position of the ancient one, watchful, afraid of the old Teacher. Cramped, tired and sleepy. Half listening to mutterings, murmurings of exhaled and inhaled breaths that sounded like words that made no sense. . . . *Mama said hide child, hide don't move and Stevie wanted a razor for his birthday and Mama said you're too young, you're only nine and he said no Mama I'm thirteen don't you remember and Mama said hide child hide don't move at all and they came in hating pretty faces . . .*

Carla sat up and picked up the pen again, then stopped. When she heard the words, they were so clear in her head, but as soon as they ended, they faded away. She wrote: "hating pretty faces. . . hide child. . . . only nine." She stared at the words and drew a line through them.

Pretty faces. Madam Westfall had called her pretty, pretty.

The chimes for social hour were repeated three times and finally Carla opened the door of her cubicle and took a step into the anteroom where the other proteges already had gathered. There were five. Carla didn't know any of them, but she had seen all of them from time to time in and around the school grounds. Madam Trudeau was sitting on a high-backed chair that was covered with black. She blended into it, so that only her hands and her face seemed apart from the chair, dead white hands and face. Carla bowed to her and stood uncertainly at her own door.

"Come in, Carla. It is social hour. Relax. This is Wanda, Louise, Stephanie, Mary, Dorothy." Each girl inclined her head slightly as her name was mentioned. Carla couldn't tell afterward which name went with which girl. Two of them wore the black-striped overskirt that meant they were in the Teacher's Academy. The other three still wore the gray of the lower school, as did Carla, with black bordering the hems.

"Carla doesn't want to be a Teacher," Madam Trudeau said drily. "She prefers the paint box of a Lady." She smiled with her mouth only. One of the academy girls laughed. "Carla, you are not the first to envy the paint box and the bright clothes of the Ladies. I have something to show you. Wanda, the film."

The girl who had laughed touched a button on a small table and on one of the walls a picture was projected. Carla caught her breath. It was a Lady, all gold and white, gold hair, gold eyelids, filmy white gown that ended just above her knees. She turned and smiled, holding out both hands, flashing jeweled fingers, long, gleaming nails that came to points. Then she reached up and took off her hair.

Carla felt that she would faint when the golden hair came off in the Lady's hands, leaving short, straight brown hair. She placed the gold hair on a ball, and then, one by one, stripped off the long gleaming nails, leaving her hands just hands, bony and ugly. The Lady peeled off her eyelashes and brows, and then patted a brown, thick coating of something on her face, and, with its removal, revealed pale skin with wrinkles about her eyes, with hard, deep lines aside her nose down to her mouth that had also changed, had become small and mean. Carla wanted to shut her eyes, turn away and go back to her cubicle, but she didn't dare move. She could feel Madam Trudeau's stare, and the gaze seemed to burn.

The Lady took off the swirling gown, and under it was a garment Carla never had seen before that covered her from her breasts to her thighs. The stubby fingers worked at fasteners, and finally got the garment off, and there was her stomach, bigger, bulging, with cruel red lines where the garment had pinched and squeezed her. Her breasts drooped almost to her waist. Carla couldn't stop her eyes, couldn't make them not see, couldn't make herself not look at the rest of the repulsive body.

Madam Trudeau stood up and went to her door. "Show Carla the other two films." She looked at Carla then and said, "I order you to watch. I shall quiz you on the contents." She left the room. The other two films showed the same Lady at work. First with a protege, then with a male citizen. When they were over Carla stumbled back to her cubicle and vomited repeatedly until she was exhausted. She had nightmares that night.

How many days, she wondered, have I been here now? She no longer trembled, but became detached almost as soon as she took her place between two of the tall windows. She didn't try to catch a whiff of the fragrance of the Ladies, or try to get a glimpse of the Males. She had chosen one particular spot in the floor on which to concentrate, and she didn't shift her gaze from it.

They were old and full of hate, and they said, let us remake them in our image, and they did.

Madam Trudeau hated her, despised her. Old and full of hate . . .

"Why were you not chosen to become a Woman to bear young?"

"I am not fit, Madam. I am weak and timid."

"Look at your hips, thin, like a Male's hips. And your breasts, small and hard." Madam Trudeau turned away in disgust. "Why were you not chosen to become a Professional, a Doctor, or a Technician?"

"I am not intelligent enough, Madam. I require many hours of study to grasp the mathematics."

"So. Weak, frail, not too bright. Why do you weep?"

"I don't know, Madam. I am sorry."

"Go to your cubicle. You disgust me."

Staring at a flaw in the floor, a place where an indentation distorted the light, creating one very small oval shadow, wondering when the ordeal would end, wondering why she couldn't fill the notebook with the many things that Madam Westfall had said, things that she could remember here, and could not remember when she was in her cubicle with pen poised over the notebook.

Sometimes Carla forgot where she was, found herself in the chamber of Madam Westfall, watching the ancient one struggle to stay alive, forcing breaths in and out, refusing to admit death. Watching the incomprehensible dials and tubes and bottles of fluids with lowering levels, watching needles that vanished into flesh, tubes that disappeared under the bed-clothes, that seemed to writhe now and again with a secret life, listening to the mumbling voice, the groans and sighs, the meaningless words.

Three times they rose against the children and three times slew them until there were none left at all because the contagion had spread and all over ten were infected and carried radios . . .

Radios? A disease? Infected with radios, spreading it among young people?

And Mama said hide child hide and don't move and put this in the cave too and don't touch it.

Carla's relief came and numbly she walked from the Viewing Room. She watched the movement of the black border of her skirt as she walked and it seemed that the blackness crept up her legs, enveloped her middle, climbed her front until it reached her neck, and then it strangled her. She clamped her jaws hard and continued to walk her measured pace.

The girls who had attended Madam Westfall in life were on duty throughout the school ceremonies after the viewing. They were required to stand in a line behind the dais. There were eulogies to the patience and firmness of the first Teacher. Eulogies to her wisdom in setting up the rules of the school. Carla tried to keep her attention on the speakers, but she was so tired and drowsy that she heard only snatches. Then she was jolted into awareness. Madam Trudeau was talking.

". . . a book that will be the guide to all future Teachers, showing them the way through personal tribulations and trials to achieve the serenity that was Madam Westfall's. I am honored by this privilege, in choosing me and my apprentices to accomplish this end . . ."

Carla thought of the gibberish that she had been putting down in her notebook and she blinked back tears of shame. Madam Trudeau should have told them why she wanted the information. She would have to go back over it all and destroy all the nonsense that she had written down.

Late that afternoon the entourage formed that would accompany Madam Westfall to her final ceremony in Scranton, her native city, where her burial would return her to her family.

Madam Trudeau had an interview with Carla before departure. "You will be in charge of the other girls," she said. "I expect you to maintain order. You will report any disturbance, or any infringement of rules immediately, and if that is not possible, if I am occupied, you will personally impose order in my name."

"Yes, Madam."

"Very well. During the journey the girls will travel together in a compartment of the tube. Talking will be permitted, but no laughter, no childish play. When we arrive at the Scranton home, you will be given rooms with cots. Again you will all comport yourselves with the dignity of the office which you are ordered to fulfill at this time."

Carla felt excitement mount within her as the girls lined up to take their places along the sides of the casket. They went with it to a closed limousine where they sat knee to knee, unspeaking, hot, to be taken over smooth highways for an hour to the tube. Madam Westfall had refused to fly in life, and was granted the same rights in death, so her body was to be transported from Wilmington to Scranton by the rocket tube. As soon as the girls had accompanied the casket to its car, and were directed to their own compartment, their voices raised in a babble. It was the first time any of them had left the schoolgrounds since entering them at the age of five.

Ruthie was going to work in the infants' wards, and she turned faintly pink and soft looking when she talked about it. Luella was a music apprentice already, having shown skill on the piano at an early age. Lorette preened herself slightly and announced that she had been chosen as a Lover by a Gentleman. She would become a Lady one day. Carla stared at her curiously, wondering at her pleased look, wondering if she had not been shown the films yet. Lorette was blue-eyed, with pale hair, much the same build as Carla. Looking at her, Carla could imagine her in soft dresses, with her mouth painted, her hair covered by the other hair that was cloud soft and shiny . . . She looked at the girl's cheeks flushed with excitement at the thought of her future, and she knew that with or without the paint box, Lorette would be a Lady whose skin would be smooth, whose mouth would be soft . . .

"The fuzz is so soft now, the flesh so tender." She remembered the scent, the softness of the Lady's hands, the way her skirt moved about her red-clad thighs.

She bit her lip. But she didn't want to be a Lady. She couldn't ever think of them again without loathing and disgust. She was chosen to be a Teacher.

They said it is the duty of society to prepare its non-citizens for citizenship but it is recognized that there are those who will not meet the requirements and society itself is not to be blamed for those occasional failures that must accrue.

She took out her notebook and wrote the words in it.

"Did you just remember something else she said?" Lisa asked. She was the youngest of the girls, only ten, and had attended Madam Westfall one time. She seemed to be very tired.

Carla looked over what she had written, and then read it aloud. "It's from the school rules book," she said. "Maybe changed a little, but the same meaning. You'll study it in a year or two."

Lisa nodded. "You know what she said to me? She said I should go hide in the cave, and never lose my birth certificate. She said I should never tell anyone where the radio is." She frowned. "Do you know what a cave is? And a radio?"

"You wrote it down, didn't you? In the notebook?"

Lisa ducked her head. "I forgot again. I remembered it once and then forgot again until now." She searched through her cloth travel bag for her notebook and when she didn't find it, she dumped the contents on the floor to search more carefully. The notebook was not there.

"Lisa, when did you have it last?"

"I don't know. A few days ago. I don't remember."

"When Madam Trudeau talked to you the last time, did you have it then?"

"No. I couldn't find it. She said if I didn't have it the next time I was called for an interview, she'd whip me. But I can't find it!" She broke into tears and threw herself down on her small heap of belongings. She beat her fists on them and sobbed. "She's going to whip me and I can't find it. I can't. It's gone."

Carla stared at her. She shook her head. "Lisa, stop that crying. You couldn't have lost it. Where? There's no place to lose it. You didn't take it from your cubicle, did you?"

The girl sobbed louder. "No. No. No. I don't know where it is."

Carla kneeled by her and pulled the child up from the floor to a squatting position. "Lisa, what did you put in the notebook? Did you play with it?"

Lisa turned chalky white and her eyes became very large, then she closed them, no longer weeping.

"So you used it for other things? Is that it? What sort of things?"

Lisa shook her head. "I don't know. Just things."

"All of it? The whole notebook?"

"I couldn't help it. I didn't know what to write down. Madam Westfall said too much. I couldn't write it all. She wanted to touch me and I was afraid of her and I hid under the chair and she kept calling me, 'Child, come here don't hide. I'm not one of them. Go to the cave and take it with you.' And she kept reaching for me with her hands. I ... they were like chicken claws. She would have ripped me apart with them. She hated me. She said she hated me. She said I should have been killed with the others, why wasn't I killed with the others."

Carla, her hands hard on the child's shoulders, turned away from the fear and despair she saw on the girl's face. Ruthie pushed past her and hugged the child.

"Hush, hush, Lisa. Don't cry now. Hush. There, there."

Carla stood up and backed away. "Lisa, what sort of things did you put in the notebook?"

"Just things that I like. Snowflakes and flowers and designs."

"All right. Pick up your belongings and sit down. We must be nearly there. It seems like the tube is stopping."

Again they were shown from a closed compartment to a closed limousine and whisked over countryside that remained invisible to them. There was a drizzly rain falling when they stopped and got out of the car.

The Westfall house was a three-storied, pseudo-Victorian wooden building, with balconies and cupolas, and many chimneys. There was scaffolding about it, and one of the three porches had been torn away and was being replaced as restoration of the house, turning it into a national monument, progressed. The girls accompanied the casket to a gloomy, large room where the air was chilly and damp, and scant lighting cast deep shadows. After the casket had been positioned on the dais which also had accompanied it, the girls followed Madam Trudeau through narrow corridors, up narrow steps, to the third floor where two large rooms had been prepared for them, each containing seven cots.

Madam Trudeau showed them the bathroom that would serve their needs, told them good-night, and motioned Carla to follow her. They descended the stairs to a second floor room that had black, massive furniture: a desk, two straight chairs, a bureau with a wavery mirror over it, and a large canopied bed.

Madam Trudeau paced the black floor silently for several minutes without speaking, then she swung around and said, "Carla, I heard every word that silly little girl said this afternoon. She drew pictures in her notebook! This is the third time the word cave has come up in reports of Madam Westfall's mutterings. Did she speak to you of caves?"

Carla's mind was whirling. How had she heard what they

had said? Did maturity also bestow magical abilities? She said, "Yes, Madam, she spoke of hiding in a cave."

"Where is the cave, Carla? Where is it?"

"I don't know, Madam. She didn't say."

Madam Trudeau started to pace once more. Her pale face was drawn in lines of concentration that carved deeply into her flesh, two furrows straight up from the inner brows, other lines at the sides of her nose, straight to her chin, her mouth tight and hard. Suddenly she sat down and leaned back in the chair. "Carla, in the last four or five years Madam Westfall became childishly senile; she was no longer living in the present most of the time, but was reliving incidents in her past. Do you understand what I mean?"

Carla nodded, then said hastily, "Yes, Madam."

"Yes. Well it doesn't matter. You know that I have been commissioned to write the biography of Madam Westfall, to immortalize her writings and her utterances. But there is a gap, Carla. A large gap in our knowledge, and until recently it seemed that the gap never would be filled in. When Madam Westfall was found as a child, wandering in a dazed condition, undernourished, almost dead from exposure, she did not know who she was, where she was from, anything about her past at all. Someone had put an identification bracelet on her arm, a steel bracelet that she could not remove, and that was the only clue there was about her origins. For ten years she received the best medical care and education available, and her intellect sparkled brilliantly, but she never regained her memory."

Madam Trudeau shifted to look at Carla. A trick of the lighting made her eyes glitter like jewels. "You have studied how she started her first school with eight students, and over the next century developed her teaching methods to the point of perfection that we now employ throughout the nation, in the Males' school as well as the Females'. Through her efforts Teachers have become the most respected of all citizens and the schools the most powerful of all institutions." A mirthless smile crossed her face, gone almost as quickly as it formed, leaving the deep shadows, lines, and the glittering eyes. "I honored you more than you yet realize when I chose you for my protege."

The air in the room was too close and dank, smelled of moldering wood and unopened places. Carla continued to watch Madam Trudeau, but she was feeling light-headed and exhausted and the words seemed interminable to her. The glittering eyes held her gaze and she said nothing. The thought occurred to her that Madam Trudeau would take Madam Westfall's place as head of the school now.

"Encourage the girls to talk, Carla. Let them go on as much as they want about what Madam Westfall said, lead them into it if they stray from the point. Written reports have been sadly deficient." She stopped and looked questioningly at the girl. "Yes? What is it?"

"Then ... I mean after they talk, are they to write ...? Or should I try to remember and write it all down?"

"There will be no need for that," Madam Trudeau said. "Simply let them talk as much as they want."

"Yes, Madam."

"Very well. Here is a schedule for the coming days. Two girls on duty in the Viewing Room at all times from dawn until dark, yard exercise in the enclosed garden behind the building if the weather permits, kitchen duty and so on. Study it, and direct the girls to their duties. On Saturday afternoon everyone will attend the burial, and on Sunday we return to the school. Now go."

Carla bowed, and turned to leave. Madam Trudeau's voice stopped her once more. "Wait, Carla. Come here. You may brush my hair before you leave."

Carla took the brush in numb fingers and walked obediently behind Madam Trudeau who was loosening hair clasps that restrained her heavy black hair. It fell down her back like a dead snake, uncoiling slowly. Carla started to brush it.

"Harder, girl. Are you so weak that you can't brush hair?"

She plied the brush harder until her arm became heavy and then Madam Trudeau said, "Enough. You are a clumsy girl, awkward and stupid. Must I teach you everything, even how to brush one's hair properly?" She yanked the brush from Carla's hand and now there were two spots of color on her cheeks and her eyes were flashing. "Get out. Go! Leave me! On Saturday immediately following the funeral you will administer punishment to Lisa for scribbling in her notebook. Afterward report to me. And now get out of here!"

Carla snatched up the schedule and backed across the room, terrified of the Teacher who seemed demoniacal suddenly. She bumped into the other chair and nearly fell down. Madam Trudeau laughed shortly and cried, "Clumsy, awkward! You would be a Lady! You?"

Carla groped behind her for the doorknob and finally escaped into the hallway, where she leaned against the wall trembling too hard to move on. Something crashed into the door behind her and she stifled a scream and ran. The brush. Madam had thrown the brush against the door.

Madam Westfall's ghost roamed all night, chasing shadows in and out of rooms, making the floors creak with her passage, echoes of her voice drifting in and out of the dorm where Carla tossed restlessly. Twice she sat upright in fear, listening intently, not knowing why. Once Lisa cried out and she went to her and held her hand until the child quieted again. When dawn lighted the room Carla was awake and standing at the windows looking at the ring of mountains that encircled the city. Black shadows against the lesser black of the sky, they darkened, and suddenly caught fire from the sun striking their tips. The fire spread downward, went out and became merely light on the leaves that were turning red and gold. Carla turned from the view, unable to explain the pain that filled her. She awakened the first two girls who were to be on duty with Madam Westfall and after their quiet departure, returned to the window. The sun was all the way up now, but its morning light was soft; there were no hard outlines anywhere. The trees were a blend of colors with no individual boundaries, and rocks and earth melted together and were one. Birds were singing with the desperation of summer's end and winter's approach.

"Carla?" Lisa touched her arm and looked up at her with wide, fearful eyes. "Is she going to whip me?"

"You will be punished after the funeral," Carla said, stiffly. "And I should report you for touching me, you know."

The child drew back, looking down at the black border on Carla's skirt. "I forgot." She hung her head. "I'm . . . I'm so scared."

"It's time for breakfast, and after that we'll have a walk in the gardens. You'll feel better after you get out in the sunshine and fresh air."

"Chrysanthemums, dahlias, marigolds. No, the small ones there, with the brown fringes . . ." Luella pointed out the various flowers to the other girls. Carla walked in the rear, hardly listening, trying to keep her eye on Lisa, who also trailed behind. She was worried about the child. She had not slept well, had eaten no breakfast, and was so pale and wan that she didn't look strong enough to take the short garden walk with them.

Eminent personages came and went in the gloomy old house and huddled together to speak in lowered voices. Carla paid little attention to them. "I can change it after I have some authority," she said to a still inner self who listened and made no reply. "What can I do now? I'm property. I belong to the state, to Madam Trudeau and the school. What good if I disobey and am also whipped? Would that help any? I won't hit her hard." The inner self said nothing, but she thought she could hear a mocking laugh come from the mummy that was being honored.

They had all those empty schools, miles and miles of school halls where no feet walked, desks where no students sat, books that no students scribbled up, and they put the children in them and they could see immediately who couldn't keep up, couldn't learn the new ways and they got rid of them. Smart. Smart of them. They were smart and had the goods and the money and the hatred. My God, they hated. That's who wins, who hates most. And is more afraid. Every time.

Carla forced her arms not to move, her hands to remain locked before her, forced her head to stay bowed. The voice now went on and on and she couldn't get away from it.

... rained every day, cold freezing rain and Daddy didn't come back and Mama said, hide child, hide in the cave where it's warm, and don't move no matter what happens, don't move. Let me put it on your arm, don't take it off, never take it off show it to them if they find you show them make them look. ...

Her relief came and Carla left. In the wide hallway that led to the back steps she was stopped by a rough hand on her arm. "Damme, here's a likely one. Come here, girl. Let's have a look at you." She was spun around and the hand grasped her chin and lifted her head. "Did I say it! I could spot her all the way down the hall, now couldn't I. Can't hide what she's got with long skirts and that skinny hairdo, now can you? Didn't I spot her!" He laughed and turned Carla's head to the side and looked at her in profile, then laughed even louder.

She could see only that he was red faced, with bushy eyebrows and thick gray hair. His hand holding her chin hurt, digging into her jaws at each side of her neck.

"Victor, turn her loose," the cool voice of a female said then. "She's been chosen already. An apprentice Teacher."

He pushed Carla from him, still holding her chin, and he looked down at the skirts with the broad black band at the bottom. He gave her a shove that sent her into the opposite wall. She clutched at it for support.

"Whose pet is she?" he said darkly.

"Trudeau's."

He turned and stamped away, not looking at Carla again. He wore the blue and white of a Doctor of Law. The female was a Lady in pink and black.

"Carla. Go upstairs." Madam Trudeau moved from an open doorway and stood before Carla. She looked up and down the shaking girl. "Now do you understand why I apprenticed you before this trip? For your own protection."

They walked to the cemetery on Saturday, a bright, warm day with golden light and the odor of burning leaves. Speeches were made, Madam Westfall's favorite music was played, and the services ended. Carla dreaded returning to the dormitory. She kept a close watch on Lisa who seemed but a shadow of herself. Three times during the night she had held the girl until her nightmares subsided, and each time she had stroked her fine hair and soft cheeks and murmured to her quieting words, and she knew it was only her own cowardice that prevented her saying that it was she who would administer the whipping. The first shovelful of earth was thrown on top the casket and everyone turned to leave the place, when suddenly the air was filled with raucous laughter, obscene chants, and wild music. It ended almost as quickly as it started, but the group was frozen until the mountain air became unnaturally still. Not even the birds were making a sound following the maniacal outburst.

Carla had been unable to stop the involuntary look that she cast about her at the woods that circled the cemetery. Who? Who would dare? Only a leaf or two stirred, floating downward on the gentle air effortlessly. Far in the distance a bird began to sing again, as if the evil spirits that had flown past were now gone.

"Madam Trudeau sent this up for you," Luella said nervously, handing Carla the rod. It was plastic, three feet long, thin, flexible. Carla looked at it and turned slowly to Lisa. The girl seemed to be swaying back and forth.

"I am to administer the whipping," Carla said. "You will undress now."

Lisa stared at her in disbelief, and then suddenly she ran across the room and threw herself on Carla, hugging her hard, sobbing. "Thank you, Carla. Thank you so much. I was so afraid, you don't know how afraid. Thank you. How did you make her let you do it? Will you be punished too? I love you so much, Carla." She was incoherent in her relief and she flung off her gown and underwear and turned around.

Her skin was pale and soft, rounded buttocks, dimpled just above the fullness. She had no waist yet, no breasts, no hair on her baby body. Like a baby she had whimpered in the night, clinging tightly to Carla, burying her head in the curve of Carla's breasts.

Carla raised the rod and brought it down, as easily as she could. Anything was too hard. There was a red welt. The girl bowed her head lower, but didn't whimper. She was holding the back of a chair and it jerked when the rod struck.

It would be worse if Madam Trudeau was doing it, Carla thought. She would try to hurt, would draw blood. Why? Why? The rod was hanging limply, and she knew it would be harder on both of them if she didn't finish it quickly. She raised it and again felt the rod bite into flesh, sending the vibration into her arm, through her body.

Again. The girl cried out, and a spot of blood appeared on her back. Carla stared at it in fascination and despair. She couldn't help it. Her arm wielded the rod too hard, and she couldn't help it. She closed her eyes a moment, raised the rod and struck again. Better. But the vibrations that had begun with the first blow increased, and she felt dizzy, and couldn't keep her eyes off the spot of blood that was trailing down the girl's back. Lisa was weeping now, her body was shaking. Carla felt a responsive tremor start within her.

Eight, nine. The excitement that stirred her was unnameable, unknowable, never before felt like this. Suddenly she thought of the Lady who had chosen her once, and scenes of the film she had been forced to watch flashed through her mind. . . . *remake them in our image.* She looked about in that moment frozen in time, and she saw the excitement on some of the faces, on others fear, disgust and revulsion. Her gaze stopped on Helga, who had her eyes closed, whose body was moving rhythmically. She raised the rod and brought it down as hard as she could, hitting the chair with a noise that brought everyone out of her own kind of trance. A sharp, cracking noise that was a finish.

"Ten!" she cried and threw the rod across the room.

Lisa turned and through brimming eyes, red, swollen, ugly with crying, said, "Thank you, Carla. It wasn't so bad."

Looking at her Carla knew hatred. It burned through her, distorted the image of what she saw. Inside her body the excitement found no outlet, and it flushed her face, made her hands numb, and filled her with hatred. She turned and fled.

Before Madam Trudeau's door, she stopped a moment, took a deep breath, and knocked. After several moments the door opened and Madam Trudeau came out. Her eyes were glittering more than ever, and there were two spots of color on her pasty cheeks.

"It is done? Let me look at you." Her fingers were cold and moist when she lifted Carla's chin. "Yes, I see. I see. I am busy now. Come back in half an hour. You will tell me all about it. Half an hour." Carla never had seen a genuine smile on the Teacher's face before, and now when it came, it was more frightening than her frown was. Carla didn't move, but she felt as if every cell in her body had tried to pull back.

She bowed and turned to leave. Madam Trudeau followed her a step and said in a low vibrant voice, "You felt it, didn't you? You know now, don't you?"

"Madam Trudeau, are you coming back?" The door behind her opened, and one of the Doctors of Law appeared there.

"Yes, of course." She turned and went back to the room.

Carla let herself into the small enclosed area between the second and third floor, then stopped. She could hear the voices of girls coming down the stairs, going on duty in the kitchen, or outside for evening exercises. She stopped to wait for them to pass, and she leaned against the wall tiredly. This space was two and a half feet square perhaps. It was very dank and hot. From here she could hear every sound made by the girls on the stairs. Probably that was why the second door had been added, to muffle the noise of those going up and down. The girls had stopped on the steps and were discussing the laughter and obscenities they had heard in the cemetery.

Carla knew that it was her duty to confront them, to order them to their duties, to impose proper silence on them in public places, but she closed her eyes and pressed her hand hard on the wood behind her for support and wished they would finish their childish prattle and go on. The wood behind her started to slide.

She jerked away. A sliding door? She felt it and ran her finger along the smooth paneling to the edge where there was now a six-inch opening as high as she could reach down to the floor. She pushed the door again and it slid easily, going between the two walls. When the opening was wide enough she stepped through it. The cave! She knew it was the cave that Madam Westfall had talked about incessantly.

The space was no more than two feet wide, and very dark. She felt the inside door and there was a knob on it, low enough for children to reach. The door slid as smoothly from the inside as it had from the outside. She slid it almost closed and the voices were cut off, but she could hear other voices, from the room on the other side of the passage. They were not clear. She felt her way farther, and almost fell over a box. She held her breath as she realized that she was hearing Madam Trudeau's voice:

"... be there. Too many independent reports of the old

fool's babbling about it for there not to be something to it. Your men are incompetent."

"Trudeau, shut up. You scare the living hell out of the kids, but you don't scare me. Just shut up and accept the report. We've been over every inch of the hills for miles, and there's no cave. It was over a hundred years ago. Maybe there was one that the kids played in, but it's gone now. Probably collapsed."

"We have to be certain, absolutely certain."

"What's so important about it anyway? Maybe if you would give us more to go on we could make more progress."

"The reports state that when the militia came here, they found only Martha Westfall. They executed her on the spot without questioning her first. Fools! When they searched the house, they discovered that it was stripped. No jewels, no silver, diaries, papers. Nothing. Steve Westfall was dead. Dr. Westfall dead. Martha. No one has ever found the articles that were hidden, and when the child again appeared, she had true amnesia that never yielded to attempts to penetrate it."

"So, a few records, diaries. What are they to you?" There was silence, then he laughed. "The money! He took all his money out of the bank, didn't he."

"Don't be ridiculous. I want records, that's all. There's a complete ham radio, complete. Dr. Westfall was an electronics engineer as well as a teacher. No one could begin to guess how much equipment he hid before he was killed."

Carla ran her hand over the box, felt behind it. More boxes.

"Yeah, yeah. I read the reports, too. All the more reason to keep the search nearby. For a year before the end a close watch was kept on the house. They had to walk to wherever they hid the stuff. And I can just say again that there's no cave around here. It fell in."

"I hope so," Madam Trudeau said.

Someone knocked on the door, and Madam Trudeau called, "Come in."

"Yes, what is it? Speak up, girl."

"It is my duty to report, Madam, that Carla did not administer the full punishment ordered by you."

Carla's fists clenched hard. Helga.

"Explain," Madam Trudeau said sharply.

"She only struck Lisa nine times, Madam. The last time she hit the chair."

"I see. Return to your room."

The man laughed when the girl closed the door once more.

"Carla is the golden one, Trudeau? The one who wears a single black band?"

"The one you manhandled earlier, yes."

"Insubordination in the ranks, Trudeau? Tut, tut. And your reports all state that you never have any rebellion. Never."

Very slowly Madam Trudeau said, "I have never had a student who didn't abandon any thoughts of rebellion under my guidance. Carla will be obedient. And one day she will be an excellent Teacher. I know the signs."

Carla stood before the Teacher with her head bowed and her hands clasped together. Madam Trudeau walked around her without touching her, then sat down and said, "You will whip Lisa every day for a week, beginning tomorrow."

Carla didn't reply.

"Don't stand mute before me, Carla. Signify your obedience immediately."

"I . . . I can't, Madam."

"Carla, any day that you do not whip Lisa, I will. And I will also whip you double her allotment. Do you understand?"

"Yes, Madam."

"You will inform Lisa that she is to be whipped every day, by one or the other of us. Immediately."

"Madam, please . . ."

"You speak out of turn, Carla!"

"I, Madam, please don't do this. Don't make me do this. She is too weak . . ."

"She will beg you to do it, won't she, Carla. Beg you with tears flowing to be the one, not me. And you will feel the excitement and the hate and every day you will feel it grow strong. You will want to hurt her, want to see blood spot her bare back. And your hate will grow until you won't be able to look at her without being blinded by your own hatred. You see, I know, Carla. I know all of it."

Carla stared at her in horror. "I won't do it. I won't."

"I will."

They were old and full of hatred for the shiny young faces, the bright hair, the straight backs and strong legs and arms. They said: let us remake them in our image and they did.

Carla repeated Madam Trudeau's words to the girls gathered in the two sleeping rooms on the third floor. Lisa swayed and was supported by Ruthie. Helga smiled.

That evening Ruthie tried to run away and was caught by two of the blue-clad Males. The girls were lined up and watched as Ruthie was stoned. They buried her without a service on the hill where she had been caught.

After dark, lying on the cot open-eyed, tense, Carla heard Lisa's whisper close to her ear. "I don't care if you hit me, Carla. It won't hurt like it does when she hits me."

"Go to bed, Lisa. Go to sleep."

"I can't sleep. I keep seeing Ruthie. I should have gone with her. I wanted to, but she wouldn't let me. She was afraid there would be Males on the hill watching. She said if she didn't get caught, then I should try to follow her at night." The child's voice was flat, as if shock had dulled her sensibilities.

Carla kept seeing Ruthie too. Over and over she repeated to herself: I should have tried it. I'm cleverer than she was. I might have escaped. I should have been the one. She knew it was too late now. They would be watching too closely.

An eternity later she crept from her bed and dressed quietly. Soundlessly she gathered her own belongings, and then collected the notebooks of the other girls, and the pens, and she left the room. There were dim lights on throughout the house as she made her way silently down stairs and through corridors. She left a pen by one of the outside doors, and very cautiously made her way back to the tiny space between the floors. She slid the door open and deposited everything else she carried inside the cave. She tried to get to the kitchen for food, but stopped when she saw one of the Officers of Law. She returned soundlessly to the attic rooms and tiptoed among the beds to Lisa's cot. She placed one hand over the girl's mouth and shook her awake with the other.

Lisa bolted upright, terrified, her body stiffened convulsively. With her mouth against the girl's ear Carla whispered, "Don't make a sound. Come on." She half-led, half-carried the girl to the doorway, down the stairs and into the cave and closed the door.

"You can't talk here, either," she whispered. "They can hear." She spread out the extra garments she had collected and they lay down together, her arms tight about the girl's shoulders. "Try to sleep," she whispered. "I don't think they'll find us here. And after they leave, we'll creep out and live in the woods. We'll eat nuts and berries . . ."

The first day they were jubilant at their success and they giggled and muffled the noise with their skirts. They could hear all the orders being issued by Madam Trudeau: guards in all the halls, on the stairs, at the door to the dorm to keep other girls from trying to escape also. They could hear all the interrogations, of the girls, the guards who had not seen the escapees. They heard the mocking voice of the Doctor of Law deriding Madam Trudeau's boasts of absolute control.

The second day Carla tried to steal food for them, and, more important, water. There were blue-clad Males everywhere. She returned empty-handed. During the night Lisa whimpered in her sleep and Carla had to stay awake to quiet the child who was slightly feverish.

"You won't let her get me, will you?" she begged over and over.

The third day Lisa became too quiet. She didn't want Carla to move from her side at all. She held Carla's hand in her hot, dry hand and now and then tried to raise it to her face, but she was too weak now. Carla stroked her forehead.

When the child slept Carla wrote in the notebooks, in the dark, not knowing if she wrote over other words, or on blank pages. She wrote her life story, and then made up other things to say. She wrote her name over and over, and wept because she had no last name. She wrote nonsense words and rhymed them with other nonsense words. She wrote of the savages who had laughed at the funeral and she hoped they wouldn't all die over the winter months. She thought that probably they would. She wrote of the golden light through green-black pine trees and of birds' songs and moss underfoot. She wrote of Lisa lying peacefully now at the far end of the cave amidst riches that neither of them could ever have comprehended. When she could no longer write, she drifted in and out of the golden light in the forest, listening to the birds' songs, hearing the raucous laughter that now sounded so beautiful.

Afterword:

About the story. We are such a godawful preachy nation, always talking about how much we do for the kids, how much we love them, how we spoil them with excessive permissiveness because we can't bear to hurt them or deny them any of life's little joys. We do Orwell proud in our expertise at doubletalk. We live a double standard in so many areas that most of us just don't have the time to listen to our own words and compare them with our actions. I am not interested in imaginary problems in imaginary times; it seems that I am too much involved in this world to create artificial ones where my own ingenuity can put things right. So I see this story as the culmination of a lot of isolated items, some big and documented, some small and private. Chicago was one of them, but only one, and not the most important, just the most publicized. What was most revolting about chicago (it will become a general usage word) was the fact that afterward a majority of over 10 to 1 Americans approved the action taken by the police. Let anyone who disbelieves my story mull over that figure.

Just as in a divorce action the cause given might be the marital equivalent of chicago, but the real reasons are small daily injustices, so the generation gap, I think, has been prodded along with small daily doses of adult irresponsibility, until now there does exist a situation that is explosive.

If you, a well dressed and apparently affluent member of the adult community enter a soda fountain, a hamburger joint, or restaurant, and sit down for service, you'll get it before the group of teen agers who were there first, although you might want only a cup of coffee or a coke and they might order several dollars worth of junk. It is not an economical issue. I've seen a saleslady turn away from a teen aged girl with her purchase in her hand, needing only to be paid for, to wait on a middle aged woman who then took fifteen minutes to make up her mind. I would have been waited on next, if I had allowed it. When I insisted that the girl be helped next, the saleslady became surly and rude. No one can show respect for my advanced age by showering disrespect on another. Okay, so it's pecking order. If it turned out that there was equality in most other areas, they could put up with this sort of thing, but there isn't.

Equality under the law. I joke. I can drive a car with a noisy muffler, and if I am stopped at all, it is only for a reprimand. My son gets a ticket for the same thing—in my car. And in the courts I can have all the legal counsel I can afford, and the state will provide more if I need help, theoretically. A juvenile is at the mercy of a judge who probably is as qualified to understand adolescents as my dear old spinster aunt.

Just as long as the kids accept our standards, we leave them alone, but let them adopt their own standards, different than ours, and there is furor. Haircuts, sandals, mini-skirts (before Jackie and her crowd made them more or less respectable) and so on. Why can't they be like us, is what the school boards are really moaning. Cut their hair, wear decent clothes, drink their gin, smoke their cigarettes, and leave that other stuff alone. We accept teens and booze and beer. There may be a little tiny bit of public outcry about a group of thirteen year olds caught at a beer party, but by the following weekend, it's a dead issue. But if it's pot! My God, call the FBI!

For sale ads feature houses with three or four bedrooms, three baths, two car garages, pools, etc. Ask about the schools: oh, double shift for the present, and the teachers are on strike right now, but we have the best parking lot available for the kids' cars. Is this love?

You see a bunch of businessmen at lunch or dinner, getting louder and louder while an indulgent management smiles. A group of college boys, or high school kids would get thrown out in a minute. The VFW can take over a town, "bomb" citizens from upper floors with bags of god knows what, and the chamber of commerce fights for the privilege of having them again. Kids get the JD treatment for the same sort of provocation.

Sorry, Harlan, I'm going on too much, could go on for pages. But this is the sort of data that sociologists deal with, not writers of fiction. At least not directly. I think this is a demented society, and one of the reasons for the dementia is our everlovin' refusal to see the reality behind our honeyed words. If we were as good as we talk about being, I'd want stock in harps. It's a whole society of Let's Pretenders, and I wish, oh, how much I wish we'd all just stop.

Introduction to

HARRY THE HARE:

Easily the most joyous aspect of putting together the *Dangerous Visions* anthologies is the discovering of new talents. Getting a flamethrower from Kate Wilhelm or Ursula Le Guin is to be expected—they're professionals with extra-special talents. But encountering someone new and unpublished, finding a story that might otherwise never have gotten into print (you'd be surprised how many fine stories by unknowns languish for years and eventually go into the trunk as the writer goes into plumbing or CPAing), is a special thrill. For one thing, it justifies the existence of the editor. Collecting either already-published stories or assembling new stories on a commissioned basis by "big names," is hardly worthy of applause or citation. But if an editor can bring forward one or two "first" writers, he can be said to have earned his share of the action and performed a noble act.

In the field of speculative fiction, helping out the tyros is a dues-paying activity held in only slightly less esteem than that of making money. I know of no other genre in which the established names—from the Asimovian/Bradburyian/Clarkesque upper echelons all the way down to last year's newcomers—break their asses with such regularity and effusiveness, to assist the fledglings. Show me, if you can, another field of freelance endeavor in which the fastest guns teach the plowboys how to outdraw them. In sf, the prevailing attitude seems to be: "A man can stay on top only as long as he can beat his own best record." There are hungry trolls clambering up our mountain every day, and inexplicably, but nobly, the Kings of the Glass Hill don't stomp them, they extend a helping hand.

In this anthology you will read quite a few new writers. Some have published in other mediums—from critical essays to poetry—and some are seeing their contributions published here as the initial appearance in print. A few—Ed Bryant, Joan Bernott, Ken McCullough, Richard Hill—have gone on to sell widely elsewhere. But the stories here were their first sales. (No, wait a minute, that's not true for Hill. Damon Knight had already bought Richard's first story for ORBIT when I met him and bought "Moth Race." This was his second sale. I want to be scrupulously honest about it.)

Jim Hemesath is a twenty-seven year old writer I met while doing a two-week Visiting Lecturer stint at the 1969 University of Colorado Writers' Workshop in the Rockies. He was one of two writers I bought for this book, out of an enrollment close to two hundred.

James Bartholomew William Hemesath was born 25 April 1944 in New Hampton, Chickasaw County, Iowa. He is ex-Roman Catholic, ex-married and ex-Marine Corps. He attended college at the Universities of Hawaii and Iowa, obtaining a B.A. in history from the latter in 1969. He is Phi Beta Kappa and won the Harcourt, Brace & World Fellowship to the 1969 U. of Colorado Workshop, as well as a Research Assistantship to the University of Iowa Writers' Workshop, 1969–70.

Apart from "Harry the Hare" and "The Box" (published in *Dare*, December 1967) he has made money at the usual mundane jobs writers seek out while waiting for the world to discover them: newspaper boy, soda jerk, food service worker in a boys' dormitory, rental housing inspector for the city of Iowa City, assistant foreman on a thinning crew in the Bitterroot National Forest in Montana; and following in the footsteps of such fine writers as John Steinbeck, Clifford Odets and Jack Williamson, Mr. Hemesath has forayed into the nitty and/or gritty working with his hands as an asphalt paver, concrete paver, on a sewer gang, and with a section gang raising track for the Chicago and Northwestern along the Cedar River.

His first contact with the Muse was during his junior year at the University of Iowa, working under Mary Carter, author of *A Fortune in Dimes* and *The Minutes of the Night*. In her fiction writing course he was required to hand in a three hundred word scene every day, and later, a short story every day, thereby proving there are other teachers of writing besides your editor who feel most theory is bullshit and the only way you can become a writer is to *write*. Mr. Hemesath insists I mention that his three favorite stories are Poe's "The Pit and the Pendulum," Shirley Jackson's "The Lottery" and "A Boy and His Dog" by your editor. He gave me no option in relating this, stating that if I really wanted to note germinal influences on him, those three needed to be entered for posterity. I found no difficulty in meeting his request. Being linked with Poe and Jackson fixes me for the rest of the week. And maybe into next week, as well.

He concludes his biographical notes with the remark that he hopes one day to write a novel that takes place in Iowa.

Of "Harry the Hare" I will only say, it is at once bizarre, funny, alarming and tragic. I suspect it is a story Ray Bradbury might have liked to've written, and one I know he will enjoy. I suspect you will, too.

James B. Hemesath

HARRY THE HARE

Inside the dimly lit movie theater, there was a muffled sound, then one of the swinging doors from the outer lobby opened, and a short, fat man began walking down the aisle toward the stage. It was early in the day, before the show had started. The short, fat man strode the descending length of the aisle, climbed the steps to the stage, and walked up close to the great white rectangle of the movie screen.

"Hello, Bijou . . . I've returned," he said softly, almost reverently. He tentatively poked a finger at the screen, and chuckled. "Nothing but a sheet of perforated plastic? Ridiculous."

"Good afternoon." The voice came from the rear of the theater. "Do you have business here? We're not open yet." The short, fat man had turned at the first words. Now he stared up and back at the rear of the theater. It was too dim back there, but now he could barely see, barely make out, something. A gloved hand rested on the hinged window of the projection booth.

"I want to see Harry." The man hand-shaded his eyes and squinted.

"He's at lunch." The window hinges squeaked. "Should be back for the matinee."

"Good. I'll wait." The man sat cross-legged on the stage. Hand-cupped his chin. Rocked. "The matinee's at one. Isn't it?"

"Why do you want to see Harry?" Two gloved hands rested on the window sill. "Are you a friend?"

"Yes," the man replied. "I've always loved Harry the Hare cartoons." Smiled. "As a child I came every Saturday afternoon. Right here. To the Bijou."

"Really? A test." The gloved hands held a piece of string. "What am I making?"

"A cat's cradle?" The man stumbled to his feet. Squinted. "Yes! That's it. A cat's cradle." Paused. "But that trick belongs to Harry the Hare."

"Most certainly. But now." The string floated to the floor. "Look at my hands. What do you see?"

"Only four fingers!" The man rubbed his eyes. "And gloves. Brown gloves." He jumped from the stage. "So that means—"

"Most certainly. I'm Harry the Hare." The gloved hands waved. "Forgive me for lying." Silence. "You know. About being out to lunch." The gloved hands became two fists. "But I must be careful. They're after me."

"Who are they?"

"My creators. The people who drew me." The gloved hands clenched each other. "The studio stopped making cartoons. I was to be buried—"

"But you escaped." The man's eyes swelled with tears. "Why do they want you back?"

"Because I'm copyrighted." The gloved hands became limp. "They own me."

"But I need you. I love Harry the Hare."

"Many people do. And they come here. Just to see me."

My name is Jack Jackson and I am a lawyer for Blue Wing Films, the former producers of Harry the Hare animated shorts. Two months ago Harry the Hare escaped from the Blue Wing Museum of Motion Picture Classics. The ensuing manhunt ended yesterday during the Saturday Matinee at the Bijou. The theater was crowded with middle-aged people.

Harry the Hare stood on the stage and I shouted, "Blue Wing Films owns Harry the Hare." I sat next to a short, fat man. He started to cry. I handed him my handkerchief. "Harry the Hare must return to the museum."

"I shall never return. The people own me." Harry the

Hare shifted his weight from one foot to the other. "The people—"

"But Blue Wing Films holds the copyright. I have called the police."

"The people need Harry the Hare. My cartoons are no longer exhibited. They only have *me*."

"I am sorry, but the law says . . ." Most of the people were crying. The siren on the police car became louder. I sat down.

Harry the Hare smiled and listened. He snapped his fingers and a scissors appeared. Then he said, "The people shall have me." And snipped off his right foot. Followed by his left foot. Both ears. And his left arm below the elbow.

I stood up and shouted, "Blue Wing Films owns Harry the Hare."

Then I sat down. The aisle was packed.

Afterword:

The first half of *Harry the Hare* was written in Iowa City sometime during the winter of 1968. The second half—the Jack Jackson segment—I wrote the following summer at the University of Colorado Writers' Conference. The very first paragraph of *Harry the Hare* belongs to Harlan Ellison. The rest I can say is mine.

The era of the big studio cartoon is past. Within the United States, production of quality theatrical cartoons has virtually ceased.

What killed the cartoon? Rising production costs. Low box office potential. And public apathy.

But I—James B. Hemesath—miss Daffy Duck, Tweety & Sylvester, and the other cartoon characters of the 1950s. They were my friends. Need I say more?

Introduction to

WHEN IT CHANGED:

I'm writing this 32,000 feet in the air, on American Airlines flight 194 to Chicago. I'm spending this flight happily broken into segments of writing introductions to stories by people I love, and by reading the advance galleys of Keith Laumer's new Scribner's novel, *Dinosaur Beach*. And with one of those wicked little coincidences that the Universe tosses at me frequently, I find something in Keith's book that sparks me into the prefatory words for Joanna Russ and her story.

The item that strikes the spark is a passage from page 48, in which two agents of a far-future timesweeping force find themselves stranded back in the Jurassic Period. It goes like this:

> "Why haven't they made a pick-up on me?" she said, not really talking to me. Her voice was edging up the scale a little.
>
> "Take it easy, girl," I said, and patted her shoulder; I knew my touching her would chill her down again. Not a nice thing to know, but useful.
>
> "Keep your hands to yourself, Ravel," she snapped, all business again. "If you think this is some little desert island scene, you're very wrong."
>
> "Don't get ahead of yourself," I told her. "When I make a pass at you, that'll be time enough to slap me down. Don't go female on me now. We don't have time for nonsense."

Now Keith is a close friend of mine, and a helluva good writer, and those of you who know he had a debilitating stroke late last year will be delighted to know he's recovering strongly, but if Joanna Russ ever got within smiting distance of Keith, I'm sure she'd belt him one up alongside his pudding-trough for those paragraphs, because they are pure-and-simple male chauvinist pig writing.

I'm not trying to start a fight here, you understand, but like newly converted Jews or Catholics, like lifetime cigarette smokers who've put down, like alcoholics now on the wagon, those of us who've spent the greater part of our lives as male chauvinists get terribly zealous in pointing out the gentlemen in our midst who are still wrong-thinking offenders.

In case you aren't aware of how insulting those paragraphs can be to a woman, fellas, consider the following:

These agents, male and female alike, are specially trained, ultra-efficient, tougher than hell, get bounced here and there through time battling a formidable enemy, as well as time itself, and yet the woman is portrayed as weak, sniveling, semi-hysterical, Puritanical, illogical, inefficient and silly. The man has to take hold and show her the way. The narrator keeps referring to himself and other males as *men*, but keeps referring to the woman as a *girl*. If Keith were consistent, he'd call himself (as narrator), and the other males in the novel, *boys*. And the most glaring evidence of the author's unconscious male chauvinism is his telling her, when she gets sappy and illogical—which I contend is out-of-character for the character—*don't go female on me.*

Ugh. Kate Millett and Germaine Greer and Mary Reinholz and, I'm sure, Joanna Russ would belt Keith soundly with their picket signs had they but access to him. I urge Keith to stay down there in his Florida sanctuary, while the rest of us, who've been "saved," try to head off the lynch party.

It all ties in so well with Joanna's story, it must be fate. Because Joanna has here written a story that makes some extraordinarily sharp distinctions between the abilities and attitudes of the sexes, while erasing many others we think immutable. It is, in the best and strongest sense of the word, a female liberation story, while never once speaking of, about, or to the subject. And it points out why I think women's lib is one of the three or four most potent and influential movements to spring up in our country during these last decades of social upheaval.

Keith and a few others may pillory me for this, but as far as I'm concerned, the best writers in sf today are the women. Most of them are represented in this volume—Kate Wilhelm, Ursula Le Guin, Josephine Saxton, Lee Hoffman, Joanna—and others were featured in the original *Dangerous Visions*—Sonya Dorman, Carol Emshwiller, Miriam Allen de Ford. Others will make their appearances in *The Last Dangerous Visions*. Now when I say I think the ladies are the best of us currently, I'm quick to add I don't even care to make the cop-out reservation that held for so many years. It went like this:

"This Leigh Brackett/C. L. Moore/Katherine Maclean/Margaret St. Clair/E. Mayne Hull (fill in the appropriate name for your own past sins, guys) is a helluva writer. She writes so good you think it's a man. You can't tell the difference."

Well, that was nonsense, too. Another glaring example of what we did to our women writers for so many years. We made them feel—and quite rightly—that their sex would lobby against their receiving serious consideration or their work being judged from the git-go on the same plane as a man's. George Sand and George Eliot were not alone in having to assume male pseudonyms in self-defense. God knows what such charades did to the talents and personal lives of not only Amandine Aurore Lucie Dupin and Mary Ann Evans but all the potential Shirley Jacksons and Dorothy Parkers against whose sex restrictions *were* placed. For no one knows how many hundreds of years in literature-in-general, and for almost fifty years in speculative fiction, we have denied ourselves perhaps *half* the great writers who might have been. By insisting that women could only write well if they wrote as men, by hardboiling themselves, by subscribing to the masculine world-view, we have disenfranchised and even blotted out an infinitude of views of our world as seen through eyes different and wonderful.

Happily, that situation is disappearing. Not nearly fast enough for me, but happening nonetheless. There is still a great deal of what was commonly referred to as "ladies' writing" going on, mostly in the major slicks intended to be read under hair dryers; but that is no more representative of the lofty level of quality attained by serious women writers than is the adolescent Ruark-muscle-flexing of stories in the "men's adventure magazines" typical of the best of serious writing being done by men. Hopefully both idioms will be recognized for what they are: sheer pandering to the lowest possible common denominators of fiction-need by women and men.

The reasons for my joy at the ever-stronger position being assumed by women writers in our genre, and my feelings that women's lib in general is a godsend not only for literature but for the world as a whole, are one and the same.

Men have had it their way for thousands of years. The *machismo* concept, the dominant male attitude, the picture of women as weak and essentially brainless, the deification of Mars as god of war and male supremacy . . . these have led us to a world of futility, hatred, bigotry, sexual confusion, pollution and despair. Perhaps it is time the women took a turn at bat. They can certainly do no worse. And while I am not unmindful that women can proliferate even these unsavory cultural attitudes (Mothers who send their sons out to battle with the admonition that they return *with* their shields or *on* them, and then pay homage to the ruins returned to them in plastic bags from Viet Nam by the display of tacky gold stars in living room windows, strike me as little better than ghouls), still I see more kindness and rationality in the average woman than in the average man.

Surely I am in the truest tradition of the Utopian by conceiving of a world saved by women, and equally surely I'm laying an unfair responsibility on women to clean up what men have sullied. (I'm reminded of the young college student who, when advised sappily by a gray-haired elder that the salvation of the world rested with her and her "more aware generation," responded with the urging that the nice old gentleman go fuck himself: why is it up to me, she demanded? You had all the time in the world and you screwed it, and now it's up to *me* to clean up your garbage dump. No thanks, dad. Her point was well taken.)

Still, I cannot escape the feeling that if women had but the oneness of purpose of the ladies of *Lysistrata*, they could end war in half a day.

Don't tell me. I know. I'm expecting a nobility of females that men certainly don't possess, and I'm expecting them all to think the same on major issues. I said I was an Utopian, didn't I?

But I can hope.

I can hope that the world, seen through the minds and eyes of women, will come to be a more pleasing and acceptable view than the one we men have proffered all these centuries. And it is this view, wholly new and different, because it comes from a different systemic orientation, that forms the core of the best new writing in sf and outside the field, by our passionate and dedicated women writers.

Not the least of whom is Joanna Russ.

Terry Carr, editor of the Specials at Ace Books, once told me that Joanna's first novel, the excellent *Picnic on Paradise*, was rejected by every major hardcover house before he saw it and snapped it up for publication. I may be wrong about the specifics, but I would be willing to bet that at least one of those hardcover editors, males all, unconsciously put the kibosh on the novel because it came from a woman. I have absolutely no evidence to back up that theory, and I don't even know to what houses the book was submitted, but I've been in this business a couple of minutes and I've encountered ingrained prejudices that are embedded so cellularly they are wholly unknown to the men from whom they leach so much fairness and rationality.

How sad and silly those editors now seem, having passed up a novel of clearly such eminence. *Picnic on Paradise* was nominated for, and missed winning by a hair, the 1969 Nebula award as best novel of that year. With her first novel, Joanna Russ found herself in the first rank of major sf talents, up against competition like James Blish, Philip K. Dick, Robert Silverberg, R. A. Lafferty, John Brunner and that year's winner, Alexei Panshin.

The promise of *Picnic on Paradise* was kept with her second novel, *And Chaos Died*, in 1970. Stronger even than her first book, it too was nominated for a Nebula, and though once again it missed copping the award (making Joanna's work for the second time a bridesmaid rather than a bride), it was clear only a matter of time separates Joanna Russ from the prizes and the greater glory.

Born in the Bronx in 1937, Joanna Russ spent most of her infanthood being wheeled around the Botanical Gardens. Of her schooling she reports, "I got into Science High School but did not go, due to family insanity, and ended my four years somewhere else by becoming one of the top ten Westinghouse Science Talent Search winners in the country, for growing fungi that looked beautiful but made my mother hysterical because I stored them in the refrigerator. I went to Cornell very conventionally as an English major, but when I got out decided to stop being a good girl, and took a Master of Fine Arts degree in Playwriting at Yale Drama School."

Joanna wrote what she calls "bad plays" for three years and then, in 1959, had her first story published in *The Magazine of Fantasy & Science Fiction*, "Nor Custom Stale." Since that time she has sold several dozen short stories to markets as diverse as *Orbit* and *Manhattan Review*. She has done copy-editing, typing and copywriting for house organs, addressed cards for Office Temporaries, worked as a secretary to an irritable psychiatrist, and finally drifted into teaching. Drifting—mostly out of desperation, Joanna puts it—she taught something she knew nothing about, speech, at a community college in New York City, and knew it was the right thing after one day in the classroom. She has been teaching Creative Writing at Cornell University for the last four years.

Joanna Russ has had four one-act plays produced: three, on one bill, Off-Off-Broadway and one at Princeton, as well as a radio play produced by WBAI, Pacifica's New York station, in 1967. Apparently feeling that there is more to the theater than the writing of "bad plays," Joanna has acted in community theater, Off-Off-Broadway productions, typed programs, run lights, sewed costumes and, one summer, she even made seventy-five pairs of Roman sandals for Joseph Papp's cast of *Julius Caesar*, for the New York Shakespeare Festival.

All of the foregoing, of course, is background to an understanding and appreciation of the woman who wrote the story you are about to read. As such, it is relevant, but hardly important. What Joanna Russ was, or what she set out to be, is not what she is.

What she is, is a fine writer, getting better every year. What she's proving—and "When it Changed" will serve in large measure to further that proof—is that speculative fiction up till now has undisputedly belonged to the men, but squatter's rights to the territory simply aren't good enough anymore. Not with talents like Joanna Russ around.

And further, she looks infinitely better in a bikini than any of the editors who rejected her novel.

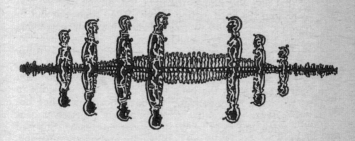

Joanna Russ

WHEN IT CHANGED

Katy drives like a maniac; we must have been doing over 120 km/hr on those turns. She's good, though, extremely good, and I've seen her take the whole car apart and put it together again in a day. My birthplace on Whileaway was largely given to farm machinery and I refused to wrestle with a five-gear shift at unholy speeds, not having been brought up to it, but even on those turns in the middle of the night, on a country road as bad as only our district can make them, Katy's driving didn't scare me. The funny thing about my wife, though: she will not handle guns. She has even gone hiking in the forests above the 48th parallel without firearms, for days at a time. And that *does* scare me.

Katy and I have three children between us, one of hers and two of mine. Yuriko, my eldest, was asleep in the back seat, dreaming twelve-year-old dreams of love and war: running away to sea, hunting in the North, dreams of strangely beautiful people in strangely beautiful places, all the wonderful guff you think up when you're turning twelve and the glands start going. Some day soon, like all of them, she will disappear for weeks on end to come back grimy and proud, having knifed her first cougar or shot her first bear, dragging some abominably dangerous dead beastie behind her, which I will never forgive for what it might have done to my daughter. Yuriko says Katy's driving puts her to sleep.

For someone who has fought three duels, I am afraid of far, far too much. I'm getting old. I told this to my wife.

"You're thirty-four," she said. Laconic to the point of silence, that one. She flipped the lights on, on the dash—three km. to go and the road getting worse all the time. Far out in the country. Electric-green trees rushed into our headlights and around the car. I reached down next to me where we bolt the carrier panel to the door and eased my rifle into my lap. Yuriko stirred in the back. My height but Katy's eyes, Katy's face. The car engine is so quiet, Katy says, that you can hear breathing in the back seat. Yuki had been alone in the car when the message came, enthusiastically decoding her dot-dashes (silly to mount a wide-frequency transceiver near an I.C. engine, but most of Whileaway is on steam). She had thrown herself out of the car, my gangly and gaudy offspring, shouting at the top of her lungs, so of course she had had to come along. We've been intellectually prepared for this ever since the Colony was founded, ever since it was abandoned, but this is different. This is awful.

"Men!" Yuki had screamed, leaping over the car door. "They've come back! Real Earth men!"

We met them in the kitchen of the farmhouse near the place where they had landed; the windows were open, the night air very mild. We had passed all sorts of transportation when we parked outside, steam tractors, trucks, an I.C. flatbed, even a bicycle. Lydia, the district biologist, had come out of her Northern taciturnity long enough to take blood and urine samples and was sitting in a corner of the kitchen shaking her head in astonishment over the results; she even forced herself (very big, very fair, very shy, always painfully blushing) to dig up the old language manuals—though I can talk the old tongues in my sleep. And do. Lydia is uneasy with us; we're Southerners and too flamboyant. I counted twenty people in that kitchen, all the brains of North Continent. Phyllis Spet, I think, had come in by glider. Yuki was the only child there.

Then I saw the four of them.

They are bigger than we are. They are bigger and broader. Two were taller than me, and I am extremely tall, 1m, 80cm in my bare feet. They are obviously of our species but *off,* indescribably off, and as my eyes could not and still cannot quite comprehend the lines of those alien bodies, I could not, then, bring myself to touch them, though the one who spoke Russian—what voices they have!—wanted to "shake hands," a custom from the past, I imagine. I can only say they were apes with human faces. He seemed to mean well, but I found myself shuddering back almost the length of the kitchen—and then I laughed apologetically—and then to set a good example *(interstellar amity,* I thought) did "shake hands" finally. A hard, hard hand. They are heavy as draft horses. Blurred, deep voices. Yuriko had sneaked in between the adults and was gazing at *the men* with her mouth open.

He turned *his* head—those words have not been in our language for six hundred years—and said, in bad Russian:

"Who's that?"

"My daughter," I said, and added (with that irrational attention to good manners we sometimes employ in moments of insanity), "My daughter, Yuriko Janetson. We use the patronymic. You would say matronymic."

He laughed, involuntarily. Yuki exclaimed, "I thought they would be good-looking!" greatly disappointed at this reception of herself. Phyllis Helgason Spet, whom someday I shall kill, gave me across the room a cold, level, venomous look, as if to say: *Watch what you say. You know what I can do.* It's true that I have little formal status, but Madam President will get herself in serious trouble with both me and her own staff if she continues to consider industrial espionage good clean fun. Wars and rumors of wars, as it says in one of our ancestors' books. I translated Yuki's words into *the man's* dog-Russian, once our *lingua franca,* and *the man* laughed again.

"Where are all your people?" he said conversationally.

I translated again and watched the faces around the room; Lydia embarrassed (as usual), Spet narrowing her eyes with some damned scheme, Katy very pale.

"This is Whileaway," I said.

He continued to look unenlightened.

"Whileaway," I said. "Do you remember? Do you have records? There was a plague on Whileaway."

He looked moderately interested. Heads turned in the back of the room, and I caught a glimpse of the local professions-parliament delegate; by morning every town meeting, every district caucus, would be in full session.

"Plague?" he said. "That's most unfortunate."

"Yes," I said. "Most unfortunate. We lost half our population in one generation."

He looked properly impressed.

"Whileaway was lucky," I said. "We had a big initial gene pool, we had been chosen for extreme intelligence, we had a high technology and a large remaining population in which every adult was two-or-three experts in one. The soil is good. The climate is blessedly easy. There are thirty millions of us now. Things are beginning to snowball in industry—do you understand?—give us seventy years and we'll have more than one real city, more than a few industrial centers, full-time professions, full-time radio operators, full-time machinists, give us seventy years and not everyone will have to spend three quarters of a lifetime on the farm." And I tried to explain how hard it is when artists can practice full-time only in old age, when there are so few, so very few who can be free, like Katy and myself. I tried also to outline our government, the two houses, the one by professions and the geographic one; I told him the district caucuses handled problems too big for the individual towns. And that population control was not a political issue, not yet, though give us time and it would be. This was a delicate point in our history; give us time. There was no need to sacrifice the quality of life for an insane rush into industrialization. Let us go our own pace. Give us time.

"Where are all the people?" said that monomaniac.

I realized then that he did not mean people, he meant *men*, and he was giving the word the meaning it had not had on Whileaway for six centuries.

"They died," I said. "Thirty generations ago."

I thought we had poleaxed him. He caught his breath. He made as if to get out of the chair he was sitting in; he put his hand to his chest; he looked around at us with the strangest blend of awe and sentimental tenderness. Then he said, solemnly and earnestly:

"A great tragedy."

I waited, not quite understanding.

"Yes," he said, catching his breath again with that queer smile, that adult-to-child smile that tells you something is being hidden and will be presently produced with cries of encouragement and joy, "a great tragedy. But it's over." And again he looked around at all of us with the strangest deference. As if we were invalids.

"You've adapted amazingly," he said.

"To what?" I said. He looked embarrassed. He looked inane. Finally he said, "Where I come from, the women don't dress so plainly."

"Like you?" I said. "Like a bride?" for the men were wearing silver from head to foot. I had never seen anything so gaudy. He made as if to answer and then apparently thought better of it; he laughed at me again. With an odd exhilaration—as if we were something childish and something wonderful, as if he were doing us an enormous favor—he took one shaky breath and said, "Well, we're here."

I looked at Spet, Spet looked at Lydia, Lydia looked at Amalia, who is the head of the local town meeting, Amalia looked at I don't know who. My throat was raw. I cannot stand local beer, which the farmers swill as if their stomachs had iridium linings, but I took it anyway, from Amalia (it was her bicycle we had seen outside as we parked), and swallowed it all. This was going to take a long time. I said, "Yes, here you are," and smiled (feeling like a fool), and wondered seriously if male Earth people's minds worked so very differently from female Earth people's minds, but that couldn't be so or the race would have died out long ago. The radio network had got the news around-planet by now and we had another Russian speaker, flown in from Varna; I decided to cut out when *the man* passed around pictures of his wife, who looked like the priestess of some arcane cult. He proposed to question Yuki, so I barreled her into a back room in spite of her furious protests, and went out on the front porch. As I left, Lydia was explaining the difference between parthenogenesis (which is so easy that anyone can practice it) and what we do, which is the merging of ova. That is why Katy's baby looks like me. Lydia went on to the Ansky Process and Katy Ansky, our one full-polymath genius and the great-great-I don't know how many times great-grandmother of my own Katharina.

A dot-dash transmitter in one of the outbuildings chattered faintly to itself: operators flirting and passing jokes down the line.

There was a man on the porch. The other tall man. I watched him for a few minutes—I can move very quietly when I want to—and when I allowed him to see me, he stopped talking into the little machine hung around his neck.

Then he said calmly, in excellent Russian, "Did you know that sexual equality has been re-established on Earth?"

"You're the real one," I said, "aren't you? The other one's for show." It was a great relief to get things cleared up. He nodded affably.

"As a people, we are not very bright," he said. "There's been too much genetic damage in the last few centuries. Radiation. Drugs. We can use Whileaway's genes, Janet." Strangers do not call strangers by the first name.

"You can have cells enough to drown in," I said. "Breed your own."

He smiled. "That's not the way we want to do it." Behind him I saw Katy come into the square of light that was the screened-in door. He went on, low and urbane, not mocking me, I think, but with the self-confidence of someone who has always had money and strength to spare, who doesn't know what it is to be second-class or provincial. Which is very odd, because the day before, I would have said that was an exact description of me.

"I'm talking to you, Janet," he said, "because I suspect you have more popular influence than anyone else here. You know as well as I do that parthenogenetic culture has all sorts of inherent defects, and we do not—if we can help it— mean to use you for anything of the sort. Pardon me; I should not have said 'use.' But surely you can see that this kind of society is unnatural."

"Humanity is unnatural," said Katy. She had my rifle under her left arm. The top of that silky head does not quite come up to my collar-bone, but she is as tough as steel; he began to move, again with that queer smiling deference (which his fellow had showed to me but he had not) and the gun slid into Katy's grip as if she had shot with it all her life.

"I agree," said the man. "Humanity is unnatural. I should know. I have metal in my teeth and metal pins here." He touched his shoulder. "Seals are harem animals," he added, "and so are men; apes are promiscuous and so are men; doves are monogamous and so are men; there are even celibate men and homosexual men. There are homosexual cows, I believe. But Whileaway is still missing something." He gave a dry chuckle. I will give him the credit of believing that it had something to do with nerves.

"I miss nothing," said Katy, "except that life isn't endless."

"You are—?" said the man, nodding from me to her.

"Wives," said Katy. "We're married." Again the dry chuckle.

"A good economic arrangement," he said, "for working

and taking care of the children. And as good an arrangement as any for randomizing heredity, if your reproduction is made to follow the same pattern. But think, Katharina Michaelason, if there isn't something better that you might secure for your daughters. I believe in instincts, even in Man, and I can't think that the two of you—a machinist, are you? and I gather you are some sort of chief of police—don't feel somehow what even you must miss. You know it intellectually, of course. There is only half a species here. Men must come back to Whileaway."

Katy said nothing.

"I should think, Katharina Michaelason," said the man gently, "that you, of all people, would benefit most from such a change," and he walked past Katy's rifle into the square of light coming from the door. I think it was then that he noticed my scar, which really does not show unless the light is from the side: a fine line that runs from temple to chin. Most people don't even know about it.

"Where did you get that?" he said, and I answered with an involuntary grin, "In my last duel." We stood there bristling at each other for several seconds (this is absurd but true) until he went inside and shut the screen door behind him. Katy said in a brittle voice, "You damned fool, don't you know when we've been insulted?" and swung up the rifle to shoot him through the screen, but I got to her before she could fire and knocked the rifle out of aim; it burned a hole through the porch floor. Katy was shaking. She kept whispering over and over, "That's why I never touched it, because I knew I'd kill someone, I knew I'd kill someone." The first man—the one I'd spoken with first—was still talking inside the house, something about the grand movement to re-colonize and rediscover all that Earth had lost. He stressed the advantages to Whileaway: trade, exchange of ideas, education. He too said that sexual equality had been re-established on Earth.

Katy was right, of course; we should have burned them down where they stood. Men are coming to Whileaway. When one culture has the big guns and the other has none, there is a certain predictability about the outcome. Maybe men would have come eventually in any case. I like to think that a hundred years from now my great-grandchildren could have stood them off or fought them to a standstill, but even that's no odds; I will remember all my life those four people I first met who were muscled like bulls and who made me— if only for a moment—feel small. A neurotic reaction, Katy says. I remember everything that happened that night; I remember Yuki's excitement in the car, I remember Katy's sobbing when we got home as if her heart would break, I remember her lovemaking, a little peremptory as always, but wonderfully soothing and comforting. I remember prowling restlessly around the house after Katy fell asleep with one bare arm flung into a patch of light from the hall. The muscles of her forearms are like metal bars from all that driving and testing of her machines. Sometimes I dream about Katy's arms. I remember wandering into the nursery and picking up my wife's baby, dozing for a while with the poignant, amazing warmth of an infant in my lap, and finally returning to the kitchen to find Yuriko fixing herself a late snack. My daughter eats like a Great Dane.

"Yuki," I said, "do you think you could fall in love with a man?" and she whooped derisively. "With a ten-foot toad!" said my tactful child.

But men are coming to Whileaway. Lately I sit up nights and worry about the men who will come to this planet, about my two daughters and Betta Katharinason, about what will happen to Katy, to me, to my life. Our ancestors' journals are one long cry of pain and I suppose I ought to be glad now but one can't throw away six centuries, or even (as I have lately discovered) thirty-four years. Sometimes I laugh at the question of those four men hedged about all evening and never quite dared to ask, looking at the lot of us, hicks in overalls, farmers in canvas pants and plain shirts: *Which of you plays the role of the man?* As if we had to produce a carbon copy of their mistakes! I doubt very much that sexual equality has been re-established on Earth. I do not like to think of myself mocked, of Katy deferred to as if she were weak, of Yuki made to feel unimportant or silly, of my other children cheated of their full humanity or turned into strangers. And I'm afraid that my own achievements will dwindle from what they were—or what I thought they were—to the not-very-interesting curiosa of the human race, the oddities you read about in the back of the book, things to laugh at sometimes because they are so exotic, quaint but not impressive, charming but not useful. I find this more painful than I can say. You will agree that for a woman who has fought three duels, all of them kills, indulging in such fears is ludicrous. But what's around the corner now is a duel so big that I don't think I have the guts for it; in Faust's words: *Verweile doch, du bist so schoen!* Keep it as it is. Don't change.

Sometimes at night I remember the original name of this planet, changed by the first generation of our ancestors, those curious women for whom, I suppose, the real name was too painful a reminder after the men died. I find it amusing, in a grim way, to see it all so completely turned around. This too shall pass. All good things must come to an end.

Take my life but don't take away the meaning of my life. *For-A-While*.

Afterword:

I find it hard to say anything about this story. The first few paragraphs were dictated to me in a thoughtful, reasonable, whispering tone I had never heard before; and once the Daemon had vanished—they always do—I had to finish the thing by myself and in a voice not my own.

The premise of the story needs either a book or silence. I'll try to compromise. It seems to me (in the words of the narrator) that sexual equality has not yet been established on Earth and that (in the words of GBS) the only argument that can be made against it is that it has never been tried. I have read SF stories about manless worlds before; they are either full of busty girls in wisps of chiffon who slink about writhing with lust (Keith Laumer wrote a charming, funny one called "The War with the Yukks"), or the women have set up a static, beelike society in imitation of some presumed primitive matriarchy. These stories are written by men. Why women who have been alone for generations should "instinctively" turn their sexual desires toward persons of whom they have only intellectual knowledge, or why female people are presumed to have an innate preference for Byzantine rigidity I don't know. "Progress" is one of the sacred cows of SF so perhaps the latter just goes to show that although women can run a society by themselves, *it isn't a good one*. This is flattering to men, I suppose. Of SF attempts to depict real matriarchies ("He will be my concubine for tonight," said the Empress of Zar coldly) it is better not to speak. I remember one very good post-bomb story by an English writer (another static society, with the Magna Mater literally and supernaturally in existence) but on the whole we had better just tiptoe past the subject.

In my story I have used assumptions that seem to me obviously true. One of them is the idea that almost all the characterological sex differences we take for granted are in fact learned and not innate. I do not see how anyone can walk around with both eyes open and both halves of his/her brain functioning and not realize this. Still, the mythology persists in SF, as elsewhere, that women are naturally gentler than men, that they are naturally less creative than men, or less intelligent, or shrewder, or more cowardly, or more dependent, or more self-centered, or more self-sacrificing, or more materialistic, or shyer, or God knows what, whatever is most convenient at the moment. True, you can make people into anything. There are matrons of fifty so domesticated that any venture away from home is a continual flutter: where's the No Smoking sign, is it on, how do I fasten my seat belt, oh dear can you see the stewardess, she's serving the men first, they always do, isn't it awful. And what's so fascinating about all this was that the strong, competent "male" to whom such a lady in distress turned for help recently was Carol Emshwiller. Wowie, zowie, Mr. Wizard! This flutteriness is not "femininity" (something men are always so anxious women will lose) but pathology.

It's men who get rapturous and yeasty about the wonderful mystery of Woman, lovely Woman (this is getting difficult to write as I keep imagining my reader to be the George-Georgina of the old circuses: half-bearded, half-permanentwaved). There are few women who go around actually feeling: Oh, what a fascinating feminine mystery am I. This makes it clear enough, I think, which sex (in general) has the higher prestige, the more freedom, the more education, the more money, in Sartre's sense which is subject and which is object. Every role in life has its advantages and disadvantages, of course; a fiery feminist student here at Cornell recently told an audience that a man who acquires a wife acquires a "lifelong slave" (fierce look) while the audience justifiably giggled and I wondered how I'd ever been inveigled into speaking on a program with such a lackwit. I also believe, like the villain of my story, that human beings are born with instincts (though fuzzy ones) and that being physically weaker than men and having babies makes a difference. But it makes less and less of a difference now.

Also, the patriarchal society must have considerable survival value. I suspect that it is actually more stable (and more rigid) than the primeval matriarchal societies hypothesized by some anthropologists. I wish somebody knew. To take only one topic: it seems clear that if there is to be a sexual double standard, it must be the one we know and not the opposite; male potency is too biologically precious to repress. A society that made its well-bred men impotent, as Victorian ladies were made frigid, would rapidly become an unpeopled society. Such things ought to be speculated about.

Meanwhile, my story. It did not come from this lecture, of course, but vice versa. I had read a very fine SF novel, Ursula Le Guin's *The Left Hand of Darkness,* in which all the characters are humanoid hermaphrodites, and was wondering at the obduracy of the English language, in which everybody is "he" or "she" and "it" is reserved for typewriters. But how can one call a hermaphrodite "he," as Miss Le Guin does? I tried (in my head) changing all the masculine pronouns to feminine ones, and marveled at the difference. And then I wondered why Miss Le Guin's native "hero" is male in *every* important sexual encounter of his life except that with the human man in the book. Weeks later the Daemon suddenly whispered, "Katy drives like a maniac," and I found myself on Whileaway, on a country road at night. I might add (for the benefit of both the bearded and unbearded sides of the reader's cerebrum) that I never write to shock. I consider that as immoral as writing to please. Katharina and Janet are respectable, decent, even conventional people, and if they shock *you*, just think what a copy of *Playboy* or *Cosmopolitan* would do to *them*. Resentment of the opposite sex (*Cosmo* is worse) is something they have yet to learn, thank God.

Which is why I visit Whileaway—although I do not live there because there are no men there. And if you wonder about my sincerity in saying *that*, George-Georgina, I must just give you up as hopeless.

Introduction to

THE BIG SPACE FUCK:

If *The New York Times Magazine* of 24 January 1971 is to be believed, this will be the last new piece of fiction you will ever read by Kurt Vonnegut, Jr.

The article said, in part, "Vonnegut says repeatedly that he is through writing novels; I took it at first as a protective remark, but then began to believe it . . ."

"After *Slaughterhouse-Five*, Vonnegut began work on a novel called *Breakfast of Champions*, about a world in which everyone but a single man, the narrator, is a robot. He gave it up, however, and it remains unfinished. I asked him why, and he said, 'Because it was a piece of—.'"

I think the word for which the *Times* writer was groping, was shit. That's s-h-i-t, entered in *The Random House Dictionary of the English Language* (Random House, New York, 1966), as follows: *n., v.,* **shit, shit-ting,** *interj. Slang* (*vulgar*). —*n.* 1. feces. 2. an act of defecation. 3. pretense, exaggeration, lies, or nonsense.

Always glad to help the *Times* through these ticklish matters.

Which language discussion points up Mr. Vonnegut's selection of title for this story. It is his own, of course, and retained faithfully from the original ms., on view at the Editor's Literary Museum daily between the hours of 12 noon and five p.m., admission thrupence. As this is the first time (to my knowledge) (I'm sure Andy Offutt or Dick Geis or Brian Kirby will correct me if I'm wrong) the word fuck has been used in a title, it becomes something of a minor literary landmark; and since the number of critics and librarians who are impressed by Names and will be drawn to this anthology because Kurt is herein will be balanced by the numbers of provincial mommies and gunshy librarians who will ban the book from their kiddies' eyes, it should be commented upon. Syntax. Blues.

Sum of comment: nice title.

Onward.

Kurt Vonnegut was born on November 11th, 1922, in Indianapolis. His first novel, *Player Piano,* was published in 1952, and I never cared for it very much, not even in its original paperback incarnation from Bantam, in 1954, as *Utopia 14.* But Kurt forgives me that.

You notice I call him Kurt, not "Mr. Vonnegut" or even the semidistant "Kurt Vonnegut." Apart from my need of sick ego to name-drop, I am *entitled* to call him by his first name. You see, Kurt and I belong to the same *karass.* Now, before I *prove* that statement, for those of you just rescued from Mohole shafts and unaware of who Vonnegut is, what he's written, and what it is a *karass,* these quotes—in explanation of the term—from *Cat's Cradle:*

(Vonnegut sets forth the religion known as Bokononism, codified by the calypso singer and philosopher Bokonon, from the Republic of San Lorenzo.)

"We Bokononists believe that humanity is organized into teams, teams that do God's Will without ever discovering what they are doing. Such a team is called a *karass* by Bokonon, and the instrument, the *kan-kan,* that brought me into my own particular *karass* was the book I never finished, the book to be called *The Day the World Ended.*" (Chapter 1)

" 'If you find your life tangled up with somebody else's life for no very logical reasons,' writes Bokonon, 'that person may be a member of your *karass.*'

"At another point in *The Books of Bokonon* he tells us, 'Man created the checkerboard; God created the *karass.*' By that he means that a *karass* ignores national, institutional, occupational, familial, and class boundaries.

"It is as free-form as an amoeba." (Chapter 2)

"Nowhere does Bokonon warn against a person's trying to discover the limits of his *karass* and the nature of the work God Almighty has had it do. Bokonon simply observes that such investigations are bound to be incomplete." (Chapter 3)

"Which brings me to the Bokononist concept of a *wampeter.*

"A *wampeter* is the pivot of a *karass.* No *karass* is without a *wampeter,* Bokonon tells us, just as no wheel is without a hub.

"Anything can be a *wampeter:* a tree, a rock, an animal, an idea, a book, a melody, the Holy Grail. Whatever it is, the members of its *karass* revolve about it in the majestic chaos of a spiral nebula. The orbits of a *karass* about their common *wampeter* are spiritual orbits, naturally. . . . At any given time a *karass* actually has two *wampeters*—one waxing in importance, one waning." (Chapter 24)

"—my seatmates were Horlick Minton, the new American

Ambassador to the Republic of San Lorenzo, and his wife, Claire. They were white-haired, gentle, and frail. . . .

"They were lovebirds. They entertained each other endlessly with little gifts: sights worth seeing out the plane window, amusing or instructive bits from things they read, random recollections of times gone by. They were, I think, a flawless example of what Bokonon calls a *duprass*, which is a *karass* composed of only two persons.

"'A true *duprass*,' Bokonon tell us, 'can't be invaded, not even by children born of such a union.'" (Chapter 41)

"Crosby asked me what my name was and what my business was. I told him, and his wife Hazel recognized my name as an Indiana name. She was from Indiana, too.

"'My God,' she said, 'are you a *Hoosier?*' . . .

"Hazel's obsession with Hoosiers around the world was a textbook example of a false *karass*, a seeming team that was meaningless in terms of the way God gets things done, a textbook example of what Bokonon calls a *granfalloon*. Other examples of *granfalloons* are the Communist party, the Daughters of the American Revolution, the General Electric Company, the International Order of Odd Fellows—and any nation, anytime, anywhere." (Chapter 42)

Essentially, that's all you need to know about what a *karass* is; and for those millions of delighted readers on college campuses, in rural ivory towers, in sunny sitting rooms, on streetcars, who've read *Cat's Cradle* and know it for the contemporary classic it has become, who may wonder why I have gone on at such length to explicate the obvious, well, let's say I did it for the three or four poor souls who have not yet found the joys of Vonnegut for themselves. And as a lead-in to a letter I have before me, dated 16 March 1963, sent from Scudder's Lane in West Barnstable, Massachusetts, from Kurt, to me, explaining why it is I presume to call him Kurt. It reads, in part, as follows:

"Dear Harlan:

"Yes, I realized before you did that you were a member of my *karass*—not the one I own, the one I belong to. I don't own or manage one."

It went on with a great deal of personal stuff we had between us, and at that point we'd never met.

How it was I came to know I was in Kurt's *karass* was in 1959, when Knox Burger, then-editor of Gold Medal Books, asked me my opinion of the stories of a certain Kurt Vonnegut, Jr., who had had a few pieces here and there in sf magazines. I had read *The Sirens of Titan*, which Dell had brought out as an original in 1959, and I remembered from 1954 a story in *Galaxy* called "Tomorrow and Tomorrow and Tomorrow" which I thought was the very best Malthusian pastiche I'd ever read. I told Knox Vonnegut was sensational, and wanted to know why he'd asked. He said he was considering putting together a collection of Kurt's short stories, even though *Player Piano* and *The Sirens of Titan* hadn't been such hot sellers. It was a brave thing to do: short story collections are traditionally poison, particularly for paperback houses, and Gold Medal had only done one or two, each time with disastrous results. But Knox was a dynamite editor, and a good friend, and he'd known Kurt since college, where Kurt was a big wheel on the campus newspaper and Knox was a wheel on the humor magazine.

So Knox asked me if I'd help package the book, and I said it would be a joy to do so, and I contacted Leo & Diane Dillon (whose artwork you'll remember from *Dangerous Visions* and the Ace Specials paperback line, not to mention the cover of almost every book I've ever written) and asked them to do the cover, and I wrote the blurbs, and Knox published it as *Canary in a Cat House* in 1961, following it in 1962 with *Mother Night* (which many hardcover houses had rejected). Why had Knox called me, rather than any one of a thousand other writers and anthologists closer to hand? Had nothing to do with my qualifications and certainly is not stated here to make me out a big *macher*. It was that I was a member of Kurt's *karass* and at that point Knox may well have been our *wampeter*.

I don't remember now where or when it was that Kurt and I finally met, but by September of 1964 we were friendly enough for me to be outraged and dismayed that the voting membership of that year's World SF Convention had awarded the Hugo for best novel to something other than *Cat's Cradle*. I sent him a telegram the essence of which, if I recall correctly, was, "The assholes suffered total brain damage and ignored the finest novel of the past twenty-five years by passing-over *Cat's Cradle*. They do themselves, sf and literature a greater disservice than they will ever know. I am ashamed for them."

His response, via Western Union, was: "Prouder of your telegram than I would be of Hugo. Much love, Kurt."

By 1967, Kurt was supposed to do the introduction to my first hardcover collection of mainstream stories, *Love Ain't Nothing But Sex Misspelled*, but something went wrong, he wasn't sent the galleys till too late, and the intro never was written. As a result—and here's *karass* again, eerily, spookily—Robert Scholes, the academician who came up with the generic title "fabulators" for a group of writers including Barthelme, Vonnegut, Barth and others, reviewed the book and gave it the most killing review I've ever had. Since Scholes is absolutely leech-like ga-ga over Vonnegut, chances are good that had Kurt been in that volume, I'd have gotten a better review. God, Bokonon and Vonnegut must have had a reason. I question not.

And most recently Kurt and I have had reason to know we're in the same *karass* because: one of my dearest lady friends, for many years, in New York, is Holly Bower. Holly grew to know Kurt from me. But never met him. Kurt moved to New York. He moved into Holly's neighborhood. Holly's friend is Jill Krementz. Holly met Kurt on the street and said hi, I'm a friend of Harlan's. They got talking. Holly introduced Jill to Kurt. Now Jill is Kurt's official photographer *(Saturday Review, Time,* etc.) and constant companion. And so it goes.

Now Kurt is ultrasuperfamous. But he's still Kurt, though shaggier. And so it goes, with our *karass:* it falls to me to publish the final short story of Kurt Vonnegut, Jr.—who wrote *Slaughterhouse-Five* and *Welcome to the Monkey House* and *God Bless You, Mr. Rosewater* and the very successful play *Happy Birthday, Wanda June.* It cannot all be merest chance. And perhaps chance will play less of a part in getting Kurt to write more stories than the *karass* of which he and I are parts. Because a talent as pure and original as Kurt Vonnegut, Jr. doesn't happen too often; to think that even a story as hilarious and incisive and deadly as this one is to be his last, is a sad-making thing.

But, as Bokonon invites us to sing:

> "Around and around and around we spin,
> "With feet of lead and wings of tin . . ."

Kurt Vonnegut, Jr.

THE BIG SPACE FUCK

In 1977 it became possible in the United States of America for a young person to sue his parents for the way he had been raised. He could take them to court and make them pay money and even serve jail terms for serious mistakes they made when he was just a helpless little kid. This was not only an effort to achieve justice but to discourage reproduction, since there wasn't anything much to eat any more. Abortions were free. In fact, any woman who volunteered for one got her choice of a bathroom scale or a table lamp.

In 1979, America staged the Big Space Fuck, which was a serious effort to make sure that human life would continue to exist somewhere in the Universe, since it certainly couldn't continue much longer on Earth. Everything had turned to shit and beer cans and old automobiles and Clorox bottles. An interesting thing happened in the Hawaiian Islands, where they had been throwing trash down extinct volcanoes for years: a couple of the volcanoes all of a sudden spit it all back up. And so on.

This was a period of great permissiveness in matters of language, so even the President was saying shit and fuck and so on, without anybody's feeling threatened or taking offense. It was perfectly OK. He called the Space Fuck a Space Fuck and so did everybody else. It was a rocket ship with eight-hundred pounds of freeze-dried jizzum in its nose. It was going to be fired at the Andromeda Galaxy, two-million light years away. The ship was named the *Arthur C. Clarke,* in honor of a famous space pioneer.

It was to be fired at midnight on the Fourth of July. At

ten o'clock that night, Dwayne Hoobler and his wife Grace
were watching the countdown on television in the living room
of their modest home in Elk Harbor, Ohio, on the shore of
what used to be Lake Erie. Lake Erie was almost solid sewage now. There were man-eating lampreys in there thirty-
eight feet long. Dwayne was a guard in the Ohio Adult Cor-
rectional Institution, which was two miles away. His hobby
was making birdhouses out of Clorox bottles. He went on
making them and hanging them around his yard, even though
there weren't any birds any more.

Dwayne and Grace marveled at a film demonstration of
how jizzum had been freeze-dried for the trip. A small
beaker of the stuff, which had been contributed by the head
of the Mathematics Department at the University of Chicago, was flash-frozen. Then it was placed under a bell jar,
and the air was exhausted from the jar. The air evanesced,
leaving a fine white powder. The powder certainly didn't look
like much, and Dwayne Hoobler said so—but there were
several hundred million sperm cells in there, in suspended animation. The original contribution, an average contribution,
had been two cubic centimeters. There was enough powder,
Dwayne estimated out loud, to clog the eye of a needle. And
eight-hundred pounds of the stuff would soon be on its way
to Andromeda.

"Fuck you, Andromeda," said Dwayne, and he wasn't
being coarse. He was echoing billboards and stickers all over
town. Other signs said, "Andromeda, We Love You," and
"Earth has the Hots for Andromeda," and so on.

There was a knock on the door, and an old friend of the
family, the County Sheriff, simultaneously let himself in.
"How are you, you old motherfucker?" said Dwayne.

"Can't complain, shitface," said the sheriff, and they joshed
back and forth like that for a while. Grace chuckled, enjoying their wit. She wouldn't have chuckled so richly, however,
if she had been a little more observant. She might have noticed that the sheriff's jocularity was very much on the surface. Underneath, he had something troubling on his mind.
She might have noticed, too, that he had legal papers in his
hand.

"Sit down, you silly old fart," said Dwayne, "and watch
Andromeda get the surprise of her life."

"The way I understand it," the sheriff replied, "I'd have to
sit there for more than two-million years. My old lady might
wonder what's become of me." He was a lot smarter than
Dwayne. He had jizzum on the *Arthur C. Clarke*, and
Dwayne didn't. You had to have an I.Q. of over 115 to have

your jizzum accepted. There were certain exceptions to this: if you were a good athlete or could play a musical instrument or paint pictures, but Dwayne didn't qualify in any of those ways, either. He had hoped that birdhouse-makers might be entitled to special consideration, but this turned out not to be the case. The Director of the New York Philharmonic, on the other hand, was entitled to contribute a whole quart, if he wanted to. He was sixty-eight years old. Dwayne was forty-two.

There was an old astronaut on the television now. He was saying that he sure wished he could go where his jizzum was going. But he would sit at home instead, with his memories and a glass of *Tang*. *Tang* used to be the official drink of the astronauts. It was a freeze-dried orangeade.

"Maybe you haven't got two million years," said Dwayne, "but you've got at least five minutes. Sit thee doon."

"What I'm here for—" said the sheriff, and he let his unhappiness show, "is something I customarily do standing up."

Dwayne and Grace were sincerely puzzled. They didn't have the least idea what was coming next. Here is what it was: the sheriff handed each one of them a subpoena, and he said, "It's my sad duty to inform you that your daughter, Wanda June, has accused you of ruining her when she was a child."

Dwayne and Grace were thunderstruck. They knew that Wanda June was twenty-one now, and entitled to sue, but they certainly hadn't expected her to do so. She was in New York City, and when they congratulated her about her birthday on the telephone, in fact, one of the things Grace said was, "Well, you can sue us now, honeybunch, if you want to." Grace was so sure she and Dwayne had been good parents that she could laugh when she went on, "If you want to, you can send your rotten old parents off to jail."

Wanda June was an only child, incidentally. She had come close to having some siblings, but Grace had had them aborted. Grace had taken three table lamps and a bathroom scale instead.

"What does she say we did wrong?" Grace asked the sheriff.

"There's a separate list of charges inside each of your subpoenas," he said. And he couldn't look his wretched old friends in the eye, so he looked at the television instead. A scientist there was explaining why Andromeda had been selected as a target. There were at least eighty-seven chronosynclastic infundibulae, time warps, between Earth and the

Andromeda Galaxy. If the *Arthur C. Clarke* passed through any one of them, the ship and its load would be multiplied a trillion times, and would appear everywhere throughout space and time.

"If there's any fecundity anywhere in the Universe," the scientist promised, "our seed will find it and bloom."

One of the most depressing things about the space program so far, of course, was that it had demonstrated that fecundity was one hell of a long way off, if anywhere. Dumb people like Dwayne and Grace, and even fairly smart people like the sheriff, had been encouraged to believe that there was hospitality out there, and that Earth was just a piece of shit to use as a launching platform.

Now Earth really was a piece of shit, and it was beginning to dawn on even dumb people that it might be the only inhabitable planet human beings would ever find.

Grace was in tears over being sued by her daughter, and the list of charges she was reading was broken into multiple images by the tears. "Oh God, oh God, oh God—" she said, "she's talking about things I forgot all about, but she never forgot a thing. She's talking about something that happened when she was only four years old."

Dwayne was reading charges against himself, so he didn't ask Grace what awful thing she was supposed to have done when Wanda June was only four, but here it was: Poor little Wanda June drew pretty pictures with a crayon all over the new living-room wallpaper to make her mother happy. Her mother blew up and spanked her instead. Since that day, Wanda June claimed, she had not been able to look at any sort of art materials without trembling like a leaf and breaking out into cold sweats. "Thus was I deprived," Wanda June's lawyer had her say, "of a brilliant and lucrative career in the arts."

Dwayne meanwhile was learning that he had ruined his daughter's opportunities for what her lawyer called an "advantageous marriage and the comfort and love therefrom." Dwayne had done this, supposedly, by being half in the bag whenever a suitor came to call. Also, he was often stripped to the waist when he answered the door, but still had on his cartridge belt and his revolver. She was even able to name a lover her father had lost for her: John L. Newcomb, who had finally married somebody else. He had a very good job now. He was in command of the security force at an arsenal out in South Dakota, where they stockpiled cholera and bubonic plague.

The sheriff had still more bad news to deliver, and he knew he would have an opportunity to deliver it soon enough. Poor Dwayne and Grace were bound to ask him, "What made her *do* this to us?" The answer to that question would be more bad news, which was that Wanda June was in jail, charged with being the head of a shoplifting ring. The only way she could avoid prison was to prove that everything she was and did was her parents' fault.

Meanwhile, Senator Flem Snopes of Mississippi, Chairman of the Senate Space Committee, had appeared on the television screen. He was very happy about the Big Space Fuck, and he said it had been what the American space program had been aiming toward all along. He was proud, he said, that the United States had seen fit to locate the biggest jizzum-freezing plant in his "l'il ol' home town," which was Mayhew.

The word "jizzum" had an interesting history, by the way. It was as old as "fuck" and "shit" and so on, but it continued to be excluded from dictionaries, long after the others were let in. This was because so many people wanted it to remain a truly magic word—the only one left.

And when the United States announced that it was going to do a truly magical thing, was going to fire sperm at the Andromeda Galaxy, the populace corrected its government. Their collective unconscious announced that it was time for the last magic word to come into the open. They insisted that *sperm* was nothing to fire at another galaxy. Only *jizzum* would do. So the Government began using that word, and it did something that had never been done before, either: it had standardized the way the word was spelled.

The man who was interviewing Senator Snopes asked him to stand up so everybody could get a good look at his codpiece, which the Senator did. Codpieces were very much in fashion, and many men were wearing codpieces in the shape of rocket ships, in honor of the Big Space Fuck. These customarily had the letters "U.S.A." embroidered on the shaft. Senator Snopes' shaft, however, bore the Stars and Bars of the Confederacy.

This led the conversation into the area of heraldry in general, and the interviewer reminded the Senator of his campaign to eliminate the bald eagle as the national bird. The Senator explained that he didn't like to have his country represented by a creature that obviously hadn't been able to cut the mustard in modern times.

Asked to name a creature that *had* been able to cut the

mustard, the Senator did better than that: he named two—the lamprey and the bloodworm. And, unbeknownst to him or to anybody, lampreys were finding the Great Lakes too vile and noxious even for *them*. While all the human beings were in their houses, watching the Big Space Fuck, lampreys were squirming out of the ooze and onto land. Some of them were nearly as long and thick as the *Arthur C. Clarke*.

And Grace Hoobler tore her wet eyes from what she had been reading, and she asked the sheriff the question he had been dreading to hear: "What made her *do* this to us?"

The sheriff told her, and then he cried out against cruel Fate, too. "This is the most horrible duty I ever had to carry out—" he said brokenly, "to deliver news this heartbreaking to friends as close as you two are—on a night that's supposed to be the most joyful night in the history of mankind."

He left sobbing, and stumbled right into the mouth of a lamprey. The lamprey ate him immediately, but not before he screamed. Dwayne and Grace Hoobler rushed outside to see what the screaming was about, and the lamprey ate them, too.

It was ironical that their television set continued to report the countdown, even though they weren't around any more to see or hear or care.

"Nine!" said a voice. And then, "Eight!" And then, "Seven!" And so on.

Afterword:

And so it goes.

Introduction to

BOUNTY:

Coups make an editor feel simply splendid. It was a coup to get a new Vonnegut story for this book. Getting a new Wyman Guin story is another (you'll read it in *The Last Dangerous Visions*). H. L. Gold, when he was editing *Galaxy*, pulled off as grand a coup as any of us: the (then) mysterious Cordwainer Smith's extravagantly memorable "Scanners Live In Vain" had appeared in 1948 in the short-lived *Fantasy Book*, and caused an immediate stir in the genre. Fred Pohl reprinted it in a Permabook paperback original in 1952, *Beyond the End of Time*. But nothing further was heard from "Smith" (a pseudonym for Dr. Paul Linebarger) until the October 1955 issue of *Galaxy* in which Gold couped everyone by presenting "The Game of Rat and Dragon," the first of many new Cordwainer Smith stories. Every other editor in the business went green with envy at Gold. Horace L. was a master at that kind of thing . . . getting great writers who'd vanished to start writing again.

Judy-Lynn Benjamin of *Galaxy* (as it is today) and I have been in competition for three years to get Catherine L. Moore to write her first new work for each of us. Thus far that charming lady has managed to elude both Judy-Lynn and myself.

Thus, following the Vonnegut coup with a Sherred coup is a soul-satisfying experience.

When Tom Sherred's exhaustively-reprinted novelette, "E for Effort," was published in *Astounding* in 1947, readers demanded *more!* But it was not till 1953 that "Cue for Quiet" and "Eye for Iniquity" appeared in *Space Science Fiction* and *Beyond, respectively*. (Both magazines are now, sadly, defunct.) And still readers clamored for more Sherred. There have been one or two others since the early Fifties, but though Ballantine issued Tom's first novel, *Alien Island*, in 1970—which I thought was poor form on Tom's part, diminishing the impact of my coup—the story you are about to read is the first new Sherred in many years, and a nice little stabber it is, too.

Because T. L. Sherred is, at core, a private sort of man, when I wrote asking for biographical material to precede his story, he sent back the following:

"My date of birth, according to my daughter who is as ornery as she is pretty, would be somewhere around 1865.

"The date of death, according to my son who does not approve of my taste in music, would be somewhere about 1932.

"I am satisfied with the accuracy of both dates."

Oh no you don't, Sherred! When I was in Detroit, I met you and found you a charming and fastidiously young-minded man, not to mention great company in Chinese restaurants on the Canadian side. So I wrote him such shifty deviousness would not suffice, and received the following:

"Shifty deviousness, indeed! A pox on thee, Ariel! I haven't been asked so many questions since I got tossed in the calabozo in several Southern states. So we'll take your questions in the order you typed them and see what comes out.

"What I do for a living? Nothing; I'm unemployed. I got laid off the same week I went to the hospital. I'll draw some disability payments as long as my doctor can legally and medically sign papers, and then I'll have to look for another job. The last one was technical writing and the one before that was engineering analysis; both were military and both jobs faded because of contract expiration. If I had my choice and were twenty years younger I'd be test pilot for a white slave crew.

"Size of family. A son who is sickeningly brilliant and is in his final year at Michigan State. A girl who is two years older—no, one—and has given me two daughters to spoil.

"I just reread your letter, and missed 'important dates of my life.' After giving the matter due thought, the day of my birth (8-27-15) comes to mind. Christmas of 1968 bears a horrid memory, also; a jolt from the Hong Kong flu came right on top of a stroke and finally convinced me that my days of boozing and alleycatting were over. I can think of no other dates that bear any significance.

"Maybe you can put this together so that I sound like a footprint on the beach of literature. I doubt it. I didn't write very much because I was too busy making a living; I only wrote when I got in a hole and needed cash. When I got the cash, of course, I had pulled out of the hole and didn't write any more and *ad infinitum*."

The only additional comments that need be entered here—there are volumes of silent comments one might make about humbleness and the way men are forced to spend their lives—are that Tom Sherred is a fine writer and it's a shame he never got in more holes, because we have little enough by his hand; and the following, dated 23 November 1969:

"Last night I was held up and slugged,
if it matters to the reader."

A final comment that will assume greater significance after you've read "Bounty," to which pleasure I now commend you.

ADDENDA:

All of the Sherred-originated material just presented came in sometime in 1968. I sat down to write Tom's introduction in June of 1971. I mailed it off with other introductions, to Doubleday's indefatigable editorix, Judith Glushanok, at three ayem of a Sunday night, air mail special delivery. Ten days later the package had not arrived in New York. I was able to reproduce most of the "lost" material from my carbons, but Tom's introduction had been made up of original pages by myself, joined with his own comments, which I had not duplicated. Panicked that the book might go to press minus one introduction, I called Tom Sherred in Detroit. I had not talked to him in quite a while, and it was good to hear his voice again. But he seemed a little lonely, and when I said he should write as much as he cared to write for the emergency introduction, to let it go at least the two pages he'd supplied previously or do as much more as he cared to do, to let his typewriter simply run away with itself, he replied, "I'm afraid those days are gone forever." We ended the conversation with Tom's promise to send what he could soonest, and I hung up with a curiously unsettled feeling.

That was on a Wednesday. On Friday Tom's biographical material came in, a revised version of what he had written two years before; and I must confess I have seldom been as touched as I was by the single page he had written. And so this addenda, and Tom's page that follows, are being added to that initial preamble.

In his covering note to me, Tom apologized for not being able to provide the two pages I'd indicated I'd wanted. His last line was, "Hell, I don't think there are two pages in *any-one's* life."

As the capsule comments that follow will testify, Tom Sherred's life puts the lie to that belief.

I only hope his penultimate paragraph is dead wrong.

"I understand I was born in 1915, just long enough to teach me that no one under 50 is to be trusted. A National Youth Administration scholarship got me into Wayne University and general economic conditions let me wander through 47 states before Alaska and Hawaii became part of the Union. I ended up in the old Packard Motor toolroom, with a belief that there were easier ways to earn a living. There were lots of ways.

"I tried technical writing (not many writers can run a planer or know what a Keller does). Then I got into the advertising business which is more profitable than anything legal. I finally decided to go straight.

"Along the way I tried science fiction which is generally fun to do and has the added advantage that, to the right editor, nothing and nowhere nohow is *verboten*. Marriage and two children set up an entirely new set of priorities, and it became difficult to think about anything besides a weekly, steady paycheck; no more, or at least very little, fiction.

"Divorce changed things around again, and I came up with *Alien Island*, a novel. It sold to Ballantine and I had the world by the tail, I thought. It took a stroke to change my mine. A mild stroke, true, but still a stroke.

"I don't suppose I will ever write again. Certainly not in the quantities or with the ease I once had, and this annoys me in a sort of abstract way. 'Bounty' is the latest, perhaps the last, I will ever write.

"I am still convinced that it was fun while it lasted."

T. L. Sherred

BOUNTY

In May, the first week there was one death. The second, there were four, the third, nineteen. The fourth week, 39 people were killed.

Most were shot by pistol, rifle, or shotgun. Four were killed with knives, two by meat cleavers, and one by a dinner fork worked methodically through the spinal cord. It was not the dinner fork that aroused comment but the evident fact that someone had finished his or her meal with its duplicate.

The Mayor said, "This has got to stop."

The Governor said, "This has got to stop."

The President, through his Secretary for Health and Welfare, said somewhat the same thing.

The Police Commissioner and Prosecuting Attorney said there would be no stone left unturned and the FBI said, regretfully, that it was a local matter.

No one ever was quite sure who was on or who was behind the Committee but the advertisement—one issue, double-page spread—had been authentic, had paid off in hard cash; within the city limits, ten thousand dollars cash for the death of anyone caught in the process of armed robbery and one hundred thousand to the estate of anyone killed while attempting to halt armed robbery.

Such an advertisement was definitely not in the public interest and every bristling aspect of the law said so. The suburban booster sheet that had originally printed the ad promised not to do it again.

But this kept on and over the weeks and a few square miles—cities are crowded in their sprawl—over two million dollars had been paid without quibble and sometimes at night secretly, because Internal Revenue considers no income tainted. Things became complex when three policemen in varying parts of the city incautiously let their off-duty holstered guns be spotted by strangers or by fellow customers in a store. Too rapidly for the innocent police to identify themselves, a swirl of action, and three men were dead—all painlessly. Further executions were eliminated by the flaunting of police badges in public, with consequent reduction of vice squad arrests.

By July, pedestrians after dark carried large flashlights and in business districts made no abrupt movements. Vigilante groups at first hired doddering men and women to hobble decoy in certain areas; later, as techniques became perfected, heavily armed and suicidal senior citizens acted as independent Q-ships and frail-looking women waited endlessly at bus stops or lugged expensive-looking packages back and forth across parking lots. Behind grocery store partitions and dry-cleaner's curtains sat or lazed volunteer part-time, full-time, and nighttime guards.

By September four hundred plus had been killed. Court dockets were clogged with scheduled homicide trials while the incidence of armed and unarmed robberies slid almost to zero. Police are forbidden to accept rewards but cabin cruisers, summer cottages, snomobiles and trips to Hawaii can be bought and paid for by midnight cash. No one dared to resist arrest.

Then the reward system was extended outstate where rates of crime had been increasing. The 11 by 14 advertising was traced to a small shop on Center Street, but the owner had moved to Winnipeg. The first to die—four men, two of them brothers—tried to hold up an outstate bank. Their dress oxfords clashed with their hunting costumes and the bank manager, one teller, and two customers were waiting.

Armed and unarmed robbery died out together with some three hundred probably-guilty persons but the Governor at last appealed for federal aid, pleading his entire legal system was breaking down. Officials of the three bordering states and Canada on the north were equally interested in his plea. Nothing was accomplished at a series of top level conferences.

In sudden succession the three bordering states had their own operating Committees, apparently unconnected with the first. Then other cities some miles away and then other states. A reliable estimate of reward money earned and paid out ran to half a billion dollars before the object was attained, as the reward system spread totally east and totally west of the Mississippi.

In New York City proper, children began to be seen playing in Central Park at dusk and even after.

With all rumors dissected, with duplicate reports discounted, and counting the death-welcoming onslaughts of unarmed applicants for free hundred-thousand-dollar survivor benefits, over the next three years the casualty list was somewhat less than automotive deaths in 1934. The fourth year there was a presidential election.

The winning candidate ran on a Law and Order platform. Two Secret Service men on inauguration day, while mingling with the gay crowd, incautiously let their .44 Magnums be seen and were dismembered quite quickly. After the first session of Congress a Federal ban on portable weapons was passed. This included weapons carried by law enforcement officers. Scotland Yard loaned fourteen quarterstaff specialists to the FBI police school and some seventeen thousand homicide cases were nolle prossed.

Montessori kindergartens expanded curricula to include judo and karate and General Motors phased out its Soapbox Derby and awarded black belts to the most worthy. *Popular Science & Mechanix Illustrated* ran a series on car-spring crossbows. Deer became an everyday sight and somewhat of a nuisance in the streets of Saginaw and Sebewaing.

At present the House Un-American Activities Committee is investigating the sky-rocketing import of Japanese chemical sets for adults.

Afterword:

Bounty could have been a much longer story, written in collaboration with Allan Hayes. Allan, a member of equally good standing in both the SFWA and the Michigan Bar and a surprisingly Puritan soul, couldn't find fast enough an eleven-foot pole not to touch it with. So it came out the way it did.

If Alfred Hitchcock were still mixed up with movies, and had a script by Robert Heinlein to start with, the opening scene might look like this:

A long shot of a woman getting off a bus at a lonely transfer point. You know it is a transfer point because a closeup shows the woman, who is at least an unattractive fifty years old in her housemaid's uniform, looking for another bus in the distance. It isn't in sight. The woman opens her purse, counts her day's wages for probably the fourth time, and looks guiltily around. She should never have exposed all that money. The villain enters, stage right; he wants the money. He gets it. He may even slap the old lady around a bit, regardless of how she cringes and pleads. Another closeup would show *him* pleading when she pulls out a .38 Banker's Special and carefully empties it into him. Then Hitchcock would show the old charwoman in the phone booth (which has until now been shown as hopelessly, tantalizingly out of reach). She dials the operator.

"Operator," she says. "Get me the police. I want to report a robbery." And she's giggling.

Introduction to

STILL-LIFE:

"Still-Life," and its thirty-two-year-old author, "K. M. O'Donnell," represent several very special things for you, me, and *Again, Dangerous Visions*. They represent, for openers, what may well be an extraordinary new kind of fiction: fantasy that becomes reality by inference. And they represent the almost pathological integrity of the typical sf writer.

On the latter matter, let me do a fast *mea culpa*. Due to the length of time it has taken to assemble this book properly—five years in the making, cast of thousands, all-singing, all-dancing, all-talking—a number of writers have suffered some rather substantial inconvenience. Dick Lupoff, whose story appears toward the end of the anthology, has suffered the most, and I'll comment on that in his introduction. But Mr. "O'Donnell" has suffered second most. He sold me this story on 11 August 1969. As I write this preface to the story, it is two full years later, and this book will be published over six months beyond *that* point. Mr. "O'Donnell" subsequently wrote a fine novel titled *Universe Day* (Avon, 1971) which I urge you to locate and purchase and read. He wanted to include "Still-Life" as a portion of that novel. Because the anthology was not yet published, and because every story in this book is an original that has never appeared *anywhere* previously, in any form, I was compelled to turn down Mr. "O'Donnell's" request that the story be included in the novel prior to publication of A,DV. I felt like a monster, but the rationale for my monstrousness was inescapable.

A,DV—like DV before it, and as TLDV will be—is a joint project. Every man and woman involved is responsible to, and benefits from, every other man and woman in the book. There will be many who will buy this book because it has a new Bradbury herein, or a new Vonnegut, or a full-length Le Guin. That clout will help Jim Hemesath and Ken McCullough and Evelyn Lief and all the other kids whose names are *not*—as yet—box office. The name "K. M. O'Donnell" is a name with which to contend. His short story, "Final War," was nominated for a Hugo and a Nebula, and has become very well known. *Universe Day* will make him many new fans. We needed the clout that could be obtained from a previously-unpublished "O'Donnell" yarn. I *had* to say no. He and I are responsible to forty-two other writers and artists, even as they and I bear that responsibility to him.

It is to his credit, and an example of the high-principled good faith that is the constant rule among sf writers (though not always the case with their publishers), that Mr. "O'Donnell" understood and revised his plans for the novel so "Still-Life" could appear here first. To our greater glory. This is hardly an unusual case, where a sf writer will suffer loss of money or prestige or convenience, rather than break his word to another member of the sf fraternity. I cannot think of many other lines of work—or other kinds of writing—where such uprightness exists. I can't think of many sf writers who'd cop to the term "gentlemen," but if states and governments acted half as well toward one another, this would be a much less twitchy world.

In case you haven't caught on, this is a deep and sincere thankyou to Mr. "O'Donnell."

And so I can stop using them, you may wonder why there are quotation marks around the name "O'Donnell." Well, it's because the name is Malzberg. Barry N. Malzberg. Under his own name he wrote *Screen* and *Oracle of the Thousand Hands* for Olympia Press in 1969, but under "K. M. O'Donnell" he has written *The Empty People* (Lancer, 1969), *Final War and Other Fantasies* (Ace, 1969) and *Dwellers of the Deep* (Ace, 1970). Why he uses the pseudonym, only Barry can say, but had *I* worked as an editor for a certain publisher whom shall go nameless whom, I'd change *my* name, too!

Mr. Malzberg was born and lives in Manhattan, married Joyce Zelnick in 1964, spawned a daughter (Stephanie Jill) in 1966, and has appeared in such prestigious collections as *Best SF: 1968, Best from the Magazine of Fantasy & Science Fiction: 18th Series, Nova 1* and most of the top periodicals in the field.

Messrs. Malzberg and O'Donnell are presently full-time freelance writers (an occupation rapidly going the way of the auk, the passenger pigeon and the Rational Man); there are a couple of writing fellowships in his background, six months in the Army, somewhat longer than that working in city and state civil services, and stints as editor of a number of magazines.

"Still-Life"—as I noted earlier—seems to me a new kind of fiction. I wish I could invent a term like "neorealistic" or "fabulorooted" the way the *literateurs* do, but frankly I cannot even devise a category. It is one of those stories that you read and find yourself thinking, "Jesus, *I* wondered about that at the time, thought what if Michael Collins up there in the Command Module got pissed off that Armstrong and Aldrin got all the glory walking on the Moon and just said, to hell with you guys, and took off." It's the kind of story that becomes reality even as it's written, that somehow carries all the past, present and future, plus future possibilities and alternate time-tracks of the *now* within itself. It is a strange and oddly unforgettable piece of fiction, and in its own special way it is the most dangerous vision in this book.

K. M. O'Donnell

STILL-LIFE

IN BED, ASLEEP, HIS WIFE

He lies curled in a foetal posture, the joint of his thumb enjambed against a cheek, his mouth open, emitting even curls of breath. In the darkness he thinks that he hears his wife cry and turns toward her, one hand reaching to curve around the fullness of her back, then he finds her flesh under his hands and grips her as if he were holding a panel of wood. "You shouldn't do that," he groans, "you shouldn't do that, you upset me, I don't know what's really going on here any more," and then runs his hands all the way down the length of her body, lingering on her buttocks, moving around the cup of her stomach and against her cunt. "Stop it," she says to him, "what are you doing? you woke me up, I was sleeping, you can't do something like this everytime you want to," but he does not hear; he is eager now, trapped in his own necessities and even though Control warned against activities of this sort during the final days before mission he finds himself quite helpless, quite stricken, as he rises above to mount her. "Oh darling, darling," he cries, "the moon, the moon," and plunges thickly into her and she says again, "what are you doing?" her voice girlish, high, suddenly pleading as if she were being pinned against a fence by a gang of strangers but it is too late, far too late for all of that and he begins to work in her, two or three limpid pulls of the prick and he is finished, the orgasm a seizure rather than a culmination and he falls from her body to his side of the bed. Even though he is still alert, he decides that it would be best for him to feign passing into an immediate sleep and so he does this, regularizing his breathing, hunching slowly into the pillow and the simulation becoming the fact he shortly does fall asleep, leaving his wife lying quietly beside him, one arm sprawled across his stomach in a gesture that might have had more meaning a few moments ago but which, for her, gives her a feeling of mute tenderness and she strokes the planes of his cheek saying "all right, all right baby, it's all right now" but for all the good this does him at the present moment she might as well be on the other side of the moon and he trapped in the damned capsule.

AT BREAKFAST, A HINT OF VIGOR

They gather for breakfast: it is the first time they have done so in several weeks because, during the last stages of the preparation, he has had to be on the grounds before 5 A.M., has, in fact, slept in the dormitory several times but now that the training has been completed and the focus of the preparations has shifted to countdown on the great ship, he is able to breakfast with his family again. He has two children, both boys, ages nine and six; his wife is 37 but does not, she is told by everyone, look it and in certain sweaters, certain postures, she can affect the breastline of a very young woman. The boys are restless and beyond discipline this morning, tossing flakes from the cereal boxes at one another, calling in high, taunting voices; it seems that they are still enmeshed in some dispute of a few days past involving, perhaps, theft. His wife attempts to calm them but he says no, no, it is perfectly all right; he does not want to interfere with routine, only try to get back into it and the younger boy says, "but how can you do *that* dad if you're going to the moon in a week?" He would answer that if he could but then the older boy says quickly, "don't be stupid, he's not going to the moon, he's just going to fly around it, they won't be ready to go to the moon for six months yet! how can you be so stupid?" and slaps the younger violently three or four times across the head. The younger begins to cry and inverts the cereal box on the table, the older starts an anticipatory cry of his own, perhaps feeling that his mother's punishment will be less if he already seems to be in agony and his wife, her face streaked and discontent, lunges from the stove to seize both of them in either hand. It seems for a moment that she is going to do a kind of qualified violence, just as she has competently done so many times when the boys have gotten out of hand, but in a quick shift of light, her face changes, becomes remote, saddens somehow and she says, "you know, I can't really take much more of this: we're supposed to be some kind of American ideal and yet I can't even control these children, I can't control anything anymore, not even *you*," and she begins to weep and he rises from the table saying "all right, everyone, look lively now, be snappy because if we have any more of this nonsense I'll sic the moon creatures on you," this has been a very effective line at some times in the past, dissolving tension toward laughter but this time they only look at him, all three, with glazed and numb expressions and feeling more than slightly ineffective, he sits again and then, unable to confront the plate of eggs, those blind eyes winking, he lunges to his feet and seizing his service cap and mumbling something about lack of consideration at the worst time he staggers from the house, reminding himself as he comes onto the street that he will definitely have to buy his wife some flowers tonight so that they can somehow smooth the damned thing over.

HIS FACE, THAT FINE PAN OF APPERCEPTION AND DOOM

His face is long and brown, slightly inverted at the eyebrows where the crest seems to go in the wrong direction; his mouth a smooth, hard line that will curve easily upward toward laughter but which fails to fold under duress. His nose seems to haunt the mouth, jutting over it at an angle a quarter of an inch short of being parodic and his cheeks are particularly fine, seeming to be etched over that intricate, delicate bone structure which is his most distinguishing characteristic. He sneezes a shade more often than the average but always has a handkerchief at ready. His eyes are deep brown and unusually penetrating. His chin is directly in proportion to his mouth. His ears contain no wax. The first time he kissed his wife, many years ago, she said that in the dimness he reminded her of a God poised to take her but they were, of course, much younger then.

IN THE CENTER, A SECURITY CHECK

Entering the huge gates he is stopped by a guard. "Don't you know what the hell is going on here, baby: let's see your identification," the guard says and then an older guard standing behind says, "you idiot, he's one of the astronauts" and the younger man pales and says "yes sir, yes sir, I'm sorry of course, go right through. I didn't recognize you for a minute; you looked like someone whose picture I saw in the newspapers and who wasn't supposed to be here," and the older guard laughs and he would laugh too but because he didn't know what the joke is (or who it is on) and is very careful not to feign involvement he only walks through with a slightly confused expression, wondering if the day can possibly be as strange in the full as it has been in the beginning.

TECHNOLOGICAL EXTRAPOLATION. EXPOSITORY DETAIL.

He is the third man on this expedition, the one who will stay in the so-called command ship while two others, younger personnel both of them, will conduct the module to within three miles of the satellite. The most recent voyage, enacted by other men, brought the module to within four miles and the next, also scheduled for others, will take it within two; in short, his is the third mission before the lunar landing itself which will probably take place somewhere around Easter Sunday if all goes well. Goes well. At first, when he learned that he would be the man to stay behind he felt vaguely shamed as if his inadequacy—or, at any rate, his lack of facility—was being exposed to the media and by implication the nation but now he feels somewhat differently: is, in fact, afflicted by fantasies about what might happen to him and the others were he to lift the ship out of orbit at a crucial time, leaving the others stranded. He knows that this falls so far from sanity that he has never discussed it with the psychiatrist nor does he really take this fantasy seriously, knowing that were he to succumb to it, his career would probably be over. Nevertheless, he knows in dreams occasionally what it would be like: an impression of wind in the windless spaces, a sensation of flight in immobility, the cries of the abandoned men like bird shrieks in his headset and as he came back all the way alone he would use the radio to tell all of them in and out of the project exactly what he thought, a performance of one to the largest audience in history. He knows that it would make his name, and there is a small chance, he sometimes admits, that he might actually do it except that he thinks he knows better, were he to attempt anything so irrational he would be cut off by mission control and would have only himself to rave to and the auditor in the silence; a portrait of madness which even a person as phlegmatic as he cannot bear. On the other hand—

HE GREETS THE OTHERS: THEY SAY GOOD MORNING

In the briefing room the two men who will accompany him are already waiting, sitting on a bench, reading newspapers. He nods hello to them and they nod back, then resume their study. He has never been to their homes nor they to his but they were picked, among other reasons, for compatibility and therefore he knows that his feelings of unease with these far younger men come only from anxiety and that once the responsibility of the voyage has settled upon them there will be no problems whatsoever.

WHILE WAITING HE HAS A RECOLLECTION

He joins them silently then: today there are to be some simulated gravity tests and also a long discussion with a board of engineers and officers who will submit to them a series of requests for special duties to be performed in orbit . . . but the schedule affecting their activities has relaxed since the emphasis has shifted toward machinery and he knows that there may very well be a fifteen or twenty minute wait before they are called. In the meantime he folds his hands and finds himself remembering the way that his wife had responded to his announcement to her, three years ago, that he had made the team after all. "What is it going to do?" she had asked, "what is it going to mean; they're going to fill you full of statistics and tell you what to say and make you do their tricks and at the end of it—if you live—they'll give you a medal and a parade and put you into public relations or something like that. It's not as if you're going up there on your own, they won't even leave you alone for an instant. I know, I know," she said and began to cry; one of her most afflicting characteristics is this tendency (to this very date) for emotional outbursts out of all relation to cause and without any apparent means of pacification; she must cry herself out at her own pace toward her own outcome. Futilely he had held her feeling, as always, clumsy and somehow irrelevant to an inner tragedy so stark and compelling that by comparison nothing which ever affected him had any dimension whatsoever . . . and finally she stopped and said, "well, I guess I'm not being very nice about this; it's a great honor of course and the boys will be very happy. At least when they get a little older and know what it means, they'll be proud of you. But I just don't see how when you come right down to it it's going to make any difference at all because it isn't anything more than them using you to put a body up there," and he had tried to explain to her then that the whole point and purpose of the selection was to arrive at the men best suited for individual initiative and intelligence and projecting a good image—because otherwise why have a selection process at all? why not merely open it to applications, first ones taken?—and that he thought she misunderstood the program. He reminded her of the many previous astronauts who had gotten into trouble in orbit in one way or the other and had had to save themselves through clear thinking and strong wills and that very likely he would have to do the same at one time or another. "Oh no you won't, it isn't anything, the challenge is only manufactured," she had said but she was calming down by then and he had been able to put the pieces of the evening together by pretending for her that he knew what she said had only come out of her fear for and dependency upon him. He had broken the news to her at a restaurant, the boys being babysat by a local college girl and when they came home they awakened them and told the news. "I guess that's good," the older had said while the youngest had stood, his whole being curled around the thumb he was sucking and only the babysitter had responded at last by saying "really? is that what happened? oh that's wonderful, I'll tell everyone, I'll tell my boyfriend," and out of gratitude he had tried to kiss her when he drove her home, feeling her slight, hard body move against his and the curve of her spine as it fit into the palm he sunk toward her back. For a moment he had passed into an illusion of copulation in this very car as being a temporary and total culmination of what had been vested in him earlier but after a moment the girl tensed and spun in his grasp, her face darkened and she said, "I don't want to do it any more: I didn't think that you people were anything like *this*," and then she left him, forcing him to drive back ruminately all the blocks of his voyage and he knew that to the extent that he had gained a space program he had lost a babysitter. (Even now, in retrospect, they seem to be very much the same thing.) When he came into the house, the youngest was screaming again and his wife was sitting in the center of this, her face perfectly white, looking at nothing, twisting her hands. At that moment he had another of those familiar emotional seizures composed of rage, pain and despair during which he asked for nothing but the strength to get past the next ten minutes after which things would be permitted to go on at whatever cost but he was afraid to look at his wife during this small, desperate prayer because he feared that if he did he would strangle her.

A BRIEF LECTURE

After some time the doors opened and the major-general who is nominally their direct supervisor comes in, nods at them and motions them to his office where they sink, three abreast, into a large couch while he sits behind the desk and to indicate that this is an informal discussion, puts up his feet. "I'm going to caution you today," he says, "on the fact that you're a credit to the nation and a spearhead or vanguard of the fight to freedom and so on but what I'm supposed to lead up to is that there is supposed to be no cursing in the capsule during the trip." On the previous expedition, of course, the junior crew member had said *fuck* while describing a landmass and although the seventeen-second transmission lag should have left ample time to kill it, the engineer on the belt somehow let it go through and there was a small flurry in the press as well as a series of larger convulsions at the television networks with a subsequent promise by the agency that such as this would never happen again.

"You do understand," the general says, "that everything you people will say is being monitored: it's being picked up, everything that comes out of that ship becomes part of the public record for all time and it's important to keep the scatology out. They can hold back transmissions, of course, but it wouldn't do us any good—would it?—to have gaps of time when they can all have the opportunity to wonder what you're saying. Now, you're grown men; all of us here are grown men and maybe we think that's asinine but it's the way it is going to be we cannot, after all, permit something like this to go on as a matter of course. One thing leads to another thing and you know what happens eventually; we'll be in the same goddamned soup that we were three years ago only worse because there are more witnesses all the time. I'm supposed to couch this in soft soap of course and tell you it's taken for granted you wouldn't want to think of cursing but I'm laying it right straight on the line. That's really all I have to say about this," and one of the younger men says "yes, I see what you're saying but how realistic is this? I mean, isn't it kind of not telling the truth, being dishonest to the experience, if we can't say it as it is?" and the general leans forward in a kindly posture and says "listen, this program is in big trouble, it's been in trouble from the start and it's only going to get worse because people, somehow, cannot believe that any of this relates to their ordinary lives if you follow what I'm saying and they don't think in terms of abstractions, only of the money so we've got to take a straight line. Cursing is just looking for public opinion trouble," and finally he wants to say something, he says, "but wouldn't that have as much to do with good public opinion as bad public opinion? I mean there must be a lot of people who wouldn't mind hearing the real stuff come over on transmission and besides that the kind of people who don't like cursing are exactly those people who don't want the program in the first place," and the general appears to think about this for a moment and then cocks his head at a different angle and says no, no, he doesn't want to hear about it any more, the point isn't relevant and in any event the word has come down from the high level, the administration itself very possibly, and so there's little that can be done other than to implement it. The astronaut finds that somehow this fills him with depression but it is not, after all, unexpected so he has nothing to say and after some time the general passes into a brief, routine reiteration of the log of the flight and then directs them toward the briefing.

SITTING HE DREAMS: DREAMING HE SITS

Listening to them, the unnecessary voices, he has a vivid apperception—one could almost call it prescience—of what his life will be like 30 or 40 years from now should he live that long; he will be sitting in a place very much like this, a small enclosure with dense walls and the murmur of men in the background and he will give his opinions on a full range of matters which he does not understand and then for a long time will listen to facts that do not interest him, simulate acts that do not involve him; a kind of perpetual dusk of the soul, in short. The fact is that he is sunken so deep into the mechanics of the program as it presently exists that he cannot conceive of a life apart from it, something which he himself does not grasp of course but which will have a large effect upon him as days go by.

The day passes quickly enough after a time and he leaves

WAS IT A SOB?

promptly at 1700 hours; at the auxiliary gate this time the
young guard knows him and salutes him with a wave but as
he walks by he hears a sound; he does not look behind him
to see what it is—he is not that kind of man—but as he
walks rapidly to his car he is not sure whether the guard was
laughing at him or whether it was merely a vagrant sneeze
that overcame the man and forced him into that high, choking
sound. He prides himself of course upon not being so reflec-
tive or sensitive that such things might bother him but finds,
driving home, that he is unable to quite dig this sound out of
his consciousness. He does not understand what the guard
was trying to express but in some way is convinced that like
it or not it all has something to do with him.

QUICK FLASHBACK: MODERN WRITING

Leaving the compound he had said goodbye to his
crewmates. "Goodbye, goodbye, goodbye," they all said to
one another and to the astronaut it is little more than a pre-
figuration of what he will hear as the lunar module separates
from command and begins its muddy descent into the lip of
that satellite. "See you again," he had said but this only after
he had long passed the guard who wept.

HE RETURNS HOME: MORE INTIMATIONS

He comes home to find himself in the middle of a serious
disruption; his older son is telling his mother "no, no, no" in
a loud voice and at least as loudly she is saying "yes, you
will!"; before he can ascertain the difficulty, there is the
sound of a slap in the hidden kitchen and then shrieks and his
wife comes into the room, her face curdled, her features re-
ceding slowly in a gelatinous mask of grief and she says, "I
simply can't stand him; I can't do a thing with him, he won't
ever apologize, he won't ever cooperate" and slightly desperate himself the astronaut strides into the kitchen and seizes
the boy (his younger is sitting in a high chair, eating pablum
and industriously working again on a thumb) and says "you
apologize to your mother or there'll be terrible trouble here,
I'll beat the living shit out of you, I mean I'm entitled to a
little peace and consideration in my own home," a little
ashamed of his language, of course, but then, after all, this is
not command post. The boy subsides from sobs to an exhaust-

ed contrition which the astronaut finds oddly moving and without a word walks in front of him to the living room, confronts his mother by the television set as some abysmal cartoon continues to squeak away and says "I apologize." "No you don't," she says, "no you don't mean a word of it so don't bother me." "Yes I do!" he says loudly and "no you don't!" she screams at him and "yes I do!" he bellows, beginning to cry and the astronaut would if he could hurl himself through the thick panes of his window for peace but there is none, none at all so he only sits down in a bewilderment of loss, not even sure what the thing is that he knows he will never have and watches the figures whirl on the screen, rockets with eyebrows blinking their way through the starry night, animals with smiles riding the rockets high into the unperceived dark.

INTO THE SEAT OF MEMORY THEY LOUNGE, WATCH THEM STAGGER

Much later, the children are in bed; his wife sits stricken on the couch, palms down and tells him that she cannot possibly think of sex this evening or even the morning for that matter, she is too tired, the tensions are too terrible. "You had it last night," she says, acknowledging that for the first time, "and maybe you forget but I don't and besides that who do you think has the real tensions here, who do you think is really putting up with the strains? not you, baby, not you; it's me." He reaches forward clumsily to touch her, to let her know somehow with his fingers that he understands and that she is still and always the girl he married but when his fingers meet her flesh it has the consistency of sweaty dough and in a vague fit of revulsion he eases her away from him, slowly, however, not to hurt her feelings. "I understand," he says, "I'm too tired myself, they take everything out of you, let me tell you the nonsense we heard today, you want to hear something, they told us that we couldn't even curse in orbit," and goes on to narrate all of that for the first time feeling that passionate and surreal horror that he knows he should have felt hours ago but now too late, too late for his wife's eyes are closing and he knows that before him—an old, cunning habit—she is miming the need for sleep so that she will not have to listen.

"Well," he says, "bed then."

IN DUE COURSE FACTORS GRIND ON TO THEIR ACCUSTOMED
CONCLUSION

He watches them in the radar, a dot and a swing, fifty
miles below, listening to the communications belt that has
now excluded him. One of the men is telling a long, labored
joke and mission control is listening with interest, encourag-
ing him from time to time to continue. The joke is aseptic
and somehow, to the astronaut, unbearable. He is not sure
what he does next. All that he knows is that the module is
streaming, streaming, all speed in the darkness, a feeling of
tearing and lurching working at him and he imagines in this
moment that he can see himself from a great distance, a
gnome in a cube speeding at enormous velocity toward the
earth. It was how he had always pictured it.

"You son of a bitch," he hears mission control say and
then the man at the desk catches his lapse and gasps, "what's
wrong? We've lost you. We have you heading earthward. Did
you," and the man's voice is a high, heavy squeak against the
walls, the dim lights, the three urinary receptacles that moved
uneasily on the floor, "did you fire the retro-rockets? *Did
you?*"

"Yes," he says, "I am coming home." He tries to shut off
mission with his left hand but the connections are one-way;
they are, as the major warned them, constantly audited and
the comptroller says, "what are you doing? What are you
doing?"

"I'm going home," he says. "I've had it. I won't take it any
more. You cannot program the universe you sons of bitches,
there are things going on outside of all of this which you cannot envision let alone understand and there must be an end
to this banality: do you understand that? It has got to end
sometime. The universe is vast, man is small, you fucking
sons of bitches."

"Crazy," he hears mission control say and he hears the
word respectfully, enjoying its admirable precision, its principle of summation, its relevance to the situation at whole. It is
the first relevant thing which mission control has ever said to
him. "Oh you sons of bitches there are stars out there you
haven't even discovered yet, how did you think you could do
this to us? We're human, human do you understand that. Oh
you bastards," the astronaut says and even for the degree of
excitement invoked his voice is remarkably level, "let me tell
you there must be an end to all of this and it better not be
equivocal."

Below him, far below him, he can hear the voices of the

two men; they are no longer telling jokes, they are no longer describing sites, they are only, in a painful high bleating not unreminiscent of the characters in the children's cartoon, begging the astronaut and mission to tell them what has happened to them. The astronaut flicks on the proper interconnection and says, "I figured I'd take a little jaunt home and then get you on the return trip. Oh you bastards. You bastards."

He will not get them, of course. The module, computer controlled, invariable to the last, will go all the way it has to go and stagger into the Pacific and there will be a recovery crew for him—because he is no less important than he ever was and maybe moreso—but for the moment, the admonition itself is enough. He folds his hands over his stomach, closes his eyes, feels the slow surge of surfaces coming over to him.

"It would all be a good deal if I could get fucked," he says then.

SEEN AS IN DISTANT FRIEZE LIKE BABYLON OR THE HOLY ROMAN EMPIRE

Much later than all of this the astronaut has a dream; he dreams that he is a character in a story which I am writing about him and as he opens his eyes to confirm what for him can only be a monumental nightmare he sees me staring at him, infinitely patient, infinitely wise, infinitely hurt, knowing everything that he will never understand and he says, closing his eyes, "but why are you writing all this? It isn't even the present let alone the future; it's the past, it all happened a long, long time ago, it's as far in the past as Babylon or the Holy Roman Empire; don't think of me, think of Centaurus, think of the moons of Ariel. I'm only a damned anachronism: why bother, why bother?" and I say to him then putting the paper away and leaning back into my own couch of torment, "of course, of course, but don't you see, you're the future too: the future and the past intermingled and there's no understanding one without the other because we are all linked together; you, history, myself, the possibility, the two of us touching for a moment in that simulation of motion known as narration and what else is there? In the long run everything is history," and the astronaut says "That's too much for me, I don't understand anything you're saying," and falls quickly back to sleep falling, to his muddled perception, into a long, long spiralling tunnel and at one end of this tunnel is the center of the earth and at the other is the moon and somewhere between the two he whirls in orbit endlessly, seeking, the fine tensors of his eyes guiding him unerringly to the other side of the planet.

Afterword:

About half of this story is mine, a fifth of it Harlan Ellison's and the remaining 30% is the property of the National Aeronautics & Space Agency which has taught us so well of the uses of metaphor in the past decade and whose future is apt to be at least as interesting as its past.

The trouble with most modern science fiction for me—make that 90% of it or upwards—is that its writers fail to tangle with the simple implications of their material and the material, due to the rather subterranean origins of the field, is often little more than the exploitation of issues for their easiest outcome. This will be changed, of course; science fiction is now unwillingly being compelled to grow up as our little lunatic asylum is being invaded by a group of attendants who, however clumsily, are taking us toward reality.

I am not really a science fiction writer—of my 20-odd published stories in the field I would say that only two or three are genre pieces and my novel, *The Empty People*, is sheer metaphor—but I know this field and care almost passionately for its possibilities and suspect that to the degree literature has any future as a viable force affecting (or afflicting) the lives of men it will be in the field of science fiction. The literary novel, with occasional brilliant one-shots excepted, is pretty well plumbed-out and category fiction, as we know it, is dying. I hope to stay around for a while to witness all the interesting things that should be happening within the next decade; with the exception of this minor morbid streak and chain-smoking, I have no bad habits.

Introduction to

STONED COUNSEL:

As with "K. M. O'Donnell," "H. H. Hollis" is a pen-name. I've had dinner with Mr. Hollis and his incredible wife, and I can state without any reservations that he is the single most enthralling dinner conversationalist I've ever encountered. He is also a man for whom one cannot feel anything less than enormous respect. I'd dwell on that, but it's so rare a feeling to get off another human being, I'd probably be talking about something too esoteric for most people to relate to. Suffice it to say, though I know Hollis's real name, substituting me for the Magdeburg hemispheres and pulling me apart by Percherons could not pry from my lips the true identity of this noble creature.

Though he has not as yet written a novel, Hollis's short stories—"The Guerilla Trees," and "Sword Game," both of which were on the final Nebula ballot for 1968, most prominent among them—have drawn to him a perceptive coterie of readers: those anxious to be in on the ground floor, so to speak, of a building talent.

The 5700 worder he here offers is a lovely thing, and quite apart from the innovativeness of its subject matter, or the lucidity with which the basic premise is pursued, I'd like to draw your attention to the writing itself. For my money, Hollis is one of the nicest stylists working in our genre today. His style is a model for those of us who rail at the limitations of linear type, who seek with almost psychopathic ferocity to expand the parameters of communication set by mere words on paper. Some of us savage the language shamefully, some of us desert and go to films or other visual media, some of us become so trickily cute we are ripe candidates for Rod McKuen's little publishing company. And men like Hollis see clearly that writing with what Flaubert called "clean hands and composure" is the answer. His stories are direct while subtle, distinct while complex, painstakingly written while seeming fluidly easy. Like the Great Art of Picasso or Astaire or George C. Scott, it all *looks* idiotically easy: until one tries it and draws grafitti or falls on one's face or makes an

315

ass of oneself in neighborhood theatrics. What I'm submitting here, is that Hollis is (if not already, then potentially) a Great Artist.

His story here will serve as my Exhibit A in contention of that position.

As for the man, what he tells us of himself reads as follows:

"H. H. Hollis is the pseudonym of an admiralty lawyer and professional Texian, with tenuous family connections to Davy Crockett and to Leander Calvin Cunningham, one of the cutthroat heroes of the Battle of San Jacinto. Born in Dallas in 1921, Hollis variously attended Ben Milam Grammar School, North Dallas High School, Southern Methodist University (B.A. Econ.) and the University of Texas (L.L.B.). Hollis was one of the rebel student leaders who struck the University of Texas for three days in 1944 as part of a series of events leading up to censure of the school by the American Association of University Professors. He is proud of being permanent possessor of a celebrated medal awarded for essays proving the South won the Civil War, of having once been described as 'the most dangerous man in Texas' by a leader of the Neanderthal Democratic Party, and of having been one of the lawyers who tried the first successful suit to desegregate public facilities in Texas. Hollis married the girl of his dreams, and although none of their friends expected the union to last six months, it has continued for twenty-five glorious, fight-filled years. Writing science fiction is Hollis' avocation. He has written, in The Forum of the Science Fiction Writers of America, that he writes science fiction for fun. He has been selling professionally since 1965, and had two stories nominated for the Nebula in 1968, neither of which bore away the palm. One of them was selected to be published in the anthology featuring the winners. Hollis is six feet tall, blue eyed, walks with a cane, and has a touch of distinguished gray at the temples. Although not as flamboyant as some practitioners of the craft, H. H. Hollis is basically as eccentric as they come."

H. H. Hollis

STONED COUNSEL

Corky Craven's cheery whistle was cut off in mid-glissando as
he turned into the ground floor entrance of the old Harris
County Courthouse. A glass door sucked shut at his back,
and the used-up air took him by the throat. When the reek of
drugs, paroxysmal sweats, and human misery surrounded
him, Craven's first impulse, as always, was to retch. His crisp
suit began to deliquesce. His fresh-scrubbed skin itched with
grime. The glorious spring morning he had left behind might
never have been.

Not for the first time, the lawyer muttered to himself,
"There must be an easier way to earn a living." With a grim-
ace, he felt the grief case in his inside jacket pocket, then
in an excess of caution pulled it out and flipped it open to be
sure it was packed with a full range of hallucinogens. Two
weeks before, he had come without scopolamine and had to
take a shot from his opponent's case. The memory shuddered
in his head. "Bastard had that scop doctored with LSD, I
know he did."

Craven stood stock still in the tiny entrance room of the
courthouse, and took six deep breaths. It was better to im-
merse oneself in the atmosphere of the old brick and granite
mausoleum at once. Otherwise the tailings of drugs and body
products in the air might produce a real nausea, and nothing
was more unprofessional than a vomiting lawyer.

In an elbow-width corridor on the second floor, Corky
found an old janitor with his head stuck inside a hearing cubicle like Pooh's in the honey jar. He joggled the old man's
elbow. "Come on, Peeping Tom, this cube's not posted for a
public hearing."

Cackling, the swamper said, "They diden finish that Dingle deevorce yestiddy. Take a peek. That Judy Halfchick, she's dreaming the balls off them two lawyers for Ole Man Dingle."

Jerking the senile delinquent's arm, Craven closed the door, but not before he had a glimpse of the three bodies twitching and shuddering, and a quick sniff of the trial mix. His nose told him they had used sodium pentothal to get under quickly, one of the mushrooms to open up the facts, and . . . something, he sniffed again, professional interest aroused . . . one of the hard drugs to keep them going.

"Hlavcek," he said. "Judith Hlavcek's her name. Counsellor Hlavcek. Clear out of here. Too much air and noise and they'll snap up to consciousness, then the sixth floor will grant a mistrial, and you'll catch hell." Smiling, he went on down the narrow hall. He heard the door behind him open, the quick tap, tap of Judith Hlavcek's heels after him. Still smiling, he thought about the trial. How well he knew what they were doing! With a three-way hookup to the fitting in each left wrist, the mark of the trial lawyer now as wigs were once, they were exchanging enough blood to assure simultaneity and homogeneity in their altered perceptions, while in the triple sensory projector they were working through the differing versions of the same story that each had absorbed from his client's brain.

Corky shook his head at Lawyer Hlavcek's clicking heels behind him. Mistrial, for sure. Lucky if she got off with a reprimand from the Grievance Committee for breaking off the hearing. All the trouble of another interview with the client. Laymen didn't stand up to drugs the way a hardened trial lawyer did, and if a client lost the thread of the story or improved it too much with his emotions, the last resort was direct ingestion of the facts. Clients had been known to refuse to give up those few cortical cells to be centrifuged and cultured and swallowed by the lawyer, and then Rule 212b came into operation. The client who refused physical preparation of the evidence to his lawyer was subject to the punitive orders of the Court all the way up to not being allowed to present his side of the case at all. Craven felt for Counsellor Hlavcek. Nothing was worse than to be wired up with a lawyer who had all the facts grooving in his cortex when you could fight back only with legal technicalities.

Judith Hlavcek's arms enwrapped him from behind. He stopped. Her soft face pressed the back of his jacket. He took a step, and she hooked one leg around his. He glanced over his shoulder, and knew, after one look at her tear-stained face, that he couldn't leave her. To hell (he thought) with the Hazlitt show cause order! He reached a hand to push open the door of a hearing cube and press the stud in the door that would light the Conference in Progress sign on the panel. He felt her hand press his shoulder. "Not that room." The voice was throaty.

Hansl Pahlevsky, his opponent in the Hazlitt case, squeezed his shoulder. Judith Hlavcek vanished, shaking her head, in the dark open door of the cubicle he had activated. Craven swallowed. "That's right. We're up on three today, aren't we? I forgot."

"Well, don't give me that 'forgot' stuff! You haven't forgot your first roach in law school."

Craven laughed. "That's right . . . we did smoke that crazy larkspur when we took legal bibliography. If it weren't for time stretching, do you suppose we could ever have got through that three-dimensional index to Corpus Juris Tertium?"

"Hell no, and I didn't get through it anyway. I got Swede Pi-Ching to drill the whole thing into my head on a packet of those morning glory seeds."

They turned into the hearing cubicle assigned to them for the Hazlitt show cause. "Why did we call him Swede? I never could figure that out."

"He claimed to have ingested the whole course of Real Property I *and* II on a hookah of Irish potato peelings. Ain't that some smoke?"

"Yeah. What ever happened to Swede?"

"He's on our embassy staff in Peking . . . trying to turn on the neo-Maoists with rectified opium. So far no smoke. Well, everybody he's allowed to meet is very conservative. They get their highs on tobacco and tea."

Craven took the grief case from his pocket and opened it on the small table provided for counsel. "Ready?"

Pahlevsky leaned his chair onto its two rear legs. "There must be a better way to work out differences than this."

"Well, we could agree to try it by using live witnesses, the way they did in the dark ages."

Pahlevsky laughed with him. "Sure, sure. Or by combat. I could take you . . . well, with a broadsword."

"Yeah, probably; but how about under demerol?"

"Oh no," Pahlevsky said. "Sleep too soon."

"All right, we've got some facts to be hallucinated. Let's go. What's your poison?"

"Let's let the Court choose."

They punched the little console on the counsel table, and got back a standby judge's rap. Taking care to do it simultaneously, each punched his preference of a trial drug into the box, and at once the binding readout came: LSD 3.

"Damn," said Craven. "That's the second time this week. I'll be psychologically addicted to this dishwater pretty soon. Trade needles, Polly?"

"Hell no," Pahlevsky replied. "Bottles."

Silently they traded vials and each loaded a tiny syringe. They made the injections at the same time, and then busied themselves with the headpiece, in which their dreams would be projected. As the walls of the cube began to swim, each opened the fitting in his left wrist and attached the tube from the blood mixer. With a sigh, Craven lay back on the couch and made himself comfortable.

At once, a parade of voluptuous beauties began to sway through his forebrain. "How can Hansl do it?" he thought. "There must be something more to his life away from the courthouse than these girls. It's always girls." As his mild disapproval turned the colors of the girls muddy, Pahlevsky's reaction made them softer, rounder, more enticing. Craven began to project thin girls at his opponent, and in a moment, Pahlevsky's girls had grown so fat and Craven's so thin that they turned into rows of binary digits. For a moment, the marching 0's and 1's were meaningless. Then Corky realized they were repeating, in Morse, "Queerqueerqueerqueerqueer . . ."

He snorted. That deep muscular contraction was reflected in the fragmentation of the digital figures, and the hemisphere of projection turned dark. It remained dark for a long time, surging with black on blackness, ignorant and irrelevant.

Craven half-dozed, turning over in the back of his head the industrial matrix of the quarrel. A poisonous effluent from an automatized factory seeped into a stream. The stream was muddy, algae-grown. He contracted his cortex, and the stream became clear and sparkling. Fish leaped over its surface, and it ran faster over the clean stone bottom.

Just as it was fixing on the projector's inner surface, a great billowing cloud of dirty water engulfed him, and with a shock, he realized he was surrounded by Hansl Pahlevsky's projection of the stream. Foul, ruined, dead, the stagnant water oozed as thick as oil into his ears and mouth. Just as it was rising to his nostrils, Craven reached back into his mind for the lovely creek he had dreamed; but it wouldn't come back into being. With a shrug of his cerebrum, he gave up on the idyllic and began to modify the picture in front of him toward reality. At least the sun could be shining. At least the water needn't stink. It supported a few carp and some turtles and, there! yes, a catfish. An older turtle appeared, sunning himself on a rock. All right, not a rock. An oil drum; but that turtle was twenty years old, at least. This wasn't dead water.

A bloated alligator gar floated belly up with agonizing slowness down the stream. Corky speeded up the current, and by a supreme effort of will, simultaneously turned the gar over, sent it swimming off, and supplied a grinning youth in ragged blue jeans who threw rocks at the gar as long as it was visible.

In another instant, the child had become a textbook cretin. His lower jaw vanished. Spittle drooled from his upper lip. He opened his fly and urinated clumsily into the stinking water.

Craven left the child growing more apelike by the instant, and widened the focus of the dream. As the whole scene appeared, the source of the water's foulness came into the foreground. A leaping, bubbling stream of phenol with a steaming ribbon of spent sulphuric acid flowed out of a drain that plainly projected from a grim concrete box. There was no identification on the front of the building, but just over the drain, a flashing neon sign said, "Fairlawn Chemicals, Inc."

Craven could feel Pahlevsky twitch physically in objection to that picture. The stones began to flow and the drain became smaller. In a sort of mental judo for which he was fast gaining a reputation in the legal community, Corky let the drain shrink to the size of a garden hose, then multiplied it in the time it took a neurone to discharge. There were ten hoses draining phenol into the creek; then there were twenty. When he had a hundred pipes pouring filth into the desperate water, he blinked his eyes and spoke to Judith Hlavcek. "Just a minute longer. I've got him on the run now."

Unfortunately, she appeared almost immediately in the foreground of the projector, tossing beer cans and the garbage of a picnic into the stream.

Craven felt himself jerking and sunfishing on his couch. "Damn, damn," he thought, "you can't look off a minute." He half-sat up, felt Judith's cool fingers press him back on the couch, saw her blow a kiss from the projector, and disappear around the corner of the factory, heels twinkling and hair fluttering. He bore down on quick cuts from the stream as it had been, with birds flying and bees buzzing, to the immense drain bubbling with the grape-soda red of phenol and the stream as Pahlevsky's clients had made it, a turgid, ugly, running sore in the land, where the only buzzes were the flies and a few hardy mosquitoes.

Although the picture wavered and shook, it held; held; held. Exultation surged in Craven, and with that momentary relaxing, there suddenly appeared a noxious herd of little people, throwing excrement and garbage into the water. For a moment, he was bemused, then he had to laugh. Catching, with devilish wit, the attitudes and mannerisms of Craven's clients, Pahlevsky had reduced them in size to fit his opinion of their moral stature, and multiplied them into a mad band of gerbils, tearing and tossing newspaper until the pond beside which they were running had been turned into a sodden, pulpy marsh. Upstream, the drain flowed water as clear as gin, sparkling and plopping into the mess Craven's clients had created.

But the picture had the fragility of satire. It wavered and shattered as the two lawyers laughed. Craven's chuckles continued to distort the projection even as he pushed it back to his stated position. He dreamingly laid on the color of the effluent as he solidified Pahlevsky's factory and its fetid drain. For a moment, he enlarged the focus, so a mile or more of the stream could be seen, because he had a subtle feeling of wrongness just out of his vision.

Sure enough, when Craven lengthened the focus, it became apparent that Pahlevsky had been at work on the peripheral aspects of the picture. The stream was not moving, and from the slope of the land, it was clear that it had never been a free flowing creek. The water was stagnant, and the effluent from the works disappeared silently into an already dead stream that hardly moved. Downriver, the really nasty character of the open sewer was reinforced by a row of privies that hung at crazy angles over the water. Craven's chief client, an expression of contentment on his face, was just emerging from an unpainted outhouse, zipping up his pants.

Corky shifted the view up so the grade of the hill showed that the flatness through which Pahlevsky looped the creek was an illusion, that there was really a fall sufficient to make the stream flow gently, and as the brow of the hill appeared, the home of Craven's client came in view. It was a magnificent mansion, in the new concrete castle style so favored by Houston architects, and had obviously cost a hundred and fifty thousand dollars. Since this projection was Craven's reprise of a factual news photograph, the house had the grainy, dot-by-dot look of a halftone; but its size and ostentation made the rickety outhouse a transparent fraud, and it vanished, along with its neighbors.

They were replaced by a smudged plumbing diagram. Pahlevsky brought up the engineer's identification number in the lower right-hand corner, and Corky saw they were looking at the actual map of the sewers adjacent to the polluted stream. Arrows of light began to dart in and out of the diagram, pointing leaks, surface traps, inefficient sewage treatment plants, and other points from which flowage of pollutants into the stream occurred.

Despite every effort of will Craven could make, his own map of the same section of the city's sewerage instantly flashed over Pahlevsky's. There was a ninety percent congruence between the two, and the projector screen flashed gold as an overlay of transparent letters from the computer monitoring the trial read out, "Stipulated." It was the first break in the surge of contention and assertion, and from that moment on would be a steady buoy around which the dreams of counsel, swirl how they might, must still flow.

Craven's back arched in a reflex he could not control, as he fought to wrest the projection back to the chemical plant. He rolled onto his side, drew up his knees and wrapped his arms around them, assuming the posture in which, from childhood, he had experienced the most vivid dreams in his real life. Pouring with sweat, he felt his eyeballs flicking back and forth and knew his brain was gathering itself for a powerful move in the legal struggle.

Another minute passed before his rapid eye movement became effective, and then he irresistibly peeled back the stone wall of the plant, accomplishing by imaginative force what he had been denied in pretrial preparation, a view of the actual workings of the inside. The ruling of the ancillary judge before whom the motion had been heard was that the plant contained trade secrets, unpatentable but valuable, which could not be revealed by inspection without working a damage on the chemical company greater than the inconvenience of hampering Craven's trial preparation.

After that motion had been acted upon, Craven had managed to locate a still operator discharged two years before by Pahlevsky's corporation, who disgorged a good deal of information. Since he was not a party to the suit, however, Corky had to take it all in verbally. A witness could not be submitted to the drugs without his consent, and the operator had been a Jehovah's Witness, with all that sect's ineradicable bias against drugs and mind alteration.

Necessarily, then, the projection Craven could achieve of the internal structure of the plant was gray, black in some areas where information was void, distorted, and shot with the wavering light of incompletion. He was still able to zero in on the massive exchanger which completed the essential operation of the plant and flowed off phenol as a by-product. From the point at which this occurred, Corky projected a simple drain without even a trap for tools and solid waste, and with its outflow directly above the surface of the stream. At that point, real information took over, and the knife edge clarity of the projection made Craven feel that he could afford to gamble on sucking new information out of Pahlevsky's mind. Eyes zipping from one side of his closed lids to the other, Craven froze the picture of the emerging drain and made the cortical squeeze that called forth the corresponding picture from Pahlevsky's brain. Even as the golden glow faded, leaving the overprint, "Stipulated," visible, Craven convulsed himself, feeling the net of his whole nervous system contract around the mental suction with which he reached for Pahlevsky's picture of the inside of the plant. With wrenching suddenness, it flowed onto the screen.

The lawyer realized the proportions he had projected were wrong, because his informant had not told him of a great, hulking complex of instrumentation and piping which occupied fully one third of the floor space. He writhed in a sine wave which terminated in a frightening click at the lumbosacral junction of his spine, absorbing the mass of stills and connections to make the pictures congruent, and was rewarded with a flash of gold and the stipulation overprint that meant he could move on to try to extract agreement from Pahlevsky on the nature of the operation.

The mind bruises and strains of making the three congruences caused both the lawyers to lie inert on their couches, flaccid puddles of flesh, while their brains drew on the web of nerves and its meaty envelope for the energy with which to go on. Inside the projector, Pahlevsky appeared, crouched on his knees, eyes covered with his hands. It was the only respite from the drugdreams: refusal to see.

For a little while, the projector flowed with neutral colors, clouds, and undifferentiated flashes from random energy accumulations along the two neuronic nets. In a slow, rhythmic repetition of patterns of energy flashes, Judith Hlavcek's face took shape, lips in Cupid's bow, eyes full forward and wide, just the way she always looked before a kiss.

Craven felt her hand on his chest, her other hand raising the hood part way. She bent gently close to him. "Polly's on his ass. Leave him snoring for a minute. You need a breather yourself."

She sat on her heels beside his couch, massaging his

cheeks. They were suffused with blood, as always when the brain was sucking every resource of the body into the dream struggle. "Listen, I'm moving Sunday, remember? Can you borrow that pickup and be there by seven? I'll give you breakfast."

With the one eye still under the hood, he saw himself sliding from a double bed into a snug bedroom where Judy, diaphanously clad, beckoned in the doorway with a skillet holding two perfectly fried eggs. "All right. I can't talk now. We're right at the major node of this hearing. I'll win it or lose it in the next dream."

Smiling, he slid back under the headset and began modifying the neurone flashes into a Morse "V" . . . "Victory, Victory, Victory," he flashed, and then suddenly brought himself up into view, right hand raised with two fingers in the Peace sign. His reply was a Peter Max colored representation of the chemical plant, somehow wearing Hansl Pahlevsky's face and body attitude. From every orifice of the factory-Pahlevsky incense poured, and the lawyer unzipped his chest to reveal a shining stainless steel precipitation tower and a circle of stainless tanks. It became clear that the tower was integral to the production process and the tanks were storing an effluent which had been made marginally profitable by increasing the volume of operations. A schematic diagram imposed itself, and it was apparent that the water used in the process was mostly recycled. What little waste there was ran off from a small drain which was enlarged so Craven could see the monitoring gauges that tested it. The water was certainly not crystal clear, but neither did it smoke and steam like Saruman's sewer.

Corky produced an overlay, "When?"

Suddenly he heard the music which Pahlevsky was quietly piping in behind this idyllic scene. It was the old prophetic song, "In the Year 2525." Craven's repulsion at this effectively indefinite postponement of antipollution equipment was so total that he actually spoke, and earned a reprimand from the judge upstairs, which slowly silhouetted itself in the projector. " 'Shit no!' is not a legal objection. Objections must be projected, not spoken."

He nearly sat up, but another gross breach of courtroom etiquette after the first might prejudice his clients completely out of the case. With an effort, he lay rigidly outspread on his couch and projected the current year's anthem, "Now! Wow! The Word Is Now!" Corky did not subscribe to the religious attitude embodied in the song, but the lyric fitted his legal position.

He could hear Pahlevsky squirming on the other couch, and there erupted on the projector's curved inner face a mad collage of the great and near-great figures of American Industrial History. Their boots crunched forests, their mouths engulfed rivers, and their nostrils drank the air in storm-sized masses; but on their shoulders and backs rose a dizzying, growing pyramid of consumers, from whose throats burst a paean of praise. Every second a vote was conducted on the life of a valley, the color of a river, or the smell of somebody's air, and production always won. Somehow, though the face of the land changed, the growing hordes following after the industrialists were accommodated. The glow that surrounded all this grew ever brighter, and out in front strode Uncle Sam, his snowy whiskers spread to the breeze, a smile of common sense and compassion illuminating his apple cheeks and twinkling eyes.

Craven contented himself with one comment. In the upper left corner of the picture he brought up Chairman Pao, not quite concealing a smile with his hand as he contemplated America burying itself in its own garbage. By a convulsive contraction of his neural net, Corky cleared the projector and wiped its color to a neutral gray. Carefully, but powerfully, he called up the congruences already of record. He had to admit the public sewer leakage, but it was minimal beside the consequences of the untrapped, unfiltered drain running the effluent from the complex of stills and cracking towers which Craven had pried out of Pahlevsky's brain. Relentlessly, he bore down on that total picture, calling up portions of it to repeat for emphasis, until Pahlevsky resignedly began to overprint, "So? So? So? So?"

Craven left the projector dripping with phenol and began to gather a picture of an undefiled stream, neither poisoned nor heated beyond the tolerance of fish, when he saw Pahlevsky erecting a projection of a plant improved by way of a large settling pond next to it. The effluent was flowing into the sludge pit, and the water which trickled through a small spillway into the natural stream was almost clear. Question marks hovered in a ribbon over the picture.

Brutally, Craven toppled a child into the settling pond. Even as its screams gurgled away, a high plank fence went up, painted so as to make it a work of art. Without hesitation, Corky sent resolute neighborhood children swarming over the fence and into the pool. Some staggered out blinded, some floated mutely on the surface, some were only scarred and frightened, but none climbed whole back over the fence. With sickening rapidity, the attorney played the record of an actual occurrence the year before, when a child had slid into the water a few meters downstream from the offensive drain. The little girl's accusing face filled the screen, filth streaming from her hair, one eye gleaming white with its destroyed sight.

Pahlevsky failed to overcome that image with the stacks of greenbacks he piled up to indicate the amount the company had paid, for Craven spread the picture in time to show that the money had been ordered to be paid only after a bitter trial . . . and a query to the computer upstairs indicated that the half-blinded child's case was still on appeal.

Now the lawyer gathered himself for a major clash. Deep in his central nervous system, primitive responses came slowly to the boil. On the projector screen, he played a diversion, the last annual meeting of the Sierra Club in Houston, at which a venerable white-haired conservationist talked with affection of that portion of the Big Thicket which had been saved from destruction. At one point in his speech, the old man lowered a screen and turning back to the auditorium, called for, "The first slide, please."

With total concentration, Craven projected on that screen a report he knew existed, but to which he had been denied access. It was a one-page outline of a low-profit marketing plan for the liquid effluent from the plant. The key, he knew, was that a plastics plant ten blocks away could utilize, almost unconverted, what Pahlevsky's people were throwing away. A pipeline would be needed for the most economical transportation of the material, and some filtering would have to be done before the slurry went into the line. The typewritten lines flowed and jumped in half-guessed projection.

Pahlevsky resisted with desperate concentration. Repeatedly a gray cloak blurred the report, skeleton-printing it with the cabalistic words, "Management Decision." Sometimes it read, "Management Responsibility."

Craven understood the point. Adding an automatic takeoff cycle to a production plan doesn't mean that it becomes economically functional. Somebody has to worry about it, somebody has to market the product, somebody has to collect for its sales, and somebody has to explain to stockholders why it doesn't fit the overall graph of their corporation's profits. But the cost of doing something right is never a legal defense to the necessity of doing it, unless the cost is economically destructive . . . and not then, if society wills that it be done. Craven kept the clamp on, and was rewarded at last with the emerging picture of the actual report which he was pulling, molecule by molecule, out of the RNA banks of Pahlevsky's brain.

There was a blinding flash of white, and when Craven could see again, Pahlevsky lay before him, naked, legs spread, scrotum open to a kick. The lawyer reeled; he was facing the classic posture of defenselessness. As the wolf defeated exposes his throat to trigger the act of mercy from a stronger wolf, Pahlevsky was exposing himself to the most punishing blow a man can absorb. He had stripped the last facade of mere objective reality from the trial, and flung on the screen the psychological crux at which the two attorneys had arrived. Craven, as a man, could not deliver the kick . . . not knowingly; but to be a professional means to do things no layman can. Craven blinked his eyes and popped his cerebral hemispheres. When he looked again, instead of Hansl Pahlevsky, Judith Hlavcek lay in the same posture. From her, it did not invite a kick.

Stumbling in the effort to peel off his jockey shorts, Craven flung himself on the woman. He was rewarded with a long scream of agony from Pahlevsky, and a great golden flash which printed on the report in see-through letters, "Defendant will install filters and organize transport, making the best contract it can with Nallard Plastics or other buyer of its effluent. After today, defendant's drain is not to be used for any runoff more polluted than rainwater. Counsel will present appropriate order."

Jerking the hood from his head, Craven sat up. With trembling hands, he unscrewed the blood mixer from his wrist fitting. Still groggy with effort, he stumbled to the toilet and basin in the corner. After relieving himself, he splashed water on his face. As usual, both shoes had been kicked off in the course of the hearing. Every stitch of his clothing was soaked with a sour sweat. The last person he wanted to face was Judith Hlavcek when she came in the door. "Don't, don't," he said, as her arms slid around him. "You don't know." He suddenly remembered the ghastly maneuver at the end of the trial, and stiffened.

"I know. I know. Whatever it is, I know it. Don't worry, funny man." She kissed his ear and slid out the door as Pahlevsky staggered off the couch, hand over mouth.

After throwing up, Pahlevsky accepted a wetted towel from Craven, and said, "You won. You draw the order." He lurched to his feet and picked up his grief case from the counsel table. "Next week we're in that three-cornered fight with Charley Kroger. Back to back?"

"Damn right. You hold him and I'll hit him."

"We'll tear both his arms off. So long." Pahlevsky dragged his soggy neckcloth into a presentable knot and went out the door of the hearing cube.

The victorious lawyer lingered for a moment, casting his mind back with mingled shame and pleasure to the memory of Judith Hlavcek on the ground. With a start, he realized that Pahlevsky had projected himself on a bed of oyster shells. Craven shuddered at the thought of the sharp shells digging into Judy's back, put his hat on his head, and went out in the hall.

Judith Hlavcek was passing by. Her face gave him a smile that managed to be both inviting and defiant. "Counsellor," he said. "How do. Who you been clawing up?"

"Just a routine bucket of blood today. And you?" She twisted her beads.

"Hansl Pahlevsky and I had it. Real rugged little dreamer, that one."

"You won. I can tell. You always talk sweet about lawyers you've defeated."

He stood stock still. She had observed him closely enough to read factual truth from his verbal smokescreens! "Oh—oh yes. Justice triumphed."

They smiled together at the old chestnut. He grimaced with effort, swallowed, and said, "I like you in that suit."

"Thank you." She looked at him with a level stare. Obviously, she was replying to the idea, rather than the statement, for her costume was just another version of the working clothes she wore every day. Serviceability, rather than looks, is required of trial lawyers' clothes. "Will I see you tomorrow, or do you have a day off?"

"Oh, no rest for the weary. I'll be here . . . see you then."

"See you."

He took the elevator to the clerk's floor to dictate the order in Hazlitt. When Craven left the front door of the old courthouse, passing by the bible open in its glass-topped stele, he saw her at the corner, under the live-oak trees. Prudently, as becomes a counsellor at law, she held a folded newspaper above her head to foil the pigeons who were settling to roost in the branches. In the mellow afternoon light, the skin of her buttocks rolled and tumbled under the glistening column of her back.

With sudden resolve, Corky cried, "Hey Jude! Wait up!" Hat straight on his head, shoes in his left hand, clothes draped over his right arm, he began to run after her.

Afterword:

A story has an independent life of its own, like a statue or a painting. It may "mean" something different, something more or less than its writer intended or expected. That is why I do not explain my stories. If they are ambiguous or polemic, that may or may not be what I had in mind. I keep all the drafts, and if it ever really becomes important (an event I find both amusing and impossible to conceive), someone can squeeze a Ph.D. dissertation out of the contradictory versions the stories went through on their way to sale. Writing is a craft to me, and craftsmen customarily enjoy what they do. I don't suffer when I write. Producing briefs and pleadings, of which I have written ten billion words, give or take a million, has freed me of inhibitions. I know perfectly well that if an idea exists, it can be expressed.

I am deeply interested in the drug culture: not just marijuana smokers, acid droppers and speed freaks, but what might be called the emancipated middle class, who save up their highs and lows by using meprobomates, bromides, nonnarcotic sleeping tablets, and even aspirin (in sufficient quantities, a pretty good tranquilizer) only to find that they can't recover the euphoria on weekends or on vacations, neither with psychic energizers nor with alcohol. Alcohol was the forbidden goody of my generation, and I have mystical feelings about the stuff. I don't see much evidence that other drugs are any more *finally* liberating than Scotch, Tequila, or Sneaky Pete, a party punch we used to make at the U of T by soaking orange peels and raisins in grain alcohol for two days before the festivities; but nothing can pervade our general culture with fear and longing as drugs do today without having something to teach us. I'm not through writing about either drugs or the law.

Introduction to

MONITORED DREAMS AND STRATEGIC CREMATIONS:

Rules have been broken for Bernard Wolfe, and frankly, screw the rules. Talk about coups! Can you dig that this book contains twenty-four thousand, eight hundred words of brand-new, never-before-published, never-seen-by-the-eyes-of-mortal-men fiction by Bernard Wolfe, one of the incredible legends-in-his-own-time of Our Times? Can you perceive the magic of that? If you can't, cup your hand around your ear and listen to the West, and you'll hear me going hallooooo among the Sequoias.

I wanted Wolfe in *Dangerous Visions* and it just didn't work out. But when I knew there would be a second volume, I assaulted his privacy and badgered and cajoled, and stole these two remarkable stories—"The Bisquit Position" and "The Girl With Rapid Eye-Movements"—away from *Playboy* and other flush periodicals that pay Wolfe three grand per story, and they are here because they were so ordained for publication by a Gracious God who takes time off from being (as Mark Twain called him) "a malign thug" once in a million years.

Bernard Wolfe edged briefly into the sf field back in 1951 with his *Galaxy* novelette, "Self Portrait," and with rare good sense (like Vonnegut, years later) scampered for dear life and a reputation in "the Mainstream."

Yet despite Bernie's fleetness of foot, the rapid eye-movements of perceptive readers caught the slamming of the door and, having been dazzled by "Self Portrait," they began asking, "Who the hell was *that?*" They found out in 1952 when Bernie's first novel, *Limbo,* was published by Random House; and for the first time insular fans who had had to put up with dilettantes like Herman Wouk sliding into the genre to proffer insipid semi-sf works like *The Lomokome Papers,* had a mainstreamer they could revere. Preceding by almost twenty years "straight writers" like Hersey, Drury, Ira Levin, Fowles, Knebel, Burdick, Henry Sutton, Michael Crichton and a host of others who've found riches in the sf/fantasy idiom, Bernard Wolfe had written a stunning, long novel of a future society in purest sf terms, so filled with original ideas and the wonders of extrapolation that not even the most snobbish sf fan could put it down.

They did not know that six years earlier, in 1946, Bernard Wolfe had done a brilliant "autobiography" with jazz great Mezz Mezzrow, called *Really the Blues*. Nor did they suspect that in the years to come he would write the definitive novel about Broadway after dark, *The Late Risers*, or a stylistically fresh and intellectually demanding novel about the assassination of Trotsky in Mexico, *The Great Prince Died*, or that he would become one of the finest practitioners of the long short story with his collections *Come On Out, Daddy* and *Move Up, Dress Up, Drink Up, Burn Up*. All they knew was that he had written one novel and one novelette in their little arena, and he was sensational.

In point of fact, the things science fiction fans never knew about Bernard Wolfe would fill several volumes, considerably more interesting than many of sf novels. Of all the wild and memorable human beings who've written sf, Bernard Wolfe is surely one of the most incredible. Every writer worth his pencil case can slap on the dust wrapper of a book that he's been "a short order cook, cab driver, tuna fisherman, day laborer, amateur photographer, horse trainer, dynamometer operator" or any one of a thousand other nitwit jobs that indicate the writer couldn't hold a position very long.

But how many writers can boast that they were personal bodyguards for Leon Trotsky prior to his assassination (or prove how good they were *at* the job by the fact that it wasn't till they *left* the position that the killing took place)? How many have been Night City Editor of Paramount Newsreels? How many have been war correspondents for *Popular Science* and Fawcett Publications, specializing in technical and scientific reporting? How many have been editor of *Mechanix Illustrated*? How many have appeared in *The American Mercury, Commentary, Les Temps Modernes* (the French Existentialist journal), *Pageant, True* and, with such alarming regularity, *Playboy*? How many have worked in collaboration with Tony Curtis and Hugh Hefner on a film titled *Playboy* (and finally, after months of hasseling and *tsuriss*, thrown it up as a bad idea, conceived by madmen, programmed to self-destruct, impossible to bring to rational fruition)? How many were actually Billy Rose's ghostwriter for that famous Broadway gossip column? How many writers faced the Depression by learning to write and composing (at one point with an assist from Henry Miller) eleven pornographic novels in eleven months? How many have ever had the *San Francisco Chroni-*

cle hysterically grope for a pigeonhole to their style and finally come up with, ". . . Wolfe writes in a mixture of the styles of Joyce and Runyon . . ." ?

What I'm trying to encapsulate with these mere words is the absolute, utter charismatic *hipness* of Bernie Wolfe, a man who knows more about everything there is to know about than any other writer I've ever met. What I'm trying to say is that his presence in this book elevates it x number of notches, even as his presence at a dinner party elevates the scene to the level of a special occasion.

Born in New Haven, Connecticut, Bernard Wolfe graduated from Yale in 1935 with a B.A. in Psychology and after a year in Yale's graduate school with an eye toward becoming a psychoanalyst, cut out and (not necessarily in this order) acted as liaison man between the Trotsky household and the commission set up by John Dewey and others to investigate the Moscow Trials, spent two years in the Merchant Marine, taught at Bryn Mawr, learned to play a vicious game of tennis, did some time in Cuba where he picked up a taste for thick (he says graceful), nasty-smelling (he says delicious), evil-looking (he says exquisite) cigars, which he can no longer obtain, due to the embargo. (This does not prevent him from constantly impaling his face with substitutes, equally as offensive to onlookers.)

Today he lives and works in the Santa Monica Mountains, overlooking West Hollywood. He lectures at UCLA, writes fiction (his latest project, working-titled *Go to the People,* is a 1700 page novel based on/focused on the Delano grape workers and their heroic *huelga*).

What he has to say for himself he says with uncommon cleverness in the Afterword to these two stories.

And with *two* stories in a book that was conceived to contain no more than *one* offering by any single writer, Wolfe broke the rules, and thereby allowed the rules to be broken for the *other* Wolfe (Gene, that is; sorry Thomas, sorry, Tom) and for James Sallis. But with stories as good as these, damn the rules.

For those purists who will say I've stretched the concept "dangerous visions" to include these Wolfepics, contending they aren't strictly—by the rules—sf . . . well . . .

Damn the rules, here's Bernie Wolfe!

Bernard Wolfe

MONITORED DREAMS AND
STRATEGIC CREMATIONS

1: The Bisquit Position

Napalm aside, he took to the idea of a month in California: he could rent a house. In a valley the size of Tom Thumb's nostril, east of Coldwater, close to Mulholland, he found a good enough cottage, redwood ceilings, rock-coped pool, sauna, terraced hillside. Place for the nerves to go loose. After a day of interviews and setting up sequences with the camera crew he could swim, take softening steam, get in a terrycloth robe to barbeque an aged T-bone or oversize lamb chops in the patio, on the hibachi. He was in holiday mood. It was a holiday when he could stay clear of restaurants and hotels, and nearby shooting wars.

Then this night he turned into his rippled tarmac lane to find the cul-de-sac overrun. Cars crowded the street on both sides to the turnabout. Attendants in red jackets, the usual college students, flashed up and down, playing musical chairs with the cars, musical cars. Hard-rock guitars jigged the air: the valley's bowl was a loudspeaker. Burble of energized voices.

There was one property of estate grandness around here, a gabled English Country structure seen in patches through stands of white birch, looking over lawns, balustraded walks, tennis courts. This place, no big thing by Beverly Hills standards but notable on an unshowy street, was diagonally across from Blake's; the party going on there was well-attended by somebodies. An indicative number of the cars bumper to bumper along the road were Cads, Lincolns, Rollses, Bentleys.

Taking the steps to his hillside perch, not especially interested in the thought he was entertaining about the fourth estate's dearth of estates, Blake was having nonadhesive feelings about coming home to the buzzing insides of a verdant loudspeaker. He felt invaded. But the invasion was so spilling, so area-wide, it sucked up his own house and head, recruiting him into the commotion, adding him to the guest list.

The sense of simultaneous violation and almost welcome suction got stronger when he reached the porch and found a woman sitting there in one of the wicker chairs. She was in a floor-length velvet gown of royal purple rifted up both sides to the upper thighs. Her face had a tennis pleasantness, her tall body was thin, not bony, so thin in the bone as to require only token fleshing to soften the skeleton's edges. This was his first impression, that she was fine of face, under a fat spiral of red-blond hair, over an elongated body whose memorable dimension was the vertical. The mesh-held thigh exposed in one of the gown's slits looked lank enough to be circled by two unexerting hands but worth a taking hold. Her green eyes were prowlers, dodged to both sides even as they looked with green insistence at and over you. She could not be much past 30.

"Hello, I'm trespassing," she said. Her voice, pitched low, had reverberances which lengthened the words. Was somewhat fogged aside from that.

"Long as you don't lie. I hate a trespasser who says he's a telephone lineman."

"I'll line all your phones, with zebra skin, if you let me stay a minute."

"Two, if you want." He took the other chair. "Don't you like parties?"

"Hate them. Especially ones I give. As hostess I get to feeling more the hostage. Over 200 people across the street drinking our champagne."

"You don't like people."

"I don't know what to do with just two or three. Hundreds make me a sprinter."

"There's a thing you can do with people in any numbers, say goodbye. Or don't invite them in the first place."

"My husband invites them. He's got a bigger supply of hellos than goodbyes. I mean, he's gregarious. Family joke. That's his name, Greg. Another family joke is, I call our place Greg Areas."

She was probably a little drunk, containing it with styled humor.

"Why don't you and your husband have a division of labor? He greets, you send them on their way."

"My trouble is," she said unresponsively, "I'm capable of just so many smiles per day. With a crowd, my quota of smiles gets used up the first 10 minutes, then I'm left with an unfunctional face."

"I'd say your face was functional."

"Oh, keeps teeth from hanging out, provides setting for the eyes, yes. But it's not going to smile any more tonight. Your face is very functional."

"Keeps siroccos out. My ears from merging."

"I see it on the news. You report wars from various places. Vietnam. Chasing Che in Bolivia."

"Yes, we're not short on wars."

"Those are the big parties, crowds invited, nobody sends them on their way. Last time I saw you you were covering, let's see, the Sinai campaign."

"When it wasn't covering me. That's a joke. They have sandstorms in the desert, not all of Jewish origin."

"You covering a war in Los Angeles?"

"The war against war, most of its general staff's out here. Doing a special report, documentary, on anti-Vietnam moves, on campuses especially."

"Some fight war while the rest fight wars. We can use that division of labor. I'd better be getting back to my own wars. Hear the enemy popping more champagne corks. Good documenting, Mr. Arborow. Many thanks for the privileged sanctuary of your porch."

Two days later he saw her again. Low-gearing to his driveway, he discovered her putting something in his mailbox. There was an eerily beautiful dog erupting around her feet, a female Siberian husky with medieval mummer's mask, eyes of glacial blue in the slant of the world's first dynasties, total grin.

"Hello there," the woman said. "I wasn't stealing your mail, I was adding to it." She retrieved her envelope and handed it to Blake. "It's an invitation to come over and drink some booze those people forgot to drink the other day."

The blatantly gorgeous dog kept jumping at her hands as at lovely bones, she kept saying, "Down, Bisk," and bucking the animal away.

"For somebody who doesn't like parties you give a lot," Blake said as he got out of his car.

"This isn't a party, just some people for drinks. When Greg heard who our distinguished neighbor was he said you had to come over and have a snort, down, Bisk. You may not be aware the word snort is still used in some circles, down, Bisk."

"Wives don't altogether approve of their husbands in some circles."

"In some circles wives get the feeling they're not engaged in a marriage but covering a war. When's the last time you approved of a war you covered? Not Vietnam, you never quite kept your lips from curling all the time you reported from there. Bisk, damn you, down, I said."

"Why's the dog named Bisk?"

"Short for b,i,s,q,u,i,t. You want to see something whorish and altogether delightful? Call her by name, then ask if she wants one of those things I spelled."

Blake leaned close to the dog, now sitting as on a throne, smiling as at a circus, and said, "Good girl, Bisk, want a bisquit?"

Bisk went out of her mind. Mouth exploded with sounds of highest romp. Tail beat a tattoo of paternosters on the tar, the pup form of rosary. Tongue came out to lavish love up the full length of Blake's jaw. Then she whipped over on her back and lay still, front paws bent and held together in the beg position, back legs similarly crooked but spread, face a panorama of flooded happiness. Her arctic blue eyes were full on Blake as she made deep, prolonged throat vowels of agony and expectancy into his face. Blake rubbed her teat-lined belly, her soft, soft neck, feeling the surge of urgent vowels inside.

"Isn't she the neighborhood tart, isn't she unbelievable," Lady of the Manor said.

Blake thought of the woman this way. The only other designation he could think of was, Master Greg's Mistress, Mum of Greg Areas.

"Is it the neighborhood style?" he said, stroking the fable-faced animal's tumulted chest above the spread legs.

"Oh, it's a mixed neighborhood, Mr. Arborow, some tarts, some creampuffs. Try to make it on Friday, won't you? The Gibsons will be dry and I can promise the small talk'll be practically microscopic. A war correspondent should be made aware that there are more wars to cover than are dreamed of in his network's philosophy. Come on, Bisk, quit plying your trade, we're going home."

The note said simply, *We're having some people for drinks this Friday at five. Is it possible you can come? We would be delighted. I give you my categorical guarantee that nobody will ask if you've seen any interesting wars lately. Do come.*

Blake was feeling broken into, potently sucked at. Mum of the Manse, Greg's Lady Lean, was named Mari Selander.

It was a manse, all right. Bucking for the apprentice-castle rating. Walls of the roomy vestibule and king-size salon were inundated with hunt and turf prints, engravings honoring marlin on the leap, woodcuts of the better known whaling ships, oils of Nantucket weltering under a nor'easter, antique wooden eagles in emblematic profile, crossed dueling pistols and sabers.

The men talking in corners over vermouthed Bombay gins had the wind-toned faces of sportsmen, the aroma of leather chairs and massages. Their wives, looking worked-over by expensive hands, in clothes built around their specifics, chatted about Acapulco and Mrs. Reagan's decorating tastes.

Greg Selander was doggedly, programmatically, the boy, under a crew-cut of iron filings. His halfback face was essentially what it had been in its third year at Princeton except for signs of going fluid at the jowls, the drinker's drip of flesh.

Mari Selander, again in velvet, cinched this time to a miraculous gaunting at the waist and falling inches short of the knee, again seemed somewhat vagued. Blake took the measure of those yearling legs that seemed to go on forever. He considered how they might be in full, urging use.

Greg Selander immediately had Blake in a gaming alcove, explaining that in spite of his appearance of the varsity athlete he'd played no football at Princeton, preferring squash and for a time shot-putting. He might have gone out for lacrosse but it took too much time, besides, lacrosse players had collisions and bad spills.

"Secret's out," Mari Selander came close to say. "You've let Mr. Arborow know he's in a den of nonconformists."

"I don't care what you look like, your looks can't dictate your action and direction," Greg Selander said. "That's the blight today, outer direction, government taking over your breathing and chewing."

Blake considered what a big man going in for football might have to do with excessive government, went back to Mari Selander's legs.

"Greg reads Reisman after his Dow and before his Jones," Mari Selander said. "Whatever takes dim view of the outside, he's for. Ask him why he takes a dim view of everything on the far side of his skin."

"Dark out there," Greg Selander said. "Dim's the one view you can take."

"That's where the masses are, out there somewhere," Mari Selander said. "They sense how many of your dark looks are meant for them. They don't elect dim viewers to office, as Barry found out."

"I was explaining why I never went in for body-contact sports, Mari," Greg Selander said. "Goldwater's a different subject."

"What's your objection to contact sports?" Blake said, looking at the wife's legs.

"Taking the dimmest view of the human race, you'd want as little contact with its units as possible," Mari Selander said. "That's why the right-of-rights play so much squash, put so many shots."

"Mari talks lefty to shake me up," Greg Selander said. "Likes to play devil's advocate."

"God and Barry have all the high-priced attorneys they need," Mari Selander said. "The devil could use a few more legal minds."

"It wasn't God incited the riots out to UCLA today," Greg Selander said. "Goldwater wasn't anywhere on the scene."

"It's because God wasn't on the scene, just the recruiter for Taybott Chemicals trying to recruit students to make napalm, that's why they had the riot," Mari Selander said. "The recruiter might as well have been Barry, Barry's a friend of napalm. Were you at UCLA this afternoon, Mr. Arborow?"

"Yes, with our cameramen," Blake said.

"What did you think of those kids chasing the Taybott man up on the roof and throwing stinkbombs at him?" Greg Selander said.

"My job's not to assess facts so much as get them."

"But you must have had some thoughts. Impressions, let's say."

"Well I thought the students' running was good and their aim fair, though spotty. I got the impression they're not opposed to body-contact games. If they'd gotten their hands on the man they might have welcomed the contact, and tried to widen it."

"I approve of you, I'd like to widen the contact, Mr. Arborow," Mari Selander said, linking her arm with Blake's. "How would it be if we sat?"

They took places with the other guests in the conversational arc before the vaulting fireplace. A fire big enough to roast a family of pigs whole was blooming in the baronial pit. When Greg Selander positioned himself to the left, Mari Selander made for the right, to balance on an ottoman no distance at all from Blake's knees. Greg Selander's reaction to his wife's scrupulous avoidance, as to her earlier baiting, seemed to be, as nearly as Blake could give it a name, scrupulous nonreaction.

Blake looked for a conversational move toward the husband which would be, by implication, away from the wife.

"Your theory that football players are Democrats to New Lefts," he said. "I wonder if a Harris or Gallup Poll would back you up."

"You'll remember the Kennedy gang played a lot of touch football," Mari Selander said.

"Touch isn't tackle," Blake said.

"Barry people are least of all touching," Mari Selander said. "Of course, Kennedy people can be all over you."

"I didn't put that forth as a thesis," Greg Selander said. "I was saying, because you've got the bootball build, and people expect you to play football, is no reason to do the thing, it's just a personal feeling of mine."

He helped himself to another Martini offered on a tray by a maid mostly starch. He had to be aware that the others had stopped their localized talk and were listening.

"If you don't like being manipulated, you don't let yourself be manipulated by eyes, either," he added as he sipped from his new drink and made a quick survey of the visiting eyes turned manipulative.

"Leaving aside the question of whether you can be handled, which is what manipulated means, by eyes," Mari Selander said, "can you in all honesty claim you were never the least bit manipulated by Barry's eyes, Greg?"

"By his ideas, policies, Mari. Which are against manipulation. By agencies, bureaus, eyes, all the outside structures. Well. War correspondent. You have one of the more interesting jobs, Mr. Arborow."

"Some people in my business say, see one war, you've seen them all," Blake said.

"Don't get that feeling from Hemingway," Greg Selander said. "He went to wars as though they were different."

"His last was different," Blake said. "Himself and himself the combatants. Toss-up as to who won."

"Lonely crowdsmanship," Mari Selander said. "Lonely crowdsmen read Hemingway for the drama of their plight, Reisman for the ideology. When not giving parties."

Blake felt his knees touching his hostess's with no initiative from his side. He moved them, crossed his legs.

"I spent an afternoon with Hemingway arguing this point,"

he said. "I said wars are so alike they get monotonous, so if you write a lot of books about war they can get monotonous. He said people die differently in different times and places, it was my thought they die more or less the same, from rocks, or arrows, or napalm."

"Or boredom," Mari Selander said. Her words were becoming runny, her green eyes, diffused.

"Hemingway died like his father," Blake said. "Tradition meant something to him."

"That's the point I can't buy," Greg Selander said, scrupulously to Blake. "Our boys in Vietnam don't die like Communists, it's for something positive and what's more, they know it."

"It's hard to tell from the body counts," Blake said. "Maybe I've been to too many."

"I've been in Vietnam myself," Greg Selander said. "I was there just last August, for the Defense Department, saw them in the hospitals, some dying. I can speak to a certain extent firsthand here."

"Eyes will handle before anybody speaks with a hand of any number," Mari Selander said. "Allowing for the deaf who use sign language. Many deaf and dumb speak firsthand."

"What were you doing in Vietnam?" Blake said.

"I'm in defense production, Mr. Arborow," Greg Selander said. "A-V-A Components, the letters are short for Aviation, we subcontract parts for planes and choppers, mostly military right now. I went over to help assess how the choppers are carrying out their missions. Naturally, I looked around."

"Greg reports the choppers are chopping fine," Mari Selander said. "Chopping some and burning some, with the help of napalm. Naturally, VC's burn differently from freedom fighters. Burn up, our fellows burn down."

"There are better things to joke about than napalm, Mari," Greg Selander said, with the air of pointing out a detail that might otherwise be overlooked.

Mari Selander looked lengthily at her husband. Her lips thinned, followed by her eyes. She pulled in a long, careful breath.

"Napalm's so unjocular," she said. "I was out at UCLA myself this afternoon. Probably in half the footage Mr. Arborow got. Hope they shot my good profile. I was one of the people chased the Taybott man up to the roof of Kerkhoff. Didn't throw stinkbombs but that was mainly because I didn't have any."

The guests were carefully listening, though not surprised.

Expecting rough games, they got rough games. It remained to be seen which passes would be completed, who would come out first in yards gained.

"You were going to the Balenciaga showing at I. Magnin's," Greg Selander said.

"Nobody throws stinkbombs at Magnin's," Mari Selander said.

"I won't go into the politics of it, Mari. Let's leave politics out. Let's just say, it's inconsistent to demonstrate against napalm in Paris and Rome clothes paid for by the manufacture of helicopters that deliver napalm."

"I could stop yelling my head off against napalm, you're right, Greg. Or you could stop being involved one way or another with napalm."

"I could. But you're fond of Rome and Paris clothes, if I didn't make the money to buy them you wouldn't like it. You don't approve of napalm but you're dressed with, in, and by, napalm." By way of footnotes, to record the minutiae that can get overlooked.

"And it burns," Mari Selander said.

"And it's self-applied, you dress yourself in the morning," Greg Selander said, still in the spirit of marginalia. "Mr. Arborow, wouldn't you say napalm in Vietnam's about the same situation as the bomb with Hiroshima? Saves more lives than it takes?"

"I'm told that," Blake said.

"I didn't ask what others tell you."

"It's tricky. I see the lives it takes and cripples, I don't see the ones it's said to save."

"But you allow for the possibility?"

"I listen to information officers' releases, and official briefings, and report what I hear. Along with what I see. Even when there's a gap between what's audible and what's visible. If you go along with McLuhan, the sights in our world are winning out over the sounds. That could mean we're being manipulated by eyes, our own."

"Not answering my question, Mr. Arborow."

"No, and I don't think I said it was."

"You could pass things along without necessarily believing or allowing for them yourself."

"I was more or less implying that."

"Mr. Arborow, are we using napalm to win a just war with the least human cost, or aren't we? You're a guest in my house and I'm trying to nail you down, for that I apologize, but with some matters we can drop amenities."

"As quick as we drop napalm," Mari Selander said.

"As quick as some throw stinkbombs," Greg Selander said. The guests were absorbed. You can't know in advance what plays will be tried and what the final score will be. It could be speculated that collision games were nothing new in this apprentice castle, and did not always concern politics.

"I'm a reporter," Blake said. "That means my best trained parts are my eyes. I'm paid not for the opinions in my head but the pictures on my trained, 20-20 eyes. I've got a surplus. Many pictures piled up on my trained eyes my employers don't want. An assortment of my firsthand sights they don't care to see, and have other people see. Very manipulative sights."

Blake was just now collecting another sight. The outrageously beautiful Bisk had wandered in and taken a seat alongside her mistress, all dripping grin under the hard-edged, archaic mask, ready to pull sleds for any who cared to travel out of gin disharmonies through whatever snowdrifts of rough games. Lady Lean had bent to whisper something in her ear Blake had heard, "Girl, sweet thing, want a bisquit?" The animal had collapsed insanely on the carpet, front paws urging, back paws validating, mouth at maximum curl to announce that anything offered was all right because catering love was the wide world's one stuff. Mari Selander was now leaning low over the dog, moving her incredibly elongated fingers up and down Bisk's two lines of nipples, whispering, "Oh, you tart, spread for all comers." Blake was trying not to see those furred legs abandoned to the air, Mari Selander's stalky legs exposed to the lap and flamboyantly parted too.

"You're still hinting rather than saying, Mr. Arborow," Greg Selander said.

"I'm saying, in stages. Five correspondents ducked this napalm assignment before the network brought me back from Sinai. I wanted to duck it, too. We all know we've stored up more sights than the network cares to distribute. Not opinions about napalm, sights of napalm. In action. Carrying out its missions. On bodies. Bodies shouting and running. Eighty-year-olds and two-year-olds shout and run the same. Napalm is the answer to the generation gap. I've been in helicopters 100 feet from the burning, shouting bodies. Helicopters you probably made parts for. You make good parts, bring a man with trained eyes to within 100 feet of the napalmed, after dropping the napalm. I feel how jellied petroleum works on bodies, how they crisp up, speeding back and forth, their sound effects, is a vital part of the napalm story, which my eyes are equipped to tell, no opinions, just pictures. I was on the phone for an hour after I got back from UCLA this afternoon, telling my home office I have to go back to Vietnam to get close-up footage on the burning, running, loud bodies. They don't see it. They think that to show these diminishing, toasting bodies right now would be playing into the hands of the enemy, as footage of the 70,000 bodies in Hiroshima would have in 1945. You asked for my opinion. My opinion is, I've got informative information on the subject of napalm on my eyes, and it burns, and I want to shout, and I'm being ordered to withhold this information, which is against my training. My first opinion is that this information all over my eyeballs isn't my private property. Your opinion and my opinion as to the privacy of some types of property may differ."

Bisk was still stretched out in total invitation, Mari Selander was still stroking her military columns of nipples.

"That's clear enough," Greg Selander said. "You claim you're a mindless transmitting belt, want to transmit everything unselectively. Meaning, you're with the rioters, ready to make things harder still for our boys dying overseas."

"You're a transmitting belt, you transmit helicopter parts mindlessly, unselectively."

"To save our boys, not kill them."

"You transmit slogans like a mindless belt, too."

"That's not slogan, that's fact."

"Not fact, press release. Look, if you defend your right to be an automaton, don't take a dim view of other automatons trying to do their job."

"Covers are off, Mr. Arborow. What's in sight is a man wants to give aid and comfort to his country's enemies."

Blake stood, feeling his drinks.

"Try stripping yourself," he said. "You know what might come in sight, to eyes trained by two minutes of history? One of the country's worst enemies, maybe. What aids and abets enemies like you is keeping back our rich footage on strategic cremating."

At this, Mari Selander did something peculiar. She'd been lost to the conversation, patting the dog as she went through two more Martinis. Now she jumped up to all her leggy, fragile height, long feet spread in challenge of everything and all.

"No more lies!" she said fever fast. "All automatons! So be it! Out from under the Balenciaga napalms! Everybody! I'll start!" She reached inside her dress with both hands, fumbled, brought the hands out again, each holding a rubber cup. "Cards on the table! All varieties of falsies! Strip, everybody! Out from under the covers! Automatons, right! All à la mode lies on the transmitting belt!" She tossed the rubber cups high in the air, a flower girl strewing modern formfast flowers. They were well aimed, they fell into the fireplace, into the fire big enough for pigs, and instantly were sprouting consequential blue flames. "Not a minute too soon! See! Blobs of lies on everybody! About to burn! Now who else's going to peel off his napalm!"

Greg Selander walked to her and said, "What are you suffering from, Mari? For once, can you say?"

Mari Selander said, "Body contact. From those I view dimly. Burns."

Blake set his glass down.

"You were right about one thing," he said to Greg Selander. "Not all wars are the same. Bodies can burn and run in ways I haven't seen. After this, attack your attackers, not strangers. And don't dress it up with politics. Thanks for the drinks and slogans."

The last picture on his eyes, breaking into him, pulling at him, was of Mistress Meager standing in the middle of the room, hands cradling sham-shorn breasts, legs planted wide in taunt more than invitation, and Bisk still on her back, legs still lax, staggered that when her dear one finally threw something it would not be tasty things to her.

Far from sleepy, Blake took a long drive, to Malibu and then on to Trancas. Twice he stopped at waterfront places for a drink, a third time to eat a hamburger. When he got back home it was well after midnight.

The light in the living room showed him objects on the floor that didn't belong there. A pair of flowered, belled slacks, woman's. Jacket, woman's. A blouse. A bra. Panties.

He heard a sound in the bedroom, more assault, beckoning.

He went there and flicked on the light to find Mari Selander stretched out on his bed, naked. No, not precisely stretched out, though precisely naked. When the light cracked on her hands elevated floppily to touch in the air over small, valiant breasts, legs bent as knees separated to the pelvis' limit of give. She waggled asking hands, stretched her mouth to make a dog's chugging sound.

"How's this for a body count."

"More casualties around here than meet the eye."

"Let's have a meeting of more than eyes, Mr. Arborow."

"Mine are meeting each other. You're an unexpected eagle in my bed."

"Know a better spread for it?"

"Spread any more and there'll be two of you."

"Animal kingdom's all botched. How come dogs are the ones to spread-eagle."

"How do other men's wives come to be doing it on my bed?"

"Easy, you've got a window in the back not nailed down."

It was a body not to be believed. Such a long, satiny stretch, no massy bulges but, oh, yes, slimmed shadowings, subtler concavities, the potential of a greyhound speediness, the promise of twine in the never-ending legs. Such a gangly want and over-readiness.

"You've got a husband across the street not nailed down."

"Don't you worry about husbands. Don't you worry. Nights I go for drives, Greg goes to bed. I parked the car two streets over and sneaked back on foot over the firebreak. Know something? There's a firebreak ends in your backyard. I take that to mean we can bring our bodies together for as long as we want and not worry about danger of brush fires. Fires we don't make by our own brushing. You come here and give me all the best bisquits. I've been long without."

"What gave you the idea of breaking in here?"

"I was looking at Greg after the people went home, which was fast. When he's boiling he doesn't say anything, just sits with a red face. I was looking at that fat football face and a thought came, I wanted somebody inside me but not him, never him, you, decidedly you. Not because politics makes bedfellows. Because fucking makes bedfellows. Come inside me, you."

"I don't think this will get Greg Selander out of the heli-copter business. I think, further, you don't give a shit what business he's in."

"Who wants your opinion? You're no opinion man. You're the reporter. Report to your brain what's craving all over your eyes from all over your bed. Be my lavish bisquit man."

"Your war I haven't been to before. All in it casualties and all casualties wearing the same dogtag."

"Don't analyze it, you correspondent, cover it."

Which, feeling somewhat tampered with, somewhat hauled, he did. Those endless legs closed, on him, all urge, going like the legs of the napalmed.

She left he didn't know when. He thought for one minute about her climbing back up the firebreak, sleek legs, product of some strong generational taffy pull, cracking the dead spines of chaparral, then he was in the sleep of the drugged.

When he opened his eyes it was after ten and he was in trouble. He shaved-showered fast, dressed without the morning swim, skipped breakfast except for a can of Snap-E-Tom Bloody Mary Mix for the tang of the tomato.

Backing down his drive, he heard sounds of running and barking. In a moment Mari developed from the crowded birches across the way, Bisk all over her heels. She made a comic hitchhiker's sign, he pulled over.

"Sleep all right?" she said.

"You'll have to ask somebody who was there."

"See how good I am for you? I slept, too, oh, did I. Like a sack of sawdust. That's better than a log. Logs sleep better when they're pulverized. Oh, how you pulverized me—"

"I can't discuss insomnia and the lumber industry, I'm late—"

"Where you going, Blake?"

"Mojave, up past Palmdale. They're putting on a napalm show."

"Take me with you, Blake? Please?"

"You'd throw stinkbombs."

"Won't, honest, Blake. Please. I get migraines when I'm alone all day and Greg's gone to Vandenburg Base for three days. To talk with the brass about chopper parts. The man of helicopter parts. Let me come, Blake. One more in your crew won't be noticed."

"There'll be some Taybott men."

"They won't know me or I them. Greg's kept me away from Taybott people for fear I'd break out picket signs. Take me and I'll tell you all about your non-helicopter parts."

"You won't get on a soapbox?"

"Or my high horse, or a low horse, or even Bisk. Bisk? Where are you girl?"

Bisk came prancing back from the driveway. She'd retrieved Blake's morning paper and was carrying it proudly in her grin. Mari accepted the paper from her.

"Can Bisk come, Blake? Please? She gets migraines when I leave her alone all day."

He waved them in.

They talked not at all on the San Diego Freeway cutting across San Fernando Valley. At moments Mari even read the paper. This was all right with Blake. He didn't want to hear about what was, or wasn't, between this woman and her husband. As for what might or might not be between her and himself, he didn't want to get into that, either, it would be a tiny pendant from what was, or wasn't, with the husband. As his brushes with women generally were.

On the run you ran into married women who were attracted to the image of man with itinerary, man just passing through, then felt martyred by the first signs of travel preparations.

As they cornered east out of Newhall, for Antelope Valley, Mari said from her paper, "VC's out to win with least human cost, too. Here's an item about their finishing off a village called Dakson, with flamethrowers."

"Cost accounting can't be the monopoly of one side."

"Double entry bookkeeping's the game on both sides. Listen. *The simple Montagnards of Dakson had only recently learned how to use matches, and flamethrowers were beyond their imagination. Then, in one horrifying hour, flamethrowers wielded by Communist troops wreaked death and destruction . . . 'They threw fire at us' was how survivors described the attack . . . 63 thatched-roof houses razed . . . Ashes blew across carcasses of water buffalo . . . Rows of bodies of women and children . . . Tiny brother and sister, still clinging to each other . . . bodies dragged from bunkers—*"

"You save lives any way you can. Don't read any more."

They were well into the desert when Mari left off scratching Bisk's unreservedly available neck to say thoughtfully, "They're not going to let you tell it like it is, not a chance."

"The Vietnam footage, you mean?"

"They won't let you put those shots in, will they, Blake?"

"How many close-ups of the skin and bone aftermath of Hiroshima have you seen, 23 years after?"

"If they hold you back, what'll you do?"

"Tell it as it isn't, or is only in propagandistically safe part, the bloodless, faceless, skinless part."

"That good enough?"

"No."

"Isn't there an alternative?"

"No."

"There's got to be."

"There's one, get a staff job on Hanoi Radio. I'd run into the same problems there, maybe worse. There's no place where they want the whole footage."

"Don't you want to hit somebody?"

"You did it for me. Your husband. More ways than one. I'm not sure he's the one to hit, but as long as you enjoy it."

"He's the one enjoys it, Blake. A good wife doesn't deprive her mate of his intensest pleasures."

"I thought you were enjoying yourself somewhat."

"In your bed I was."

"Long before."

"Don't make a big thing of how I took off after Greg, Blake. I was drunk, that's all."

"Think about this, drunk comes in four parts, jocose, morose, bellicose, comatose. You start on bellicose and end on bellicose. You're fixated on fight even when much less than drunk. Your private war is peculiar, each shooting the other to make him happy."

"Public wars may involve some of that altruism, too. Was I bellicose with you?"

"You're a smart enough strategist not to start offensives on two fronts at once. Remember Hitler."

"Tomorrow the world. Today there's you."

"Today there's the Taybott people, don't try to make them happy, all right?"

This was a proving ground for some types of field and air ordnance. Deep in the desert a Mekong Delta jungle hamlet had been reproduced, a cluster of huts, camouflaged underground hideouts, ammunition dumps, snipers' perches under thatched roofs and in trees. Taybott technicians and Marine Corps officers, Air Cavalry men, were on hand to explain how the insurgent's installations had to be got at, to cut their deadly fire, when our troops moved into such hostile areas.

Technicians and officers explained that no hostile personnel would be indicated here, not by mannequins, not by dummies, not by cutouts. The reason for this was, today's mission was to show things being destroyed, not, primarily, people, so our troops could move in without bitter casualties. The emphasis, for purposes of this demonstration, was on things, not people. The implications, though, had much to do with people, ours. If things designated as military targets could be knocked out, caves, dumps, perches, many American lives would be saved, Asian ones, too, in the longer view. The point was that traditional weapons were of little use against the guerrilla refuges, since they couldn't be seen and located. Therefore the invention and use of napalm. Today's show would point up how vital to our overall goal of saving lives the new anti-guerrilla weapon, napalm, was. The technicians and officers hoped Blake, as anchorman of this news team, would see the logic in this emphasis on things, with the overtone of vastly lowered casualty lists, meaning, people.

Blake said he saw the logic. He wondered, all the same, if such a show was entirely realistic without a hint, through the use of dummies, or cutouts, that a hamlet of this type was inhabited by people, noncombatants who might be in the line of fire.

The officer in charge, Colonel Halbors, said there were no villagers shown precisely because the targets of napalm missions were things, along, of course, with whatever hostile troops might be manning the things, and to show villagers would shift the emphasis from things to people. He hoped Blake appreciated the logic behind featuring the military mission and not dwelling on incidental casualties among civilians, which had been wildly exaggerated, especially by the enemy and those naive about military exigencies. This being, it should be kept in mind, war.

Blake said he appreciated it, yes. He just felt that as a reporter he ought always to be looking for the whole picture.

As he spoke he was watching Mari, who stood to one side holding Bisk tight by the leash. She was chewing on her lips, her eyes were fixed, but she kept her mouth shut.

The cameramen left for shielded blinds from which they could shoot at a variety of angles. Blake, Mari, and the rest of the crew were led to the concrete bunker a distance from the mock-up village, a structure mostly underground but with a viewing slot some two-feet wide, protected by a wide concrete overhang. Colonel Halbors came with them, to explain the operations step by step. There was the rouping of unseen helicopters from some part of the sky.

After some minutes Colonel Halbors signaled through an intercom that stage one, the approach, could start. At the same time he pressed a button on his control panel. Instantly large glare-orange arrow markers swung into sight in and around the village, pointing to the hidden installations which were the targets in this mission, rather than people.

Certain things, not people, had to be sought out and destroyed, Colonel Halbors said. Artillery and air-to-ground missiles could not do the job. The idea was to watch how napalm got in there and did the job, to save lives, as well as rout the enemy and deal him a costly blow.

The thrum from the sky had been getting louder, now three helicopters came into sight, approaching from the black, broken-spined mountains. Mari was still biting on her lips. Suddenly, she stood.

"Colonel," she said, "did you happen to read the paper today?"

"Yes, yes, I did," Colonel Halbors said, surprised. "Why do you ask?"

"Did you happen to read the item about VC's knocking

out the whole village of Dakson with flamethrowers, people along with things?"

Blake was waving to her to sit down, she remained standing.

"I did. What is your point?"

"My point is, the VC doesn't attack mock-up villages, it attacks real villages, as we do. In these attacks they don't pretend to separate people from things, they say people are things, that's what war is, and that's how we act in war too, when we go into villages not mock-up but inhabited. The VC's honest, at least, they say there are no people in war, can't be, there's only things, except a lot of them walk around on two legs—"

Colonel Halbors' face was hard. He said, "Are you trying to say we annihilate whole local populations as the enemy does, purely and simply for the sake—"

"Colonel, when you drop napalm on a whole village, and the village is full of people, not mannequins, not mock-ups—"

"Hold it right there, Miss," Colonel Halbors said in command voice. The helicopters were now circling over the village. He spoke into the intercom, saying the drop could begin, as Mari fought off Blake's efforts to get her back in her seat. "Now. Did I hear you right? You were actually saying—"

"Colonel, the survivors at Dakson said, they threw fire at us. Colonel, in the real hamlets, not pretend ones, we throw fire at them. Can you tell me how from their point of view one thrown fire is different from—"

The words were still coming from her mouth when a small, energetic body, a jackrabbit, went arcing fast across the desert on the near side of the village. Heading for the village, with mathematical, measured bounces.

At this moment Mari stopped talking and screamed. Screamed again. Shrilled, "My God! Here! Bisk! Back, Bisk!"

There was Bisk on the desert, going fast toward the village. The rabbit was streaking across the sands, Bisk was streaking after it.

Blake saw what had happened. In her outburst, Mari had been gesturing strongly at Colonel Halbors, with her hold on the leash relaxed. Bisk, seeing the rabbit, had simply pulled the loop off her fingers and dived out through the viewing slot. The leash was trailing after Bisk as she flashed along, the happy hunter.

"Happened so fast!" Mari bubbled. "She goes crazy when something on four legs moves fast! Bisk! Please! Bisk, girl!"

"Colonel," Blake said fast, "can you possibly, is there any chance—"

"Started," Colonel Halbors said, pointing. "Can't call back what's dropping."

He was right, objects were descending from all three helicopters.

The rabbit, Bisk hot after him, was tearing around the bamboo huts, Mari, face come apart, was halfway through the bunker opening, trying to climb out. Blake took her by the hips, slender, boyish roundings, well remembered, pulled her back.

"Nothing to do," he said, holding her down on the bench. "Easy now. You'd get yourself killed and that's all."

Mari was shaking, looking around, wild-eyed.

"You couldn't give up your war," Blake said, holding her. "If there's a casualty, it'll at least have a different dogtag."

Black objects from the helicopters were dropping on things, not people. One by one, things belched up, and out, in flame.

An ammunition dump gushed flame. A sniper's platform in a tree spewed orange. A machine-gunner's blind, hidden with piled brush, erupted in an all-directional lick. Huts kept popping flashes of flame, here, there, everywhere. Bisk kept dogging the rabbit between the igniting huts, full speed.

"Bisk—you—come—back—here!" Mari screamed from the deeps of her lungs.

The rabbit shot into view around the corner of a hut, Bisk inches from his heels. At this moment the hut metamorphosed, as by the push of a button, from structure to flame, and at that moment, Bisk metamorphosed. One second, running dog, next, standing flame.

She'd skidded to a halt, frozen as in a stop-action movie. Through his binoculars Blake saw how she stood still, puzzled, how she turned to bite the attacker all over her body to find her jaws closing on flame.

She looked everywhere overhead, as at sneaky birds, as she burned. She found no explanations, the big birds in the sky only burred, in a language that to her was only loudness. Burning, she turned her eyes at last toward the bunker, to the one source of all correctives, to all impedings and harassments, Mari.

Mari moaned, pushed again toward the opening. Blake pressed hard on her shoulders.

"Don't look," he said, forcing his body in front of her to block her vision.

Bisk stood motionless, looking to Mari, a fire with four legs. Now she did the only thing she knew to do, when the ultimately wanted was not forthcoming, flopped over on her back in the bisquit position. Paws flabbed over chest, barely in touch, were burning, paws stretched wide were burning.

She begged, she burned, mouth totally open for the ultimate bisquit, a cessation of heat, of being eaten by enemy with no bulk or outlines. Eyes still looking to Mari.

"Put your mind on something else," Blake said mechanically, blocking Mari's eyes.

The choppers rattled away. It was two or three minutes before Colonel Halbors judged it safe for Blake to go out, provided he was careful. The other members of Blake's crew took Mari's arms to hold her back.

When Blake got to Bisk, the colonel right behind, the dog was still alive, still burning in places, still on her back in position of ask, still asking.

Flames flicked from her belly, forehead, one foreleg. Black smoke came from these points as from other points where the flames had subsided. Bisk was diminished. In places, instead of fur, dark smoking patches. In others, no flesh, bone bared within the charring.

All fur and flesh were gone from the soft, soft neck. Lower jaw gone, except for the armature of surprisingly frail bones.

Left eye gone. What had been eye was black hole, smoking. Above this hole, where the fuzzed brow had been, small flames fighting to live.

Bisk's right eye, intact, looked straight to Blake, with all its uncomprehending blue. Asking all the questions.

The asking front paws were charred, bones showing, flames eating vaguely, afterthoughts, about the remnants of paws. An end to heat, this haphazardly cremated animal from a vanished dynasty of the icecaps, displaced monarch of remote snowlands, was saying, as the cremation continued.

Remnant of mouth, ringed with small flames, leftover mouth was in total crazed grin to total crazed environment, which must in the end relent and produce the bisquit of bisquits, a taking back of cannibal heat. The inch by inch cremation continued.

"Need a gun," Blake said. "One around?"

Colonel Halbors shook his head. Much napalm here, no guns. "Terrible thing to happen. You'll turn this footage over, I assume."

"Network decision, I don't make policy. There's got to be a gun somewhere."

Colonel Halbors shook his head. "Would you rather I confiscated all your reels?"

"What're you afraid of?" Blake was looking everywhere. "Shots of one dog burning'll give you another Dien Bien Phu?"

"You can't leave this area with that footage, Mr. Arborow."

"All right, you get it."

The nearest hut had just caved in, its understructure was creeping with spent flame and smoking. The supports on which the hut had rested were four-by-fours, good. Blake ran over and pulled a charred beam free, a four-foot length. He ran back, holding the beam by one end.

"Couldn't even save the film. Be cool again," he said to the dog, and brought the beam down as hard as he could, on the head.

Bisk jerked, her head shook, then her good eye settled on Blake again, asking. Manipulating him full force with the eye.

"Go home to snow, Bisk. What's so worth seeing out here. You've got the whole picture."

He swung again, with all his strength.

Bisk's body shook, the eye rolled away, came back, gelled again, held steady on Blake, asking.

"Leave us to our leashes, Bisk," Blake said, and swung again.

The magnificently blue eye quivered, began to take the dim view, then dimmer, then closed altogether, and Bisk was cool again, as finally, Blake thought, with luck, with luck, we'll all, the invaded and the sucked, all bisquit wanters, be free from burning.

2: The Girl With Rapid Eye Movements

On the night of April 22, when I got back from lecturing to FANNUS (For A New Novel Undergraduate Society) on

Hemingway ("A Psycho-Statistical Survey of the Broken Bones in Papa"), my answering service gave me a cryptic message. From Kid Nemisis, pronounced Quentin. Call no matter what the hour. There was no way to call at any hour, the number he left was wrong. The harpie at the other end said in Placidyl tones that she didn't know any Quentin, and if she did she'd turn him in for what, considering he was a friend of mine, must be his main activity, child molesting. I said she had no grounds for assuming I was in a child molesting ring since the people I molested on the phone sounded 300 years old, and senile. She said she wasn't too senile to know that molestation professionals will practice on anybody when there's no child around, to keep their hand in, in what she wouldn't say, being a lady. I said if she was a lady any one of the Gabor sisters was Miss Twinkletoes, and asked if anything she kept her hand in was mentionable, a question I hinted was in order about any member of her sex, lady or not, who went to sleep before nine. She said if she could get within reaching distance of me she'd show me what she'd dearly love to put her hand in, my mouth, and rip out my filthy degenerate's tongue to use for a pincushion.

Enough of this conversation. I reproduce its high points mainly to show how frayed nerves everywhere are getting, maybe due to Vietnam. What made me boil was not the old hellhag's tone but Quentin's typical sloppiness in leaving a wrong number, urgently.

I didn't call him the next morning. I gave him until noon to feel urgent enough to call me. When my curiosity peaked and threatened to zenith, I dialed his home number. The phone rang a dozen times before he answered; his voice seemed to have its origins at the bottom of a barrel, out of a mouth brimming with molasses. More simply put, out of a mouth in a molasses barrel.

"Gordon, zow, I'm desperate for sleep. Can I ask what this is in reference to?"

"Your call last night. Its reference."

Time went by.

"You're crazy. I didn't call you."

"You mean my answering service is hallucinating?"

"They probably make up calls so you won't feel nobody cares. No kidding, they really said I called?"

"And gave the impression lives were at stake. And left a number to call back. A wrong number, as a result of which I was treated to a long string of insults from somebody I don't even know."

More time passed.

"That nibbles, Gordon. Dhzz. I remember calling Cedars of Lebanon, zhmm, yes, and the L.A. Times Information Desk, right. But you, uh, uh."

"Reconstruct the circumstances. Where were you?"

"Some friends' house off Laurel Canyon, I've told you about them, The Omen. May be pertinent that we were stoned to a tilt, the third time down, and I have the impression I still am. We were really stretched out on this grass."

"I take it you're not talking about a lawn."

"Maybe Forest Lawn. Where I believe I still am, hear embalmers coming, hypo needles jingle. Gordon, I'd be greatly in your debt, which I'd be willing to settle for money, a sizable amount, if you'd stop cross-examining me and let me get back to sleep. You get so goddamn cross when you examine."

"I don't let people go back to sleep after it's established that in the course of a social evening they've placed calls to Cedars and Times information. Especially when I learn that in their thinking I was on a par with a great hospital and a foremost metropolitan daily.

"I'll see you're stoned, Quentin, out of town, if you don't clear this up. Why did you call the hospital and the paper?"

"See, now. Oh. There you go. It was about cracking knuckles."

"Sure."

"See, we were sitting around, listening to records, and we got to cracking our knuckles, first I did, then everybody. First in time with the music, then not. Then somebody said, what makes a knuckle crack. We got to discussing it. That's a scary thing to discuss, Gordon. The more we got into it, the more we realized we're not so brainy. Your knuckles are more a part of you than Jean-Paul Sartre, say. We know all there is to know about Sartre, not the first thing about our own knuckles that we've been hearing all our lives. If I don't get some sleep my teeth'll fall out. What makes knuckles crack, Gordon?"

"Bending your fingers backward is the usual cause, Quentin."

"I know what you *do* to bring it about, what I'm asking is *why*. See, we got into it, and we were absolutely in the dark as to the mechanisms. We started to get panicky. It's like first hearing your heart without any prior warning you've got such a loud organ. You feel you've been invaded by enemy aliens. That was when somebody said, call Cedars, get some staff doctor who could give the professional view. Nobody there would talk, and that's supposed to be a hospital serving the public. If an institution looks out for the public, wouldn't you think it would have some interest in preventing panic? You know what runaway panic can lead to in these times, once it spreads."

"So you tried Times Information."

"Gordon, it's the right of the public to be informed, and the duty of a newspaper to give information. The Times people got very wiseass. Said sleep it off and when we woke we wouldn't be stampeding about knuckles or any joints. That kind of sneery talk is a cover for ignorance."

"So then you called me."

"Did I?"

"You'd better remember before I make liverwurst out of your knuckles." It occurred to me that I should have said Knucklewurst, but this was no time for anatomical niceties. "Think, now."

"Let's see. Hnng. Don't threaten my knuckles, Gordon, I resent it. About that time there *was* something else. See, now. Fmmp, it's coming, I was scared stiff, I was sweating. Somebody said, *Gnothi seauton.* I said, that's Greek. Somebody said, yes, Greek for, Know thyself. Somebody said, the essence of the Greek philosophers' wisdom was, Know thyself, and if you don't even know what makes the sounds in your knuckles how much can you claim to know about thyself. Somebody said, well, if doctors and newspapermen can't help, and if philosophers try to study thyselves, call some philosopher. Somebody said, Sartre's a philosopher and he's never written a line with any insights about knuckles. Somebody said, Sartre's no test, existentialists study alienation, so naturally he'd be more interested in fractures than in joints. Somebody said, they don't list philosophers in the Yellow Pages, even under Thyselfhelp. Sure, course, that's how it went. Ah, right. I said, I know a philosopher, older man thinks about everything and has looked into all human phases quite deep. Somebody said, well, Christ, give him a call, and I guess that's when I called, Gordon. It's not so important now. It can wait, now that I look it over. What's important is that you stop shaking your fist at my knuckles and I get back to sleep before I have a heart attack, Gordon."

"Not just yet. The answer, in case you're interested, is synovial fluid."

"What, Gordon? Synovia? The flamenco guitarist? He flew what?"

"That's Segovia, not Synovia, besides, we're discussing fluids, not musicians. The cracking has to do with synovial fluid."

"I'm not going to sit here and have an hour discussion about fluids, Gordon, laying the groundwork for a coronary, my God. I don't care how gorgeous a philosopher you are, when I bring up bones, don't change the subject to fluids, Jesus. I'm begging, Gordon, I've got to get some sleep before I turn blue."

"You were in a panic last night. The panic could come back, you'd better know about this. Synovial fluid is a colorless, viscid lubricating juice. It has in it a mucinlike substance. It's secreted by the synovial membranes of articulations, bursae, and tendon sheaths. Its purpose is to prevent a lot of scraping in the sockets when you move their parts. This fluid is found in knuckles, as well as knees, elbows, hips, and so on—"

"Gordon, what, for Christ's sake, would this or any fluid have to do with the cracking sound I've been referring to?"

"I wouldn't know about that, Quentin."

"Ah. Znnk. Huh?"

"I haven't looked into that end of the thing yet, I've had other matters on my mind. I'm just saying that if you're really serious about Gnothi seauton, you have to know about the synovial fluid in thyself, your most intimate greases, that's a starting point—"

"You dirty, rotten, miserable, miasma-jawed, thumbsucking—"

All things considered, including the evenness of the score, plus my dazzling outburst on the workings of the skeletal hinges, which told me I didn't Gnothi much about my own seauton because I never guessed I had such information in my head—all things considered, this seemed the logical time to hang up.

I'd known Quentin Seckley for what is usually called the better part of a year, but I won't call it that. The part of a year in which you know Quentin, whatever number of months it embraces, is not the better part.

Beware of wellwishers. Often they are people wishing themselves wells, oil or gas, to be obtained through your good offices, in extreme cases over your dead body, so they can flash a lot of money in your face. It was wellwishers of this type, I think, who suggested that after 20 years of writing I should have the profit of teaching writing to the youths. Everybody thought I should be put in touch with the electric new generation. Nobody stopped to look into the matter of my insulation.

I listened. When I was offered a lectureship in creative

writing at Santana State, close by Los Angeles, I took it. My subject, it turned out, was recreative rather than creative writing. Some students took the course for refreshment, as they'd take gymnastics or folk dancing, or a butterscotch float. Others were hard at work composing meticulous re-creations of Joyce, Hemingway, Kafka, J. P. Donleavy, Dylan Thomas, not to mention, though I'm obliged to, O. Henry and Albert Payson Terhune.

Quentin, a New Yorker who'd arrived at Santana after being expelled from four eastern universities, sometimes for unplanned pregnancies, sometimes for plans to synthesize STP in undergraduate chemistry laboratories, was the exception. He had no interest in writing for diversion, he was concerned with one thing only, writing for money. Neither was he moved to write imitations of well-known prose, he didn't care to write prose at all. What he began to inundate me with were rock-and-roll lyrics.

An intimate of psychedelic musicians, Quentin was composing lyrics for one of their groups, for, if it worked out, money. Two of his songs had already been recorded, with results closer to a thud than a splash. He was taking my course, he explained, to learn how to write better rock lyrics. He accused me of deliberately perpetuating the generation gap when I pointed out that, even if "better rock lyrics" was not a contradiction in terms, lyricism of any order, very definitely of this electronic order, was not within my expertise. Quentin had concluded that I was a philosopher of cosmic scope, an authority on you name it, and as such the best guide for rock-lyricism. Lyrics are made of words, aren't they? I was a word expert, wasn't I? Well, then? Why, except out of orneriness, plain and simple withholding, wouldn't I instruct him in bettering his lyrics so he could better his income?

To show the magnitude of the problem he posed to me and to literature, not to mention the English language, I will give here one of his efforts. Its title was, *After You Get Your Troubles Packed, Don't Send Dat Old Kit Bag to Me*. It went this way:

> *Fire come down the mountaing*
> *   Burn up all yo house an goods*
> *Fire come adown the mountaing*
> *   Burn away yo house an goods*
> *Yeh, dat fire roll down fom de high country*
> *   Smoke up all yo tangible assets*
> *But you kin give us a smile, a smile, a smile*
> *Iffn ye'll curl up yo lips t'other way*

After you git all yo troubles awrapped in dat
*   ole kit bag*
What's the idee mailin em to me?
Wouldn't send dat greasy load to Care Packages, naw
Whaffo you parcelpost dat mess to me? Huh?

Connin man took all yo money
*   Meddlin man took off yo wife*
Connin man abscond wid yo money
*   Meddlin man hep hisself to yo missus*
O fasttalk man walk away wid yo savings
*   Meddlesome man partake of yo better half*
Now you kin give us a grin, a grin, a grin
Jess curl up yo mouf t'other way

"See some way I can improve it?" Quentin said the night he showed me this work.

"Yes, burn it in the first fire that comes down the mountaing. If the fire doesn't come down, go up after it."

"Come on, I'm really finding my own voice here."

"Losing, I'd say. Mountaings. I take that to be your best rendering of Ozark hillbilly. The deses, doses, and dems could be Old South Uncle Remus, or Brooklynese, I'm not sure which."

"Little of both."

"A little of either would go a long way, Quentin. Kentucky mountaineer, Dekalb Avenue, blackface patois, backed with sitars, that's not a voice, that's glossolalia. They call this the gift of tongues but with you it's a curse. Many of your tongues should be tied."

"Jesus, these are sounds I maybe didn't hear around my family's dining table in the Silkstocking District, but I've heard them on records, and records are part of my environment, and my environment's part of me. Am I supposed to be a snob and assume only my Junior League and stockbroker family talks right?"

"Quentin, right now you're talking more like a Silkstocking than a combination stevedore-cottonpicker-moonshiner. Silkstockings should have some place in the linguistic sun along with Leatherstockings."

"Mr. Rengs, think about this, when I'm talking to just one person I don't have to sound like more than one person. In song lyrics you're talking to a whole lot of different people so the trick is to be democratic and sound like all of them."

"All who never went beyond third grade? Why not address

a few college graduates, too? Or does your kind of democracy ban the literates?"

"Look, there's a theory behind this. Most things never melted like they were supposed to in this alleged melting pot. It's time we at least let the different languages and styles of talk melt down a little."

"Melt is one thing, fracture's another."

"I know, things liquefy when they melt, have to be hard to fracture. You're confusing fluids and bones, I wish you'd stop that, Mr. Rengs."

"If you don't stop pestering me with schizoid lyrics, Quentin, you'll see some real confusing of fluids and bones, this minestrone will be confused with your skull."

We were at that point sitting in the House of Gnocchi, a ghastly Italian gag-and-vomit on Santa Monica Boulevard in Hollywood. It was so far from being a restaurant, or any food dispensary for humans, the gnocchi should have been used to plug leaky faucets and linguini served in a trough. Quentin had insisted on taking me to his favorite eating place to discuss his writing problems, which he felt were inadequately covered in class.

"Mr. Rengs, you're pretending to be above this language mix that's happening today. That's hiding behind the generation gap."

"You're not mixing words, Quentin, you're dismembering them. Let's examine your last statement. How can anybody hide behind a gap? That's like saying, he camouflaged himself in a vacuum, or, he took refuge in a quantity of nothing."

"Quantity of nothing. You just made my point. What's a gap, by definition, but a ditch, and what's a ditch but something with nothing in it, no things, no people? If there aren't any people around in the ditch, well, there's nobody to see you, so you can hide damn efficiently."

"Logic, Quentin. No people around, no reason to hide."

"What I mean is, there aren't any people *in* this ditch, they're lined up on both sides."

"In that case, the ditch would have to be very wide, say 10 miles, before it could be used for hiding purposes."

"Well, the way you're digging at this particular ditch, it'll be 10 miles wide in no time."

"Whatever the dimensions of a gap, Quentin, you can't hide *behind* it, the best you can do is hide *in* it."

"I can't buy that, Mr. Rengs. If a tree falls in the forest and there's nobody there to hear it, is there a sound? That's philosophy, now don't deny it. By self-same logic, if you're using a ditch for hiding purposes, and it works, that means there's nobody close enough to see you, so who knows if you're in the ditch, or behind it, or under it?"

"Whenever I'm within 10 miles of you, Quentin, I'm in the soup, not behind it, or under it, and I'm not referring to this minestrone, which isn't soup, it's sheepdip."

Over a zabaglione that tasted like detergent Quentin made a sudden announcement. He said, "The Omen are interested in the Mah Own Tang lyric." I said I was not aware that he had also written a song saluting his own body odor. He said he still had reference to the kit-bag lyric in which there was mention of the article Sir Edmund Hillary was always going up. I said, "When the subject is one omen the verb must be is, watch those singulars and plurals." He informed me that The Omen were very singular but happened to be several people, they were a raga-rock recording group, some folk-hard material, too, but mostly raga, featuring sitars and tablas.

I was just becoming aware of the trend among recording groups to use common nouns in the singular as appellations for a collectivity. It was a source of concern to me that in time this might lead to a new vocabulary of aggregate nouns: a jefferson airplane of draft dodgers, a grateful dead of tambourinists, a loving spoonful of schizophrenes, a vanilla fudge of juvies, a holding company of dropouts. Now, it seemed, we had to allow for a new and still more worrisome formulation, an omen of hecklers.

"One thing you're overlooking," Quentin went on, "this song is a takeoff, and as such a howl."

"A titter, maybe. To those who know the old song you're taking off."

"You know it."

"No, I don't."

"Don't give me that, you just mentioned it."

"It was my race unconscious talking."

"Your race prejudice, you mean, against the race of everybody under 30. All right, let's see how prejudiced you get against some lyrics not in the language mix. Here."

He handed me a page with scribblings on it at all angles. I could decipher only two bits:

> suppose on the day of days
> when comes the savior
> to lead us way upstairs to best behavior
> his name is mao
> will we gao?

And:

> if hell is hot
> what's the temperature of heaven
> seven?

"I can't go into these political and theological questions on a sick stomach, Quentin," I said. "The zabaglione is giving me ptomaine, I think."

"Ptomaine," Quentin said, quickened. "There's a great word to work with. Gives me an idea for a takeoff number about the trots tourists get when they go someplace like Spain. This is inspired. *Ptomaine in Spain Falls Rainly in the*—"

Everything considered, including the sharp pains in my stomach, that seemed a good time to go to the men's room.

Not long after this takeoff of a dinner, the kind that will make you take off for even the worst ptomaine zones of Spain, Quentin asked if he could stay with my class in the second quarter. I categorically refused, on grounds that, though he was up to many possibly stunning activities with words, none could be related to writing or the English language, my two areas of competence. Quentin didn't fight. He simply said that maybe I ought to let him into some of my areas of incompetence and maybe they'd shrink. My answer was, my areas of incompetence had been too hard come by, I couldn't give them up. To match that, he decided there was something he couldn't give up. Me. When class ended for the quarter, Quentin went right on. Deprived of me on campus, he showed up almost daily on my doorstep, with batches of lyrics. Once I ventured the thought that his lyrics were for the birds, for example, goonies. He informed me that The Byrds wrote their own lyrics, his efforts were mainly for The Omen. I came to see that an omen custom-made for me had been installed centrally in my life. In the person of Quentin Seckley, relentlessly, ominously, filled with song.

Days after the conversation about knuckles and their sound effects, my phone rang. A girl at the other end said, "Hello, Mr. Rengs? Would Ivar by any chance happen to be there?"

This voice sounded blurrily, adrenalizingly, familiar. It immediately made my tongue ache at the root.

"Ivar?"

"This is Mr. Gordon Rengs, isn't it?"

"Yes, and there's nobody named Ivar here. I don't know anybody named Ivar. Take that as boasting if you want."

I was nipping at the tip of my tongue with my fingers, as though to pull it out. This was annoying on several counts: I pride myself on having no tics, I had no reason to pull my tongue out, this interfered with my talking. The girl's voice held bad echoes. That pulled at my tongue through my fingers.

"There's some mixup, Mr. Rengs. You're the Mr. Rengs teaches at Santana, aren't you? You're a good friend of this fellow I'm trying to locate, his collaborator."

"I am? On what?"

"Lyrics, of course. You write those great lyrics with him. You know."

"Lyrics? What type?"

"Hard, folk, country, jazz, raga, any rock lyrics they need."

"I see. You're looking for Quentin Seckley."

A pause.

"Quentin what'd you say? Huh? I don't know any Quentin."

Simultaneously I bit my tongue viciously and remembered this voice, the bite in it when vicious.

"Miss, I have no dealings with an Ivar. I don't do business with Quentin Seckley, either, but from time to time, when he holds a gun on me, I point out the shakier lines in his songs, the Parkinsonian ones."

Another pause.

"Mr. Rengs, could I trouble you to describe this Quentin?"

"Yes. Sandy hair down to the eyes. Looks like shredded Naugahyde. Decided stoop, slight list. About five-ten. Mole on right cheekbone. Sneaky air. Writes his lyrics for The Omen. Also—"

"That's Ivar. Well I'll be."

"I'll join you, if there's room. What do you want Quentin for?"

"Well, he was supposed to sleep with me, it was made very clear it had to be promptly at three, and he hasn't shown up, and they're all asking questions."

"All. How many are there?"

"Well, all the regulars, six, at least. They've been waiting for an hour for us to get started, they don't like to just sit around."

"Who does? I'm curious as to where you got my name."

"Well, Ivar, Quentin talks about you and what a help you are in his writing. I knew you teach at Santana, and right now I'm out here at UCLA, of course, so I called UCLA Administration and they had a Santana faculty directory—"

"You're at UCLA? That's where Quentin was supposed to, ah, join you?" I thought about synovial fluid. Flamenco guitar in the background. No sitar.

"Sure, that's where we always do it. It wouldn't work out anyplace else, this is where they've got all the apparatus. So, in short, you don't have any idea where he might be, Mr. Rengs?"

"None. Unless he's found some other place where they have the apparatus."

"Not likely, Mr. Rengs, you don't find machinery like this any old place. Well, case you hear from him, would you tell him call in right away to the Sleep Project. It's very important, he's throwing our whole schedule off."

"Sleep Project. Certainly. I'm sorry about your schedule."

Yet another silence, potently pulsed.

"Mr. Rengs, I know this sounds crazy, but would you do something for me?"

"Miss, of course you'd want to get back on schedule, it's only natural, but I have a very complicated lecture to prepare for tomorrow, it deals with the quantity and quality of broken bones in the collected works of Hemingway, did you know that in his first 49 stories alone there were 28 cases of physical mangling, 15 involving legs, 5 hands, 4 groins—"

"No, what I want to ask is, would you say some words for me? I'm beginning to remember something about the name Quentin. Would you do me a big favor and just say the words, Hello, is Quentin there?"

"First say some things for me. Child molester. Filthy degenerate. Rip your tongue out. Pincushion."

The longest pause yet. Calibrated with emotional exhalations.

"Well I'll be triple flogged. You're the man called me the other night."

"You're the 300-year-old lady."

"When I'm woken up from a deep sleep I sound about 600. See, knocking myself out like I do on class assignments and all the hours at the Project in addition, by dinner I'm beat, so some nights I just take a pill after dinner and crawl into bed. Wow, I'm sorry I spoke that rough way to you, Mr. Rengs. I had no idea who it was, you can appreciate that. Also, I'd never heard of any Quentin, I knew the fellow in question as Ivar Nalyd. Oh, oh. Wait a minute. How'd you happen to get my number that night? What gave you the idea of calling me to locate him under any name?"

"I had a message to call him. The number he left was yours."

"Now that's real funny, Mr. Rengs. First, he's never been to my place, second, I never gave him my number, though God knows he's asked over and over, why I hardly know this guy, just see him at the Project and sometimes talk about rock lyrics and that's all. My number's not listed and my friends don't give it out, they know how I insist on my privacy. This is in the category of weird."

"Yes. Tell me, could you in any way be linked in Quentin's mind with the idea of cracking knuckles, Miss—I'm afraid I don't know your name."

"Victoria Paylow, Mr. Rengs. Vicki. What's this about knuckles?"

"Could Quentin connect you in any way with the matter of cracking knuckles, Vicki? That was the subject on his mind the night he left your number."

"Knuckles. Boy. This is insanity of the top echelons. Wearing a derby. I never got into knuckles with him, not in any deep way, that's the truth. I never discuss much of anything with him, about all we do when we're together is sleep. But awhile back I did have some kind of a dream about cracking knuckles. More than one, maybe. It's mostly gone but I remember the loud sounds like pistols and how they scared me close to bald. But where'd Ivar, Quentin, get any thoughts about knuckles? Not from my dreams, that's for sure, we're under strict rules not to talk about our dreams. Well. Would you have any idea why he has two names, Mr. Rengs?"

"No, but the question might be refined. Why does he go to school at Santana under one name and sleep, participate in sleep projects at UCLA, under another?"

"It does seem fastidiously demented, Mr. Rengs. You have any theories about it?"

"Hard to say, Vicki. It could have something to do with keeping fluids and bones separate, he has strong feelings about—"

"No. This has got to stop. This is blue-ribbon lunacy. Somebody's ransacking my brains."

"Did I say something to upset you, Vicki?"

"Fluids and bones, I'll be triple napalmed. That's a theme that crops up time after time in my dreams. Offhand I don't remember any particular dream but it keeps turning up. It's against all rules to tell the contents of our dreams so where's he get off slinging around my dream language? If there's stuff like that in my memory banks, how come he can crack them? I swear—"

"If I find out anything I'll certainly let you know, Vicki, I have your number—"

The following day, after lunch, Quentin rang my bell. He had another ream of lyrics with him. I threatened to send all his lyrics to the CIA if he didn't give me a full explanation of the name Ivar Nalyd. The explanation was not what I would call simple, nor, in the last analysis, or any analysis, very explanatory.

Ivar was nothing but Ravi spelled backward, in honor of Ravi Shankar. Nalyd was a reversal of Dylan, in honor of Bob D., not D. Thomas. Quentin wrote all his songs under this name. He was afraid that if his family got wind of his income-producing activities, his father would cut off his allowance. Quentin held the view that any family as loaded as his should make allowances for a son busy in the arts, so any income the son produced would be gravy rather than bread and butter. Buttered bread is enhanced by gravy.

How, I wanted to know, was he safeguarding his allowance by passing himself off as Ivar Nalyd with such as Victoria Paylow?

He gave several starts. He tabulated his fingernails. He hummed for a time, in sitar glides.

"Victoria Paylow, I believe you said."

"That is correct."

"What would you be knowing about this young person, Gordon?"

"That she knows you as Ivar, and sleeps with you at UCLA with six people looking on. There's a fair amount of apparatus involved, I gather."

"Where'd you come across Vicki, Gordon?"

"She called here yesterday. Looking for you. You've got to learn finesse in dealing with the opposite sex, Quentin. When you make a date to sleep with them and don't show up, they worry. So do all the people standing around."

"Damn it, I called in and left word with the Project secretary that I couldn't make it, she must have forgotten to tell them. The Omen were rehearsing for a record date and I had to be there in case they needed some lyric changes. Listen, how come Vicki was calling *you* to track me down?"

"Would it occur to her that you might be at home, when you write lyrics around the clock with your collaborator?"

"Collaborator?"

"She has the distinct impression that that's my function in your life, Quentin."

"I never used that word, Gordon, I swear it, all I said was, you're kind of editor with my stuff. I'm searingly sorry she bothered you, Gordon."

"She has to be set straight, Quentin. She must be made to

understand that I'm not your collaborator, you're my con-
taminator. Now. Two more things need clearing up. First, why
you leave this girl's number for me to reach Quentin at,
when she knows you as Ivar. Second, regarding this Sleep
Project, what, exactly—"

"Who left Vicki's number for anything, Gordon? Are you
completely crazed?"

"I direct your attention to the night of the cracking knuckles, Quentin. You left a number for me to call. It was Vicki's
number. Vicki said she'd never heard of a Quentin, which
was true. What would lead you to do such a rabid—"

"Syllogism serenade sweatshirt. This is a bummer. I was
stoned, that was the thing, I must of plain forgot she knew
me as Ivar. Oh, so no wonder you thought it was the wrong
number. I get it now. Bllb. It was a slip on my part, from
being stoned. Leaving that number altogether was a slip, if I
did it. Grrz. I had the thought in the back of my head of
going over to her place, that much I know. I was cracking
my knuckles and getting tensed up and the urge was on me
to drop over to Vicki's, I don't know why. The thing with the
knuckles just naturally made me think of going to Vicki's. I
guess, being stoned, I just translated going there as being
there, mixed up the wish and the result, so I left her number
without realizing what I was doing. I really meant to drive
over there but instead I passed out—"

"How did you know her address and phone number? She
tells me she wouldn't give them to you and she's not listed—"

"Not in the phone book, no. But she is in the personnel files
at the Project. I've had the idea of paying her a visit for
some time, Gordon. I've had my eye on her at the Project,
been building up some major urges about her. I'll confess
something. The urges got so major, I hung around the Project office one day until the secretary got called out, then I
sneaked a look in the filing cabinet, located Vicki's personnel
record and memorized the salient facts. Look, it's complicated. I'd have to reconstruct the whole situation for you.
Where it begins is with the Sleep Project—"

"I'd better know about that, too. Just try to spare me the
details, such as why they need a secretary."

"You don't know about the Project, Gordon? Ah, then.
None of this can make any sense to you, that's obvious.
That's where I met Vicki, at the Project. They found out we
sleep well together, for some reason, so they schedule us to
do it together, for reasons they won't explain. I use the name
Ivar Nalyd over there for the same reason I use it on my
songs—"

"Let me see if I'm following. You get paid for your activities at the Project?"

"Sure, Gordon, why else would I be putting in all that time? Sure, I get good hourly rates, so does Vicki. So, see, because I make money there, I figured, better do it under the alias, so my old man won't hear about it and stop the allowance. Listen, I've got to take off now. Due at the Project. How about coming out with me and see the setup for yourself, it's wild! Dr. Wolands likes visitors. Gordon, this is a whole new approach to a crucial human function. Look at it this way, here's a thing you do every day of your life, yet you're a blank about it. It's like your knuckles cracking, the most intimate thing and you don't know what's going on. They're studying every aspect at the Project, they go into it real deep, it'll open your eyes . . ."

I had to go, of course. There were witless laminations between Quentin and Vicki, not as many as he would like, more than she warmed to. They made a leaky sandwich which had insinuated itself into my life, leaking from all sides. I felt a need to trace it to the bughouse short-order kitchen in which it had been put together, called, for some reason, the Sleep Project. To get this picture straight, I would have climbed any Mah Own Tang Quentin led me up. Followed him into any unhinged heaven, even if the temperature was seven. Had his name been Mao, I'd still gao.

As we drove along, Quentin told me something about Victoria Paylow. Graduate student at UCLA in history. Doing Master's thesis on the sadomasochistic aspects of late medieval sorcery, demonology, witchcraft, black masses, and alchemy. Played good guitar. Carried guitar around to play and sing Omen numbers to herself at odd moments. Adored Omen songs, particularly their lyrics, particularly those lyrics written by him, Quentin, Ivar. Her enthusiasm for said lyrics so intense as to suggest she had a big yen for him which she was trying to cover up by refusing to give him her phone number. Very vital presence to have sleeping next to you. Increasingly, the focal point of the increasingly agitated dreams Quentin was having at the Project. More spectacularly stacked than the Queen Mary.

"Quentin," I said cautiously, "about the night of the knuckles. If I recall, you said you started the cracking, then the others joined in?"

"That's the way it went, yes."

"Do you remember why you started it? What train of thought you were in when you began bending your fingers?"

"Oh, I was thinking about Vicki, I guess. These days a major part of my thinking is about Vicki."

"Can you recall what you were thinking about her, exactly?"

"Mmp, well, I guess I was thinking about her skirt. She wears this miniskirt to the Project, see, actually it's more micro than mini, a figleaf stretched just enough to wrap around is what it amounts to. I devote a lot of thought to that flyspeck of a skirt, that iota of a skirt, what you might call that soupcon of a cover, just this side of bareass. I was thinking about that little-as-the-law-allows garment, then about reaching for some scissors, then beginning to snip at the skirt with the scissors. Yep, that's about the sequence. I was cutting away, and humming. And thinking, get this, about the La Brea Tar Pits, thinking they should be called the La Brea Arm Pits, though they're between the legs, and laughing to myself. Then there was this voice. Her voice. I was imagining it, of course, remember I was some miles from my skull from this rich grass. The voice was loud, deep, and aggressive. Deeper than a bass. It said, you keep that up and I'll give your hands a whack that'll turn your knuckles to mush. Those are the exact words. The liquid threat first, then it said, fool around like that and I'll crack your knuckles in half, plus each and every other bone in your body. The fracture threat. At that, you can bet, I dropped the imaginary skirt and then the imaginary scissors. All because of this imaginary voice, full of melts and breakages, which rattled my ears. That was when, sure, I began to crack my knuckles. Say, I'm glad you asked this question. It clears some things up. No wonder I got scared from the cracking. Actually I was already scared from the voice's threats against my knuckles."

"So you'd say the nervous cracking stemmed from some prior thoughts, imaginings, about Vicki."

"Gordon, I not only would, I just did."

We rode a while longer.

"Have you ever noticed, Quentin, how often references to fluids and bones come into your conversation?"

"I don't know. Plenty of people talk about fluids and bones, they figure in everybody's life."

"In yours more than in some, I'd say. You like to keep your fluids in one category, your bones in another, and it annoys you when people get the categories mixed. I mention it because just now, when you remembered about this voice, you quoted it as threatening to hammer your knuckles to mush. The concept of reducing your osseous materials to liquid form would seem to disturb you, I think that's a reasonable conclusion. Do you link this concept in any way with Vicki?"

"That's a big batch of silliness, Gordon. True, the threat was in Vicki's voice, but I was hallucinating, the voice was in my head, not coming from the outside."

"True, but it was your head that, after originating the words, put them in Vicki's mouth. You were the author, but it seemed important to put quotes around the words and attribute them to Vicki."

"Gordon, I don't know where you're trying to get with this line of questioning. What's the whole question of solids and liquids got to do with Vicki, anyway?"

"I don't know, Quentin. But I have to ask you to stop cracking your knuckles and put your hands back on the steering wheel before you kill us both."

Scientism is not for me. What are called the laws of Nature I take as gossip. They tell us a balloon filled with hot air rises because of Boyle's Law, specific gravities, etc. I know different. I know that the balloon goes up because the sun sucks it up. How do I come by this information? By empathy, because my own head is often subject to the sun's powerful suction, is heliotropic, so much so that my neck and shoulder muscles are pulled tight a good deal of the time, to keep my head in place. Medical men tell me this is neurotic tension but I know it for a healthy attempt to keep the organism in one piece. The migraine sometimes produced by this muscle strain is healthy, too, the head's reassuring signal, in the only language it has, that it's very much with me against all cosmic sabotage. Again, think about the peculiar behavior of water when the temperature drops below 32° Fahrenheit. This has always struck me as a highly emotional, and sick, reaction to unpleasantness, like the rigidification you see in certain advanced cases of schizophrenia. Well, science puts the stress on matter, art, on manner. This is probably not news to you.

The point is that I understood no part of the laboratory Quentin led me into. The large main room was laced with wires and cables leading to wall panels on which dials jigged and styluses twitched across revolving drums. Off this central room was a row of cubicles visible through wide walls of glass. Each contained a bed, plus a desk with a typewriter on it. In several of the beds people, men and women, were fast asleep. Electrodes were taped to assorted parts of the sleepers' bodies, including their skulls. Technicians in white smocks sat in the main room, following the electronic messages being sent out by the sleeping parties. In one cubicle a man in pajamas, apparently just come awake, sat at the desk, typing energetically.

This, Quentin informed me, was the Sleep Center, where that crucial human activity, sleep, was being investigated from every angle, probed to the bottom. It was only in their waking hours, Quentin let me know, that men allowed themselves to be separated by the artificial barriers of color, ethnics, politics, ideology, hunger, territorial imperatives. In their repose all men were one because all slept, and slept alike. Sleep, you might almost say, was humanity's least common denominator, because most common, indeed, universal. Sun makes men aliens to each other and, thus, themselves. Night unites. Mankind could open itself to, and assert, its true physiological community only with eyes closed. The Sleep Project, by ferreting out the true race-wide nature of sleep, was going to show all men their mutuality. The way to a lasting One World was to be revealed to us by that least likely leader, Morpheus, plus his right-hand men, his buddies, Somnus and Hypnos. In Thanatopsis our eyes would for the first time be opened. We would in the end cast off our false gods and pay full respect to His Worship Nod, the Sandman with his ingratiating sands. Something like that. He was very likely going to write a song about it. I couldn't follow the argumentation because I was getting sleepy.

The chief psychologist had joined us during this impromptu lecture. He nodded his approval of the explication by Quentin, now Ivar Nalyd, who, he said, was this lab's champion sleeper, though sometimes carried away in his poeticized claims about the lab's work. Quentin introduced us. The man in the starched smock, truncated, coaly-haired, crisply managerial in manner if pudgy in matter, was Dr. Jerome Wolands. Dr. Wolands greeted my name with the precise opposite of somnolence. He took in so much air so rapidly, I expected all the Pentel pens in his breast pocket to pop.

"Gordon Rengs!" he said. "No! You can't be!"

"I wish they'd told me sooner," I said.

"Gordon Rengs! This is an occasion!"

"For me to leave immediately, unless you calm down."

"No! Fantastic! I've read every word you ever wrote!"

Quentin, Ivar, took this as an occasion, not to leave, not to fall asleep like a champion, simply to put in something obnoxious. He said, "Doc, if those are the only words you've ever read, you're in trouble."

"I'm serious, Mr. Rengs," Wolands said. "In fact, it was a

book of yours, *Messages, Hints,* that led me to study psychology."

I was not pleased with the undercurrent that he might have been led to psychology to figure out why he read me. Quentin had another interpretation: "I get your meaning, Doc. That book kept putting you to sleep, so you went into the psychology of sleep, to stay awake."

"No, this man's work kept me awake nights," Wolands said. "He raises so many questions about how and why men claw at each other, up to the level of shooting wars, I turned to psychology to find some answers, and get my sleep again. Well. We're certainly honored a man like you should take an interest in our investigations, Mr. Rengs. Believe it or not, through our studies of sleep we're learning a considerable amount about how and why people provoke each other."

"It's a provocative approach," I said. "What's the basic idea, that if you make people sleep a lot you'll cut down on wars?"

"It's not the sleepers who make wars," Wolands reminded me.

"Not while they're sleeping, anyway."

"Mr. Rengs, well-rested people don't hit each other, asleep or awake. If we can get the insomniacs dozing off again, and improve the repose of the tossers and turners, you see how that ushers in a new epoch. The next great slogan may be, Sleepers of the world, unite! Conceivably that's the only way men can ever forge the true communitas, in sleep. If we can just get them to sleeping soundly again, and that's not a reference to snoring—"

This loonily utopian dissertation on the politics of sleep was interrupted by the arrival of a bouncy, bubbly, extravagantly larded girl, the lab's runner-up sleeper, the one contender to Ivar's title. Victoria Paylow, of course. Carrying her guitar. She stretched outsize blue eyes at me in the very act of winking broadly. I was disturbed by this capacity of hers to enlarge her optic diameters in the process of a signifying contraction. How she managed to convey openness, readiness, a lusty receptivity, with a very literal narrowness of outlook, I don't know. It seemed a trick, in a totally unexpected area, for blending fluids and bones.

She was, in fact, wearing a miniskirt that had the proportions of an iota, even a soupcon. It did, in fact, invite thoughts of scissoring. Ivar was, in fact, studying it in a scissory silence.

"Hi, Mr. Rengs," she said, her two-way-stretch voice as elastic as her eyes. I considered the emotional gamut of a female who could make dock-walloper threats to rip out tongues one minute, utter a chirpy Future Farmers hi the next. "You come down here to see some world-champ sleeping?"

"I like to observe people who are outstanding in any field," I said.

"We don't do it standing," she said. "Doing it on your feet is for amateurs."

"If you keep on standing around, Mr. Rengs will question your professional standing," Wolands said. "Hop to it, kids."

Quentin and Victoria waved to me and slipped out a door. Very soon they reappeared in two of the vacant cubicles, adjoining ones, now dressed in pajamas. In a businesslike, practiced way they arranged themselves in their respective beds and lay still while lab assistants attached wires to all parts of their bodies, including their heads. They seemed unaware of each other and us. Wolands explained that they were in audio-visual isolation: blank wall between them, the windows we looked through were one-way glass. Soon they were alone, eyes closed. Soon after, they were asleep, as Wolands thought he proved by calling my attention to the movements of dials, gauges, meters, and recording styluses.

"You're going to see some very special sleeping here today," Wolands said. "Ivar and Vicki have real gifts for this. More than they know. Interlocking gifts."

I recalled that Quentin had a good deal of Irish blood in him. Vicki had a colleen sauciness about her. I refrained from saying that this might be the lock of the Irish.

"Do you appreciate the full significance of what's going on here, Mr. Rengs?"

"Something that'll wreck the music world? Ivar writes lyrics, you know. I can't believe he writes what he does in a waking state. I assume he creates them when he's asleep."

"It goes far beyond lyrics. Have you heard talk about our recent discovery, REM sleep?"

"You've discovered a new kind of sleep?"

"No, brought to light a very, very old type. REM means Rapid Eye Movement, Mr. Rengs. Every 90 minutes or so our subjects show signs of intense neural-cortical activity. Their alpha brainwaves energize and their eyes begin to move fast, as though watching something. They are watching something. A dream, which accounts for the sudden jump in cerebral energies. The typical sleep pattern is to dream every 90 minutes, Mr. Rengs, in other words, to show high alpha-wave and REM activity every 90 minutes. Part of our job here is to wake certain subjects after each REM episode and get them to write down as much of their dream as they remember. We're learning revolutionary things about dreams. That they take place several times a night. That they release clamoring unused energies in the brain which, unless drained off during the alpha-REM phases, would in short order make us psychotic."

"I don't follow this. If Ivar's a champion sleeper, that means he has a lot of REM episodes a night. If these are supposed to drain off potentially psychotic energies, why does he go on writing psychotic lyrics?"

"He may write fewer of them than you think, than he thinks. Can you keep a secret, Mr. Rengs?"

"As well as I can keep a distance. I'm a champion distance keeper. My one failure is with Ivar."

"It's absolutely essential that Ivar and Vicki have no inkling of this. You mustn't breathe a word of it, it could destroy the stupendous thing that goes on between them. Stupendous in the sense that it comes out of their torpid states, stupendous also in that it leaves us scientists stupefied. Mouths hanging open. Come with me, please."

He led me to an office off the main room, whose door he unlocked with three different keys. He proceeded to some filing cabinets which had to be opened with multiple keys, too. He brought out two thick dossiers, one with Ivar's name on it, the other with Vicki's. He showed me the contents of both dossiers, stacks of papers on which the dreams of both subjects were typed, each item dated. Each dream record had stapled to it the related alpha-wave, pulse, respiratory, skin-electricity, and other readings.

"I can best make my point by asking you to match a few of these records, Mr. Rengs. Take Ivar's dream sheet for any given day and compare it with Vicki's for the same day. Compare, first of all, the times recorded for the REM episodes."

I took the top sheet from each collection, dated two days before. Vicki's first dream was timed as beginning at 3:47. Quentin's first one got under way at 3:49. Vicki's second one started at 5:31, Quentin's at 5:32. I glanced at some other sheets from both piles. The correspondences seemed to be of the same order.

"They dream together?" I said.

"Not quite," Wolands said, eyes in a high glint. "You will note that there's always a gap of two, three, or four minutes between the starting times. They're close, but not neck and neck, especially at the beginning."

"Vicki always starts before Ivar?"

"Now we're getting somewhere, Mr. Rengs! Yes, the sequence is invariable, Vicki takes the lead, Ivar very soon falls in! The sensational point is that, each and every time, day in and day out, Vicki's alpha-REM burst *triggers* Ivar's! Isn't it enough to make your head swim!"

The swimming in that portion of my anatomy was more localized than that. Each of my own eyes was trying to do the Australian crawl away from the other.

"Then their alpha-REM patterns are related as to chronological form. Is there any indication that there's a give-and-take in content, too?"

"Spoken like a true scientist, Mr. Rengs! I'm proud of you! Yes, indeed, that's the hammerblow question! And as for the answer, it's a piledriver! I mean, yes, absolutely, quite so, staggeringly so, in each and every case Vicki's dream sets off Ivar's, then colors and seeps through all its content! The psychic traffic so far has been all one-way, from Vicki to Ivar, never the reverse! It's her unconscious dictating to his all the way, much as he tries to fight it off! In this give-and-take Vicki gives and Ivar takes, takes, takes! Just read a few of the dreams for the same time slots and see for yourself!"

I picked a page from Vicki's pile at random. It was dated sometime in March:

Mound of human bones, melting, making puddles. Some rock musicians on it, rehearsing. Sitar player resembles Ivar, hair like overcooked linguini. I say fingers too stiff, you need more liquid sound. He says, show me how. I pull sounding board off sitar. Sit, put hollow sitar between legs. Open 13th Century illuminated book, manual on witches' concoctions. Read recipe for brew to dissolve bones: to contents of whale's small intestine add 7 owls' beaks, 5 hyenas' tear ducts, 13 bats' eyes, pinch of pulverized tarantula legs, sprinkle of finely ground rhino spleen, etc. Mix in ingredients, stirring slowly. Drone proper incantation: if Hell's a boil, a boil, a boil, what's the temperature of the Shiny One's Rotunda, I wunda, zero or unda? Brew begins to steam. Sitarist says, I make hard-rock sound for the people, you're putting me on. I say, no, I'm going to put you in. To show him how it works, I take human shinbone from pile, drop it in brew, bone dissolves with a hiss I say, that's the sound you should make, very soft rock. He hides his hands, screaming, get out, you don't make soup out of my knuckles, bitch of the Styxian kennels. I say, if you know where I live, why're you always trying to get my address and phone number? I add, what could you do if you came calling anyway, you with your already mostly soft bones? He says, never mind the insults, sticks and stones may break, but. I say, drop around to my place, buddy, I dare you, the Styx that runs through my house'll break all your bones, soften them up, anyway. I grab his arm and shove it into the brew, up to the armpit. It dissolves with a hiss. He stands there with one arm gone, socket still steaming, says, now how do you expect me to play that sitar? I say, try your toes, if they're still hard enough, but why make hard sounds when soft becomes you more ...

I located Quentin's corresponding dream. It had started to register less than two minutes after Vicki's got under way:

House of Gnocchi. Having dinner with Vicki. Steaming bowl of stracciatella (spinach and egg drops) in front of her. She asks if I wouldn't like her to dip my knuckles in her soup to make them soft like the rest of my bones. I tell her to stop talking crazy. She says if I don't want her to fix my knuckles up why take her to a place like House of Gnocchi, which means knuckles, gnocchi as a matter of fact are soft farinaceous knuckles. She stirs her steaming soup with a spoon. This makes me hide my hands behind my back. She says my bones are brittle from trying to be so hard and would feel better with some lubrication, get soft, their natural state. I ask why when subject of bones comes up she always puts in something about fluids. She says my bones have tendency to go watery by themselves, don't need her help. She says she'll illustrate. She drops a breadstick in her steaming stracciatella, it goes soggy and begins to shred. I yell at her, breadsticks and breadstones can't break my bones, and she can keep her goddamned address and phone number. As I'm about to rap her with my knuckles, idea for a lyric jumps into my head. Along these lines: If hell's hot, what's the temperature of heaven, seven? She says, how long you think you'd last at my house, anyway? I say, there's nothing so threatening in a kennel but fleas. She says, how about in a House of Nyooki, Nyooki, Nyooki? I quick shove my hands behind my back again ...

I put my own hands behind my back. Their palms were

sweating in the manner certain novelists call profuse. My thoughts spiraled down to a crucial date, April 22. I was not sure I wanted to, but I began to search through the records for the dreams of that day. I found them:

Vicki:

Cauldron between legs. I'm enormous, cauldron's enormous. Mixing a black, viscous brew, enormous bones swimming in it. Fumes smell like tar. Singing usual incantation in basso profundo: Fire roll down from the mountaing, the mountaing, the mountaing, cook up my good brew, burn up his house, burn up his goods, soften up his bones, cook up my melting brew. Ivar appears. He's tiny. Looks up, says, why you sing about mountaings? I say, because I'm a Kentucky hill-woman, cooking up my home remedies. He says, don't you know any other songs, I don't like that song. I sing something else from my repertoire: If on Deliverance Day, when comes the Saver, to bring us Up There where They got the High Flavor, his name's Ho Chi Minh, will we dig in? He says, what you cooking there? I say, stuff to keep your knuckles from cracking. He says, does this remedy have a name? I say, sure, we call it La Brea Arm Pits. He says, that stuff won't melt any bones, look at all those bones in there. I pull some out, mastodon thighs, saber-tooth tiger fangs. I say, you a mastodon or saber-tooth, that your bones won't melt down? He says, I got your address and phone number from another source, you witch. I say, don't you call or come around, with your easy melted bones. He says, that won't work, keeping that big mess of black threatening remedy between your legs, it won't remedy me. I begin to sing another song: one'll con off all your money, another'll meddle away any wife you got, cause where you should be ossicle you are or will be all lappy treacle. To show him his problem, I crack my knuckles, they sound like pistol shots, frighten me. He begs me to stop. I crack harder. He gives a terrible cry and dives head first into the steaming tar . . .

Day and date with this, Quentin:

Going up steps to Vicki's place. Not invited, she's re-fused me the address, but I wheedled it out of our sitar player who sells her pots and pans and is operative for

CIA. Pick the lock, go in. She's cooking in the kitchen. I ask what she's making. She says, Shrimps Remedie, old Alsatian delicacy. I ask why so many bones in this stew if it's a shrimp dish. She says those are just Master Don's knuckles for flavor, because she likes high flavor, that's the saver, only she pronounces it saber, and says it's toothsome. I say, Don who? She says, Don Juan, that's spelled, W, A, N, Don Wan. She says maybe you haven't heard but Don Wan always sucked his knuckles. Rest is very vague. Recall just bits and pieces. She sings a lot. One song has the line, Ho, G-Men. Another is some kind of folk number with the repeated stanza, Mah Own Tang. She beats out time on her knuckles and asks if I wouldn't like to have my shrimp remedied. I say, sure, and to get away from that terrible drumming from her knuckles I jump into the big bowl of delicious-smelling steamy chocolate between her legs with the crisped nuts floating in it. Going down for third time I hear her singing, Ah-men, Ah-men, I try to yell to her that we're known as Omen, but it's too late, only make bubbles in this chocolate that smells and tastes like tar. I feel my right arm coming off. I tell myself, I'm drowning in Mah Own Armpit and tar is Mah Own Tang ...

I put the typewritten sheets down. I had to, they were getting soaked through in my hand. I said, "I see. It's some kind of devilish ESP."

"We're not prepared to give it a name," Dr. Wolands said, "but we give it our fullest attention."

"Her unconscious seeps, you said? Steamrollers. Rips to shreds."

"All we know is, when they're lying in adjoining rooms, fast asleep, there's some terrifying traffic through that wall."

"Missile launchers and 105's. You were saying they don't provoke when they're asleep?"

"Not in a way that breaks bones, Mr. Rengs."

"Bones don't get broken, no. But melted, all over the place."

"They harden again, by the time they're needed. As they don't in, say, Vietnam—"

Wild sounds from the central room. Quentin's voice bellowing something. Vicki screeching a counterpoint. A crash, a splintering, more yells. Someone shouting for Dr. Wolands, Dr. Wolands.

Wolands looked disoriented. Loud noises were not the order of the day in this citadel of sleep. Again, the bellows, the shrillings. Wolands hurried out, with me close behind.

The commotion was coming from Vicki's sleep chamber. It had an amplified, metallic quality because it was reaching us in the main room through the lab's sound system.

Quentin had gone amok. He had apparently broken out of his own cubicle and into Vicki's. He had smashed Vicki's guitar over Vicki's head, it was resting now on her shoulders with her head poking up from the ruins of the soundbox. He had two clumps of her long reddish hair in his hands and was pulling demonically at them, twisting her head from side to side. His eyes were bugged out in a mammoth raging. His gaped mouth appeared to be on the verge of producing foam.

He thundered, "Liar, am I! A liar, huh! I'll show you, you bitch!"

She was trying to push him away, yelling back, "Cut that out! Quit it, now, you ultimate maniac!"

There were several lab assistants in the cubicle, trying to take hold of Quentin. He kept kicking and shouldering them away, with the strength of ten, of demons.

"Show who writes my words, you scabby she-hound!" Quentin boomed terribly, in day-of-reckoning tones. "Going to write the whole oration for your funeral, right now, on your scummy skull, in my own handwriting, every word, you refugee from the verminest kennels! Had just about all I'm going to take from you, understand! Insults and more insults till I'm up to here! They're gonna break your bones, not mine, reject of the garbage hounds!"

She screeched, clawed at his hands. He kicked more attendants away.

"What is it, what's this insanity?" Wolands spat at the nurse hovering over the electroencephalograph drums.

"I don't know! It was like an explosion!" the nurse sputtered, palms tight to her cheeks. "They both had REM episodes, close together as usual! We woke them when the energy levels went down, as usual! They went to their desks, as they always do, they began to type, then Ivar began making faces, he seemed to be getting angrier and angrier as he got more awake, then all of a sudden he jumped up shouting vile words, and rushed into the corridor, and broke into Vicki's room carrying her guitar, he must have picked it up in the dressing room, and before anybody could stop him—terrible, horrible!"

Wolands looked grim. "I half saw it coming," he said. "I sensed it, to a degree. I just didn't know it would be this soon, and preferred to believe—"

"Make wisecracks about knuckles crack!" Quentin roared. "Go ahead! Here's more crack for you, you apprentice bitch!" He whacked his hand, knuckles leading, across her left cheek, then her right, at the same time scattering more attendants.

"You're a great big shipment of stenchy suet and that's why you've got to go hitting your betters!" Vicki ground out at him, shutting her eyes tight against the slaps, struggling to pull free.

"Here's some suet'll knock your teeth out!" Quentin blasted, cracking her in the mouth. "Want to see how your teeth crack? Listen!" Crack, he went. "Want some teeth melted down? How's this for melt!" Crack, again.

"We can't just stand here, it's not right!" the nurse groaned.

"No, you prepare a hypo, strongest tranquilizer, strongest dose," Wolands said. "Get it ready and stand by. We'll stop this one way or another."

He rushed into the corridor, me close behind. We eased our way into Vicki's crowded cubicle. Quentin was practically pulling poor Vicki off the floor by those ropes of hair, those two red asps, trumpeting, "Where're your shitty magic brews now, huh! Put some on your scalp that'll keep it from peeling off, that's an invitation, you great boiler of bones!"

"All your stiff's in your fingers, that's why the knuckles crack, let's see you do something with a girl with something besides the big noise fingers!" Vicki splatted back at him.

Wolands signaled to the assistants to close in on Quentin again, with us reinforcing their flanks. They made a concerted grab for him, as Wolands and I tore his hands away from Vicki and pinned them to his sides. He writhed, he did the exercises of the serpent. We had to stay well behind him to avoid his snapping teeth.

"Now, Ivar, you're getting worked up over nothing," Wolands said at his most syrupy. "You've simply misinterpreted, lad."

"Easy, friend," I said into Quentin's ear. "You said the hourly rates are good here, keep them happy."

"You don't know the extent of their diabolism, Gordon," Quentin panted. "They're giving me the worst kind of injections, in the head, while I sleep."

"We'll give you the best injection, lad, you'll sleep the sleep of the righteous," Wolands said, helping to steer Quentin out to the corridor and back into his own cubicle.

We got the squirmy boy down on the bed and held him

down. The nurse was immediately there, giving him the hypo while we all cooperated in keeping his arm still.

"Now I know what's going on here," Quentin puffed into my face. "They're trying to see how many pieces they can break me into, that's the project. Somnial suggestion, Gordon, I've read about it. The minute I'm asleep they start piping that she-devil's voice into my ear, with all kinds of cackling witch suggestions, to make me dream their programmed dreams, and study how far they can go programming my dreams before I break down into a howling maniac entirely, somnial input, I had inklings of it before but I closed it out of my head but today it exploded in my head and I got their number, I already had her number, didn't have to wait for her to give it, got it elsewhere, would of gone there and showed how much stiff but passed out, today got theirs, whole scheming bunch . . ."

His voice was trailing off. Whatever the nurse had pumped into him, it was powerful.

"They couldn't pipe her voice or anybody's in your ear," I said into his ear. "Feel around, there's just no apparatus for it under the pillow or anywhere. Besides, I was watching when you went to sleep, I didn't see any signs of any such piping."

"No sense looking for apparatus," Quentin said sleepily. "Got it hidden well. Inside tubes of bedstead behind walls somewhere. Pipe her hellcat's poisons up through pillow into my head so I dream against myself and they wait to see how long before I fall apart start raving. Put stop to this once for all. Gordon. Enough's enough."

His voice faded altogether and he was asleep. He began to snore immediately in soundest sleep.

"What's got into him?" I said to Wolands. "Too much Vicki? He got too big a dose of her infiltrations and began to sense a plot?"

Woland's face was serious. He pulled the sheet of paper from Quentin's typewriter and studied it, frowning.

"I've got an idea what happened, got to go to Vicki's room and check it out," he said. "Would you mind waiting for me in the file office, Mr. Rengs? I left the door open. Wait there, I'll bring along the evidence in a moment."

In a matter of minutes Wolands joined me, carrying the dream records typed by the tandem sleepers. He placed them on the desk, side by side, for me to examine.

"Before you read the texts," he said, "look at the starting times registered on both alpha-REM graphs. The clue is there."

I did as he suggested. Vicki's dream, if the styluses were right, had started at precisely 3:47.91, Quentin's at precisely 3:47.91.

"No gap at all," I said. "This time they did start neck and neck."

"The evidence is indisputable. I've wondered many times if this would happen, and if so, when, but I never dreamed, if you'll forgive the word in this context, it would be so soon, and the results so violent. As a matter of fact, I've even had a careful study of the time differentials made, to ascertain if they indicated any trend. There certainly was a trend. It wasn't straightline, there were waverings and backslidings, but we found an undeniable overall curve. Downward. When they began sleeping together, their dream initiation times were as much as five and six minutes apart. Slowly, and jerkily, the gap came down to four minutes, then three, then two. It was a mathematical certainty that in the end the gap would close, they would be identical starters, but we couldn't say when. Today, as you've seen, the gap was closed. With a bang, and a variety of whimpers."

"What does this tell you about his going berserk?"

"You've read samples of their earlier dreams, Mr. Rengs. You know his were never just mirror images of hers, he was resisting, fighting off her imposed content, distorting her symbols, cloaking, reshaping. But the resistance was going steadily down. In the last days his dreams have echoed hers much more strongly and nakedly. This explains why the gap was narrowing between their starting times. Because his unconscious was fighting hers off less and less, his dreams were triggered more and more rapidly by hers. As he became more and more her slave in point of time, so he did in the dream content."

"And today the gap is wiped out altogether. Meaning his resistance is wiped out?"

"I see no way to avoid that interpretation."

"If that's so, wouldn't his dream be an exact duplicate of hers, with no distortions, colorings, reshapings?"

For answer, Wolands slid the two typewritten sheets closer to me. Not wanting to, I read.

Vicki:

A classroom. Subject, musicology. Various instruments on display on pedestals. Students in kneepants and Eton collars are members of The Omen, plus Ivar. Lecturer is myself in academic robes but wearing tall conical hat with arcane symbols on it, plus an assortment of musical

signs. I say, students, today our subject is lyrics. Students
begin to take careful notes. I say, lyric derives from the
word lyre, name for the old string instrument, the hand-
held harp, which was used in olden times to accompany
vocalized words. I take down the lyre from its pedestal.
I strum its strings. I say, the member of this class who
calls himself a lyricist is a lyre, spelled, l-i-a-r, pronounced, liar. Because he claims to write original lyrics
and only steals them from his collaborator. I say, I will
now introduce the collaborator, who is not a liar but a
true lyricist worthy to be accompanied on the lyre. Will
our guest lecturer Mr. Gordon Rengs please come in.
Mr. Rengs steps in, wearing a leopard-skin loincloth,
more a jockstrap. I say, Mr. Rengs will now favor us
with a few words on the musical potential of the human
knuckles as an accompanying instrument. Mr. Rengs
says, friends, music lovers, the melodic and harmonic
capacities of the human knuckles are limitless, if they
are in good condition and emit rich, resonant soundings,
not the unpleasant cracklings of the over-dry and hence
brittle, those who at their hardest may crack and shat-
ter. Allow me to demonstrate with one of my own com-
positions. He begins to sing, Fire come down the
mountaing, burn up all you house an goods, striking rich,
resonant background chords from his knuckles with
some xylophone hammers. He says, there is an individual present in this room who claims he strikes songs like
Mah Own Tang from his own richly lyrical knuckles but
I can attest that his knuckles only crack, as the two brittle bones crack in Hemingway, and, in short, that I
wrote this song, as I write all his songs, and he is an
ooze pretending to be a monolith, and only plagiarizes . . .

It went on and on. Vicki had been dreaming lavishly today. I felt I had read quite enough. With some reluctance I
turned to the twin sheet.

Quentin:

   Lecture hall. Some class in musicology. Lots of instruments standing on pedestals. All The Omen and me
present, in short pants and wide starched collars with big
bunched ties. Lecturer is Vicki, wearing doctoral robes,
high cone-shaped hat with magic and music symbols all
over it. She says, today our subject is lyrics. We begin to
make notes. She says, lyric derives from the word lyre,

name of an old string instrument, the hand-held harp, which they used in ancient times to accompany vocalists. She takes the lyre down from its stand. She runs her fingers across the strings. She says, the member of this class who calls himself a lyricist is a lyre . . .

I felt an ache at the base of my tongue, as though it were being pulled at hard. I said, "Yes, I guess you could call this a breakthrough."

"A break through and down," Wolands said.

"This is what I get out of it. Ivar may have some potency doubts. I suspect this because one night, April 22, he was having heated erotic thoughts about Vicki, and decided to go to her place and establish his virility, but instead smoked a lot of marijuana and passed out, maybe to avoid the challenge. Let's say it's so. All right. Vicki senses this shakiness in him from the beginning. Out of her own malicious needs, she goes after this weakness in him, real or imagined. Her unconscious goes after it. Her dreams zero in on this sore spot, week after week. Today they score the full bullseye, all the fight's gone out of him . . ."

"I would say that's very acute, Mr. Rengs. To the extent that he's an avoider, she's an attacker, their whole sequence of dreams shows that. And this afternoon, when he had no more defenses left, no more energies to ward off her gibes, and her dream crashed into his full force, he felt invaded. He knew such a terrible dream had to come from somewhere. It was out of the question to name himself as the source. So he decided it was all trickery, we were in an elaborate plot against him, using sleep suggestion, piped-in voices, and so on. He's right to suspect there's some sort of psychic breaking and entering, of course. What he doesn't know, because we haven't been able to tell him, is that the footpadding is exclusively of the mental order, without electronic tricks."

"There's one thing I don't understand. Why has she got me parading through her dream as a lyric writer in a loincloth—"

"The best person to ask about that is Vicki, Mr. Rengs. She's down on the campus waiting for you. She thinks it's important that you two talk."

In parting I said, "You may have to revise your ideas somewhat. The worst wars may originate in dreams."

He countered with, "Come, come, Mr. Rengs, you're not going to argue that Ivar and Vicki are typical dreamers."

"Maybe not. But they're typical, if highly energized, in-fighters."

"That's precisely why we must study them in depth, Mr. Rengs. Thanks to the rich network of underground channels open between them, they afford us a rare opportunity to get some electroencephalographic and other insights into that most American of phenomena, togetherness. Don't you think they're the ideal mutually tuned couple? Perhaps, if we can learn enough about these two, we'll come to appreciate that togetherness can be one of the weirdest and wildest variants of total war, if not its prime source. . . ."

Her face was covered with bruises, but she was in good spirits. As soon as we found a place on a bench, she said, "I don't blame Ivar for any of this."

I said, "That's broadminded of you. Whom do you blame?"

"Nobody, Mr. Rengs. The setup in the lab guaranteed that it would come to this sooner or later, I see that very clearly now."

"How, exactly?"

"I'm not a fool, Mr. Rengs. I know now that what they're really studying, at least as between Ivar and me, is some kind of ESP, and between Ivar and me there's damn plenty."

"How do you know that?"

"I've got a head to think with. And plenty to think about, after today. I don't have to see Ivar's dream records to know there are correspondences between our dreams, overlaps, echoes back and forth, that just can't be explained by any kind of communication other than the extra-sensory. For example, the songs, incantations, whatever you want to call them, that show up in my dreams. Don't you suppose I recognize how close they come to the lyrics Ivar keeps turning out for The Omen? I sing about what's the temperature of the Shiny One's Rotunda, zero or unda, only I never breathe a word about this dream to him, yet he comes back with, what's the temperature of heaven, seven. Such reverberations need explaining, don't they?"

"And your explanation is?"

"ESP, Mr. Rengs, there's no two ways about it. It's only a question of which way the ESP traffic goes, him to me or me to him. I'm dead sure of the direction now, it's him to me all the way. And that's the reason you showed up in the dreams today. In mine, and I suppose in Ivar's, though there I'm just guessing."

"You're losing me, Vicki. How would ESP from Ivar to you bring me in?"

"I've got the whole picture now, Mr. Rengs, I assure you. You're his collaborator! He's boasted about it often enough when I've complimented him on his lyrics! He uses the word collaborator so he can claim a creative association with a distinguished writer and teacher like you, but what he's hiding with that puffed-up boast is that you really write those great lyrics and he just steals them and puts his name on them! He's an impotent scribbler but he gets a big creative potency from you, because you're nice enough and generous enough to let him take all the credit! Well, he's got to have a lot of secret guilts about that sleazy lie, which color his dreams, and, in reflex, mine. Today those guilts just shot up and took over his dream. He was making a naked confession as to his plagiarism in his dream, and it spilled right over into mine. Of course, he couldn't acknowledge that the terrible revelation in that dream came from him, and spilled out to me. He had to claim it originated with me and was fed in some tricky way *into* him. And, of course, had to deny it was based on fact. We know the technical word for that, projection, sneaking your own guilts out and into others. So he came roaring after me, to beat me up for his own sleep admissions. But listen, I know I'm right about how the traffic goes. I know because of the inspired lyrics that come out of a clod and a dud like Ivar. They come up in you, a vastly talented man. He takes them over. They get fed into my dreams, even ones he's still working on, ones I haven't heard yet and couldn't possibly know. So what I'm saying is, there's a flow of rich psychic material *through* Ivar, and into me. Coming, if you want to name the source, from *you*. I know the logistics here, Mr. Rengs. Ivar's only a transmitting belt, for the marvelous excitements and incitements from you to me. That's what I wanted to say to you. When there's that much wild flow from one human being to another, they ought to face the fact and consider its meanings . . ."

The ache at the root of my tongue had become a nagging pulse. This was a new situation to me, the Muse accusing the a-mused of plagiarism, or having a ghostwriter.

"I think you're exaggerating the sizes of my emotional exports, Vicki. To begin with, I really contribute very little to Quentin's lyrics, you must believe—"

"Come on, Mr. Rengs. Really. How's a klutz like that going to come up on his own with a shattering thought like, comes the savior, to lead us upstairs to best behavior, and if his name's mao, will we gao? There's a kind of genius in that. I can tell a klutz from a genius."

"You should also be able to tell that this genius of mine does not produce such inspired lines in my own writing. These references to klutzes, Vicki. I'd like to get into that a little more. You seem to feel that Quentin is somewhat deficient in fields other than lyric writing. For example, why do you make so much of his knuckles? Their fragility, and so on?"

"Oh, that started with something simple. Once in the lab, while we were waiting to be called, just to pass the time, because he's not exactly an inspired conversationalist, I said something about Hemingway. That's it, he'd told me you were scheduled to give a lecture to the Santana branch of FANNUS on all the broken bones in Hemingway, and that interested me, so I said, that's right, it's a panorama of fractures, the males in Hemingway were always getting their bones broken, and having severe potency troubles too, so maybe the broken bones were as much symbols as anatomy. I said, Robert Jordan in *For Whom the Bell Tolls* can't finally make it with Maria because they shot his leg into splinters at the bridge, but Jake Barnes can't get together with Lady Brett in *The Sun Also Rises* because his tool of the male trade was shot off in the war, and didn't it add up to the same thing finally? That's when I first noticed this funny habit in Ivar, how he began to suck on his knuckles like they were candy, and the color in his cheeks was high. I said to him on that occasion, what are you trying to do, dissolve your knuckles? His color got higher and he said something feeble-mindedly irrelevant, something about, well, on the subject of sucking, you smoke and I don't. He's really a nowhere conversationalist."

"Coming back to today's dream, Vicki. The dream you feel Quentin originated and passed along to you. What's your thought as to why Quentin would bring me on the scene dressed in a loincloth?"

"Nothing to it! You're the creator, he's the copycat and snitcher! The creative one's the potent one, right! The source of all the flow! The male in the loincloth's the walking epitome of potency, whereas the snotnose plagiarist is a kid in kid's sissy clothes who can do nothing with his puny little pencil but sit there while the real man talks and take impotent notes! It's so plain, no wonder the dumdum had to jump me and give me a working over! On the assumption that this humiliating picture was sent out by me, not you, of course."

"I see."

"Another thing I've been dying to ask you, Mr. Rengs. How come you know so much about synovial fluid?"

I bit my tongue hard, at precisely the point where it was still sore from my biting it some days before.

"Do I?"

"Plenty. See, the other afternoon Ivar and I were chatting for a minute, and when I remarked about his cracking his knuckles so much he said it had something to do with synovial fluid. He said you'd explained the whole thing to him, that it has mucinlike ingredients, it's secreted by the synovial linings of bursae, articulations, and tendon sheaths. Well, I give you my word, that hit me hard. When I was an undergraduate I was set on being a doctor so I took the pre-med course, a lot of classes in physiology and such, so I know all about synovial fluid, but I wondered how a nonscientist would know so much. Where did you pick up all this technical information, Mr. Rengs?"

"Here and there, I guess. Anybody who's a writer browses a lot."

"You might know the name of the fluid, yes. But all that detailed information about bursae and articulations and mucin? It just doesn't figure, bright as a man like you must be."

"Vicki, I once was friendly with the flamenco guitarist Segovia. He was a pre-med student before he gave up science in favor of his first love, the guitar. We spent many evenings together, talking about this and that, he gave me a lot of medical information that's stuck in my mind. Forgive me, it's been stimulating talking to you but I must go now, lecture to prepare—"

"You going to lecture any more on the statistical distribution of broken bones in Hemingway? I'd sure like to hear you talk about that."

"No, I've about covered that, what I'm tackling next is a more fluid subject, the incidence of ptomaine in the 19th-century literature of the Iberian Peninsula."

"Ho. Wowie. Now that's irrevocably wild, Mr. Rengs. I had a dream way back there about ptomaine and Spain, one of my first dreams, if you don't believe me ask Dr. Wolands to look it up in the records. If you needed any more proof about the traffic between you and me and its direction—"

"Yes. Goodbye, Vicki."

"See you around, Mr. Rengs."

"Right. I'll be the one wearing the loincloth."

I'm sorry to be breaking a prime rule of the writing game. Everybody knows about the so-called obligatory scene. If you've been building to a confrontation, laid the groundwork for a showdown, you're obliged, it's said, to carry through. This is known as going from premise to payoff. Now, in this REMMY story I've been telling, so full of rapid eye movements, there are certainly the seeds of one more encounter between Victoria Paylow and myself, a bang-up, all-out, full-bodied encounter in which all foreshadowed can come to, well, pass. The encounter never took place, I'm obliged to report, and that's the extent of my obligation. It makes no difference how rapidly you're eyeing me. This is the point where make-believe and the undoctored particulars part company. On the stage, for example, you have to stick with your premises to the neatly packaged end. In real life, you can vacate any premises any time you want. This is the great advantage of actuality over art, and why many people prefer it. All I'm saying is, being more interested in guarding my hide than weaving a plot, I was under no obligation to come face to face with Victoria Paylow again, and didn't.

There was one more phone call, however. The voltage flow being, I hardly have to note, from Vicki to me. I mean, she was the one who placed the call, and made the major waves, I assume of the alpha order; arousing much REM in me.

"Mr. Rengs, I just wanted to tell you I got a new guitar, the Sleep Project paid for it, I'd love to show it to you."

"Vicki, you're half my age."

"So? Does that make me half your weight? Height? Body heat? Itch?"

"It makes me twice as old as you."

"I'm for all that separates the men from the boys. So I can get to the men without stepping around the boys and wasting valuable time."

"Don't you care about the generation gap?"

"I care about people who know how to hop it. Neither party has to travel the whole distance. I could meet you halfway. Or at any bar you care to name. For that matter, at your apartment. Say in about 15 minutes."

"You're a fluid always ready to call a cab."

"A good ossicle's hard to find. It's worth some road work."

Behind every successful man, we're told, there has to be a woman. Yes, but a miniskirted graduate student of the incantatory arts with a guitar slung over her shoulder? Robert Graves may be right about the fount of all poetry being the primal Mother-Mate-Mistress-Muse, the chesty White Goddess fancied up with asps and corn shucks. But must she be putting all the words, every last one, in our mouths? What are we, then, sending stations, echo chambers?

I had a wobbly picture of Vicki and myself lying side by side, togethered in bliss, her unconscious dictating all my books to my unconscious. I thought about her, in some ESP-oriented future, having legal claim to my royalties. Suing me. For plagiarism.

"Vicki, you may be a fluid, but you're acting like several petrified forests on the move. Which, I'll make no bones about it, petrifies me. Which, I don't have to point out to your sharp mind, is not a good state for your purposes. My calcifications and your liquefactions, I'm afraid, are destined to remain forever unjoined. That's about the hard and the soft of it."

"You're a flinty man, Mr. Rengs. That's what I like about you."

"You're the sort of lymphy girl I vastly admire, Vicki. At a distance."

"A gap?"

"Agape."

"I hear The Omen's recording a new number Ivar just wrote, something called, *Ptomaine in Spain Falls Rainly in the Plains*. Now, Jesus, Peter, Paul, and Mary, doesn't that prove—"

"My cup runneth over. With a grateful dead of migraines, a loving spoonful of cold sweats, a holding company of grand-mal seizures. I wish you and your whole generation well, and godspeed, without traffic jams. Good-bye, Vicki."

Leopard skin. Ho. Syllogism serenade sweatshirt. Hm.

Afterword:

I haven't paid much attention to science fiction but the last time I thought about it, 11:43 P. M., October 29, 1948, I didn't think much of it.

It was a particularly smoggy day in Los Angeles. I wasn't in Los Angeles, I was in Greenwich Village reading a self-complacent report in the Herald-Trib on Angelenos about to breathe their last and observing with no complacency whatsoever that my window sills, desk, typewriter, manuscripts, and therefore, by logical inference, my lungs, were beady with soot.

I remember what thoughts went through my head. That the poisoning of air, earth and all living creatures was not an invention of the writers of sf. That this infestation of a whole planet, quite beyond the wildest imaginings of sf writers, had been brought about altogether absentmindedly, as the merest byproduct, by the scientists. That science, in other words, turned out much better fiction than sf ever could.

That was when I stopped thinking about sf and began to pay attention to science. As a writer of non-sf fiction I know how to go to the source.

I saw the bad joke being staged when, on the occasion of our first landing on the moon, the "experts" asked to telecomment on the event were two deans of sf. They spoke emotionally, while, I imagine, the entire scientific community snickered, about how they had both prefigured this moon voyaging in their sf novels.

All they had prefigured was the physical displacement of human beings from earth to moon, which meant that they had prefigured nothing. Not the diversionary nature of the gala, to take our minds off the unsatisfactory results of the displacement of U. S. citizens to Vietnam. Not the vomitous showbizz inanity. Not the PR milking of the solemn moment by Tacky Dick, the everybody-wants-to-get-into-the-act circus atmosphere. (Nixon had his PR reasons, of course. He badly needed to have his oily image associated with some real estate in the cosmos on which there was no static-making and bolixing Ho.)

Not, certainly, the later commercial exploitation of the astronaut program, which began to suggest that the whole NASA spending spree was by way of giving enough big-science panache to Scott Carpenter so he could do all those commercials for Standard Oil pushing their fake F-310 gasoline additive as the surefire cure for air pollution, lumbago, and, possibly, impotence.

The sf deans may have thought science had vindicated them but all it had done was show up the "avantgarde" fictioneers about science for the stragglers behind reality they always are. I continued with profit to go on not thinking about sf.

This is by way of getting it straight that the two stories presented here are not sf. They are fiction, to be sure, about matters that embrace certain scientific considerations, but they are not sf, whose premise is that science embraces all matters and that therefore any sf work, which is about nothing but science or the superficialities of science deftly skimmed off, is by definition about everything. SF is in the nature of things about things, sometimes disguised as people. A very different kind of fiction becomes necessary when you're interested in people not reduced to things.

These stories should not be taken as anything more than finger exercises. It's sometimes relaxing and restorative for

writers to do a story with the little finger after long periods
of working with both fists. I can tell you from long experience that it's hard, and very tiring, to do any extended typing
with both hands balled into fists. It results, among other
things, in a lot of misspellings.

These stories are in a minor, though I would hope not altogether trivial, key. One thing they are trying to say is that
you can't get any fiction of consequence out of science unless
you gain enough elevation over the subject to see that science
is not coterminous with the human condition, however much
its increasingly demonic and mindless energies seem
nowadays to be devoted to curing that condition through the
process of elimination. Which, to be sure, would eliminate
science, too. But it takes somebody more or other than a
scientist or sf writer to see that. It also requires a science-
freed eye to see how plain fucking boring much of science is,
a concept foreign to both scientists and sf writers.

"The Bisquit Position" has to do with the reactions of a
handsome Alaskan malamute to napalm—not the concept
of napalm, the experience. Napalm is a direct product of
science, again, one the sf people didn't manage to dream
up in the head before the scientists got it sizzling in, and on,
the flesh. The attitude of a goodlooking, intelligent dog to the
experience of napalm, not the concept of it, does. I contend,
go somewhat beyond the purlieus of sf, particularly since the
sf people, being so busy writing their highly imaginative TV
scripts for "Lost in Space" and "Star Trek," seldom get
around to expressing much of an attitude toward napalm.

This is a story much more about Vietnam, even, in the
end, about human attitudes toward meat both human and animal, than about napalm and, therefore, science. Sf writers
don't seem to be notably up in arms about the U. S.-stage-
managed bestialities in Vietnam. They don't seem to get into
politics much at all.

You'll never get science to stir up any real social conscience in scientists, they're much too busy smashing society
and its environs under various military-industrial-complex
contracts. But if science doesn't generate some pretty hot politics in sf writers they're clearly cases of tails wagging dogs.

That rule can be broadened. If consciousness in general
doesn't bring out some damned booming politics in writers in
general, especially in these deadened times, the proof is in
that said writers are unconscious.

"The Girl With Rapid Eye Movements," on the other
hand, is a facetious, though perhaps not entirely beside the
point, treatment of the thesis that rock lyricists, who put

themselves forth as the free-est minds and souls, really dictate their lyrics to each other. The medium through which the dictation takes place (in this case, anyhow) is ESP during a period of REM, or deep-sleep dreaming, for both parties, which does put us in the realm of science of a sort. (In other more frequent cases the medium for the dictation is plagiarism, which can account for some very rapid eye movements indeed.)

Somewhat below all this horseplay I am concerned, I think, with the ways in which officious parties of various sorts are now beginning to monitor our dreams, having run out of daylight activities to break and enter. The monitoring devices, again, are derived from the new sciences of eavesdropping and peepingtometry, so I suppose for this reason too we might say the story at least brushes the science world, before recoiling in utter disgust.

But the heroine of this story is both prescient and indifferent to science, having at her disposal means of reaching into other people's heads, particularly male ones, that came into being long before the wheel. She is, of course, none other than Robert Graves' White Goddess, whom I have taken the liberty of dressing in see-through blouse and tie-dyed bellbottoms.

One of the most discouraging things about scientists—as about the sf writers who dog them around hoping to catch a dropped idea—is that they've so completely lost sight of the W. G. who inspires us all as to imagine they themselves are responsible for their fancy and fevered imaginings. Now you know and I know it just doesn't work that way. I'm not giving you the dismal cliche about behind every successful man stands a woman. I don't know what self-respecting woman would be caught dead behind the scientists and sf writers of today. But some dire presence, some hag form of the proud old Muse, one of the Gorgons, Medusa, say, maybe all three Furies, has got to be tickling these people from behind. They just couldn't be the unassisted authors of their dread works. Nor can I see why they'd claim to be. If I had anything to do with work like that I'd sure want to claim some collaboration.

I suppose we can't blame the scientists too much for this blind spot; they're too busy with their military contracts to look upward or backward, let alone inward. But sf writers are definitely to be faulted for such oversight. The Pale but Potent Lady, Graves has made very clear, inspires all art, for those who can open themselves to the communion. It's the sf writers' blindness to this Faded Femme Fatale, inherited from the scientists they so venerate and panhandle from, that prevents their work from being inspired. The droppings from science may give a writer thin fomulas to play with; the electric emanations of the Unpushy Muse might give him fervor.

Orwell's *1984* is taken by many to be a classic work of sf. The one thing we know for sure about *1984*, whatever else in it may hold your masochistic interest, is that it has nothing whatsoever to do with the year 1984 we'll all too soon be encountering.

Orwell—and Bradbury after him—could extrapolate into the future no horrors more shivery than thought control and book-burning. We know now that thought has less and less to be controlled because it is being less and less engaged in. As for books, they won't have to be burned. Right now unsold paperbacks by the millions are being sold to road contractors to be used as fill under freeways.

The way to get rid of troublemaking printed matter is simply to make more and more narcolepsis-producing films, up to the point at which all the image-makers and imager-consumers will sleepwalk to the polls to elect Marshall McLuhan president by acclamation.

Repression is not in the future so much as more and more celluloid. Why scare people with horror stories about books being burned? Pretty soon you're not going to be able to give them away.

I have somewhat arbitrarily given this brace of stories the overall title of "Monitored Dreams and Strategic Cremations" because I think science is working very hard to make for us a world of collectivized dreaming and stepped-up missionary work—in other lands and on the home front, too—with updated weapons of instant cookery. Thanks to science, and the aura of untouchability given to it by sf, they'll be programmatically charcoaling our outsides (in the name of making the world safe for the ants, or some up-and-coming virus) while systematically trespassing on our insides (in the name of data collection, census taking, keeping the computers well-fed). This, or something very like it, is what capitalism offers us as it enters its amuck, apocalyptic phase.

Science has from the beginning been what it most spectacularly is now, the handmaiden of capitalism. Sf has all along been the handmaiden of, as well as the parasite on, science. This is a treason to the profession of writing, which in its serious forms can be a handmaiden of nothing but disdain for, and assault upon, that-which-is.

They will, of course, improve their dream monitoring in

order to make their cremations more strategic. With the technical assistance of the for-anybody's-hire scientists. And the gleeful sidelines cheers of their sf votaries.

Those subversive enough to go on reading instead of living other people's lives out in the movies can do something to stymie the scientists. All they have to do is stymie the governments and social systems that harness the scientists to do their proliferating monitory and cremational work. Stymie, in this context, means, quite simply, overthrow.

I mean, the decade ahead has got to be a period of the most radical mass politicalization and polarization. Now, as in the thirties, we are emerging from a time of sexual revolt, that is, bohemianism, into a time of political revolt, that is, social revolutionism. Put another way, the bohemianism of the sixties, paralleling that of the twenties, is beginning to be bristlingly politicalized, in a way that promises to make the farthest-left politics of the proletarianized thirties look like amateur night.

Sure as shooting, and I use the term advisedly, revolutions are going to come in wholesale lots in the years ahead. Whether or not they win and, further, manage not to degenerate or grow fatcat, will depend in large measure on whether enough people stop living ersatz lives in the movies, and filling their heads with the irrelevant muzzy junk of sf, and lose their awe of scientists, who are an integral part of what has got to be overthrown. And turn to reading again, that is, reading in the realm of ideas, rasping ideas, incendiary ideas, which would mean a boredom, finally, with sf, which is simply films, formulas, honed mindlessness put on the printed page in place of literature.

I have a dangerous vision. I have a dangerous vision. I have a dangerous vision. I see capitalism once and for all overthrown; truly overthrown, not just replaced with a new power structure just as fawning upon scientists and just as exploitative of them and their fake charisma as ever was the old. The only kind of socialism or communism I'm interested in is one that makes science and scientists look a little bit ridiculous, to be humored, maybe, but never taken in by; never catered to, always kept in their place. Humanism—and if communism isn't humanism, as Marx and Engels defined it, it is nothing—is incompatible with scientism.

And so, an end, finally, finally, to the reactionism that is at the heart of sf, all technology-worship. An end to all the soupy mysticisms that, whether they mean to or not, bolster the slobbering profit economy, all low-level intellectual hand-maidens to the Great God Mammon.

And, of course, to this slime of a capitalist terminal-case order that breeds such scientist slaveys and sf hangers-on—what a bonus.

One of the most peculiar of all the superpeculiar facets of the "sf writer generality" is that so many of our most outstanding writers live life-styles that are the very antithesis of what their stories deal with. I'll give you a couple of f'rinstances.

Isaac Asimov writes some of the most far-flung fictions ever conceived by the mind of mortal man (and I'm not just referring to *The Sensual Dirty Old Man* by "Dr. A."). But he won't fly in airplanes. Space journeys to the far side of the Universe he dashes off with his left hand, but his right trembles like a spastic's when he nears a 747.

Robert Silverberg has written novels in which tri-vid and holograms are commonplaces, yet until recently he wouldn't have a TV set in his house.

I won't name any names, because I don't feel like belittling my friends, but if pressed to the wall (like if for instance you had my mother and were holding her as hostage in the matter) I could rattle off the names of a dozen top sf writers whose stories deal exclusively with the living habits and mores of worlds-of-tomorrow, who write with familiarity and detail that borders on minutiae, of the dress and speech patterns of the world of the future. Yet every one of them dresses as though it was the early 1940's, and they speak slang straight out of *Studs Lonigan*. They even vocally put down the creature comforts provided by the technological wonders their stories have predicted. It is as if they conceived of those wonders as worthwhile only as long as they were figments of the imagination; but let them become realities and they are treated with the contempt usually reserved by writers for one of their number who hits with a bestseller.

And so now, with the new generation of sf writers emerging, many of whom are living life-styles the older and more reserved members of the clan might call "pointless" or "counter productive" because they resemble too much the way of the hippie, we have the first of the sf writers to come to us not from pulp magazines or hardcovers or even the mainstream . . . but from television.

The first sf child of his times, David Gerrold.

David Gerrold, *né* David Jerrold Friedman, got his break writing for *Star Trek,* the television series so popular a few years ago. He wrote for that series a segment titled "The Trouble with Tribbles" that was marked by inventiveness, humor of the whacky Henry Kuttner sort, expertise in the medium of visual effects, and professionalism of a high order. I assure those of you writers who put down scriptwriting as a bastard form of the art, that it is a highly complex, very demanding and difficult medium in which to work. I wish I had a dollar for every Big Name sf writer who thought he would just waltz into TV scriptwriting, and a month later, right around pick-up&cut-off time, was slid out the studio gates on his Big Name backside. So when I say David Gerrold's first time out was marked by expertise and professionalism, I am not just whistling Apartheid.

David sold "The Trouble with Tribbles" in 1967. It was nominated for a Hugo award in the category of Best Dramatic Presentation by the World Science Fiction Convention (held in Berkeley in 1968), and came in second behind another *Star Trek* script, which is pretty fair for a first-timer. At that convention, incidentally, the ancient and onerous fan custom of auctioning off an hour of a writer's time—the monies to be donated to the convention sinking fund—if you have attended a sf convention you know the word "sinking" is used advisedly—was once again pursued. Your editor was auctioned off for seventy-two dollars, Gerrold was auctioned off for twenty-two dollars and one of his furry little tribbles was auctioned off for twenty-two dollars *and fifty cents,* which says something about the market value of six foot tall, one hundred and fifty pound, brown-haired, hazel-eyed *Star Trek* scenarists, as compared to useless balls of fluff. But then, no one ever denied that *Star Trek* "trekkies" are bats from the git-go.

Moving right along . . .

Since the unseemly notoriety attendant on airing of his script, David (born an Aquarian on 1/24/44) sold other teleplay treatments and episodes to *Star Trek,* most of which never got past the preliminary stages. The sanity and ethics of some of the *Star Trek* production personnel has frequently been called into question, but in this case the lucidity of their caution and good sense shines through like a nova.

Surging forward from this impressive career opener, David struck forcefully on several creative fronts:

He was hired to write a film treatment for Robert A. Heinlein's *Stranger in a Strange Land* and was fired (David swears) for doing it right. That is, the "producer," a Hollywood type gentleman who'd bought the book because his girl friend had read it, though *he* hadn't, fired David when our Gerrold told him to take his girl friend's ideas for the way the movie should be written and jam them up his, her, or both their nether apertures in the key of C#. (He was also hired to develop an original screen story titled *Whatever Happened to Millard Fillmore?*) As of this writing, neither film has seen release, though Gerrold has.

He sold a plethora of stories to magazines and original anthologies, including Harry Harrison's NOVA and A,DV. The story you are about to read was David's third or fourth submission. He first submitted a very long, incredibly moronic thing called "In the Deadlands." Very dumb story. Full of pages of pseudo artsycraftsy nonsense like this:

The men tramped all that day.

    Tramp.

        Tramp.

            Tramp.

                Tramp.

                    Tramp.

   They tramped into the night.

And that's all there'd be on the damned page. I'd have had to pay him five thousand dollars for the use of the silly thing, just on page-count alone. No, we are much better off with the story herein offered. Besides, it's a goodie.

He wrote novels and sold them. *The Flying Sorcerers* (originally titled "The Misspelled Magishun") in collaboration with Larry Niven, published in August of 1971 by Ballantine. *Yesterday's Children*, bought but as of this writing unpublished by Dell. Spring 1972, *The Space Skimmer*, from Ballantine and a book of short stories, still untitled. *When Harlie Was One*, from Ballantine, late 1972, and a sequel to *The Space Skimmer* in early 1973. Additionally, a first hardcover sale: to Random House: *The Man Who Folded Himself*.

He edited anthologies. The much-touted and long-awaited *Generation*, from Dell, featuring new writers; and *Protostars* from Ballantine.

All of this while working full-time as a clerk in a liquor store. Now tell me Gerrold doesn't have all the credentials for being a *great* science fiction writer!

But all kidding aside, folks . . .

David recently returned from a five-month stay in Ireland. He lived in a suburb of Dublin called Dun Laoghaire, just four blocks from James Joyce Tower and a few miles from fellow expatriate sf'er Anne McCaffrey. He swears he had nothing to do with feeding the Protestants to the Catholics.

Let's see, is there anything else you should know about Gerrold? Mmm, yeah, a few things.

• He graduated from San Fernando Valley State College in 1967 with a B.A. in Theatre Arts, and prior to his graduation attended Los Angeles Valley Junior College where he majored in Art and Journalism, and then University of Southern California majoring in Cinema.

• His professional career began in 1963 at the age of 19 when he produced a ten-minute animated educational film called *A Positive Look at Negative Numbers* for which he wrote the script, did the animation, inked and painted cels and therefrom received honorable mention for same from the Educational Film Library Association.

• He plays the violin. Not terribly distinguishedly.

• He is an alumnus of the Zeta Beta Tau fraternity, out of which your editor was hurled in 1954 at Ohio State University, and about which your editor assures you nothing good can be said. Scratch two points for Gerrold.

• In 1968, when he received his Hugo nomination, he was 23 years old, the youngest active member of the Writers Guild of America, the guild of the Hollywood TV and film writers.

And finally, about this story, and its acquisition, the following must be said, merely to keep Gerrold in his place. Next to your editor, whose ego problems have been diagnosed in detail by no less a psychiatric authority than the European sf novelist Stanislaw Lem (whose conclusions about me terminate just this side of my being incarcerated as a dangerous psychopath), David Gerrold has an egomania terrible to confront. When he offered this story for publication, though it was worth the same money offered to all other authors in the book, I insisted he take one-third the rate, just to break into A,DV. It was an act of love and compassion, not parsimoniousness, I assure you.

For without these little acts intended to bring David back to Earth regularly, with a background and a promise of wonders such as David has already shown, he would be barely tolerable.

I know you will read this story, bearing these facts in mind, with reserve and dispassion. And when you tell him how much you liked it, do it left-handedly.

After all, we have to live with him.

David Gerrold

WITH A FINGER IN MY I

When I looked in the mirror this morning, the pupil was gone from my left eye. Most of the iris had disappeared too. There was a blank white area and a greasy smudge to indicate where the iris had previously been.

At first I thought it had something to do with the contact lenses, but then I realized that I don't wear lenses. I never have.

It looked kind of odd, that one blank eye staring back at me, but the unsettling thing about it was that I could still see out of it. When I put my hand over my good right eye, I found that the eyesight in my left was as good as ever and it worried me.

If I hadn't been able to see out of it, I wouldn't have worried. It would have meant only that during the night I had gone blind in that eye. But for the pupil of the eye to just fade away without affecting my sight at all—well, it worried me. It could be a symptom of something serious.

Of course, I thought about calling the doctor, but I didn't know any doctors and I felt a little bit embarrassed about troubling a perfect stranger with my problems. But there was that eye and it kept staring at me, so finally I went looking for the phone book.

Only, the phone book seemed to have disappeared during the night. I had been using it to prop up one end of the bookshelf and now it was gone. So was the bookshelf—I began to wonder if perhaps I had been robbed.

First my eye, then the phone book, now my bookshelf had all disappeared. If it had not been that today was Tuesday, I should have been worried. In fact, I was already worried, but Tuesday is my day to ponder all the might-have-beens that had become never-wases. Monday is my day to worry about personal effects (such as eyes and phone books) and Monday would not be back for six days. I was throwing myself off schedule by worrying on a Tuesday. When Monday returned, then I would worry about the phone book, if I didn't have something else of a more pressing nature to worry about first.

(I find that pigeonholing my worrying like that helps me to keep an orderly mind—by allotting only so much time to each problem I am able to keep the world in its proper perspective.) But there was still the matter of the eye and that was upsetting me. Moreover, it was *distorting* my perspective.

I resolved to do something about it immediately. I set out in search of the phone, but somewhere along the way that too had disappeared, so I was forced to abandon that exploration.

It was very frustrating—this distressing habit of disappearing that the inanimate objects had picked up. Every time I started to look for something, I found that it had already vanished, as if daring me to find it. It was like playing hide-and-go-seek, and since I had long ago given up such childish pastimes, I resolved not to encourage them any further and refused to look for them any more. (Let them come to me.)

I decided that I would walk to the doctor. (I would have put on my cap, but that would have meant looking for it and I was afraid that it too would have disappeared by the time I found it.)

Once outside, I noticed that people were staring at me in a strange way as they passed. After a bit, I realized that it must have been my eye. I had forgotten completely about it, not realizing that it might look a bit strange to others.

I started to turn around to go back for my sunglasses, but I knew that if I started to look for them, they too would surely disappear. So I turned around and headed once again for the doctor's.

"Let them come to me," I muttered, thinking of the sunglasses. I must have startled the old lady I was passing at the time because she turned to stare at me in a most peculiar manner.

I shoved my hands into my coat pockets and pushed onward. Almost immediately I felt something hard and flat in my left-hand pocket. It was my sunglasses in their case. They had indeed come to me. It was rewarding to see that I was still the master of the inanimate objects in my life.

I took the glasses out and put them on, only to find that

the left lens of the glasses had faded to a milky white. It matched my eye perfectly, but I found that, unlike my eye, I was quite unable to see through the opaqued lens. I would just have to ignore the stares of passersby and proceed directly on to the doctor's office.

After a bit, however, I realized that I did not know where I was going—as I noted earlier, I did not know any doctors. And I most certainly knew that if I started to search for the office of one, I would probably never find it at all. So I stood on the sidewalk and muttered to myself, "Let them come to me."

I must confess that I was a little bit leery of this procedure—remembering what had happened with the sunglasses —but in truth, I had no alternative. When I turned around I saw a sign on the building behind me. It said, "Medical Center." So I went in.

I walked up to the receptionist and I looked at her and she looked at me. She looked me right in the eye (the left one) and said, "Yes, what can we do for you?"

I said, "I would like to see a doctor."

"Certainly," she said. "There goes one down the hall now. If you look quickly, you can catch a glimpse of him. See! There he goes!"

I looked and she was right—there *was* a doctor going down the hall. I could see him myself. I knew he was a doctor because he was wearing golf shoes and a sweater; then he disappeared around a bend in the corridor. I turned back to the girl. "That wasn't exactly what I meant," I said.

"Well, what was it-you meant?"

I said, "I would like for a doctor to look at me."

"Oh," she said. "Why didn't you say so in the first place?"

"I thought I did," I said, but very softly.

"No, you didn't," she said. "And speak up. I can hardly hear you." She picked up her microphone and spoke into it, "Dr. Gibbon, puh-lease come to reception . . ." Then she put down her microphone and looked at me expectantly.

I did not say anything. I waited. After a moment, another man in golf shoes and sweater came out of one of the nearby doors and walked over to us. He looked at the girl behind the desk and she said to him, "This gentleman would like a doctor to look at him."

The doctor took a step back and looked at me. He looked me up and down, then asked me to turn around and he looked at me some more. Then he said, "Okay," and walked back into his office.

I asked, "Is that all?"

She said, "Of course, that's all. That's all you asked for. That will be ten dollars please."

"Wait a minute," I said. "I wanted him to look at my eye."

"Well," she said, "you should have said so in the first place. You know we're very busy here. We haven't got time to keep calling doctors down here to look at just anyone who wanders in. If you had wanted him to look at your eye in particular, you should have said so."

"But I don't want someone to just look at my eye," I said. "I want someone to cure it."

"Why?" she said. "Is there something wrong with it?"

I said, "Can't you see? The pupil has disappeared."

"Oh," she said. "So it has. Did you look for it?"

"Yes, I did," I said. "I looked all over for it—that's probably why I can't find it."

"Maybe you left it somewhere," she cooed softly. "Where was the last place you were?"

"I wasn't anywhere," I said.

"Well, maybe that's your trouble."

"I meant that I stayed home last night. I didn't go anywhere! And I don't feel very well."

"You don't look very well," she said. "You should see a doctor."

"I already have," I said. "He went down that hall."

"Oh, that's right. I remember now."

"Look," I said. I was starting to get a little angry. "Will you please get me an appointment with a doctor?"

"Is that what you want—an *appointment?*"

"Yes, that is what I want."

"You're sure that's *all* you want now? You're not going to come back later and complain that we didn't give you what you want?"

"I'm sure," I said. "I'm not going to come back."

"Good. That's what we want to be sure of."

By now, everything seemed to be all wrong. The whole world seemed to be slipping off sideways—all squished together and stretched out and tilted so that everything was sliding down towards the edge. So far, nothing had gone over, but I thought I could see tiny cracks appearing in the surface.

I shook my head to clear it, but all that did was to produce a very distinct rattling noise—like a very small walnut in a very large shell.

I sat down on the couch to wait—I was still unable to think clearly. The fog swirled in thicker than ever, obscuring everything. Visibility had been reduced to zero and the controllers were threatening to close down all operations until the ceiling lifted. I protested, no—wasn't the ceiling all right where it was?—but they just ignored me.

I stood up then and tried to push the ceiling back by hand, but I couldn't reach it and had to stand on a chair. Even then, the surface of it was hard and unyielding. (Although, I was close enough to see that there were numerous cracks and flaws in it.)

I started to push on it again, but a strong hand on my shoulder and a deep voice stopped me. "Lay down on the couch," she said. "Just close your eyes. Relax. Lie back and relax."

"All right," I said, but I did not lay on my back. I lay on my stomach and pressed my face into the hard unyielding surface.

"Relax," she said again.

"I'll try," I said, forcing myself.

"Look out the window," the doctor said. "What do you see?"

"I see clouds," I said.

"What kind?"

"What kind???"

"Yes. What kind?"

I looked again. "Cottage cheese clouds. Little scuds of cottage cheese clouds."

"Cottage cheese clouds—?" asked the doctor.

"Yes," I said. "Cottage cheese clouds. Hard and unyielding."

"Large curd or small curd?"

"Huh?" I asked. I rolled over and looked at her. She did not have on golf shoes, but she was wearing a sweater. Instead of the golf shoes, she had on high heels. But she was a doctor—I could tell that. Her shoes still had cleats.

"I asked you a question," she rumbled in that deep voice of hers.

"Yes, you did," I agreed. "Would you mind repeating it?"

"No, I wouldn't mind," she said and waited quietly.

I waited also. For a moment there was silence between us. I pushed the silence to one side and asked, "Well, what was it?"

This time she answered, "I asked whether the clouds were large curd or small curd."

"I give up," I said. "What are they?"

"That's very good of you to give up—otherwise we'd have to come in after you and take you by force. By surrendering your misconceptions now you have made it so much easier for both of us."

The whole thing was coming disjointed and teetered precariously on the edge. Bigger cracks were beginning to appear in the image and tiny pieces were starting to slip out and fall slowly to the ground where they shattered like so many soap bubbles.

"Uh—" I said. "Uh, Doctor—there's something wrong with my eye."

"Your I?"

"Uh, yes. The pupil is gone."

"The pupil is gone from your I?" The doctor was astounded. "How astounding!"

I could only nod—so I did. (A bit too hard perhaps. A few more pieces came flaking off and fluttered gently to the floor. We watched for a bit.)

"Hm," she said. "I have a theory about that. Would you like to hear it?"

I didn't answer. She was going to tell me her theory whether I wanted to hear it or not.

"The world is coming to an end," she whispered conspiratorially.

"Right now?" I asked, somewhat worriedly. I still hadn't fed the cat.

"No, but soon," she reassured me.

"Oh," I said.

We sat there in silence. After a bit, she cleared her throat. "I think . . ." she began slowly, then she trailed off.

"That's nice," I said, but she didn't hear me.

" . . . I think that the world exists only as a reflection of our minds. It exists the way it does only because that's the way we think it does."

"*I* think—therefore *I* exist," I said. But she ignored me. She told me to be quiet.

"Yes, you exist," she confirmed. (I'm glad she did—I was beginning to be a bit worried—and this was the wrong day for it. The last time I looked this was Tuesday.) "You exist," she said, "because you think you do. And the world also exists because you think it does."

"Then, when I die—the world ends with me . . . ?" I asked hopefully, making a mental note not to die.

"No—that's nonsense. No sane and rational man believes in solipsism." She scratched at her eyeball with a fork and went on.

"When you die—*you* cease to exist," she said. "But the world goes on—it goes on because everybody else who's still alive still believes that it exists. (The only thing they've stopped believing in is you.) You see, the world is a collective figment of all of our individual imaginations."

"I'm sorry," I said stiffly. "I do not believe in collectivism." I unbent a little so as to sit up. "I am a staunch Republican."

"Don't you see?" she said, ignoring my interruption. "This mass hallucination that the world is real just keeps on going because of its own inertia. You believe in it because that's the way it was when you first began to exist—that is when everybody else first began to believe you existed. When you were born, you saw that the world followed a certain set of rules that other people believed in, so you believed in them too—the fact that you believe in them just gives them that much more strength."

"Oh," I said. I lay there listening to her, trying to figure out some way to leave gracefully. My eye was starting to hurt and I couldn't see the ceiling any more. The fog was rolling in again.

"Look at the church!" she said suddenly.

"Huh?" I said.

"Look at the church!" she said it again, insistent.

I tried to. I lifted my head and tried to look at the church, but the fog was too thick. I couldn't even see my toes.

"Look at it," she said. "*Faith* is the basic precept of religion—faith that what they're telling you is true! Don't they tell you to have faith in the church, that faith can work miracles?!! Well, I'll tell you something—it can! If enough people believe in something, it becomes reality!"

By now, my eye was throbbing most painfully. I tried to sit up, but her strong hands held me back. She leaned closer and whispered intensely, "Yes! It's true. It is."

"If you say so," I nodded.

She went on, "Fortunately, the church long ago abandoned miracles in favor of conservatism—now, it's fighting to preserve the status quo! The church is one of the last bastions of reality—it's one of the few things holding back chaos!"

"Chaos?"

"Yes, chaos."

"Oh."

"The world is changing," she explained. "Man is changing it."

I nodded. "Yes, I know. I read the newspapers too."

"No, no! That's not what I meant! Man is changing his world unconsciously! More and more people are starting to believe that they really can change their environment—and the more they believe it, the more drastically it changes. I'll give you an example—fossils!"

"Fossils?"

"Yes, fossils. Nobody ever discovered any fossils until people started believing in evolution—then when they did start to believe in it, you couldn't turn around without tripping over fossils."

"You really believe this?" I asked.

"Yes, I do!" she said intensely.

"Then it must be so," I said.

"Oh, it is," she agreed and I knew that she really did believe it. She made a very convincing case. In fact, the more she talked, the more I began to believe it too.

"Why did you tell me all this?" I asked.

"Because we're in great danger. That's why." She whispered fiercely, "The world isn't changing uniformly. Everybody is starting to believe in different things and they're forming pockets of non-causality."

"Like a pimple?" I offered.

"Yes," she said and I could see a small one forming on the tip of her nose. "It works this way: a fanatic meets another fanatic, then the two of them meet with some other people who share the same hallucinations and pretty soon there are a whole bunch of fanatics all believing the same thing—pretty soon, their delusions become real for them—they've started to contradict the known reality and replaced it with a node of non-reality."

I nodded and concentrated on wrapping a swirl of the fog securely around me.

"The more it changes, the more people believe in the changes, and the stronger they become. If this keeps up we may be the only sane people left in the world—and we're in danger—"

"They're outnumbering our reality?" I suggested.

"Worse than that—all of their different outlooks are starting to flaw the structure of space! Even the shape of the Earth is changing! Why, at one time, it was really flat—the world didn't turn round until people started to believe it was round."

I turned round then and looked at her, but she had disappeared into the fog. All that was left was her grin.

"But the world is really pear shaped," I said. "I read it in *Scientific American*."

"And why do you think it's changing shape?" The grin asked. "It's because a certain nation is starting to believe that it's really bigger than it is. The Earth is bulging out to accommodate them."

"Oh," I said.

"It's the fault of the news media—television is influencing our image of the world! They keep telling us that the world is changing—and more and more people keep believing it."

"Well," I said. "With the shape of the world the way it is today, any change has got to be for the—"

"Oh, God—not you too! All you people keep talking about the world going to pieces—falling apart at the seams—"

And then even the grin was gone.

I was left there. I was also right. Other people had begun to notice it too. Great chunks of the surface *had* gone blotchy and holes had appeared in it. More and more pieces were falling out all the time, but the waters had not yet broken through from the other side.

I poked my finger through one of the holes and I could feel the soft gelatinous surface behind. Perhaps it hadn't completely thawed out yet.

So far, nothing had been accomplished about my eye—not only was it beginning to ache something fierce, but my I was beginning to twinge a bit also and I had a feeling that that too might be going opaque.

"Have you found yourself yet?!!" one of the speakers in the park demanded. (I hadn't even looked—and remembering my previous experiences with looking for things, I certainly was not going to initiate any kind of a search.) I walked on.

Farther on, there was another speaker—this one on a soup box. "We should be thankful for this great nation of ours," the speaker woofed and tweetered, "where so many people are allowed to believe in so many different things."

I rubbed at my eye. I had an uneasy queasy feeling that great cracks were opening in the ceiling.

"Anyone can get up and speak for his cause—any group can believe in anything they choose—indeed we can remake the world if we want to! And in our own images!"

Things were teetering right and left—also write and wrong.

"But the truly great thing about it," he continued, "is that no matter how much we contradict each other, we are all working together for the common good! Our great democratic system lets us minimize our differences so that we can all compromise ourselves. Only by suggesting all the alternatives to a problem can we select the best possible solution. In the long run, this ultimate freedom and individuality will help all of us to achieve the most good for the most people!"

It sounded good to me.

When I got home, the workmen were just finishing with the wallpaper. It was amazing how solid the surface looked once all the cracks and flaws in it had been covered with a gaudy flowered facade.

I could no longer tell where the plaster had given way—and the bare surface of the understructure had disappeared into the fog. Indeed, the only thing was that the ceiling seemed to be much lower than before.

I paused long enough to stroke the cat. He waved as I came in. "Like—hello, man," said the cat. "Give me a J."

"I can't. I'm having trouble with my I."

"Well, then give me a dollar."

"What for?"

"For a trip," he said.

"Oh." I gave him a dollar, waited for the trip.

He dropped the bill into his mouth, lit it, picked up his suitcase and quickly rose to a cruising level of thirty thousand feet. Then he headed west. I did not quite understand this. The fog had gotten much worse and the controllers were just not letting any traffic through.

There had been something I had wanted to ask, but I had forgotten it. Oh, well—it couldn't have been very important. But I wish I could figure out—

The man on the TV was a Doctor. He sat on top of it with his feet dangling in front of the screen (his cleats were scratching the image) and said that the drugs were destroying the realities. Drugs could destroy a person's sanity by altering his perceptions of the world until he could no longer perceive reality at all.

"Just so long as it doesn't change what he believes in," I muttered and turned him off. Then I turned him out. It was getting late and I wanted to get some sleep. However, I did make a mental note not to have my prescription refilled. Already the wallpaper was peeling.

In fact, by now, only the framework of the structure is left, and it looks like it's made out of chocolate pudding. Maybe it is. Perhaps it *is* the drugs. Maybe they *are* altering our collective fogments—but I haven't noticed anything.

Afterword:

I've often wondered just what the difference is between a

madman and a politician. I suspect it has something to do with the number of followers that either has.

For instance, what would Mao-Tse-Tung be without 700 million Chinese under him? Just another cranky old man.

I remember once seeing a cartoon showing a psychiatrist looking out of his office window at an arriving patient. There below him, on the street, was a royal coach drawn by four ornately harnessed thoroughbreds. There was a coachman, two footmen, and a very regal looking set of guards—all very loyally aiding a man dressed disturbingly like Napoleon.

That cartoon says it better than any set of words. When we start taking our madmen seriously, we're in trouble. Look what happened when Germany started listening to a deranged paper-hanger.

Too many of our insanities are tolerated because they are harmless on an individual level—but multiply them by a millionfold and you have a nation that is culturally sick. These things stem from each individual's conception of himself—which he arbitrarily assumes to be the nature of the world as well. These conceptions are haphazardly picked up during youth—along with all of the other opinions, neuroses, hangups and etceteras common to the human animal.

(Sometimes I wonder how some people can do some of the things they do to impressionable children—don't they realize it's not the child they're hurting, but the adult who will stem from that child? Ah, but that's a rhetorical question—)

As yet, there doesn't seem to be any way to prove that any one person's set of conceptions, opinions, neuroses, hangups and etceteras are any more correct than anyone else's set— let alone sane. (Define sanity.)

Keeping this in mind about all human beings—and especially those who consider themselves *leaders*—I ask, shouldn't we concentrate on ascertaining just what the questions are before we decide on the answers?

Introduction to

IN THE BARN:

More than any other writer, Piers Anthony is responsible for there *being* an *Again, Dangerous Visions* and a forthcoming final volume in (what has now become) a trilogy. I talked about it a bit in the general introduction to this book, but I think it bears repeating here, in Piers's own little section preceding "In the Barn," which is very much the kind of *story* that was being sought when DV was first conceived.

In the introduction to David Gerrold's story, which you've just read, if you're dealing with this literary entity sequentially, I noted that David had come to sf not through the traditional channels accepted by the old-line *afficionados*, but via TV, a totem and a route of his times. Rather than struggling up through the pulp magazines, writing crap at a penny-a-word for ten years, or pounding out witless action paperbacks for a grand-and-a-half (for four months' work), Gerrold got his break into sf paid handsomely for a different *kind* of dreaming. But not till he had written those penny-a-word stories for the magazines—in some ways lesser work than his TV script—was he accepted by the cadre. The mass of sf readers and fans are a fickle people. They don't take to newcomers all that quickly, though the editors and their fellow-writers do. The fans seem loath to raise to the heights too quickly, those new writers constantly banging on the doors and breaking the windows of the house of sf glory.

Most frequently, the fans will have known about a writer for some time, will have followed his life and his career, particularly if he started out in the ranks of fandom, writing for the amateur magazines, finally selling a story here, a story there. And eventually, when a fan turned writer has paid sufficient dues in the eyes of the omniscient observers, they will grudgingly admit him to the ranks of the professionals, even though he may have been selling for ten years. It is a peculiar kind of peer-group acceptance, and it's as Robert Silverberg once said: for that kind of writer, his public progress in the craft is like that of the Chambered Nautilus, the cephalopod that moves though the various rooms of its shell

till it emerges and dies. In effect, it carries its past on its
back. So, too, do sf writers who have to win the approbation
of sf fans. The fans never forget. They find it difficult to deal
with the reality of a writer *today,* as he is. They see him still
as eighteen years old and trying to effect the metamorphosis
from amateur to pro. It can be a killing thing, forever shadowed in the eyes of one's "audience" by the ineradicable record of what one has been. Some writers never outgrow the
need to win the praise of that tiny coterie of vocal fans. And
there are writers in our genre whose work has been stunted
forever because fans did not want them to move forward,
change, expand. If you doubt the truth of these remarks—and
I await with a certain stoicism the inevitability of fan magazine
response to these harsh criticisms of The Faithful—you need
only ask Isaac Asimov how he feels when fans tell him the
best thing he's ever written is "Nightfall," published in 1941,
years before the first of his hundred-plus books. You need
only ask Philip K. Dick or James Schmitz or Robert Heinlein
or any of the many other writers who avoid contact with
fandom, why they have chosen to absent themselves from
close contact with organized fans and their publications. You
need only ask Kurt Vonnegut why he fought so hard to have
the words "science fiction" disassociated from his work. That
is, if you can track them down.

Only rarely in our field does a writer emerge quickly and
totally, like Athena from the forehead of Zeus, whole and
complete, writing the way he or she wants to write, and giving very little of a damn for the opinions of the fans with
their frequently already-formed conceptions of what is acceptable in the genre.

It happened with Sheckley, and it happened with Ursula
Le Guin, and it happened with Lafferty, and it happened with
Norman Spinrad, and it happened with Tom Disch . . .

And it happened with Piers Anthony.

He came into being between the closing of *Dangerous
Visions* to contributors, and the book's publication. In that
one year—1967—Piers Anthony's *Chthon* (pronounced
thōn) was published by Betty Ballantine (whose antennae for
new writers are supersensitive and almost always amazingly
accurate) and was an immediate sensation. It was nominated
for both the Hugo and the Nebula in that year, and though it
missed copping the awards, the name Piers Anthony was suddenly a first-rank one. His work began appearing in all the
top magazines, and more important, what he wrote was
talked about. He became a focal point of controversy, and
when his contentiously exciting replies to critics began ap-

pearing in the fanzines, it was apparent here was a man who was willing to stand toe-to-toe with all the self-styled little literary dictators, and punch the shit out of them when their opinions were muddle-headed or impertinent or uninformed. And often when they weren't.

I met Piers A. D. Jacob at Damon Knight's 1966 Milford (Penna.) Writers' Workshop, and while it took some time till later for us to become what each of us would call "friends," we developed instant respect for one another. I know I did for him, and he assures me the reverse was true. Though I don't recall Piers ever raising his voice at that workshop—a situation in which obsidian idols would become hysterical— his presence was felt, and he had the strength of personal conviction to attack with solid literary judgments some of the gods in attendance. When we all went out to dinner at one of the lesser dining spas in Milford, Piers ordered a special vegetarian meal (with some difficulty), and my respect for him increased at the manner in which he handled the remarks and stares of his fellow writers. It was clear that Piers was his own kind of man, that he had decided in what way he could best support the kind of life he felt he needed to enrich himself, and in the most laudatory senses of the word he was a "strange" man. In some ways he is the most interesting of all the interesting people who write sf. The fascination of the man, incidentally, carries over strongly into his work, and—if I can be pardoned equating the writer with what he writes —where his soul resides in life has much to do with the depth of his stories.

In any case, Piers was too late for DV, but he wrote a very long, very perceptive review of the book for one of the fanzines, and in it he mentioned that if there was to be a sequel, he would rain fire and brimstone on me if he was overlooked. At that point, contemplating no companion volumes, I regretted having closed the book just before the advent of Anthony, because I was deeply impressed by *Chthon*.

And later, when Larry Ashmead shunted my little red wagon onto the spur leading to A,DV and it became obvious I should not repeat anybody who'd been in the first volume, I started drawing up a list of writers I wanted in this book. The first name on the list was Piers Anthony. He seemed to embody all the qualities necessary for an appearance in a book intended to carry forward the ideas of DV: he had come to prominence during the period of "the new wave" (God forgive my use of that phrase), he wrote in a style and with a verve peculiarly his own, he had a sound grounding in the disciplines of the best sf of the past, he was outspoken, his themes were fresh and different, and he was brave.

So I solicited a story from him.

He sent me a manuscript titled "The Barn" and I liked it very much. I made a few suggestions for revision and wondered if he'd mind adding "In" to the title.

Here, in part, was his response, included with this introduction to the man himself, as a (hopefully) interesting insight into how an editor and a writer can work together.

October 14, 1968

Dear Harlan,

When I saw the ms of "The Barn" back, I knew my work had bounced ... yet again, and of course that particular piece had no real hope of publication elsewhere. You had nicely preserved the ms by backing it with cardboard, though, and used your own envelope. I had enclosed postage but not envelope because I had figured you would want the story. Ah, well, and I took the story out—and discovered that the cardboard was instead a six-page cardboard-colored letter *accepting* the story. You bastard, you shook me up again.

Business first: can do. You ask for revision *not* deleting the meaty portions, but intensifying them by increasing the protagonist's personal involvement. You are talking my language. Fact is, the version of the story I showed you I knew was sketchy, because I concentrated on the brutality, the shock value. As it stood, I did not consider it high-class literature—yet it seemed to me it could be improved quite a bit by filling in more on the hero (?), Hitch. His own background, a frustrated love affair, some kind of emotional parallel to what he saw in the barn—but I didn't do it a) because it would have lengthened the story, that might already be unacceptable because of what it described, and b) because it would have required additional work and craftsmanship, and I've put my full skill into my work only to have it bounced by all markets too many times already. One does hesitate to open his vein too far if he suspects his blood is draining not into a patient clinging to life but a rank sewer.

OK—it seems to me now that we see eye-to-eye on this story, that lengthening and strengthening of personal involvement will not be effort wasted on you, and I shall go to it. You suggest that Hitch might fuck (that word won't be used in the story: not because I'm prudish, but because it would strike at a different cerebral level than I'm aiming for in this story) her, and feel an attachment. So what I have in mind is to run through the sick scene—hand-milking, and temperature, heated erection (what *is* the term for perpetual and painful erection? I needed it for this story, couldn't remember it, and couldn't find it listed. I thought it was peripeneurises or some such, but found no such word in my dictionary. Damn frustrating, to know the word exists but not be able to pinpoint it.) pretty much as before, then have the contact with Iota, the teen-aged breeder, be too much. . . .

Main reason I stick to novels now is that I have yet to fail to sell an sf novel, yet still can not sell more than about one story in five, though it is the same skill applied to each form. Seems as though the magazines are determined to bounce anything with any reasonable spark of originality or imagination—but let's not get back into that gripe. You proved the truth of any complaints I might make when you published DV. (You know, I haven't seen any other editor claim he *would* have published "Riders of the Purple Wage" either. They still claim it is a wide-open market, but they don't mention that . . .)

You say you created A,DV just for *me?* I find that hard to believe. How about this: you are afraid that if you *don't* include me, I will review it again . . . anyway, whatever the weight of various factors, I'm glad you had the first and will have a second. The field does need this type of shaking up. Even more, the field needs the replacement of about four magazine editors . . . but that's another matter. You realize, I trust, that you won't be able to come up with another "Purple Wage," and that all the people who condemned *it* will then condemn *you* for not duplicating the feat? Yeah, you know.

Lastly, the baby. She's a year old now, been walking since 9½ months, has shoulder-length hair, is impossibly cute. My prejudice, of course—except that everyone who sees her agrees. Name is Penelope—"Penny"—kind of you to inquire. I can't do much writing on the days I am taking care of her (my wife works 3 days a week, thus I work the remaining 4), but should be able to handle the "Barn" revision this coming weekend. You should be hearing from me again, then, in about a week.

Sincerely,
Piers

And then, just five days later, I received the following . . .

October 19, 1968

Dear Harlan,

   Here, 4,000 words longer, is "In the Barn." I incorporated your notions and mine, and have what I believe is a superior version. I have not proofread it, so there will be typos etc., but I wanted to get it out to you as soon as possible. Hurricane Gladys passed by here in the last day, and we were without power for 17 hours, so portions of the manuscript were typed by kerosene lamplight.

   This revision helped take my mind off a different problem. Four days ago I had a call from the last publisher I submitted my novel *Macroscope* to, Avon. He was ready to offer an advance of $5,000 without significant revision . . . but it turned out he hadn't read the last 90 pages. Since those very pages made another publisher change its mind, I advised him to finish the ms, then make his offer again if he still felt the same. He said ok, he'd call back in a day or two . . . and that was the last I heard. Ouch! Did I scare him off?

Piers

   As it turned out, Piers had not scared off Avon's editor, George Ernsberger, and *Macroscope* was published in 1969 to mixed, but controversial, reviews.

   In the last few years Piers has run afoul of the Recession-produced wearies even longer-established, bigger-name writers have come to know. (We can thank Messrs. Nixon, Agnew, Mitchell, Rogers *et thugs* for that condition of life: possibly the most innovative method yet devised for "balancing the economy." They may balance it so well that within a short time we'll all be back on the barter system, which might not be a bad idea at that. Anyhow . . .) Yet he has continued to write, and his work continues to be marked by vigor, innovation and a commendable fearlessness.

   I think "In the Barn" will surprise, delight and possibly even shock a few of you; but whatever its final judgment by critics and posterity, it holds for this editor the essence of what this book attempts to do in advancing sf and the fiction of the imagination.

   As for the man behind the story, I include here his autobiographical musings, in many ways as fascinating as the stories they helped produce. Friends, I give you Piers A. D. Jacob.

   "I was born in Oxford, England on August 6, 1934, thus (I think) beating out John Brunner for the honor of being the first contemporary sf writer to be born in that particular locale by about six weeks. Both my parents graduated from

Oxford University, which is why I happened to be there at the time. They both went on to obtain Ph.D's in America, while I went on to become an, er, science fiction writer. Happens in the best of families. I lived in England to about the age of four, when I joined my parents in Spain. They were doing relief work under the auspices of the AFSC (American Friends Service Committee), feeding milk and food to the hungry children during the Spanish civil war. I believe my father, Alfred Jacob (brother, that fouls up my pseudonym, doesn't it) was head of the Spanish AFSC relief project. When Franco took over, things became dubious; my family's sympathies were with the Loyalists, who lost that war. One day my father disappeared. After several days he managed to smuggle out a note, and thus was documented what the new government had denied: he had been thrown in jail. One of those holes with a trench for sanitary facilities and no separate bathrooms for the female prisoners: the sort you read about in novels but don't really believe exist. They *do* exist. He got out, but the agreement was that he would depart the country. That spared the Fascists having to admit they had made a mistake. I don't know what happened to the stores of food for the starving children after that, but I doubt they went where intended. We boarded the *Excalibur* (this is from memory, so I don't guarantee ship or spelling, but I think that's it) and steamed for America in August, 1940. It happened to be the same ship and the same voyage that the Duke of Windsor made, going to the Bahamas. Remember, he was King Edward VIII of England, who reigned for less than a year until he abdicated in order to marry an American divorcee. I had my sixth birthday on that voyage, celebrated by a cake made of sawdust (they were short of party supplies: WW II, you know) and a harmonica present. I played the latter endlessly, and I wonder to this day whether the one time King of England had to grit his teeth at the interminable racket.

"School in America was no fun. I attended five schools while struggling through first grade, flunking it twice. Those first grade schools were in five states, too: Pennsylvania, Vermont, New Hampshire, Maine and New York. If I were to judge states by that sampling, I would rate Pennsylvania at the top, New Hampshire in the middle, and the rest at the bottom. In New York they were trying to teach me to pronounce my words correctly—not realizing that it was *my English accent* they were attempting to eradicate.

"College was a kind of paradise. All the food I could eat (and I ate more than any person my size I know, without gaining weight) and almost complete freedom. It was a no-grade system, so there was no class pressure except the student's own desire to learn, and my desire was not particularly strong at first. Much of that freedom was wasted, as I did not achieve puberty until age 18 and did not shave until 21, but I did learn the essentials, as demonstrated by the fact that I got married upon graduation. For my thesis I wrote a science fiction novel, at 95,000 words the longest thesis in the history of the college until that time, 1956. It never sold, but years later I reworked one segment of it for a contest and won $5,-000. I was drafted into the army in March, 1957, took basic at Ft. Dix and Survey training at Ft. Sill, Oklahoma.

"The army was not paradise. I, as a pacifistically inclined vegetarian, barely made it through basic (about a third of my cycle *didn't*—illness, mostly). They called me "No Meat." When the time came for me to make PFC they pulled a battery rank-freeze. I went to the battalion C.O. and next day exactly one PFC stripe came down: mine.

"In 1959 we moved to Florida, where we stayed. We had medical problems, so that we were married eleven years before we had a baby survive birth. Our first, Penny, came in 1967, and our second, Chery, in 1970; both bright, cute little girls well worth waiting for. Penny walked at 9½ months and spoke 500 words by 18 months; not sure I can do as much myself, some days! We're basically settled and happy, and now I've even conformed to the writer's image by growing a beard.

"My writing career has been similar to other aspects of my life. I wrote on and off for eight years before selling my first story late in 1962 for $20.

"I have sold stories to all the major sf magazines in this country (hard to count exactly, because some have been republished as portions of a novel)—a score or so, I guess. Eleven novels at this writing, with four more on the market, and more in progress, since I earn my living by writing. They range from juvenile sf to pornographic fantasy, though my ultimate aspiration is to write straight history. Six have sold in England, and I have a few translation sales: Holland, Germany, Japan.

"Titles of novels: *Chthon* (Ballantine 1967); *Sos the Rope* (F&SF, Pyramid, 1968, contest winner); *The Ring* (with Robert Margroff; Ace Special 1968); *Omnivore* (Ballantine 1968, SF Book Club 1969); *Macroscope* (Avon 1969); *The E.S.P. Worm* (w/Margroff; Paperback Library 1970); *Orn* (serialized in *Amazing* magazine, 1970; Avon 1971? SF Book Club 1971?); *Hasan* (serialized in *Fantastic* magazine, 1969-

70; bought by a book publisher but written off without publication in 1971); *Var the Stick* (Bantam 1971?); *Prostho Plus* (the dental series novelized; Berkley 1972?); *Neq the Sword* (Bantam 1972?). Question marks indicate my guess when they will be published. One novel, *Chthon,* was in the running for both Nebula and Hugo, but made neither; *Macroscope* was on the Hugo ballot but lost, and one of the dental stories, "Getting Through University," was also on the Hugo ballot."

Piers Anthony

IN THE BARN

The barn was tremendous. It was reminiscent, Hitch thought, of the red giants of classical New England (not to be confused with the blue dwarfs of contemporary farming), but subtly different. The adjacent fences were there as usual, together with the granary and corncrib and round silo and even a standard milkhouse at one end. To one side was a shed with a large tractor and cultivating machinery, and to the other were conventional mounds of hay. But the curves and planes of the main structure—a genuine farmer could probably have called out fifty major and minor aspects of distinction from anything known on Earth-Prime.

Hitch, however, was not a connoisseur of barns, EP or otherwise; he was merely a capable masculine interworld investigator briefed in farming techniques. He could milk a cow, fork manure, operate a disc-harrow or supervise the processing of corn silage—but the nuances of bucolic architecture were beyond him.

This, mundane as it might appear, was it: the site of his

dangerous inter-earth mission. Counter-Earth #772, located by another fluke of the probability aperture, and for him a routine investigation into a nonroutine situation. Almost a thousand Earth-alternates had been discovered in the brief decade the aperture had operated reliably, most quite close to Earth-Prime in type. Several even had the same current U.S. President, making for rather intriguing dialogues between heads-of-state. If, as some theorists would have it, this was a case of parallel evolution of worlds, the parallels were exceedingly close; if a case of divergence from Earth-Prime (or if EP represented a split from one of the other worlds—heretical thought!), the break or series of breaks had occurred quite recently.

But only Earth-Prime had developed the aperture; only EP could send its natives into alternate frameworks and bring them back whole, live and sane. Thus it claimed the title of stem-world, the originator, and none of the others had been able to refute it. None—yet. Hitch tried not to think too much about the time when a more advanced Earth would be encountered—one that could talk back. Or fight back.

On the surface, #772 was similar to the other worlds he had visited during past missions, except for one thing. It was retarded. It appeared to have suffered from some planetary cataclysm that had set it back technologically thirty years or so. A giant meteor-strike, a recent ice-age—Hitch was not much on historical or geological analysis, but knew that something had severely reduced its animal life, and so set everything back while the people readjusted.

There were no bears on #772, no camels, no horses, sheep or dogs. No cats or pigs. Few rodents. Man, in fact, was about the only mammal that remained, and it would be centuries before he had any overpopulation problem here. Perhaps a germ from outer space had wiped the mammals out, or a bad freeze; Hitch didn't know and hardly cared. His concern was with immediacies. His job was to find out how it was that livestock was such an important enterprise, dominating the economics of this world. Barns were everywhere, and milk was a staple industry—yet there were no cows or goats or similar domesticants.

That was why he now stood before this barn. Within it must lie the secret to #772's sinister success.

So—a little innocuous snooping, before the official welcome to EP's commonwealth of alternates. Earth-Prime did not want to back into an alliance with a repressive dictatorship or human-sacrifice society or whatever other bizarrity might be manifested. Every alternate *was* different, in some obvious or devious manner, and some were—well, no matter what Io said, that was not his worry. She liked to lecture him on the theoretical elements of alternistic intercourse, while cleverly avoiding the more practical man-woman intercourse *he* craved. In the months he had known her he had developed a considerable frustration.

Now he had to make like a farmhand, in the name of Earth-Prime security and diplomacy. A fine sex-sublimation *that* promised to be! He could contemplate manure and dream of Iolanthe's face.

He kicked a clod of dirt and advanced on his mission. Too bad the initial surveyor had not taken the trouble to peek into a barn. But virgin-world investigators were notoriously gun-shy if not outright cowards. They popped in and out again in seconds, repeating in scattered locations, then turned their automatic cameras and sensors over to the lab for processing in detail while they resumed well-paid vacations. The dirty work was left to the second-round investigators like Hitch.

Behind the barn were long corrals extending down to a meandering river. That would be where the livestock foraged during the day. But the only photograph of such an area had evidently been taken of a cleanup session, because human beings had been in the pastures instead of animals. Typically blundering surveyor!

No, he had to be fair, even to a first-rounder. The work *was* risky, because there was no way to tell in advance what menaces lurked upon an unprobed alternate. The man might land in a cloud of mustard-gas or worse, or in the jaws of a carnosaur, and pop back into EP a blistered or bloody hulk. He had to keep himself alive long enough for his equipment to function properly, and there was no time to poke into such things as barns. Robotic equipment couldn't be used because of the peril of having it fall into inimical hands. The first investigator of #772 probably had not even been aware of the shortage of animals, nor would he have considered it significant. Only the tedious lab analysis had showed up the incongruity of this particular world.

Still, that picture was unusual. Maybe it had been a barn-yard party, because in the foreground had been a splendidly naked woman. The farmers of #772 evidently knew how to let off steam, once the hay was in!

Once he got home, *he* was going to let off steam—and this time sweet Io would not divert the subject until well after the ellipsis.

He was very near the barn now, but in no hurry. His mission could terminate suddenly therein, and natural caution restrained him.

Transfer to #772 had been no problem. A mere opening of the interworld veil, a boost through, and Hitch was in the same geographic area of another frame of reality. When he finished here, a coded touch on the stud embedded in his skull would summon the recovery aperture in seconds, and he would be hooked back through. He was in no danger so long as he kept alert enough to anticipate trouble by those few seconds. All he had to do was make his investigation and get the facts without arousing suspicion or getting into trouble with the locals. He was allowed no weapon other than a nondescript knife strapped to his ankle, per the usual policy. He agreed; imagine the trouble a lost stunner could cause . . .

So far it had been deceptively simple. He had been landed in a wooded area near a fair-sized town, so that his entry had not flabbergasted any happenstance observer. That was another fringe benefit of the initial survey: the identification of suitable places for more leisurely entry. It wouldn't do to find himself superimposed upon a tree!

He had walked into that town and filched a newspaper. The language of #772 matched that of EP, at least in America, and he read the classified section without difficulty. Only the occasional slang terms put him off. Under HELP WANTED were a number of ads for livestock attendants. That was what he was here for.

No bovines or caprines or equines or porcines—what *did* they use?

The gentleman farmer to whom he applied at break of day hadn't even checked his faked credentials. Hitch had counted on that; dawn was rush-hour for a farm, and an under-staffed outfit could hardly be choosy then. "Excellent! We need an experienced man. We have some fine animals here, and we don't like to skimp on supervision. We try to take good care of our stock."

Animals, stock. Did they milk chickens or turtles here? "Well," Hitch had said with the proper diffidence, "it has been a little while since I worked a farm. I've been traveling abroad." That was to forestall challenge of his un #772 accent. "Probably take me a day or so to recover the feel of it, to fall back into the old routine, you know. But I'll do my best." For the hour or two he was here, anyway.

"I understand. I'll give you a schedule for my smallest unit. Fifty head, and not a surly one among them. Except perhaps for Iota—but she's in heat. They generally do get frisky about that time. No cause for alarm." He brought out a pad and began scribbling.

"You know the names of all your animals?" Hitch hardly cared about that inconsequential, but preferred to keep the farmer talking.

The man obliged, smiling with pride as his pencil moved. "All of them. None of that absentee ownership here—I run my farm myself. And I assure you every cow I own is champion-sired."

Cow? Hitch suspected that the labman who had made the critical report on #772 had been imbibing the developer fluid. No bovines, indeed! For a damn clerical error, he had been sent out—

"And if you have any trouble, just call on me," the farmer said, handing him the written schedule and a small book. "I'd show you the layout myself, but I'm behind on my paperwork."

"Trouble?"

"If an animal gets injured—sometimes they bang against the stalls or slip. Or if any equipment malfunctions—"

"Oh, of course." Yes, he could see the man was in a hurry. Perfect timing.

It had been *too* easy. Now Hitch's experienced nose smelled more than manure: trouble. It was the quiet missions that were most apt to boomerang.

He glanced at the schedule-paper before he entered the indicated cowshed. The handwriting was surprisingly elegant: 1. FEEDING 2. MILKING 3. PASTURE 4. CLEANUP ... and several tighter lines below. It all seemed perfectly routine. The booklet was a detailed manual of instructions for reference when the need arose. All quite in order. There were cows in that barn, despite what any half-crocked report had said, and he would verify it shortly. Very shortly.

Why, then, did he have such a premonition of disaster?

Hitch shrugged and entered. There was a stifling aroma of backhouse at first, but of course this was typical. A cowbarn was the barniest kind of barn. His nose began to adapt almost immediately, though the odor was unlike that of the unit he had been briefed in. He ceased—almost—to notice it.

He paused just inside the door to let his other senses adapt to the gloom and rustle of the balmy interior. He faced a kind of hallway leading deep into the barn, lined on either side by stalls. Above the long feeding troughs twin rows of heads projected, emerging from the padded slats of the individual compartments. They turned to face him expectantly as he approached, making gentle, almost human murmurs of an-

ticipation. This morning the herd was hungry, naturally; it
was already late.

At the far end was the entrance to the "milkshed"—an
area sealed off from the stable by a pair of tight doors. Short
halls opened left and right from where he stood, putting him
at the head of a T configuration. The left offshoot contained
bags of feed; the other—

Hitch blinked, trying to banish the remaining fogginess.
For a moment, peering down that right-hand passage, he
could have sworn he had seen a beautiful, black-haired
woman staring at him from a stall—naked. A woman very
like Iolanthe—except that he had never so much as glimpsed
Io in the nude.

Ridiculous; his more determined glance showed nothing
there. His subconscious was playing tricks on him, perking up
a dull assignment.

He faced forward with self-conscious determination. The
episode, fleeting and insubstantial as it had been, had shaken
him up, and now it was almost as though he had stagefright
before the audience of animals.

As his eyes adjusted completely, Hitch felt a paralysis of
shock coming over him. These were not bovine or caprine
snouts greeting him; these were *human* heads. The fair features and lank tresses of healthy young women. Each stood
in her stall, naked, hands grasping the slats since there was
room only for the head to poke through. Blondes, brunettes,
redheads; tall, petite, voluptuous—all types were represented.
This group, clothed, could have mixed enhancingly into any
festive Earth-Prime crowd.

Except for two things. First, their bosoms. The breasts
were enormous and pendulous, in some cases hanging down
to waist-level, and quite ample in proportion. Hitch was sure
no conventional brassiere could confine these melons. They
were long beyond cosmetic control. It would require a plastic
surgeon with a sadistic nature to make even a start on the
job.

Second, the girls' expressions. They were the blank, amiable stares of idiocy.

Milkers . . .

For some reason he had a sudden vision of a hive of bees,
the workers buzzing in and out.

He had seen enough. His hand lifted to the spot on his
skull where his hair covered the signal-button—and hesitated
as his eye dwelt on the nearest pair of mammaries. Certainly
he had the solution to the riddle; certainly this alternate was
not fit for commonwealth status. Quite likely his report

would launch a planetary police action, for the brutal farming of human beings was intolerable. Yet—

The udderlike extremities quivered gently with the girl's respiration, impossibly full. He was attracted and repelled, as the intellectual element within him strove to suppress the physical. To put his hand on one of those . . .

If he left now—who would feed the hungry cows?

His report could wait half an hour. It would take longer than that for him to return to headquarters, even after the aperture had been utilized. Time was not short, yet.

Hitch opened the instruction book and read the paragraph on feeding. Water was no problem, he learned; it was piped into each cell to be sipped as desired. But the food had to be dumped into the trough by hand.

He returned to the storage area and loaded a sack of enriched biscuits onto a dolly. He wheeled this into the main hall and used the clean metal scoop to ladle out two pounds to each individual. The girls reached eagerly through to grasp the morsels, picking them up wholehanded, thumbs not opposed, and chewing on the black chunks with gusto. Hitch noticed that they all had strong white teeth, but could not determine why they failed to use their thumbs and fingers as— as thumbs and fingers. Why were they deliberately clumsy? Yes, they were healthy animals . . . and nothing more.

He had to return twice for new bags, keeping his eyes averted from the—empty?—right-hand hall lest his imagination taunt him again. He suspected that he was being too generous with the feed, but in due course breakfast had been served. He stood back and watched the feast.

The first ones had already finished, and a couple were squatting in the corners of their stalls, their bowels evidently stimulated to performance by the roughage. His presence did not seem to embarrass them during such intimate acts, any more than the presence of the farmer restrained a defecating cow. And these cows did seem to be contented. Had they all been lobotomized? He had observed no scars . . .

Idly, he sampled a biscuit. It was tough but not fibrous, and the flavor was surprisingly rich. According to the label, virtually every vitamin and mineral necessary for animal health and rich milk was contained herein. Only those elements copious in pasture foliage were skimped. Rolling the mass over his tongue, he could believe it. He wondered what kind of pasture was available for such as these; surely they didn't eat grass and leaves. Were there vegetables and fruits out there among the salt licks?

Now he had fed the herd. The cows would not suffer if he

deserted them, since the shift would change before they became really hungry again. He had no reason to dawdle longer. He could activate the signal and—

Again his hand halted short of the button. Those bobbling teats reminded him of the second item on his schedule: milking. He knew that real cows hurt if they did not get milked on time. These—udders—looked overfull already.

Damn it, he hadn't sacrificed his humanity when he obtained his investigator's license! The report could wait.

And, a small insidious voice taunted him, there was that vision in the T-hall stall. There *could* be a naked girl in there, obviously. One that did not resemble these pendulous cows. A—virginal type . . . that looked like Iolanthe.

That was the real reason he couldn't press the stud yet. He could not leave until he screwed up the courage to check that stall—thoroughly.

He reviewed the manual, glad for the moment to revert to routine. It seemed there were six milking machines for this wing: suction devices with vacuum-adhesive conical receptors. He opened the milking room and trundled one machine up to the first milking stand and flipped the switch. It hummed.

He hesitated before undertaking the next step, but the instructions were clear and he reminded himself that a job was a job. The prospect, he had to admit, was weird but not entirely onerous. He unbolted the first gate—the entire front of the stall swung open—and approached its occupant cautiously with the milking harness.

She was a tall brunette, generous of haunch and hair as well as the obvious. To his surprise she stood docilely while he attached the harness: fiber straps around neck and midriff and the chest just below the arms, with crosspieces down the back and between the breasts. The last was tight because the mammaries hung against each other like full wineskins (so it wasn't a contemporary image; nothing more apt came to mind) but he got it into place by sawing it through. The whole was designed to keep the cow from jumping off the stand or fidgeting too far from the milking machine, though Hitch doubted that the harness would withstand a determined lunge. These animals were well-trained, and required only gentle guidance. He hoped.

He had an unbidden vision of the cow careering about the barn, mooing, he trying ineffectively to brake her by clinging to one milk-slick protuberance. No!

He fastened the clasps and led her to the stand. This was a padded ramp with a cutaway in the center for the bulk of the milking machine and hooks for the termini of the harness.

The girl mounted it without instruction and placed her two hands knuckle-down on the front section and her knees on the back, so that she straddled the machine. Her breasts depended enormously, reaching down just beyond her elbows. The brown nipples were tremendous, and Hitch observed flecks of white on them, as though the very weight of milk were forcing the first squirts out.

He brought up one milker-cup and placed it over her right breast. It was shaped to accommodate the expanded nipple in the center, with a special circular flange of flexible rubber. The outer cone adhered by suction, its slightly moist perimeter making the seal perfect. He attached the left cup, turned the dial to MILK and stood back to watch the proceedings.

The feeder-cones covered only the lowermost surface of each breast, though they would have engulfed the architecture of a normal woman. They seemed to be efficient, regardless; the machine generated bursts of shaped suction that extracted the fluid quickly and cleanly. He could see the white of it passing through the transparent tubing, and hear the squirts of it striking the bottom of the covered pail as the breasts jumped to alternating vacuum. One-two! One-two! the rhythm was compelling, the pulsing whiteness suggestive of an interminable seminal ejaculation.

It's only milk! he reminded himself. But, unbidden, his erogenous zones were responding.

The girl masticated a chunk of hard cracker she had preserved, cudlike, in her cheek and waited with a half-smile. She was used to this, and glad to be relieved of the night's accumulation.

Only forty-nine to go! He left her there and proceeded to the next with considerably enhanced confidence. Cows were cows, after all, whatever their physical form.

By the time he had the sixth stand occupied, the first cow was done. He unhooked the brunette, whose bosom was now sadly slack, led her to the door in the far side of the milk room, and removed the halter. The front center strap came away from between dangling ribbons of flesh. How much had she been good for? Two quarts? A gallon? He had no idea of the prevailing standards, but presumed she was an adequate milker. She skipped outside with a happy twinkle of buttocks, her hair flouncing. From this viewpoint, beautiful.

Before he closed the door he observed that there were great piles of apples and carrots and what looked like unshelled peanuts in the yard. The girl was already scattering them about, not yet hungry enough to do more than play with her food. And there *were* salt-licks, down beside the stream.

The following hour was hectic. It took him, once he got the hang of it, about thirty seconds to place each cow and attach the milker, and about fifteen seconds to turn her loose again once drained. But more time was required for those farthest from the milk room, and every five cows he had to replace each machine's weighty bucket. As a result he was kept hopping, and the attention he spared for each individual became quite perfunctory. Dairy farming was hard work!

Sweat rolled down his nose as he placed the final capped bucket on the conveyor leading to the processing section of the barn and put the hoses and cups into the automatic washer/sterilizer. Milking was done, the stock pastured—last time he had looked, they were roughhousing amid peanut shells and splashing in the shallow river—and he could go home with a clear conscience. Whatever pay Hitch had earned so far in this world the owner could keep, courtesy of Earth-Prime. The man would need all his resources, when the EP police action commenced!

Whom was he fooling? He wasn't even close to making the return trip to Earth-Prime. He still had that stall to check. If there were a woman there, and if she did resemble Iolanthe—well, this *was* an alternate world. Many, perhaps most of its people could be identical or very similar to those of Earth. *There could be an Iolanthe here!*

Perhaps one more available than his own . . .

He closed his mind to the thought again, not caring to face its ramifications all at once. Anyway, there were concrete, mission-inspired reasons for him to remain here longer. For one thing, these milkers were obviously virtually mindless, rendered so by what means he could not tell. But they could not have freshened so voluminously without first having been bred. That meant calving, and not so very long ago—and what had happened to the babies?

Naturally his report would not be complete without this information. This was too blatant a situation to investigate casually. He had almost come to think of human beings as animals, during the rush of the milking, but of course they were not. This barn represented the most serious breach of human rights ever encountered in the alternate worlds, and it wasn't even in the name of war or racism. These were Caucasian animals—*girls!* he reminded himself furiously. How great was the total degradation of liberty, worldwide? Were there Negro and Mongol cows, or were other races used for brute-work or sport or . . . meat?

He had to discover much more, but he could not break loose and wander around the rest of the barn without a pretext. That would attract attention to himself all too quickly. And he did not *want* to poke into the right wing ... yet. He would have to continue his chores in a routine manner—and keep his eyes and ears wide open until he learned it all.

Next on the schedule was cleanup. He read the manual and discovered that this was not as bad as it might have been. The girls were naturally fastidious, and deposited their intestinal refuse in sumps provided in the corner of each stall. He had merely to activate the section fertilizer pump and flush each residue down its pipe, checking to make sure that no units were clogged. The smell from the vents was not sweet, but no direct handling was required.

Theoretically, however, he was supposed to check first to make sure the bowels were well-formed and of the proper color, consistency and effluvium, since nonconformity was an early signal of illness. If suspicious, he was also to probe for worms or bloodclots before flushing a given deposit. There was a special pan and spreader fork for this purpose. Nevertheless he ignored this instruction and flushed each sump without looking or sniffing closely. There were limits.

"Duty ends where my nose begins," he muttered.

He completed the cleanup circuit and could no longer avoid the problem of the T offshoot. Now that the main stable was empty, he could hear sounds from this wing. It *was* occupied! Anxiously he reviewed his schedule. The facts were there, obvious the moment he chose to look. The occupants of this section were special cases: items to take care of after the routine chores were accomplished.

He set himself and approached the wing. *There could be an Iolanthe here*—a stupid one.

To his relief and regret, the first stall contained a sick cow. She lay on a pallet along the side of the stall, a shapely blonde whose mammaries had diminished to merely voluptuous stature. He could tell they had shrunk because there were stretch-marks on them defining the grandeur that had been. Yet at this moment her bustline would have strained an EP tape measure.

There was a note that she had to be milked by hand, so as not to contaminate the equipment (even through sterilization? fussy, fussy!) and the milk disposed of. She would be tapered off entirely, then bred again when fully recovered. Her temperature had to be checked to make sure her fever remained down. Her name was Flora.

He had not paid attention to the names until now, though they were printed on the crosspiece of each gate. His ignorance had facilitated impersonality and blunted the horror of this monstrous barn. Now—

Hitch peered through the slats and surveyed this new problem. Milk her by hand? Take her temperature? That meant far more intimate contact than hitherto. He delved into the manual. Yes, the procedures were there . . .

Well, one thing at a time. He entered the pen with a small open bucket. "Up, Flora," he said briskly.

She looked at him with a disturbing but illusory semblance of intelligence, but did not move her torso. Damn the humanization wrought by knowledge of her name! He simply could not think of her any longer as an animal.

"Flora, I have to milk you," he explained. The anomaly of it struck him afresh, and he wondered whether he should not get out of this world right away.

No, not yet. He would never be satisfied if he left without verifying that vision of Io.

Flora continued to lie there on her side, one leg pulled up. Her hair fell across her face and curled over one outstretched arm, and he noticed how neatly it matched the hue of her pubic region.

He looked in the book again. "Milking a supine cow by hand . . ." the instructions began. Nothing like a complete manual!

He propped the bucket under the upper nipple and took Flora's breast in both hands. The feel of it gave him an immediate erection, despite everything he had seen during the mass-milking. It seemed he had been sight-anesthetized but not touch-anesthetized; or perhaps it was the fact that this was a true breast by his definitions rather than a gross udder, despite the stretch-marks. Or maybe it was simply the name. Had he known any blondes called Flora?

Was there a black-haired cow named Iolanthe?

In the line of duty . . .

He centered the nipple and squeezed. Nothing happened. He tried again, more positively, and succeeded in producing a translucent driblet. One milked a bovine-cow by squeezing the neck of the teat shut and applying more gentle pressure with the remainder of the hand so that the milk had only one exit, but the human breast was structured differently. It took him several tries to accomplish anything substantial and he was afraid it was rough on her, but Flora did not move or make any sign. Once he took hold too far back and feared he had bruised one of the internal glands, but she merely watched him with sad gray eyes.

The job was inexpert and messy, but he managed to get

several ounces into the bucket and probably several more on the two of them and the floor. It didn't matter; the point was to relieve the pressure, not to extract every tantalizing drop. *Why don't I just put my mouth on it and suck it out?* he thought wickedly. *Who would know?* But he remembered that the milk was supposed to be bad.

He poured the hard-won liquid down the disposal sump, flushed it, and tackled the nether breast.

"What have they done to you?" he asked rhetorically as he worked. "What makes you all—pardon the expression—so stupid? No woman on my planet would tolerate what I'm doing to you now." But he wondered about that as he said it; probably there were some types who—

Flora opened her mouth and he thought for a horrifying moment she was going to reply, but it was only a yawn. There was something funny about her tongue.

Now he had to take her temperature. The book cautioned him to insert the thermometer rectally, because the normal animal was apt to bite anything placed in her mouth. As if he hadn't done enough already! He had pulled some weird stunts as an interworld investigator, but this was breaking the record.

Still, she was ill, or had been, and it would be neglectful to skip the temperature. It had been neglectful to skip the feces inspection, too, he thought, but somehow it was different now. More—personal.

"Over, Flora," he said. "I can't get at you from this angle." He opened the supply box nailed to a wooden beam and found the thermometer: a rounded plastic tube about half an inch in diameter, eight inches long, with a handle and gauge on the end. The type of rugged instrument, in short, one would use on an animal—a patient that might squirm during intromission. There was a blob of yellowish grease on the business end.

When she still did not respond, he set the thermometer carefully in the feeding trough and tried to haul her about by hand. He grasped her around the middle and hefted. Her slim midsection came up and her well-fleshed leg straightened, but that was all. She was too heavy to juggle when uncooperative. He eased her down, leaving her prone on the pallet. It would have to do. At least the target was approachable, instead of aimed at the wall.

He recovered the thermometer and squatted beside her. With the fingers of his free hand he pried apart the fleshy buttocks, searching for the anus. It didn't work very well; her hindquarters were generous, and her position squeezed the mounds together. He succeeded only in changing the configuration of the crevice. He could probably open the spot to view by using both hands, but then would not be able to insert the thermometer. Finally he flattened one buttock with his left hand and guided the tip of the instrument along the crack with his right, leaving a slug-trail of grease. When he judged he was in the right area, he pushed, hoping the slant was correct.

There was resistance, she squirmed, and the rounded point jogged over and sank in. He was surprised at the ease with which it penetrated, after the prior difficulties. He let the stem shift until the angle was about ninety degrees and depressed it until he estimated that the tip was a couple of inches deep beyond the sphincter. He readjusted himself and settled down for the prescribed two minutes.

God, he thought while he waited. What was he doing in this stable, with a naked buxom woman stretched out, he straddling her thighs and his clammy hand on her rear and jamming a rod up her rectum? His own member was so stiff it was painful.

To have you like this, Io—your dainty, chaste, aseptic little ass—

The seconds stretched out, incredibly long. He wondered whether his watch had stopped, but heard it still ticking. What would he tell the boys, in the next post-mission (post emission?) bull-session? That he had been milking cows? Surely they would laugh off the truth. Truth was a fleshy buttocks and a dizzy feeling.

The time, somehow, was almost up, and he began to ease out the thermometer. At that point she moved again, perhaps in response to the withdrawal, climbing to her knees with her head still down. He had to follow quickly to prevent the tube from ramming too far inside, and almost lost his balance. But the new position flung open her buttocks and revealed to him the thermometer's actual point of entry.

Not the anus. Well, it probably didn't make any difference. The temperature couldn't vary that much between adjacent apertures. Carefully he drew the length of plastic out and checked the gauge. It reached the "normal" marker exactly.

"Flora, you're mending," he announced with his best bedside manner, averting his gaze from the intriguing view presented. "You'll be spry again in no time."

Perhaps it was the pseudo-confident tone. She rolled over, her breasts creased from the pallet, and smiled. He retreated into the passage and ladled out a pound of the special sick-animal crackers. It had been rough, for more reasons than he cared to think about.

The next occupied pen was going to be worse. It was the one in which he had seen—the girl. The one he had avoided until this moment. The one that fastened him to this world.

There could be an Iolanthe here.

He peered at the instructions before taking the plunge. This cow was in heat, and had to be conducted to the bull for mating. The handbook had, he discovered, a sketch of the barn's floor-plan, so he knew where to take her. "It is important that copulation be witnessed," the book said sternly, "and the precise time of connection noted, so that the bull can be properly paced."

Hitch took the last step and looked in, his pulses driving. It was not Iolanthe.

Just like that the bubble burst. Of *course* it wasn't Io. He had seen a black-haired girl in poor light, and his mind had been on the black-haired girl he knew at home, and the similarity of names—his stiff member had pinned the image to the desire.

This was a yearling—if that were the proper description. In human terms, about sixteen years old and never bred before. Her breasts were slight and firm, her haunches slender but well-formed, her movements animate. She paced nervously about the pen, uttering faint squeals of impatience. Her glossy hair flung out, whipping around her torso when she turned. She was, if not Iolanthe, still a strikingly attracttive specimen by his definitions, perhaps because of her fire. The others had been, comparatively—cows.

Naturally a woman in heat would have sex appeal. That was what the condition was for. Mating.

Her name, of course, was Iota. The farmer had mentioned her specifically, and Hitch had made the connection, at least subconsciously, the instant he saw her first. "All right, Iota, time for an experience you'll never forget," he said.

She spun to face him, black pupils seeming to flare. Then with a bound she was glued to the slats, her high young mammaries poking through conically. Her breath was rapid as she reached for him. Could she, could she be—

A younger edition of Iolanthe?

Some interworld parallels were exact, others inexact. Iolanthe, Iota—both Io, as though they were sisters or more than sisters. Iolanthe might have looked like this at sixteen.

Ridiculous! It was just a mental phenomenon, a thing anchored to his yearning. A thousand, a million girls looked like this at this age.

He had a task to do. He would do it.

"Easy girl. Stand back so I can open the gate. You and I are going to the bull-pen."

As if in answer, she flung herself back and watched him alertly from the far side. He unlatched the gate—strange that these girls were all so dull they could not work these simple fastenings themselves, even after seeing it done repeatedly—and stepped inside with the halter.

Immediately she was on him, her lithe body pressed against his front, her arms clasped about his chest, her pelvis jerking against his crotch in an unmistakable gesture. She was in heat, all right—and she figured him for the bull!

And he was tempted, as her motions provided a most specific physical simulation. Recent events had heightened his awareness of his own masculinity, to phrase it euphemistically. What difference would it make, to the owner, exactly *who* bred her? All they wanted was the milk when she freshened. And this whole foul system would be thrown out when the Earth-Prime troops—correction, law & order expediters—came. The chances were she would never become a milker anyway.

He looked into her eyes and read the mindless lust. Never had he perceived such graphic yearning in a woman. She had no brain, only a hungry pudendum.

She was, after all, an animal, not a human being. Fornication with her would be tantamount to bestiality, and the concept repelled him even as his member throbbed in response to the urgent pressure of her vulva.

"Get away from me!" he cried, shoving her roughly aside. God! They had even reduced women to animal cycles, in lieu of human periodicy. To control freshening, no doubt, and forestall restlessness at inconvenient times. There would be no mooning in the absence of male company, this way, except for those few days when the repressed sexuality of a year or more was triggered.

She hunched against the wall, tears coming. He saw that her emotions were human, though her mind was not. She felt rejection as keenly as anyone, but lacked the sophistication to control or conceal her reaction.

He had been too harsh with her. "Take it easy, Iota. I didn't mean to yell at you. I *wasn't* yelling at you!" No—he had been shouting across the worlds at Iolanthe, who had teased him similarly for so long. Arousing the urge, but unavailable for the gratification. The difference was that this time *he* had called it off. Taking out his suppressions on this innocent wanton who could not know what drove him.

She peered at him uncertainly, her face bearing the sheen of smeared tears. He lifted the harness and shook it. "I have to put this on you and take you to the bull. That's all. Do you understand?"

Still she hesitated. How *could* she understand? She was an animal. The tone of his voice was all she followed.

Or *was* it?

The animals here were incredibly stupid, considering their human origin. Obviously they had been somehow bludgeoned into this passivity. Drugs, perhaps—the biscuits could contain a potent mix. Probably most of the subjects finally gave up thinking; it was easier just to go along. But what of a young one? Her metabolism might have greater resource, particularly when she was ready to mate. To be in heat—it was the animal way to be in potent sexual love. Powerful juices there, very powerful. Counteractants?

But more: suppose an individual succeeded for a time in throwing off the mind-suppressant? Started protesting?

What was the reply of *any* tyranny to insurrection? The smart cow would keep her mouth shut, at least in the barn. She would conform. Her life depended on it.

Iota might not be stupid at all. She might be doing exactly what was expected of her. Concealing her awareness.

She was still damned attractive in her primeval way.

She had been watching him with that preternatural alertness of hers, and now she approached him again, cautiously.

He set the harness over her shoulders and reached around her body to fasten the straps. "Can you talk?" he whispered into her ear, afraid of being overheard. He doubted there were hidden mikes—that would not be economically feasible for a retarded technology like this—but other farmhands could be in the area.

She lifted her arms to facilitate the tightening of the clasps. A thick strand of hair curved around her left shoulder and the inside arc of her left breast. She was not as scantily endowed as he had thought at first; he had merely become acclimatized to the monstrosities of the milkers. She was clean, too, except for the feet, and there was an alluring woman-smell about her.

"Can you talk, Iota!" he whispered more urgently. "Maybe I can help you."

She perked up at the sound of her name. Her breathing became rapid again. She rested her forearms against his shoulders and looked into his face. Her eyes were large, the irises black in this light. But she did not smile or speak.

"You can trust me, Iota," he said. "Just give me some sign. Some evidence that you're not—"

She closed her arms gently around his neck and drew him to her. Again her breasts touched him; again her hips nudged his groin. The woman-smell became stronger.

Was she trying to show him that she comprehended, or was it merely a more careful sexual offering?

What difference did it make?

He had fastened the straps long since, but his arms were still about her. He slid his hands across her smooth back, down to the slight indentations above her buttocks. She responded, putting increasing pressure against him.

What the hell.

Hitch looked about. There was no one in the stable, apart from the cows in the special stalls. He tightened his embrace and carried her upright into her own compartment. "You want to get bred, OK," he muttered.

He put her down in the straw. She yielded to his directions, eager to oblige. He kneeled between her spread legs, released his belt and opened his trousers, watching her. Then, unable to restrain himself any longer, he put his left hand on her cleft to work the labia apart. The entire area was slick and hot. He transferred the hand to his own loin, supporting the weight of his body with the other hand as he descended, and guided himself down the burning crevice and in. He was reminded strikingly of the manner he had placed the thermometer not long ago. There didn't seem to be any hymen.

He spread himself upon her, embedded to the hilt. He tried to kiss her, but the position was wrong and she didn't seem to understand. What opportunity would she have had to learn about kissing?

He had expected an immediate and explosive climax, but was disappointed. Iota had a dismayingly capacious vaginal tract; he could neither plumb the well to its depth nor find purchase at its rim. He realized belatedly that cows would naturally be selected for ready breeding and birthing. Entry had been too easy; there was no internal resistance, no friction.

After all his buildup, he couldn't come. It was like dancing alone in a spacious ballroom.

She lay there passively, waiting for him to proceed.

Angry, now, he pulled back, plunged, withdrew and plunged again, his sword impaling only phantoms.

And felt his weapon growing flaccid. "Bitch," he said.

But it was the bovine, not the canine, image that had unmanned him. It just wasn't in him to fornicate with a placid, mindless cow.

She looked up at him reproachfully as he disengaged and covered up, but he was too disturbed to care. "Get up, animal. You want bull, you'll *get* bull."

She stood up and he took hold of the harness leash and jerked her forward. "Move," he said firmly, and she moved. There was, it seemed, a trick to handling animals, and he had mastered it out of necessity. He was becoming an experienced farmer.

They traveled down long dim corridors to the bullpen, she tugging eagerly at the leash and seeking to poke into side passages. She had forgotten the frustration of the recent episode already. Obviously she had never been in this section of the barn before, and curiosity had not been entirely suppressed along with intelligence. She *was* stupid, of course; otherwise he would not have failed with her.

He didn't know much about lobotomy, but this didn't seem like it. Yet what technique . . . ?

The bull was a giant of a man, full-bearded and hirsute. His feet and hands were crusted with callus and there was dirt on his belly. His tremendous penis hoisted, derrick-like, the moment he winded Iota, and he hurled himself around his large pen. Only the stout double harness and chained collar that bound him to the far rail inhibited his savage lunges. He stank of urine.

Hitch loosed Iota and shoved her into the pen. He was anxious to have the bull cover up any guilty traces of his own abortive gesture.

She was abruptly hesitant, standing just beyond the range of the man-monster that reared and chafed and bellowed to get at her and bucked awesomely with his tumescence. She wasn't afraid of him, though his mass was easily twice hers; she was merely uncertain how to proceed in the face of so much meat.

She made as if to step forward, then withdrew. She was trying to flirt! Hitch found quick sympathy for the bull, allied with his own apprehension. "You idiotic tease, get over there!" he cried at her.

Startled, she did.

The bull reached out and grabbed her by one shoulder, employing the same five-fingered mitten-grip Hitch had observed with the cows. Iota spun under the force of it, thrown off-balance, and the bull caught at her opposite hip and hauled her in to his chest backwards. He clubbed her so that she doubled over and rammed his spurting organ into her narrow cleft, thrusting again and again so fiercely that her abdomen bowed out with each lunge.

That was the treatment she had been waiting for! She hadn't even been aware of Hitch's effort, thinking it only the preliminary inspection.

Then Iota tumbled to the floor, stunned by the impact of the courtship but hardly miserable. She was in heat, after all, and now that she had found out what it was all about, she liked it. She lay on her back in the soiled straw, smiling, legs lifted, though Hitch was sure she would suffer shortly from terrible bruises inside and out. What a performance!

The beast was on her again, this time from the front, biting at her breasts while trying to get into position for another assault. His organ glistened moistly, still erect.

"Get that heifer out of there!" someone shouted, and Hitch started. It was another farmhand. "Want to sap our best stud?"

Hitch ran out into the pen, wary of the bull, and caught hold of one of Iota's blissfully outstretched arms. It was obvious that she would happily absorb all the punishment the creature chose to deliver. A festoon of white goo stretched downward from the bull's penis as he made a last attempt at the vanishing target. Then Hitch hauled Iota across the floor until they were entirely out of range of the monster and stood her on her feet. She was still dazed as he reharnessed her, not even wincing as the strap chafed across the deep toothmarks on her breast.

The other farmhand glanced at him as they trooped by, but did not say anything. Just as well.

About halfway back, Hitch remembered that he had forgotten to post the time of service on the bull's chart. He decided not to risk further embarrassment by returning for that errand. The bull seemed to have sufficient pep to go around, anyway.

Iota was dreamily contented as he returned her to her stall, though there was a driblet of gluey blood on one leg. Apparently there *had* been a hymen . . . Well, she was out of heat now, and she wasn't a virgin heifer any more!

There was trouble in the final stall. He had been so occupied with the prior chores on the schedule that he hadn't bothered to read ahead, and now he regretted it. He had just witnessed, per instructions, a copulation, and it was as though gestation had occurred in minutes. This next cow was delivering!

She lay on her side, legs pulled up, whimpering as her body strained. There was something funny about her tongue too, as it projected between her teeth. Was there a *physical* reason these animals never spoke? The head of the calf had already emerged, its hair brown like that of the mother. Hitch had thought all babies were bald. All *human* babies ...

Should he summon help? He was no obstetrician!

But then he would have to explain why he hadn't notified anyone earlier, and he had no excuse apart from carelessness and personal concupiscence. Better to stick with it himself.

Odd, he thought, how one could become committed against his intention. This laboring cow was not really his problem, and she belonged literally to another world, yet he had to do what he could for her. The activities of this brutal barn were as important to him at this moment as anything he could remember. Even its most repulsive aspects fascinated him. It represented a direct personal challenge as well as an intellectual one. Iota—

As the cow struggled to force out the massive bundle, Hitch skimmed nervously through the manual. Good—the stock was generally hardy, and seldom required more than nominal supervision during parturition. Signs of trouble? No, none of the alarm signals itemized were evident. This was a normal delivery.

But the text stressed the importance of removing the new-birthed calf immediately and taking it to the nursery for proper processing. The mother was not supposed to have any opportunity to lick it down, suckle it or develop any attachment.

And how about the father? How about *any* observer with a trace of human feeling? It was as though he *had* impregnated a cow, and now his offspring was being manifested. He had failed with Iolanthe, he had failed with Iota, but he still had something to prove. Something to salvage from this disaster of a world.

The cow heaved again, and more of the balled-up calf emerged. There was blood soaking into the pallet, but the manual assured him callously that this was normal. He wanted to *do* something, but knew that his best bet was noninterference. He was sure now that a human woman could not have given birth so readily without anesthetic or medication. In some ways the animals were fortunate, not that it justified any part of this. That large, loose vagina—

"What's going on here?"

Hitch jumped again. The voice behind him was that of the owner! For an experienced investigator, he had been inexcusably careless about his observations. Twice now, men had come upon him by surprise.

"She's birthing," he said. "Routine, so I didn't—"

"In the *nightstall?*" the man demanded angrily, his white hair seeming to stand on end. It was the way he combed it, Hitch decided irrelevantly. "On a bare pallet?"

Oops—he must have missed a paragraph. "I told you it's been a while since I—the other farm didn't have separate places to—"

"That farm was in violation of the law, not to mention the policies of compassionate procedure." The owner was already inside the stall and squatting down beside the laboring cow. "It was a mistake, Esmeralda," he said soothingly. "I never meant to put you through this here. I had a special delivery-booth for you, with fresh clean straw and padded walls . . ." He stroked her hair and patted her shoulder, and the animal relaxed a little. Obviously she recognized the gentle master. Probably he came by the stables periodically to encourage the beasts and grant them lumps of sugar. "In just a moment I'll give you a shot to ease the pain, but not just yet. It will make you sleepy, and we have to finish this job first. You've been very good. You're one of my best. It's all right now, dear."

Hitch realized with a peculiar mixture of emotions that it wasn't all acting. The farmer really did care about the comfort and welfare of his animals. Hitch had somehow assumed that brutality was the inevitable concomitant of the degradation of human beings. But actually he had seen no harshness; this entire barn was set up for the maximum creature comfort compatible with efficiency, with this backward technology. Had he misjudged the situation?

Under the owner's sure guidance the calving was quickly completed. The man lifted the infant—a female—and spanked her into awareness before cutting and tying off the umbilical cord. He wrapped her in a towel that materialized from somewhere and stood up. "Here," he said to Hitch, "take it to the nursery."

Hitch found himself with babe in arms.

"All right, Esme," the owner said to the cow, his voice low and friendly. "Let's take care of that afterbirth. Here—I'll give you that shot I promised. It only stings for a second. Hold still—there. You'll feel much better soon. Just relax, and in a moment you'll be asleep. In a few days you'll be back with the herd where you belong, the finest milker of them all." He looked up and spied Hitch still standing there. "Get moving, man! Do you want her to see it?"

Hitch got moving. He did not feel at all comfortable carrying the baby, for all his determination of a moment ago to help it in some way, but that was the least of it. Its cries, never very loud (did they breed for that, too?), had subsided almost immediately as it felt the supposed comfort of human arms, and probably that was fortunate because otherwise the mother would have been attracted to the sound. But this removal of the baby so quickly from its parent, so that it could never know a true family—how could that be tolerated? Yet he was cooperating, carrying it down the dusky passages to the nursery.

The fact that he had witnessed its arrival did not make him responsible for it, technically—but the baby had, in more than a manner of speaking, been given into his charge. His prior mood returned, intensified; he *did* feel responsible.

"I'll take care of you, little girl," he said inanely. "I'll keep you safe. I'll—"

He was talking like a hypocrite. There was very little he could do for this baby except put it in the nursery. He didn't know the first thing about child care. And—he was no longer entirely certain that he *should* do anything specific if he had the opportunity.

He had been ready to condemn this entire world out of hand, but in the face of this last development he wasn't sure, oddly. This breeding and milking of human beings was shocking—but was it actually evil? The preliminary report had remarked on the strange peacefulness of this alternate Earth: computer analysis suggested that there was no war here, and had not been for some time. That was another riddle of #772. Was it because those who ruled it were compassionate men, despite the barbarity of their regime?

Which was better: to have a society peacefully unified by a true segregation of functions—men-men vs animal-men—or to have every person born to contend so selfishly for the privileges of humanity that all succeeded only in being worse than animals? Earth-Prime remained in serious jeopardy of self-extermination; was that the preferred system to impose on all the alternate Earths too?

#772 did have its positive side. Economically it functioned well, and it would probably never have runaway inflation or population increase or class warfare. Could it be that with the breakup of the family system, the human rights and dignities system, the all-men-are-created-equal system—could it be that this was the true key to permanent worldwide peace?

He had not seen a single discontented cow.

By taking this baby from its mother and conveying it to the impersonal nursery, was he in fact doing it the greatest favor of its existence?

He wondered.

The nursery caught him by surprise. It was a cool quiet area more like a laboratory than the playroom he had anticipated. A series of opaque tanks lined the hall. As he passed between them he heard a faint noise, like that of an infant crying in a confined space, and the baby in his arms heard it and came alive loudly.

Hitch felt suddenly uneasy, but he took the squalling bundle hastily up to the archaically garbed matron at a central desk. "This is Esmeralda's offspring," he said.

"I don't recognize you," the woman said, glowering at him. Epitome of gradeschool disciplinarian. He almost flinched.

"I'm a new man, just hired this morning. The boss is in with the mother now. He said to—"

"Boss? What nonsense is this?"

Hitch paused, nonplussed, before he realized that he had run afoul of another slang expression. This one evidently hadn't carried over into #772. "The owner, the man who—"

"Very well," she snapped. "Let me see it."

She took the bundle, put it unceremoniously on the desk, and unwrapped it. She probed the genital area with a harsh finger, ignoring the baby's screams. This time Hitch did flinch. "Female. Good. No abnormalities. Males are such a waste."

"A waste? Why?"

She unrolled a strip of something like masking tape and tore it off. She grasped one of the baby's tiny hands. "Haven't you worked in a barn before? You can't get milk from a bull."

Obviously not. But a good bull did have his function, as Iota's experience had shown. Hitch watched the woman tape the miniature thumb and fingers together, forming a bandage resembling a stiff mitten, and something unpleasant clicked. Hands so bound in infancy could not function normally in later life; certain essential muscles would atrophy and certain nerves would fail to develop. It was said by some that man owed his intelligence to the use of his opposable thumb . . .

"I haven't been involved with this end of it," he explained somewhat lamely. "What happens to the males?"

"We have to kill them, of course, except for the few we geld for manual labor." She had finished taping the hands; now she had a bright scalpel poised just above the little face.

Hitch assumed she was going to cut the tape away or take a sample of hair. He wasn't really thinking about it, since he was still trying to digest what he had just learned. Slaughter of almost all males born here . . .

She hooked thumb and forefinger into the baby's cheeks,

forcing its mouth open uncomfortably. The knife came down, entered the mouth, probed beneath the tongue before Hitch could protest. Suddenly the screams were horrible.

Hitch watched, paralyzed, as bubbling blood overflowed the tiny lip. "What—?"

"Wouldn't want it to grow up talking," she said. "Amazing how much trouble one little cut can save. Now take this calf down to tank seven."

"I don't—" There was too much to grapple with. They cut the tongues so that speech would be impossible? There went another bastion of intelligence, ruthlessly excised.

With the best intentions, he had delivered his charge into this enormity. He felt ill.

The matron sighed impatiently. "That's right, you're new here. Very well. I'll show you so you'll know next time. Make sure you get it straight. I'm too busy to tell you twice."

Too busy mutilating innocent babies? But he did not speak. It was as though his own tongue had felt the blade.

She took the baby down to tank seven, ignoring the red droplets that trailed behind, and lifted the lid. The container was about half full of liquid, and a harness dangled from one side. She pinned the baby in the crook of one elbow and fitted the little arms, legs and head into the loops and tightened the fastenings so that the head was firmly out of the fluid. Some of it splashed on Hitch when she immersed the infant, and he discovered that it was some kind of thin oil, lukewarm.

The baby screamed and thrashed, afraid of the dark interior or perhaps bruised by the crude straps, but only succeeded in frothing redly and making a few small splashes with its bound hands. The harness held it secure and helpless.

The matron lowered the lid, checking to make sure the breathing vents were clear, and the pitiful cries were muted.

Hitch fumbled numbly for words. "You—what's that for? It—"

"It is important that the environment be controlled," the woman explained curtly. "No unnecessary tactile, auditory or visual stimulation for the first six months. Then they get too big for the tanks, so we put them in the dark cells. The first three years are critical; after that it's fairly safe to exercise them, though we generally wait another year to be certain. And we keep the protein down until six; then we increase the dose because we *want* them to grow."

"I—I don't understand." But he did, horribly. In his mind the incongruous but too-relevant picture of a bee-hive returned, the worker-bees growing in their tight hexagonal cells. His intuition, when he first saw the cows, had been sure.

"Don't you know *anything?* Protein is the chief brain food. Most of the brain develops in the first few years, so we have to watch their diet closely. Too little, and they're too stupid to follow simple commands; too much, and they're too smart. We raise good cows here; we have excellent quality control."

Hitch looked at the rows of isolation tanks: quality control. What could he say? He knew that severe dietary deficiencies in infancy and childhood could permanently warp a person's mental, physical and emotional development. Like the bees of the hive, the members of the human society could not achieve their full potential unless they had the proper care in infancy. Those bees scheduled to be workers were raised on specially deficient honey, and became sexless, blunted insects. The few selected to be queens were given royal jelly and extra attention, and developed into completely formed insects. Bees did not specialize in high intelligence, so the restriction was physical and sexual. With human beings, it would hit the human specialization: the brain. With proper guidance, the body might recover almost completely from early protein deprivation, but never the mind.

EP had researched this in order to foster larger, brighter, healthier children and adults. #772 used the same information to deliberately convert women to cows. No drugs were required, or surgical lobotomy. And there was no hope that any individual could preserve or recover full intelligence, with such a lifelong regime. No wonder he had gotten nowhere with Iota!

He heard the babies wailing. What price, peace?

"And," he said as she turned away, "and any of these calves could grow up to be as intelligent and lively as we are, if raised properly?"

"They *could*. But that's against the law, and of course such misfits wouldn't be successful as milkers. They're really quite well off here; we take good care of our own. We're very fortunate to have developed this system. Can you imagine using actual filthy *beasts* for farming?"

And he had milked those placid cows and had his round with Iota . . .

He left her, sick in body and spirit as he passed by the wailing tanks. In each was a human baby crying out its heritage in a mind-stifling environment, deprived of that stimulation and response essential to normal development, systematically malnourished. No health, no comfort, no future —because each had been born in the barn. In the barn.

He could do nothing about it, short-range. If he ran amok amid the tanks, as he was momentarily inclined to, what would he accomplish except the execution of babies? And this was only one barn of perhaps millions. No—it would take generations to undo the damage wrought here.

He paused as he passed tank #7, hearing a cry already poignant. The baby he had carried here, in his naivete. Esmeralda's child. The responsibility he had abrogated. The final and most terrible failure.

A newborn personality, bound and bloody in the dark, never to know true freedom, doomed to a lifelong waking nightmare . . . until the contentment of idiocy took over.

Suddenly Hitch understood what Iolanthe meant by integrity of purpose over and above the standards of any single world. There were limits beyond which personal ambition and duty became meaningless.

He stepped up to the tank and lifted the lid. The cries became loud. He clapped his free hand to his ankle, feeling for the blade concealed there. He brought it up, plunged it into the tank and slashed away the straps.

"Hey!" the matron cried sharply.

He dropped the knife and grabbed the floundering infant, lifting it out. He hugged it to his shirtfront with both arms and barged ahead. By the time the supervisor got there, Hitch was out of the nursery, leaving a trail of oil dropplets from the empty tank.

As soon as he was out of sight he balanced the baby awkwardly in one arm and reached up to touch the stud in his skull.

It was risky. He had no guarantee there would be an open space at this location on Earth-Prime. But he was committed.

Five seconds passed. Then he was wrenched into his own world by the unseen operator. Safely!

There was no welcoming party. The operator had merely aligned interworld coordinates and opened the veil by remote control. Hitch would have to make his own way back to headquarters, where he would present his devastating report. Armies would mass at his behest, but he felt no exhilaration. Those tanks . . .

He held the baby more carefully, looking for a place to put it down so that he could remove the remaining strapfragments and wrap it protectively. He knew almost nothing about what to do for it, except to keep it warm. But the baby, blessedly, was already asleep again, trusting in him as it had before though there was blood on its cheek. The mutilated tongue . . .

He was in a barn. Not really surprisingly; the alternate framework tended to run parallel in detail, so that a structure could occupy the same location in a dozen Earths. There were many more barns in #772 than in EP, but it still didn't stretch coincidence to have a perfect match. The one he trekked through now was an Earth-Prime barn, though, an old-fashioned red one. It had the same layout as the other, but it contained horses or sheep or—cows.

He walked down the passage, cradling the sleeping baby—*his* baby!—and looking into the stalls. He passed the milkroom and entered the empty stable, noting how it had changed for animal accommodation. He couldn't resist entering the special wing again.

The first stall contained an ill cow who munched on alfalfa hay. The second was occupied by a lively heifer who paused to look soulfully at him with large soft eyes and licked its teeth with a speech-muted tongue. Had she just been bred? The third—

Then it struck him. He had been shocked that man could so ruthlessly exploit man, there on #772. It was not even slavery on the other world, but such thorough subjugation of the less fortunate members of society that no reprieve was even thinkable for the—cows. When man was rendered truly into animal, revolt was literally inconceivable for the domesticants.

Yet what of the animals of *this* world, Earth-Prime? Man had, perhaps, the right to be inhumane to man—but how could he justify the subjugation of a species not his own? Had the free-roving bovines of ten thousand years ago come voluntarily to man's barns, or had they been genocidally compelled? What irredeemable crime had been perpetrated against them?

If Earth-Prime attempted to pass judgment on this counter-Earth system, what precedent would it be setting? For no one knew what the limits of the alternate-universe framework were. It was probable that somewhere within it were worlds more advanced, more powerful than EP. Worlds with the might to blast away all mammalian life including man himself from the Earth, leaving the birds and snakes and frogs to dominate instead. Had it been such intervention that set back #772?

Worlds that could very well judge EP as EP judged counter-Earth #772. Worlds that might consider *any* domestication of *any* species to be an intolerable crime against nature . . .

Iolanthe would take care of the baby; he was sure of that.

She was that sort of person. Prompt remedial surgery should mitigate the injury to the tongue. But the rest of it—a world full of similar misery—

He knew that in saving this one baby he had accomplished virtually nothing. His act might even give warning to #772 and thus precipitate far more cruelty than before. But that futility was only part of his growing horror.

Could he be sure in his own mind that Earth-Prime had the right of it? Between it and #772 was a difference only in the actual species of mammal occupying the barn. The other world was, if anything, kinder to its stock than was EP.

No—he was being foolishly anthropomorphic! It was folly to attempt to attribute human feelings or rights to cows. They had no larger potential, while the human domesticants of #772 *did*. Yet—

Yet—

Yet what sort of a report could he afford to make?

Afterword:

The name inscribed over the bullpen is HARLAN, though the description is not necessarily physical. I was one of those who supposed his intellectual scrotum contained two jellybeans, but I learned that there were, after all, nitties in his gritty. Thus I applauded the potency of the first DANG VIS and clamored for admission to the second.

Why? Why:

Our field of speculative fiction, like our nation, like our world, becomes too complacent at times. Originality and candor are not always sought, not always appreciated, even when the need becomes critical. At such times there may be no gentle way to fertilize the willing medium; we have to call upon a bull-editor, a rampaging volume, and irate authors such as these you read here. Perhaps even so the mission will fail—but we must, must try. For it is in the expansion of our horizons, including especially these literary and moral ones, that our brightest future lies.

In the Barn is intended to be a shocker, of course. It could have been told without the, if you'll pardon the expression, vulgar detail. But the real shock should not stem from the portrayal of acts every normal person practices. It should be this: this story is a true representation of a situation that exists widely in America, and in the world, and that has existed for millennia. Only one detail has been changed: one form of mammal has been substituted for another in the barn.

Does human morality *have* to be defined in terms of humans? Is it impossible for us to recognize the inherent rights of nonhuman creatures? Surely, if we can show no more respect for cows, for chickens, for pigs, for any animal or color or philosophy—no more respect than this—surely we have defined our own morality unmistakably.

Other SIGNET Science Fiction You Will Enjoy

☐ **THERE WILL BE TIME by Poul Anderson.** Only a natural-born time traveler stood between man and a future which could destroy human civilization.
(#Q5401—95¢)

☐ **THE OTHER SIDE OF THE SKY by Arthur C. Clarke.** Twenty-four stories of man's first outposts among the stars. (#Q5553—95¢)

☐ **MOON OF MUTINY by Lester del Rey.** Set in the early days of the moon's colonization this exciting novel tells of one man's escapades in space. (#Q5539—95¢)

☐ **THE BLACK CLOUD by Fred Hoyle.** Earth was menaced by a power from beyond the stars and older than time.
(#T5486—75¢)

☐ **THE MAN WHO SOLD THE MOON by Robert Heinlein.** The daring adventures of the bold men of tomorrow told as no other can by the ever popular Heinlein.
(#Q5341—95¢)

☐ **METHUSELAH'S CHILDREN by Robert A. Heinlein.** The dean of space-age fiction tells the provocative story of Earthmen compelled to wander the distant stars because they have been blessed with extraordinary life spans. (#T4226—75¢)

SIGNET Science Fiction You'll Want to Read

☐ **ROGUE QUEEN by L. Sprague de Camp.** From out of the sky came the magic. From out of the hive came the queen. (#Q5256—95¢)

☐ **THE HEIRS OF BABYLON by Glen Cook.** After the bombs had stopped, there was still . . . THE WAR! (#Q5299—95¢)

☐ **THE OTHER SIDE OF TIME by Keith Laumer.** When time runs backward, can a world be recaptured? Imperial Intelligence Agent Brion Bayard had to find the answer to this question, for if he failed, the Imperium and all the known universe would vanish. (#Q5255—95¢)

☐ **WHO CAN REPLACE A MAN? (Best Science Fiction Stories of Brian W. Aldiss) by Brian W. Aldiss.** Fourteen of the best stories by one of Britain's top science fiction writers. "A virtuoso performance."—Saturday Review (#T5055—75¢)

☐ **ELEMENT 79 by Fred Hoyle.** A noted astronomer and science fiction author leads an excursion into a fantastic—but scientifically possible—future universe in this engaging collection of stories. (#Q5279—95¢)